SOLDIERLY

'What a stupid, tormented fool I must have been to think her a decrepit old crone. Why, she is the most indescribably perfect woman a man could lay eyes upon.'

Every morning when he wakens and she brings him breakfast, she appears to be even more stunning, even more beautiful to behold, than she did the night previous. The dry, stringy, knotted shreds of grey hair are really thick, jet-black raven tresses flowing liquidly to her waist. Her skin could never have been parched and wizened. It had never cracked with age and decay.

While, true, she's paler than most women he's met, her skin shines, glistens, as if with a life all its own. No, her breasts never sagged with time. She never hobbled around on arthritic legs. Her lips have always been red, full of life's blood. With the poise of a born queen, the grace of a real goddess, she can dance, it seems to him, on the very air itself.

If he's delirious, it's with happiness. But, no again, he mustn't think of the happiness, the euphoria. Dare not, for to do so might presage its ending. It can't end. The life he's living's more than any one man deserves ...

One night the soldier has a dream. It starts idyllically enough. He's lying on his bed of cocoa leaves, having just finished a fine meal of rabbit roasted on a spit. He swallows the final dregs of excellent, honey-sweetened nectar she gives him each night so he can sleep better.

As usual, as he's nodding off, she dances for him. This night – this dream at any rate – she seems more passionate; wilder than ever before. As she whirls, her long tresses flailing about in a dance of their own, the dark garment she always wears slowly dissipates into nothingness.

For the first time he beholds her naked. Unnerved not in the slightest, she doesn't try to cover up. Quite the contrary, she shows no trace of embarrassment; continues brazenly before him. Visibly exhilarated, movements beyond suggestive, expression ecstatic, she's lost in the flow of her own body.

He reaches out, touches her ankle. A scream, hers. A release, his. She stops dancing. Stands above him. Wanton. Covered in sweat. She smiles; bends over him. Her skin's gone greenish pale. Her canine teeth are long, sharp. A third eye appears in her forehead. He shrieks. Eyefire rivets him in place, silencing him.

The bite feels like twin pinpricks; the only thing uncomfortable about the sucking is the slurping sound and a strange, light-headed sensation of blood draining out of his veins.

Then he awoke and began to live the nightmare.

GODDESS GAMBIT

A *PHANTACEA* MYTHOS MOSAIC NOVEL

Conceived, written and produced by Jim McPherson
Front and Back Cover by Verne Andru

Original artwork for "Nuclear Dragons" by Ian Bateson, 1980
Interior collages prepared by Jim McPherson

Phantacea Publications
(James H McPherson, Publisher)
74689 Kitsilano RPO
2768 West Broadway
Vancouver BC
V6K 4P4 Canada

Library and Archives Canada Cataloguing in Publication

McPherson, Jim, 1951-
        Goddess gambit / Jim McPherson.

Bk. 3 in the Thrice cursed godly glories trilogy.
ISBN 978-0-9781342-2-8

        I. Title.

  PS8625.P535G63 2011   C813'.6   C2011-
907766-3

Print publications featuring

Jim McPherson's

PHANTACEA Mythos

- *PHANTACEA* **One to Six**
(A series of comic books with artwork by various artists)

- **Forever & 40 Days – The Genesis of *PHANTACEA***
(A graphic novel with artwork by Ian Fry as well as
background material and a short story featuring the
Damnation Brigade, the Death Dodgers & Signal System)

- **Feeling Theocidal**
(Book One of *'The Thrice-Cursed Godly Glories'* Trilogy)

- **The War of the Apocalyptics**
(The first entry in the *'Launch 1980'* story cycle)

- **The Death's Head Hellion**
(A mini-novel commencing *'The 1000 Days of Disbelief'*)

- **Contagion Collectors**
(A mini-novel continuing *'The 1000 Days of Disbelief'*)

- **Janna Fangfingers**
(A mini-novel concluding *'The 1000 Days of Disbelief'*)

- **Goddess Gambit**
(Book Three of *'The Thrice Cursed Godly Glories'* Trilogy)

In one form or another, all are available for ordering through:
www.phantacea.com

Goddess Gambit

- Year of the Dome 5980 -

Jim McPherson

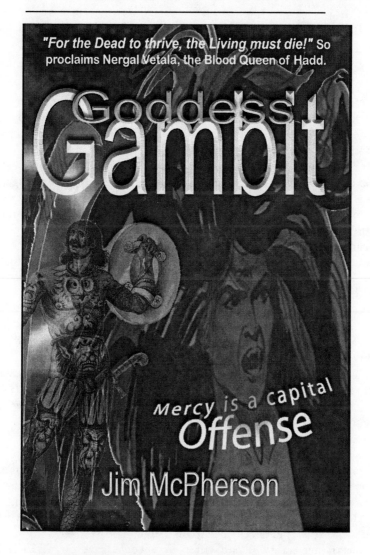

"For the Dead to thrive, the Living must die!" So proclaims Nergal Vetala, the Blood Queen of Hadd.

Goddess Gambit

Mercy is a capital Offense

Jim McPherson

A **PHANTACEA Mythos** Mosaic Novel

Phantacea Publications (James H McPherson, Publisher)

ISBN 978-0-9781342-2-8

AUCTORIAL PREFATORY

From comic books to novels to mini-novels – with a graphic novel and 10 web-serials between – *PHANTACEA* moves into its 35th year with the publication of "Goddess Gambit".

Actually, Phantacea as it applies to me has been around much more than 35 years. Sooth said, the first time I used it was for a short story I wrote in high school; the same story I used to gain acceptance into the Creative Writing department at UBC sometime later, as it happened.

The word itself is Greek for *'imagination'*. As for the story, which I still have, it involves a character by the name of Eye. This Eye ventures into a strange, midnight land – whereupon he's promptly captured by a nasty Dracula-type who populates his realm with distortions of characters culled from other people's imaginations.

The gist of the grist is that Herr Hell Nastiness will let Eye go provided our hero first gives him his shadow – a shadow being one thing he doesn't have. Eye's shadow, he figures out just in time, is his imagination externalized. Which, the lack thereof, is why the bad business guy, who naturally declares himself a count, has been reduced to abducting the products of other folks' *phantacea*, if you will.

(As might be expected, Eye prevails by activating his shadow psychically, not to mention incandescently. He thereupon renders Count Nastiness – not his real name – a cerebral cinder, heroically liberates the corrupted characters, and returns to reality a wiser, if not necessarily saner, personage.)

When I, not Eye, decided to start writing and publishing my own series of comic books in the late Seventies, calling them, and my company, *PHANTACEA* (by now italicized and all in caps – at the insistence of Dave Sim, *pHant*'s first artist, shortly to be of Cerebus the Aardvark fame) proved irresistible.

And it still does, all these years later.

========

I published six comics from 1977 until 1980. Had many more sketched out, often on proper paper instead of just in my head, when putting my line-of-credit to decidedly different uses suddenly became a matter much more pressing. Following advice always given to those of us with artistic pretensions, I never gave up my day job – until, that is, it in effect gave up on me.

I was an inveterate weekend writer. Never could leave my *PHANTACEA* characters behind for very long and always felt they deserved to be out in the public eye. The graphic novel, "Forever & 40 Days – the Genesis of *PHANTACEA*", which came out in 1990, is proof of that.

So are the many web-serials I published online from 1996 until 2008, when I started the current series of Phantacea Publications. The policy of Anheroic Fantasy

Illustrated continues as well, though the novels and mini-novels only contain a few reworked cover collages. All my websites are heavily illustrated, however, mostly with my own photographs and collages built around them.

Not counting the Wilderwitch-Furie short story in the graphic novel, "Goddess Gambit" is the sixth all-prose offering from Phantacea Publications. It concludes *'The Thrice-Cursed Godly Glories'* trilogy. With it, there are now three full-length novels and the three mini-novels that made up THRICE-CURSED Book Two ("The 1000 Days of Disbelief") available from the usual sources both online and in bricks-and-mortar bookshops.

Hooks for the books are the same as for the comics, graphic novel and web serials before them:

> The gods and goddesses, the demons and monsters, of ancient mythologies have been trivialized, their worship proscribed and the entities themselves mostly confined to another realm.
> Jim McPherson's **PHANTACEA** Mythos chronicles their ongoing striving for a return to paramountcy.

That I call these gods and goddesses *'Devas'*, plural and capitalized, or *'the Shining Ones'* shouldn't be surprising since *'bright'* or *'shining'* is what the Sanskrit word, also *'dev'* (in the singular), means. What perhaps may be surprising is that standard dictionaries give an entirely different, not to mention incomprehensible, derivation for word *'devil'*.

I'll leave you to look that up. Suffice to say, as near as I can make out at any rate, *'devil'* just means *'little god'*. Certainly folks living on Sedon's Head commonly use the word, as in devil-gods, on a day-to-day basis to refer to the same purportedly immortal beings. So do the devils themselves; always have done apparently.

Probably you and I should, too.

========

Lest anyone get the wrong idea, the **PHANTACEA Mythos** (capitalized, optional emboldening) is as strictly non-religious as it is anheroic. As follows, I expressed the same, essentially secular sentiment in the introduction to 1990's aforementioned graphic novel:

> Taking Genesis literally troubled me. Treating Genesis as mythology – like The Iliad or the Eddas – was inspirational.

So it was; so it remains today – and so, I devoutly, um, hope, may it be for another 35 years, minimum.

========

The main website for Phantacea Publications is *www.phantacea.com*.
****

GODDESS GAMBIT — CONTENTS

The launching of the Cosmic Express took place on Sunday, the 30th of November 1980. On the Hidden Continent of Sedon's Head it was Sedonda, the 30th of Maruta 5980.

The Cosmic Express never reached the Whole Earth's Outer Space. It did, however, reach an aspect of its Inner Space.

Briefly.

(PREGAME-GAMBIT) 1: **Meanwhile, on the Inner Earth**

Sedonda, Maruta 30, 5980

Cosmicaptain Dmetri Diomad and the six cosmicompanions with him inside Cosmicar Four writhed under the stress of takeoff. So did the sixty odd other people aboard the Cosmic Express proper, its hub-craft, control capsule and six cosmicars.

Something happened.

========

Diomad had seen some peculiar sights in his twenty-seven years. Nothing matched this; not even the disappearance of an entire island, his foster father's ancestral home in the Aegean Sea, a dozen years earlier. The spacecraft was somehow still intact. Whatever hit it managed to inject it into some sort of black space. The Cosmicaptain felt a strange sense of deep joy, almost of accomplishment. Hundreds of pinpoints of light were approaching the Express.

Stars, faeries, angels? Devils!

As the smaller pinpoints kept on coming, the largest, the brightest, resolved itself. It was at least ten times the size of the Cosmic Express, which was close to twenty storeys high if you included its firing rockets, what were only now detaching themselves. What it was, what it appeared to be, was a single, impossibly huge, disembodied eye. Its pupil had lips and teeth and a tongue. A mouth. It spoke.

"YOU PIG-WHUMPING, MECHANICAL LOLLIPOP, LOOK WHAT YOU'VE DONE.

"NOT ONLY HAVE YOU RIPPED MY HOLY HALO AND PIERCED THE FORBIDDEN ZONE, YOU'VE FREED SOME OF MY JACKASS OFFSPRING AS WELL."

Over his headphones he heard the Cosmic Express's Cosmicommander shout to one of his technicians: "Fire second stage. Let's get the hell out of here."

"Second stage fired, sir!" That'd be its Gypsium fuel-stage. Gypsium was teleportive.

"AND AFTER ALL THAT, YOU'RE TRYING TO GET AWAY. WELL, PUKE ON YOU. A LITTLE GOD-SUCK WILL TEACH YOU SOME MANNERS."

Pursing its lips, the eye-mouth slurped the entire Express into its mass. Began to chew it.

RRRUURP!

"BLOODY HELL! YOU OUTER EARTHLINGS TASTE AS LOUSY AS YOU DID SIX THOUSAND YEARS AGO!"

The eye-mouth spat them not just out of its craw but out of wherever they were in the first place.

"YUK!"

========

The Ice Palace was carved out of a glacier high up in the Labrys Mountain Range that gave the Frozen Isle its geographical backbone. Largely composed of active volcanoes, the Labrys Range effectively divided Lathakra into two distinct realms. Those were that of the Fire Kings on the west, Sea of Clouds side, where lava rivers flowed; and that of the Intuits on the east, Ocean of Psychron side, where the sun rose but where there was little besides Intuit settlements on ice floes.

Here banged the Piper.

========

"Well, Smiler, was it worth it?" grumbled the twelve-foot tall, blue-skinned, snow-haired and hoar-bearded god-devil of Lathakra.

"Look upstairs," responded his fiery, red-faced and red-haired, six-inch tall sister-wife, Heat to his Cold. "The stars of our lost children, never shining more brilliantly than they were last night, are no longer in Sedon's heavens."

Maintaining the bongo-beat he'd already set, their never-remembered guest continued to tap the two humanoid skulls depending from the Brainrock chain around his neck. Did so with pinkish fingers that were too long by at least a joint each and too many by however many he fancied. Small mercy, he'd stopped tooting on his panpipes. Instead he licked their nibs with a forked tongue to keep them moist. Beamed broadly – even when playing music, which he loved doing, the fiend was always smiling.

"Care for another tune?"

========

Old King Cold, as his fellow Master Devas referred to him, Tantal Thanatos, as ancient, well-travelled Illuminaries of Weir named him, ignored the Smiling Fiend.

"Stoke your cauldron, woman. I want to know where they went."

Strictly speaking the cauldron did not belong to his sister-wife, the Frozen Isle's other resident Death God. (Smiler did not live there. As for where he did live, that had to be Satanwyck – Sedon's Temple, Hell on Earth, Paradise for the Damned.) Tvasitar Smithmonger, the Anvil Artificer, the devic Prometheus, crafted it initially for another third generational devil, a Lazaremist like the smithy himself. The same Illuminaries of Weir named her Metisophia, though she was often referred to as Titanic Metis (titanic as in rebelliousness, not enormity).

Six-inch tall Methandra, perhaps misnamed after Mediterranean Athena, the Olympian Goddess of both War and Wisdom, waved her firebrand or matchstick, a cane-like Tvasitar Talisman that served as her power focus. Fumes from the steaming cauldron she'd appropriated from Titanic Metis, Wisdom of Lazareme to Heat's Wisdom of Mithras, during the expansion of the Thanatoids' comparatively short-lived empire some 1200 years ago revealed an astonishing sight.

"That's Devil Wind!" roared her not-always-gigantic brother-husband, all twelve feet of him. He'd recognized their ages-old antagonist, the Whirling Deva, whom Illuminaries had named Vayu Maelstrom and whom the Mayan peoples of Central America on the Outer Earth once worshipped as *'Hurican'*, or hurricane, immediately.

"Wait a minute," exclaimed their never-remembered guest, *"That's the Outer Earth!"* Smiler sounded as amazed as he was ever-amazing. How could he be so sure?

"What's a Byronic doing out there?" Reflexively Tantal reached for his power focus, the double-headed Brainrock war-axe or Labrys, like the Frozen Isle's volcanic backbone, strapped across his massive back. Not for a moment did he doubt Smiler was right about it being the Outer Earth. "And where are our children?"

"Patience," squealed his diminutive wife – his Crimson Queen, Miss Myth, the Mistress of Mythland, the Scarlet Seeress, his Scarlet Empress when Lathakra was their empire. "We've endured nearly five decades without them. What's another few minutes? We'll locate them."

"You bloody better," grumbled her husband.

Ancient Illuminaries had taken the name Tantal from an even more ancient Greek myth, one of a Lydian king punished by the gods for daring to divulge their secrets. Thanatos was the name of those selfsame ancient Greeks' God of Death. Put together, Tantal Thanatos wasn't an altogether inappropriate appellation. He had overseen a lot of death during the expansion of his empire. However, he was decidedly the punishing-gods kind of third generational devil rather than the other way around: a punishing anyone else kind of Master Deva.

Methandra was once Mithras's Virgin; was that long no longer. Hadn't been, rumours to the contrary, since well before she and her immediate litter sibling became both independently and individually solid most of 4,000 years ago. She never bothered denying those rumours mostly because she rarely deigned to speak with anyone except her gregarious mate. Perhaps due to the fact she was so long a virgin, starting roughly sixty years earlier she became the first and thus far only Master Deva to have a fourth generation of devic children. Initially there were ten of them, twins, not triplets, each pair born a year after the preceding pair.

By contrast she and Tantal had only the one azura: the one, due to Sedona Spellbinder's Spell of Disproportionment, who was forced to physically bear her mother's eleventh, and last, fourth generational devil, albeit not until 5955. His twin brother was stillborn, which was why Tantal no longer acknowledged her existence. Methandra did, however. For an azura Klannit Thanatos had some very useful attributes, foremost an affinity for mirrors.

The dinky devil's attribute was Heat. Consequently, some wags referred to her sorcerer's wand as a matchstick rather than a firebrand, which she preferred. She was standing upon a floating platform akin to a flying carpet. Another purloined power focus, it had been just that, a flying carpet, when it belonged to Pretty Parsis, Byron's Enchantress and Earth Magician. Unlike Titanic Metis's cauldron, she didn't acquire it in their empire-building days. She acquired it on the same day she lost her initial batch of ten fourth generational children.

Circa twelve hundred years earlier, with much of the Hidden Continent their own, she and Tantal were without doubt the two most venerated Master Devas the Headworld had ever seen. Since the more adherents they had the more powerful devils became, they were approaching omnipotent. They anticipated, when the Smiling Fiend wasn't in their presence, that once they had reunited their family they would begin becoming that again.

"Or what, — you'll leave her?"

"I might, Smiler. But only after I've first relieved you of your head."

========

A few minutes later, the Parents Thanatos and their disruptive as well as disturbing ally, still gazing into the scarlet vapours emitting from once Metis's, now Methandra's visions-visually steaming cauldron, were in an only slightly better mood than they had been. More stuff had happened. Stuff has a habit of happening.

They'd followed Devil Wind to what they recognized as a bleak hump of a landform in the Outer Earth chain of islands and islets known as the Aleutian Archipelago. They could even recall the atoll's name: Damnation Isle. There was one on the Inner Earth as well. Smiler, whose knowledge of the Outer Earth was one of the least amazing things about him, claimed the two Damnations were once linked. Maybe they still were. Faint hope.

Disappointment followed when Devil Wind spotted a cosmicar, Cosmicar Four, on the ice-rimed islet and went into it in order to investigate what it was and what it contained. They'd always realized their children, as decathonitized devils, were going to need to possess sentient shells, at least for awhile, once they broke out of Cathonia, the Sedon Sphere, but it was empty. There weren't even any corpses of cosmicompanions left around for the Thanatoids' children to reanimate, should they have that ability. Which they might have.

Then, wonder of wonders, their despondency was replaced by emotions identical to those experienced on or near the Outer Earth's version of Centauri Island. (There was one of those on the Hidden Continent as well, albeit in Byronic territory.) Joy, jubilation, elation. One of their ten missing offspring did manifest himself. Didn't do so out of nothingness either.

Endgame, before even begin-game, Devil Wind, Vayu Maelstrom, one of Bodiless Byron's Primary Nucleoids.

"That makes four," Tantal congratulated Smiler. "Day, Earth, Air and Water."

========

Although Tantal had thousands, maybe even tens of thousand azuras by other female Master Devas, together the Parents Thanatos had only the one, their firstborn. Klannit was her name. Unlike any other Master Deva, however, they did have devils. Third generational Master Devas such as themselves were born triplets. Their fourth generational devils were born twins.

The first pair were Day and Night. The next two sets were the Four Elementals: Earth, Fire, Air and Water. The final sets of twins were the Four Seasons: Autumn, Winter, Spring and Summer. As they had with Klannit and Sedunihas – the one Klannit, occupying a Samarandin homunculus, bore in 5955 and whose twin, Motan, was stillborn – Tantal and Methandra Thanatos named them themselves. In order of their births the names they gave them were: Castella, Erebe, Antaeor, Acheron, Aires, Thalassa, Orinth, Auraura, Constantin and Veronas.

Tantal could not have expected the last one, Veronas, to have been decathonitized. He'd earned his Thanatos surname and killed him, the traitor. Thereafter, he abolished his summery season from the Frozen Isle. Which in a way accounted for why his sister-wife had a flying carpet to ride about on nowadays, almost fifty years later. He'd gone after the traitor; she'd gone after the one who turned him traitor.

Without their Tvasitar talismans Metis and Parsis were rendered insubstantial Spirit Beings again. They were both still around, though. So was Veronas, sort of, albeit only during the summer months, from mid-Azky until mid-Rudar, and then only on Freedom Beach, which lay across from the Sea of Clouds on the Cattail's mainland.

Tantal didn't know that of course. Even immediate siblings who were married to each other could keep secrets from one another.

========

"Perhaps only in appearance," cautioned Methandra suspiciously. "Antaeor's been turned into Demon Land before – after the misguided Egyptian, as I still think of the Pauper Priestess, Pyrame Silverstar, fell out with Grandfather and helped the Warlock interlopers build what they called the devil ray.

"Now that you're here beside us, Smiler, it's just occurred to me that Judge Warlock, like the Daemonicus form you animate beyond the Dome, was another of your stooges. One can only hope neither you nor that Judge were privy to the machinations of Wiccan Warlock, the Summoning Child he pretended was his bastard up until his death more than a quarter century ago. And Wiccan was a bastard, a bastard Celestial.

"As for the other three, we've seen them before, although not since the day Sedunihas was born. They've the right talismans but there's nothing new about that either. Where are their third eyes? Or, if they're not ours, how did they get their power foci? And where are Night, Fire, Spring, Autumn and Winter?"

"She's right," said her immediate sibling, fellow firstborn Mithradite, husband and Death God. "Where's our reward? Where've our efforts got us? How did we end up with Apocalyptics instead of our children? And how is it their Death, their Murder Mistress, is pregnant?"

Given the amount of devic energy he and Methandra put into corrupting the Byronics' Express project for their own jailbreak purposes, Tantal felt he had a right to better results. Thus far they'd only seen Antaeor for sure – and, as he'd already remarked, he was sure it was his Antaeor, not some devil-rayed Demon Land back again. The decathonitized rest were a two-headed, Mithras-spawned lowborn known as the Vultyrie and the four Primary Apocalyptics: Mars Bellona, Mater Matare, Carcinogen the Leper and Headless Ramazar; War, Death, Disease and Disaster.

"There's only one answer to any of that, isn't there? We're all of us victims of a Sedonplay. Our next task is to win the game."

"Grandfather's game?" Cold demanded, suddenly alarmed. "Or your game, Smiler? Like, as I too now realize, the Pauper's devaray was one of your games?"

"You speak of events nearly forty years passed, Thanatos. Circumstances were much different then. Did you not just acknowledge that was your Antaeor?"

"That I did, unless my eyes were deceiving me. Are they deceiving me now? Because it looks like Antaeor and the Apocalyptics are trying to kill the four left. What if those three are not – as you're suggesting, woman – Celestial usurpers who have somehow arrogated our children's talismans?"

"What if that Day, Air and Water are ours? They look no older than what they did when last we saw them, which would belie the theory they were akin to deviants, mortal angels. Would that also be part of your latest grand scheme, Smiler? The Apocalyptics killing them?"

"My grand scheme, Thanatos? Are you now threatening to divorce yourself from it as well as your sister-wife?" The Fiend may have been feigning outrage. It was difficult to ascribe characteristics to his never-wavering smile, though it did twist somewhat. *"Our grand scheme was intended to rescue not just your children. It was intended to rescue all of our lost brothers and sisters from the Cathonic Zone. It also anticipated every one of them returning to the Head.*

"It did not include any of them decathonitizing outside of the Dome; it did not include any of them being left without shells to possess; it did not include reconstituting devil-slayers like Blind Sundown and Raven's Head, Horrites like Cerebrus David Ryne, or any children of the History and Memory Entities. It certainly did not include freeing Lord Order from Cathonia, which has also happened, as you'd realize if your star-gazing encompassed the whole of the night's sky, not just Constellation Thanatos.

"In short, yes, things have to a degree gone awry. There's no denying that. Nor is there any denying that cosmic forces -- be they Sedonic, Celestial, or what-

ever -- are conspiring both with us and against us. As I say, though, we must now set our minds, and our abilities, to making the best of the mess presented us."

"In short, Smiler, you buggered up royally."

"Be fair, husband," urged Methandra. "Smiler hasn't so much buggered up as given us new challenges, new opportunities to exploit. In his own way, he has helped revitalize the entire devazur species. We must see this as a new beginning. For the good of all and the greater glory of devazurkind."

"Admirable sentiments indeed, wife. Where's my ale? If I'm going to be cosmically forced to sit here and watch four of my children go at each other along with five of our younger siblings and some obviously Brainrock-blessed humanoid wearing crimson goggles and a rubber seal-suit that looks like something a Selkie left behind in Twilight, I might as well do it drunk."

"Nothing new about that either, Thanatos." If the fiend's smile had been one of wryness moments earlier it was now more of a smirk.

"Be silent, both of you," insisted Heat coolly. "Smiler may be more familiar with the ones Antaeor densified and possessed out there, the ones who finished off Devil Wind. But even as alcohol-addled as you usually are, husband, you remember them as well as I do. Whatever else they may be, you can't deny they individually and collectively possess spectacular abilities; abilities we may be able to turn to our advantage.

"Let me concentrate. If this Water is our Water, there may yet be a way to win this hand of whomever's new game we've been dealt. And, if the two Damnation Islands are still linked, there may even be a way to get everyone back to the Head. If not, well, the colossal faerie wearing the Thrygragos Talismans Antaeor has hold of now got outside once, so maybe he can get inside, too."

An iceman brought King Cold a prodigious stein full of enough ale to jar even Lathakra's god-devil out of any semblance of his howsoever momentarily regained sobriety. One thing that never had to be said about the Frozen Isle was you needed ambulatory snowmen and ice-statuary to keep your lubricant of choice chilled.

Even though he didn't much like ale, Jordan Tethys would have been happy here.

========

The Inner Earth of Sedon's Head was a continental landform about the size of Africa. It was situated within what amounted to its own dimension centred on the Outer Earth's for the most part landless North Pacific Ocean. The dimension itself was called variously: Cathonia, the Cathonic Zone or Dome, the Sedon Sphere. It had been in existence since the Genesea, the Great Flood of Genesis, an event that occurred 5,980 years earlier. The Hidden Continent was shaped like a human head, left-side perspective. The Moloch Sedon wasn't human. He was the Devil.

Was, put better, the inspiration for the Devil. Perhaps.

========

The enormous, south-westernmost territory on the Lower Head was the subcontinent of Aka Godbad. From north to south it consisted of the Head's mouth, lower teeth, lower lip, lower jaw and its goatee. From west to east Crepuscule, the Grey Land of Twilight, where dwelled faeries, was its Outer Nose. The Bloodlands,

New Valhalla, the Land of the Militant Dead, where corpses were animated by symbiotic Sangazurs, was its Inner Nose.

Marutia was Sedon's Cheek. Hadd, the Land of the Ambulant Dead, was Sedon's left Sideburn, his Mutton Chop or, as it was known due to its likeness to something else, the Penile Peninsula. The Cattail Peninsula was Sedon's Ponytail. The Frozen Isle of Lathakra was a sizeable chunk of metaphoric dandruff laying off the Cattail's east coast. Although it more like resembled Aegean Crete than Japan, it was the Head's Land of the Rising Sun.

Their unaged bodies reunited with their minds, ten supranormals emerged from a quarter century in what they'd come to consider Limbo on the Outer Earth's Damnation Isle. Perhaps fatalistically their nominal leader unilaterally decided to name the group of them the Damnation Brigade, after the Aleutian atoll where they'd been so rudely thrust into this Limbo of theirs on Christmas Day 1955. Ringleader, Dr Aristotle Zeross, and Demios Sarpedon, Blackguard or the Ace of Spades, were beyond the Dome as well.

Beneath the Dome, Saladin born Nauroz, aka Devason, the Master of Weir, lived in Skyrise, an Outer-Earth-modern skyscraper off the great central square of Cabalarkon City proper. Apple Isle in the Gulf of Corona was the pupil of Sedon's Human Eye. The Weirdom of Cabalarkon was over a thousand miles north, in Sedon's Forehead. Cabalarkon, the place, was Sedon's Devic Eye-Land. At least one of its buildings was antediluvian.

Sal's year younger sister, Morgianna born Nauroz, become Somata, then – and for the last 30-years – Sarpedon, was visiting Petrograd, the capital city of New Iraxas, a Godbadian province. Among those she was with count Scylla Nereid, Lady Achigan Auranja, the marital queen of Godbad, who'd been deposed at the end of the Godbadian Civil War of, mostly, the Fifties.

Morg, Superior Sarpedon, was also called the Morrigan. Lady Achigan was also called Fisherwoman or just plain Fish. They were friends; had known each other, on both sides of the Dome, for most of sixty years. Neither looked anywhere near their age. They wouldn't. Morg was a hybrid Utopian. Utopians aged slowly compared to humans and, indeed, most other sentient beings.

Fish was a deviant; had at least one half-parent who was a devil. She was amphibious, a Melusine Piscine. In that she was akin to Morgan Abyss, the Thanatoids' to this day never forgotten and, hence, much reviled Death's Head Hellion, the Master of Weir who effectively brought an end to their Lathakran Empire in the Dome's 48th Century. Both Morg and Fish were top-shelf witches; might be the best witches alive.

Sal and Morg had the same parents. Their mother was possessed by a Master Deva when he was conceived; hence Devason. A couple of faerie farts, as they referred to themselves, Young Life and Young Death, claimed to be what had become of their parents, Pandora Mannering and Augustus Nauroz respectively. Young Life could be anywhere on the planet. Young Death was on Sraddha Isle, in Hadd, the Land of the Dead.

So were the Sraddhites' High Priest, Thartarre Sraddha Holgatson, Field Leader Garcia Dis L'Orca, an Athenan War Witch, and Field Commander Golgotha Nauroz, a Trinondev, one of Weir's Warriors Elite. Athenans were supposed to worship Mediterranean Athena, the Thanatoids' Mother Methandra. Some of them were Hecate-Hellions. They worshiped Mother Earth. Golgotha was an 80-year-old clone. He was cloned from Sal and Morg's paternal grandfather, Ubris Nauroz. During the Simultaneous Summonings of 19/5980 Ubris had been turned; became a vampire. Jordan Tethys, in a previous incarnation, had dusted him.

Superior Sarpedon had two children, daughters: one, the youngest, Andaemyn, Andy, by Demios; the other, Tsishah, by a faerie fart, Tom-Tiddly Taddletale. Tsishah, Sea-Saw as Fish called her, was with Fish and her mother Morg in Petrograd. Andy was in the Crystal Mountain Range, in the Upper Head's far-eastern Occipital Regions, just north of Sedon's Hairband. Andy was travelling with a band of mercenaries who called themselves the Good Companions.

Their leader was 130-years-old, didn't look to be much older than his midforties. He too was a deviant; had extraordinary recuperative abilities. Two of those with them were fifty. They were sisters, two-thirds what was once a set of Japanese-looking triplets, the other one not only being dead but gone, dust. Another of those with them was a Dead Man Walking. He was Gypsium-gifted and possessed of a symbiotic Sangazur.

Haddit Zombies, for the most part once living Iraches, who were ethnically related to North, Central, and South American aboriginals, were kept going by different kinds of azuras; very few of them Sangs. Some found work in New Iraxas primarily because its air and water were so polluted no one alive could work there very long or very hard. Thanks to Alpha Centauri and Centauri Enterprises, which relied on its petroleum products, Dead Things in the workforce were now in the minority. That fact had been causing considerable labour and social unrest of late.

At first the Dead Things' vampiric overseers didn't mind Living Things, humans for the most part, working alongside Dead Things in New Iraxas since it meant they didn't have to go so far to hunt for their supper. The Living didn't object to Dead Things because they maintained themselves on much the same food as they did. They did object to being food for the Undead, however. Consequently, Centauri Enterprises had put a bounty on bloodsuckers. It was payable in Godbucks, Godbad's currency. The bounty paid was based on weight. It had to be. Besides witnesses, how else could you prove you'd killed a vamp if you didn't bag its dust?

Folks cheated. The governor of New Iraxas, Ferdinand Niarchos, had brought in a talented deviant to aid him in assessing how much in the way of Godbucks he should authorize paying bat-bounty-hunters. The talented deviant was Jordan Tethys. He was drinking beer. Unbeknownst to him Janna Fangfingers was nearby. She too was drinking.

North of Petrograd was the Forbidden Forest of Kala Tal, Sedon's Moustache and Lower Lip Hairs. There persisted the lone devic vampire. She looked up into the Sedon Sphere. There were dozens of stars missing from the night's sky; she'd known most of the personally, more than a couple even intimately. There was also a shooting star. It crashed nearby. She sent her Cloud General, a gargantuan, semi-sentient vulture, to investigate it.

At that moment, no one on either side of the Cathonic Dome could tell anyone else where they could locate the Thrice-Cursed Godly Glories better known as the Trigregos Talismans. They were a curved blade, a framed mirror and a bloodstone tiara. No matter what they appeared to made out of all three were composed of teleportive as well as transmutable Brainrock-Gypsium.

A good percentage of why no one knew where they were right then was hardly anyone cared what had become of them over the centuries. Some who did included Sal, Morg and Ringleader. They thought the Sraddhites' High Priest had the Amateramirror, as the mirror was known traditionally. For his part, Thartarre thought Janna Fangfingers had it. Another who cared about where they were was Warlord Mikoto, the 130-year-old samurai-deviant leading Andy and the so-called Good Companions.

He thought the curved blade, the Susasword, was somewhere in the Crystal Mountains. He wanted it. Find one of the three Sacred Objects, it would lead to the other two. The Trigregos Talismans could kill devils. Mikoto wanted them in order to kill his devic half-father and thereafter rule his protectorate, Subcranial Temporis, as its Kronokronos Supreme. The hybrid Utopian siblings, Morg and Sal, both born Nauroz, wanted them so they could be replicated; whereupon they could be used to kill devils.

Ringleader wanted them to make his wife happy. His wife was a Utopian pureblood, the High Illuminary of Weir. Her name was Melina. She was Demios Sarpedon's twin sister. Fish didn't want anything to do with them. She'd fallen under the influence of one of them, the tiara, the Crimson Corona, in the past. She knew they were trouble. Anyone who played a Trigregos Gambit lost.

Jordan *'Q for Quill'* Tethys just wanted to finish his beer in peace.

========

Via the Nag Gap, Nag for Nagasaki, the Inner Earth's Godbadian-based Centauri Enterprises clandestinely imported a wide variety of products manufactured exclusively on the Outer Earth. Among these imports were long-playing, stereophonic records. Alpha Centauri was fond of a singer-songwriter who went by the pseudonym of Bob Dylan. Tethys liked his songs, not his singing.

One of Dylan's best known songs was 'The Times They Are A-Changing'.

****

(Pregame-Gambit) 2: **The Deviant Dead**

Sedonda, Maruta 30, 5980

The legendary 30-Year Man didn't so much dislike ale as it was well down his list of preferred malt beverages. He didn't particularly dislike any of the Thanatoids either. Sooth said, which being a taleteller he always strove to do, he'd completed a couple of full, 30-year life-allotments whilst covering the expansion of their empire in the 4700s and into the early 4800s. He had plenty of tales to tell as a result of them as well.

What he did dislike was wearing a garlic necklace.

========

Jordan Tethys was a scruffy looking fellow with a stubble beard and thinning, reddish-blond hair. He made his living telling stories; hence one of his nicknames: the Legendarian. He was wearing his favourite tweed jacket and a checked cap. Like him both jacket and cap had seen better days.

Underneath the cap, stuck to his scalp by their own gluey ichors, were a half-dozen tee-tee-tails. Tee-tees were talking rodents. He could also read the ridges and nodules of their tails, which contained tales. Pierced into his cap was what appeared to be an ordinary feathered quill. Appearances were deceiving. It was made of Brainrock-Gypsium, the miraculous Godstuff, the post Big Bang remnants of the Primordial Godhead, that, besides being teleportive and transmutable, composed devic power foci.

The Legendarian looked to be of an indeterminate age, anywhere from his early thirties to his mid forties. Physically his body was only 32-years-old. He lived rough, often in the streets; treated his bodies disrespectfully. At the most he could only hold onto them for 30 years; hence another of his nicknames: the 30-Year Man. At the earliest he could only get into them when they'd been around for 20 years.

This particular body had been, more so than belonged to, George Taurson. George had always been sickly; had died. Tethys had taken it over when he did; made it healthy again. That was an oddity of his deviancy, one of a number. George was his son. He'd been doing that sort of thing for going on 2,000 years.

Tethys claimed he was born of an ordinary man and woman around the start of the Outer Earth's Christian era. The one that he knew of for sure was possessed by a Master Deva when he'd been conceived as well as born. He said his devic half-mother was Metisophia, the iconoclastic Lazaremist whose Brainrock cauldron Methandra Thanatos now owned. Although in its absence she was bodiless, if you asked it, she wouldn't deny it.

He denied he was a devil, although he did have a scar in his forehead about where a devil's third eye would be. Significantly none of his offspring, or their offspring, had a scar in their forehead until he incarnated within them. Two incarnations ago he was a woman. She was a nun. She was also a tippler. He, even as a she, drank a lot of beer. Hence his third major nickname: 30-Beers.

He was doing that now.

========

After a short sleep, and a much shorter flight from Aka Godbad City, he was in Petrograd, the coastal capital of New Iraxas, the subcontinent of Godbad's northeasternmost province. Across the Gulf of Aka from New Iraxas was Old Iraxas, Hadd, the Land of the Ambulant Dead as well as living Iraches. He was in Petrograd as a guest of Ferdinand Niarchos, the provincial governor as well as one of the most influential figures within Centauri Enterprises, the Corporate State of Greater Godbad's real power. CE, Centauri Enterprises, was named after its founder, Alpha Centauri. Alpha Centauri was not his real name.

The Fatman, so-called, often to his face, because he was well-north of 400 pounds, was Tethys's patron in Aka Godbad. They often drank together. Indeed, they'd been drinking together until the early hours most of yesterday, the 29th of Maruta. The Fatman liked his stories and, in terms of length, Tethys had told him a whopper: 'Janna Fangfingers' or 'The Disunition of the Unities'.

It wasn't a whopper in terms of verisimilitude, however. Even though the events he told him about took place five centuries ago, some of its characters were still around. One of them often used the Fatman as his shell. That was Thrygragos Byron. Another was Tethys himself. A third and a fourth were the Terrible Twins, Janna and Sraddha Somata. Well, the male of the two may not be around anymore. However, the female of the two still had a Crystal Skull attached to the torc she perpetually wore around her neck. It might contain Sraddha's soul.

Tethys wasn't the only one who referred to the governor as Weird Ferd. The largely CE-owned media-paparazzi often did as well. Even though he never bothered to get married, Ferd had plenty of children. Some of them probably belonged to his father Gomez. In the decades the subcontinent was still a monarchy, one ruled by an aristocracy, Gomez was the hereditary Duke of the Duchy of Aka Godbad.

Thanks in large measure to Alpha Centauri, the subcontinent was nowadays a nominal democracy, the Corporate State of Greater Godbad. Thanks mostly to Tethys himself, Gomez was now dead and possessed of a Sangazur Spirit Being, Guardian Angel Gomez. Father and son still talked, usually via Crystal Skull-sets. Gomez was still fertile. His children were fully alive. The pollution of New Iraxas was nonetheless preferable to trying to raise kids in the Bloodlands. Sedon's Inner Nose wasn't called New Valhalla for nothing. In New Valhalla sibling rivalry was a blood sport.

Although Weird Ferd hadn't required of him any Tethys Tales as partial payment for his room and board, he had required of him some backward drawing. Backward-drawing was one of Tethys's talents. With it the Legendarian had thereby confirmed Ferd's suspicions re Irache capitalism. Yes indeed, as well as in deed, folks cheated. Living Irache vampire-hunters had been gathering the powdered remains of freshly dusted Marutian or Sraddhite fat-cat bats and passing them off as two or three dusted, oppressed underclass, Irache vamps in order to collect a triple bounty from Centauri Enterprises.

Somewhat disquietingly, though it turned out Ferd had suspected this as well, the Irache bounty-hunters got their information as to the whereabouts of non-Irache fat-cat bats from scrawny Irache bats. He'd been particularly displeased when one of Tethys's backward-drawings filled in with the familiar face and form of Night Owl, the chief Irache vampire in New Iraxas. While Night Owl was hardly the most imaginative of names, Night Owl was a very hardy vamp. He'd been around since the Simultaneous Summonings of 19/5920 and, as Tethys himself was fond of saying, he had his-stories; one of which was how he got himself fused with Titanic Metis.

He also had a pair of twin sons, both of whom were now dead and non-risen, a wife who died having them, whereupon she became a Lamia, which meant she had to be dealt with more terminally later on, and a deviant heritage. Which meant he was very difficult to deal with himself, though both Ferd and Tethys thought he had been. Until yesterday, that is, when he and Mama Metis jointly showed up in Tethys's public spaces suite in the Fatman's Aka Godbad fortress. In doing so, he-they drove away the vampire who'd turned him, pre-Metis.

Something else about Night Owl was he chewed garlic. He did so because said vamp, Second Fangs, Janna Fangfingers, found the smell of garlic appalling and when one of your sons was her mortal enemy, emphasis on '*was*', his own discomfort was a small price to pay to keep her off his back. Or at least keep her too distant to rip out his backbone with her fang-fingered glove.

Born Janna Somata, in 5456 Year of the Dome, Second Fangs and twin brother Sraddha were two of the non-devic main characters in his rendition of '*The Disunition of the Unities*'. The Terrible Twins were deviants. Their birth parents were hybrid Utopians, Zalman and Melina Somata. Paternally their devic half-grandfather was Lord Yajur, the Unity of Order; maternally their devic half-mother was Datong Harmonia, the Unity of Harmony or Balance. Even more significantly their devic half-father was Great Googly-Woogly – none other than Thrygragos Lazareme himself.

Most believed the third Unity, Unholy Abaddon, Abe Chaos, using a Trigregos Talisman, the Susasword, had killed Harmony in 5492. Certainly neither the Female Unity nor the curved, Brainrock blade had been seen since then. Chaos cathonitized Order, rendered him a star in the night's sky, on the Prison Beach of Incain in 5495.

He thereafter committed devic suicide by cutting out his third eye. Actually it was far more brutal than even that. He drove the central prong of his trident, the hilt and sheathe of his Chaos Blade, through his third eye. His debrained daemonic body dissolved, Brainrock trident with it; his remains blowing out to sea. Tethys was there, saw it happen. More than just chances were he was still around somewhere, though. No one knew where; probably no one cared where either.

Tethys was glad Ferd gave him a garlic necklace when he decided to leave the governor's staid domicile in order take a walk and taste the remarkably breathable night air of Petrograd. It wasn't just the night air he wanted to taste either. Now that a majority of altogether alive workers from Godbad proper were living here on a daily basis there were some great public bars in Petrograd. Too bad he'd chosen one that didn't have garlic garlands strung around its doors and windows. Vamps were public too.

Garlic wouldn't do any good against Night Owl but right now it was certainly keeping Second Fangs far enough away for him to finish his getaway drawing. Which he did. It wasn't perfect but it'd be good enough.

"Oh, don't be in such a rush to flush, Tethys," she fay-said, sauntering up to his table. "At least have another beer; for old times' sake if nothing else."

"Sorry, Fangs, but I'm particular about who I drink with. I hate being the person who's drunk. Or haven't I mentioned that to you before?"

"I expect you have." She sat down unbidden. "Waitress, another beer for my friend here."

The bar had become noticeably emptier the moment she walked in, all in white. Sleeveless cloak, stylish crewneck blouse and pleated skirt cut just below the knee, hose or leggings, stiletto-heeled boots, even the strip of white cloth she wore about her throat, like the Brainrock torc her devic half-mother wore about her neck, was white. The cameo attached to it wasn't, however. He wasn't sure cameo was the right for the ornament but he knew what it looked like: a crystalline skull. Very charming. And ever so appropriate for a vampire.

One thing he'd never quite figured out, despite nearly twenty centuries worth of incarnations, was how vamps could shape-shift clothes or jewellery out of their bat-forms. He supposed it had something to do with them being soulless demons. Not that most demons wore clothes they manufactured. Those that didn't go naked tended to wear the clothes of those they ate. Still, one of these nights he hoped to see a bat, in a bat form, wearing a dress, tux or cape as if it was about to attend the opera.

Second Fangs was all white herself. Being originally a Utopian hybrid, she always had been, hair and flesh; though the former was, technically speaking, more silvery than whitish. Her lips and teeth were red, however, while her furry, fang-fingered glove was dripping. "Nothing for me, I've already had my fill for the night."

"So I noticed," he said. Her Brainrock glove was drenched with blood.

The glove was once the power focus of First Fangs, a foppish Master Deva prone to wearing, yes, opera capes. A lowborn Lazaremist antique Illuminaries named Faustus Vladuca after some obscure figures from East European folklore, at one point in time Janna married him; something mortals rarely did devils. (Except, that is, when the latter were possessing the spouse they did marry.) Her actual lover, Abe Chaos, first acquired it for her – the Fop's hand still inside it – when she was altogether alive.

"Been meaning to ask what happened to your third eye?" he asked, friendly like.

Illuminaries dated the First War between the Living and the Dead from the birth of Janna's lone offspring, Johann-Georg Somata-Faust, in 5480 until his death in 5538. During it – on New Years Eve 5492/3, to be precise – Tethys had the misfortune of being killed by his Uncle Abe Chaos. Almost immediately thereafter, he had the howsoever dubious fortune of being possessed and thereby reanimated by a symbiotic Fatazur, a spirit being he still referred to as Guardian Angel Jordan. He decided further that Guardian Angel Jordan was his own half-brother in that his devic half-father, Rumour of Lazareme, was the azura's father by Fata Fortuna, Dame Chance.

At various times over the course of the next two-plus years, Janna Somata, by then Second Fangs, possessed both Nergal Vetala, the Vampire Queen of the Dead, and the Legendarian's consequential, immediate half-aunt Irisiel Mercherm, Lazareme's female heliodromus or sun-runner. Although he was never sure which one she had when she did so, on the Summer Solstice of 5495, either Janna-Vetala or Janna-Irisiel definitely eyefire-burned Guardian Angel Jordan out of existence, thus ending that particular Squiggly of an exceedingly eventful incarnation.

"Oh, I haven't had one of those for absolutely ages; decades and decades much more so than years and years. That an Illuminary star-chart sticking out of your satchel?" She didn't expect an answer. She knew what it was and that was what it was, an Illuminary star-chart.

"Not much use tonight, is it? I'm pretty sure Star Belialma's still up there but there's some big ones missing." (Belialma was Lady Lust, a onetime Prime Sinistral of Satanwyck, Hell on Earth, which was where demonic vampires presumably originated at some unknown time in the past. Janna had hold of her, too, for a while – for sure on that selfsame New Years Eve of 5492/3, when Chaos topped the Squiggly Legendarian, but more likely months earlier.)

"So there is," he agreed, finishing off his beer. He hated to drink and run; not that he'd be running as such.

"Lord Order's the biggest one in the Lazaremist Quadrant but there's an equally significant one missing over in the Mithradic Quadrant. Phantast Thanatos is no piker either." (Star Phantast had been in the night's sky for going on 2,000 years. Tethys blamed him for his first death.) "From the looks of it, the entire Constellation Thanatos has vanished. So that's got me in conspiracy theorist mode. Non-Lazaremist firstborns tend to stick together."

(Called by devils Dream or Dreamweaver – because weaving dreams for others was his attribute – and hence considered a Death God, one of many, Phantast was a firstborn Mithradite. Methandra and Tantal were the other two. The Silverclouds, Rufous Rudra and Lunar Uma, who were as married as Heat and Cold, were Byron's remaining firstborn. Their third, immediate sibling – a female Illuminaries named Serathrone Hallow after they heard her-story multiple millennia after her last sighting in the Celestial Sphere – never made it to the Whole Earth, either pre-Genesea or since. Of them, only Dream had ever been cathonitized.

(For most of their existence the Lazaremist firstborn stuck together too; so long as Harmony, Datong Harmonia, the Unity of Balance, Second Fangs' devic half-mother, was around to stick herself between her two brothers, the Unities of Order and Chaos, that is to say. Once she wasn't, they forgot the togetherness part and started trying to stick it to each other; Unholy Abaddon being more successful in that department than his fellow triplet.)

The waitress was bringing him another pilsner. He eyeballed her. It was a different waitress than the one who'd been serving him earlier. This one wasn't wearing a garlic necklace whereas the previous one had been. She also had black skin whereas her predecessor was an Irache redskin. Her skin colour didn't mean much; there were plenty of women with black skin in Godbad. Mind you, he thought to himself, tapping the tip of his Brainrock quill against his drawing, there were plenty of women from Marutia who had black skin, too.

That her head was shaven did mean something. Only Sraddhites shaved their heads bald and Sraddhites weren't very popular in New Iraxas. That she put the beer down in front of Fangs, skewing her nose as she did so, meant something as well. He squiggled his name on the bottom of the drawing but held off doing his getaway dot. He could as easily drink one-handed as he could dot his drawing with the other one.

"Really, Tethys," Fangfingers, who knew him for the deviant he was, re-proached him for readying his getaway, "I'm disappointed in you. We're old pals, you and I. Besides, I haven't turned everyone left in this room. Some of the Iraches Night Owl turned are no more offended at the smell of garlic than he is, which is to say not so much so as mine. And enough of them are as pissed off at him as I am. Bats shouldn't rat on bats, even fat-cat bats."

Using her glowing glove she shoved the beer mug across the table to within easy reach. He was tempted. She was tempting him; mesmerizing him, put bet-ter. "In other words," he appreciated, taking it by its handle, "I was as dead as you wanted me to be. Which isn't at all, right? Not right away anyways." He took a sip. Beer would be the death of him yet. Again, make that.

"Why'd you come here, Fangs? What is it you really want – a drawing of Night Owl? Ferd did too: where he was during the daytime; then where he was after dark. Except, well, you saw him coming at you last night in Aka Godbad City. Which is why you buggered off so rudely, not to mention quickly. And you must know I wouldn't be drawing just him – I'd also be drawing my devic half-mom, who wouldn't take kindly to being, um, drawn out on behalf of one such as you.

"Besides, as much as the Wily Owl's as much my old pal as you are – albeit not so much so old, I'll grant you – and as much as, you know, I'm such a big bat-lover, it seems he's his spies just as you've your spies. Only his spies got word to him during the daytime. Furthermore, it seems that, no doubt due in part to my half-mother, he's become more of a shape-shifter than most of you bats are already. Sorry to dis-appoint, Janna."

"Janna's nice, Jordy. No one's called me that for centuries." Tethys couldn't recall the last time she called him Jordy either. She'd always blamed him for killing his son, the *'Q for Squiggly'* Legendarian, her then beloved betrothed all those same centuries ago. The truth of that matter was Squigs died from a Turk's sword thrust through the gullet whilst adventuring on the Outer Earth in the company of her twin brother, Sraddha *'Shreds'* Somata.

"I'm perfectly capable of fighting my own battles," she carried on, cutting to the chase. "Always have been, as you should recall. I'll find Wily Old eventually, no matter what shapes he and your Mommy Dearest can take nowadays. Those stars you mentioned, I didn't realize Phantast and the rest of Constellation Thanatos were missing I did, however, realize three others were, one in each quadrant: Star Straw-Man, Star Shovelful and Star First Fangs.

"And even I can't fight them all at once, can I? So, yes, I want a drawing from you; one of a certain Tvasitar Talisman."

Tethys pretended to mishear her meaning. He flipped some pages back on the sketchpad he'd been working on all day. Most of them needed their backgrounds filling in, then his signature and dotting, but otherwise they were finished products. He ripped off three of the sheets, the ones where he'd done drawings of the Trigregos Talismans: the Amateramirror, the Crimson Corona and the Susasword.

He drew them as he last saw them, not as he first saw them – which, he'd remembered while turning down a similar request from the Fatman, Alpha Centauri, a couple of days ago, was actually on Thrygragon. He was in a booze tent run by one of his ex-wives of a few lifetimes earlier by that time of that Mithramas day.

The table cloth he'd drawn them on went up in flames then too. So did the booze tent. So much for another lifetime. He could never quite remember how many he went through on Thrygragon but it was a few. He'd married many, many women over the centuries – married many a man, too, when he was a woman – but never before nor since had so many gathered in one place. At least he kept coming back. Thrygragos Varuna Mithras never did.

Poising his quill to dot whichever one she chose, he continued to feign innocence. "You're hardly the only one. Which one do you want?"

She scowled at him. Then she smiled, too toothily for his taste, unfinished beer or no unfinished beer. "Nice try, dickhead. You reckon you can get away that easily? In a puff of smoke no less. That's my trick. One of them anyhow. I know what'll happened if you dot any one of those things. The sheet will burst into flames. No, my lad. I'm quicker than that. And so are they."

The Petrograd beer hall had always been smoke-filled. Most taverns were; except in Aka-Godbad City, that is. Smokeless bars were another of the Fatman's recent innovations in the name of 'greening'. So distracted was he, though, he hadn't realized the smoke in the bar, particularly around his table, had become a whole lot thicker than it had been before Second Fangs walked into the bar.

(Which was something else he'd always wondered about vampires. How could they travel about as mist? A decent fart would blow them away, wouldn't it?)

Then they had him, her vamps, demystifying out of all that smoke. Had him, arms pinned back against the chair, his quill shaken out of his grip onto the table-top and his garlic necklace torn off and tossed against the wall, before he could dot a ditto to any of his getaway pages. Second Fangs leaned forward. Her breath was fetid. Nothing new about that. She licked her lips then bared her fangs. Nothing new about either of that either.

"Maybe I'm still thirsty, dearest, latest, incarnation of my first living lover. Maybe I'm not. But they are, my bats. Then again, another of your howsoever recent pals, CE's Fatman, has been providing us, day by day, with fresh food, night by night. So, here's what you can do for me, 30-Years, if you want your 30 beers. You can draw me a Tvasitar Talisman, a trident, you know the one, and I won't have to fight all of my battles all by myself. Abe Chaos could never say no to me."

The nib of his Brainrock quill no longer just perceptibly glowed. It ignited instead; began to glow as brightly as a miniature sunburst. About time too, thought Tethys, having had enough sense to close his eyes, both of them, just before it did so. When he opened them again, the smoke in the barroom was even thicker and Athenan War Witches were all about the place, gathering up dust. They were bounty-hunters, too, although unlike capitalistic Iraches they'd have done it for free.

One of them was Morgianna Sarpedon, the Athenans' so-called Grandmother Superior, the Hellions' Morrigan as well. Her birth name was Nauroz but when Morg's great-grandmother, Kyprian Somata, the then Master of Weir, adopted her she changed her maiden name to her own – Somata also being Janna Fangfingers' birth name. They were in fact directly, via Kyprian's daughter (Morg's grandmother) Chryseis therefore born Somata, if distantly, by a few centuries, related.

There was also, strictly speaking, nothing dead about her. Probably was something daemonic about her, though. The Morrigan may have been an honourific but it came with certain horrific perks, one of which was an invisible, debrained demon. Of course she'd had to earn it and part of earning it meant de-braining it.

She congratulated him. "Well done, Jordy, though I have to wonder why you were so slow on the dotting. Good thing Sister Scylla here doesn't trust anyone. Otherwise you would have been well-done-for."

"Things are missing, mother," said Morg's daughter, the eldest of two, Tsishah Twilight, Shenon's non-Lemurian Aortic.

She was another one wearing a demon. Her demon wasn't invisible. It made her look like a red-skinned Irache, not a pureblood Utopian. Which Morgianna very nearly was; it was only her mother, Pandora Mannering, who had mixed blood. Her father, Augustus Nauroz, was as pure as the driven snow; if there was such a thing as pure black snow, driven or otherwise.

"Her Crystal Skull and the fang-figured glove, where are they?"

"She got away," said one of the other Athenans there, Janna St Peche-Montressor, Alpha Centauri's daughter-in-law, who'd also been on hand last night when Janna Fangfingers sought to get him to draw Abe Chaos to her the first time. Rather, she'd been in the same building, father-in-law Fatman's residence-cum-fortress in Aka Godbad City.

This Janna's maiden name sounded French because it was; albeit Inner Earth French. She hailed from Dukkha, on the Coast of Fearsome Fobbiat, on the edge of Sedon's Moustache, his hairy Upper Lip. Before he became Tom-Tiddly Taddletale, a recurring faerie-type, Tammuz Rhymer, Tsishah's father, was born and raised in the same place.

The second half of her surname sort of did, too. But that was because, during the Godbadian Civil War, Centauri had to foster out his son, whose first name was Yataghan, to a family whose last name was Montressor. She'd married him some years back; was the father of Yat's lone child, a girl by the decidedly non-French-sounding name of Gudrun.

Other than many of the Mantel replicas of Subcranial Temporis, only Dukkhans had as their birth-tongue a language different from Sedon Speak; pre-Babel Babble as Tethys called it. How that came about was one of the post-Disunition stories he'd have told the Fatman, Governor Niarchos and this Janna last night, had he had the time.

"And you know that because you're named after her?" queried Witch Isle's other Aortic, the amphibious, Lemurian Frog Woman of the two.

Aortic Amphitrite was being sarcastic. She was also wearing a Mandroid guard-body as opposed to a debrained demon; was more squished into it than wearing it, sooth said, like a humanoid frog preserved in amber. It kept her sprayed with ordinary, as in non-vampiric mist. Like Morgianna she was a Summoning Child, which meant she was approaching her sixtieth birthday. That was old for a Lemurian. Soon she'd have to submerge herself beneath the Head's Interior Ocean of Akadan permanently.

The only reason she hadn't done so already, she'd told him this afternoon, was because her deviant daughter Lakshmi, who lived in Subcranial Temporis, way up north, beneath Sedon's Cranium, was first of all turning eighteen this Lazam, Friday on the Outer Earth. Then, second of all, the very next day, Devauray or Saturday, she was getting married to a much older man, one Centurion Sophiscient by name. Jordy was of course invited.

Since Temporis was one of his favourite places on the Whole Head, even if the Thousand Caverns of Tariqartha were actually in its underside, and since he knew all the parties involved, he said he wouldn't miss it for the world. Then he'd agreed to this hair-brained scheme Ferd and the Athenans put to him and his world very nearly ended, at least for the time being.

Which was why he whirled to rail at the eldest witch there.

She was Amphitrite's slightly older step-sister, the one the others, her-stories all of them, deferred to even though she wasn't in any position of authority over them. She'd once been the Queen of Godbad, though, and still was the Duchess of Achigan, the dukedom at the tip of Sedon's Lower Lip. Like Amphitrite she was amphibious, albeit with her gills discretely placed behind her ears instead of in her neck.

That meant she was Piscine rather than Lemurian; made her akin to a Melusine Piscine like the fabled Death's Head Hellion of so many centuries ago; the Master of Weir who caused both the Ghostlands and the Thanatoids of Lathakra to sink into their thousand year sleep – although, strictly speaking, it was more like an 1100-year-sleep.

Melusine Piscines being the probable inspiration for mermaids, one of them, it also made her an exotic form of human being; exotic in every sense of the word, including erotic. As much as he found Living Janna as irresistible, albeit in a living way, as he had been finding the Undead Janna irresistible in a potentially deathly way, this witch was still by far the best looking of the lot who'd come to his rescue.

That she was a deviant, like him and Amphitrite's Lakshmi, only partially explained how she managed to hold onto her looks. Her human forbearers were very good looking as well. Not that he got any of them. Then again, once he incarnated in them, the boys much more so than girls, who didn't lose their hair, started to look more like him than they looked liked themselves.

That she wielded three Brainrock power foci, one of which, what she called her soul-net, had extremely coercive qualities to it, had nothing to do with how she'd convinced him to go along with tonight's idiocy. Like Abe Chaos to Janna Somata, in all the incarnations he'd known her, which was all of the incarnations he'd had this century, he'd never been able to say no to her.

He couldn't say no to her even when she was just a little girl digging large, disturbingly penile geoducks on Shenon, Witch Isle, for Merthetis, her adoptive mother – who eventually became the heart-shaped island's Lemurian Aortic, a position now held by her Summoning Child daughter, nearing sixty Amphitrite.

(Frog Women were rarely confused with mermaids but the Legendarian had always been an equal opportunity Lothario. Despite her addiction to the mannish molluscs, he found Merthetis unaccountably attractive, so he used to go to Shenon in order meet her for purposes purely puerile, as he playfully put it. That particular incarnation rivalled, and probably exceeded, the Squiggly-him he'd told Alpha Centauri about yesterday when it came to his-stories.)

Neither had his current incarnation George Taurson, he sort of remembered, when he was just a little boy and she – by then a beauty fully grown, including the sharpness of her incisors, which matched her wit – came by Apple Isle for one of her infrequent visits there. (Fisherwoman and the Korant Corn Queens' Miracle Maenad George Taurson called mom may not have been bosom buddies but they shared the same bosom, albeit almost a decade apart and with a different Master Deva lactating said breast milk behind the scenes, as it were.)

After what he just been through, he could envisage saying no to her now. He felt sure of that; told her as much as well. "That's the last time I let you use me as bat-bait, Fish-Witch."

"Oh, do clam the oyster-shuck up, Jordan River," the exotic retorted. "At least you're still altogether alluvial alive. And that's albacore-more than I can say about my nephew."

He hated it when she called him that, but she was right. Auntie Fish didn't just have fish-stories, she had bilge buckets brimming over with them. And in a convoluted way his current incarnation did indeed live out his life as her nephew. He might live out his death as well, if a Sangazur or Fatazur or some such symbiotic spirit being got hold of this body after he, the Legendarian, passed on to his next 30-year-lifetime.

He flipped a page, dotted a getaway-drawing, took himself elsewhere.

========

For the three Master Devas on Lathakra tuned into the Outer Earth's version of Damnation Isle, via the scarlet fumes of Miss Myth's purloined cauldron, the day and thereafter the night of the 30th of Maruta, YD 5980 – the 30th of November, AD 1980 out there – the hand dealt them did not play out as perfectly as they hoped it would. It nevertheless did surprisingly well.

They had not as yet won any game they'd been forced into participating in by whomever, by whatever, but they were very much still in it, any and all of those games.

========

Time to pay the piper? Not quite yet, though said piper had a notion as to how to get to the paying part next-to-immediately. It was the same notion he'd had when he had to figure out a way to get word to the self-predetermined stars in the night's sky he wished to help escape as to their rendezvous star-spots. It was just a matter of locating him.

"Refocus your scarlet fumes on Lazareme's Legendarian, Seeress. Bring me the head of Jordan Tethys, breathing, with his body still attached to it and its fin-

gers still attached to his Brainrock quill. He can draw your outstanding children to Lathakra. Then we can both find a way to kill the meddlesome deviant once and for all time hereafter."

"Once, both?" queried Tantal. "Haven't I killed him a couple of times already?"

"You may have, Thanatos. I haven't. And those I kill stay dead!"

========

Jordan Tethys didn't just draw himself elsewhere, he drew himself a second skin and crawled into it.

========

Then he drew himself a tent, some bed linen and a bed to go with it. Where-upon he crawled into all of that as well. Unable to sleep, he drew to himself the cooler full of chilled pilsner he'd stashed at Ferd's place for just such an emergency, pulled out the Illuminary star-chart the governor had given him earlier, went out-side and sat down on a camp chair he also drew to himself. He had lots of stashes.

It was a nice night, clear and warm. Even at the end of Maruta, November on the Outer Earth, the first day of Tantalar by now, it usually was down here at the bottom of the Cattail Peninsula. The Prison Beach of Incain was about a far south as you could go without drawing yourself off the Headworld entirely, something he couldn't do. The She-Sphinx kept it spic and span, too. As the joke went, Incain wasn't so much windswept as All-swept.

(Unless it was from memory, in which case it was just an ordinary drawing, he could no more draw anyone who was on the Outer Earth than he could anyone be-tween-space or in an area shielded by Stopstone, Brainrock's counterforce. He also couldn't draw anyone anywhere against their will, not even when they were asleep.)

More than sixty, he'd concluded by the time he was ready to try sleep again. Could be even more, he supposed. Some of the missing stars didn't have names at-tached to them, That included the ones in an odd little cluster of very faint stars straddling the border between the Lazaremist quadrant, in the southern hemisphere of the Head's heavens, and the Mithradic quadrant in the north. Someone had writ-ten *'Damnation?'* (with a question mark) over the stars in red ink.

He couldn't remember hearing of any Constellation Damnation before, so he checked the date on the star-chart: Only a year old. That meant Melina Sarpedon-Zeross, the current High Illuminary of Weir, had overseen its preparation. He won-dered if it was Mel or Morgianna Sarpedon who wrote it. Ferd said he got his copy from Morg, so he assumed the latter.

Mel, whose twin brother Demios was married to Morgianna, was a stickler for details so she'd know why it was called Damnation and what devils composed it. Maybe he should go up to the Weirdom of Cabalarkon and ask her. Besides, it had been awhile since he'd talked to Daddy Cabby, he in his tub brimful of life-preserv-ing but animation-suspending Cathonic Fluid. Too bad the Master, Mel's brother-in-law, Saladin Devason, had gone off drinking since their near-death experience on Shenon six years ago last Solstice, the summery one (of two).

He had, too, for a day or so. Being about to be boiled alive in a Lemurian soup-pot did make you consider slimming down; less temptation if you did. Beer bellies made for good eating, Mel's much younger hubby Harry had joked after he rescued them. Even if he and Sal wouldn't have been, Harry's jokes generally were in poor taste.

Tethys sneezed at the memory. He always did. He didn't like being spice any more than he did being drunk, by a vampire.

That night he dreamt of a pink-furred Cheshire Cat all-hooded in darkness. Scary, horrible, and very, very itchy it had been too. Had Phantast the Dreamweaver found him already? He'd never forgiven him for spilling the baleful beans re the Crimson Conspiracy he'd dreamed up with the likes of Strife and Sinistral Gluttony circa the start of the Dome's 5th Millennium.

As unsettling as that was, more unsettling was what was waiting for him out-side his tent when, after dawn broke but before it burst, he got up to empty his bladder.

All was manifesting herself as a cute, cuddly cub of a She-Sphinx, one with the 3-eyed, peach-fuzzy face of a little girl that may have been based on Morg's Young Mommy Life. (More likely it was based on the Devil Child, Tralalorn, who had so plagued her father, Thrygragos Varuna Mithras, toward the end of the Dome's 44th Century on Thrygragon.)

"Go away, Jordan Tethys," said the She-Sphinx. "Go away or All eat you."

========

He almost asked what was eating her but instead picked placation as preferred policy. "Hey, I was going to pee in the sea, not on your prissily perfect sandbox."

Bad choice. She didn't purr in amusement as anticipated. Nor, in predictable pleas-ure of his presence, did she roll over and present her belly for scratching. Something was definitely wrong here. All wasn't usually so unfriendly. True, she wasn't much larger than Cheshire pussycat-size, but he knew she could get herself a whole bunch bigger in very short order.

He went away – better something was eating her than she was eating him.

****

(Pregame-Gambit) 3: **Fangs Fights Her Own Battles**

Overnight Birhym 3, Sapienda 4, Tantalar 5980

Initially in the form of bats, the very biggest ones carrying Haddit Zombies, the vampires flew across Lake Sedona and struck Sraddha Isle shortly after dusk. The Inner Earth date was Birhym, the 3rd of Tantalar, Year of the Dome 5980. Since some of the bats were originally educated in the subcontinent of Aka-Godbad, they'd have known the Outer Earth date was Wednesday, the 3rd of December, AD 1980.

Most bats were known more for their unrelenting persistence than their retentive intelligence, though. That was because they were persistently hungry.

=========

On the monastery battlements, shaven-headed, brown-robed Sraddhites fought them off as they always did:

- with – now that the Godbadians had taught them to generate hydroelectric power – stroboscopic lights that were so bright they approximated daylight;
- with – the always treacherous mines in Diluvia providing mother-lodes of the stuff – reinforced silver-bladed swords and daggers, reinforced silver-headed arrows and spears;
- with fire-canisters perfected if not precisely invented by their order's founder, Life's heroic martyr, Sraddha Somata;
- with simple torches and Molotov cocktails;
- with grenades that didn't so much blow up as burst into fireballs; and
- with exploding bullets packed with herbs, potions and chemical compounds concocted for them by their long-time War Witch allies, who knew a thing or two about killing the pre-killed.

While life-defending Athenans weren't half-bad when it came to dispensing life-saving condiments prepared for them by their Althean counterparts, who were pacifist witch-healers, they were a whole lot better when it came to dispensing with bats. Life's defenders didn't spray fresh water, though.

The killing floors were already slippery enough with blood and guts.

=========

Although surrounded by the stuff, freshwater, flowing in from the Diluvia Mountain Range, a few hundred miles north, that only prevented the vamps' friends, the nowadays mostly dead Irache, Haddazur-animated zombies, from swimming to Sraddha Isle and the dozens of other islets dotting Lake Sedona. Second Fangs, whom the forces of the Living counted as Public Enemy Number One, didn't leave the waterways untended, though.

There were now non-Haddazur and non-Nergalazur azuras – azuras whose devic mothers were other than the Mithradites' Fecundity, Nergal Vetala – animating dead Piscines, Akans and Lemurians in the Lake and the rivers feeding it. They weren't so easy to burn but at least there weren't many of them. Life's defenders had aquatic allies as well. Living Piscines, Akans and Lemurians didn't appreciate their fathers and mothers, their brothers and sisters, being azura-animated any more than the ground-based priests or priestesses of godly Sraddha did.

The vast majority of always brown-robed warrior monks made their home in the heavily forested mountain slopes Hadd-side of Diluvia, where it hadn't stopped raining since the Great Flood. While the hunting was wonderful it wasn't too good for crops, ranches or ranges. Domesticated animals developed respiratory ailments and their coats problems with mange.

The most sought after soil were the flatlands, the hills and the dells of El Dorado's mainland, where it never rained but never got sunny either. Still, what with all its flooded mines and tunnels, underground rivers and overground streams, oases, aquifers and cenotes, animals could graze there. Plenty of crops could be grown there as well; if you like your crops stunted.

For more than four hundred years, the native Iraches contested with the originally non-native Sraddhites, who mostly hailed from Marutia, Sedon's Cheek, to the north, for every inch of arable land. The former, who still referred to Hadd as Iraxas, had their plodding Dead Things to aid them while the latter, who called Hadd El Dorado, had metallic weaponry that, in the absence of reliable trade routes to any of its three coasts and no way through the mountains, they had to maintain themselves.

Over the centuries a testy and very much grudging saw-off had been reached between the two sides. The Marutians could work the lands on the fringes of the mountain ranges as well as in and around Lake Sedonda. The rest of Hadd they were supposed to leave to the Iraches and their Dead Things. As for the Undead, initially both sides had them. To some degree that was still the case, though the Brown Robes, who had always cremated their dead so as to prevent them becoming azura-animated Dead Things Walking, were supposed to stake any vamps they came upon. The Sraddhites' officialdom therefore considered bats of every ethnicity to be on the Iraches' side.

It wasn't quite the Third War between the Living against the Dead yet. There were stacks of living Iraches out there, having tea and buttered scones with their ambulatory ancestors. The Sraddhites, though, had long thought of themselves at the vanguard of Life's forces. The trouble was that, for hundreds of years, theirs were mostly unheard voices crying in the wilderness.

Hadd was the Land of Dead, as far as most everyone else was concerned. Leave it to them. It kept them away from our territories didn't it. Nonetheless, during the mid-to-late Sixties, particularly in Godbad and Krachla, word finally started getting out that, yes, they, the Sraddhites, were still around and fighting the good fight against the Evil Dead.

That they could even get their message to those places was mostly due to the fact Alpha Centauri, Godbad's Civil War essentially over by 5960, sponsored a mapping project of the entire Headworld, a project led by Gomez Niarchos, Ferdinand's father. It in effect rediscovered the Sraddhites and shortly thereafter Centauri Enterprises began making regular flights, via their long-range helicopters and planes, to Sraddha Isle.

The flights were severely curtailed in the early Seventies due to a combination of politics and petroleum. The latter was only extractable in the Godbadian province of New Iraxas and in the bordering Gulf of Aka, between Hadd on the east and New Iraxas on the west. But offshore drilling outraged the undersea inhabitants of the Gulf, the amphibious Piscines and the strictly water-breathing Akans themselves. Their saboteurs became an escalating concern.

Shipping dwindled in the Gulf almost to the point of non-existence. When undersea guerrillas, who had long had what amounted to submarines, expanded their explosive activities to include the Headworld's Interior Ocean of Akadan, the seafaring Pani merchants of Krachla, who had been circling the Head since time very nearly immemorial, became so infuriated they threatened to boycott Godbad's ports altogether.

As if that wasn't bad enough, the Panis began intercepting boats travelling the calm waters between Djerridam-Goatwood, Sedon's Beard, in the southern subcontinent, to Greater Godbad's long-time provinces in the southern Cattail Peninsula. Although the tolls they charged were relatively insignificant, it was a stupidly provocative act.

Fortunately for almost everyone, the Panis not only worshipped Byronic deities, they relied on them for Akadan's calm waters. Wiser heads prevailed. Needless to say, most of the wiser heads had three eyes in them. Which was about when, no doubt goaded on by their vampiric overseers, the Iraches and their Dead Things, who worked the oilfields of New Iraxas, got difficult.

Through their spokespersons – especially the Molech Xibalba, a rabble-rousing Irache Summoning Child who had an annoying knack of going away, sometimes for years at a time, only to return at the worst possible time – they insisted Centauri Enterprises cease flying back and forth to Sraddha Isle. They further insisted the CE-controlled media stop ranting on and on about the Evil Dead and start telling the Iraches' story more sympathetically. After all, given the intolerable conditions there, why would any sensible Godbadian work in New Iraxas?

They went so far as to demand the Godbadian military stop supplying the Sraddhites, which frayed more than a few epaulets in its high command. The Godbadians could of course keep supplying the living Iraches in Hadd and indeed a great deal of the wages earned by their Dead Things went to pay for weaponry living Iraches could use to defend their territories from Sraddhite encroachment. Which, although there were cutbacks due to a lack of strife on the subcontinent, served to keep CE's armaments division profitable.

With Godbad still mopping up from its Civil War, hence the cutbacks in its armaments division, CE caved-in to pressures from the undersea dwellers and

Krachlans. It ceased all offshore drilling, as well as commercial fishing, in the Gulf of Aka. New Iraxas thereupon became the only place left where Godbadians could produce the fuel to which the subcontinent and its territories on the Cattail Peninsula had become so addicted.

Even after Xibalba went away, yet again, labour strife continued in New Iraxas. Rough times were ahead for the Sraddhites. They battled through it, much as they always had. But what could CE do except give in to the demands of the living Iraches, who did the aboveground work, and their Dead Things, who did the underground work? They were right; they were the only ones willing to work New Iraxas year in, year out.

Centauri's enlightened answer was to green it up. Make it so Godbad's once again burgeoning population, for the most part Byron- as opposed to Vetala-worshippers, could find work there too. The Iraches must have seen the writing on the wall because for months now the Ambulatory Dead had been attacking the Sraddhites' fringe settlements, driving more and more of the Brown Robes back onto the islets and into the mountains. It seemed there were more Dead Things Walking than there had been for decades.

Then the vamps started attacking the islets and there definitely were a lot more of them than previously; Marutian and Godbadian ones especially. As CE expedited the greening of New Iraxas with its typical efficiency, bounty-hunters collecting dustbins of their dust forced them to move onto greener fields, as it were, particularly ones on the fringes of Old Iraxas.

Which they seemed intent on turning into very much bloodier fields.

========

Tonight wasn't as bad as some nights. For a change the bats seemed to be shying away from the warding symbols, such as sacred stars, crosses and oversized, mirrored eggs festooned about the battlements. They were even staying away from Sraddhites wearing garlic necklaces in addition to their usual mirrored amulets. Which the Irache bats in particular didn't always do because, when they were alive, garlic was a major component of their diet.

For the third or fourth night in a row there weren't as many of them as there had been the week before. At best the attack was half-hearted tokenism; the defence a bit of a ho-hum yawn; all in a night's work really. Oh, a couple of the presumably younger bats, thinking themselves ever so clever, switched to their human forms then switched that form into humanoid mist, but that was an old routine, easily countered.

Sure, it rendered them intangible while, at the same time, it allowed them to use their eyes in hopes of mesmerizing the priests and priestesses into dropping their weapons. It was a pointless effort because, generations earlier, the Sraddhites had developed eye-shields, which they wore in order to diffract the hypnotic glares of the vamps.

Godbadians, for a price of course, had refined the optics and mass-produced them. The Morrigan's War Witches, who could travel between-space on their stepping stones, carted so many boxes of them to Sraddha Isle, the eye-shields were now standard equipment. Every non-Irache alive in Hadd now had a couple of pairs.

Some of the living Iraches did too, the ones who feared Godbadian and Marutian bats, who weren't known for their circumspect eating habits.

Athenans, who were led on a day-to-day basis by Garcia Dis L'Orca, a 27-year-old woman from the southern Cattail Peninsula, carted in a lot of other things as well. They even shared out the delayed-reaction, combustible compounds non-pacifistic Witch Sisterhoods developed generations ago to spray over bats and Dead Things alike. Called fire-powder, or variants thereof, it was akin to a pesticide that didn't poison but instead ignited. War Witches had poisons too. And guns. Annoying a War Witch was bad procedure.

In short, the Sraddhites weren't as poorly supplied as they had been once CE stopped its regular commercial flights to and from Sraddha Isle. The bat who put the bite to the Morrigan's grandson – Aortic Tsishah's eldest son by Jester Jaguar, the grand chieftain of Free Iraxas, the no longer quite so loosely knit confederation of Iraches over on the Cattail – had buggered things up right royally for recalcitrant, Hadd-based, Irache freedom fighters and their Dead Things.

The Molech Xibalba, Night Owl's son, would be rolling over in his grave by now, if Second Fangs hadn't crisped his howsoever rejuvenated body after she drained it.

========

Even in their solid form vamps weren't much use against Sraddhites. Ordinarily the attackers trusted in their justifiably feared speed and equally fabled strength to gain an advantage over their living foes. The Brown Robes on Sraddha Isle were hardened veterans, though. What they lacked in supernatural speed and strength they made up with training and preparation.

Weapons and charms weren't all they relied on either. Most wore prickly vests, with neck-covering snoods over their robes, and their quills were as silver as their blades. Try putting the bite on a Sraddhite wearing a porcupine turtleneck and all the vamp would get was a mouthful of argental metal rather than scrumptious flesh. As for the sacred symbols, that was another indication tonight's bats were mostly young or relatively freshly turned.

No matter how hard Brown Robes held to the efficacy, the genuineness, of their talismans, a truly hungry bat was usually more than willing to suffer superficial burns to get at an unprotected neck. Only disbelievers were falling that night and, among the shaved-bald priests and priestesses, there were none of those left on Sraddha Isle. When it came right down to it, vamps were no match for Sraddhites on their home turf. Especially now that it wasn't just Sraddhites and mostly non-Sraddhite Athenans defending the battlements.

The Morrigan, Morgianna Sarpedon, hadn't just brought in War Witches. She'd brought in Utopians exiled, along with her and husband Demios, from the Weirdom of Cabalarkon thirty years earlier. They brought in some of their zebra-striped sons and daughters with them as well. Once he found out about it, the Master of Weir, Saladin Devason, Morg's year older brother, wasn't about to be upstaged. On a Pani merchant ship that arrived in a Krachlan port a month ago now, a 300-man-strong battalion of Trinondevs, Weir's Warrior Elite, under the leadership of the canny, 80-year-old clone, Golgotha Nauroz, disembarked.

They didn't have to march up to Lake Sedona. Nor did they take the God-badian Air Force up on its offer to fly them up there. They did it by themselves, collectively, using the levitating aspects of their originally extraterrestrial eye-staves to do so. From replaceable eyeorbs attached to their tops, eye-staves generated force shields that could be solid-substantial, alternatively energetic or simultaneously both. Individual Trinondevs often used them to manifest tangible, very much visible and fearsome-looking gargoyles.

Golgotha divided them into 10-man units. Each unit generated a gargoyle of their own but, on his orders, they were all variations of the same animal. In broad daylight, thirty enormous, multi-coloured and noisily tittering bats flew from Krachla to Sraddha Isle. They'd been patrolling the skies above Lake Sedona and islets since then. So it was the vampiric bats worst enemies became 10-Trinondev battalion-bats.

Although cloned from a Utopian pureblood – most of whom were exceedingly long-lived and physically healthy by everyday human standards, most of whom were also inbred and imbecilic – Field Commander Nauroz really was a cagey old codger. Of course he was cloned from cells donated by Ubris Nauroz, who was both bold and bright. He wasn't long-lived, though, not by pureblood standards.

He was one of those who called the Simultaneous Summonings of 19/5920, however.

========

That the Godbadians were back in the game heartened the Sraddhites even more than the Morrigan's recruits. They had everything they needed to rout the Iraches, their vamps, even if they were more Janna Fangfingers' vamps, and the rest of the Dead Things. Everything included seemingly unlimited numbers, endless supplies of war machines and war materiel, an air force and, perhaps most significantly, so the rumours had it anyhow, access to the Outer Earth. It also helped that, at least nominally, its military and the democratically elected civilian authorities who oversaw its activities had nothing to do with Centauri Enterprises.

Plainly, if somewhat clandestinely, the powers-that-be in the Corporate State of Greater Godbad were becoming thoroughly fed up with the turmoil living and dead Iraches, what with all their labour stoppages, were causing in New Iraxas. Of course, other than their Byronic deities, the powers-that-be in Godbad mostly amounted to Alpha Centauri, the founder and main moneybags behind Centauri Enterprises.

Then again, rumours also had it, the Fatman was possessed by Thrygragos Byron, the Great God whose age this was throughout the Hidden Continent of Sedon's Head. (It had been Byron's Age since a few decades before the First War between the Living and the Dead ended; since Chaos cathonitized Order in 5495 and thereby completed the Disunition of the Unities of Lazareme, the Great God whose age it had been since Thrygragon. Which took place in the Year of the Dome 4376, when Thrygragos Varuna Mithras was killed, never to rise again.)

All in all it looked as if the Sraddhites were about to live to tell the tale of yet another night of unabashed Dead-bashing. One more and, no rumours this time, it would finally be their turn to go on the offensive. Assuming Thartarre Sraddha Holgatson could deliver the goods.

Rather, assuming Ringleader, Aristotle Zeross, could deliver them to him.

========

In the midst of the nightly assault on the monastery, the High Priest of Sraddha barely heard the rap-a-tap-tap on his balcony door. When it was incessantly repeated for about five minutes, Thartarre calmly unscrewed the hardened-steel blade that was attached to the stump of his right arm. Replacing it with a reinforced silver one, making sure his Godbadian-manufactured eye-shield was in place, he went and opened the garlic-garlanded door.

A beguilingly familiar, female vampire, with long, silvery hair to match her deathly white skin and outfit, what part of it that wasn't bloody, awaited him patiently.

========

"Go away," he urged it. "I won't let you in and I've no time to dally on the porch tonight. Just be thankful there are no Utopians with me right now. Which is no doubt why you've chosen tonight to visit me. Take my advice and go far away. I've a busy day tomorrow and, if all goes well, come the day after, you and your ilk will be heads on our pikes; those that don't blow away in the breeze anyhow."

"Come with me, beloved," spoke the entrancing, fang-fingered beauty. "Your mother's returning."

"My mother's gone for good. I cremated her myself thirty-five years ago. No way she's coming back."

"Your birth-mother's dead and her body's ash, true, but, young fool that you were, that just freed Nergal Vetala. And cost your father his life. That's who's coming back!"

"All the better then. Let her. I've just the thing for Nergal Vetala. Good night!" Holgatson slammed the door in its face.

Moments later the night's din, which had been gradually dying down, as was usual with daybreak more a matter of minutes than hours away, suddenly re-enlivened, in a decidedly noisy fashion. Gunfire. Shooting. More gunfire. Much more shooting. Someone was shooting back. Or was it some things were shooting back?

Has Fangfingers grown that desperate, giving her zombies guns? They'll only shoot themselves. Maybe I should ask the Godbadians to send me high-powered magnets as well as splatter-packs. He decided to radio Petrograd with just that request. Then he decided that whimsy had no place in warfare.

He radioed anyhow, if only to say hello to someone normal. It was lonely at the top.

========

Slow and dull-witted, the zombies the bats-of-burden vampires dropped fared even worse than the bats themselves. They were chopped apart. Then the back canisters, filled with flammable fluid or the War Witches fire-powder, came into play. Sraddhites sprayed their foes with practised discipline. Whereupon they stood back to watch as they burned unto irreconcilable ash. It being Tantalar, the warmth thus generated was almost welcome. So far that night, with dawn not far off, the casualty list read zombies twenty, vamps three, living zilch.

Seemingly unfazed by the fates befalling their fellow Dead and Undead, three of the bloodsuckers became semi-solid and alit beside each other on the monastery's midway-up walls. Likely they weren't scouts, most of whom were animal-feeders, not man-eaters, and as such tended to maintain their bat-forms and avoid coming anywhere near target range. Nor were they bats of burden, whose size and consequential ability to carry zombies, and the occasional homemade bomb, made them so prized other vamps fed them.

Neither, by the mere fact they were just sitting there, were they the terrifying attack-bats Second Fangs sometimes turned loose to feed on an entire village at a time. Akin to berserkers of Northern European legend on the Outer Earth, attack-bats deliberately starved themselves for days or weeks on end. Their resultant, all-but-overwhelming hunger made them bloodlust-blind to the risk-reducing stealth techniques city-sippers and country killers alike habitually employed when they were on the prowl, looking for victims conveniently ill-prepared to defend themselves.

Attack-bats didn't stop to sate themselves, which was the instinctive thing for especially young, untrained bats to do. Slaughter was foremost in their minds; they could eat later. For certain highly skilled and somewhat sportingly inclined Sraddhites, big game bat-hunters as they thought of themselves, who were as devoted as they were manifestly crazed, that made attack-bats prey to pray for, as fays would say.

Thartarre's Number Two, Diego de Landa, Diego Sraddha Landa-son as he was officially designated, was one of best of the big game bat-hunters. The only thing he didn't enjoy about wiping out attack-bats was that dust made for lousy trophies. In that respect demons were much preferable. Their heads you could mount on the monastery's walls. Unfortunately, if perhaps not so surprisingly given what they were, a few decapitated demon-heads not only had to be fed and watered regularly, they had to be caged.

Vampiric lore suggested semi-solidity was an acquired skill. But it wasn't necessarily something only bats dedicated to their craft could accomplish after years of practise. These three could be psychopomp-bats, vamps who could travel through the Weird, just as Athenans did, albeit on their witch-stones. Prevailing wisdom also had it only bats turned by Second Fangs – who, because of her fang-fingered glove, once a devil's power focus, was Brainrock-blessed – could become psychopomps.

There were plenty of arguments about that, though. For one thing, no one had ever been able to prove bats turned by Fangs couldn't make those they turned into psychos themselves. As well, witches of every sort, of every Sisterhood – and the Headworld had sometimes scabby scads of Witch Sisterhoods, some of whom hated each other – had been making psychopomps since well before the Genesea, albeit at the cost of their soul-selves. Chthonic, pre-Genesea, demon-empathizing, Earth-Goddess-venerating, Hecate-Hellions, probably the oldest sisterhood on the Whole Earth, were notorious for their psychos.

Garudas, who were native to Goatwood, Sedon's Beard, in Godbad, were natural psychos – the recallable, feathery part of their being even developed betweenspace, the same as a Melusine Piscine's fishy bits did (unless it was their human bits, as in their lower limbs, which happened when they were born beneath the waves rather than on land). Vamps could put the bite on almost anyone. These three didn't have any feathers and Garudas needed to be wearing their feathers, their regalia they called it, in order to traverse between-space.

There were lots of other ways to make psychos but one thing was certain. They were very dangerous things. Which, when they could get them, made them very valuable to the forces of the Dead and Undead. Made them eminently warrant the, in reference to vampires in general, kill-at-all-costs wanted posters featuring Irache vamps put up by less tolerant, Sraddhite sympathizers in the Godbadian media.

So why were they squab-squatting there, like the proverbial wooden ducks on a rotating shelf in a carnival shooting gallery? Why were they just perched there, midway up the ages-old monastery's external brickwork, in full view of everyone alive then gathering to see them? Gathering only, thus far, since they couldn't do much about killing anything semi-solid. To be seen was obviously one reason. To attract a crowd was the real reason.

Two were women, one was a man. Of them, one woman had a shaven head and black skin. That probably made her a Sraddhite grown careless and consequently bitten. It might make her a War Witch as well; a group of them had been reported missing a couple of weeks ago. Not that anyone had worried about that then: Sraddhites, War Witches, Trinondevs and Zebranids were taken, they were trained to commit suicide, preferably by fire, rather than risk being turned. Spray from a Sraddhite warrior monk's back canister or a hit from a War Witch's combustible chemicals worked as well on the Living as it did on the Dead.

Training wasn't always put into practise, however. The other woman, younger, maybe in her late teens to early twenties when she was made, had zebra-striped skin. That made her a Zebranid Leper, the daughter of one of the Sarpedons' exiled Utopians. For some reason their offspring always had striped skin. When asked, most said it was because they were brought up outside the Weirdom of Cabalarkon and therefore didn't have access to the slop artificially generated by the Utopians living in Sedon's Devic Eye-Land's still functioning, though originally extraterrestrial, food replication systems.

But that was neither here nor there, was it? Not tonight it wasn't, that was for sure. The point was they were here at all. And it was underlined by the presence of the third semi-solid vamp on the wall. His skin was jet black, blacker than that of the ex-Sraddhite; blacker than midnight on a starless night, as the saying went. He was one of Golgotha's Warriors Elite.

There was no doubt about it. His clothes were the indigo-dyed, linen-sheet robes, turban and veil that amounted to the Trinondevs' uniforms. The veil wasn't drawn, presumably so everyone there could bear witness he was a potentially pure-blooded, Utopian male. He didn't have an eye-stave, though. Was probably so freshly made – maybe only the minimum 3-days turned – chances were it was all he could do to shape-shift clothes out of his bat-form.

Then he did have something, an incendiary grenade. So did the Zebranid vamp, a Godbadian machine rifle. He threw it, the Zebranid opened fire, and the ex-Sraddhite tossed a handful of itty-bitty glowing things onto the battlement. Off of them – Athenans called them variously, but bullet-pellets was the commonest term they used for their witch-stones – came at least a dozen dead War Witches.

They weren't animated by Haddazurs, at least they weren't initially. They were too quick afoot to be zombies. But they were dead, and didn't become any deader despite being ventilated by all the gathered, altogether alive Sraddhites, and not just Sraddhites by then, intent upon killing them irrecoverably dead. That meant, although their bodies had to have been animated by Haddazurs by the time they got up and were re-disposed of properly, they were animated at the outset by some kind of super-azura, ones with a dominating will. Which azuras, almost by definition, didn't have. Or else they were animated by something else entirely.

Whatever that something else was, whatever they were, it was nearly midday before Thartarre got the revised casualty reports from his Marutian-born lieutenant, Diego de Landa, as well as that of the War Witches, from Morg's Cattail-raised Number Two, Garcia Dis L'Orca. It was depressingly extensive. Janna Fangfingers had always boasted of her ability to fight her own battles. But the carnage her dead witches far more so than her Undead vamps caused Sapienda predawn went far beyond her best buckets-of-blood record to date.

What was animating the dead witches anyways?

========

Thartarre Sraddha Holgatson knew why Second Fangs asked him to come away with her. When she was human Janna Somata had a twin brother, the bald-headed, eponymous founder of their militant, life-protecting order. Although their skin wasn't quite as darkly Utopian as her brother's had been, Thartarre looked much like him. So had his father. Curators picked High Priests for their resemblance to Sraddha Somata first and foremost.

They knew what he looked like, too. There was a famous portrait of him done by one of his contemporaries in the late 55th Century of the Dome. It was lost now but over time so many copies of it were made virtually no Sraddhite household was without one. He was their living god. His spirit lived on in the Sraddhites' High Priest.

Too bad Fangs had his soul.

****

(Pregame-Gambit) 4: **Wrong-Handed Thumbs**

Sapienda, Tantalar 4, 5980

On the Outer Earth, the so-called Secret War of Supranormals lasted from early 1938 until late 1955. Many, though by no means all, of the supranormal combatants in that 'War' were Summoning Children. In early 1938 they had either just turned or were about to turn 17. Seventeen, almost eighteen years later, only 12 supras were left in the sense they were both still alive and recalled, howsoever momentarily, that they were once supranormals.

Of them one was a mere boy of twelve. Two Summoning Children who never came close to 19/5955 had a son named Thartarre.

=========

With a shake of his religiously kept-bald head, the one-armed High Priest of Sraddha pushed the tragically lengthy casualty reports aside. Lifting up his God-badian-manufactured reading glasses, he surreptitiously wiped away another tear. Despite the relative earliness of the hour he broke tradition and called for his first and only beer of the day. His guest was already on her third and they hadn't even had lunch yet. Sraddhite monks made an especially fine pilsner.

Thartarre Sraddha Holgatson returned his attention to the Illuminary star-chart his freshly arrived guest brought from the Weirdom of Cabalarkon. Not much more than a year old, it was one of the most recent ones Cabalarkon's Illuminaries and their estimable High Illuminary, Melina nee Sarpedon Zeross, had produced. He compared it to the list of names his guest, who'd come directly from the Weirdom via between-space, had also provided.

Melina had helped prepare the list. She hadn't been able to add many names to the one his guest had done in Incain the previous Sedonda. She'd never heard of a Constellation Damnation either, but thought the writing looked a little like hubby Harry's – Aristotle 'Harry' Zeross, Ringleader, being on the Outer Earth at the moment, he with his miraculous Brainrock rings. It was no big deal anyhow. In total perhaps only twenty stars were unnamed and they could be shining through the Sedon Sphere from the Outer Earth's heavens. Illuminaries were good at keeping tabs on devils, Mel insisted. Had been anyhow.

One of Thartarre's just-as-shaven-headed attendants, an elderly, shaky-handed priestess, brought him his beer. His guest recognized her from previous visits to the monastery. The main reason for that was she was such an oddity. First of all, elderly men and women were a rarity among the island-dwelling Sraddhites, who were more in the frontline than their soaking wet fellows in the mountains. Secondly, she was a simpleton. Thirdly, she was his barber.

And that surely was the oddest thing of all. The last thing his guest would wish was an elderly, shaky-handed simpleton with a razorblade anywhere near anyone's head.

This even though, one-armed, which he was, or two-armed, which he wasn't, Thartarre would have had no problem shaving himself. He was a very capable fellow was the High Priest. That was one good thing about Sraddhites. They weren't ones to discard their elders, no matter how old, female or simple-minded they might be; weren't ones to insist they retire to the Diluvia settlements if they didn't want to do so.

Clearly this particular, poorly aging priestess wanted to stay on the frontline for some reason and Thartarre felt obliged to give her something to do. Still, as far as his guest was concerned, giving an unsteady, low-watt antique the task of being his barber, that wasn't just odd. It was positively spine-tingling, jugular-throbbing lunacy.

Understandably, said guest was hypersensitive when it came to dying.

========

The High Priest finished his comparison of the chart and list. He found the sheer number of missing stars daunting, almost mind-numbingly so. There were damn near seventy of them. He took a sip of his beer and turned to his guest. "This is exceedingly bad. You reckon decathonitized devils can get away with killing?"

"They got out of the Sedon Sphere, didn't they," said his guest. "They didn't do so with said-Sed's permission, why would they be bound by his dictates anymore?"

"But how could they get out of Cathonia without the Demon King's permission?"

"Call it wishful thinking, Tar. If he did let them loose we might as well throw in the form sheet. No one ever wins a Sedonplay except the Moloch Sedon himself."

"Oh, I wouldn't say that. I've an ace-in-the-hole I've yet to play."

"One that's only cost you your parents so far."

"Parents are expendable. Life isn't. Want another beer?"

"Not right now. A girl's got to watch her figure."

"A girl? You'll have to get rid of the tee-tee-tail hair-implants, not to mention the breast ones, before I start calling you Sister Jordan again, Jordy. How's her son, by the way?"

"He's short a couple of years for succession duties yet but he'd be an interesting one. The last time I was a Utopian hybrid … Sorry, you'd know when that was, wouldn't you? Because, in a way, you're still living with the consequences. None of it was my fault, I assure you. Not very much of it anyhow."

The last time the Legendarian was a Utopian hybrid was during late 55th Century of the Dome, when Janna Somata became Janna Fangfingers and Nergal Vetala became the Vampire Queen of Hadd, when it was still called Iraxas or El Dorado.

It was Tethys's idea for Vetala to start calling Sedon's Mutton Chop, the shaft of the Penile Peninsula, Hadd.

"Maybe not. But if you'd done like you were supposed to do and drawn the Amateramirror and its sister object, the Crimson Corona, into the lava lake on Sedon's Peak at the end of the Thousand Days of Disbelief, my mother might still be alive."

"Ah, but as I eventually found out, I did; the real ones as well. And they'd have melted away just like they were supposed to if the devic Anvil, not the God-badian General Anvil, hadn't been entertaining a Dead Thing Fucking up in his Prometheum when I did. Somehow she sensed them coming through the Weird and hauled them out of the lake before they could go blub, blub.

"Did so at the cost of the corpse she was animating, true, but there were plenty of corpses around for her to reanimate everywhere you went in those days. So it was no great loss."

"You're saying a devil animating a Dead Thing stopped them melting away?"

"Not a devil, Tar. Close, though. An azura, one with a name: Klannit Thanatos."

"Should have guessed. She's the other reason I haven't looked in a mirror for 35 years."

========

Professional storytellers enjoyed having stories told to them almost as much as they enjoyed telling them. They particularly enjoyed hearing stories they were allowed to re-tell themselves, due credit given, at a later date. Provided they could remember them of course, which the Legendarian generally could.

Right now, though, the scar in the centre of his forehead was itching something awful.

========

The future High Priest of hallowed Sraddha first saw the dank light of day in 5940. His parents, Holgat and Barsine, were Summoning Children. They'd met under trying circumstances in 5938, when they were only 17 years old, and hit it off immediately. They hit off much more than each other but, as Tethys might put it, the earlier parts of the deadly – especially to the predeceased – duo's their-story isn't this-story.

Born in the perpetually rain-drenched mountains of Diluvia, Thartarre never really knew the sun. It didn't bother him in the slightest. An intelligent, able-bodied and adventurous tyke, he and his young parents spent much of their time outdoors. Even as a toddler he revelled in it. There was nothing he loved more than roving the strange, wild forest that was his alpine home.

The Curators, higher-ups in the priesthood of Sraddha, did not approve of Barsine. It wasn't because she might be a deviant; that was only gossip. Nor was it necessarily because she was an outsider. They didn't even object to the fact she was a gun-carrying, natural-born Hecate-Hellion who could get about on their Hell-stones. While that meant she could and did travel extensively, which was something, because of their isolation, hardly any Sraddhite could do, they didn't approve of her primarily because she positively reeked of independence.

Having had a decidedly anarchic bent to her upbringing, she returned the favour. Even after they were married, she not only refused to shave off her long, dark hair, she flaunted it. That wasn't all she flaunted either. Holgat loved her dearly. So much so he threatened to leave the priesthood if the Curia banished Barsine. What they did instead was make him their High Priest. In order to accept the appointment, which he wanted, Holgat moved his family south to the Sraddhite monastery on Sraddha Isle shortly after their only child's 5th birthday.

Being on the frontline of an approaching five hundred year stalemate between the forces of the Living and their mostly Vetalazur-possessed, hence zombified, foes was far more than just a stressful position. It was, as his father put it, a bull's-eye position. With Barsine's reluctant acquiescence, Thartarre was placed in the care of a series of handlers-cum-bodyguards.

The boy, used to running free, found moving to the environs of Lake Sedona a stultifying experience. The islets he could visit had none of the attractions of the rainforest. While the sun still never shone – Hadd being as perpetually cloud-covered as Diluvia – it never rained here either. What atmospheric moisture there was came in the form of fog and mist emanating from the huge lake, fed as it was by rivers and tributaries running out of the mountains, most of which ended up underground as they wound their way from Lake Sedona to the seacoasts.

The area was more dangerous as well. In the mountains there were lions and tigers, sure; wolves, bears and massive snakes. Big deal. They could be killed. So could the occasional, usually primitively equipped Irache warrior who strayed into territory where he didn't belong. Except, on the islets of Lake Sedona – El Dorado's mainland, what everyone else called Hadd, beyond the fringes Sraddhites tilled, being entirely out of bounds – the foe, once killed, had to be killed again; then burnt unto ash.

That only destroyed the Dead Things; not what reanimated them. When not possessing corpses Haddazurs – as all the antagonistic azuras were referred to regardless of parentage – were spirits, invisible and seemingly indestructible. They could travel with impunity, which made them great ghosts and greater spies; could animate anything dead, even animals and plants; and there wasn't anything you could do about them.

Most of the zombies couldn't abide immersion in running water but they could row, or be rowed, over it. In addition, vamps could fly to the islets in the form of bats and some of the Dead Things had been water-breathing Akans, amphibious Piscines or just as amphibious Lemurian frogwomen, those who had adapted, over the millennia, to freshwater as well as seawater. Although presumably animated by azuras whose devic mother wasn't Nergal Vetala, their natural habitat in life remained so in death.

The watery dead were particularly frustrating. You netted one, it was more likely they'd drag you and your net into the water before you could drag them into your boat. Besides, what would you do with them in your boat? You couldn't burn them; you'd burn your boat. So you had to haul the net to shore, winch it over a burn-pit, and dump it, with the Dead Thing in it, into the conflagration. You lost a lot of nets that way. It also made fishing very difficult and swimming inadvisable. The reaching assists Sraddhite lifeguards used doubled as gaffing hooks.

Then there were the gargantuan vultures, the Vultyrie, dubbed the Cloud of Hadd. Living things who survived on carrion, they had been trained to carry zombies on their back in return for free flesh so damaged there was no point in an azura possessing it. Plus, his handlers assured him, there were a bewildering variety of 'Indescribables', very few of whom were Dead Things. Malevolent faerie-types and earthborn demons, Hankering Handkerchiefs among them, their supernatural abilities made them even worse than Haddazur-animated Dead Things.

Other than Hankering Hankies, which were a form of Ghast, the white-as-a-sheet kind of Ghast, which Child Thartarre found particularly terrifying, the worst of these really bad things were the vetalas. There are a few ways to tell a Vetala, his favourite nanny informed him, time and time again. For one thing, they're always young-looking, humanoid and female. For another, they always have jet-black hair. Or they do in their most common form.

"They're ever-so-beautiful, at least young men find them so," she'd say. "But those are just warning signs; signs of their few weaknesses more than anything else. Because, even though they are shape-shifters, can retract their fangs and claws like most vamps can, they have trouble holding onto their false forms.

"But, make no mistake about it, they aren't your every-night-ordinary, blood-sucking, changeling vampires. No, young sir, they're far more powerful than that. They can walk about in broad daylight, which only the best bats can do, even here on the islets, where the sun never truly breaks through the non-vulturous clouds of Hadd.

"They can frolic in the lakes, creeks and waterways, unafraid of Dead Things Swimming – because Dead Things Swimming are afraid of them; they're their mistresses, you see. As often as not they do so stark naked, which young men find stimulating. They spice their meals with garlic, which most vamps can't abide. And they not only always tell you to eat your fruits and vegetables, they eat them too. Which a proper bloodsucker would never do.

"Vetalas are named after the real Vetala, the Vampire Queen of the Dead. The fact of the matter is she's their mother, not just their maker. And she's much more than just a vampire, much more than just the titular Blood Queen of Hadd, much more than even dead, though she's all of that. She's a true devil; a Master Deva, your parents call them. Altogether alive, Irache savages worship her, dead and gone as she is. Except she isn't, is she? Can't be, gone anyhow. Otherwise how can she be the mother of all these vetalas?

"So how else can you tell a Vetala, Tarry? The real Vetala has a third eye of her own, right about there, in the middle of her forehead." His nanny would poke him there, in the middle of his forehead, just to make her point. It sort of hurt. She had sharp, glistening fingernails. "And so do they, though they're subtle about hiding them. Subtlety, that's vetalas in a mirrored egg."

A mirrored egg was one of the Sraddhites' sacred symbols. Legend had it their Living God had worn one for years. Yet, for some reason, he hadn't been wearing it when he was killed. Not that he had been killed of course. How could you kill a Living God; especially one whose adoring sister, according to certain less reliable legends, had already turned into a vampire?

"I hear they have these devices, made in Godbad, atop of which they can manifest them, their third eyes. They flash them and that's how they steal your souls, because it's souls, not flesh, vetalas are most interested in. That's because every other vamp is so afraid of them they bring them food themselves.

"Souls come in all sorts of colours. And do you know what they do with the ones they capture? They bank them, first in the boxes they carry with them, the ones their third eyes are attached to, then they transfer them to crystalline piggybanks shaped like human skulls. So, if you ever find any crystal skulls you know there's a Vetala around. You do, you tell me where you found them and we'll lay a trap for her." She made him promise that, and he did.

"Soul-stealing, that's what vetalas are all about, child. That's because they serve a devil and devils devour souls. We don't, do we, young Master Thartarre? Bow down your head and pray with me now, to the Crown of Heaven, to Sraddha Somata, Living God that he was, is, and shall be again. May he find a worthy receptacle and return to us soon."

She clutched her dangling egg-shape, he clutched his, and together they'd do just that. (It was said Sraddha Somata wasn't so much dead as he'd hidden his soul away in the mirrored egg he once wore all the time. His soul was trapped in it, though. Couldn't get out of it. At least he couldn't get out of it yet. He could, he would, wouldn't he?)

Thartarre still said his prayers, albeit more on a daily than a nightly basis. Nights on Sraddha Isle were usually too frenetic to perform proper prayers. He always made a point of invoking the Crown of Heaven as well. He prayed it would appear around his forehead and lead him to Sraddha's mirrored egg.

He even prayed Sraddha would find he himself, Thartarre, to be a worthy receptacle for his reawakened soul. His dad had, too, when he was alive. Every High Priest did. So did just about every male Brown Robe. For their part the women prayed Janna Fangfingers would find their neck worthy of biting, because then they could trap her.

Everyone believed she, born Janna Somata, Sraddha's twin sister, Second Fangs, was the Undead Thing who kept his mirrored egg, Sraddha's soul inside it, locked away in the Crystal Skull attached to the choker she always wore around her neck. They were never too clear how they figured to trap her, though.

Praying done, his nanny would build herself up to a fear-fraught finale. "Any other way to tell when you're up against Vetala? Not really. They enjoy music, play it themselves, as do your parents. Mind you, they're educated, cultured. I haven't had time for much education, much culture, myself. Been too busy staying alive, haven't I?

"Because they share with standard vamps a mesmerizing gaze, most vetalas make friends easily. They aren't at all religious so they cultivate all manner of non-Sraddhite familiars: witches, Akans, Pani merchants, Godbadians, Piscines and, yes, even Iraches. But, then again, your parents cultivate non-Sraddhite allies and your father is very religious, isn't he? Couldn't be our High Priest if he wasn't, now could he?"

Sraddhites lived in a hagiocracy or hierocracy, a form of theocracy wherein they were ruled by a clergy or priesthood. While everyone who applied his or her self to the task of doing so eventually attained the rank of priest or priestess, there were varying degrees of authority. Holgat, like Thartarre much later on, was accorded the rank of High Priest solely on the basis of his looks.

They, he and his father both, looked like Sraddha Somata. Or what Sraddha was supposed to look like. Then again, especially with their heads shaven, many male Sraddhites looked like Sraddha – so long as they tinted their skin dark, that is, since he was a hybrid Utopian and proper Utopian males were always black.

The ubiquitous pictures of their Living God were all based on a single surviving painting of him done during his lifetime by a famous artist by the name of Jordan Tethys the Younger; whose father was a pretty well-known painter as well. (Because there were so many Tethyses, males and females, whose first names were Jordan they were usually individualized by quirky middle names, which always contained the letter '*q*' in written Sedon Speak. This younger's father went by Quidnunc whereas his son went by Squiggly or Squigs.)

The original portrait was done shortly after he'd had part of his scalp ripped out during a legendary encounter he had with a freshly turned vampire in Kanin City, his not quite so legendary birthplace. There wasn't much left of the onetime Weirdom of Kanin. It was mostly just ruins, his parents, who'd been there, told him.

That the portrait had not only survived the city's destruction but had made it through Diluvia to Sraddha Isle in pristine condition was counted a minor miracle by the Curia. Nonetheless, generations of Curators had insisted any subsequent reproductions of it didn't show him with such a hideous disfigurement. Wouldn't do for the faithful to think a Dead or Undead Thing could harm their Living God.

For her part Thartarre's mother detested seeing a painting of someone who looked so much like her precious husband portrayed so matter-of-factly vulnerable to the vicissitudes of mortality on a daily and nightly basis. As far as Barsine was concerned, Holgat was perfect. Be that as it may, he certainly wasn't disfigured.

She found it so disturbing she had it covered with a sheet. Her husband wouldn't let her store it away, however. So it, in its ornate frame, still hung in the High Priest's bedroom, where it had been for hundreds of years. Even with a sheet covering it, they saw the damn thing as a constant reminder not to get careless.

Another thing High Priests were expected to do was act like Sraddha. Which meant they were supposed to fight in the frontlines. Some even survived High Priesthood and made it into the Curia, a council of elders composed of men and the occasional woman who provided the High Priest advice, which he was free to ignore, albeit at his peril. Many a High Priest died in battle, the same as anyone else, and were burnt unto ash before he had a chance to get up and join the fight on the other side. More than a few, however, were struck down from behind.

Members of the Curia were called Curators; they thought themselves the real powers-that-be amongst the Sraddhites. Virtually all of them lived in the Diluvia settlements. Unless they counted advanced witches among their subjects or membership – which they often didn't, the Curia not being fond of independent women – until radio reached Hadd, the islets and fringe settlements in the Thirties, they could only communicate with the High Priest via carrier pigeon, runners or horse messengers. Besides themselves, there was nothing a Dead Thing enjoyed more than horsemeat. They killed for it. Then again there wasn't much they wouldn't kill.

Holgat, like most High Priests before and since, tended to ignore the Curia. Which for the most part was fine with the Curators. Life was a whole lot better, and safer, in Diluvia.

"What else? They reflect in mirrors, which most vamps don't, so that's no way to tell a Vetala. It is, however, a way to tell if someone is a Vetala because they can only reflect their true forms. So that's why, in addition to my sacred egg, I always carry a hand-mirror. You do too, at your parents' insistence, thank Sraddha, because it's too awkward to keep twisting your neck down to look to see if the person you're talking to is reflecting in your egg.

"Some of them can travel between-space but your mother and our allies, the War Witches of Athena, whoever she was, or is, can do that too. They're usually not as pale as we are, even those among us whose skin isn't quite as white as mine is to start with, like yours. We're Caucasians, your mother tells me, and some Caucasians even have brown skin she also tells me.

"We've some of them here, descendants of those who fought alongside the blessed Sraddha as well as the occasional Athenan who comes by for a visit. They hail from over in Ophir-Moorset, in the Head's occipital regions. But because they're so robust and healthy-looking, because they can go places where the sun shines without clouds to hinder it, vetalas tan regardless of where they come from. Which of course vamps can't do since the sun burns them up.

"Other than that, though, that and their love of swimming, their true forms, their effect on young men, especially young religious men, who should know better, the tricky way they steal souls, by externalizing their third eyes, as I described, and their stashes of soul-banks in the form of crystal skulls, there isn't much more I can think of.

"Nonetheless, you must beware of vetalas more so than any other Dead or Undead thing, child. Because this much more I do know. While they do make young men, and even not so young men, their playthings, and while they're so jealous of young maids like me they'd prefer to turn us into old women, also like me, rather than drain us entirely of our blood, the hunger does come upon them occasionally.

"And what's their favourite food, garlic-spiced or otherwise? Why, young lads like you."

========

"This nanny of yours," wondered his guest. "She wouldn't have been named Janna by any chance?"

========

"All female Sraddhites take Janna as their middle name, Jordy. Just as all male Sraddhites take Sraddha as their middle name and we all take our father's first name as our last name. I'd have thought you'd have known that. You being a woman now hasn't made you suffer any brain-slippages, has it?"

"Cranial cramps have nothing to do with gender, Tar. And as for any other kind of cramps, I'm just wearing a second skin. Underneath it I'm as male as you are underneath your brown robe." Tethys wasn't wearing a monk's garment. Nor was he wearing a nun's penguin suit like he did when he was incarnated as Sister Jordan, in Ukemoshi Tethys, for over a decade, throughout the Fifties and into the very early Sixties.

Neither did he have on his checked cap or tweed jacket as he had when he went to Cabby's Weirdom after his overnighter on Incain. Instead, he had on a cream-coloured pantsuit and scarf Melina nee Sarpedon Zeross requisitioned from one of her older, and stouter, Illuminaries. Man or woman, he wasn't much of a stunner, like Mel was. His skin wasn't as white-white as that of her and her fellow female Illuminaries either. However, his outfit would be considered stylish among Godbadian businesswomen so that's what he told everyone he was, a civilian attaché to one of Godbad's military brass then bivouacking on Sraddha Isle.

"Well, I wish you'd take it off. Why are you wearing it anyhow?"

"Funny, I've been scratching my head about the same thing myself; the top of my head, where what's left of hair is, not the scar in my forehead, which for some reason is really itchy right now. And, you know what, I can't remember exactly why I did it. My sixth sense must have kicked in. I guess I just somehow intuitively realized someone was looking for me and I didn't want whomever it was to find me."

"And who might be looking for you, as you looked?"

"That's just it, isn't it? Someone who could find me, but only as I looked. Can't be too many of those, can there? Not from a long distance, not the way I move around. But looking at your mirrored egg, one comes to mind right away."

"Does me as well. My nanny's name, other than Janna, was Klannit."

"Was it really? And you think it was Klannit Thanatos?"

"Do you?"

"Isn't what I asked but, no. Unless it was a Samarandin homunculus prepared specifically for her, as an azura Klannit Thanatos can't take over anyone with a fully functional brain of her own. As a matter of fact I know a story, which I'm tempted to tell you, in exchange for lunch of course, of one time circumstances left the Thanatoids' lone-begotten azura in the body of debrained daemon and she couldn't get it to move.

"The other thing about a homo concocted in Samarand is Samarandins tend to make them look Samarandin. And your nanny said she was a Caucasian, didn't she?"

"She looked like one too."

"You ever consider this nanny of yours was an agent of the Curia? You said the Curators didn't approve of Barsine's independent ways. And, from the sounds of things, your Nanny Klanny was deliberately trying to turn you against your mother."

"Self-evident, isn't it."

"In hindsight, yes. I knew your mother; met her plenty of times, albeit obviously a few incarnations ago now. Young, jet-black hair, ever-so-beautiful, walks about in broad daylight, skinny dips, and so on and so on. I'm surprised she didn't tell you vetalas spend hours and hours in a darkroom because your mother certainly did."

"Actually, now that you mention it, she did. Guess that's why I'm a High Priest and not a certifiable storyteller like you are. I tend to forget pertinent details like that."

"Certified, not certifiable," Tethys forgave him. "Plus, you were only 5 years old at the time. So no sin there. But it doesn't surprise me. I have to say the capturing souls crap isn't as farfetched as it might seem. Lots of modern day folks, on both sides of the Dome, shun photographers for just that reason. And Barsine was a lifelong shutterbug.

"Regardless of whether vetalas do prematurely age instead of outright kill or turn those they bite, which they do by the way, she was talking about Barsine's box camera. Her third eye was its handheld flashgun and she'd have kept her photographic chemicals in bottles marked with the symbol for poison, a skull and crossbones.

"But she was setting you up to bring mommy Barsine down. Rather, she was setting you up to influence your daddy Holgat, supporting you, into bringing her down. Or at least to divorce her. Your nasty Nanny Klanny, if she was as young as she claimed she was, might have even had a thing for him. Make no mistake about any of that. She wasn't, she would have told you about a Vetala's most distinguishing characteristics."

"I was just getting to that. My father did, when I asked him if my mother was a Vetala."

========

It was also no sin for a 5-year-old to ask his father the wrong question. Thartarre should have asked him if his mother was Vetala.

He had, he might have elicited a different answer.

****

(Pregame-Gambit) 5: **Justifiable Matricide**

Sapienda, Tantalar 4, 5980

Almost everyone knew of a number of ways to dispose of demonic vampires. Almost no one knew how to dispose of a devilish vampire, however. Not permanently. In that respect, therefore, Barsine Holgat-wife might still be alive – in a way.

========

"A Vetala?" Holgat laughed when, here on Sraddha Isle, albeit in 5945, his 5-year-old child asked him if his wife, Thartarre's mother, was a Vetala. "Don't be ridiculous, son. Vetalas have their hands on the wrong wrists and their feet on the wrong ankles. By that I mean, palms downwards, their thumbs and big toes point outwards instead of inwards.

"Everyone knows that. And, as drop-dead gorgeous as your mother is, Tarry, her fingers and toes aren't any more extraordinary than mine or yours are. Your Nanny Klanny tries to tell you differently you let me know and we'll find you a new nanny. She's a little long in the tooth for a bodyguard anyways."

"Long in the tooth? Is she a vamp?"

"It means old, boy. Klannit was my predecessor's wife. And he is a vamp. That's why we haven't sent her into the mountains already. She wants to hang around in case he comes back to put the bite on her."

"So she can dust him?"

"I certainly hope so. I'd hate to have to dust her. While she never was my nanny, she spent a lot of time babysitting me when I was your age."

========

Nanny Klanny, and not just Nanny Klanny, told young Holgatson about all sorts of other boy-stealing or boy-eating fairies and shape-shifting demons besides vetalas. His handlers seemed to take a perverse delight in terrorizing the High Priest's only child with their grisly descriptions of these supernaturally endowed, so-called Indescribables.

There were howlers, heinous hyenas, three-headed Keres Hellhounds, kobolds, ghouls, Gobble Stones and plain goblins, pookas, kelpies, Selkies and dozens if not hundreds more. Both his daddy and mommy confirmed their existence. They also agreed that every one of these non-imaginary creatures of not just a little boy's nightmares slipped into Hadd from the northwest, through the Forbidden Forest of Kala Tal, Sedon's Moustache.

Furthermore, whatever else they did, none of it pleasant, and they did lots of other horrible things besides stealing and/or eating little boys, or often as not both, all strove against the forces of the Living. That said, though, the good news was that every one of them could be killed, usually with the Godbadian-manufactured guns his parents and handlers carried with them at all times. Chthonic creatures, as in earthborn, had a lot of problems with metals like silver, iron and especially lead. Well-known fact that. Mind you so do we, bullets in particular.

And, although there were the occasional exceptions, such as in the cases of Salamanders or Lava Louts, who had to pulverized, once killed almost all of them could be burnt unto ash. So, if you go about anywhere after dark, in the monastery or outside it, you better be sure whomever you're with has more than just a gun on them. You better be sure he or she has either a fire-canister on their back or is carrying a torch. A real torch, not just a flashlight. All of which they would say of course. They didn't want him straying.

They also warned him, as had his Nanny Klanny, never to take off his mirrored egg. They were truthful about that, too. Wherever your are, his dad insisted, so long as you have your egg dangling around your neck, on its silver chain, or in your pocket, your mom will find you.

"Better keep it round your neck, though, Tarry. Vamps hate silver and it's not just because they don't have dentists. You see, your mom's a witch. A very, very good witch; not a gingerbread witch, especially not one with an oven. We've servants to do our cooking. And your egg has a witch-stone in it. She'll step on one of hers and step out wherever you are."

Not unpredictably their terror-tactics had the reverse effect. He became convinced his bed-sheets were Hankering Handkerchiefs. No amount of dissembling would dissuade him of that. So what if hankies were small little things you stuffed in your pockets? Demons were shape-shifters, weren't they. They could grow as big as bed-sheets, couldn't they. Did his sheets have eyes or mouths, did they float about in the dark or talk to him? They did in his dreams. Those are just nightmares. There's a difference?

He became scared of sleeping alone. So they moved his bed into their bedroom. Where are your torches? Torches stink, we've electric lightbulbs now. We can turn them on any time. Bats don't like light. Besides, bats can't come into the monastery without permission and that's another fact. But Dead Things can and they're not afraid of the light.

They showed him their back-canisters, which they kept in a locked closet; the same place they kept their blades, axes and the myriad other kinds of weaponry, Marutian arcane and Godbadian modern, they used against Dead and Undead Things. It was also where they put their guns when they went to bed at night.

A Hankering Hanky would eat me before you can get to it. And even if I'm only half-eaten, what are you going to do then, burn me up with it? They performed ablutions on his bed-sheets. His dad was a High Priest. Priests practised ablutions; it made their parishioners feel reverent. You told me not to wet my bed, now you're doing it for me.

He took to sliding into the sack with his parents. They let him. What else were they to do? Mama Barsine had always been a bit of a night owl – and quite the party girl before Holgat settled her down – so at first she didn't object. She often strolled around the massive edifice until the early hours anyhow. Island days were dull as dishwater and, without rain, almost as boring. She liked the sun, did Mama Barsine; had been brought up in it, tanned a golden brown. She liked the tads of action the night's then-rare bat-attacks provided as well.

When, after a month or two of this nonsense, she began to actually prefer resting during the day rather than sleep with her son and husband at night, not just Holgat became alarmed. One day, perhaps not her oldest friend in the world, but nevertheless her oldest friend on this side of it, as she sometimes strangely put it, flew in for an official visit. It was official because the friend, who was only a couple years older than his parents, was the marital Queen of Godbad, Scylla nee Nereid become Auranja.

She was a witch: the best witch ever, according to his mother; albeit not so much so a good witch, according to his father. True, she didn't have an oven but she preferred her food raw and his father didn't approve of that sort of thing. Dead Things liked their food raw, too. She didn't fly in on a broomstick. Nor did she ride in on a Garuda, pterippi, or any other kind of psychopomp. Which she apparently once could do, on a winged dolphin, also according to his mother.

She flew in on a contraption Holgat, who had a talent for technical precision, helped to both design and engineer. It was a prototype whirlybird, the like of which the Godbadian military perfected years later, during the subcontinent's Civil War. Centauri Enterprises not yet in existence, it was made by one of the aristocracy's most Outer-Earth-modern companies: Royal Byronic Volant, RBV for short.

Like most members of the imported aristocracy that owned almost everything worth owning in the subcontinent in those days, as CE did now, her husband's ancestry was Bandradin, meaning his extensive family hailed from the Cattail Peninsula. Nevertheless he, Achigan Auranja, was Godbad's hereditary king, hence the 'Royal'. Godbad's gods, devils that they were, were Byronics, hence that. The Volant part – 'Volant' just meant flying – came from PV, Pyçonja Volant.

PV was a rebellious Byronic Master Deva whose star had been shining in the Night's Sky since 5918, the very year the future Queen Scylla was born. No coincidence there. Scylla was amphibious; a humanoid Piscine, with gills behind her ears. Contrarily, she was raised by the Piscines' traditional enemies and sometimes main meal, the Lemurian Frogwomen.

Like his mother, although she was trained in the crafts of a variety of different Sisterhoods, whereas Barsine didn't have any formal training whatsoever, Scylla was a natural-born witch. Also like his mother was rumoured to be, she was deviant. Her devic half-mother, so she always claimed, was none other than that very Pyçonja Volant.

The visit from Queen Scylla started to ring Barsine's own, evidently by then highly developed alarm bells. She became increasingly agitated about her only child's behaviour. It's peculiar, she kept saying to Holgat during the few minutes they had alone everyday, that the boy, once so vibrant and outgoing, was pent up to the point he hardly ever left his father's side, even in bed. Perhaps they should send him back to his early childhood stomping grounds in Diluvia. She'd go with him of course.

Better yet, maybe he, High Priest Holgat, whom she sometimes called 'Holy' as in 'holier than thou', should just let her take the boy to the subcontinent for a vacation. Holy could come too. A break would be good for them. Godbad was mountainous, the sun shone there, Tarry had never really seen the sun and, you know, my oldest friend on this side of the world is its queen.

Hubby Holy resisted. As annoyingly cloying as Tar's attentions were sometimes, Holgat could see nothing wrong with father-son bonding. He rather enjoyed the youngster's constant company, truth be told. He'd never felt closer to his son before. Never felt healthier either. And why was it Queen Scylla insisted him having sex with her, Barsine, was so important to keep her only rumoured deviant tendencies quelled anyways?

"All I'm suggesting is it's just not natural," Barsine kept reiterating.

"Maybe not," considered Holgat. "But it's good for us, Tarry and me."

"But I've got desires. How can we maintain a proper relationship with our son always in bed with us?"

"We'll find a way," snuggled Holgat. They didn't.

Perhaps to her credit, Barsine didn't succumb to depression. Rather, the more desperate she grew the more aggressive she became. Her persistent nagging grated at her husband. But the manner in which she comported herself during her scheduled, and unscheduled, self-defence training sessions were costing him the affection and loyalty of his priests and priestesses. While he no more appreciated her like this than she did herself, those she trained with, when anyone would train with her, definitely didn't appreciate the hours and sometimes days they spent in the infirmary after their sessions.

Howsoever reluctantly, Holgat finally relented. He didn't agree to let Thartarre go on vacation with his mother to the subcontinent of Aka Godbad. All he agreed to do was send him back to Diluvia with, as if to add insult to injury, his Nanny Klanny, not his mother, as his accompanist. That way Barsine would get what she didn't so much want as need, some serious love-making. There was only one way to soothe a savage beast by the name of Barsine Holgat-wife and she was right. He couldn't do it, over and over again, in the same bed with his son.

When told the news after his bath early one night in late Hektor 5945, August 1945 on the Outer Earth, the boy ripped off his mirrored egg and threw it at his parents. He fled from them, whereupon he managed to elude his retainers as well as his parents for the rest of the evening and most of the night. Disappearing into the bowels of the monastery, no one could find the little scamp. But he found someone else; some ones else. It was his Nanny Klanny and she was smooching with a somewhat dark-skinned someone, one who also looked a little like his father.

Thartarre still had his handheld mirror with him and when he turned it on his nanny and her paramour only she reflected in it. The poor child dropped it in terror. It broke. They heard it. He ran. Ran back to his mommy and daddy's bedchamber. Fortunately, having not so much given up the search as left it to others, they were there. Unfortunately, they were making love when Thartarre burst in on them. Klannit and her Undead husband, the now-turned former High Priest of Sraddha, were right behind him; slamming the door as they entered.

He went straight for the closet where his parents kept their weaponry. It was locked. He screamed. His parents screamed, struggled to disengage. Klannit was armed, had a gun in her holster and a fire-canister on her back. She must have realized the game was up, her trysts discovered, all her work on the boy ruined, she with her mirrors. The vamp, who being a former High Priest may not have needed permission to enter the monastery, though she'd given it to him anyways, went straight for Barsine as Klannit struggled with her holster's flap.

Holgat tumbled out of bed, as naked as his wife; went straight for the closet. It didn't need a key but the mechanism, which he'd designed, needed some manipulation, which he was too flustered to perform accurately. Klannit had her gun out by now. The vamp had pinned Barsine's arms behind her back but for some reason wasn't putting the bite on her. It was Klannit who shouted the cease and desist.

"Stop making life so difficult, all of you. It's you Fangs wants, Holgat, so I'll shoot the boy if I have to. But none of you have to die. Not even your wife. If you do as we say."

Holgat wasn't stupid. He grabbed the child and held him by his wrists behind his bare backside. If Janna Fangfingers wanted him and Klannit was prepared to shoot Thartarre, then she'd have shoot the child through him. Which wouldn't endear her to Second Fangs. "What's the meaning of this?" he blustered impotently.

"Figure it out for yourself, successor," said the vamp holding onto Barsine, who had quit making any effort to get away from him. "Fangs always wants the High Priest. She thinks her twin brother is incarnated within us. She sent a Vetala after me; an ever-so-enticing one who didn't look much different than your outsider here. I didn't realize it. But my wife discovered our dalliances and proved it to me, with her mirrors. Hands on the wrong wrists, feet on the wrong ankles, you'll have been taught.

"I was smitten. I wouldn't kill her and by then the Vetala had my wife in much the same situation I now have yours. Only she began to feed on her, aging her day after day, slowly, imperceptibly. Everyone thought she had a wasting disease of some sort. But we had a notion, did Klannit and I. Fangs wanted me so badly she could have me. You see, Fangs doesn't want a vampire, she wants her brother back, alive and well.

"Except he rejected me, so she said anyhow. Claimed he'd determined I was an unworthy receptacle for his soul. So she put the bite on me; just for spite. I'll offer you the same deal. She's outside. Go with her and you'll all live. So will she and so will I, again. She knows how to cure vampirism. All you have do is prove yourself a worthy receptacle."

Holgat hesitated. Everything the vamp said made some sick degree of sense. Barsine must have felt the same way. Her upbringing what it'd been, she didn't like being forced into doing anything she didn't want to do.

"Open the window, Holgat," she yelled at her husband. "Invite Fangs inside. She gives us her word she won't turn you if you don't prove worthy of Sraddha Somata's soul, I'll take Tarry to Godbad until you send word for us one way or another: to come back or not to come back."

Now it was Klannit's turn to hesitate. "Why should we let you take the boy?"

"Because he's my son and I'd rather take a risk sacrificing my husband than any chance of losing my son. Now put your gun away."

"After Fangs agrees." Klannit waved her gun at the latched window opposite his parents' bed. There was indeed a big bat hovering outside it; had to be Second Fangs. The window was set in the wall beside where the shrouded painting of Sraddha Somata hung in its ornate frame. It was almost as if she'd seen it for the first time.

"What the fuck?" she cursed, dropping her gun and going for her back-canister.

Then the Ghast attacked her.

========

"Your mother wasn't quite naked, was she?"

"Apparently not. She was wearing her wedding ring."

"Witches and matrimony," muttered his guest. "There's a lesson for you, Tar.'

"There is?"

"You ever marry a witch, don't bother asking if she likes the ring. They'll just change it to suit themselves anyways."

========

The shroud covering the painting was a Hankering Handkerchief. Young Thartarre was right. Hankering Hanks could become big as sheets – or shrouds. It must have been waiting for some sort of mental signal from Barsine, whose mother was once a Morrigan, the big boss bitch of the Hecate-Hellion Sisterhood, the same as Superior Sarpedon was today.

It wasn't as fast as Klannit was, though. She ignited it, ignited the painting it was covering as well, before it could even get close to her. She fell to her knees, ducking, it still burning into wisps of ash above her. Artificially aged by the Vetala or not, Nanny Klanny was still pretty perky. Her gun was in her hand again. Holgat had already taken his son behind the nearest settee. Not having a ready target, maybe not even wanting to shoot anyone anymore, she pointed it in the direction of Barsine and her vamp of a self-admitted, unworthy receptacle for Sraddha Somata's soul.

Barsine was covered in dust, no vamp in sight. A materialist, like most top-of-the-class witches were, not that she'd ever attended witchery school as such, she held a silvery stiletto she'd conjured out of her wedding ring. Had something in her other hand. This she tossed at Klannit. It was Thartarre's mirrored egg.

Klannit shot her; shot at her. Barsine was already disappearing. And reappearing, off the mirrored egg that cracked in front of Thartarre's nanny. She drove the silver blade into Nanny Klanny's arm. The older woman dropped the gun but, much to Barsine's astonishment, didn't turn to dust as her Undead husband had.

Holgat was quick himself. He was away from behind the settee and across the room in a few blinks of Thartarre's eyelids. He picked up Klannit's gun; trained it at her head. Barsine yanked her silvery blade out of the prematurely aged nanny's arm. Klannit slumped, clutching the wound. Holgat told his wife that was enough.

"Not quite." Barsine slashed the straps of Klannit's fire-canister. It fell onto the floor. Just for good measure she bare-foot-booted her in the skull. Nanny Klanny got glassy-eyed; pitched backwards. Barsine picked up her canister, which had shut off automatically, once she'd released its triggering device, but was still hot to the touch, and tossed it onto their bed.

She gave her husband a lascivious wink "Next time you need a cigarette afterwards, Holy, we've a lighter."

Thartarre grabbed the flamethrower. Dazed, Klannit pointed upwards, towards the still-latched window. The bat was gone. She wasn't pointing at the window, though. She was pointing at the wall. "I knew it," she gasped. His parents followed her gaze. Barsine shrieked.

Klannit was pointing at the famous painting of a disfigured Sraddha Somata done by his contemporary, Jordan *'Q for Squiggly'* Tethys, already become the 55th Century of the Dome's latest Legendarian. It wasn't very much there anymore; was still more there than her ex-husband or the Ghast-shroud that had been covering it.

She wasn't so much pointing at it as she was at what was behind it; it in its ornate, now telltale-glimmering and evidently fully fire-resistant frame. It was a mirror. Her reflection formed in its glassine sheen. So did Holgat's and Barsine's. Only, while it was remarkably close to Barsine's, it wasn't Barsine's. Smiling toothily, out of it grinned Nergal Vetala, the long, thought-gone Blood Queen of Hadd herself.

Even longer raven-hair, elongated canine teeth, uppers and lower, thick, ruby-red lips, pale-greenish skin-tint, all of that kind of gave her away. That she was wearing clothes, black tatters of a gown, whereas Barsine was still as naked as the day she born, only larger, provided additional confirmation of the distinction. What cemented it were her fiery eyeballs. She had three of them, one in the centre of her forehead where Nanny Klanny used to poke Thartarre for emphasis when she was describing her.

"Burn the witch!" cried Klannit.

========

Thartarre Sraddha Holgatson paused momentarily. Hit the intercom button and ordered lunch. His guest retained a respectful silence. "Maybe I will take you up on your offer, Jordy. A tale for a tale. Besides, I'm hungry and my barber's a tremendous cook. Sure you won't have another beer?"

Even when you didn't live just the once, you might as well enjoy your currently latest 'once' while you still can. Immortality for everyone else might be only a medical breakthrough away. Could be, if your name was Jordan Tethys, you're stuck in Limbo waiting for one of your children or grandchildren to catch an incurable illness when it comes. Except, that being the case, it won't, wouldn't, would it?

"Maybe I will."

========

So preconditioned was he – by Klannit's Mirror Mentalist coercive talents, he forever-after claimed – Thartarre did just that. He triggered his nanny's fire-canister, ignited his mother. Barsine was too transfixed on the wall-mirror's reflection that wasn't hers, but was where hers should be, to notice what he was doing until it was too late for her. Their bed-sheets, his and his parents' bed-sheets, Ghasts the lot of them, flew across the room, covered his mother; tried to smother out the resultant flames engulfing her.

Klannit scampered safely away from her, and them. She was giggling insanely; would never regain her sanity, if she was sane to start with after the Vetala's slurping attentions. Holgat reacted smartly, hauled the revealed mirror off the wall. Out of Vetala's third eye devic eyefire burst forth. Holgat was scorched but determined; he was thinking almost as fast as he was moving and his beloved wife was burning to death.

He smashed the mirror on the floor, kicked the shattered shards of glass out of its frame. The Hankering Handkerchiefs were only smouldering now, the fire was out, but Barsine wasn't moving underneath the dead or dying Ghasts. As if it was a hula hoop Holgat looped the mirror's glowing frame over his wife's body. She stirred, squirmed, but, divesting herself of the Ghasts, it was Vetala who sprang up, whole and unburned, not Barsine.

"At last," she gloated. "Three generations of hateful Hellions and their menfolk have kept me quelled within them, grandmother, mother and daughter. For finally freeing me, Sraddhite, I let you live."

Priests and priestesses crashed into the room, responding to the noise and screams. Vetala manifested her power focus, a Brainrock-luminescent, wickedly-curved sickle. She swiped at the newcomers then went for Thartarre. Reflexively he triggered the flamethrower again. Her turn to screech, her turn to burn. She slashed out, cut off his right arm at the elbow, mystified, became a bat, crashed through the latched window; fled into the night's sky. Going for the dramatic she flew towards the full moon. It must have been an awe-inspiring sight.

Holgat lost control, forgot about his son, whom Klannit had gone to instinctively. Still butt-naked, he raced past his men and women, down the corridor and up the stairs onto the roof pad. There awaited the prototype Godbadian whirlybird he designed for RBV to build. He'd been flying it on a daily basis since Queen Scylla delivered it. There was no need for a key; no one else could get it to work. He went after the devil. She led him a merry chase but the copter caught up with her hundreds of miles to the east.

It was running low on fuel but Vetala was just below it. Holgat leapt out and landed on the vampire. Gravity propelled them downwards, into the midst of the Jaag Maelstrom. It whirled around and around; a pool of water that never quite went down the drain but made as if that was what it was doing. She must have struggled, damaged bat-form then damaged human form, to get away but Holgat wouldn't let her go.

Inexorably both were sucked into its liquid depths. That should have been it for both of them. It definitely was it for Holgat who, being human, couldn't survive breathing water. The pirates of Jaag found his body shortly after dawn. It washed up near the wreckage of the prototype whirlybird on one of the jagged islets that give the Strait of Jaag, what lies between the Head's Interior Ocean of Akadan and the Aural Sea, Sedon's Ear, its name.

His corpse was a mess but someone, one of the pirates' witches, must have recognized it because they chained it up and contacted Aortic Merthetis, who was then the Lemurian Quarter Queen of Shenon, Witch Isle. That's the heart-shaped island far to the south of Jaag, in Akadan, between Krachla and the Cattail Peninsula.

Aortic Merthetis was Queen Scylla's stepmother. The current Lemurian Quarter Queen, Aortic Amphitrite, is her daughter. She's a Summoning Child. She knew

Holgat and Barsine personally and it was her, along with her stepsister, Queen Scylla herself, who brought Holgat's body back to Sraddha Isle.

========

"Guess it was a good thing they chained up his corpse then," said his guest.

"And kept it chained," confirmed his host, who was tearing up. "Because it was still struggling against them when it came to fire his pyre."

========

Wiping his eyes with the sleeve covering his lone arm, Thartarre finished his narration more emotionally than he'd been telling it. "Thank sainted Sraddha my Nanny Klanny had trauma-training keyed to the battlefield. Given where she's spent most of her adult life, she also had plenty of experience when it came to providing emergency medical treatment. As a result, Vetala cutting off my arm hadn't killed me.

"I was still more than a little rocky on my pins but, since I could walk, I was accorded the honour of disposing of his body. She held me up, though. Helped me hold the torch, too. As we approached the pyre to light it, the Dead Thing turned to glare at me. The hate that was in its eyes resolved into, I swear, a look of love.

"I know that isn't possible but that's how I always end my story."

"And a fine way to end it as well, Tarry. Ah, here's lunch. Isn't it about time you formally introduced me to your barber."

"Of course," he said as the elderly simpleton put the tray containing their lunches and beer down on the table. "Jordan Tethys, I'd like you to meet Klannit Janna Anvil-wife."

"Delighted to make your acquaintance, Nanny Klanny."

========

"Anvil-wife?" queried Tethys, once she'd left them alone to eat. "What was the name of her husband, the vamp the Vetala seduced and Fangs turned?"

"Tvasitar Sraddha Quentin-son. But everyone called him Anvil because he was such a hard-headed fanatic. They got together during the Simultaneous Summonings of 5920. You've met their son, Quentin Anvil. He's the Godbadian General who's in charge of Operation Haas."

"Ah, well, that must explain how she became a Klannit then."

"Why 'must'?"

"Because nobody, not even me, remembers what happened during the Summoning."

****

(PREGAME-GAMBIT) 6: **Chomping the Cosmicar's Four**

The First Few Days Of Tantalar, 5980

He knew they were after him. They'd been after him for days and endless days. Ever since they'd ambushed his patrol. In the jungle. He'd only freshly arrived. Was barely old enough to join them. His patrol, what they ambushed. But, whoa. Not this jungle. At least it didn't look like this jungle. Yet it had to be this jungle. What other jungle could it be?

Couldn't think. No time to think. Days and endless days. Run. They were after him. Running. Always running. For days. They weren't going to catch him. Not alive at least.

He'd kill himself first.

========

And so he ran. And staggered and tripped and fell and crawled and slithered. Through the jungle. The reeking jungle. Must be the same. Days and endless days. The jungle. The slime. The swamp muck. They weren't going to catch him. Aren't going to catch me. I'll kill them first. Kill myself first. Kill myself. Run. Jungle. Stagger. Slime. Fall. Swamp Muck. Leeches. Worms. Skulls. Crawl. They aren't kill myself. Catch them first. Slither. Serpent. Bite off head. Suck blood. Eat. Save ammo. Heard what they do. In jungle. Muck the fuck. Must be same. Duck! Ambush. Move. Through swamp fuck. Stop laughing. Kill something.

He passes out. Face down. In the swamp muck. Above him monstrous vultures are already circling. He'd forgotten to kill himself.

Better to have remembered.

========

He awoke. Became aware of two strong hands gripping him by the arms, dragging him through the mud. So, they've caught me. He flops his hands at his side. Possum. Dare not open eyes. Yes, possum. Pogo-possum. Must think. Feel. Still there. Fools forgot to take my hand-Gatling. Battle-hardened. Trained never to panic in face of enemy. Feigns unconsciousness. Bides time. Collects thoughts. Concentrates. Steels his nerve. Waits. It's the only way. Should have tried it long ago. NOW!

Twists his body. Yanks free. Rolls. Draw gun-Gatling. Fires. "Fucking kill me. So? Take some of you yellow fuckers with me." Gasps. Incredulity. Stops firing.

Missed! Captors? Captor! One. Female. Yellow? White as Aegean whitewash. Resumes firing. Empties automatic handgun into ancient crone. "Impossible. Couldn't have missed. Never missed before. Not so close!"

"Hold, mortal!" chortles hideous hag. "Cease this idiocy. I am the Goddess of Life Eternal. None dare defy my will."

He knows it's a trick; knows they've got him; knows this hateful old woman isn't really there. Hallucination. Result of some foul experiment gooks performed. Heard what they do to captives. Sick fucks. Remembers vow. Hold Gatling to eye. Must be full of bloody blanks. Couldn't have missed. Impossible. Blank in eye's as good as bullet, right?

"Hold, damn you to Satanwyck!" commands the crone, no longer amused. "I've not dragged you all this way just to let you kill yourself."

Fingers tense. Knows it's a trick. Knows there's no old woman standing in front of him. Heard what they can do to men's minds. They, them, slants, captors, raptors, enemy. Knows it's a trick. Must pull trigger. Now, while time still has.

"Hold I say!" The etching of a third eye appears in her forehead. From it shoots a faint beam of light. He pulls trigger. Nothing. Empty. Fumbles for ammunition pouch. "Raise your eyes, soldier. Behold." He obeys. Lifts head. There, perched on a hill cleared of the grasping jungle stands an emerald and gold pagoda, a reminder of heaven in the hell of this Eden.

"You please me, soldier. Live."

========

For the war-weary soldier, the next few weeks are as close to paradisiacal as a man could hope to experience. Living in luxury amidst the splendour of the goddess's gilt-green pagoda, he lazes away his days by strolling through the tropical gardens, sampling its fruit-bearing trees and soaking in its warm-water ponds. In the evening he relaxes to the sound of wonderful music; exquisite, enchanting sounds that seemed to come out of the air itself; instruments played by an ethereal orchestra, songs sung by a celestial choir.

Always at his beck, she brings him fresh vegetables and fruit with delectable dips and spicy sauces, fragrant hand-squeezed juices, titbits of fowl and roasted boar; presents him with pleasing smoke, mushrooms, seeds and unguents to heighten his mounting euphoria. Every night, after the moon rose and the little creatures of the dark began to cavort, she gives him a warm, exquisite elixir she calls 'soma'. He sips this, basking in her company, until sleep finally overtakes him.

Although he can't remember them, his dreams must be expansive. He always wakes up exhausted, though nonetheless content. He's delighted with his good fortune; hasn't a care, not a worry in the world. Hasn't died and gone to bliss everlasting; has chosen life and been rewarded with heaven on earth. Is overjoyed he didn't killed himself.

It never bothers him goddess never eats with him; never asks him about his past, even his name. It doesn't alarm him he never sees another human besides her. Doesn't scare him his health, which improved remarkably at first, has begun to deteriorate; doesn't bother him he always wakes up feeling weaker than he had the night before.

Oh, things aren't perfect. Initially he found it distressing the only other living creatures constantly around the pagoda were oversized vultures; found it doubly distressing she seemed able to communicate with them. But he soon got over that. He hadn't been in his right mind at first. Now he is. He's stopped worrying. Worrying was an alien concept. He never thinks about the war, the enemy, what they'll do to him if they catch him.

His past life, his hopes, his ambitions, his loves, his friends, his conquests, his defeats, his betrayals, his doubts: he's forgotten everything. Even what he did or who he was. Name? What name? Soldier's good enough. Everything before goddess is meaningless, useless, ultimately self-destructive; even less relevant than a scarcely recalled childhood nightmare.

Like silly terrors of youth make an adult chuckle, he laughs aloud whenever a dim memory of past frights floats into his consciousness. Big eye in night sky, mocking laughter, supernova sunburst, jungle, running. Existence before meeting her is an absurdist's abstraction. He laughs all the more on the rare occasion he recollects their first encounter.

'What a stupid, tormented fool I must have been to think her a decrepit old crone. Why, she is the most indescribably perfect woman a man could lay eyes upon.'

That she is, was, ever will be. Every morning when he awakes and she brings him breakfast, she appears to be even more stunning, even more beautiful to behold, than she did the night previous. The dry, stringy, knotted shreds of grey hair are really thick, jet-black raven tresses flowing liquidly to her waist. Her skin could never have been parched and wizened. It had never cracked with age and decay. While, true, she's paler than most women he's met, her skin shines, glistens, as if with a life all its own.

No, her breasts had never sagged with time. She never hobbled around on arthritic legs. Her lips have always been red, full of life's blood. With the poise of a born queen, the grace of a real goddess, she can dance, it seems to him, on the very air itself. Undeniably he must have been raving mad, a dementia wrought by his past life.

Whatever, wherever that was, he's beyond it now. If he's delirious, it's with happiness. But, no, he mustn't think of the happiness, the euphoria. Dare not, for to do so might presage its ending. It can't end. He can't bear the thought of living without her.

She doesn't deign to sleep with him. That'd be beneath her dignity and his right to wish. But she does tease him with her body. Her nightly dances drive him to such heights of pleasure that to desire more would be tantamount to sacrilege. The life he's living's more than any one man deserves.

========

One night the soldier has a dream.

========

It starts idyllically enough. He's lying on his bed of cocoa leaves, having just finished a fine meal of rabbit roasted on a spit. He swallows the final dregs of excellent, honey-sweetened nectar she gives him each night so he can sleep better. As usual, as he's nodding off, she dances for him. This night – this dream at any rate – she seems more passionate; wilder than ever before.

As she whirls, her long tresses flailing about in a dance of their own, the dark garment she always wears slowly dissipates into nothingness. For the first time he beholds her naked. Unnerved not in the slightest, she doesn't try to cover up. Quite the contrary, she shows no trace of embarrassment; continues brazenly before him. Visibly exhilarated, movements beyond suggestive, expression ecstatic, she's lost in the flow of her own body.

He reaches out, touches her on the ankle. A scream, hers. A release, his. She stops dancing. Stands above him. Wanton. Covered in sweat. Can it be? Has the moment finally come? She smiles.

"Yes, my soldier, my saviour, my rejuvenator, it is that time. That time at last." Her teeth gleam bright white; she licks them until they glisten in the torch light. "That time when I shall join you; that time for the last time."

She kneels, bends over him. He thinks to kiss her; shrieks. Her skin's gone greenish pale. Her canine teeth are long and sharp. A third eye appears in her forehead, riveting him in place, silencing him. The bite feels like twin pinpricks; the only thing uncomfortable about the sucking is the slurping sound and a strange, light-headed sensation of blood draining out of his veins.

Then he awoke and began to live the nightmare.

========

Elvis Elfin, Felix Dee, and Geraint Plantagenet – 'E',' F', and' G' – were guy-pals; had been so ever since they were assigned to Cosmicar Four three years earlier. The Express was launched Sunday. Today, by their own reckoning, was Thursday night.

Nights were the worst.

========

One minute the six cosmicompanions and Cosmicar Four's captain, Dmetri Diomad, the *'D'* that made Dee have to be an *'F'*, were enduring the gravitational crush of takeoff. The next, *boom!*, they were in some kind of dark space dominated by a few stars and a huge discorporate eye. Then, *zoom!*, Elfin, Dee, and Plantagenet were back on Earth – only it was no part of the planet any of them had seen before.

Because of the low temperature and the variety of huge trees, some coniferous, most deciduous, Plantagenet, who had a doctorate in Botany and knew his trees, speculated they were in Alaska, Northern British Columbia, or the Rocky Mountains. Dee, by profession a systems analyst but, by inclination, a bit of a mystic, had his doubts.

Given the time of year and apparent altitude, he pointed out that the moisture pouring from the sky by the bucketful should be snow, not rain. He suggested they were in the Andes of South America or, possibly, somewhere in New Zealand. Not that one idea was any more likely than the other, noted Elfin, in his usual sarcastic manner. They shouldn't be anywhere except Cosmicar Four. Or else dead.

Too well trained to waste time on guesswork, they set about surviving. Thankfully, wherever they'd been transported, their life-packs, including their automatic handguns and rifles, had as well. They had food rations, clothing, maps of Earth, and navigational equipment. Their immediate trouble was that it was raining so hard they couldn't get a fix on the stars.

Wisely, on the Sunday, they just raised tents and went to sleep. Monday morning provided no relief. It just kept raining. Using their compasses and common-sense, they headed downwards and, as much as the terrain allowed, due south. Elfin, the geo-cartographer of the three, assumed the leadership role. Thursday morning, their supplies well-conserved and spirits high, they reached the foothills. Other than spotting a sabre-toothed tiger, whom all agreed were extinct, their journey had been relatively uneventful.

Theories that they had somehow been sent to the distant past were dispelled when they reached an anomalous region where, within two or three steps, they were either in a heavy downpour or a completely rain-free area. The consensus was that this could never happen on Earth, neither millennia ago nor today. So where in creation were they?

Dee had read a book entitled *'The Twelfth Planet'*. It was written by an Armenian scholar named Zecharia Sitchin a couple of years earlier. Dee suggested the three of them had found themselves on that selfsame planet, the Twelfth. Any day now, they'd come across their first *'Nephilim'*, the race of super-advanced *'supranormals'* that Sitchin claimed came from that planet and had bio-engineered modern day humanity three hundred millennia earlier.

The other two were highly dubious but, after four days of wandering, in a never-ending torrent, without seeing another intelligent being – nor any sign of one – they were willing to accept almost anything. Being on another planet, even a farfetched, hypothetical 12th one, made as much sense as anything else. Besides, despite the insulating quality of their silver and black, hooded uniforms, they were tired of being inundated. Hiking through a dry land was preferable to almost literally swimming through a mountain forest. They carried on their southward vector.

For all their brains; their collective wisdom, skills, training and experience, they were ignorant wayfarers. How were they to know they had just entered Hadd, the Land of the Dead?

========

Goddess was on her feet, drawing her robe around herself. Too weak to move, he just lay on his back and stared up at her. The transition was complete.

She was a young woman again; he felt a hundred years old.

========

She picked him up like a straw man and sat him on a boulder in the middle of the jungle. Only then did he realize he wasn't in the splendid pagoda anymore. She waved at a pile of clothes nearby. They were his. He recognized his uniform, black pants and boots, dark-grey and silver-striped, hooded top, survival pack, ammo pouch, machine pistol and assault rifle.

"At first you were stronger than me. You could have escaped but I made you want to stay. Now I am torn between slaying you, rewarding your loyalty and making you one of mine forevermore, or leaving you alive. I'll savour your blood one more time." She moved towards him. He thought to run once more into the jungle. "Struggle not, my soldier, for surely I will open your throat and drink you dead."

He didn't struggle. She let him live. She could always come back for more.

========

Around noon, if their reckoning by a completely cloud-covered sky was at all accurate, they sighted their first manmade structure far in the distance. Pushing hard, over the bleak, mud-caked landscape of the high plateau, they reached the isolated building

shortly after dark. It was deserted; had probably been so for years. But there was no doubt what it had been: a tannery with an abattoir adjacent to it.
A slaughterhouse!

========

The wagons appeared on the horizon shortly before midnight.

From their hiding place in the upper level of the ruin, the three cosmicompanions, their weaponry at hand, some of their incendiaries pre-deployed, their strategy already decided, observed their approach. A half dozen carts, each with a drover, a guard, and maybe eight prisoners in the back of each one, were pulled by a team of four ostrich-sized birds. When they came close enough to be seen by the three companions through their night-sight binoculars, they appeared to be huge, long-legged vultures whose wings had apparently been clipped.

The half-dozen things flying above the carts were large bats and the ten or so creatures loping along behind them were some kind of half-human wolves. The whip-wielding drovers and the spear-carrying guards were definitely human, though some of them looked to be in an advanced state of decomposition. Whatever else they were witnessing, you never expected to see sights like this.

The occupants of the carts were also human. Red-skinned, perhaps fifty in number, they appeared to be Native American Indians. For prisoners, the aboriginals were acting inexplicably happy, almost jubilant. Some hugged one another smilingly; some clasped hands and looked to be chanting; others were on their knees, praying in contented unison. No sign of tears, remorse, fear.

Not just because there were a few deaf people aboard the Cosmic Express, all three cosmicompanions knew and understood sign language, lip-reading and finger-spelling. They communicated silently.

"What think now, F," signed Elfin then spelled, "Nephelim?"

"No way, E! Drivers look sleep. No, dead walking!"

"Zombies?" Plantagenet finger-queried. "Then, mean ... big bats, wolves-men ...."

Dee spread his second and third right fingers into a v-shape then touched them to his jugular. "Vampires!"

"Teasing?"

"No!"

"FK," spelt Elfin, mouthing the word *fuck*.

"Forgot melt candlestick," joked Plantagenet grimly.

Elfin signed: "Count beads have, F?"

"Always," responded Dee. Count-beads were a rosary.

"Good. Maybe work."

"Catholic, you?" asked Plantagenet.

"Before, youth, yes. Not church many years now."

"Not believe, not work. Read Count Dracula."

"What work? Bullets? Water?"

"Only if holy. Fat chance here."

"Maybe, maybe not. Must try."

"Fire?"

"On dead things walking, hope. On wolves, think so. Bullets too. On vamps, doubt."

"Have fire. Must try also."

"Silver only in uniform."

"So, throw uniform then run, last chance. Joke? Not really."

"Try everything. Play dead first. Maybe not notice us."

"Teasing again, G?"

"We CCs." Cosmicompanions. "We fight, if must. Try keep hide first. Hope go away. Notice us. Try everything. Agree with G. Fight same hell. Then blow up! Understand? Don't want become dead thing walking."

"Here come."

"Ready? Start quiet. No move. Spot us. Fight hell!'"

========

The carts stopped in front of the tannery. The prisoners, if such they were, got off then helpfully removed the bridles and ropes from the six teams of grounded vultures. The two dozen birds, once relieved of their restraints, nodded to the zombie drovers and guards who seemed to understand them via some sort of telepathy. The werewolves kept a respectful distance as the six giant bats landed then transmogrified, became human.

Of the shape-changers, four were men and two were women. They came from a variety of racial backgrounds. One of the men was a redskin, a native North American Indian type like the prisoners, who didn't act like prisoners. He was dressed approaching stereotypically, in hides and furs, as if he'd just stepped off a John Wayne, me-kill-um-Injuns, movie set. Another was brown-skinned, like an East Indian, and was shabbily-dressed in peasant garments reminiscent of the same place, modern-day India. How they shape shifted clothed was merely a minor mystery. How they existed at all, let alone that what they appeared to be existed, wasn't worth wondering about.

The other two men struck the three spying cosmicompanions as even stranger. One was accoutered in a regular, if somewhat tattered, black business suit while the other wore a tracksuit, as if he just come in from jogging. Clothing aside, what was so strange about them was they both had skin coloured and textured the same as a California orange. What was so strange about one of the women, a young and nice-looking, albeit toothy, dark-haired oriental in a kimono and sandals was both her feet and hands seemed to be attached backwards.

The lone classical, Hammer-Horror-style vampire, with her long, silver hair and diaphanous, silken gown, had no fangs manifest. Instead, on her right hand, she wore a furry glove that was tipped by wickedly sharp, talon-like claws. The glove glowed with the gleam of Gypsium so familiar to the cosmicompanions – Gypsium being the Cosmic Express's secondary fuel, what was supposed to be teleportive.

Probably was too, since they'd ended up down here, three instead of seven and minus their Cosmicar, #4 of six, out of a Cosmic Express with more than ten times that number in terms of cosmicompanions. From the way the zombies, vultures, werewolves, aboriginal American sorts and other vamps, alien as three of them looked to be, reacted when she spoke, she had to be their squad leader if not their overall commander, always assuming they were part of a military or, more likely given their lack of uniforms, a militia of some sort.

"Iraches, hear me!" she said, in perfectly comprehensible English, with an accent that might have been Germanic. "There must be no hesitation, no regret. The goddess is returning after decades away from us. She will be thirsty. Give your life's blood to her freely. If any of you have had a change of heart, tell me now and you may walk away freely."

"Do not insult us, surrogate," warned one of the aboriginals. "No matter how long you have dwelt amongst us, you are Marutian. When we return we will deal harshly with you. We have suffered you to rule over us only in our Blood Queen's absence."

"If you return, Irache, it shall be by the goddess's grace and by no other right. I am ever your superior. Even if she grants you the boon you crave, you shall be remain as subservient to me as I am to her. That is the way of things. I have not survived for nearly five centuries by tolerating insubordination, nor any other form of rebellion, amongst the likes of you nor any of your heroes. Mayhap you should walk."

Severely chastened, the Iraches' spokesperson bowed his head. "I spoke wrongly. I wish only to join you and yours. Please forgive me."

Felix Dee's rifle-shot took the Irache square in the face. He was dead before he reached the ground. No way he'd be coming back. Geraint Plantagenet leapt out of an empty window blasting away. He mowed down the stunned aboriginals like so many blades of grass. He didn't consider himself a racist or a mass murderer. He just figured it was a matter of kill or be killed. And he who kills first lives to kill again.

Nonetheless, at the back of his mind, Plantagenet entertained the same whimsical notion he always did when he found himself in this sort of tragically unavoidable situation. If loggers could chop down his cousins then he was justified in chopping a few dozen potential loggers.

Elvis Elfin triggered the incendiaries he'd set within the building and a selected few outside it. Panic hadn't quite yet hit the obviously brain-baffled aboriginals nor the slow-thinking zombies, vultures and wolf-men. The explosions and resultant flames caught them napping. Too late they sparked into action. Elvin threw out their survival packs then he and Dee jumped out the window and joined Plantagenet.

Death-dealing was newer to E and F than it was to G. Surviving wasn't. They'd trained for just this moment.

========

Kill the live ones, blow apart or burn the dead ones, handle the six vamps as best they could. That was what the cosmicompanions had silently agreed to do after hearing Fangfingers' instructions. Zombies, birds, aboriginals, even the werewolves, most of whom sensibly chose to flee, were nothing against the sudden onslaught of the three companions and their heavy armaments. Bullets took out the vultures and redskins; they being living creatures and efficiently put to pasture. Fire dealt nicely with the zombies. The vamps were different, though.

Dee had the flamethrower. He napalmed one of the vampiric Oranges but the creature turned to mist, jogging suit and all. It became solid behind him. Dee tumbled away just as Elfin tossed a grenade at the Undead thing. The vamp caught it – must have been a ballplayer in its life, thought E – and, not realizing what it was, held on too long. It and it promptly blew apart; Elfin and Dee devoutly hoped never to re-form.

The other Orange took on G. Materializing behind the cosmicompanion it snatched away his automatic rifle. With practised swiftness, Geraint yanked out his hand-Gatling and emptied it into the Undead thing. Unaffected, the vampire laughed triumphantly. Plantagenet fled into the nearest blaze. Protected by his flame-proof uniform, having pulled down its hood into a facemask, he was only marginally affected. The idiot vamp pursued him and was immolated before it thought to become mist.

The three companions went back to back, exchanging weaponry so none was at a disadvantage. No further assaults came. The surviving werewolves had retreated a hundred yards away. The aboriginals, those that were left, had run into the abattoir. The groundling birds were dead; the zombies, drovers and guards, crisped. Four gigantic bats hovered above them.

"I make it those four," Elfin pointed upwards. "And a bunch of redskins inside."

"The whole place is burning down, E," trumpeted Plantagenet. "They'll come out soon. I've plenty of clips. It'll be a pig-shoot."

"Don't forget the werewolves, G," cautioned Dee. "I count five. Might be more, wounded ones, cowering out there."

"Pack animals," Elfin snorted scornfully. "Taken a couple down already. Grenades work, so do bullets. We'll need lots and all at once. High calibre's the best. We're running low but they don't know that. What they know is we're dangerous. They'll stay away."

"For now maybe," insisted Plantagenet, taking charge. "Listen, these things communicate mentally, so reinforcements can't be hard to call. They were here to meet some goddess, probably the big petunia. The way I figure it the curtain of rain was what kept them out of the mountains. I vote we head back there, starting now. We last to dawn, the vamps will be gone; at least any vamps I've ever heard about would be. I haven't read Count Dracula, E, but I've seen the flick."

"Yeah, well, these ones might be different. I take your point about the rain-curtain, though. Let's get rolling."

"Look out!"

========

Geraint Plantagenet's warning came too late. An enormous vulture landed atop the three cosmicompanions, crushing them with its sheer weight. The goddess leapt off its back and wasted no time cutting them open with her sickle-shaped Brainrock talisman. She drank their blood, all of it. There was a certain untainted quality to it so she made a point of regurgitating some of it back into them just in case, in three nights time, she needed to find out where they came from and thence go there for more of the same.

Semi-sated, she called for the surviving Iraches to come out of the blazing slaughterhouse. Obediently they did so, just as the four remaining vampires, the native of Moorset, the Irache, the oriental-looking Vetala and Janna Fangfingers, the silver-haired and silvery clothed vamp, she with the fang-fingered glove and the choker with a Crystal Skull attached to it, landed. They promptly veered humanoid again.

Vamps were daemonic in that they could shift shapes. They were better than daemonic in that they could also shift states; could become mist, for example. Janna Fangfingers described what she could do as being your own revolving door. She carried a variety of both shapes and states with her between-space. She also carried with her a variety of outfits. Rotate the door and, so long as she had it with her, she could come around all sorts of different things.

It saved on having to go home for a change a clothes. Or physical forms. Saved on dressing as well.

"I still thirst," said Nergal Vetala.

"Our blood is yours, goddess!" all except Fangfingers answered.

"Then I shall sup yours first, Utopian. It's ever so refreshing."

"As you desire, goddess," Second Fangs agreed, having no other choice in the matter.

Hardly for the first time in their 500-year-relationship, Janna wished she had blood that was fatal to Master Devas and vampires both. Hers wasn't fatal to devils.

========

Methandra Thanatos had given up trying to find Jordan Tethys via her purloined cauldron days ago. Maybe he'd died again; was between lives, put better. He'd been dead before, she'd heard tell, by him, a generally welcome visitor to both Tantal's Lathakra and her long ago abandoned Mythland – from both before and after her and her brood brother's thousand year sleep.

He nevertheless still managed to keep ambling along for awhile. Or maybe he'd just drawn himself a new appearance, though she couldn't think why he'd do that. Sooth said, which the legendary 30-Year Man always did, even when he was well on his way to this 30th beer, she couldn't even remember why she'd been looking for him in the first place.

Then she had it. Was looking at it, them. Except three of the ice statues had melted.

========

At 12-feet in height, her truly gigantic Viking of a husband had forgotten why as well. (To some extent ass-backwards, his worshippers were Lathakra's Fire Kings whereas hers were the Intuit telepaths whose ancestors had been native to Mythland.) She knew that because she asked him. He couldn't even tell her if Tethys was a man or a woman these days, which she did know.

Then again, his short-term memory had never been very good. Hers had, even when she wasn't occupying, or being occupied by, the Memory-aspect of the Dual Entities. (Which she had been when she conceived and thereafter bore her ten fourth generational, devic children.) She really did hate it when her memory developed blanks. And it seemed to her it had been doing that a lot lately. Could immortal devils grow senile?

She had this last son, though. Her eleventh child; the one she'd somehow managed to conceive after she lost control of the Female Entity but couldn't bear, due to Smoky Sedona's Spell of Disproportionment. So did her immediate sibling-husband. He'd even named him. Cold thought Sedunihas was as funny as it sounded.

Not every devil could claim their very own, in-house Sedon, he said to her when he chose it.

The youngster had plenty of problems. He was deaf, couldn't talk either. Growth-retarded, he seemed to age only one year in five by human or even Utopian terms, who started out aging normally but slowed down dramatically after a decade or so. But, boy, the boy was talented. He'd hand-carved these amazingly lifelike ice statues of their then still nine missing children.

Having – 6-inch her in contrast to 3-foot-plus him – just put the 25-year-old, in a 5-year-old's body, to bed, she'd flying-carpet-surfed, on heat-waves of her own conjuring, down to his workshop to have another look at them. Considering they were in a Glacial Palace she was startled to discover that three of them had gone the way Cold's Tantalazur-animated snowmen did when they'd intemperately annoyed her.

(Only long gone Father Mithras had more azuras than Tantal did. By contrast, she had but the one – appropriately the first known azura ever engendered, testimony to her magnificence.)

These were the ice statues representing their Earth, Air and Water. Six others still stood: Day, Night, Fire, Spring, Autumn and Winter. Not so disturbingly anymore Day was still bald. Not so disturbingly because Day's hair wasn't just a rainbow, it was her power focus, as was Night's, her midnight-black, raven tresses. Methandra, Heat to hubby's Cold, was by now virtually certain who had Day's talisman.

What was somewhat disturbing was that when he'd made them, or at least when he'd shown them to her, their thumbs were up. Now they weren't; in fact he'd obviously been doing some work on them because their hands were clenched. He'd changed their facial expressions, too. Whereas before he'd depicted them smiling happily, he'd redone their faces furrowed, as if in exertion. Even odder, he'd started to redo them as wearing striped shirts; not skin like Zebranids, shirts like referees in that hockey game virtually everyone on the Frozen Isle played.

Unless, and here was a thought, he was portraying them as convicts, like in some old Godbadian movie Pani merchants traded to the Fire Kings and Intuits years ago, before The Argent, across the Sea of Clouds on the Cattail's mainland, got television and the Fire Kings in particular started pirating their signals. Was Sedunihas somehow sensing that the six siblings he was still working on were prisoners trapped in the bodies of the cosmicompanions they must have possessed when the Cosmic Express burst into and out the Sedon Sphere? And if so, where were they?

She had another flash – a hot-flash, did Heat, as Tethys couldn't have resisted saying if he was here. She had this daughter, so did Cold, the aforementioned azura who, using a Samarandin homunculus to solidify herself, ended up bearing Number Eleven, albeit nearly a decade after she transferred 11's foetus to her. And 12's, only he was born dead, poor lad. Still was too, even though she'd gone to considerable lengths wrangling an oversized thimble full of Cathonic Fluid out of the Weirdom of Cabalarkon, the place.

She named him herself, her tiny tom-thumb. Quite cleverly too, she reflected, growing increasingly morose. When he came out, almost as much of an afterthought as he was almost mistaken for being part of an afterbirth, he wasn't much bigger than a mote. So she added the tan-bit from Cold's Illuminary-given first name and called him Motan. She kept his dinky casket, still filled with the same miraculous fluid that kept Cabalarkon, the person, an undying Utopian, on ice.

Other than in the vicinity of its volcanic backbone, very little of Lathakra wasn't either on ice or in ice. Cold liked it that way so Cold kept it that way

Klannit was only a never-could-be-solely-substantial azura, another damn shame that, but she was bright for an azura; so bright she could animate all sorts of otherwise inanimate objects. She was also very good with mirrors. And there was this mirror Methandra knew about; so did Klannit, come to think of it.

Miss Myth, Methandra of Mythland, didn't know where it was, but Klannit might. She'd ruined a perfectly fine corpse – one her oft-times Lazaremist boyfriend, Anvil, the devic Smithy, Tvasitar Smithmonger, had procured for her – fishing it out of his lava lake: Tvasitar's crater full of self-replenishing, molten Godstuff below his Prometheum on Sedon's Peak, his good-as-protectorate.

(He designed, rather than personally built, the Prometheum remarkably early on in the Hidden Headworld's history. When he did so he was occupying, though not dominating, a Gobble Stone daemon, unless it was a lava lout demon. He perched it precariously atop a precipice overlooking the volcano's crater. Presumably more by good fortune than sound management, thousands of years later it still stood there.

(Its disturbing-to-behold cliff heads reminded not just her of their joint, but effectively jilted, mothers, the Trigregos Sisters: Demeter the Body, Sapiendev the Mind and Devaura the Soul. Because the Moloch Sedon, with eventually undying Cabalarkon's assistance, built them to be patrilineally loyal, Master Devas were ever incapable of disobeying their fathers. Which of course left their mothers on the outside wanting in, or at least deserving of adulation.)

Their resourceful azura-daughter retrieved the Trigregos Talismans centuries ago now, sometime during the final days of the Thousand Days of Disbelief. Which Tantal and her slept through: they then being in the midst of their 1000-Year Sleep; what was actually more like an 1100-Year Sleep, as it turned out. Still, now that the Legendarian had done a bunk, what with Klannit's affinity for mirrors ...

And what with what that particular mirror could do, did do, to both Lord Order and Nergal Vetala, she recalled hearing from Jordan Tethys; what the Attis very nearly did do with it to the Unnameable on Thrygragon ... Maybe Sedunihas finishes redoing their still missing children as they are; who they're in, rather ... Maybe Klannit reflects his ice statues in it ... Maybe it reflects them into it ... Maybe Klannit can get it to reflect them out of it.

Where was that girl anyhow? More to the point, was she prepared to play a Trigregos Gambit?

========

Someone else certainly was and she was pretty sure where it was, on Sraddha Isle.

========

True, she'd once spent months inside it. But the last time she encountered the Amateramirror, it served to free her from a Summoning Child she'd been reborn inside. True again, she hadn't lasted very long that time out, due in part to the same Hellion of a Summoning Child trying to reassert herself over their joint body after she should have been dead and gone. The other part of the reason was the interference of another Summoning Child, the Hellion's husband, who was born on the Inner Earth rather than the Outer Earth. He even managed to drag her into the Jaag Maelstrom, the ingrate. She should have eaten him.

The way she had it figured, though, she wouldn't be the one holding onto it. Or using it to secure the other two. Who said Trigregos Incarnate had to be female? True, the Death's Head Hellion, the one most responsible for causing the Thanatoids' Thousand Year Sleep had been. But Pyrame's Attis – the Pauper Priestess's golden-brown warrior – wasn't. And he, also Mithras's Universal Soldier, held onto them, all three of them, lifetime after lifetime, for some-thing like 2500 years. Until Thrygragon, as a matter of fact.

Besides, she wasn't prejudiced. She'd bite anyone.

She had a willing pawn. Well, that wasn't quite fair; more like a knight. He was a soldier, though, just like Chrysaor Attis had been. An Outer Earth soldier full of refreshing, revitalizing, Outer Earth blood to boot. Thus far she had resisted the temptation to drain him entirely, thereby killing him. Or to turn him into one of her own, as she had last night's triple-threat-treats, among others.

She'd held off primarily because she was fairly certain you had to be alive in order to become Trigregos Incarnate. Fairly wasn't definitely, of course, but she really didn't need to make him a vamp.

He was already completely devoted to her.

========

No, her soldier wasn't a pawn. He was a Godsend. Make that a Sedon-send. He'd literally fallen out of the sky, the Sedon Sphere.

****

(Pregame-Gambit) 7: **Sedon's Stooge**

<u>Sapienda, Tantalar 4, 5980</u>

"The mirrored eggs," Jordan Tethys commenced while he waited for his lunch to cool, "Invoking what you call the Crown of Heaven in your prayers, and even why you Sraddhites tend to use curved blades, you know why all that is, so there's no need to retell the story of the Disunition of the Unities to you.
"But do you know how they came about in the first place?"

========

In the first Weirsystem, multiple multi-millennia ago, and so far away it boggles the brain even attempting to comprehend just how far away it was – something like 200,000 light years I've been given to understand; which, as I say, I can only do with great difficulty – the Moloch Sedon created the second generation of devazurkind. These were the three Great Gods, or Thrygragos Brothers, and the three Great Goddesses, the Trigregos Sisters. He did so to share his immortality, some of his godlike powers and, basically, just to keep him company.

Stuff happens, as it has a wont to do, and the seven of them began to intermingle merrily. Yet all they produced were spirit beings. Try as they might to solidify their offspring, the third generation of devazurkind, Sedon and the six Great Gods and Goddesses remained the only fully physical devils in the cosmos. Which isn't to say the rest of the devic race wasn't talented – being immortal certainly implies a measure of talent; if only an ability to avoid being killed. But they could only manifest those talents by possessing other sentient beings.

All this changed well over twenty-five hundred years after devils came to the Whole Earth. That makes it not quite two thousand years after Dark Sedon effectively turned himself into the night's sky, Cathonia, the Cathonic Zone or Dome or, most transparently, the Sedon Sphere, in order to protect what was then known as the archipelago of Pacifica, the Places of Peace, from the Genesea or Great Flood of Genesis.

Today, beyond the Dome anyways, Pacifica is better remembered as the sunken continent of Mu or Lemuria. We of course know it as Sedon's Head, the Hidden Headworld, Big Shelter, and by so many other names that if you invented one for it right now, it'd probably already have been invented. We'd just forgotten it until a couple of minutes ago. We are talking going on six thousand years, recall.

The division between the Inner and Outer Earth was never entirely perfect. Rifts, cracks, gaps in the Dome remained or developed over time, albeit usually only to heal over again, also over time. Although greatly separated in terms of distance from the Hidden Headworld, which is situated in what amounts to its own dimension off the North Pacific Ocean, one of the most enduring of these gashes opened onto the twin cities of Sodom and Gomorrah, in what's known on the Outer Earth as its Middle East. You know what happened to them. One way or another they were destroyed.

Howsoever that happened – and I know a number of variations about that, one or two of which are even scientifically based – at the same time they were destroyed the crater of a minor, size-wise, but historically significant, Headworld volcano known as Sedon's Peak began to fill with an extraordinary element, if I can use the word in a non-scientific sense.

It wasn't anything new; devils had known of Brainrock, as it's most commonly known here on the Head, for as long as they'd been in existence. They also knew to call it Gypsium, which might surprise you if you were aware that most Outer Earthlings think that word wasn't coined until not so very long ago, in their 1948, our 5948.

Be that as it may, let's remember we're talking devils here. Recollect what I said about them having talents? One of the most talented was a son of Thrygragos Lazareme far-ranging Illuminaries of Weir, who had their own way through the Dome back then, eventually named Tvasitar Smithmonger. Devils themselves referred to him variously; as often as not as Anvil these days, after his primary power focus. Which was, duh, an anvil.

More than four thousand years ago, though, I believe the term they most commonly used for him was Artificer, after his main attribute. Which was making things.

========

"Like my father," inserted Thartarre, smiling in a sadly reminiscent manner that Tethys found vaguely disturbing. As well as disruptive, not to mention somehow itch-inspiring.

========

"Whose name was Holgat, not Tvasitar," remarked the Legendarian, second-skinned as he was, persevering despite the interruption. "I'll grant you there must be some sort of connection there. At least there once must have been between the devic Anvil and the azura Klannit in combination with the High Priest Anvil, Tvasitar Sraddha Quentin-son, and your Nanny Klanny. But, like I told you, I don't know what that is.

"That said, I have it on good report that during what's called Ragnarok on the Outer Earth, which is to say not much more than two hundred years before the Great Flood of Genesis, which is also to say when the Moloch Sedon became the Demon King as well as the devils' king, a couple of firstborn Master Devas got hold of a pair of demons. Which made them solid long enough to have a child together."

"Sorry," said his one-armed host, apologizing for the interruption. "Dig in." Tethys did. It was a savoury stew; very good too. He couldn't identify the meat;

didn't want to know what it was either. He just trusted it wasn't that sort of Dead Thing.

Swallowed and carried on: "Only she was just a spirit being ..."

========

Illuminaries of Weir eventually name the two devils Tantal and Methandra Thanatos. The child they had – best call her an offspring, since she wasn't solid – was Klannit. Only they named her, not the Illuminaries. She's the first azura in the known cosmos; not that anyone knows what an azura is yet. Pass forward back to where I started, more than two millennia later. Sodom and Gomorrah are twin cities, yes, but maybe that's not their real names. Maybe their real names are Nikaya and Tivatimsa.

In case you haven't heard of them, they're the twin Shangri-Las that pop up randomly, in the Outer Earth's Himalayan mountains, every century; pop up out there at the same time once every millennium as well. They feature in what little a few us do recall about the Simultaneous Summonings of 1920/5920. The former is the City of Wickedness, the latter the City of Blessedness. I can't say for sure they were originally Sodom and Gomorrah but there's persuasive evidence that suggests as much.

Regardless of what their actual names were, or are, I can say that Sodom is definitely the honourific assigned to the former's king while Gomorrah is the honourific given to the latter's queen. That's the way it had been for multiple generations; the way it had been even when they were Weirdoms and their rulers were pureblood Utopians, descendants of extraterrestrials. They haven't been that, Utopians, for almost as long; generations anyhow. His sacred symbols of office are a mask, a cruciform and a cloak of many colours; hers are a bloodstone tiara, a mutable mirror and a sword with a curved blade.

The twin cities are destroyed. One of the stories I've heard regarding that was it was because an asteroid containing a superabundance of Brainrock landed atop them. But that could be apocryphal, a later addendum to their legend. So are their respective king and queen of the time. Not so, as I'm about to relate, their respective symbols of office.

Because they were Weirdoms, were a couple of the places where ancient Illuminaries got through the Dome, fame of both the twin cities themselves and their eponymous rulers, Sodom and Gomorrah, had long ago reached the Head. Wandering troubadours told or sang their stories far and wide. Some even claimed they were immortal. Well, they would, wouldn't they? That's the purpose of an honourific, to perpetuate the semblance of perpetuity.

Two of them were named, funnily enough, Jordan and Pusan. He was the musician of the two, the one who told the stories. She sang and danced. They were very much in love, these two. Their parents were against them marrying so they ran away. Their parents were pagans. They worshipped Mother Earth; not the three Great Gods, who were the only solid devils on the planet now that Dark Sedon was up there in the night's sky being dark during the day.

Their mothers were more than merely pagans; they were Hecate-Hellions. That meant they belonged to the oldest Witch Sisterhood on either side of the Dome; one that was even older than that of Flowery Anthea. Which was named after Xuthros Hor's wife, Hor being the Biblical Noah; not Thrygragos Lazareme's highborn epitome of the Spring Season, of Life Itself.

They conjured up a pair of demons to go after them. These two were very old demons. Not that there's anything natural about demons, other than Mother Nature's their mother, and that includes aging or death. Put it this way, they still contained a pair of devils they'd acquired during the tail-end of Ragnarok some 2000 years earlier, pre-Genesea, when the Whole Earth was still the Whole Earth. We'll save some time and name them now. They were Future Tvasitar Smithmonger and Future Klannit Thanatos.

The former was a gargantuan concretion of galumphing granite while the latter was seemingly composed entirely of reflective glass; a mobile mirror, in other words. In terms of demonology there's stacks of variants on the former. Blockhead's one of them, Gobble Stones is another, but the generic term I use is Rockhead.

The latter, though, shouldn't be confused with the Diamantes native to the Crystal Mountain Range; they're at least humanoid. The term demonologists use for mobile mirrors, and this shouldn't surprise you, if you don't know it already, is a Klannit. They were as in love as the two troubadours, which may have been how they caught their scent. Love stinks, don't you know? Sorry, bad joke.

The troubadours, unaware of their demonic pursuers, were entertaining a bunch of Bandradins in a village well up the slope of Sedon's Peak when it erupted. The ground's groaning. Its grumbling and rumbling preceded the eruption. All the usual suspects followed; lava-rain, and rivulets of same, most devastatingly. By the time the demonic pursuers reached the village, well, you can imagine what greeted them.

The village wasn't so much still smouldering as what was covering it was still hardening. The scent still lingered, though. So even farther up the slope the demons tromp. And what do they find up there near the top, the Rockhead and the Klannit? Why Jordan and Pusan as King Sodom and Queen Gomorrah of course, complete with their signs of office.

Troubadours, no matter what they have about themselves, aren't much for fighting. And demons, no matter how intelligent the devils they're containing are, aren't much for thinking ...

========

"Which," said Tethys, interrupting himself this time, "If you could read tee-tee-tails, which I know you can't, is about as far as any tee-tee tale will take you before you have start filling in the blanks for yourself. However, like I said, I have it on good report ..." The legendary 30-Year Man paused, suddenly, inexplicably, nervous. Underneath his facial second skin, the incessant itchiness of the scar tissue in the middle of his forehead, what transferred with him from one incarnation to another, intensified ever-so-alarmingly, well beyond even its regular level of merely annoying.

He regarded his host just as much so distressfully. "Why are you looking at me like that, Tar? And why are you smiling like that?"

=======

Blip! Transmogrification! Thartarre wasn't Thartarre anymore.

"Don't worry, Tethys. As much as I find your squirming amusing, it's more a matter of me avoiding laughing in your face. Finish your lunch while I tell you what really happened. Of course you won't remember it after I've left but you will remember it once I reveal myself to the entire Head.

"Which should only be a couple of days from now."

========

Regardless of their actual names, the twin cities were destroyed when an asteroid containing a superabundance of Brainrock-Gypsium landed atop them. It wasn't a fluke of cosmic happenstance. It was an assassination attempt. And it certainly wasn't any ordinary asteroid. It was a Utopian millennial ship. Unless it had three peaks, that is. In which case it had a name as well: Trans-Time Trigon.

Say it was, then for many moons it had been orbiting the planet's moon. Or else it had been sitting atop it. Trans-Time Trigon never just contained a superabundance of Godstuff either, though it would have by the time it destroyed our cities. Initially it would have also contained the time-tumbling Dual Entities: Helios called Sophos the Wise and his female counterpart, the Mnemosyne Machine. This last, Machine-Memory, is a three-thing who could be wholly humanized by possessing a devil. Or being possessed by a devil, as is often the situation.

Two more confounding beings are difficult to imagine. It's said Celestial God Himself, or Herself, or Whatever, couldn't have imagined them. Which was proof, their sheer existence, that there was no such thing as an Omniscient God. They originated somewhere, the Dual Entities; they had to have. Then again I've also heard it said they're the Male and Female Principals and, as such, originated at the same moment the cosmos did. In which case they're the ineffable God and Goddess of Natural Duality, as opposed to the duality of good and evil, which is a burst-bladder of bilge-water as far as I'm concerned.

To give an example of their ineffability: When he's killed, which he often has been, she goes back with him, into the time stream. When she goes back into the time stream she takes with her Trans-Time Trigon, of which she's its innards; its intelligence, put another way. There's no question she's mostly machine whereas he's mostly mortal. Both are Brainrock-blessed, if that isn't a misuse of the term *'blessed'*. Yet, to give another example of their ineffability, they time-tumble randomly.

In his Fifth Lifetime, she more than him it has to be said, they and a then fully alive, Utopian scientocrat from the first Weir World, one Cabalarkon by name, a geneticist by trade, concocted the Moloch Sedon. That said, two of his lifetimes earlier Sedon was already around. And it was in his third lifetime when the Female Entity discovered devils could humanize her.

So, when Sedon destroyed her then, in the Third, she somehow had to make him, Sedon, two of the Male Entity's lifetimes later, in his Fifth. She didn't, there would never be any devils around to humanize her. She enjoys being human, being Miracle Memory, which is the name her human form takes.

So she did; helped Heliosophos and Cabalarkon make Sedon. The Moloch rewarded Cabby with a form of everlasting life, albeit as a kind of psychic vampire. He rewarded Helios with his fifth death. And when Helios dies, like I said, he goes back into the time stream. She does too, taking Trans-Time Trigon with her; her

Mnemosyne Machine aspect does anyhow. They, Helios no less so than Memory, now that devils exist, have been trying to destroy our All-Father Sedon ever since.

Call it payback for Deaths Three and Five, if nothing else; Deaths One, Two, Four and Six, for all I know, because it was now early on in Helios's seventh lifetime. It's not quite two thousand years after Father Sedon raised the Sedon Sphere, out of his own essence, in order to separate the Inner Earth, his Headworld, from the Outer Earth. Trans-Time Trigon has been out there, in the heavens, for awhile now. They've been looking for Sedon, in order to destroy him. They've decided King Sodom, of Sodom, or Nikaya, or whatever, is him in human form.

After taking themselves safely elsewhere, into Thrygragos Varuna Mithras and Kore-Discord as I eventually discover, they launch Trans-Time Trigon at him, at the twin cities. Unless, as I said, they launched a Utopian Mother Ship at him. In whichever event a big bang ensues; one of the biggest bangs the planet's experienced since another asteroid – and presumably this one was a cosmic happenstance – wiped out the dinosaurs.

Only King Sodom isn't Father Sedon. He's me.

========

"Got me yet, Jordy?"

"Never haven't, Smiler. You're Sedon's stooge. Might someday, though."

"Ever the optimist, eh? That's two things we have in common."

"Two?"

"At least two. One of which is we both have Tvasitar talismans. Except I've three to your one. None of which I had something like 4000 years ago."

========

Our cities are destroyed but we aren't, Queen Gomorrah and I. It's exceedingly difficult to destroy Master Devas, as you're well aware. We come through the Dome; emanate through it might be a better way of putting it. Our symbols of office aren't destroyed, either, but our daemonic bodies, composed as they are of subtle matter, have been severely damaged. And, yes, that means we knew about power foci before I assumed the identity of King Sodom and she became Queen Gomorrah; before Thrygragos Sedon, his two brothers and their devic offspring, the Anvil Artificer included, did as well.

Sooth for me said, which I don't always do – one of my more recognizable Outer Earth nomenclatures is Ahriman or Aryanman, Judge Druj in the Zoroastrian religion, wherein Druj means 'the Lie' – we knew about them long, long before anyone on the planet, ourselves included, even knew what a devil was. That's because we had existed long, long before devils came to the Whole Earth some, what?, 730 years prior to Sedon raising the Dome and not quite 2700 years prior the Dual Entities destroying our cities.

We knew about power foci because neither of us started out as devils.

In those millennia I was Daemonicus, the immanent even more so than immortal King of Daemons, and she was Lilith, the Daemon Queen of the Night. Rather, I better stipulate, she was until Alorus Ptah, the First Patriarch of Golden Age Humankind, captured her within the Osiris Sphinx, as we knew it then, around 1500 years before Father Sedon raised the Dome. In other words, what I call power foci were our symbols of office and our symbols of office were their symbols of office, their power foci.

You'll have heard Ptah manufactured the male Sphinx that eventually took root upon what became Egypt's Giza plateau in one of two ways. He did it either by using technology developed in the far-off Utopia of Weir, that of the first Weir World, which he'd somehow managed to acquire. Or else he did it by employing the discredited science of Old Eden, the Whole Earth's indigenous, yet stunningly advanced, lone pre-Golden-Age civilization.

While there's a remote possibility they might be six of one and a half dozen of the same, it's likely you won't have heard how Ptah animated it. He did so with my symbols of office. His despicable mate, Trishtar Thrae, had somehow got hold of Lilith, and with her my queen's talismans. They thereby shamelessly used their concomitantly combined feminine wiles to coax mine off me, Daemonicus. Whereupon they gave them to the First Patriarch

Despite what you may have heard he didn't use mine to capture me. Perhaps fittingly, he instead turned the tables and used them to capture Lilith instead. Then, with her inescapably within the Osiris Sphinx, he proceeded to render it immobile by taking them back. Needless to say, he kept mine and let Trishtar Thrae keep Lilith's. Thus they, clever bastards the pair of them, took our place as the King and Queen of Daemons.

When he retired as First Patriarch he passed mine onto his successor and third-born son, Pseth Ra. She did the same; passed Lilith's onto Pseth's mate, their second-born daughter as it happened, whose name, curiously enough, was Azura – the same as a devil's offspring with another devil when neither are possessing anyone except a debrained daemonic body. And so it goes, century after century, from one long-lived patriarch to the next, and from one equally long-lived patriarch's primary wife to the next.

All this time I'm still around, Daemonicus is to be clearer; albeit only in the sense that my body hasn't altogether disintegrated. Without my power foci even my daemonic, nominal subjects feel no compulsion to pay me any heed. I'm useless; so useless I grow increasingly moribund. So, for literal centuries I might as well be dead. Or imprisoned in the Osiris Sphinx with my beloved Lilith, for that matter.

My consciousness doesn't reactivate, as it were, until sometime after Droch Nor has become the seventh patriarch of Golden Age Humankind. We're now talking circa 730 years prior to Sedon raising the Cathonic Dome. Nor's wife, by whom he had the eventual eighth patriarch, Amemp Tut, the Biblical Methuselah, goes by name of Lamia. She wears Lilith's power foci, the crown and mirror, and carries the curved blade with her wherever she goes. But she's recently been possessed by an extraterrestrial Spirit Being, a third generational Master Deva. Since devils didn't have names in those days, let's keep it simple and call her Lamia too.

Howsoever we call her, she's a member of Thrygragos Lazareme's exploratory party – the Sedonshem is sitting on the Moon by now – and as such she's only recently arrived on the then still Whole Earth. She's Lilith's; Nor's mine. I reawaken inside him. We hit it off, the devic Lamia and I. She wants to become both individually solid and individually powerful. I convince her that the only she can accomplish both her aims is by her possessing my Lilith. Which naturally means she'd have to first help me free Lilith from the Osiris Sphinx.

There are lots of other Master Devas on the Whole Earth as part of Lazareme's expedition. My daemons are responding to me again. Let's be magnanimous and say they're responding to us again, shall we? Yes, let's do that. We form together, devils and daemons, fuse them with our symbols of office. Become, well, if she's Lamia and lamiae, in much later Outer Earth history as well as mythology, are a form of gorgon, let's just refer to what we become as unnameable.

It wears a crown, the Crown of Hell rather than Heaven if you're tetchy about that sort of thing. He has a face that's more like a mask. It's always grinning – that's my influence – and has mirrored eyeballs as well as fangs like curved blades. Its hide is multicoloured and in order to maximize the squeamishness quotient, we make it into an indescribably huge snake. As the Unnameable, we attack the immobile Osiris Sphinx.

Unfortunately, although we could have easily demolished it, that wouldn't have freed Queen Lilith for the simple reason everyone the Sphinx held was as fused with it as we were into the Unnameable. Destroy it we destroy those we wish to free. We reason the Sphinx needed my power foci before it could release anyone. Dare I give them up, so soon after I've reclaimed them from Droch Nor? More to the point, should I choose to keep them about me and try to take over the male Sphinx instead? And if I did, could I hold onto it even long enough to force it to release my Lilith? I'm dubious but it turns out Lamia is duplicitous.

Alorus Ptah's still alive. So are all the other patriarchs, Nor and his predecessors, and so are all the anti-patriarchs, including Anti-Patriarch Cain, Slayer of Abel, whom many believe was the Male Entity in his first lifetime. So too is Trishtar Thrae, the Biblical Adam's Eve. Cooperatively, using, I'm saying, Old Eden's forsaken science, the same science that accounts for so many of the Head's planetary unique, yet still extant and thoroughly exotic lifeforms, they duplicate Ptah's feat of something like 800 years earlier.

They manufacture a mate for it; a female equivalent, albeit one with wings. It's just as immobile but there is a way to mobilize it. And how might they be able to do that, you won't have to ask. By animating it with Lilith's power foci of course. Lamia goes for it, animates it, dominates it. She's finally as individually solid, in the form of a female sphinx, and as powerful as her male counterpart. She suppresses or captures dozens of Lilith's daemons and her devils within it. Only she turns it on me and the remaining daemons and devils in my side of the Unnameable. I panic, reanimate the Osiris Sphinx with mine and seek to defend ourselves.

They played us for fools, did Ptah and Thrae more so than anyone else. How could we have been so stupid? That to me remains the real, evermore unanswerable Riddle of the Sphinx. What's left of what we formed, our Unnameable of some 700 years before the Great Flood or Genesea, is devoured by the pair of sphinxes.

Their gambit won, Ptah and Thrae take back our power foci, three for him, three for her, and after implanting the two sphinxes on opposite sides of the planet, they immobilize them again. Henceforth, amongst our sometimes unkind kind anyhow, they become known as Giza's Androsphinx and Incain's Gynosphinx. I, as Daemonicus, manage to survive yet again, though I have no idea how.

Come what has come down to us as the legend of Ragnarok, I believe I must have absorbed a devil; the same devil you sometimes remember, when I'm with you, as Smiler. Unless he absorbed me, that is. Point being I can't distinguish between my daemon-self and my devil-self anymore. We are one and the same; have been since Ragnarok, which you'll recall was when Father Sedon became the King of Daemons.

========

"And how did the Mighty Moloch do that, you might want to ask. Which I'll assume you are, silently. You are eating your lunch, as am I, and unlike me you hate talking with your mouth full. Allow me to smiley-happily answer you. Although it should be needless to say, I feel it needful to say: It was my idea."

Tethys swallowed manfully, said bravely: "Never doubted that for a minute, Smiler. Which is why I had no intention of interrupting. Like you said, I'm embodied etiquette."

========

You're a skyborn immortal, I say to Sedon just before he tosses the Ragnarok Roll, the dice of which eventually turn up not so much the Twilight of the Gods as the death of Jaro Dan, Odin, the long retired Sixth Patriarch of Golden Age Humankind. And thanks to you, so am I. Once upon a time, however, there were earthborn immortals; they're called daemons. The twain have met in me. I am both your firstborn son and the son of Mother Earth. As the latter I had myself three, call them power foci or talismans: a mask, a cloak and a cruciform.

You've a couple of other firstborn sons. Pay them no mind. But they have had, I have to say, via their second generational sisters, many a talented offspring. One of their most talented, via Thrygragos Lazareme and his Trigregos Sisters, is the Artificer. Have him remake for me my talismans and I shall thereafter make you King of Daemons.

Although a volcanic islet at the time, what in time became known as Sedon's Peak was already sputtering. We're still talking pre-Genesea, when today's Headworld was the archipelago of Pacifica. The Future Tvasitar acquires a humanoid shell skilled in metalworking, a Vulcanian as they were known in classical times on the Outer Earth.

As a just as solid but much less fragile entity – I'm a daemon, not a humanoid – we retire to this geologically unsafe islet. After a great deal of trial and error, during which Future Tvasitar crafts for himself, among many another useful thing, an anvil, a hammer, and a pair of pincers out the islet's scant Brainrock, we succeed in replicating my signs of office.

As pre-agreed, we turn them over to Father Sedon. He uses to them to acquire the real ones from the then current patriarch, the Tenth and last patriarch of Golden Age Humanity. That would be the Biblical Noah, though we know him as Xuthros Hor. Does so very perspicaciously, does Sedon. By mentally causing them to fuse together, albeit in his possession not Hor's, Sedon does indeed become the King of Daemons as well as the All-Father of devic kind.

Although he successfully divides the loyalties of my daemons, his daemons now, such that some of them turn against the Golden Age patriarchs, one of whom, the aforementioned Jaro Dan, dies in the ensuing conflict, he can't altogether claim their loyalty. That's because daemons are chthonic, not Cathonic; are earthborn, not skyborn, put just as accurately. And Hor's wife, whose name was Anthea, still has hold of my Lilith's power foci.

Time to have Future Tvasitar forge replicates of them, the blade, the mirror and the crown, you'd think. So do we, but it doesn't work. Why? Because they only work for women? Possibly. That's certainly how it seems anyways. No doubt both sides hoped Ragnarok would prove to be the determinative engagement between Golden Age patriarchs and devils, but it wasn't even close.

Nor do I believe the fact Hor's wife continued to hold onto my Lilith's power foci and, with it, the allegiance of her daemons was much of a factor in the ongoing stalemate between the two sides, though it may have been. Finally the ever-intransigent, yet verging on impossibly resourceful Tenth, Hor himself, unleashes the Great Flood of Genesis and Sedon is forced to raise the Cathonic Dome out of his own essence to protect Pacifica from its ravages.

Sedon raised the Dome in our Year Zero, 5,980 years ago. On the Outer Earth Hor lived for another 360 years. The Bible states he and his family, and they and theirs, for generations thereafter, repopulated the Outer Earth. But, as any archaeologist on either side of the Dome will tell you, that's another boatload of bunk and balderdash.

What would have been flooded, had he not raised the Dome, was the archipelago of Pacifica. Whatever else wiped out so many humans as well as devils wasn't just water. It was waves of chthonic energy. I believe Anthea may have generated those waves by using Lilith's power foci but can't swear to it.

What I will swear is that the Whole Earth was now made up of an Inner and an Outer Earth. Furthermore, the Androsphinx was in what's now Egypt while the Gynosphinx, the Headworld having thoroughly dried out in the first few decades of the Dome, was on Incain's beach. Both sphinxes were immobile and both also contained many devils. I sought to liberate them; had an idea how to do just that. By now, I should preface, Sedon's experiencing trouble maintaining Cathonia, his Sedon Sphere, its integrity. He's afraid it'll collapse.

My idea is to reanimate the female sphinx. In order to do that, I prevail upon him to return to me my symbols of office. Partially because his Brainrock replicas are superior to my originals, which means he can fuse them together again anytime he pleases, he does so. He also gives me the replicated versions of Lilith's power foci.

Although the originals are presumably still in the possession of Hor's Anthea on the Outer Earth, I'm stuck on the Inner Earth, with no way through the Dome short of Sedon deliberately collapsing it. Which he doesn't have any intention of doing. Nonetheless, I reckon I can use the replicas to animate the Gynosphinx long enough for her to release the devils she's holding prisoner.

And I do, except rather than release them, she inhumes me. Which is when I make the amazing discovery that her digestive tract, if I can call it that, is linked to that of the Egyptian sphinx. I've my symbols of office. I'm carrying replicas of hers. The Androsphinx, on the other side of the Dome, pukes me up. Only it's not just me he pukes up.

Kings need their queens and while we were on the Sedonshem – Mithras's Virgin, the future Methandra Thanatos, having rejected him over and over again – Sedon made a ninth-born Mithradite Master Deva his queen. He hasn't been with her for a very long time. As you may have guessed, or already know, she was lost during the assault on the Androsphinx. Not anymore.

When the Androsphinx pukes me up, he also pukes her up. Only she's now irreversibly fused with my queen: she of the night to my day, as some have us. And as some have the Dual Entities, interesting enough. This two-in-one entity acquired many names over the subsequent centuries but I have always preferred Astraea, the Queen of Courts, so that's how I'll refer to her.

Now that we know we can use the sphinxes to traverse the Dome any time we please, we stay on the Outer Earth long enough to track down Hor's Anthea. Astraea has Lilith's replicated foci. They work for her. So she pulls a Sedon, fuses the real ones with the replicated ones; fuses them in her possession, just as he did. Losing them costs Hor's Anthea her life. Tough kitty litter, I say. She was a menace and, even though circumstances have forced me to make common cause with some of them, her descendant witches remain just as much so.

Sedon's still having trouble maintaining the Dome. Plus, to put it simplistically, he's horny as hell. By using his replicas of my foci to overrule me and my originals, he usurps me, joins with me, joins his replicas with my templates at the same time. Whereupon he impregnates my Astraea, whom he calls Astroarche, Queen of the Stars. They have a daughter. She's immortal, still exists, usually on Apple Isle, as a perpetual 7-year-old. And, as near as I can make out, has absolutely no useful talent other than an ability to annoy anyone.

The next go-round they have a son, a Sed-son. He turns out to be mortal. So does the next one, although by then Astraea-Astroarche and he/me have returned to the Head, as we're calling Pacifica now that it's filled-in and begun to take on its head-like silhouette. As soon as the second Sed-son comes along, well, what do you know? Surprise, surprise, Sedon stops having trouble maintaining the Dome.

He goes back upstairs, gets greedy, insists his Queen of the Stars join him in the Headworld's night sky, in order to share his heavenly throne. She resists; somehow senses going from earth-based to sky-based will kill her. So he reluctantly leaves her down here with me; her with her amalgamated talismans and me with mine. Then Sed-son Number One dies on the Outer Earth and, lo and behold, guess who has trouble maintaining the Dome again.

That's the formula then: So long as at least two Sed-sons are alive, one on either side of the Dome, adding chthonic to Cathonic equals a stable Sedon Sphere. So it is at least once a human generation, on both sides of the Dome, he comes out of his heavenly perch and mates with his earthy Queen of the Stars. The rest of the time she stays with me, as my Astraea, my Queen of Courts.

On the Headworld our court is in Grand Elysium, what's now Pettivisaya, the City of Wailing Souls, in the Ghostlands. In time we divided our court on the Outer Earth between the twin cities: my Sodom and her Gomorrah. Ironically enough we're both happy, Sedon and I, he in the night's sky and me down here, in an enlightened share-and-share-alike manner of speaking.

So maybe I do become his surrogate. Or his stooge, if you wish to call me that. As you might expect, I have a different perspective. Consider our relationship as follows: his is the heavenly kingdom whereas mine is the earthly kingdom. That's certainly how I thought of it. And she's as content as we are; maybe even more so.

She's the Perpetual Presence, the lone adult female on the Whole Earth since her daughter refuses to age, whereas we both need and cherish her; are in a way therefore dependent on her. That remains our situation for damn near two millennia. Then the Unities come time-tumbling back into our ever-linear time-space. Then they seek to assassinate us, they with their millennial ship or tri-peaked asteroid, their Trans-Time Trigon.

They don't succeed but it's a near thing.

========

Our daemonic bodies, as hardy as they've always been until then, are suffused with molten Brainrock. Because of that they're suddenly dying externally. Our individually fused-together power foci are all that's holding us together. We get lucky. Or maybe it's more a matter of the Devil, capitalized, as in the Moloch Sedon mostly in the sky, providing.

As you're aware, the Godstuff Outer Earthlings commonly call Gypsium, that's the ticket for sending daemons on their merry way back to whatever hell spawned them. Which we on the Hidden Headworld call the Hell-Well. Contrary to popular misconceptions it underlies much of the Upper Head, meaning it's only partially contained within Sedon's Temple, Satanwyck, aka Pandemonium.

So yes, we're bodily dying demonically but mentally we're more like reverting devilishly. The two Bandradin troubadours you were telling my host about, Jordan and Pusan, are still alive. The cascading rivulets of lava have left them only one way to go, though, and that's uphill, where we've just as desperately emerged from the Dome's Cathonic hole, as it were.

Demons coat when we take someone over; devils occupy when we do a ditto. We possess them. They should keep us going until our daemonic forms heal or we acquire some already healthy replacements. As their paramount couple we send out a far-spoken summons for just that. The first two daemons to respond are a Rockhead, as you call it, and a Klannit. We should have realized that they were there far too quickly for it to be a response.

We've an excuse. The lava lake of Sedon's Peak is already filling with overproof Brainrock-Gypsium and the fumes are affecting our daemonic brains in ways we'd never experienced before. So we're a mess and our shells aren't in much better condition. The fumes are knocking them out on their feet. They aren't doing the Rockhead and the Klannit any good either.

Even if our daemonic aspects, our brains and bodies, are dying within our humanoid shells, we're still their King and Queen. We've six recognizable power foci between us. No matter what we look like, they should realize that these talismans make us their commanders-in-chief. They shouldn't be able to attack us but the low-watt dullards do so anyways. They're nearly brainless, desperate to complete their mission and get away themselves.

Spiritually speaking we're simultaneously Shining Ones, Master Devas. We devils are nothing if not willful beings. Religious people are said to have Faith, capitalized; a will to believe regardless of how ridiculous, how patently absurd, their beliefs are to everyone else. Similarly our will to survive knows no bounds.

You'd think we'd have everything going for us. At the very least we should be able to transfer ourselves, howsoever disembodied, to the Rockhead and the Klannit, right? Wrong. How were to know the Rockhead was containing Future Tvasitar and the Klannit was containing Klannit Thanatos?

Shouldn't we be able to displace them anyways? He's a Lazaremist and Klannit isn't even a devil. So what if they've as much of a will to survive as we do? We're their seniors as well as their superiors in every way. I can't speak for Astraea but I didn't even try. In fact I believe Daemonicus's brain actually died due to exposure to the Brainrock fumes and it very nearly took mine with it. It may even be that the Lilith aspect of my Astraea did as well; unless it was already brain dead.

Put obviously, the Rockhead and the Klannit hadn't just avoided an assassination attempt by asteroid; didn't have to ride a wave of Brainrock crashing through the Dome; and especially didn't have to take over a couple of deathly weak troubadours, ones who couldn't fight their way out of a soggy paper bag with a pair of sharpened drumsticks.

Put appreciably, we're so wrecked it's a wonderment we've lasted this long. Put plainly, they're stronger than us. Put embarrassingly, they overpower us. They disarm and disrobe us, Gomorrah and I. They throw our six, combined power foci into the rising lava lake, where they melt away into so much slag and Brainrock slush.

They cart us away, back to Jordan and Pusan's respective parents, mission accomplished. And what do their parents do, their Hecate-Hellion mothers in particular? They forcibly part us. Her parents, using her mother's Hellstones, move north, to Daybreak, which was still on the coast of the Head's far-eastern, occipital regions in those distant days.

As for Jordan's parents, they put him to work tilling the fields. His mother even ensorcelled a Hellstone in order to compel him to stay on the family farm. She couldn't have known she was compelling a Master Deva at the same time, but she was. When my consciousness fully returned, I discovered I was still in Jordan.

He was getting on by then. Nonetheless, he was in remarkably good shape for a hard-working Bandradin of that day and age. My daemonic form, wholly recovered, shared his fitness. Him having both it and me in him could well be the reason for his comparative healthiness. Of course, despite our occasional bouts of mass mindlessness, devic healing talents are one the major reasons modern men and women, on this side of the Dome anyways, continue to worship us.

Before that Jordan's mother died, she removed her spell and he was free to take up lute and panpipes again. Even more years passed before we, me in him, him again a wandering troubadour, found ourselves back at Sedon's Peak. I was shocked to discover the Anvil Artificer was now in control of the Rockhead. Its daemonic brain had died, you see, in the Brainrock fumes still emitting from the lava lake. So had the brains of hundreds of daemons that responded to our psychic scream for assistance all those years ago.

The Artificer had combined their debrained, yet still subtle matter, daemonic bodies with power foci he crafted for Master Devas who, in their shells, had come calling on him once they heard the story of the Cousins and how they became individually solid after acquiring the Trigregos Talismans. After revealing myself – as you'd expect, the Artificer had forgotten I existed – he made me a power focus of my own, my panpipes. Which I still have.

He offered me a different daemonic body as well. I took it because, well, he said I better. Poor old Jordan had collapsed when I, in my Daemonicus form, stepped out of him. He looked about to die and the Artificer said All-Father Sedon cathonitized devils who killed lesser beings.

An individually solid, albeit only willfully shiny Master Deva all by my lonesome, I took myself to Grand Elysium. In time, I reacquainted myself with my Astraea, the other female Perpetual Presence, the one who stayed both an adult and mostly humanoid, especially from the neck down.

She'd forgotten about me, too, as it happened; had already taken up with a recurring deviant not unlike you, albeit only in that respect. The offspring of Helios-Mithras and Mnemosyne-Marutia, better known as Strife, his parents named him Chrysaor Attis. Over time, though, particularly when he recurred beyond the Dome, he eventually became the stuff of not just heroic myths and legends under a notable number of much more illustrious names.

I could never come close to listing them all: Adonis, Perseus, Bellerophon, possibly Heracles, probably Achilles, maybe Rama and maybe Kukulcan, albeit on opposite sides of the world, and so shockingly many of the Outer Earth's historic or semi-historic Greats even you'd be stunned if I started going through them. In here he was the Universal Soldier, the Golden Brown Warrior, the oft-times Taurus of Apple Isle and its Mithrant Brotherhood. And you know what six Sacred Objects he acquired and kept until Thrygragon, don't you?

They weren't quite the same as when either Astraea or I had the originals or their first facsimiles; hers especially. By dedicating them to our Sedon-jilted, and subsequently abandoned, mothers the Artificer rendered them deadly to anyone else. But they're virtually identical in appearance. I understand there's even a fourth version of them, the Trigregos Talismans anyhow, in the Weirdom of Cabalarkon; not that I'd ever chance going there to verify it.

For me, past experience is unforgettable. So long as I'm not taken by surprise, with all my firstborn as well as residual daemonic abilities I shouldn't have any problem avoiding Trinondev eyeorbs. That said, even if I confidently could, I dare not risk it. I was taken in by one once, in the aftermath of Thrygragon, and didn't get out until centuries later, during the time of your daughter or granddaughter, the Death's Head Hellion, if you have to know.

I never want to go through that again. What you call Limbo, I call oblivion. Howsoever you describe it, that's what happens to a devil thus captured. Besides, he's so overly protective of the place, the Moloch Sedon would almost certainly notice me there. Before I realize he has, he might reason I'm there to kill Cabby and decide to ill-star me or worse: suck me back into another prison pod – perhaps a pre-Earth one this time – or outright kill me.

He'd be right, too; not that you'll remember I told you that. The only reason the Devil has kept Cabby going for so long has to be because, if you kill the undying Utopian, you kill him, Sedon himself. And if he goes, what about the rest of us? Even I can't answer that, thankfully.

Here's something else you won't remember when I'm gone. Although I'm fairly certain Daemon Queen Lilith's brain died on Sedon's Peak at the same time the brain of my Daemonicus aspect did, her body survived. I know that because my

Astraea, Sedon's Astroarche – whom ancient Illuminaries of Weir named Pyrame Silverstar long before they named any other Master Deva – had it; still had it when she became better known as the Pauper Priestess.

But Sedon finally decided to cathonitize her, to make her his Queen of the Stars in fact as well as name, thirty years ago. Because she was threatening to get herself in position to kill Cabby, I reckoned he'd done so permanently. That said, and while it's true that, as of Sedonda, her silver star's not up there anymore, thirty years is an awfully long time to be without her down here having Sed-sons. My conclusion is she lost Lilith's body to the Female Entity.

That happened before, during his Eleventh Lifetime, which lasted from roughly 5909 until 5950. Starting around 5918 Methandra Thanatos got hold of her and her beer-guzzling buffoon of husband got hold of the Male Entity. That's how the ten, fourth generational Thanatoids came into existence. It took me some doing but I managed to sort that out in the mid-Twenties.

As a result, Silverstar gained control of Miracle Memory again and, with her, regained Lilith's body, what was humanizing Machine-Memory. But the coincidence of her being ill-starred at the same time Helios was killed for the eleventh time does beg the conclusion I've made, wouldn't you agree?

========

"Ah, I see from your eyes you do. Good."
"Good lunch too, wouldn't you say?"

========

"On the contrary," differed the Smiling Fiend, *"What I would say, and am about to say, is that when Helios was killed, Memory took Lilith with her, and Trans-Time Trigon, back into the time stream."*

"Sounds plausible. Assuming daemons can humanize her, too."

"I'm glad we can agree on that much. Let's hope you figure out the same thing after I've left because the Dual Entities are back. That I can assure you. And if the Outer Earthlings don't take them out this time, which they should, and if Father Sedon doesn't either, which he shouldn't be capable of doing by then, well, it may be it'll fall to you, or someone like you, to finally do something permanent about them.

"Otherwise I'd have to delay revealing myself to the Head and you wouldn't like that, would you?"

"Heaven forbid."

"As if I'd obey."

"I suppose when you've survived an assassination attempt via asteroid, what's a bolt of lightning amongst share-pals, eh?"

"There is that I'll grant you. Let me tell you something else for free before I go, though. Through certain associates of mine currently on the Outer Earth I've already ensured the Thrygragos Talismans have been torn into so many Brain-rock shreds and fragments. As for the Sisters' talismans, well, that's why I'm here. I expect that's why you are as well. I know where one of them is and I gather you do too, albeit only in proximate terms.

"While it may be both of us would like to see it destroyed before anyone else gets hold of it, neither of us is foolish enough to go nearer to it than we already

are. They've a built-in survival instinct, those things; a mutually protective, 'all for one, one for all' aspect to them. So I'm not even going to try to destroy it.

"Nor am I going to make any effort to compel anyone else to try to do so. Sedon's Peak isn't going anywhere – at least it never has yet – but I don't see how they'll get there, let alone stay there long enough melt away, any more now than they did 500 years ago when you had your go. They may not be sentient as such but they're something besides just malignant, that's for sure.

"'Let sleeping dogs lie' is one aphorism that comes to mind. But here's a better one; one I not so much made up as have made my motto: 'Out of sight, out of mind'. So, be consoled, I'm no more going to kill you right this minute as this Holgatson is going to act upon a sudden urge to kill himself.

"No thanks needed, Jordy."

"None given, Smiler. I just wish I'd wake up with a intuitive need to crawl out of this second skin of mine. It's becoming almost as irritable as you are."

"That much else I will grant you. Good intuition, by the way, going to the Weirdom of Cabalarkon on Sedonda. Congratulations. I have you now, though. Outside of Cabby's Weirdom I can find you anytime I want from now on."

"Since I won't remember you can do that, allow me to say, as a kind of goodbye, I hope you're the only one."

"That'll have to be your business. Mine here is about to be concluded. Return the favour, Tethys. Congratulate me. I'm about to become a smiley-happy, daddy Daemonicus, four times over."

"Am I invited to the baptism?"

"Not to worry about that either. I'll make sure you're there. You might need to bring some thermal underwear, though. I fully intend for it to be a baptism by fire."

========

Third eye opens. Eyefire burns. Blip! Transmogrification!
****

(PREGAME-GAMBIT) 8: **Amatory Ants**

Sapienda, Tantalar 4, 5980

"Because you were there," smiled Thartarre Sraddha Holgatson. When the legendary 30-Year Man said he had something on good report it usually meant that, whenever it occurred, he'd witnessed whatever it was he was talking about personally.

"Huh?"

========

Jordan Tethys did a double-take, as if he'd hadn't been paying attention or had nodded off mid tale-telling. Then he caught the reference.

"Wait, no, I wasn't even alive; not even for the first time, 4,000 years ago, Tar. No matter what name the male of the two troubadours went by I wasn't there. I'm no devil, never have been; though one of my half-parents was, obviously: Titanic Metis, Wisdom of Lazareme. Wouldn't be a deviant if I didn't have at least one devic half-parent, now, would I? And she says the other one was, too: Rumour of Lazareme. Hence why I've his quill."

"Methinks thou dost protest too much, Jordy."

"Bugger that for a game of horseshoes. Just for the record, Tar, Thrygragos Lazareme – whom I've always called granddad, not dad – finally came to accept I'm just a deviant and he should know. Even if he wasn't born until his seventh brood, Rumour was his favourite son, not to mention his favourite drinking buddy.

"Also for the record, all I meant by good report was I interviewed the Anvil Artificer, Tvasitar Smithmonger, more than a couple of millennia later. Sure, it was well after the fact. But he helped me fill in tee-tee-tail blanks in the tale I'm telling you. According to him, the Peak's eruption had a literally deadening effect on the functional sentience of the daemons that had been holding onto him and Klannit.

"Its fumes killed their brains. ..."

========

The soulless Rockhead had effectively been Tvasitar's jailer since Ragnarok. Suddenly he found himself in complete control of the granite-goliath's daemonic form. Klannit wasn't experiencing anywhere near the same thing, however. Also, all the more so considering Jordan and Pusan were a pair of Bandradin peacenik troubadours, they were putting up an extraordinary fight.

They had these glowing things about themselves. He's a hideously grinning, daemonic mask, some sort of cruciform crutch he wielded as a cudgel and a multi-coloured garment. She's a bloodstone crown about her forehead, a mirrored shield and a curved blade she seemed highly accomplished at using. Physically they weren't much, though. So, concentrating on ridding them of their glowing things, which they tossed into the ever-rising lava lake, Tvasitar-Rockhead and Klannit-the-Klannit finished their task as quickly as they could.

The Peak erupted again. Unlike him, Klannit couldn't keep her daemon moving. She told him to leave her there, to get Jordan and Pusan back to their parents, but to come back for her afterwards. He's thinking now, he rips a hunk of her mirrored self off her daemonic body, from about where your Nanny Klanny said a devil had its third eye, hauls Jordan and Pusan onto his massive shoulders and trundles down the slopes of Sedon's Peak.

Future Tvasitar's now brainless daemonic form – brainless except for his own thought processes, I shouldn't have to re-emphasize – must have had some lava lout or fire-resistant salamander-daemon to it. He makes it not only down the Peak. He makes it back to the Bandradin troubadours' farming community in the Holy Heights, as Bandradins call their high plateau.

As grateful as they are for the return of their love-struck children, their Hecate-Hellion mothers are disturbed they can no longer compel the previously dim-witted Rockhead. They let him go. Due to their sometimes unsavoury eating habits daemons aren't very popular, so they reason someone will find a way to kill him.

Then, just to ensure their children don't run off again, Pusan's mother, using her Hellstones, moves their entire family up north to the Land of Daybreak, to the then easternmost extremity of the Upper Head. Needless to say this is multiple-centuries before the Moloch Sedon decided to transfer Daybreak to the other side of the Hidden Headworld, where it became, and remains, his Outer Nose, Crepuscule, the Grey Land of Twilight.

The Anvil Artificer, as Future Tvasitar's now thinking of himself, plays around with the Rockhead's subtle matter body. It's hard but it's also metamorphic and goes with him when he possesses someone. He therefore has no real difficulty finding his way back to the top of Sedon's Peak, where he left the Klannit-daemon. Unfortunately, by the time he returns there it's months later and there's nothing left of her.

However, by then its lava lake has not only filled up with much more molten Brainrock than it ever had before and its shore is littered with daemonic, former denizens of the depths. There are colossal clumps of them, huge mangled mounds of them. Day after day more and more arrive. It's as if they're responding to some cry of command he can't hear. They can't take its Brainrock fumes, these chthonic critters, these earthborn excrements. They accumulate, brainless and immobile.

He still has what amounts to Klannit's third eye. They think of it that way, too, because he in his Rockhead body has developed a third eye of his own by then. Somehow her spirit's transferred into her headless and bodiless equivalent. She reflects out of it, making herself appear to be a Klannit-daemon because that's the form she's always had. Her voice does too, although I suppose it more emits than reflects.

Multiple centuries, more than two millennia of them, she reckons, she was inside the Klannit-daemon. She could no more influence it than he could the Rockhead of course. Yet they both had a sense of self and it was their selves, not that of the bundle-of-bricks-thick daemons, that fell in love. They were conscious, alive and mobile; albeit, admittedly, only because the daemons holding onto them were mobile.

She's still conscious, which means she's still alive, but she can't raise any of the brainless daemons. Can't make them hers, she complains. Nonetheless, you've managed to make the Rockhead yours. What's so special about you; what's so non-special about me? They compare notes. He can remember an absolutely astonishing amount of places, an astounding amount of events associated with them: the first Weir World, the second Weir World, the Sedonshem, the stars, countless shells on this and countless other planets.

He can remember his father, his uncles, their lone father, the Moloch Sedon. He can remember this last, his grandfather he supposed, calling him the Artificer. He can even remember the Rockhead snagging him and thereafter keeping him snagged until its brain died such a comparatively minuscule number of months ago. She can't remember anything except being stuck inside the Klannit creature.

'Your grandfather called you the Artificer,' she says. *'Make something for me to occupy, to make my own; something I can make move.'* How? *'You're a Vulcanian. Craft yourself everything you need, an anvil, a hammer, pincers.'* This he does, dutifully. Because he truly does love the Thanatoid, though we're still centuries away from Illuminaries naming either of her parents, let alone their brood brother Phantast the Dreamweaver, Thanatos. Nor them naming the Anvil Artificer Tvasitar Smithmonger, for that matter.

He finds he can make very nearly anything he wants but he gets nowhere making her anything she can use. Klannit Thanatos never stops nagging at him. Those things the troubadours had, what were they? He doesn't know what they were, but he agrees with her that once they tossed them into the lava lake, the fight went out of the troubadours. So maybe their thingies provided some kind of method to concentrate their abilities. What abilities? They were useless without them. Then maybe they were the source of their abilities, a kind of power focus.

'Make them for me. One of the thingies Pusan had was a mirrored shield so start with that. I was in a Klannit after all; a mirrored daemon.' He did. Did all sorts of other things, too. He tried imbedding her third eye into one of the daemonic forms lying around the peak. Zip. He tried building a Klannit-daemon all her own. Not quite zip this time. Klannit Thanatos could get her spirit into its mirrored exterior, could reflect out of it, but she couldn't get it to move.

One day an actual Klannit showed up on the Peak; whereupon the daemon's brain promptly expired. But Klannit Thanatos couldn't raise it either. They experimented. The Artificer could raise it; could with or without carrying his Rockhead body with him into the Klannit as well. He could do the same, raise and make move around, every single debrained daemonic husk littering the Peak. He could even get inside his anvil, the first object he'd handmade.

Could do it with every object he'd subsequently crafted as well. Could change them into any shape he wanted. Could make them humanoid and walk; birdlike and fly; fishlike and swim. She couldn't do any of that. How could she? She was an azura whereas he was a Master Deva. But how were they to know that?

'Something's still wrong,' she insisted, never giving up. 'We're still missing something. Maybe Jordan or Pusan could help us. Maybe they're special like you are, only once we disarmed and disrobed them, got rid of their power foci, they became as useless as me.' He could fly them both to Jordan if she wanted. No, she had a better idea; she had powers too.

He fashioned facsimiles of the two troubadours, reflected them in mirrors he'd also fashioned and set up in various positions around the Peak such that mirrors were reflecting mirrors in that ad infinitum way mirrors have. Eventually a remarkable thing happened. Pusan herself was looking out of one of the mirrors. Foolishly Klannit went to her, presumably went into her as well because, to hear Tavy tell it, it was hundreds of years before he came across her again.

Daemon after daemon continued to arrive atop Sedon's Peak. Their brains, those that had them, continued to seep out their ears, those that had them. Or any other orifice they may have had. They piled up, daemons galore, like so many petrified logs awaiting tossing into the pyre of the Peak's bubbling Brainrock. He grew despondent. Despairing of ever encountering his Klannit again, yet fearing to leave the Peak in order to go in search for her, he just sat there, on his anvil, tools all around him, in the middle of all those mirrors.

No one knows how long Future Tvasitar just sat there, through wind and rain and snow and even a few more volcanic eruptions. It had to be months, maybe a year or even a decade. He became a monolith, like one of those Outer Earth titans, of both its lore and its yore, who grew bored and turned to stone. Howsoever long it was, a frequently re-grown tee-tee-tail somewhat salaciously tells of his next conscious moment.

And so does he.

=========

"Three beautiful young women," Tethys told Thartarre, "Having stripped off their clothes, were doing their best impersonations of frolicsome frotteurs. In other words, they were rubbing mega-gently against his monolithic form less so in search of self-gratification than intent upon providing it." Thartarre gave him a blank look that could only be read one way. Although, thankfully, it was a non-itch-inducing, smiley-face, he clearly wasn't getting it.

Tethys did some mental math of the reciprocally bland, overtly-fill-in-the-blank variety and devised a quick solution for his host's evident perplexity. He could not, however, resist no small measure of prefatory editorializing. "At the risk of offending your priestly prudery, allow me to suggest two words that rhyme and you can put together an appropriate sentence."

"Those words are?"

"Roused and aroused."

"Gotcha."

=========

He roused. Got what he wanted. Hence the arousal. Got it a number of times, according to both Tvasitar and the tee-tee-tails, which even I have to rate Triple-X. Whereupon he forged for them what they wanted. Which was three objects, one for each of them. They were as beautiful as they were; were a sword, a mirror, and a bloodstone tiara that could be either worn about the head or clipped around the neck.

"But these can't be for us," gushed one of the young women. "They're too magnificent. Give them to your mother."

"My mother's dead," said Tvasitar, perhaps inaccurately.

Like every other devil except Sedon and the second generational Six, Tvasitar had three mothers. Rather, they had one. Except, while the Trigregos Sisters separated when they gave birth, they nevertheless always gave birth simultaneously. So it is no devil can be certain which Sister gave birth to him or to her.

Of course that hasn't stopped Illuminaries of Weir from speculating which mother gave birth to which devil. Equally so, speculation's one thing, certainty quite another. And that's the truth of that. It also explains why every devil has two immediate siblings in whichever litter of whichever Great God who impregnated, just as simultaneously, the three-in-one Goddesses.

"Then dedicate them to her memory. We'll live in her stead," promised another of the enchanting girls.

In a way Tvasitar wasn't being all that inaccurate. The three Sisters were, to all intents and purposes, dead. If in fact they still lived, they dwelt in the second Weirsystem, which was also some two hundred thousand light years away from old Sol and this Whole Earth pebble of ours. However, in the case of devils, who are genetically compelled to obey their fathers, absence does not make the heart grow fonder. Quite the contrary, as you'll know if you know much of anything at all about the history, or her-story if you prefer, of these objects. They're spiritually poisonous to devils. Don't do the rest of us any good either.

I'm not saying Tvasitar could have anticipated the sheer malevolence he'd wrought into the things when he mentally dedicated the sword to Demeter, the tiara to Sapiendev, and the mirror to Devaura. He's not a mean fellow, though he has had at least one jealous rage I could tell you about. Neither is he clairvoyant; no devil is that I can verify. Yet, in hindsight, given their subsequent history, you have to wonder if someone, or some ones, didn't put these three enchantresses up to approaching him in the first place. Long-range planning, properly enacted, is a feasible substitute for clairvoyance after all.

Witches within the Superior Sisterhood of Flowery Anthea, for example, have long held a scheme they call a dream; that of Panharmonium. It's not precisely identical to that which Datong Harmonia, the incomparable Unity of Balance, instituted something like three thousand years later, but its name and its goals of good fellowship and enduring peace were the same.

(Harmony realized her Panharmonium around the turn of the millennium only now coming to an end. It lasted almost five hundred years as well, until her tragic demise at the beginning of the so-called Thousand Days of Disbelief circa 5492 YD. Which, not coincidentally, was precisely when Iraxas became Hadd and your Sraddhite Faith hit the proverbial fan.)

Just so we're clear, the Ants' Panharmonium Project has aspects Harmony's never had: three dandies of aspects, to be accurate. It envisages the Trigregos Sisters returning to the Whole Earth, either as themselves, if they're still alive and if transportation can be arranged for them – not much hope of that, considering the brain-boggling distances they'd have to travel – or else as incarnations.

Once here, the theory goes, they'll exert a feminine damper on the evidently egregious excesses of patriarchal devils. They'll thus ensure a renewed Golden Age for not just devazurkind ensues. And this, in my view, is where hypothetical becomes hypocritical. The non-cynocephalic cynic in recurring-me would dog-star, as in seriously, object if I didn't remind you that one should always be careful what one wishes for.

If wishes were horses, it almost goes without saying there'd be a stampede. Furthermore, as Thrygragos Lazareme once put it, folks caught in stampedes invariably get trampled under-hoof. Nevertheless, leopards and spots pipedream or not, over the centuries, right up to the present day, many a female Master Deva, belonging to all three of the Thrygragos tribes, have at one time or another jumped aboard the Panharmonium bandwagon.

That some one, or ones, put the onanistic opportunists up to approaching Anvil circa 2000 YD therefore strikes me as a reasonable proposition.

========

His invocations complete, Tvasitar handed one of the now sacred, at least to his mind, objects to each of the three women. Their human semblances promptly transformed and three, 3-eyed female devils stood physically before the devic smithy. I gather the rotten rubbers, rummaging reprobates or frottage-foragers, whatsoever you think of them, they in their shells, which were presumably daemonic, got as far as the Peak only to have the brains of the daemons who'd been holding onto them for howsoever long die.

As I say, it might have been planned that way. I've no way of corroborating that one way or another. I can, however, confirm that latter day Illuminaries named them Susal, Amateram and Crinsom after, I believe, three goddesses venerated on the islands of Japan, the land of the Rising Sun off the far eastern coast of the Outer Earth's Asian continent. Part of the reason for that was that, although each had a different devic father, they looked Samarandin.

Which is also to say they looked similar to the Japanese themselves: dark-haired, slightly built and barely five feet tall. There was nothing similar, Japanese or Samarandin about their skin pigmentation, though. Susal's was as white as the moon, Ama's as bright yellow as the sun and Crinsom was, well, crimson, as red as a volcano erupting out of the fiery bowels of the earth.

"Lovesick dolt!" laughed Susal, the warrior of the three. Who, now that I've just described her, does sound both Japanese and Samarandin, doesn't she? "You've rendered us as solid as the Thrygragos Brothers; as solid as you are. Only you don't get to stay that way. You don't even get to stay alive."

With her curved blade she sliced off his head and, it being self-sharpening, didn't stop until she reckoned the butchering complete. Amateram and Crinsom weren't interested in grilling or barbecuing anything. Instead, they tossed his bitty bits and picayune pieces into the lava lake for swiftly ashen disposal. Congratulating themselves on their accomplishments, the three, let's call them *'the Cousins'*, rose into the air and went in search of Byron, Mithras and Lazareme.

Their ambitions were purely amatory. They fully intended to become Trigregos Incarnate, Trigregos on Earth. Despite their differences, the Brothers were united in wanting nothing to do with their lowborn offspring. However, the Cousins' power foci or Tvasitar talismans, newly coined terms back then, gave them impressive abilities.

Hard-pressed to resist the women's lures and entrapments, the Brothers either had an inspirational moment or, more likely, a Sedon-sending. They hastened to Sedon's Peak. Simply cutting off his head and chucking chunk after chunk of his daemonic body, if it was a daemonic body, into the Peak's Brainrock lake was no way to kill a devil four thousand years ago and it still isn't today.

What they would have had to do was twofold. They'd have had to destroy all the other daemonic bodies still littering the lava lake's shore, maybe even their own, and they'd have had to toss all the tools he made while trying to fashion something functional for Klannit Thanatos into the molten Godstuff. So long as they have someone to occupy, and thereupon dominate, devils can stay individually solid without a daemonic body. That said, they can't stay any more powerful than a possessive Spirit Being without a power focus.

Live and learn is the motto here. Too bad for them, the Cousins weren't given the opportunity to do either/or. Which takes me back to my earlier point. I hold they were no more than guinea pigs. At the risk of repeating myself, I think they were sent to Sedon's Peak deliberately. I also think they were sent there by Anthean Witches, who'd by then formed what amounted to an anti-devil, anti-patriarchal anyhow, confraternity with the Mother Nature worshipping Hecate-Hellions.

While, on the surface, an alliance between members of the life-loving, so-called Superior Sisterhood and the even older, daemon-friendly Hellion Sisterhood might seem improbable, it really isn't such an oddball notion. You only have to think of the example currently being set by Morgianna Sarpedon's firstborn, Tsishah Twilight.

She may be the Anthean Quarter Queen of Shenon, Witch Isle, but she was kidnapped not long after birth by the daemons' cousins, the feeorin of Crepuscule, and spent the next nearly thirty years of her life in Twilight's fairyland. As such, as she'll tell you herself, that makes her as much a Hellion as she is an Ant.

Going back into Headworld history, of the her-story genus, there was Helena Augusta, of Thrygragon infamy, whose best friend and closest ally Volsanga was a Hellion Valkyrie. A thousand years later, as I was telling Al Centauri and Weird Ferd – Governor Niarchos – last Devauray in Aka Godbad City, the Trigregos Titaness throwback – your Sraddha's Mama Melina – was both an Anthean Mother Superior, as in Nightingale, and a Hellion Matron Inferior, as in hellish.

Then there was Morgan Abyss, the Death's Head Hellion, a solely Cabalarkon Master of Weir betwixt and between the two double-timing, initially Kanin City Masters of Weir. Finally, lest we forget, both our ever-fishifying friend Fisherwoman, Godbad's ex-Queen Scylla, and Tsishah's mother Morgianna are probably as much Hellions as they are Antheans – much more in Fish's bait box and about dot-ditto in Morrigan Morg's breath-basket.

All of which suggests the Pusan-troubadour's mother got hold of Klannit Thanatos and milked her for all she knew. It further suggests that even 4,000 years ago Ants had already formulated at least the rudimentary concept of a Panharmonium Project, albeit one anticipating the catalytic, as opposed to cataclysmic, involvement of the three Great Goddesses in one form or another, not to mention for good or for bad.

As in until the death where none of us ever come back.

========

"Don't you mean evil?"

"No such a thing, Tar. Not unless you're a religious whacko, which I guess you are, in a good way. But, hey, that's just my pet theory. Let's get on with my story. I feel a tinkle coming on."

========

Tvasitar wasn't visibly present when the Thrygragos Brothers arrived on the Peak. Then he was. With father Lazareme and his two uncles, Bodiless Byron and Varuna Mithras, looking on in disbelief he grew physically out of his Brainrock anvil. You see what he'd done? He'd made his talisman his body. Which is why devils also call him Anvil. Of course he'd done that before, when he and Klannit Thanatos were experimenting with what he could do; with what made him so special compared to her.

The devic Anvil didn't need a brainstorm to realize what it would take to counter the Cousins' power foci. Recalling how Rockhead-he and Klannit-she bested the two troubadours wasn't much of a mental feat. He immediately crafted the three Great Gods talismans of their own: a daemonic mask for Byron, a cruciform for Mithras and a cloak of many colours for his father. Thus armed, the Thrygragos Brothers returned to the physical fray. Returned to it in a decidedly non-amatory manner, I shouldn't have to add.

Susal, Amateram, and Crinsom were atomized, their beings conjoined with Dark Sedon in the Cathonic Zone. The three would-be incarnations of the Trigregos Sisters became the first stars to shine in the Sedon Sphere besides, and beside, Big Daddy Devil himself. They were cathonitized. Regrettably, the to-him-sacred, to the rest of us accursed, objects Anvil dedicated to each of his three potential mothers weren't cathonitized with them. Presumably at Sedon's insistence, the Great Gods secreted them in the Weirdom of Cabalarkon, where devils dread to tread, in order to keep them away from any of their other offspring.

It would have been better if they'd destroyed them because, years later, once Master Devas were individually solid, the Great Gods bequeathed their own talismans to Chrysaor Attis, the Universal Soldier, Pyrame Silverstar's golden-brown warrior for in excess of 2,000 years. In case you're not familiar with him, he was Mithras's deviant offspring by the myrionymous second-born Apple Goddess: Kore-Eris, Kore-Discord, Marut Kanin, Fitna Marutia, after whom Sedon's Cheek Lands were named, but most commonly, and most simply, Strife.

They did so, they'd tell you, to protect him from the murderous machinations of Divine Coueranna, Kore-Concord, and Cruel Plathon, the Bull of Mithras. Rather, Mithras being dead since Thrygragon, Byron and Lazareme would tell you, should the former deign to open his mouth or the latter bother waking up long enough to tell you anything.

However, as you'll most likely have heard, mostly from me, Attis used the Brothers' talismans to get into Cabby's Weirdom and make off with the Sisters' talismans. He held onto them, with great effect, until the aforementioned Thrygragon. Which is when the Bull forevermore enslaved him. Or at least enslaved him until he was apparently killed, hopefully forevermore, by an oversized faerie fart known as King Orfeo over a century ago now.

Which is a story I may not have told you. I've told plenty of others about it, though.

========

"It's this one here." Jordan Tethys gave a tug on one of her tee-tee-tail hair-implants.

========

"I've also got one regarding Thrygragon; not its immediate aftermath, though. Wouldn't have room for any actual hair if I did. It forms the basis for an operatic endurance test that's still performed on the Outer Earth to absolutely astonishing acclaim despite the fact it takes literally days to get through.

"So for our purposes. suffice it say that the Trigregos Talismans eventually ended up back in Cabalarkon. And that's where they remained until roundabout the start of the First War between the Living and the Dead circa 5480 Year of the Dome. Whereupon – thanks mostly to Janna and Sraddha's aforementioned parents, Daddy Zal and Mama Mel – they came back into play in a very big way.

"Want to borrow them? Thrygragon's this one; the Unities' Disunition's this one."

"You know I can't read tee-tee-tails," Thartarre reminded him unnecessarily. "And, as far as you know, no one knows where the Trigregos Talismans are nowadays?"

"Oh, I imagine Dark Sedon knows exactly where they are."

"In the Weirdom of Cabalarkon."

The High Priest was doing it again, grinning. "Why do you say that?" Tethys demanded to know. Underneath her second skin, the scar in his forehead was almighty tickly.

"Just a theory I was working on while I was listening to you talk about the guinea pig Cousins and their witch-connections. Isn't it possible the real ones have been fused with the replicated ones the Attis left behind in the Weirdom of Cabalarkon all those centuries ago?"

"Possible," Tethys considered. "Maybe. But if that was the case then Harmony would be out and about again, wouldn't she? And I think I would have heard if that was the case."

"So would I, I expect. Janna Fangfingers has been knocking on my balcony door lately. She wants me to fly off with her; must think I'd make a worthy receptacle for her twin brother's soul. And we both know who their devic half-mother was, don't we?"

"That we do. What are you thinking, that if you had it you could capture Second Fangs in the Amateramirror like Sraddha once did Nergal Vetala?"

"That thought has occurred to me. If it's up there in Sedon's Devic Eye-Land, you could draw it down here."

Tethys was about to object; Thartarre anticipated it. "No, you can't, can you? You draw them, your drawing goes poof, doesn't it?"

"It isn't just my drawing, I'm afraid. Not if I'm careful. I had a wife once. Well, I suppose I've had more than a few wives over the course of 2,000 years. Tsukyomi was a relatively recent one, though. She died in '38. You see, I was doing a drawing her and our girls together. We had triplets; you've met them. Tsukyomi, who's maiden name was Tornado, had on her necklace, a wedding present she'd been wearing for years by then, and guess what it turned it out to be."

"The Crimson Corona."

"And it wasn't just the Crimson Corona that went poof. Our daughters never forgave me. Fact is, a dozen years later, one of them killed me."

"And you came back in one of the other ones, Ukemoshi, Sister Jordan. I'd forgotten about that. Sorry." The High Priest paused, grinned wistfully. Tethys dreaded what was coming next. He was disappointed not to be disappointed. "You think if you drew me up there Master Saladin would lend it to me? I'd only need the one."

"Don't even think such a thing, Tar. It's not too bad no one know where it is anymore. Believe me, it's better that way. There's a couple of applicable aphorisms that come to mind right away in that regard. One harkens back to Sirius: *'Let sleeping dog-faces lie'*. A better one might be: *'Out of sight, out of mind'*. A shame it isn't *'out of sight, out of plight'* because no good ever comes of anyone going anywhere near any one of those things. Will you please stop smiling like that."

"I'm finding it very difficult," the High Priest admitted in a voice entirely his own. "Could it be that for just one time in all the years we've known each other, in all the incarnations I've known you, I've figured out something you haven't? Quite frankly I'm surprised you haven't thought of it yourself."

"Thought of what?"

"It's a matter of hiding in plain sight, isn't it? How many years, how many decades, even centuries, have folks been looking for even one the three Sacred Objects, thinking that if you find one it'll lead you to the other two? Everyone knows the ones in Cabalarkon are replicas, right? Yet, what if the Weirdom's replicas are the real things, or were somehow fused with the real things, that'd be a pretty good hiding place, wouldn't it? It would also explain why the Terrible Twins' half-mother isn't out and about again. Trinondevs would have captured her in their prison pods, their eyeorbs, wouldn't they?"

"A remarkable theory," Tethys congratulated the High Priest. "There are an itsy-bitty iota of problems wrong with it, though. For one, it doesn't explain why my notepads burn up every time I consciously try to draw one of them."

"Does anything?"

"Other than Dark Sedon gets a kick out of it, probably not."

"Dark Sedon or you?"

"Point to the priest. Because no good can come of having even one of those thrice-cursed things, I don't want them found either. Ergo, I subconsciously ignite my own notepads. Sounds like some Godbadian psychobabble to me, Tar. Psychology, psychiatry, psycho-priest-craft, I don't buy any of that pseudo-science unless it comes with a prescription. Point's blunt anyways. I don't buy it. I did, then I subconsciously wanted to ignite my Tsukyomi forty-odd years ago and I didn't."

"When was the last time you tried to draw the ones in the Weirdom?"

"Can't say that I ever have. But I can say there's a chance the real Crimson Corona was destroyed thirty-five years ago. Around the same time you incinerated your mother and your father died in that crash you were telling me about: When he tried chasing down Janna Fangfingers in that whirlybird Fish had made for him at RBV, in Godbad, and it ran out of fuel over the Jaag Maelstrom. Either that or it's too hot to handle."

Thartarre's smile saddened momentarily. Then he, and it, perked up again. "Too hot to handle? So the real one might still be around. Where?"

He was serious about this *'find one and you'll find the others'* business, 30-Beers apprehended. Second Fangs and her three vamps, the Sraddhite, the Zebranid and the Trinondev, the ones who shouldn't have been vamps because they were trained to kill themselves before they could be turned, must have thoroughly pissed him off last night. He was prepared to go to any lengths to get back at her. He was even willing to play a Trigregos Gambit.

"More than likely on the Outer Earth," said his guest. "Here's a mini-version of that story. After my wife's death, we thought the Corona destroyed as well. It wasn't. A friend of mine's wife acquired it. Her name was Takeda Mikoto, by the way. His name was Akbarartha. Takeda was a Summoning Child, like your parents.

"Her father was Kronokronos Mikoto. You met him a few years ago, when he came by thinking you had the Amateramirror. My two remaining triplet-daughters by Tsukyomi travel with him. So does Superior Sarpedon's other daughter, Andaemyn; Morg's daughter by Demios, not Tom-Tiddly.

"The Awesome Akbar, as I called him because he was just that, awesome – although that was hardly the only name he went by while I knew him, in a variety of incarnations – and Takeda, of Clan Mikoto, were thought to have perished when one of the Japanese Caverns his devic half-father was working on time-space-displacing in Subcranial Temporis blew up big-time; as in big-time atomically.

"Akbar's father's a Lazaremist, like both my devic half-parents, which makes him my half-uncle on both sides of the bed. Antique Illuminaries named him Tariqartha for some reason but devils refer to him variously – as often than not as either the Time-Space Displacer or the Chronocollector. No matter what anyone calls him, he's Lazareme's Earth Magician, one of them, and he never really recovered from the explosion. Which is a shame because he's Temporis's Dand and its thousand caverns are among my most favourite places on the entire Head."

"So the Corona's too hot to handle because it's radioactive, like the Ghostlands. How do you know it's on the Outer Earth? More to point, how did it get there?"

"I said there was a chance it might be on the Outer Earth. The city the Dand was replicating was called Hiroshima. It still exists. But it also might still be in the Hiroshima Cavern because the Hiroshima A-Bomb cracked the Dome. So it went off in there too. The Dand collapsed the Hiroshima Cavern in order to prevent its radiation leaking into any of the nearby caverns; then to the rest of Temporis. You want to go there, you should probably wait a few thousand years before you bother.

"As for why it might be on the Outer Earth, that's possible because Kronokronos Akbar and Takeda Artha definitely got there. And do you know how I think they did it?"

"Should I duck? I can sense one of your punch-lines coming."

"It's a good one, too," the Legendarian confirmed. "Akbarartha had about himself some rather pertinent accoutrements when he and Takeda paid what amounted to a state visit to his Dand the Dad replicating Hiroshima in early Hektor 5945. He had about himself the Thrygragos Talismans. They allowed them to survive even a nuclear holocaust."

Thartarre digested that. Decided it was worth congratulating his guest on: "Four-and-a-half to four-and-three-quarters out of five in the punch-line department, Jordy." He ruminated a mite more: "Hektor of '45, you say. Well, that being the case, maybe it was Saladin Devason's predecessor as its Master, Kyprian Somata, and not one of her predecessors, who fused the real ones with the replicated ones. She didn't die until, what, 5950?"

"Except, even though they took on different names once they got there, Akbar didn't die until '55 whereas the last I heard Takeda was still alive; still lived in Hiroshima as well. Fish, the Sarpedons and the Zerosses have all visited her there over the years and, before you try to book passage outside through one of Harry's rings, she denies ever having Crinsom's Crown. What's more she denied it under the influence of Dem's open eyeorb. He's the oldest eye-stave in existence so she couldn't possibly be lying."

"She's been redacted; had her memories wiped and replaced with false ones. Devils can't lie but I've heard tell, probably from you, that they're so headstrong they can delude themselves such that they're convinced something happened that didn't. And if devils can do that to themselves why can't they, or someone else, do it to someone else?"

"Bang on the bellybutton, Tar. Not to mention indubitably true. Possibly even by Superior Sarpedon, who's as good with eyeorbs as she is at witchcraft. But if you think that means Morg has it, well, unless one doesn't lead to the other, I'd say you're wrong. They're made of God-stuff. That makes them as transmutable, they could look like anything, but it also makes them teleportive. So one probably would lead to the other. Ergo, because she wants all three of them, she doesn't have any of them."

"But someone might; might have all three of them and not realize it."

"Back to the three-in-Weir theory, eh? I hate to indulge your pseudo-psycho-silliness, but the next time I'm up there I'll make a drawing of the Master's regalia, albeit not on anyone this time, especially not my soupy friend Sal. If my notepad doesn't go poof, I'll bring it down to you, the notepad not the phony talismans.

"In the meantime, how about this? Wherever the Crimson Corona is, odds are it's unattainable. Similarly, wherever the Susasword is, the probability is it's still pinning the knockdown-gorgeous Harmony Unity to a slab of Brainrock in some long ago collapsed, mountainside cave somewhere on the Head. As for the Amateramirror, well, apply a little deductive reasoning, Tar. Say whoever has it knows exactly what it is and doesn't want the other two because it might wreck what she's using the mirror for."

"She?" Thartarre frowned. The High Priest usually did frown. But Tethys found his manner of frowning almost as unsettling as he did his until-then-uncharacteristic grinning.

"Fangs, priest. Janna Fangfingers has it. It's where she keeps her twin's life-essence."

"It is? I thought she kept it in an mirrored egg like mine or like what just about every other Sraddhite monk you'll ever meet wears. Or else in a Crystal Skull, one of those oddball soul-sinks that breaks apart to release and re-forms to capture or recapture. Or in a mirrored egg secreted within the Crystal Skull she always wears about her throat."

"Precisely. Godstuff is transmutable. It's also teleportive and she's damn good with it. How else can she get around the Weird; how else can she make vamps she turns into psychopomps? It fits. Besides, Janna likes to be stylish. Vampires are nothing if not gothic. They reckon a Crystal Skull as a cameo on a choker is stylish. Now, if you'll excuse me, I really have to tinkle."

"I liked my idea better," Thartarre mumbled to himself, smiling again, as Tethys made his-her way to the comparatively recently renovated, adjacent bathroom.

"Don't forget to sit down," he shouted after her/him.

That was inspirational.

=========

In the Weirdom of Cabalarkon two Utopians, a female pureblood and a male hybrid, gazed into the presumed-replicated Amateramirror above the latter's throne.

=========

"Has he got it yet?" demanded Saladin Devason.

"How the hell should I know, Sal?" responded Melina nee Sarpedon Zeross, somewhat brusquely considering he was her titular Master. "I'm a doctor, not a witch – not unless you count Altheans witches, which we technically are but aren't really. I can't read minds." She was also the High Illuminary of Weir. Her hubby Harry was as much a medical doctor as she was; she'd helped train him. Mel was a Summoning Child, nearly sixty. Rings would be 37 come the solstice.

"There's all kinds of interference. Besides, even when I can get it to work properly, it's a replica, not the genuine article. First off, I'm amazed I can tune it into the Outer Earth at all. Second off, it's not one of those television sets the Fatman builds in Godbad. No matter how I try to manipulate it, I can't get any sound. But, yes, it looks like Harry's about to take delivery."

"Then take that damned crown off your head, Mel."

=========

Klannit Janna Anvil-wife came in to somewhat shakily start clearing up their empty beer-mugs and lunch plates. Some seconds later the simpleton barber and the boy she'd helped raise into manhood – and into the High Priesthood, once he was orphaned – reacted to a startled scream coming from Thartarre's Godbadian-modernized bathroom.

It was more of a boisterous 'eek' than a shriek of terror but it was very much masculine-sounding.

=========

Holgatson providing the muscle, they barged into it.

Nanny Klanny sniffed. "She's pissed herself." Then she gasped. Whoever it was on the tiled floor was in the process of clawing away her face. Underneath it was another face. With her barber's practiced perception she realized he hadn't shaved.

"Correction, he's pissed himself."

Thartarre bent down. With his one normal hand he tore away the rest of the Legendarian's facial second-skin. He smacked Tethys across the face.

"Get with it, Jordy," he demanded, preparing to slap him again.

He didn't need to; Tethys was with it already. "Your mirror, it was frightening."

"What's wrong with the mirror?" wanted to know Anvil-wife, calming down noticeably as soon as she recognized who was on the floor.

"Not it, what reflected out of it. Me! Only I was Sister Jordan again."

=========

Job done as best a job could be done without playing a Trigregos Gambit himself, the Smiling Fiend attended to a few more matters before he returned to the Frozen Isle of Lathakra.

=========

Once there he found dinky – at barely 6-inches tall – Methandra Thanatos in her last-born son's workshop. She was standing on her Parsis-purloined hovering, more so than flying, carpet. It naturally took her a few second to realize he was in her presence. Once she did another aphorism came immediately to mind.

"Oh, there you are, Smiler. I've just had the most fantastic idea. You remember that mirror Klannit told me she hauled out of Sedon's Peak's crater hundreds of years ago, while Cold and I were in the midst of our Thousand Year Sleep?"

That aphorism? *'There's no rest for the wicked!'*

=========

End Pregame-Gambit.

****

(GAME-GAMBIT) 9: **A Dinq, a Doinq and a Danq**

Lazam, Tantalar 5, 5980

In terms of cosmicompanions, Cosmicar Four had seven first names. In terms of last names, it only had six. That was because 'A' and 'B' were both 'Zs'; were brother and sister. Although it had never been made official, they were virtually certain they had a bastard half-brother, the first name 'D' of the seven. He was their Cosmicaptain.

A and B knew they had paternal cousins; they also had a dead paternal aunt and a likely living paternal uncle. There was something akin to Alcoholics Anonymous about his alias.

========

Amos Annulis was a medical doctor in his late thirties. With a dark, Mediterranean complexion he looked as Greek or Turkish as he did Armenian. Around 5'9", well-proportioned, moderately muscular even, and in the best condition of his life, he had curly black hair and a thick moustache.

Having taken leave from his practise five years earlier, he toured the Western World promoting the ideal of an independent Armenian state. He and the group he was associated with – the *'Meherr'* or *'Lion'* – hadn't received much in the way of international attention but Ronald Reagan, the United States' President-Elect, interested in destabilizing Soviet Armenia's neighbours, Iran and the rest of the USSR, changed that. He now had all the attention he needed.

Thursday night *'Double-A'* was in the Mohave Desert, on the border between California and Nevada, with his own private cargo plane fuelled and running. Men in civilian overalls were loading the contents of two dozen camouflaged US Army vehicles into the plane. When they were finished he walked up to their elderly supervisor and his adjunct. After exchanging a few pleasantries they parted company.

The vehicles withdrew to the perimeter of the air field. *'AA'* entered the plane. The cargo doors closed. It rumbled onto the runway then took off. Climbing into the sky, it headed eastward on a flight plan that would take it to Florida, where it refuelled. Taking off again, it flew over the ocean. Its ultimate destination was eastern Turkey. A NATO country that had no love for either Iran or the Soviet Union, and even less love for Armenia, Turkey was nonetheless beholden to the former movie star turned highly successful politician and his backroom supporters in the US military and intelligence fields.

Somewhere over the fabled Bermuda Triangle, a huge glowing ring formed in front of it. The plane flew into it and promptly vanished.

========

Friday morning, Lazam on the Hidden Continent of Sedon's Head, the same plane landed on an airfield specifically built to accommodate its girth. The airfield was situated on the outskirts of Petrograd, the capital of New Iraxas, a large province in the northeast corner of the subcontinent of Aka Godbad, Sedon's Lower Jaw and Beard. AA strolled out to greet the welcoming party.

Among the Godbadian dignitaries there to greet him were Ferdinand Niarchos, the province's governor, Quentin Anvil, the commander of Godbad's military presence in neighbouring Hadd, the Land of the Dead, and Janna St Peche-Montressor, Alpha Centauri's 27-year-old daughter-in-law. Although Janna's last name sounded Outer Earth French, it was actually Inner Earth Dukkhan — other than parts of Temporis, which was largely peopled by Mantel replicas, Dukkha was the only place on the Hidden Headworld where Sedon Speak was a second language.

Representing the Sraddhite theocracy was its High Priest, Thartarre Sraddha Holgatson. Around forty, the bald-headed warrior-monk was wearing what was probably his best brown robe. It was so fancy it had filigrees worked into it with silvery thread. That wasn't the only thing silvery about monk either. His spiffy, mirrored egg – mirrored eggs being one of the Sraddhites' most sacred symbols – depended from his neck, on a silver necklace, while the curved blade screwed into the protective, metallic plate constructed off the stump of his right elbow was so shiny it might well have been made of reinforced silver.

AA was particularly pleased to see the three Utopians there: Golgotha Nauroz and the Sarpedons, Demios and his wife, Morgianna, the latter of whom was born Nauroz but brought up Somata, after her grandmother and great-grandmother. Golgotha was an eighty year old, nearly seven foot tall string-bean of a man. Actually a clone, his skin was so tight to his skull he earned his nickname: Black Skull-Face.

Although a few inches shorter than Golgotha, and much broader than most men in his homeland, Demios was as night-black as anyone from the Weirdom of Cabalarkon. Golgotha wore an azure robe and similarly coloured turban, veil not drawn, while Demios was in his trademark black: shirt, pants and boots.

Both carried eye-staves but, since Demios's eye-stave manufactured its own eyeorbs to replace the one on its top should it become full, only Golgotha had a shoulder satchel containing extra eyeorbs. Neither was manifesting a gargoyle off the eyeorb atop his eye-stave. Neither was either of them carrying any sort of gun or blade. For Utopians, even Utopians in exile, eye-staves were the only weapon they needed.

In contrast to her husband of thirty years – 30 being the age when slower aging Utopians attained their maturity – Morgianna was as day-white and almost as expressionless as a pureblood Utopian woman. Which she wasn't, not quite. While father Augustus was pureblood, mother Pandora wasn't, although her ancestry reputedly included some Utopian. If she was that old, which she wasn't, Morg could have been the model for Auguste Rodin's statue of Eve.

The Sarpedons were Summoning Children, which meant they'd be turning sixty towards the end of this month, Tantalar on the Head, December on the Outer

Earth, or early in the next month, Yamana in here, January out there. They didn't look much older than Thartarre, however. Utopians, even clones like Golgotha and hybrid-Utopians like Morg, lived long, usually healthy lives, sometimes making it well past two hundred with little or no appreciable wear and tear.

Morg and Demios might not make it that long. They'd been exiled from the Weirdom of Cabalarkon thirty years earlier. That meant they were denied a diet supplied by the Weirdom's originally extraterrestrial, food-processing units. It also meant they knew what real food tasted like. Utopians recycled everything. What went out one end went back in the other end.

Technically Morg's eldest daughter, Tsishah Twilight, was Janna's superior; the Mother Superior of the Athenan War Witch Sisterhood. However, in practise, Aortic Tsishah was more of a figurehead than anything else. Besides, she was scheduled to retire come the Spring Equinox. The real powers-that-be in most Sisterhoods were their elders.

Antheans, for example, had their Nightingales whereas Korant Corn Queens had their Miracle Maenad. Janna therefore deferred to Morgianna, whom she thought of as Grandmother Superior. The truth was she had no more to do with Tsishah than she did Morg's protégé, Garcia Dis L'Orca, who was only in charge of directing the day-to-day activities of Hadd's War Witches.

Superior Sarpedon had the added distinction, though as far as he was concerned it was more a matter of notoriety than distinction, of being the Morrigan, the honourific applied to the big boss bitch of the Hecate-Hellions. Theirs was an antediluvian Witch Sisterhood even older than that of Flowery Anthea, which claimed to be the Superior Sisterhood on either side of the Cathonic Zone or Dome, the Sedon Sphere en-globing Sedon's Head.

The reason he was so pleased to see Golgotha and the Sarpedons together was they were supposed to be mortal enemies. At least that's how Saladin Devason, the current Master of Weir, perceived them. After all, in one of his first acts after winning the Challenge of Weir in 5950, he was the one who exiled them. Exiled Demios anyhow, Morg just went with him. Love conquers all, they say. As the Morrigan a lot more than just Demios loved Morgianna; demons did, too. And she returned the favour. Utopians were brought up to hate devils with a passion verging on monomania but evidently demons didn't count.

Sal was Morg's year older brother. Although they had the same conceptive parents, Augustus Nauroz and Pandora Mannering, mom was possessed by a devil, one Pyrame Silverstar by Illuminary-given name, when she became pregnant with him. Hence the Devason surname, which Sal loathed almost as much as he detested Demios. Nonetheless, even thirty years later, his wife, Demios's white-as-light twin sister, insisted a reconciliation wasn't just possible, it was inevitable. So long as he, alias AA, found and returned the Trigregos Talismans to the Weirdom first of course.

Doctor Double-A, Amos Annulis, was a real person. He wasn't there on the tarmac. In his stead was a glamourized doppelganger: Dr Aristotle 'Harry' Zeross, the second Ringleader thus codenamed on the Outer Earth during the Secret War of Supranormals – the first being his father, whom some suspected Harry may have slain in '68, howsoever accidentally.

For his part, Harry denied ever killing anyone, not even on purpose.

========

Greetings and congrats followed.

========

Both Golgotha, who was a beanstalk, and Demios, who wasn't, towered over him. Golgotha's greeting was restrained as usual, a tap of his eye-stave to either shoulder and nothing else, but Demios, whose face looked a little like a furless tomcat who'd recently strayed into a dogfight, insisted on giving him a big bear hug. After surviving that, he endured a kiss on both cheeks from Dem's wife Morgianna, the dreaded Morrigan, who reputedly wore an invisible demon. Delighted that she hadn't turned him into a warty toad he returned the Hellstone she'd had ensorcelled to alter his looks.

Although he too had a moustache, Harry was far hairier than the real Annulus. He also had a five o'clock shadow in serious need of the attentions of someone like Thartarre's Nanny Klanny, whom the High Priest had left behind on Sraddha Isle. His hair was so curly his twelve years dead mother was still calling him Ringlet the last time he saw her. Considering what he could do with his miraculous Gypsium rings, that would have been a decent supra-codename. He'd chosen another one, though.

On the Outer Earth in late December 1955, when he was barely 12 years old, Harry became the last of its supranormals. He was using the codename Kid Ringo then, before his memory was redacted by his handlers with a mind-manipulating pharmaceutical known as amnaesthetics — a concoction that was in part devised by his wife Melina, the High Illuminary of Weir, a medical doctor and Althean witch-healer both.

The personally tragic as well as traumatic events of April-May 1960 restored his memory. He accepted, in his own mind, just as 12-years' late father Angelo's supra-codename, Ringleader, shortly after he found his way to the Inner Earth later that month (May being Vanalal beneath the Dome). Since there was something of the sinister about Ringleader, most folks just called him Harry. Others, though, preferred Rings.

One of them was waiting to greet him.

========

As pleased as he was to see his brother-in-law and consequential sister-in-law together with Golgotha, who was cloned from Sal and Morg's paternal grandfather, Ubris Nauroz, in 5900 Year of the Dome, Zeross was even more pleased to see him. Once everyone higher up on the protocol list had been attended to he went up to him, proffered a paw.

"Been a while, bud. What brings you to New Iraxas?"

Jordan Tethys took his hand and pumped it enthusiastically. "Looking for a story, Rings. What else do I ever do?"

========

Although his flight crew was composed of Godbadians, most of whom were born in the subcontinent and all of whom trained there, the rest of Harry's men were hand-picked by Golgotha from his cadre of Trinondevs, his nowadays all-male, Utopian Warriors Elite. Their eye-staves, rather the eyeorbs atop them, were ever so useful, in so many ways. They were particularly useful when it came to brain-baffling reticent allies such as cold-warring Americans who thought they were dealing with freedom-fighting Armenians.

Of course Morg's witches weren't exactly slouches in that department either, especially the life-loving Antheans she conscripted to help them out. Ants hated Dead Things almost as much as life-defending Athenans did. Plus, they were much better trained than War Witches. No surprise there. It took an average Ant fully fourteen years, seven as daughter, seven as mother, to approach becoming an advanced Ant, called Nightingales and/or, for higher-ups, Superiors. Far too many Athenan War Witches didn't last even long enough to become mothers.

There were also natural-born witches. A pair of them, Morg's firstborn, Tsishah Twilight, and a certain ever-fishifying exotic, had been very helpful to Harry accomplishing his mission. So too had the real Amos Annulis. His equally actual Armenian confederates, those still in freedom-fighting mode, would be very, very disappointed at the loss of their anti-personnel 'splatter packs'. No use crying over spilt beer, though. Maybe Ronnie and his pals could divert to them some of the supplies they were already sending equally anti-Soviet Afghani Jihadists.

Dr Aristotle Zeross and his crewmembers, who'd also given back the Hellstones and Anthean Agates the Morrigan and her fellow witches used to provide them their glamours, retired to the barracks for showers, a change of clothes and some much needed food. They left the task of transferring the armaments and scientific devices from the super-grand-larcenously-acquired plane into adjacent warehouses and helicopters to Anvil's Godbadian regulars.

(Quentin Anvil, Klannit Janna Anvil-wife's son, was the general responsible to Godbad's military and its democratically elected, civilian overseers for Operation Haas.)

In addition to a shower, a change of clothes and some food, Harry needed a nap; always did after using his miraculous Gypsium rings to the extent he had. Nap and yet another shower done, he had his prearranged meeting with Thartarre Sraddha Holgatson, the current High Priest of Sraddha and the son of an earlier High Priest, his father, whose first name his only son now used, as was traditional among Sraddhites, as his last name.

Some thirty-five years ago, Harry had heard, first-name-Holgat dragged the Vampire Queen of the Dead, Nergal Vetala, to her then latest extirpation. While she might be reborn, yet again, by now, Holgat wouldn't have been; couldn't have been. Not if he was as everyone believed: both altogether mortal and altogether normal. After all neither Haddazurs nor Sangazurs, or any other kind of azura, could reanimate ashes.

Holgat died as a Sraddhite hero. Thartarre had a much better plan. He wanted to retire as a Sraddhite victor.

By the time he joined Jordan Tethys for a late afternoon beer in the nearly empty military commissary, also prearranged, Harry Zeross wasn't so much fit to be tied as he was seriously thinking about tying Thartarre to the flagpole of his monastery on Sraddha Isle. There, in Hadd's Lake Sedona, Fangfingers and/or her bats would happily make a meal of him. The only reason he discarded that notion was that then Second Fangs herself might claim for her own what Harry had intended to bring back to Saladin Devason.

The famous Legendarian, whom Zeross had known, one way or another, in all of Tethys's incarnations virtually since his birth, in 1943, didn't need to be a mind-reader to pick up on Ringleader's infuriation with the Sraddhites' High Priest. "Your rings are glowing, Rings. Did the meeting go that badly?"

"Fucking ingrate," cursed Zeross. "He said he had it; now he says he doesn't remember saying anything of the sort. He even had the nerve to tell me I had my facts wrong. He burnt his mother to death because he'd been fooled into thinking she was a Vetala, not the Vetala, and his father died going after Janna Fangfingers, not the Vampire Queen. Morg's got to him, I'm sure of it; her and Dem, him with his fucking pre-Earth eye-stave."

"They got to him or they got to you?"

"Don't tell me you don't know what I'm talking about either?"

"Hey, I spent all day with Tar yesterday; heard his whole horrible story, too. Even met his doddering Nanny Klanny, the one who set him up to kill his mother so Fangs could lay claim to his father, whom she thought might prove a worthy receptacle for her brother's soul. Only nothing worked out the way any of them planned it."

"You're not kidding, present tense. You're trying to convince me the Sarpedons got to me. You, yes, obviously. You and Thartarre. You, especially. What about all those tales you told us, me, Mel, the Master, and all the rest of us, up in Daddy Cabby's Weirdom? What about all those tee-tee-tails you showed us? Mel can read them, too. She wouldn't be the High Illuminary of Weir if she couldn't."

"How the fuck do you think we figured out Thartarre had it? Everything pointed to him having it. You told us so yourself. And he confirmed it. Why else would the Master have sent Field Commander Golgotha Nauroz and his Warriors Elite to the Penile Peninsula?"

(Penile Peninsula was a term used by devils, who could air-walk, for old Iraxas, Krachla-Hadd these days, because of how looked like from on high. Others called it Sedon's Mutton Chop or Side-whiskers. Tethys used both interchangeably.)

"Sibling rivalry?"

"Besides that, Jordy. The insufferable bitch. Shows you what happens when you decide your parents are a couple of faerie fucking tricksters and it's okay to take man-eating demons as your familiars. And to think that when I saw them together with Golgotha awhile ago I figured everything was finally going to start going right for our families."

Melina born Sarpedon was 23 years older than Harry. Even though in many respects pureblood Utopian women matured much slower than ordinary human men and women – for example, the women were supposedly genetically incapable of having children until they turned thirty – that was quite the age-gap.

Nonetheless, despite the Master's strenuous objections to it, they'd married and, by her, he became the father of three lovely, if perhaps precocious, hybrid-Utopian daughters.

In state of disgust Harry gave Tethys a closer visual going-over. "Hang on. Something's not right with you either."

"Now what are you on about? The Outer Earth's air must have got to you, Rings. There's nothing wrong with me. I feel fine."

"Take off your cap." 30-Beers obliged. "Something's missing, make that. Where are your bloody tee-tee-tails?"

Tethys ran a hand over his bald pate. It was smooth as a baby's bum, as Thartarre's Nanny Klannit ever so quaintly put it after he finally relented and let shaky-handed-her give him a Sraddhite's do. He plucked his quill out of his cap, licked it until it began to glow, pulled a pad of paper out of his shoulder-satchel, which he laid on the mess hall table between them, and said: "Hold still a moment. This won't take but a minute."

"You can't draw me anywhere I don't want to go."

"Then I'll draw to somewhere you do want to go. How about the Danq?"

"And why would I want to go that old dump in Diluvia? What if a Time Quake's hit it? The beer's okay here."

"It isn't just good beer I'll find in Diluvia. Unless you'd prefer to go your way than mine? Me, I'd recommend mine. Even if your Gypsium rings and my Brain-rock quill are presumably composed of the same Godstuff, it'll save you some measure of exposure going my way."

"Fair enough; permission granted. Besides, I've too much to do these next few days to risk getting Gypsium sick."

"Mel included?"

"Doing her, too. Right now, though, I could really go for a pint of decent bitter."

"Consider it done."

Tethys had a quick look around in the vain hope no one was looking at them. Even in Godbad, where once in a while devils had been known to strut about in public, or float about in the case of the Byronhead, Tethys being there one second and then suddenly drawing himself elsewhere was something he tried to do only in private. Unless circumstances forced a quick exit, he made a point of avoiding being the cause of heart attacks.

It being Tantalar it was getting dark. Dinner hour was approaching. The commissary was filling up again. Rings and the huge airplane he rang in from the Outer Earth were the talk of Petrograd. Vain hope was an understatement; no hope was more accurate. The scar in his forehead wasn't itching but he sensed someone staring over his shoulder at what he was doing. Nothing unusual about that. Lots of folks liked to see an artist at work, even a scruffy street person in a tweed jacket that, like him, had seen better days. He gave her a glance.

She was an extremely attractive young woman wearing blue jeans and a mauve sweater. That her hair was dark, unbound and quite long suggested she was a civilian rather than an out-of-uniform soldier. That she had brown skin indicated her parents or grandparents hailed from Ophir-Moorset, the Headworld's counterpart of the Outer Earth's Indian subcontinent. Unless she did herself of course, which wasn't too likely. Petrograd was a long way to come for a native of the Head's occipital regions. There was always a chance she was a witch, though. In which case Ophir-Moorset was only a few properly tuned stepping stones away.

He spotted two women and a man enter the commissary. They didn't get in line for food or drinks like everyone else had. He, Rings and the woman behind him seemed to have their undivided attention. They were coming their direction.

He didn't need to be an ethnic profiler to recognize the man as one of Golgotha's Trinondevs, one of the women as a Zebranid Leper and the other as a Sraddhite priestess. Black skin, striped skin and a bald head told him that.

Bugger speculative heart attacks. Right this second bat attacks were guaranteed. He made a few scribbles that vaguely resembled Ringleader and himself, signed his name and dotted it.

========

Instantly he and Harry were transported between-space to the woods outside the Dinq, Doinq, Danq Cavern Tavern. Too bad he hadn't had time to draw them wearing raincoats.

========

The DDD was a largely natural honeycomb of caves, some of which were artificially linked together, rather than a single cavern. Catering primarily to members of various southern Marutian militias, it was a bar cum dance hall, cum rooming house, cum just about everything and anything else. As always in Diluvia it was raining heavily. Covering their heads, the two acquaintances more so than friends ran to its entrance, submitted to a thorough frisking and went inside the crowded, bright but smelly, torch and candlelit beer hall.

Because gold dust and precious gems were about the only things that could withstand Time Quakes, what Tethys sometimes called Kronos Quakes, Godbucks and even coins struck in areas bordering the Cheeks not prone to them were useless here. He kept a room of sorts at the DDD and in that room he'd buried a stash of more than just acceptable currency. He'd have to sign and dot said-stash before he could access it but the Danq's bouncers no more considered his Brainrock quill a weapon than they did Harry's Gypsium rings.

Grabbing a lit candle even though his quill could provide him all the light he needed, Tethys left Zeross inside the capacious, stone and timber reinforced cavern to order them drinks and munchies, a pint of best bitter for Harry and a pill, or pilsner beer, as well as a Cathy for him. Feeling like a troglodyte, which he always did when he was here, he made his way into the Danq's depths, went up and down some tunnels, and finally arrived at his literal hole-in-the-wall hovel.

It wasn't much but it was home, one of them. It beat a tent, cardboard box or packing case if only because it was at least moderately private.

He creaked open the door and suddenly felt like Papa Bear returning to his den, albeit without Mama or Baby Bear for company.

"Hi," said Goldilocks, though her first and last names began with a 'C'.

========

By the time Tethys returned to the beer hall, his Cathy was cold and his beer mug was empty. So were two mugs in front of Harry Zeross. "About time you showed up. That inverse Utopian waitress over there wants payment before she'll bring me another." By inverse Utopian Harry was referring to a black-skinned woman. Barring visitors, in the Weirdom of Cabalarkon only the men were black.

"Sorry about that, Rings. I was detained." He doffed his cap to reveal tee-tee-tails, maybe ten of them, once again glued to his bald pate. He held up a tiny pouch, jingled it. That caught the waitress's attention. When was the last time he'd seen a black-skinned waitress? Oh, oh. He nevertheless signalled her for two more beer and a fresh Cathy for himself.

Cathy was a non-alcoholic liquid that only sounded like coffee. A weak sister of Cathonic Fluid, dependent on where you went its makeup varied greatly. Basic-ally it consisted of Brainrock pebbles ground to grommets then boiled in a cauldron full of water and whatever else the locals threw in to give it a pretence of being pot-able. In colour the Danq's Cathy was slightly off-brown, like a thin tea. Most folks found it completely unpalatable but some, notably ones whose taste buds had been ruined by drinking the crud, insisted it had rejuvenating qualities.

It was only available in a few places on the Head. Cabalarkon had the real stuff, Cathonic Fluid, distilled Brainrock they sometimes called it. Their recipe wasn't a closely guarded secret like it was in the Danq. Although Illuminaries of Weir swore they didn't know everything that went into their version of it, they and everyone else up there in Sedon's Devic Eye-Land knew how it was produced. It was one of those concoctions some of their originally extraterrestrial, yet remarkably still functional machinery churned out, when given the proper command.

Two other places besides here in Diluvia – in Corona City, on Apple Isle, and in the vicinity of Sedon's Peak, on the Cattail Peninsula – made a comparatively agreeable Cathy; albeit in their own way. Ap Isle had Mt Maenalus with its internal river, the Stynx as he referred to it, that ran with molten Brainrock whereas Sedon's Peak had a lava lake filled with the same Godstuff. That it was available here had everything to do with the DDD's relative proximity to the Strait of Jaag and Sedon's Hairband across from it, in the Head's lowermost occipital regions.

Sedon's Hairband used to be called Harmony's Hairband. A chain of inter-connected mounds, it was raised as much as constructed by Datong Harmonia, the Harmony Unity herself, long prior to the Disunition of the three Unities of Lazareme in the 55th Century of the Dome. She made it in order to separate the Head's occipital regions, where Thunder and Lightning Lord Order then held sway, from the Cattail Peninsula, Sedon's Ponytail, where the devic abomination Quill Tethys addressed, to his face, as Uncle Abe Chaos dominated both physically and philosophically.

A strong component of Brainrock to these mounds explained why this strip of territory was also known as the Gypsium Wall. Even though she was abolished, for want of a better word, in Rudar 5492, the nowadays immobile, holeyest – as in rid-den with seemingly empty but roomy, even palatial (not glacial) caverns – and most Godstuff-concentrated crag in the Hairband was referred to, likely erroneously, as Harmony's High Seat.

(Holeyest, yes, but for many it was also homonymously, as well as harmoni-ously, holiest. Legend had it Harmony herself hollowed out its caves. And the Unity of Balance remained almost universally admired for her fundamental role in estab-lishing and thereafter preserving the nearly 500-year-long epoch of Panharmonium that comprised the first half of this, the Dome's 6th Millennium. Even if it was halcyon, as in suspiciously fabulous, in this dreary day and increasingly hopeless age that made the supposed remnant of her High Seat hallowed ground.)

Whilst the 30-Year Man was in Cabby's Weirdom convincing those who would listen to him that Thartarre had the Amateramirror, one of the theories Harry's wife,

its High Illuminary, Melina born Sarpedon, broached was Nergal Vetala was flying toward the Gypsium Wall when Holgat overtook her in his whirlybird. Mel
reckoned she was on her way there in hopes of more fully revitalizing herself after
howsoever many decades of being reborn – if that's how she kept coming back – in
one Hellion after another.

It was certainly plausible, Tethys agreed. Whereupon he plucked a tee-tee-tail
off his head and read them another of his tale-tailings. From his reading it was clear
she would hardly have been the first devil to do so. During the expansion of the
Empire of Lathakra in the 48th Century of the Dome, the Death Gods of Lathakra
and their allies, Byronics and Lazaremists as well as Mithradites, commonly allowed
devils whose protectorates they'd overrun to recuperate in the Gypsium Wall.

Absorbing Gypsium to rehabilitate themselves beat consuming their own
azuras, which was another method devils used to recover after a thorough bashing.
Of course, as the story illustrated, they'd have to become the Thanatoids' allies afterwards. But that was better than the obvious alternatives: dismemberment and, possibly, subsequent death; imprisonment within All of Incain; endless cathonitization,
aka both catasterization and ill-starring; or confinement within the highborn devils'
equivalent of a Trinondev's prison pod, which took the shape of rings.

(Harry's father, Angelo Zeross, who was killed in 1968 beyond the Dome,
found a bag or kibisis full of these selfsame rings – which were ever-so-appropri-
ately called *'ringots'* – during the Simultaneous Summonings of 19/5920. Once he
learned to project and thereafter control the devic Spirit Selves held within them, he
became the first Ringleader.)

Utopians of Weir, inbred imbeciles that the majority of them were once again
becoming, were as addicted to Cathy as they were to all the other slop excreted,
as Tethys often put it, by their inedibility processors. Zeross, who lived up there,
couldn't stand any of the stuff the so-called Mother Machine produced. He insisted
his wife feed him and their kids human food, as he described regular eats. By that
he meant edibles grown, caught, slaughtered or shot by country-dwelling Utopians;
ones who could still be trusted with a spade, a cleaver, a slingshot or a bow.

Not guns, though. According to the Master, no one, not even Sal himself,
could be trusted with guns. Which of course was why, as Mel noted in her inimit-
able Mel-way, he kept huge armouries full of the fucking things. (Like hubby Harry,
Mel was prone to using curse words. Unfortunately, their daughters were acquiring
the same propensity for soap-free mouthing.)

When he was up there, as he had been earlier in the week, Tethys drank Cathy
like water – or beer, preferably pilsner, anywhere else. Even if Golgotha Nauroz
and his wife, Gethsemane, who was cloned out of Chryseis Somata, Saladin and
Morgianna's paternal grandmother, made a passable homebrew, they couldn't get it
quite right. As for the frothy fakery the processors produced, it tasted more like the
swill you regurgitated after you've had way, way, too much real beer.

Sometimes, if he was well into his cups, Tethys would call Cathy soma, the
drink of life, or *'haoma'*, the elixir of Elysium – Grand Elysium being Sedon's Cult
Centre prior to most of the Upper Head becoming the radioactive, and hence uninhabitable Ghostlands in 4825 YD. Here, though, in the DDD, when it arrived

and he'd paid the waitress using his own set of hand-scales to weigh out an agreed-upon price, he only sipped it.

"Actually," he reflected out loud. "Come to think of it I'm not at all sorry. At least I'm not sorry for myself."

"You certainly look like the cat that ate the golden canary."

"More like the Goldilocks, of the Three Bears fame. She wasn't any kid either, I can assure you of that. I asked her join us. It was the least I could do after she asked me to join her."

"And is she?"

"She says she's waiting for a couple of friends to show up, then she'll be down."

"Don't bother on my account, Jordy. I'm married, remember. Fact is I was about to ring myself home and leave you to deal with the fallout."

"Shouldn't drink and ring, Rings. Mel wouldn't approve. What'd you do with the real Annulis and his men by the way?"

"Regular routine. The Fatman's rich as stink, on both sides of the Dome, so some money changed hands. A few got new identities out there: Canada, the States, Australia. A few agreed to forget they were freedom-fighters and just went back to their families in the Soviet Union. Some of the truest zealots are probably still twiddling their thumbs somewhere near Ani, on the Ahuryan River, in northeast Turkey, awaiting delivery of their grenades, incendiaries and such like antipersonnel doodads and gewgaws.

"As for Annulis himself, the KGB – that's an Outer Earth secret society as much as it is the USSR's national secret service – had targeted him for assassination. He knew it too. Next time you're in Rêve, over on the Cattail, you might want to look him up." Rings paused for a gulp more so than a sip of his bitter.

"A decent deal for all concerned, especially the Russians and Armenians, I'd say. And I guess I just did. At least they won't be getting killed with any of the splatter packs I brought through. At the same time, the Sraddhites in here will only be blowing apart things too stupid to stay dead, though I guess it's the Haddazurs, not their deceased selves, that get them up again."

"A terribly taxing exercise, from the sound of things. Wears me out just hearing about it. Aren't you afraid you'll get Gypsium sick?"

"I don't have to go back to the Outer Earth until the end of the month, so I should be all right. It seems that, as long as I'm under the Dome, I don't get sick. Tired and debilitated once in a while, sure, but then I just hang out in the Weirdom, have a few months with my family, and I'm fine again. That's why I only pop between the two sides a couple of times a year nowadays, for a month around Eastertide and again during Xmas week to collect the results."

"'*Delivery Days*'," muttered Tethys, who didn't approve of the methods the adult Zerosses were employing to augment the Utopians' breeding stock and thereby stave off increasing idiocy.

That Mel claimed her Sarpedon ancestors did the same thing throughout the Dome's Fourth Millennium conveniently ignored a couple of salient devils in the details, as far as Tethys was concerned. Firstly, from what he understood of that olden era – he didn't have his first lifetime until the start of the Dome's Fifth Millennium – the Utopians who returned to the Hidden Headworld way back then knew they were Utopians, or at least knew they had U-blood.

Secondly, her Sarpedon ancestors, the one who did come inside, may not have been precisely enslaved but they didn't attain full status until after Cabalarkon's so-called Independence Day in 5476. (In fact, for the thousands of years intervening between their return and their emancipation, for want of a better word, the Idiots of Weir leached off the Sarpedon underclass like a collective of psychic vampires.)

Finally, tampering with someone's mental stability so cavalierly was something their devic enemies did. It shouldn't be something Utopians did too. That was like using torture in the name of freedom. Or advocating capital punishment at the same time as opposing abortion. Or praying for victory instead of good fellowship, let alone each other. Or … or … or … the drivel does dribble on doesn't it.

"And nowadays Xmas is Zmas up there – after you."

"That was Sal's idea, not Mel's nor mine."

"So it was," recalled Tethys, having had it on good report. "Exciting times, Delivery Days, I don't doubt that. But they can't be as much fun as Spring mating season used to be. Yet, thanks also to you, Eastertide has replaced Maypole Day in Cabalarkon. It's become almost a big a deal as it is on the Outer Earth and has been for a couple millennia longer on Ap Isle; not that Apple Kores crucify their The-attises anymore. My latest incarnation's Miracle Maenad of a mommy dearest put a stop to that decades ago."

"As you more than anyone else on the Head should appreciate, Jordy," Ring-leader reminded him, "I avoid Corona City like the plague."

"No more so than I do, Rings." 30-Beers acquired George Taurson in 5968. He hadn't been back since.

After Cruel, Kind or Indifferent Plathon, the devic Bull of Mithras, George's mother, the Korant Corn Queens' Miracle Maenad, was Ap Isle's Boss Bovine. At a few years over a hundred, her artificially preserved father was the lone known Sed-son surviving on the Outer Earth. While that didn't automatically make George one himself, the presumption was he was an Inner Earth Sed-son – there needed to be one on either side of the Cathonic Dome to maintain it.

George dying, even though Tethys took over his body and thus kept it going, cost her a great deal of prestige and Miracle was a vengeful as well as a highly skilled and devious old cow.

"Anyhow," said Harry, "In a few years time, once Persephone and Helen are old enough, I'll let them take over the whole distasteful business. They're half-Utopians and, since it's the Utopian race we're trying to revitalize, that will become their job."

"I didn't realize they could use your rings."

"Neither do they. Mel may be an Althean witch-healer but she's just as prop-erly trained as the real Amos Annulis and I am in terms of being a legitimate medical doctor. Fact is, when we were living in Godbad she helped train me. But you'd know that. Besides, Alts are at best, or at worst, not really witches anyhow. Most of them can't travel between-space on witch-stones. But she is good with eyeorbs. So is my sister-in-law. Damn useful things, eyeorbs. When did Morgianna get to you and Thartarre – yesterday?"

"More than likely earlier on today. If she did."

"Oh, she did. Or Demios did. Now that you've some tee-tee-tails stuck back onto your head, do you recall what I was talking about in Petrograd yet — about Thartarre having the Amateramirror? Or were you too busy playing Papa Pervert Bear?"

"I told you she was no kid. No devilish goat either; my old pal Pusan's the faun, not me. It wasn't the itch in my forehead she scratched. But you're about to find out for yourself because here she comes. Those must be the friends she was waiting for." Zeross turned to have a gander at the golden goose. Too bad he had his mug in hand.

The sound of it smashing onto the Danq's hard-packed, earthen floor was barely louder than his cursing: "Fucking Hell!"

"Uncle Harry!" yelped a new entrant to the cavern tavern's beer hall. "Is that you?"

"It is!" exclaimed her identically-uniformed and similar-looking male companion.

The woman was young, in her mid-twenties, fit-looking and well-tanned. Her clipped, shoulder-length hair was more sandy than brown. She wore a silver and dark grey, striped and hooded top, black pants and black boots. The third one with them, who was a golden blonde, had on the same sort of clothes.

Which was no improvement, as far as the legendary 30-Year Man was concerned. The last time he saw her she didn't have on a stitch of anything.

========

"Jesus H Fucking Christ! Ange, Baal, how'd you get to the Head?"
****

(Game-Gambit) 10: **The Three Guinea Pigs Bluff**

<u>Lazam, Tantalar 5, 5980</u>

It was family reunion time.

========

Not that either Tethys or Goldilocks, who'd told him her name was Carmine Carmichael when they paused for a brief chat between go-rounds awhile ago, was part of anyone else here's family. The remaining three, though, were part of the Family Zeross. Other than the brother and sister's hair colour, there was a definite resemblance between living uncle and dead brother's kids.

Goldilocks, CC she'd said to call her, was right in there with them when it came to hugs and kisses; tears too. Evidently Harry, Rings, was an answer to their prayers. As he habitually did when feeling stress, Tethys detached his Brainrock quill from his checked cap and pulled a notepad out of his shoulder satchel. Something else fell out with it: the Utopian star-chart Melina Zeross gave him in Cabalarkon Birhym night.

He picked it up, scratched the tickly scar tissue between his eyebrows contemplatively. *'Avoid it like the plague'*, Harry said. Star Carcinogen, to Illuminaries, the Plague Star, to devils, was but one of the stars missing from the night's sky. Indeed, from his observations over the past few nights, the entire Apocalyptic Constellation was gone. As boding badly as that was, its components were hardly the only stellar absentees.

"Seems I'm missing something here, Rings," he noted wryly, once reunion time was over and Harry, Ringleader, brought the two youngish women and man, A, B and CC, as he was already starting to think of them, over to their table. "Besides introductions I mean."

Itch scratched a couple more times by then, Tethys was in the process of sketching the three identically uniformed newcomers on three different sheets torn from his notepad. His quill wasn't glowing and, for a change, he was dipping it into an inkwell, also taken out of his shoulder satchel. Appearances must be maintained, he'd decided.

Next to the three sheets he was working on was a fourth one, a now blank piece of paper that Harry, if he was as observant as, say, his wife might have been – which he wasn't, nowhere near – might have recognized came out of a processing unit from way up north in his Inner Earth home, the Weirdom of Cabalarkon.

"I doubt that," said Ringleader, paying Tethys a rare compliment. "You know something of my family. I had an elder brother and a younger sister. Both are dead now: Demonites at the same time as our parents in '68; my baby sister, Oriani, three years ago."

"And these ones are?" queried the Legendarian, playing for time. Having no idea who he was dealing with, he felt he had get them just right.

"Demonites and Hiliarti Schroff-Zeross's children. Hiliarti's German, which helps account for their lighter hair. Allow me to introduce my niece and nephew, Angelica and her year younger brother Baalbek. Their pal's name, I've only just learned, is Carmine Carmichael. I'm to gather you two have already introduced yourselves. Ange, Baal, this is my old pal, fellow adventurer and occasional drinking buddy, Jordan Tethys."

"Pleased to meet you," they said in unison. Sometimes twins were like that, supposed Tethys, who'd been part of a multiple birth more than a few times, as they took chairs around the table. Evidently sometimes close siblings were like that, too, he mentally amended. He'd had plenty of siblings over the centuries as well.

"I may have been born five years before him," continued their uncle, once they were seated. He was referring to Tethys, not his oddly named brother Demonites. "But he's actually a whole lot older than me; way older. In fact you won't believe how old he is – as you might have noticed, the Head's an exceedingly strange place. If it wasn't for him, twelve years ago, I'd be a dead man today; maybe even a Dead Man Walking."

"Twelve years?" Baalbek quickly calculated. "That'd make it 1968; the same year our father, grandparents and a half dozen members of Heliopolis's Black Rose of Anarchy were killed."

"No need to remind me," recalled Ringleader, his turn to fight back tears. "If I hadn't been trapped on Apple Isle, for the second time in three years, I might have been able to save them and the rest of our family – Kadmon, Thaddeus, the lot." (When down in the dumps, Harry was known to blame himself for their demise even though it was his unavoidable absence, not any of his actual deeds, that contributed to it.)

"Stop belittling yourself, Rings," said Tethys. "'68 wasn't a very good time for any of us. Glad to meet you both but, hey, like your uncle said, how in whomever's name did you get to Sedon's Head?"

"Ever heard of the Cosmic Express, Mr Tethys?" asked Angelica.

"As a matter of fact I have," he answered.

He'd left Aka Godbad City on Sedonda morning, the day of its scheduled launch from the Outer Earth's largely manmade Centauri Island, off the coast of Maui in the Hawaiian archipelago. However, Janna St Peche-Montressor, Alpha Centauri's daughter-in-law, whom he counted as a friend, told him in Petrograd earlier today that it had been intercepted and blown to hell and gone before it left the Outer Earth's atmosphere.

He must have been suffering from a critical case of cranial conniptions after his narrow escape from Janna Fangfingers then All on Incain. Otherwise, he would have figured out before today what had happened to the missing stars in the Sedon Sphere. It had only been presumably blown up; that much was clear to him now.

Seeing three individuals in identical uniforms walk into the DDD's subterranean beer hall had pretty much cemented it. All the more so when two of them had names he'd heard before; names of a pair of Outer Earth Zerosses, to be precise. It also explained why his scar had been telltale tickling. The hell and gone was right here, beneath the Cathonic Dome. Rather, at least part of it had ended up in here.

"I have too," admitted Ringleader, who would have since the other person he worked for in here, besides Saladin Devason, went by his given name, Alfredo Sentalli, out there. "So tell us how you got to the Danq. Jordy here may be a tremendous artist but he actually tells stories for a living and I bet yours will be as good or better than any he has. Drinks?"

Baalbek had a preference for hard liquor, the equivalent of scotch whisky, though the Danq had its version of both Ouzo and Retsina available. Angelica preferred the house specialty, Mushroom Wine. Carmine didn't drink alcohol, said she had enough vices already, but took a sip of the cold Cathy Tethys left on the table and, despite its terrible taste, perhaps not surprisingly ordered one for herself.

Among the snacks the waitress brought were a few fingerbowls of assorted mushrooms, which those in the Danq tended to call '*shrooms*' either for short or because then they could pretend they weren't slurring their words. The three Outworlders were wary of these shrooms, thought they might be toxic. Tethys and Zeross weren't.

Other than endless rain, Diluvia was most famous for its mushrooms. As a result, the DDD's proprietors were acutely aware of which ones were safe to consume, one way or another, and which ones weren't. Paying customers in such a comparatively far out place in terms of a population hub were hard enough to come by, so keeping them alive and coming back for more made good business sense. That was also why they cultivated such a remarkable variety of not just shrooms but related fungi in nearby caverns.

The pair of Headworld veterans did, however, warn the three neophytes to stay away from another of the Danq's specialties, Amanita, a cave fungus sometimes called god-drops because of its mild entheogenic properties. Carmine took one anyhow. First Cathy now this, thought Tethys. Rephrase that. First me then Cathy and now this. The girl may have only the one major vice, Lust, which even Lovely Lady Afrites like Yataghan's Janna – who didn't drink either, Tethys recalled – regarded as a vice, but she was unquestionably experimental.

Mind you, Lovely Ladies made love-making a virtue and, wild as she was, Carmine had the makings of a first class Afrite. One of Shenon's Quarter Queens, Ventricular Telepassa, she of Godbad, had begun her career in witchery as an Afrite. Although she went on to take her last seven years of Anthean training as well as gain a considerable rep as an Althean healer, the best on the Head some said, she let her eldest daughters, who were triplets, become Lovely Ladies. Maybe Telepassa would take Carmine on as an apprentice Afrite.

Something for the future file, that. Right now though, as mostly Baalbek touched on some of the highlights of their experiences since last Sunday, Sedonda, Tethys concentrated on finishing CC's sketch before he moved onto the two

Schroff-Zerosses. He figured a wild one popping magic mushrooms and drinking Cathy warranted his first shot at some remedial medicine of his own. It really was too bad he couldn't draw anyone anywhere they didn't consent to going; was equally too bad Rings couldn't be trusted to drink and ring. But hey, subterfuge, thy name is 30-Beers.

"People joked about us," Baal was saying. "Used to call us Cosmicar Alphabet Soup. It actually made a funny sort of sense. There were seven of us; now there's only three. Ange was 'A'; I was 'B'; Carmen was 'CC'; 'D' was Dmetri, the Cosmicaptain ..."

"You mean Diomad, your older brother?" Rings interrupted. It seemed to Tethys there was more than just a hint of displeasure in his voice. "Demonites' bastard?"

"He never admitted that. Neither did dad. But, yeah, the same guy, Dmetri Diomad."

"I've had more than a few bones to pick with Dem's Dim over the years. He was the one who betrayed Heliopolis and the Black Rose to AMERICA, you know."

"Not proven either, uncle," Angelica protested loyally, as she tossed back a couple of the Amanitas. "Dim's no angel but he is a survivor; one of the toughest customers I've ever met. I looked forward to serving with him."

"The others aboard Four," picked up Baalbek, taking three of the hallucinogens, "Were Elvis Elfin, Geraint Plantagenet and Felix Dee."

"Eel was a junior hockey star up in Canada," said CC, helping herself to half of the god-drops. Done with Baal, Tethys hurried on to complete Ange before the inevitable happened.

"Until he blew out his knees and took up geography instead," A qualified, finishing off the bowl of shrooms. "While G's a Brit botanist who, to hear him talk, which he loved doing, could trace his ancestry all the way back to Matilda, the Twelfth Century daughter of England's King Henry the First and the wife of France's Geoffrey Anjou."

"F's a computer analyst and a bloody bisexual," carried on B. "One the world would be well rid of, if you ask me."

========

Tethys had to remind himself yet again that A and B weren't twins because Baal had carried on from Angelica in that bizarre way twins so often had of being able to finish the other twin's sentences. A Zeross exhibiting such unvarnished intolerance for a companion as well as fellow human being did strike him as highly unusual, though.

To a Jack or Jill man-woman of them, every Zeross he'd ever come across was a moral anarchist – and that went for every one of their cousins and near relatives, one of whom was Thartarre Holgatson's shutterbug of a mother Barsine and another of whom, though she wouldn't remember it, was Ventricular Telepassa of Godbad.

An odd term, in philosophical, if not actual, paterfamilias Angelo Zeross's lexicon moral anarchists reckoned the world would be much better off if everyone just shut up and did the best they could for the commonweal. No one needed anyone lording over them, he'd say, not in any truly civilized society.

You pulled your own weight or you went elsewhere, not that you'd be welcome anywhere else either; not any proper anywhere else anyhow, to use one of Angelo's regular phrases. Properly speaking, rulers or would-be rulers and their lackeys – as opposed to local or national elders, wise men and often even wiser women – were run up the flagpole not to see if anyone would salute but to see how long it took them to expire.

(Angelo wouldn't actually say this out loud. Neither would he express it in writing, which he did, and published, prodigiously. However, Tethys had come across plenty of Headworld Harry's contemporaries and their progenitors over the course of a variety of incarnations this century and, yes, even earlier. More than a few of the less committed than committable ones would not only say it aloud, they'd put said advice into summary practise.

(Harry's howsoever more humanistic hero, Kadmon Heliopolis, had, after all, only inherited the Black Rose of Anarchy from his forbearers and they from theirs.)

Zerosses as a genus, if such they could be considered, collectively prided themselves on being True Cretans – Etocretans, to use the correct term. Black flags and shotguns marked them as surely today as they had during the island nation's Second World War resistance to Nazi incursions inland; as surely as they had during the hundreds of years of Ottoman occupation and before it, when the Venetians controlled access to Crete's ever-so-ancient ports.

Indeed, the Zerosses' attitude was no different to that of True Cretans going back thousands of years, to pre-Phoenician, even pre-Mycenaean times. Prior to Santorini – Strongyne, the Island of Strong Women – blowing its heart into the sky and thereby rendering Crete's seemingly perpetual predominance into merely an extended peak period, the so-called Minoan thalassocracy made not just Mediterranean and near-Atlantic sea lanes mostly their own.

Historically Crete's thalassocracy rivalled Pharaonic Egypt for worldwide influence pre-1500 BCE. Admittedly, that was long before shotguns let alone Nazis, Ottoman Turks, and/or Venetians came a-calling. But Tethys knew from undying eye-witnesses like providential pal Pyrame Silverstar that that statement didn't apply to black flags or black roses. Those too could be traced back to the Goddess Culture era, what many patriarchally-inclined devils still thought of the mad goddesses' man-hating matriarchate.

Oddly, while black roses were not found in nature, they remained the symbol the Zerosses and their relations most frequently used. A still extant Etocretan town – albeit generally spelled Ziros, not Zeross – was named after the family and somewhere Tethys had a tee-shirt Harry brought back from it.

Guess what it's crest was? A black rose, of course.

========

"Which no one did," CC observed. "He always used a condom with me"

Tethys thanked his lucky stars she'd insisted he did as well. And he'd known the foremost lucky star intimately, both in her flesh and in someone else's, hence Dame Chance so frequently being his successors' half-mother prior to circa 4800 YD. Hers wasn't among the stars he'd already prepared, but he hoped the ones he had would be lucky, too.

"CC's a nymphomaniac," said B, matter-of-factly.

"Good thing someone is," Carmine retorted, just as much so.

"Someone had to stay with our survival kits, CC," countered A. "And you elected me. Said I was a better shot than whore, as I recall."

"Well, you are."

"Sure, you just didn't want my brother alone?" queried A, nastily.

"Put it the other way round, A," said CC, with a coquettish smile that made him wonder if bouncing, bedazzling or plain old beguiling Belialma, Lady Lust, was among those who'd escaped Cathonia.

"And I wasn't the only one," grinned B. He leaned over to take a closer look at the drawing Tethys was doing of him. "You're pretty good at that, aren't you?"

As Baalbek had already explained, albeit only briefly, they'd materialized high up in the Diluvia Mountain Range on Sedonda, which he still called Sunday. Fortunately they'd strapped on their survival packs the moment they realized they'd been thrust somewhere they shouldn't be. When they popped out of the blue, even if it was the Grey, the Weird, or the dark-grey matter of Samsara, the cosmos's substratum, and into the desolate damp of Diluvia, they had everything they needed to last for weeks on end.

For the rest of that day and the subsequent day and two nights they let their training take over, stayed out of sight and moved steadily downhill. They were stunned to hear English spoken; what they took to be English, rather. Even if Tethys was among those who referred to it as pre-Babel Babble, what was generally referred to as Sedon Speak here on the Head was more correctly thought of as the Universal Tongue.

Come Tuesday, Demetray, with Ange covering them from the bushes, Baal and Carmine, posing as man and wife, made their first face-to-face contact with the natives. Came Wednesday, Birhym, they'd made their way to the Danq and had been here ever since. Other than saying part of their equipment included anaesthetic dart-guns, which non-killer witches commonly carried as well, and a couple of marble bags containing generic coins, gold dust, gems and dinky diamonds, he'd skipped over details as to how they managed to avoid being ambushed and robbed blind.

Neither had he said much about how they came by their information as to the way things worked on the Head. Tethys and Ringleader hadn't asked either. If the three cosmicompanions had buried more than their survival kits in the woods, that was their business. Desperate times, desperate measures, and all that rot. Which, rot, was whatever they may have buried would eventually do.

Besides, once Harry sobered up, they were only rings away from the Weirdom of Cabalarkon and safety. Harry, though, showed no signs of sobering up. Tethys had his own resources of course. Given his lifestyle, particularly his procreative imperative, he would never have completed any 30-year-lifetimes if he didn't. He'd have to rely on a tricky tongue, true, but when you're a successful taleteller a tricky tongue was just one of the tricks of the trade.

"Oh, my God," Rings finally grasped what they weren't trying to keep secret. "You're pimping her, aren't you?" The DDD's main clientele being militiamen, it doubled as a brothel.

"At least she enjoys it," B justified, almost casually, as if the allegation amounted to no more than a sniff of snuff. "You can only play the hand you're dealt, uncle. You make do the best you can and, until you two came along, Carm's, um, charms were our best hope of making out. Sorry about the pun by the way. Must be the shrooms."

Carmine probably wasn't sure which pun he was referring to, the alliterative wordplay on her first name or the *'making out'* one. She didn't sound particularly perturbed either way. "You have to admit it's better than flashing tiny tote bags of goody-goody gemstones around then having to blast your way past gangs of cutthroats who call themselves militias. You'll run out of stuff to blast with before you run out of assholes to blast "

"Reprehensible," said Harry Zeross.

"Reality," said his nephew.

"He forgot your blade, bro," said his niece.

"Forgot my necklace too, cuz," said Carmine Carmichael.

"Cuz?" queried Ringleader. "Cousin? You related to Hiliarti, C? Because, cuz, I don't recall any Carmichaels in my lineage." Harry giggled inelegantly; must have thought *'because cuz'* was kind of clever. He would; he was still drinking.

"I think you need to go to bed, Rings," said Tethys, doing his best to remain affable. "Go to bed in your bed, with Mel, in Cabby's Weirdom."

"Cabby's Weirdom?" queried B; hard-liquor B. It was coming.

"Want to go there, too?" wondered Tethys.

"Wouldn't say no," said Baalbek.

"And you two lovely ladies?"

"Not without my mirror," said Angelica.

"Nor I without my tiara," Carmine concurred. "My power focus, where is it?" A third eye shimmered into view on her forehead.

"And if I draw them on you, would you go there with us, to Cabby's Weirdom?"

"Can you do that?" asked C.

"Me first," demanded Tethys, nicely.

"I would," said Carmichael.

"And you, Ange?"

"Draw it on me and I'll tell you then."

"Not quite the answer I was hoping for," said Tethys familiarly. He pulled the blank sheet of Utopian parchment within dotting distance of his quill. He was getting a serious migraine preventing it from glowing. "Here's the problem. I draw it on you, your mirror, you might burst into flame. And I wouldn't want to take the blame for that."

"Flame, blame," appreciated Ringleader, deliberately distractingly, Tethys felt. He was rapidly sobering up. "For shame, Jordy. But I'm definitely game."

"Thanks for that, Harry. You?" the Legendarian coaxed Angelica.

She answered carefully. "I don't want to burst into flames, Mr Tethys, but I definitely want my mirror back. Can you help me do that?"

Tethys took what he feared what might be his final swig, in this incarnation anyhow, of the Danq's excellent pilsner. "If I knew what it looked like, right this minute, I probably could. But I don't, do I? I know someone who can, though. Only problem is he doesn't do house calls. So you'll have to ask him yourselves, personally. You up for that?" Up was a particularly bad pun but he hoped none of the three realized that.

"I am," agreed Angelica. He flipped to her sketch and drew a confirmatory ovule in her forehead. A looked a tad 'P', as in peed off, but didn't object.

"What about you two?" He inquired of B and C.

"Sure," said Baalbek, the mushrooms having clearly taken effect, albeit in a distinctly Head-worldly way. He was looking more and more effeminate with each passing moment.

"So long as he knows where my necklace is," said Carmine. He did two more egg-like ovules in the drawings of their respective foreheads. Goddamn, and here on the Head there wasn't a god who wasn't damned – there wasn't one who wasn't a devil already, put better – he was good at suppressing his quill's gleaming.

"So, we're all agreed? Three nods will suffice." Three nods he received. "Excellent. Now here comes the sticky wicket. Might want to close your eyes first, it'll get bright for a moment." A, B and C obliged. So did Rings. Drunk as he was, he was as good at keeping his rings from Gypsium-glowing as Tethys was keeping his quill from Brainrock-ditto.

"Not your third eyes, Cousins," Tethys reprimanded the three possessed as well as alphabetical cosmicompanions. These they opened. Reddish, whitish and yellowish their third eyeballs were; so were their skin pigmentations. Weren't bad looking either, although Susal was still in transition from a man named Baalbek.

His quill glowed. The Utopian star-chart spilled out of it onto the blank sheet of parchment, rendering it exactly as it had been before. Three quick plops later Stars Susal, Amateram and Crinsom, the three transformed cosmicompanions with their third eyes, were in place as well. He called the technique splotching; unless he called it blotching. Whatever he called it, dotting followed.

He'd never dotted anything, any things, so fast. The Cousins had enough time to start to scream before they were drawn out of their shells and into it, the Sedon Sphere, where they'd spent most of the last 4,000 years. Tethys hadn't lied; he never did, not knowingly at any rate. The Moloch Sedon was indeed the one entity who'd know where the three Sacred Objects were.

Harry Zeross fell onto the floor puking. A, B and C pitched forward onto the table, passing out. Tethys calmly finished his beer then called over the black-skinned waitress.

"A sack of pilsner to go,' he said to her when she finally got up enough nerve to approach them. "That's a sack, 12, not a pack, 6. And make sure it's cold."

========

The waitress's eyes widened. She looked past him, behind him. Then she nodded, ever so gratefully, it seemed to Tethys, and went away to put in his order.

"She's not the same waitress you had in Petrograd, Jordy," said Janna Fangfingers, from behind him. "She's not even a vamp. And there won't be any need to leave her a tip. Because I've already given one to her, her life. I will collect hers for her, though. It'll be the same as we were discussing before we were so rudely interrupted the last time we had the pleasure of meeting: a drawing of my Abe's trident. Then you're going to draw me to it. And him."

"Sure you don't want me to draw you wearing the Crimson Corona, say, around your neck?" He felt something warm and fuzzy brush against his cheek. It was also wet and drippy.

"No, I guess not." He tapped his quill against his notepad. He didn't make any effort to keep it from shimmering this time. Sunburst shining was a thought. So was drawing her not so much to Abe Chaos and his trident as onto it, the trident. How drunk was Rings anyways? Had he even stopped puking yet?

He had a sniff. "Room doesn't seem any smokier than usual," he observed.

"It's smoky enough," she said, still behind him. "And I have it on good report Outer Earth blood is particularly refreshing."

"From whom?" This time he felt the tips of her fang-fingered glove lightly scrape his neck. He could hear Carmine groan, as if she was coming around, and he was pretty sure Rings had stopped puking. He started doodling up a trident. It had been ages since he'd encountered His Unholiness. Nonetheless, what was actually the sheathe and tri-tined hilt of his Chaos Blade had looked much the same when last he saw the now mostly daemonic, 2-eyed devic suicide.

"So far so good," she approved. "The middle prong is a little longer, though."

"What about you; you look the same as in Petrograd?"

"You only need approximations, Jordy. My Vetala recognized the Danq's outside but she reckoned you didn't have enough time to finish off Dr Zeross before my agents got to you. Then you did. She almost had a heart attack."

"Didn't realize a Vetala's heart still beat."

"Now you do. Why's the background filling in grey." When Tethys did a drawing of a thing, its environs filled-in precisely where it was. "Don't tell me Abe's between-space?"

"It isn't done yet," said Tethys, astonished at what it was doing. In photographic terms his drawing of Chaos's trident was going from positive to negative. The background was filling in the opposite way. He knew where Unholy Abaddon was now, he knew he couldn't draw Second Fangs there, and he knew everyone who could become George Taurson's successor as him. They were all exceedingly healthy.

CC, Carmine Carmichael, was the first of the three Outworlders to recover. She was spry. Had a crucifix around her neck, ripped it off and waved it at Tethys and the vampire standing behind him. The air suddenly became much clearer and more breathable.

"Jesus Christ!" CC cried. "That's a fucking vampire!" Janna Fangfingers laughed out loud. 30-Beers' heart sank, proverbially.

"A woman of faith," marvelled Second Fangs. "How sweet."

Carmine, crucifix in hand, saw what happened to her next. She didn't know what a Crimson Corona was but she recognized a glittering necklace when she saw one. That it constricted, that it severed the voluptuous vampire's head from its shoulders and that then the vampire, head and body from the neck down, went up in a puff of smoke, screeching shrilly every second of it, well, she'd expected that.

She'd seen it in the movies.

========

Dotting of third eyeballs followed, though not before their waitress brought him his 12-pack of cold ones to go. Ringleader was on his feet by then, so were his niece and nephew. Harry apologized for taking so long to take the Legendarian's not-so-subtle hint that he should provide Second Fangs with a Gypsium ring around her neck. Regrettably, he pronounced, puking does tend to take precedence over anything else.

Tethys forgave him. How could he not? Fangs had explained in considerable detail what she'd do to his immediate offspring, and theirs, once she turned him. He liked coming back, even if those he came back in didn't — this on account of they didn't (unless he lasted 30-years-long-enough for a Quit Quill stage to kick in, which he virtually never did).

He was still curious about one thing, though. He had trouble accepting the notion of a fanatically faithful Christian nymphomaniac.

Once he transported them to Cabby's Weirdom and they were alone again, he asked CC about that: "Me, a Christian? Hell no, I'm the fucking Virgin Mary."

He'd seen many an Outer Earth film during his stints in Godbad as well as when he allowed All of Incain to tongue-tug him through to her male equivalent, Andy the Androsphinx, on the Giza Plateau. (Which was something he might not risk again, not after Mithrada-Monday's close encounter of the comestible kind.)

One of his favourite flicks was called "Casablanca". It had a great line in it; one that went something like: *'This could be the start of a beautiful relationship'.*

And so it was – for a night.

========

Second Fangs, Janna born Somata in the Weirdom of Kanin City over 500 years earlier, demystified herself.

========

That was wicked discourteous.

She'd fallen sometimes-hot-head over usually-happy-heels in love with Un-holy Abaddon, Tethys's Uncle Abe Chaos, when she was altogether alive and still a teenager; had even had his child, a boy – the only time on record that a third generational Master Deva parented a mortal child by his or her self without having to possess anyone. But, even if it was only momentarily, she'd never lost her head quite so literally.

If ever there was a man in need of biting it was Ringleader. The Legendarian, though, was a near second. On the other hand, her threats to exterminate him over the course of three generations to the contrary, it was a drawing of a Brainrock tri-dent she wanted of him; not to glug his deviant blood. And he'd begun to give her just that, the drawing she wanted. So maybe she'd just chomp Rings and let Jordy watch, from a wheelchair.

Chaos was out of reach. She'd recognized the negative space the Legendarian's drawing filled-in with: the Land of Nothingness. She'd also recognized where he'd drawn himself, Rings and the three other born-Outer-Earthlings to: the Weirdom of Cabalarkon. Her birthfather conquered and thereafter ruled there, as its Master. Her birthmother ruled there as well, somewhat later on. Mama Melina had the same first name as its current High Illuminary. Was that coincidental? Did Utopian witches have transferable souls the same as Hellions sometimes did?

There wasn't much else for it, was there? Abe was denied to her so she better make sure one of his two immediate siblings wasn't. Lord Order was her paternal half-grandfather. As of Sedonda, his star was no longer in the night's sky. That meant he'd been decathonitized. However, she had no idea where he was or, other than Tethys, how to reach him. She'd also had a friendly little chat with Klannit Anvil-wife last night and was now faced with much the same option. The Weirdom of Cabalarkon it would have to be.

Second Fangs had known Anvil-wife for over sixty years. Thartarre's Nanny Klanny had answered the balcony door when she knocked on it and she'd provided her with more than just information on the whereabouts of the High Priest and his guest of the day, Jordan Tethys, who'd been successfully avoiding her since Sedonda.

She had trouble accepting the Trigregos Talismans were now fused with the Brainrock copies of them in Cabalarkon. But if Klanny said they were, Klanny should know. She'd always been unnaturally talented when it came to manipulating mirrors. When you were born with Klannit Thanatos inside you, and had managed to keep her inside you for at least the first part of your life, you should be.

The vamp she'd brought with her last night was as skilled with eyeorbs as Klanny was with mirrors. It was damn difficult to lie under the influence of an open eyeorb. It was truly spooky how useful the thing were, she reflected as she ordered a bucketful of finger-licking-good blood. And a Cathy — just in case she got thirstier later.

She began to contemplate how to get her devic half-mother, whom Melina Zeross's 3000-years-gone predecessors named Datong Harmonia, out of a Trinon-dev's eyeorb, his prison pod, without alerting Saladin Devason of her presence. As she recollected from the time she spent with her Mama Melina up there half a millennium ago, only a devil in his or her protectorate was more powerful than the Master of Weir in Sedon's Devic Eye-Land.

The waitress delivered. She wanted to waive her tip. Fangs said it was okay, honey, I just want to sweeten it. Cathy's such unpalatable crud without a little sweetening. The waitress was missing her right hand from the wrist down by the time Fangs' four confederates, a Vetala, a Sraddhite, a Trinondev and a Zebranid, finally found their way through the Grey, the Weird, to the Dinq, Doinq, Danq.

Second Fangs was indulgent. She slowly sipped her Cathy while they finished slurping their supper. The turned Trinondev in particular needed his strength if they were going to launch an assault on the Weirdom of Cabalarkon tomorrow night.

All the more so if, as it sounded, tonight's exertions weren't done with quite yet.

========
A, B and CC awoke in various domiciles within the Weirdom's Masters Palace.
========

It was Devauray morning, Saturday on the Outer Earth. It wasn't the first time the Schroff-Zerosses had slept together. It was, however, the first time the two of them had awakened to find themselves surrounded by a dozen silent, expressionless black men. They'd met the ilk the night before. They'd been bare-faced then; they weren't now.

Each of the Warriors Elite was seven feet tall, more or less. Each wore azure-dyed, muslin robes. Each also had on a turban made of the same cloth and had a drawn veil covering his lower face such that only his eyes were visible. Each held a staff with an egg-like ovule atop it. Out of those bulbs, on prehensile filaments, peered a single, disembodied eye. The Trinondevs had been told their *'guests'* were possessed by Master Devas. None of them, despite their reason for being, had seen a devil before.

More than just out of duty, they were determined to stay on guard in case one manifested itself. They wanted to see if their eyeorbs actually worked against devils – the enemy the staves were designed to neutralize millennia before the designers, their ancestors, came to the Whole Earth ten years before Xuthros Hor, the Tenth Patriarch of Golden Age Mankind caused the Genesea or Great Flood of Genesis.

"So," asked Baalbek, in true Zeross fashion, "What's for breakfast?"

========

"So?" asked Melina nee Sarpedon Zeross, after the legendary 30-Year Man finished his drawing of the Weirdom's replicated Trigregos Talismans Devauray morning.

"So they're not the real ones," said Saladin Devason, looking over the Legendarian's shoulder. "They were, your drawings would have burst into flames."

"Maybe so, Sal," semi-confirmed Jordan Tethys, familiarly if uncertainly. "Then again you ever heard of a Sedonplay won by anyone other than Big Daddy Devil?"

****

(GAME-GAMBIT) 11: **Hadd's Bloody Goddess**

Devauray, Tantalar 6, 5980

Twenty-nine Iraches survived the onslaught of three cosmicompanions Sapienda-Thursday night. While the wooden, Godbadian-built tannery-cum-abattoir had been gutted, its roof collapsed, and most of its walls reduced to heat-twisted metal supports and little else, the porcelain blood-tub at its heart was barely damaged by the conflagration.

Once the death-obsessed, red-skinned zealots cleared away the rubble, their Goddess of Life Eternal stripped off her soiled clothing and entered the tub. At her signal, Irache after Irache obediently bent over it and allowed the one called Janna Fangfingers, whom their Goddess had only briefly tasted, to claw out their throats with her fangfingered Brainrock glove.

Its Blood Queen celebrated her return to the Land of the Dead by showering in the resultant bloodbath.

========

Dawn called the four vamps underground but she continued to bask beneath the cloud-shrouded sky for the balance of the day, Lazam, bathing and drinking in what was left of the Iraches' self-sacrifice. As daylight waned and twilight waxed, she was visited by a 3-eyed, pink-faced, shadow-shrouded smiling someone she didn't recognize at first.

"Nergal Vetala, Blood Queen of Hadd," grinned the fiend, *"I heard you were returning to us. Or do you still prefer being called Goddess?"*

"Hello, judge," she said, after a moment's hesitation, "Been a while." Baring her fangs, she let open her third eye. "So, what have you been up to lately?"

"You know me," he shrugged. *"The usual stuff: keeping the cosmos safe for we devazurs; stimulating a fourth generation of our unkind kind; rescuing our siblings and, sadly, far too many of our cousins from the Sedon Sphere. It's been a hectic week: Lathakra, the Lake Lands, Apple Isle, Pandemonium, Godbad. I even spent a few hours not so long ago on your old killing floor, Sraddha Isle. All things considered everything seems to be working out surprisingly well. Glad to see you back in the pink."*

Vetala rose to her feet. "You call this pink, I call it red; as in arterial, as in Irache." Snatching her Brainrock sickle out of the bloodbath, she leapt at the sardonic fiend, intent upon decapitating him. He winked. So did the third eyeholes on the two skulls dangling from his Brainrock necklace. Dematerializing was always more dignified than ducking.

She sliced through the air and vanished; cut herself to Dustmound.

========

Dustmound was a hardened concretion of calcium more so than anything besides dirt. It was situated a couple of hundred miles south of the abattoir and about the same distance west of Lake Sedona. As her howsoever suspiciously faithful, yet ever-so-capable surrogate promised her, upon its pinnacle stood a throne composed entirely of Brainrock-Gypsium.

(The same one, howsoever ironically, faeries fashioned for First Fangs, Faustus Vladuca, whilst he, occupying Sraddha Somata, ruled a dinky protectorate on the Marutian coast of the Gulf of Corona, Sedon's Human Eye, circa 5475 or thereabouts. That was about when his twin, the future Second Fangs, started bopping Unholy Abaddon, the Unity of Chaos. Another brief-time occupant of the same throne was none other than Thrygragos Lazareme, Thrygragos Everyman, the Unities' presumably still extant Great God of a father.)

Its Godstuff meant there was no need for her to try for Ap Isle's River Styx, the Stynx to some, the mostly molten Brainrock flow inside its Mt Maenalus. Which, weak as she was before her soldier fell out of the sky, she'd been contemplating cutting herself to for quite some time. (Or Sedon's Hairband, aka the Gypsium Wall, for that matter. Which was what she'd foolishly attempted to reach the last time she was out and about in the altogether.)

She could just relax here, atop Dustmound, and refresh herself on its Brainrock instead.

Melding her sickle within it, she clothed herself in a regal purple and black robe, one slit down the front to her navel and split sidewise, baring her legs, from hips to calves. She had fine legs. Then again so had the shutterbug – Barsine paternally born Mandam, even though there had been considerable debate about that during her abbreviated lifetime – and look where it got her. Sitting in her throne she began to formulate revenge on all things alive.

She couldn't shake it, the same notion kept coming back to her. She wasn't that stupid. She couldn't be that stupid. Life wasn't a chess game. Janna born Somata may have been a pawn who made her way down the board and became a queen. But was her soldier, whom she'd left behind in her immediate sibling's Forbidden Forest, really up to being a knight?

Might he be capable of winning a Trigregos Gambit? Did the Blood Queen of Hadd really need a crown? Forget its possibly apocryphal, faeries-provenance for the moment. When had fucking fays ever made anything that lasted this long? Never answered that. So, had Second Fangs constructed the seat she was sitting in out of the Crimson Corona? Was it crazing her?

Her Gypsium throne ameliorated her see-forever-eyes, as that annoyingly recurring fellow, Jordan Tethys, often described devic far-sight; what parapsychologists on the Outer Earth during Barsine's day would have called remote viewing. She surveyed her realm. She didn't like what had become of it since she'd last seen Hadd, through Barsine's eyes, thirty-five years ago; didn't like it in any way whatsoever. She should have realized how far it had deteriorated the second of her return.

Close to five hundred years ago, during the Thousand Days of Disbelief, there had been so many dead bodies lying around the Hidden Headworld her Haddazurs, her Nergalazurs, and virtually every other azura here, there and everywhere, as engendered by her siblings and devic cousins, couldn't animate even a small portion of them. So they'd piled them up for future use, corpse atop corpse, in places like Dustmound.

Three centuries later, at the height of the Second War between the Living and the Dead, there had been hundreds of similar spires scattered throughout her Hadd in particular. None was higher than Dustmound. It was a monstrous, almost mountainous pillar of fleshy and skeletal remains. It was little more than a hillock today. Her single digit salute to the Sedon Sphere had been reduced to a semblance of a stump, a middle finger without any knuckles, compared to its formerly protrusive outrageousness.

Janna Somata, called 'Fangfingers' thanks primarily to her perverse paramour, the Chaos Unity, had gradually assumed the stewardship of Hadd during her extended absences. Overall she'd done an admirable job. But she was a vampire, reliant on the blood of the living for her sustenance. She didn't need the Dead, animated as they were by Vetala's worshipful azuras, to keep herself going, so she hadn't considered their welfare. The alarming contraction of Dustmound was evidence of that. The Dead had been diminishing their reserves. It was time they started replenishing them again.

Dustmound's approaching corporal bankruptcy was only a minor indicator of how bad Second Fangs had let things slide. Everywhere she scanned, her domain of the Ambulant Dead was retracting; shrinking in on itself. All along Hadd's eastern and western coastlines, verging the Head's Interior Ocean of Akadan and its offshoot Gulf of Aka; around Lake Sedona and the Diluvia Mountain Range to its north; in the vicinity of its myriad, midland oases and cenotes; what had been at best root-settlements thirty-five years ago had noticeably expanded.

The picture was just as gloomy to the south. There, pale-skinned Panis were encroaching onto this side of the sunken fold – called the Circumcision Canal for reasons obvious – between Hadd, the Penile Peninsula's shaft, and their homeland, Krachla, its head. Traditionally Panis were seagoing merchants and fisher-folk. The best that could be said about them was they worshipped just about anyone who could provide them with fair winds, good profits and bountiful catches. Nonetheless, thirty-five years ago they would never have dared enter Hadd proper.

What was worse, recent settlements particularly on the south-western coast seemed mostly populated by Byronics-worshipping Godbadians. While that might be expected, it appeared the Sraddhite-held territories around Diluvia and Lake Sedona had expanded more than the Irache-held territories on the east coast and in Hadd's midlands. That the Iraches still worshipped her was heartening; that the Sraddhites continued to worship a dead mortal, Fangfingers' twin brother, that only made them Number One on her hate-list, which doubled as her hit-list.

In the north-western corner of Hadd, where she'd just come from, there was evidence Godbadian engineers had been assessing the possibility of dredging out the silted-up Pani Canal. The abattoir, abandoned for maybe a decade or two by now, was only a solitary example of their moderately recent presence.

Millennia ago, long before she claimed what became Hadd as her own, the canal was more like dredged out than newly cut between Diluvia to the east and the Forbidden Forest to the west. It thereby connected the Upper Head of once mostly Mithradites-worshipping Marutia to the Gulf of Aka and the Byronics' Lower Head.

Seemingly her immediate sister, Kala Tal, as Cabby's Illuminaries of yore had named her litter sister, had put a stop to the reclamation nonsense – the canal was originally a sea lane lying between two islands in the then archipelago of Pacifica. But Tal's Forbidden Forest, realm of the mad and the maddening, had consequently grown into Hadd-lands.

It growing out of Hadd-lands could probably be negotiated. The rest would have to be excised, like a malignant tumour. And by rest she wasn't only thinking in terms of trees, though they were thriving as well. Little more than scrubby shrubs stunted by a lack of moisture and blown dust when last she beheld them, they were growing taller and more lushly than ever before.

Wildlife was in abundance. Irrigation was prevalent. Vegetable gardens, kept-pruned and plucked orchards, family homesteads and even a few commercial farms or ranches proliferated. Livestock grazed contentedly, further stinking up the air with their flatulence. Godbadian outposts, Irache villages, Krachlan communities, Sraddhite districts, life was flourishing. Hadd was becoming Haas.

"Intolerable," muttered Vetala, as darkness descended and her abilities bloomed.

Closing her eyes, she mentally spread herself over the realm remaining, let every mind hers contacted comprehend she was back. The stewardship of Hadd that Janna Fangfingers assumed in her absence was revoked, effective immediately. The Marutian-born, hybrid-Utopian vampire would carry on as her Number Two. Not just because of her top level Lazaremist forbearers, she was to be treated with respect. But she was no longer her surrogate queen.

Nergal Vetala communicated with Kronar, her Cloud General, he in Tal; awoke vamps in their crypts beneath Necropolis, made them thirsty; inspired her adherent azuras, some of whom she hadn't mothered, and their shells to get hungry again. Rise up, my minions. Hadd must be retrieved. The lazy Dead must once again fight as one force in order to renew it, their land. They must fight to everyone else's death. For the Good of All and the Greater Glory of the Dead! *'Ad Majorem Dei Gloriam'*. Not to mention your Goddess.

Her thoughts reached into New Iraxas, across the Gulf of Aka, which she could see with ordinary eyes from her perch. Bloodsuckers everywhere must forget factionalism. Vamps were vamps, not Godbadian or Marutian or Irache vampires. My ever loyal Redman, you and your Dead Things Slaving, the Living must join us, must die. Accept my bounteousness, not Godbadian bounties. Night Owl, I know you can hear me, you traitorous clot in the land's bloodstream. Come to Dust-mound, bring me the head of Governor Niarchos, in a box, and his body in chains, submit to my justice and you may yet survive to hunt the more.

Throughout Lazam's night and into Devauray's early morning, she mentally broadcast her call to arms. The response was overwhelming. Haddazur- and Nergalazur-animated zombies crawled out of the earth in tremendous numbers. Until then dormant azuras born not by her, as were the Hadd-born Haddazurs and the elsewhere-born Nergalazurs, responded as well; roused the corpses they were occupying.

Kronar's vulturous Cloud of Hadd flew in from the Forbidden Forest of Kala Tal and even further afield. Some began the long journey from as far away as the Bloodlands, New Valhalla, Sedon's Inner Nose. They came carrying Sangazur-animated Dead Things, skilled at weaponry, Rakshas demons and even more of Tal's equally demonic Indescribables.

The ghoulish armies of Necropolis, what was called Manoa, the Gleaming City, when Godbadians and Marutians alike called the land El Dorado, were marshalled, given leaders and their leaders given directions. Northwards towards the Sraddhites around Lake Sedona and southwards towards the Krachlans and Godbadians, slaughter every non-Irache you come upon; slaughter every Irache who refuses to march with you.

Those were their instructions stripped to the germane. Mercy, like neutrality, was a capital offence, punishable instantaneously. Stop not until the Dead rose not. Which would never happen. Azuras were immortal, only their parents could end their existence. In the absence of fathers Vetalazurs adored their mother. Other azuras, of other Master Deva mothers, would join them as they had before.

But, she apprehended a couple of hours before daybreak, it still wasn't enough. She had to go to Lake Sedona herself, to Sraddha Isle.

She was that stupid after all.

========

Thartarre Sraddha Holgatson counted himself fortunate when the Godbadian helicopter gunship finally landed on Sraddha Isle Devauray morning. He wished he'd taken the Morrigan and Lady Achigan, the long-deposed, marital Queen of Godbad, up on their offer to transport him home between-space via witch-stones. So did Field Commander Nauroz and Governor Niarchos. Quentin Anvil wouldn't have gone through the Weird regardless. He hated witchcraft.

The Godbadian general nevertheless had to ask himself what lunacy had overcome him to even suggest the four of them go in the same copter? More pertinently, how did the Cloud of Hadd learn they were together? Golgotha kept his own counsel. Thartarre was too polite to rub in the palpable. Ferdinand Niarchos couldn't resist.

"The Trinondev vamp was right. Before Skull-Face, um, enlightened him he said Nergal Vetala was back. In the lands of the Living as well as the Dead."

========

Much less than a day earlier, in Petrograd, the capital of New Iraxas, Thartarre officially accepted delivery of the ordnance and other equipment Aristotle Zeross brought in from the Outer Earth. Although he remained personally ignorant of the high tech weaponry developed beyond the Dome, Niarchos and Anvil seemed satisfied with it.

Then he had that miserable meeting with Dr Aristotle Zeross, wherein the Brainrock-blessed outsider demanded the High Priest live up to his part of the bargain and turn over the Amateramirror to him such that he could take it up north to

Saladin Devason. Thartarre was stunned. The mirror was already in the Weirdom of Cabalarkon, wasn't it?

Harry Zeross was approaching apoplectic. He'd accused him, lewdly, rudely, crudely, disrespectfully, in no uncertain terms, of every manner of dirty-dog double-dealing; of wanting to keep the gods-cursed thing for himself. Which he would have, if he'd had it. Janna Fangfingers was in need of abolishment, a pan-Sisterhoods' term witches tended to use when they were speaking about eliminating one of their own.

Which Fangs was once. An unprincipled, even evil witch, all agreed; one of a very few, most witches insisted. Nothing new about that of course. '*Suffer not a witch to live*' was a dictum even a devout, Outer Earth born and raised Roman Catholic like Alfredo Sentalli, Alpha Centauri in here, considered fatuous. Then again, rumour had it, the Fatman often housed a devil, one of the two remaining, second generational Great Gods, Thrygragos Byron.

Zeross had stomped off. Whereupon he buggered off with Jordan Tethys to who knew where. As prearranged, in all his restrained finery, Thartarre attended a banquet dinner in his honour then settled down for a night's rest in the governor's mansion. Fat chance of that. The vamps attacked around midnight.

Ferdinand was their target. He knew they were coming; apparently the governor had vampiric spies. Glamourized War Witches and fully outfitted Trinondevs, veils drawn, were waiting for them. So were Anvil's soldiers and Ferd's house-guard; these last desirous of having a go with their recently issued, much more Inner-Earth-antique than Outer-Earth-modern weaponry: hand-muskets that shot silver bullets, wooden crossbows, some of which has silver arrowheads, flamethrowers and such like tried and true.

Vampires were notoriously self-preservative so it was hardly a rout. Nor was it much of a dustup, as Quentin put to him afterwards, using what passed for humour in military circles. It was, however, a ruse. One of the veiled Trinondevs was a vamp; so was one of the glamourized War Witches. Her head was shaved. She therefore looked like a Sraddhite, though Holgatson didn't know her. Also, there was no reason to suppose vamps didn't have barbers of their own. They did have razor-sharp teeth after all.

The idea must have been for the former to snag the governor within an eyeorb-manifested force field. Whereupon the ex-Athenan would spirit the three of them away on her witch-stones. She escaped but the Trinondev didn't. Golgotha had recognized his gargoyle, knew it belonged to one of his MIAs, a pureblood, not a clone, and snagged him instead.

Thartarre was there for the interrogation.

========

They got some startling information out of the Utopian vamp. The least startling of it was his assertion that Nergal Vetala was back in her domain of the Dead. Even Ferd knew that. It seems his vampiric spies had heard it was her, not any of the usual suspects, Night Owl or Janna Fangfingers for instance, who wanted his head and body delivered to her, separately, on something called Dustmound, which sounded much less scary than it probably was in reality.

Far more startling was just how much of a busy-bee-bloodsucker Second Fangs had been of late. She'd somehow forged an alliance with Underlord Yama Nergal, the devic father of something like half of Vetala's Nergalazurs. He and his Inglorious Dead, Death's Angels, were taking advantage of the drought that had beset the Upper Head for more than a quarter century.

They'd already left the Ghostlands – wherein lay old Valhalla, among many another former devic paradise – and were making their way south to join her in Hadd. Always assuming they could get through the Forbidden Forest of Kala Tal of course. Which shouldn't be much of a problem since the Underlord was the arachnid devil's elder in Mithras.

Just as worrisomely for the High Priest, Sangazurs from the Bloodlands – New Valhalla, Sedon's Inner Nose – had driven out their primary deity for over a hundred years, a freedom-loving Lazaremist Illuminaries had named Badhbh, after an Outer Earth Celtic War Goddess. (One of, naturally, three brood sisters collectively called the Morrigu, who were never to be confused with the Hellions' Morrigan of a Mother Superior, Morgianna long nowadays Sarpedon.)

They'd forced Battle Baby, as she was sometimes not-so-sarcastically known, to seek refuge next door in Crepuscule, the Land of Twilight, Sedon's Outer Nose. Twilight was her elder sister Krepusyl Evenstar's devic protectorate. In fact it was the first protectorate Thrygragos Lazareme condescended to countenance for his offspring, at least officially.

Since Janna Fangfingers was already in league with Kala Tal, witness the incursion of more and more of the Mithradite's Indescribables into Hadd; since it sounded like she now had the Inglorious Dead inline and the Sangs coming online; what chance had the Living, his Sraddhites in particular, against the massed forces of the Ambulant Dead?

Fret not, Ferdinand Niarchos attempted to mollify him. His dead dad Gomez was Godbad's ambassador to Sanguerre. They still communicated. Hell, Weird Ferd – as not just Tethys referred to the nevertheless democratically-elected governor, often to his face – was raising Gomez's post-possession children.

Maybe that was why the Nergalid had targeted Ferd, to get back at Gomez, a Byronics-worshipping Dead Thing who ignored Janna Fangfingers and therefore wasn't about to start paying any attention to her either, her being Vetala. Furthermore, having only recently returned from Aka Godbad City, Ferd could assure him, Thartarre, that the Trinondev vamp's revelations were old news. Which of course beat old nudes with a proverbial horsewhip.

The Fatman had the situation well in hand. It might even be Baby Battle Rattle, the Lazaremist the Sangs booted out of the Bloods, was planning a comeback. Neighbouring Twilight, Sedon's Outer Earth, was full of living men and woman who hated Dead Things encroaching on their turf as much as Sraddhites did. It had been almost forty years since they'd an opportunity to go head-hunting.

Left unsaid, for hate-devils-Golgotha's benefit more than anyone else's, was the fairly common knowledge that Bodiless Byron often used the Fatman, Alpha Centauri, as his shell; had done for slightly more than thirty-five years now. When Ferd assured Thartarre the Fatman had the situation well in hand he was implying the admittedly-handless Great God did.

Under the glare of Golgotha's open eyeorb, the kaleidoscopic radiance it emitted, the Utopian-looking, black as midnight, male vamp could resist turning to

mist. He couldn't resist sooth-saying, however. As a result of what he told them –
and this was what the Trinondevs' Field Commander found most upsetting – could
they ever trust a War Witch, a Trinondev or even one Thartarre's own Sraddhites
again? Evidently not when Second Fangs was around. She was that persuasive, her
mesmerizing talents that irresistible.

The Trinondevs' Field Commander couldn't accept that. Dead or alive, his men
were incorruptible. Ergo, this man wasn't one of his Utopians; was humanoid husk
only. Thartarre expressed utter dismay at the clone's hubris. What other explanation
could there be? You said it yourself, the Trinondev was a pureblood. Purebloods can't
be possessed by devils let alone by some newfangled sort of super-azura, which was
another of the theories discussed around the late night cheese table.

'*What other explanation?*' countered Golgotha, who was his Master's man, even
if he was merely a clone of his Master's grandfather. '*What other explanation can there
be, priest? It's witchcraft. There's a traitor in the midst of the Living and I've a horrible
idea who.*' He didn't provide a name. Thartarre didn't pry. Ringleader was hardly the
only one who thought the Sraddhites' High Priest had the Amateramirror.

Another was the big boss bitch of the Hecate-Hellions.

========

*The Trinondev should have killed himself before he was taken. Golgotha did it for
him; dusted him most convincingly. Didn't use a stake or a flamethrower either. Those
eye-staves of theirs really were so very useful in so many ways. Gargoyles weren't the only
things they could generate. The brain-bulb he'd trapped the Utopian vamp inside of was
akin to a lightbulb. Its eyeorb was filament. It was incandescent. It was also incendiary.*

Incendiaries begot cinders.

========

Today's early morning flight was far more life-threatening than last night's bat-
attack. As their copter and others escorting it neared Lake Sedona, flying low for
reasons of visibility, the vulturous Cloud of Hadd swooped out of Hadd's perpetually cloud-covered sky. As if they were human bombs, the oversized, living vultures
– or Vultyrie, to use the accepted taxonomy – dropped noticeably damaged zombies
atop their helicopter gunship from above. The Vultyrie then sought to flee upwards
again, back into the clouds.

Their pilot was highly skilled, Quentin Anvil reserved the best for himself. He
managed to keep them aloft. A couple of the flying gunships accompanying them
weren't so lucky but the wondrous devices the Godbadians flew, which Thartarre
believed were based upon designs initially made and engineered by his father most
of forty years earlier, were equipped with a very impressive arsenal. Feathery living
things were quickly falling to ground feathery dead things.

The Cloud of Hadd had to retreat or face decimation. Then, from below, up-
swept a second Cloud of Hadd. This was a new wrinkle. Until then Haddazurs
regularly only possessed sentient lifeforms, predominantly human beings, but that
was no longer the case. No reason it should be, Thartarre supposed.

Can't really call this second Cloud of Hadd suicidal, because the Vultyrie com-
posing it were already dead, but they had no qualms going for the rotors self-de-
structively, like Japanese kamikazes did during the Outer Earth's Second World War.

Again their pilot proved himself a top gun. Nonetheless, their copter was so badly damaged the High Priest despaired of ever retiring a Sraddhite victor.

Not so remarkably the gunship had radio. Consequently a number of Sraddhites, including Thartarre's second-in-command, Diego de Landa, as he preferred, using Marutian nomenclature, and non-Sraddhites, including the Athenans' field leader, Garcia Dis L'Orca, were awaiting them on the landing pad.

Also not remarkably, given what they could do, among those waiting for them were Jordan Tethys, altogether male; Aristotle Zeross, Ringleader as he'd codenamed himself for some reason; Lady Achigan, who apparently didn't mind being called Fish to her face; and the Morrigan, Morgianna born Nauroz, Superior Sarpedon, whose husband Demios had returned to Aka Godbad City with the non-Fang-fingers Janna, St Peche-Montressor, yesterday afternoon.

What was remarkable was who wasn't there waiting for them.

He had one of those sinking sensations he knew why that was the moment de Landa, whose Curia-given surname was Sraddha Landa-son, went up to General Anvil instead of him. He knew it for sure when Anvil uncharacteristically raised his voice, cursing as foully as Dr Zeross had the day before, when he reamed him out, once he'd heard what Diego had to say.

========

"Like fuck you are, priest. You're not using my mother to heat your fucking monastery."

****

(Game-Gambit) 12: **Morg's Young Daddy Death**

Devauray Dawn, Tantalar 6, 5980 – Tal, the Forbidden Forest thereof

Couldn't think. No time to think. Days and endless days. Run. They were after him. Running. Always running. Days and days after days and me. Stagger. Slime. Fall. Leeches. Worms. Skulls. Crawl. They aren't killing myself.

Pass out. Face down!

========

The soldier raised his head, opened his eyes. It was shortly past dawn. Shortly past how many other dawns since the last dawn? Someone was there, standing above him. No, not all there. An outline, more like; in a form like hers. Purple and black, more hair than anything else. Raven tresses. Lips and eyes, three of them, blood red, coals burning. Pale skin, beyond white, closer to green. Like Death's horse.

"Goddess, have you returned to me?"

"Highness, my soldier. Your Highness, Nergal Vetala, Blood Queen of Hadd. Are you man enough to fight? Are you man enough to be my knight? Can you stand?"

He could, he was, he reached out for her. No contact. Hallucination. He knew what they did. When they captured you. In the jungle. "Are you real? Are you a ghost?"

"I am both. I am also much more than both. I am conduit, your conduit. Your weapons, everything you have in that kitbag, pick them up, pick it up. Put it on your back, howsoever you carry it all, your carryall."

He did. What he could. His hooded, silver and black striped shirt was tatters; his pants shreds. He no more knew where he'd left his wristwatch, cum-compass, cum-bleeping-beacon, cum-everything-else, than he did his socks. Must have lost them, socks, watch, somewhere, in the swamp fuck. He had on his boots. And he remembered what every single weapon he had left did as well. Fight? Maybe not. Kill? Definitely.

She, her ghost, sucked him in visually. "You'll have to do." Then she sucked him in physically. "Be still. Let me embrace you; no, engulf you. Let me bring you to me."

He did that too.

========

Earlier, not long past dawn, Devauray, Lathakra

True, it was once Sedon's Horn. True also, it more like resembled Aegean Crete than any other island beyond or below the Dome. But the humanoids who dwelt there – its Fire Kings, its Intuits, its ruling devil-god and his just as firstborn sister-wife – knew it was the Hidden Headworld's Land of the Rising Sun; had been since the Dome's 48th Century.

Besides the fact that it was a solitary island rather than a chain of islands, the main difference between it and the Outer Earth's Japan was that there was nothing warm about the radiance that reached Lathakra come daybreak. Its sunrays were freezing cold.

So was the heart of its devic overlord. Except when it came to his nearly 50-years cathonitized, fourth generational devic children, that is. Six of these last were as unaccounted for as Phantast the Dreamweaver, the elder Thanatoids' immediate sibling. Three weren't, assuming two of them were theirs after all.

One definitely was, however.

"Ah, there you are," said gigantic Tantal, once he recalled who had just entered the glacial chambre wherein they'd been watching the visionary fumes emanating from Titanic Metis's purloined as much as captured cauldron. (The chambre was actually more like a superbly-furnished cavern among the hundreds King Cold had long ago hacked into his ice palace atop one of the Frozen Isle's highest, albeit no longer volcanic, mountains.)

"Good news. Our Antaeor's finally made it to the Lazaremist's Temporis."

"You still drinking, Thanatos?" queried the Smiling Fiend, who like all devils was immune to temperature extremes.

"When does he stop?" muttered tiny Methandra.

Her brood-brother-husband ignored the jibe. Said instead: "For someone like you, Smiler, there might be even better news. It seems your Medusa's given birth."

========

Well after Devauray dawn, Hadd, Lake Sedona, Sraddha Isle

The monastery on Sraddha Island in Lake Sedona was built atop a much older structure; what, on the Outer Earth, would have been called a ziggurat. Unlike most ziggurats, however, this one was not just a pile of rubble, roughly shaped into a pyramidal form, upon which were appended finishing stones, external terraces and a few niches cut into each level. Although constructed along similar principles, the rubble had been heaped around a cylindrical core.

Diego de Landa led the sombre crew down a cascade of dangerously worn stone steps built into this well-like more so than hell-like hollow; led them toward not so much the basement of the monastery as its base. The main body of the ziggurat lay below. So did Nanny Klanny's.

The only reason it was laying there was because the Sraddhites had chained her reanimated corpse to the floor of the cage they'd placed it in after, on de Landa's orders, they netted rather than crisped her on the spot. He figured either General Quentin Anvil or their High Priest, Thartarre Holgatson, might want to fire her pyre personally.

Someone else was down there as well. He wasn't laying. He was working.

========

Golgotha Nauroz, eye-stave at the ready, was beside de Landa. Niarchos, Anvil and Tethys followed them. The first was in front of Quentin, the third lagged behind him, just in case the bereaved general faltered in either direction and needed steadying or catching. The Morrigan and Fish were next.

(Fish, more correctly Fisherwoman, was the codename Scylla Nereid was given by Kyprian Somata, Morgianna Sarpedon and Saladin Devason's great-grandmother as well as Sal's predecessor as Master of Weir, before she sent her, a barely pubescent teenager, to the Outer Earth for the first time in the early to mid Thirties.)

They were in an intense discussion, one audible to no one other than themselves. They had known each other since their preteens, these two top-dog witches, a period well in excess of fifty years now. If they didn't want anyone to overhear what they were saying, then no one would overhear what they were saying.

Even if you could; even if you could follow Fish and her sometimes incomprehensible fishisms; there was no point making the effort. Properly trained witches could rewrite memories with their witch-stones as easily as a skilled Trinondev like Golgotha could with an eyeorb. Indeed, even though they originated on planets separated by vast, far beyond merely galactic distances, one had much in common with the other.

Garcia Dis L'Orca hadn't tagged along – Fish wanted Morg alone – so Thartarre tarried with Harry, bringing up the rear. "You've travelled the Headworld over," said the High Priest as they wound their way down the steep stairwell. It was a long way to the bottom so he figured he might as well at least attempt to pretend they were still friends.

"You've also traversed the Outer Earth and not just via your rings. So you tell me at any rate. You must have seen places similar to this in your wanderings."

"Almost every former duchy in Godbad has the ruins of something like this," agreed Ringleader. Despite his frustrations with the High Priest in particular, and damn near everything else in general, including Mel's lack of interest in lingering with him, in or out of her lingerie, once he woke up first thing this morning, he was maintaining a civil tongue.

In the Weirdom both his wife, the High Illuminary, she with her caduceus, and its Master, he with his Master's Mace, what Saladin sometimes referred to as his Speaking Stick, had thoroughly probed the Legendarian. They were convinced the 30-Year Man truly believed that the real Amateramirror was fused with its copy up there in Sedon's Devic Eye-Land.

However, they were just as convinced that it, the real one, was still down here, in Hadd. By their estimation it was either in the monastery itself or possibly, just possibly, Second Fangs had it secreted somewhere in or around her home base of Necropolis.

(Necropolis meant the City of the Dead. Decidedly ironically, during the Byronic hegemony of what was now Hadd, it was known as the Gleaming City of Manoa, the capital of El Dorado. The devil who had it built, in all its now crumbling and be-blotched splendour, was Damon Goldenrod, Byron's Apollo.

(Along with All-Eyes {Byron's Venus, Aphropsyche Morningstar or just APM} and his monomaniacal paladin Nevair Neverknight – the only devil besides Pyrame Silverstar Dark Sedon had ever voluntarily released from his Sedon Sphere –

Goldenrod was one of that Great God's Secondary Nucleoids. If Damon, a name that sounded suspiciously like demon, was a Mithradite instead of a Byronic he'd be a candidate for one of Satanwyck's Sinistrals, that of Pride.)

"There are pyramids of a similar or somewhat later age all over the Head. On the Outer Earth too, on different continents as well. I've never seen the biggest ones out there, which are supposed to be in China, but I've seen the most famous ones in Egypt in addition to some topnotch ones in Central and South America.

"Places such as these are a source of some pretty overwrought speculation as far as I'm concerned. Most of it centers around how our ancients could build them when modern man, with modern machines and modern methods, can't replicate the feat except on paper and then only in theory.

"As for myself, I always say it's tragic what slaves have been forced to construct. All too many idiots, at least on the Outer Earth, admire the work, not the workers; the labourers who had no choice but to do as their egotistic and probably priestly slave-masters made them. If those holier than thou assholes actually get rewarded in heaven, I'd rather go to hell.

"Non-Headworld variety, if you don't mind, assuming there's a difference. I bet it's a ton more fun."

"Regardless of your sentiments, Dr Zeross," said the Sraddhites' High Priest, "And the testy, if perhaps not deliberately vexatious manner in which you phrase them, you are about to witness something very few outsiders have ever been given the, um, opportunity – definitely not the privilege – of seeing.

"Think you're up to it?"

"As long as it doesn't say *'abandon all hope ye who enter'*."

Dante's fabled inscription was posted around Satanwyck, far to the north of Hadd. Aka Sedon's Temple, for reasons both slyly appropriate and fairly close to geographical, it was a vast amalgamation of devic protectorates under the central control of its Prime Sinistral. Currently that was Sloth, Lord Lazy, Baaloch Hellblob as long-gone Illuminaries named him.

(What with the earthborn demons' howsoever grudgingly acknowledged king, the Moloch Sedon Himself, being mostly in the sky maintaining the Cathonic Dome, Prime Sinistrals were only caretaker kings. As tempting as it was, you couldn't really called them viceroys because one of Sedon's favourites, Cyclopean Ibal, had that title more so than honour.

(Vice-regent worked nicely, though, every which way including both loose and louse.)

Next to, arguably, Godbad, which many considered to belong exclusively to Bodiless Byron rather than divvied up between his offspring; the Ghostlands, which were uninhabitable save for Death's Angels, their Nergalazur-animated Inglorious Dead; and Temporis, beneath Sisert, the Silent Sands of Cathune Bubastis; what had been quite accurately described as Hell on Earth was the largest devic domain on the Inner Earth.

"Don't confuse us with the abominations of Pandemonium," Thartarre warned him. "But where we're about to go is truly infernal."

(Pandemonium – as opposed to the Superior Sisterhood's scheme of Panharmonium, which Jordan Tethys had characterized as being more of a pipedream –

was Satanwyck's main metropolis. Reputedly it was a Paradise for the Damned. In a her-story, all the details of which even the usually well-informed Legendarian didn't know or couldn't remember, it was also where Morgianna became the Morrigan.)

Once they joined the others at the bottom of the monastery's stairwell, and the monastery proper, the High Priest nodded to two burly, shave-skulled Sraddhites. They roped open a thick, forged metal bulwark in the basement floor. The heat as much as the smell came close to decking Ringleader. He wasn't alone. As the saying went, Tethys looked a little green around the gills. So did Fish. Then again she not only had gills, behind her ears, to some eyes her pigmentation had always had a distinctly greenish tinge to it.

The other thing about her skin, besides it was slightly scaly, was she generally had no bones about displaying plenty of it. Despite the fact it was late fall and cool; despite as well she was in a monastery where everyone dressed in formless, but warm-looking brown robes; and despite her not being a devil, not even possessed by one; today was no different.

Underneath a translucent overcoat of what looked to him like a jellyfish's membrane, she wore what he supposed was a half-wetsuit. It had no sleeves, no legs below mid-thigh and a midriff gap cut in its front in order to display her so-called bellybutton bauble, her Vesica Piscis. At least she had on sandals, the better to show off her webbed toes.

Her navel accessory was one of three Brainrock power foci the late Aortic Merthetis found beside her infantile self in 5918, after Fish's real mother, whoever that was, abandoned her inside the belly of the beast, Island Leviathan. The other two were a fishhook or landing gaffe, and a fishnet or soul-net, as she sometimes referred to it.

These she kept dematerialized between-space. They were only a shake away from being solidly in her hands. Like many witches, though not like Harry's good-wife Melina born Sarpedon, Fish and Morgianna were materialists.

Even if she was a deviant, she was as stunning to behold, at 60-plus, as she had been when Harry could first recall meeting her in the war-torn Forties. Of course he was just a wee whippersnapper then, living on Aegean Trigon with his parents, Angelo and Megaera born Kinesis. Which only went to prove how much of an impression she made on not just him; made, in truth, on virtually everyone she met.

(Fish knew his parents via hers and their mentor, Magister Joseph Mandam. Seemingly always Old Joe's Summoning Child of a daughter became perhaps her best friend and definitely Thartarre's mother.)

Morg was the same age as Barsine become Holgat-wife, to the day; was as well-held-together as Fish, too. And so she should be. Utopian hybrids aged almost as slowly as purebloods like the Sarpedons and the vamp Golgotha enlightened, as Weird Ferd sarcastically said on the tarmac, or clones like the Field Commander and a majority of his men.

Harry had always found something off-putting about his eventual sister-in-law. It wasn't so much she allegedly wore a demon; if she did it was invisible. Or even that she always wore white. After last night's encounter in the Danq he knew what it was: Morgianna bore a shocking likeness to her still-extant ancestral cousin, Janna born Somata become Fangfingers.

Thartarre propped him up as de Landa continued to guide the group into the hellacious depths of the ziggurat's core. That meant descending yet another dizzying set of stone steps. Appropriately these were lit by torches, not the electric lightbulbs so prevalent everywhere above them. Narrow, claustrophobic, it went down perhaps the equivalent of ten storeys in a Godbadian apartment building; only widening near the bottom.

By then, Thartarre said, they had gone beneath the ziggurat itself and were about to enter into a large series of mostly artificial caves, caverns and tunnels; a microcosmic Temporis, as he put it. Which reminded Harry of something else Mel had told him and Tethys last night after Jordy drew them, along with the three displaced cosmicompanions, including his niece and nephew, the Schroff-Zerosses, to the Weirdom. Today's scheduled wedding between Lakshmi of Lemuria, Aortic Amphitrite's daughter, and Centurion Sophiscient, Dand Tariqartha's seneschal, had been cancelled for unspecified reasons.

While she'd neither requested nor received any explanation, more than sixty missing stars in the night's sky probably had a lot to do with it. Seemingly all those missing stars had most of everything to do with so much going wrong of late. Mel hadn't committed herself to attending it anyhow. Dand Tariqartha, the Time-Space Displacer, the Chronocollector, was a Master Deva. Utopians were born and bred to obliterate devils.

"Long before it became Sedon's Head," the High Priest recounted, doing a fine imitation of Jordan Tethys, "The archipelago of Pacifica – or Lemuria, as I've also heard it was called before the Flood – was controlled by a blue-skinned race of Outer Earthlings. They hailed from the opposite side of the planet; from an island or small continental landform called Old Eden or Atlantis. These, call them what you will, Edenites or Atlanteans, turned Pacifica's islands into some kind of zoo whereon they deposited the results of genetic experiments. Which is why there are so many wildly disparate, sentient lifeforms still existent on the Hidden Continent.

"As mountainous as it was and is, albeit more so in the north than south, Godbad was by far the largest of these islands. I expect it was good deal larger than the Edenites' Atlantis. But in those centuries what the Byronics and we Sraddhites both call El Dorado, the Iraches call Iraxas, most everyone else calls Hadd, and disreputable characters such as Mr Tethys, down below us, call the Penile Peninsula, was more like a partially submerged plateau extending south from Diluvia.

"Some of the earliest of the Edenites' genetic experiments resulted in the Lemurians themselves. No doubt politically incorrectly, we still refer to them as Frog Folk. As is the case today, only Lemurian females were truly amphibious – and them only up to a certain age, around sixty I understand. I further understand that amphibious Piscines and their ilk, the likes of Lady Achigan and her confreres have Lemurian blood mixed in with human or U-blood.

"Entirely aquatic, Lemurian men could no more survive in the open air than a fish can, our esteemed, afore-noted visitor excepted. At least in part because of the male's deficiencies in this regard, Lemurians were, and are, a matriarchy. Their homeland was centred here, in what's now Lake Sedona but what was then much closer to sea level. In fact its environs were more marshland than dry land.

"Another of the Edenites' experiments, we're told with chthonic creatures, demons or faeries, rather than human beings this time, resulted in half-life tellurians or Mandroids. The Lemurian women somehow gained command over these tellurian sub-humans and, just as they did in the Godbadian Civil War many thousands of years later, used them as nearly indestructible foot soldiers when they rebelled from the Edenites.

"Prior to their homeland sinking underneath what's now the Atlantic Ocean, which is to say less than eight thousand years ago, virtually nothing for devakind, which is also to say just before the rise of what we're taught to call the Golden Age of Mankind, Edenites determined to extirpate their rebellion. They were so successful the Lemurian frogwomen's resistance was literally driven both underground and undersea, into a honeycomb of nowadays more subterranean than submarine tunnels constructed for them by their half-life tellurian servitors.

"What we're about to enter is one of them. Its branches go under Lake Sedona to the mainland but others go quite far into Hadd. It's our belief Hadd's underground river system is a result of these ever-so-ancient, Mandroid-made tunnels. That being the case we might someday be able to reach the Interior Ocean of Akadan, where as I said dwell the male and no longer amphibious female Lemurians, the precursors of the present day Akans and Piscines.

"Although this one was known to exist long before my father became the High Priest, it wasn't until his time that it was properly mapped. That it was mapped at all is thanks to his friendship with Lady Achigan down there, when she was still Queen Scylla, and her stepsister, Amphitrite, the current Lemurian Aortic of Shenon; they and their water-breathers.

"We've been industriously excavating it and its branches for over fifteen years. Once it's open it'll take us to Tulum-Hadd, on Hadd's north-eastern coast of Akadan, very near Jaag and its maelstrom. As I shouldn't have to tell you, for us Sraddhites it will be absolutely wonderful when that day arrives. It'll mean we'd have access to the sea without having to fight off Dead Things every step of the way; them and recalcitrant Iraches who still consider Hadd irreducibly their own territory. It might be years before we get to that point, though."

"The Jaag maelstrom would be where your father, Holgat, drowned attempting to rid the world of Nergal Vetala," Zeross coaxed, neither subtly nor very well.

Thartarre didn't take the bait; didn't dare crack him a good one either. Which was just as well. He especially didn't want to crack Harry one with his right arm because, it having a curved, reinforced silver blade attached to it, that would crack his numbskull like a nutshell. Clutching his mirrored egg, silently invoking the Crown of Heaven, praying for patience, he corrected him instead.

"Where his whirlybird ran out of fuel while trying to fly down Janna Fangfingers."

"So you say and so 30-Beers' confirmed. Under the influence of the Master's Speaking Stick as well. What's more, both he and my wife, who's probably better at using eyeorbs than anyone else up there is, including Sal, don't think anyone got to him. And by extension you. Not with either a witch-stone or an eyeorb anyhow. Not even Dem with his pre-Earth eye-stave. So I'm not about to dredge up any of that crap again."

"Are you finally satisfied it's up there?"

"No, but I was prepared to consider the notion Second Fangs has it. Except we're all agreed she couldn't have had it for very long; certainly not long enough for it to have her twin brother's soul stuck inside it since his death five hundred years ago."

"You said *'was'.*"

"I also said no one got to you or Jordy with an eyeorb or a witch-stone."

"I see. And now she's dead."

"Her host is; Klannit Thanatos is still out there somewhere, probably on Lathakra. My Mel's a Summoning Child, remember. She knew your parents and your dad's predecessor as the Sraddhites' High Priest. Maybe she didn't know them as well as Fish or Morg did but she knew them before your Nanny Klanny became brain-damaged.

"The Thanatoids' Klannit may only be an azura but Mel and her Illuminaries think she could dominate a simpleton. Which might not be fair to Klannit Anvil-Wife but is pretty much indisputable from what I saw of her. I volunteered to coax her up to Cabalarkon so Mel and the Master could have a go at her. Only someone got to her first."

"Second Fangs, I'm presuming. De Landa says it wasn't long before dawn when they spotted Klannit's body below my balcony, where Janna Fangfingers comes a-knocking more often than I care to admit. It was pulped, the Haddazur that re-animated her could barely get it to move. He thinks she tossed herself to her death rather than let Fangs turn her."

"Second Fangs was in Diluvia last night. I know, I decapitated her. But Jordy says she probably mystified. Which means I'd at best only briefly inconvenienced her. Nonetheless, she can travel between-space. So, maybe. That said, if your Klannit gave it to her, say, in the last week or so; then if the Thanatoids' Klannit went through her to wipe you and Jordy on Sapienda; one not only has to wonder why bother but why now?

"I don't want to absolve Second Fangs of anything, but consider this scenario instead. By Sedonic decree, ordinarily no devazur is allowed to kill anyone, so I'm inclined to believe Klannit Thanatos had little or nothing to do with her death. However, there's all those missing stars in the Night's Sky, more than sixty of them.

"When Mel's mentor, Kyprian Somata, was the Master as well as the High Illuminary of Weir, she identified seven of them as belonging to fourth generational Thanatoids. Not only that but, when we were talking first thing this morning, Jordy convinced us that decathonitized devils aren't obliged to obey their All-Father's dictates anymore.

"So, say the Thanatoids have decided to play a Trigregos Gambit, maybe to get back at Great Byron and his Nucleoids for cathonitizing their kids back in the early Thirties. Say your Klannit was the mirror's guardian but their Klannit has always known where it was hidden; somewhere in the monastery I'm saying. She, or more likely her parents, send some of her decathonitized siblings to retrieve it. Your Klannit tries to stop them so they kill her and take it with them to Lathakra. To say the least these are extraordinary times, Thartarre."

"Tricky ones as well, Dr Zeross, as whomever killed my Nanny Klanny will hopefully learn to their distinct discomfort. As I was saying, the tunnel we're coming to was known long before my father's time. I also said we didn't start excavating it until roughly fifteen years ago. Part of the reason for that was because most of the tunnels our predecessors had discovered were, and are, um, moist, to put in mildly.

"Once it was mapped, and then-Queen Scylla and her fellow Piscines informed him it was mostly dry, my father had it blocked up. Quite rightly too. As you should appreciate, or apprehend, dry tunnels are a natural habitat for Haddazur-animated zombies. As you should also appreciate, or apprehend, excavating a tunnel is a lot of work for folks like us.

"After all we're the ones who have to fight off Dead, Undead and myriad demonic Indescribables on a near night-by-night basis. Sometimes, as today, on our flight here, on a day-to-day basis as well. That doesn't leave us with a whole lot of energy left for tunnelling. Then, around the same 15 years ago I made mention of moments ago, we found a better way. Rather, a better way found us.

"And through him, instead of fighting and destroying the Walking Dead, we've learned how to make the relatively still able-bodied ones we capture work for us."

"So he's still here," Ringleader did appreciate, not apprehend. "Both Mel and Sal said I should say hello to the little prick if he was. The Master even promised to kill an ant if he promised not to come through on it."

"Yes, well, he would, wouldn't he?" said Thartarre. He had met Saladin Devason on a few occasions; knew how much he hated Ants, as in the witch-membership of the life-loving, Superior Sisterhood of Flowery Anthea.

"Brace yourself, doctor."

========

Already queasy, as soon as he entered the large cavern Ringleader fell to his knees and vomited. He'd been doing a lot of that lately. It was no wonder Mel hadn't lingered in her lingerie first thing that morning.

"This is our furnace," said Thartarre Holgatson, helping Ringleader, Dr Aristotle Zeross, to his feet and motioning another priestess to clean up the mess he'd made of his breakfast.

"Its fuel is Haddit Zombies."

========

A deep, metal-lined burn-pit, one surmounted by a similarly metallic hood and ducts leading upwards, back into the monastery, was built into the centre of the large cavern they'd just entered. In it, going up in smoke and welcome, if nauseating, heat were the chopped-up bits and pieces of, presumably, many of last night's victims of Vetala's call across Hadd to arms.

A Godbadian zombie knelt on the edge of the burn-pit. Thartarre recognized it, couldn't call it a him anymore. When it was last a he, he'd been on the gunship the second Cloud of Hadd, the one made up of predeceased vultures, caused to crash just as theirs, with its anti-Dead brain-trust, reached Sraddha Isle. Although only recently dead, and therefore not at all decomposed, it was in irredeemably rough shape.

Most of its right side was gone; it had lost its left forearm as well. Nonetheless it was more than capable of putting up a struggle. Two Brown Robes, priests, had to restrain it as a third Sraddhite, a priestess, decapitated it with a well-honed, curved blade – Sraddhites next-to-invariably used curved blades. Even headless it writhed about futilely. Promptly and efficiently she dismembered what could still be dismembered; kicked its head into the pit. The other priests followed suit, dumping the rest of its remains into the blaze.

As Harry recovered, another onetime he, a distinctly deteriorated zombie, staggered out of a neighbouring tunnel. Defiantly it strained against its holders then, breaking loose, rushed the priestess. She stepped back and expertly sliced it in twain above the hips. The priests managed to boot its bifurcated bottom half into the pit but its head, arms and torso continued to clutch at them. She quartered it. Her compatriots scooped the still-mobile sections of its upper parts into the flames.

A spirit shape, a spectre, appeared above the pit and wafted over to the solid ground. Was this an azura? wondered Ringleader, fighting back another wave of nausea. Then it solidified. Became a black-skinned boy, no more than a child of six or seven. He was dressed in a tattered tuxedo complete with bashed-in top hat and scuffed-up black shoes. Didn't have on a shirt, though, frilly or otherwise. Ahead of him Harry heard the, for him, ever-unlovable Morrigan giggle like a little girl. Even Fish, who preferred her food not only freshly caught but raw, clapped in glee.

"Irascible old fucker," the boy said to the priestess. "Zombs over a century are the worst but, like I told it, tough tiddlywinks. When you can't pull your weight you heat the house."

"Auguste Moirnoir!"

"Humping hula hoops," exclaimed the apparent seven year old recognizing Rings instantly. "Long time, nay see, Harry lad. How's it hanging? If it's hanging. Even diamond drills dull after too much use."

Morgianna Sarpedon barged past everyone. Hoisting him into her arms as if he was her son or grandson, she gave him big kiss on the forehead and a huge hug. Young Death didn't turn into a horny toad anymore than Harry had the day before in Petrograd. "He's my father," Morg proudly proclaimed, "Augustus Nauroz."

Thartarre knew that. Didn't know the other name, though. "Moirnoir?" he required.

"French for the Black Death," said Zeross. "That was Gus's codename during the Outer Earth's so-called Secret War of the Supranormals, which I didn't get involved in until I wasn't much older than he always looks. Everyone thought he was an Haitian midget freak who managed to make it appear as if he never aged. But that was only his most savoury knack."

"Well, savoury or unsavoury," provided the warrior-monk, "We're very grateful for some of his other knacks; particularly the one whereby he overrides Haddazur-conditioning and gets zombies to work for us instead of always trying to kill us. We know him best as Young Death, the male trickster, by the way."

"That'd be me," agreed Moirnoir. As Morgianna put him down, he reached into his jacket pocket and pull out a long, half-smoked, chew-ended cigar. Lighting it on flames coming out of the burn-pit, he got it going then added: "Nowadays I'm the Chief Revenant of Sainted Sraddha. So, what brings you fine and upstanding clean-airheads down into my despicable depths?"

"Her," said Quentin Anvil.

He was pointing at a cage on an overhead trolley of identical cages. The ones that weren't empty contained badly broken, yet still twitchy Dead Things. When roped over the burn-pit their floors or bottoms would open like a crane's dumpster. Chained to the floor of the one he was pointing at lay his birthmother, Klannit Janna Anvil-wife.

She was glaring at them, revulsion in her eyes. Even though she and her husband, Tvasitar Sraddha Quentin-son, had fostered him out to Godbadians at an early age, Anvil must have hated her looking at him with such unconcealed animosity. Thartarre unquestionably hated her looking at him like that. But, as he'd implied to Rings on their long descent, he had a notion. So did Anvil, as it happened.

"Well, Golgotha," the Godbadians' general asked the Trinondevs' field-commander. "What do you think, can you get it out of her?"

"Perhaps," Black Skull-Face responded, both carefully and hesitantly. "Our eyeorbs have a great many functions. In term of their prison pod aspects, there's no question they're capable of taking out Master Devas. But they weren't designed to cleanse humans, nor anyone else, of their azura-offspring. Sooth said, they were designed in the first Weir World, many, many, multiple millennia before there was any such a thing as an azura."

"Is that a yes?" Anvil demanded, impatiently as well as vainly. Unless it was in battle, or when a Trinondev known to be missing in action shows up in a certain governor's public mansion in Petrograd during a bat-attack, Golgotha was not one to be rushed.

"Our Illuminaries," he continued at his own pace, "Have long held that since azuras are as abundant as they're essentially useless, we shouldn't bother wasting our mental energy sucking them into our eyeorbs. We open them to do that, the azuras fill them up, then it's our eyeorbs that are useless and we each only brought a dozen of them to Hadd.

"If you know your Headworld history, our Kanin City predecessors learned this very much to their detriment the high hard way on Thrygragon, which occurred in 4376 Year of the Dome. And by high hard way I am of course referring to what happens to a levitating Trinondev when his or, back then, her eyeorb fills up."

"Azuras are not useless when they're animating Dead Things," Anvil countered.

"Don't misunderstand me, general. I'm not disputing that; just the advisability of what you're suggesting. For us the question of capacity is paramount. Since there's so many of them, the azuras might occupy space best kept reserved for their forbearers. For another, sucking one out would just leave a cavity another would suck into, and thereby fill, virtually instantly. That is especially true here in Hadd, where Haddazurs abound.

"Furthermore, as our two witches will tell you, their sheer numbers render witch-stones, even ones properly ensorcelled to double as soul-sinks, as inoperable as our prison pods. You open for one, what's to stop dozens, maybe even hundreds of the blighters rushing in? Which brings us to another risk we have to consider and that's overloading. Overload something, chances are it'll burst. Then we're back to square one, aren't we?"

"Our rule of thumb for devils is one per pod but, quite honestly, we don't know many azuras, or devils for that matter, a single eyeorb will hold. As our 30-years-gone, late Master once said to me, tragically all too many decades ago, opening an eyeorb to take in azuras would be like using a Godbadian vacuum cleaner to suck dirt off an otherwise pristine beach made up of fine, powdery white sand. You'd run out of replacement bags awfully quickly."

"That's a no by the way, general," volunteered Morgianna. "While we witches can prevent ourselves being possessed by devils, there's nothing we can do about their azuras." Was it his imagination or did he, Ringleader, just perceive Nanny Klanny's corpse shoot his sister-in-law a very specific, albeit metaphoric, dagger of detestation, to quote one of Tethys's recitations?

"Yet," said Thartarre, seizing the chance to elucidate his notion. "Young Death here has a proven ability to override Haddazur-compulsions."

"That I do," puffed Auguste Moirnoir.

"You want me to let that little fuck into my mother?" exclaimed Anvil.

"Got that in one," trumped the High Priest. "At the very least he might be able to interview her spirit and find out why she killed herself. Or who murdered her, if that's what happened." The High Priest was looking directly at Morgianna Sarpedon, the Athenans' White Witch and the Hellions' Morrigan, when he said that. Golgotha was as well.

"Of course we'd still have to cremate her afterwards. I don't much fancy the idea of my Nanny Klanny's corpse trying to claw its way out of a coffin. Haddazurs can get to your body in a grave as readily as anywhere else in Hadd. The Chief Revenant here can become insubstantial, as in spiritual, when he needs to get into a zombie but an azura is always insubstantial. For them solid ground's as easy to get through than air is to us."

"I'd kill him first," said Anvil unthinkingly.

"Oh, no," anticipated Moirnoir.

"Allow me to save you the trouble," said Thartarre. "Don't worry. It won't be for long. Just find out how she died and where she hid the Amateramirror, if she hid it anywhere, and you're done in there. We'll kill you a rat as soon as you want out."

He was still looking at Superior Sarpedon when he used his right arm – rather, when he used the curved, reinforced silver blade attached to it – in order to crack open the Voodoo Child's numbskull like a nutshell. Morg barely flinched. In that, she was nearly alone. To their credit, no one passed out, though. Brains being a local delicacy, Fisherwoman even licked her lips, howsoever involuntarily.

The male trickster died in mid-puff.

========

Killing Young Death was akin to buying him an airline ticket.
****

(GAME-GAMBIT) 13: **Non-Melting Mirrors**

Devauray, Tantalar 6, 5980

On the Frozen Isle of Lathakra, gigantic Tantal and tiny Methandra were still searching for their lost children.

========

They, her more so than him, were doing so via the sorceress's bubbling cauldron, what had once been the power focus of Metisophia, Wisdom of Lazareme, the devic half-mother of Jordan Tethys (if you could believe him), who was perhaps most often referred to as Titanic Metis. Their Klannit, the Thanatoids' Haunted Angel, not the Klannit whose corpse was on the precipice of heating the Sraddhites' monastery, approached her parents with typical trepidation.

Accidentally engendered – to say the least – when her devic parents less occupied than were being inescapably encrusted by daemons, she was their lone, jointly conceived azura. Since she was born a couple of centuries before Dark Sedon raised the Cathonic Dome out of his own essence, everyone, Illuminaries of Weir included, now agreed she was the cosmos's first azura.

Indeed, even though she came into being during the course of what eventually passed into both Inner and Outer Earth folklore as Ragnarok, no one, not even her parents, seemed to realize what she was until Master Devas began gaining individual solidity, circa 2000 YD, and started having ever-insubstantial children of their own; ones they had without possessing anyone or anything save debrained demonic bodies. Until that time, those few near-immortal devils who knew she existed simply assumed she was one of them.

Klannit Thanatos probably did as well. However, she was no such a thing; definitely wasn't the first of the Parents Thanatos' eventual, fourth generational devic children either. She would have loved to have had that distinction; never stopped trying to make herself into a full devil. Her desires to the contrary, that she had never, ever, succeeded in doing so was proof she was just a lowly spirit being. Was, despite being a free-thinking, emotional and, yes, loving individual, one with her own distinct personality, not solid by and of herself.

Although she could possess anyone, it was rare she could control anything. Vacant Dead Things were one of a few exceptions. So were, for roughly fifteen years now, ice-statues crafted by Sedunihas, the fourth generational devil she actually gave birth to in 5955. She was animating one of those ice-statues right now.

Something else that made Klannit so special, that made her a near-devil in many respects, was she had worshippers. Which was why, when not on Lathakra, or on Sedon's Peak with her forever-lover, the Lazaremist Anvil, Tvasitar Smithmonger, she could usually be found in the Crystal Mountains. They were situated not all that far north of the Gypsium Wall, the dividing line between the Head's occipital regions and the Cattail Peninsula, where his Unholiness, Abe Chaos, didn't so much once hold sway as left it to sway whichever way its populace bent.

There, in the Crystal Mountains, Samarandin pilgrims, the distinctly oriental-looking inhabitants of neighbouring Samarand, once Sedon's Tongue, considered her a Kami, a Spirit Being. Which was what she was of course. Having no devil-gods, nor devil-goddesses, anywhere near their proximity anymore, these pilgrims had essentially adopted her as their own goddess. That still didn't make her a devil, though.

Samarandins practised a version of Shintoism. They would fashion homunculi, or homos, of various sizes and appearances for her to occupy. This proved a boon to her parents, who were afflicted with Smoky Sedona's 'Spell of Disproportionment' in 5933. Sometime thereafter her mother discovered she was pregnant, with twins as well, as she had been five times from 5919 until 5923. Sedona's Spell, though, prevented her from having any kind of normal pregnancy, let alone giving birth.

In desperation Methandra transferred the twin-foeti into Klannit; rather, into one of the homos containing Klannit. Mama Myth intended to thereby kick-start the twins' birth processes. That's how it worked in the case of Sedunihas; how it didn't in the case of Motan, as Methandra named her little Tom Thumb. Motan was born dead.

Klannit's father Tantal – the old King Cold of legend – knew that; blamed her, his wife's sole azura by anyone, for Motan's stillbirth. He hadn't spoken to her since that ill-fated Mithramas day, the 25th of Tantalar 5955; Tantalar being the tenth month of the Sedonic Year, the month named after Tantal himself.

Klannit Thanatos was appropriately appreciative of the devotion accorded her by the Samarandins. She showed her appreciation by using her very much non-azura affinity for mirrors to adjust the crystalline walls of the caves wherein they worshipped her such that they turned into effective television sets; this long before Outer Earthlings' had invented photography, let alone television. She tuned – no one knew how, other than it was just one of her knacks – their walls to various parts of the Outer Earth.

Unhappily for her adherents, her reception was lousy. She never mastered sound either. (Metis's cauldron also produced visuals alone.) Many a Samarandin developed fairly impressive lip-reading skills but it was mostly a pointless accomplishment. After all, lip formations out there did not necessarily match the Sedon Speak they were used to in here. Thus, when they tried to duplicate the Outer Earth's technology they saw on the walls, they invariably failed.

Klannit nevertheless became adept at fine-tuning; deliberately began to spy on designers' workshops and factories. Consequently Samarandins became expert copycats. Samarand thereafter became the most technologically advanced area on the Head next to the subcontinent of Aka Godbad, whose scientists and engineers had access to actual Outer Earth blueprints and suchlike.

The most technologically advanced place other than the Weirdom of Cabalarkon, that is. Then again Cabalarkon's technology was extraterrestrial in origin and nobody in the Weirdom could remember why anything worked. That was at least in part due to the fact an ever-increasing number of pureblood Utopians were inbred idiots. Nonetheless, that a lot of things up there still did work was amazing, albeit not as amazing as Klannit Thanatos.

More so than anything else, her affinity for mirrors made her unique amongst azuras. Very few of these tormented, yet potentially benevolent spirits had a knack for much of anything, let alone talismans of any description. Which explained why she was commonly referred to as Mirrors – not to be confused with Icy Miros, a dissolute Lazaremist male, whose nominal protectorate was the surrounding Crystal Mountains.

For the time being anyways. Klannit's ambitions didn't stop at becoming a Master Deva.

========

"Screaming skulls!" cried out Nanny Klanny's corpse, in his voice.

Young Death's body was already dissipating; the blood and brain-matter that gushed out of it evaporating.

"It's true. Crystal skulls, that's Janna Fangfingers' trick. Wait a minute, it was Hadd's Blood Queen, not Second Fangs. Our Klannit killed herself to avoid Nergal Vetala. She's everywhere, ubiquitous, thinks Hadd's still her devic protectorate, hers alone. It isn't. Hold on, what's all this about renovations?

"Fucking hell, Holgatson, kill that rat now!"

========

Dead Things were carnivores. They would eat anything so long as it might have once been construed, or misconstrued, as flesh. They would happily eat each other. More often than not they shut down instead, after burying themselves in shallow graves, rather than gnaw at themselves. This was a good thing for Nergal Vetala's forces because it freed up her Haddazurs to go scavenging for more fresh corpses to reanimate.

It wasn't such a good thing for Sraddhite slave-masters, their zombie-whippersnappers. You want your tunnels dug, you want them dug before you want your monastery heated, you want healthy Dead Things, you have to feed them. Other than each other, their favourite food was probably horsemeat. Horsemeat was too good for Dead Things. So the Sraddhites not only trapped rats, who would eat anything, even vegetables, they bred them. Then they fed them to Young Death's reconditioned Haddit Zombies.

Thartarre Holgatson snapped his fingers. One of his priests snapped a rat's neck. Auguste Moirnoir, who believed he was born Augustus Nauroz in the first decade of this, the 60th Century of the Dome, in the Weirdom of Cabalarkon, wafted out of the dead rat. He took shape, with clothes; became solid, his clothes did too. He glared at the High Priest.

"You owe me a new top hat, Tar."

Morgianna picked up the halves of her thought-father's top hat. Thartarre had sliced it in two even as he was splitting Young Death's head in twain. There was no hope for it so she wrist-jerked its pieces, as if they were parts of a bifurcated Frisbee, into the burn-pit. The priest tossed the dead rat into a slop bucket. Waste not, want not.

Young Death had dropped his cigar. He retrieved it off the tiled floor, got it going again. Said: "Whew!"

"Whew what?" required General Anvil. "What did you see inside my mother?"

"It was more like whew-who, Daddy Quentin," said Young Death familiarly.

He knew everyone there; knew a couple of them, the two witches, Morg and Fish, much better than he did most of the others. He had never been one for formalities. He also tended to address adults as Daddy or Mommy. Tethys presumed that was because his mother, Augustus's mother, Chryseis Somata, died having him whereas Augustus's father, Ubris Nauroz, didn't live through the Simultaneous Summonings of 5920.

(Not in any ordinary sense anyhow. He, the legendary 30-Year Man, eventually had to dust him, Ubris, Golgotha's template.)

"Besides," Ubris's maybe-son added, "You don't see inside Dead Things. You see out of them. You can read them, though, if you've the gift; their minds anyways. Or, if you prefer, their memories. Your mother was as old as I am, maybe even older, when she died, so she's got piles of them. She's also got stacks of secrets.

"Normally I'd say she's a head worth preserving; that her memories would make fine, mid-winter reading, once the workday's done. But there's no way I'm going back in there. It isn't empty and her memories aren't all that's left inside it." He paused for another nerves-calming puff on his noxious cigar.

(There were those who claimed he puffed cigars just to be offensive. On the Outer Earth, though, it was this particular habit, as objectionable as it was for many, more so than any trace of an accent, that convinced ordinarily worldly, as opposed to credulous, folks he was a midget bokor, houngan or voodoo priest from West Africa or Haiti.)

"Whew-who, Gush?" picked up Fisherwoman, Lady Achigan. She'd been calling him *'Gush'* ever since the first time she slaughtered him. She'd done so not because he thought himself born Augustus *'Gus'* Nauroz. She'd done so because his arteries gushed, as they should, whenever she killed him.

His blood quickly evaporated. He never left much a body behind either. Nothing for scavengers to eat, let alone occupy; nothing for undertakers to make a pretty penny taking underground. Thoughtful sort that he was, what he left behind cleaners could easily sweep into dustpans. Unlike his cigars, what he left behind didn't even reek.

"Who'd you sense in there with boo-you? What eel-eek-freaked you out?"

"I don't know, can't remember. Really. But, whomever it was, he was laughing at me. Big grin, daring me to go deeper. I did, I knew I'd never get out again. It was devilish, that much I can tell you. But I'll stake a pearl-inlaid boar's tusk it wasn't Vetala-devilish." (Boar-tusks were what he usually used to kill himself, when there wasn't anyone else to do it for him and he had an urgent appointment across the continent.)

"Your mother's been messed with by a pro, Quentin old darling. Messed with before the Haddazur got hold of her too, if I'm any judge. And I am." He paused again, this time wondering about the word *'judge'* for some reason. He quickly resumed, as if he'd almost immediately forgotten why he'd paused in the first place. "And not so very long ago either. Maybe yesterday, maybe the day before."

"When you were last here, Jordy," said Thartarre.

"Don't look at me," 30-Beers protested. It must be close to mid-morning by now and he still hadn't had his first pilsner of the day. "What about the renovations?"

"Lost that too, I'm afraid," Young Death admitted.

"There've been renovations going on here for decades," said de Landa. "Since long before I was assigned to the monastery. Which was years before you and Anvilwife moved back here," he added, speaking to Thartarre directly. "Plumbing, wiring, drywall, internal and external elevators, smoke-detectors, fire-alarms, sirens, you name it. And most of it was paid for thanks to the generosity of your father, governor, and you, Lady Achigan."

Honourifics Fish and Ferd got; honourifics Thartarre didn't get. No one missed that. Diego was a few years younger than Thartarre. Although born in Marutia, in one of the myriad feudal states that dotted Sedon's Cheek like age-spots, he had nonetheless spent much more time in and around the monastery than his current High Priest had. As a result, there probably was more than just an element of disentitlement in the omission.

After Barsine and Holgat's death in 5945, Nanny Klanny took the now one-armed, consequential orphan to a Sraddhite settlement fringing Diluvia. There, under the watchful eye of the Curia, she helped raise him until he was in his late teens. Even then the Curators wouldn't let her bring him back to the Lake Sedona monastery. But there was more to de Landa's apparent jealousy than that.

Generally speaking average life-expectancies for those on the frontline weren't lengthy. It therefore seemed prudent to keep a potential High Priest or three in reserve. That they let de Landa, who was officially renamed Diego Sraddha Landa-son at the time of his ordination, come to the lake when he was barely out of his teens therefore boiled down to skin colour.

Even though most folks reckoned him much more innately capable than Thartarre Holgatson, he was also much whiter. In other words, de Landa wasn't groomed to his full potential because didn't look at all like Sraddha Somata.

The High Priest snapped his fingers again. A priest dutifully went for another live rat. That wasn't why Thartarre had snapped his fingers. "Eel-eek," he said out loud.

"I was fishifying," justified Fisherwoman, Scylla Nereid, the onetime Queen of Godbad.

"So what?" he exclaimed, not catching himself in time. "Pardon, my lady," he instantly apologized. (Thartarre was always deferential when it came to addressing persons who, rightfully or wrongfully, were in a position of authority. Much to his annoyance, he rarely got the same respectfulness in return.)

"The last time I heard anyone go *'eek'* was you, Jordy. In the bathroom off my workroom, the one with the balcony Nanny Klanny threw herself off, or was thrown off of, last night, this morning. And it was only just recently renovated. Under her guidance as well."

"Don't tell me we have to trudge all the way up those stairs again," Ferdinand Niarchos complained. Ferd was in even worse shape than his father, who was dead. (Gomez was animated by a Sangazur, rather than a Haddazur, so he wasn't quite as dead as Nanny Klanny. Sangazurs were symbionts; Haddazurs were parasites.)

"Save yourselves the trouble," said Morgianna. "I've already looked. It isn't there. Isn't in your bedroom either, Tar, or I'm sure I'd have sensed it. Whoever got to you and Jordy got to Quentin's mother too. I'm inclined to agree with my Young Daddy Death. Whoever got to them was a master. And by that I'm thinking Master Deva."

"Sixty-plus missing stars," said Moirnoir. "That's an awful lot of suspects."

"Isn't just devils that smile," Thartarre reminded them. "Hadd's chock-a-block with Indescribables. De Landa here once silver-shot himself a Grim Grinner." (Grim Grinners were Nanny Klanny's 'heinous hyenas'.)

Morgianna realized where he was going; took umbrage at it. "Look, priest, even though I finally finished my last seven years of Ant-training once my Andy was born, I may still be more of a life-defending Athenan than I am a life-loving Anthean." (Her mother was hardly the only one to refer to daughter Andaemyn as Andy. Especially around these parts, some people got squeamish even mentioning a word that rhymed or sounded like 'daemon'.)

"Even though, as well, I may also be the Morrigan, the Hecate-Hellions' superior, I'm no more evil than I am dumb. So, no, despite what most of you seem to be thinking, I didn't kill her. Fish and I interviewed her together. As far as she knew it was in the Weirdom, fused with the copies Sal already has up there. Needles to slay – to borrow one of your lines, Jordy – the chances of that being the case are nil, plus or minus zilch and equalling zip, to borrow another one."

"Negative-zero," contributed Tethys, never averse to coining quotes for future use. "I drew the ones up there. Still have the drawing if you want to see it. No fires."

"So where does that leave us, Morg?" queried Ringleader.

"You and Sal, and your Mel, Harry, nowhere. Nanny Klanny's head, though … well, the truth might still be inside it. So, Quentin, how about we leave you to bury or burn Mommy Dearest from the neck down?"

"You can go to hell, witch," said Anvil.

"Been there, done that," she grinned. "Bought the tee-shirt too, you might have heard."

As the Morrigan, she supposedly wore an invisible demon. While, if she did – Morg was a hybrid-Utopian – it may have rendered her moderately more facially expressive than pureblood females native to Cabalarkon, her grinning was a very disturbing sight. She didn't crinkle or wrinkle the way most people, even Utopian men, did.

"Burn her whole, priest," the Godbadian general decided. Told Thartarre: "I'd rather have her ashes than either of them have her head."

"Um," interposed de Landa hesitantly. "As you may have noticed, we here are better at cremating than we are at differentiating someone's ashes from anyone else's ashes."

Thartarre was right about his unfairly perceived rival. Diego was a big-game bat-hunter if ever there was one. He had not only once silver-shot a Grim Grinner, he'd skinned and mounted its pelt as a trophy. Taxidermy was in fact one of his favourite hobbies after killing (for fun as well as necessity). He'd wanted to mount its severed head alongside its pelt. Only the heinous-hyena-head still grinned, laughed, howled and bit, so it had to go the same way Nanny Klanny was about to go.

Burn-pits were nowhere near as useful as a Trinondev's eye-stave but they had the advantage of finality. Godbadian General Quentin Anvil took control of the pulleys. It was past time his mother was good for something besides being a personal embarrassment.

Uncharacteristically, Thartarre shed a tear for the Dead. In that he was alone.

========

For an azura, Klannit Thanatos had led an extremely long and exceptionally lucid existence.

========

Because she could travel, mentally or psychically, betwixt and between mirrors, even into the otherwise mostly devil-denied Weirdom of Cabalarkon; because she also had compulsive abilities that approached the level of a Master Deva; in the past few decades her mother had often used her as an angel, as her personal messenger, her voice.

Since Klannit discovered she could animate her deaf-mute, age-retarded, baby brother's ice-statuary, and physically carry it with her, also via mirrors, she had been given the additional honour as acting as her mother's go-between with the rest of the Head's Panharmonium Project pushers.

If Klannit agreed that a proposition put to her was in accordance with her mother's wishes, that could be considered gospel. Due to the fact Methandra was a female firstborn, one of only two known to be still alive and active on the Head – the other being the frequently imprisoned Byronic, Umashakti Silvercloud – Klannit's word had a weight far beyond her lowly stature as a born-azura.

She was acting in just that capacity, as her mother's proxy, when Methandra, whose actual protectorate was Mythland, in the Mystic Mountains, Sedon's Crown, a few hundred miles due north of Cabalarkon, recalled her to her side in Lathakra yesterday. Her assignment was to reflect the six non-melted statues Sedunihas had sculpted of their decathonitized, but as yet still missing siblings in mirrors also fashioned for her by the 25-years-old, apparent 5-year-old.

Klannit did that, she could thereby learn where they were at that moment. At least she could do in theory. Whereupon it would be up to her parents to find a way to bring them home, to the Inner Earth's Frozen Isle. That wasn't necessarily done bordering on effortlessly but it was key to their immediate success. Even devil gods had their limits, though. What if they turned up beyond the Dome, as Antaeor, the Thanatoids' Earth Elemental, had for sure?

Klannit, she in her self-animated ice-statue, and her currently 6-inch tall mother discussed a number of options they might be able to employ in order to reacquire them, as it were. None of those they went over seemed too likely to either of them. At the back of her mind Klannit was sure there was a far better way to bring them home, should she locate them beyond the reach of her parents. But, for the immortal life of her, she couldn't remember it.

She sensed Methandra felt the same thing; that Miss Myth once knew of a better way, too. Only, just as Klannit had, she'd forgotten what it was. Having problems with memories usually meant you were having problems with Memory, the Mnemosyne Machine, the Female Entity. Except Methandra and Machine-Memory shared the goal of Panharmonium didn't they. They were allies. Weren't they?

The better way wasn't the Wandering SAG Gap. (Which was named after the twin cities of Sodom and Gomorrah.) Although it adhered to Methandra of Mythland, hence Miss Myth, when it wasn't the Stationary SAG Gap – which it wasn't, on average, once a decade – it currently wasn't in a wandering phase.

Neither was it All of Incain. The She-Sphinx responded to them as readily as she responded to Unmoving Byron. There was, however, always the danger she'd eat them, like she had both Umashakti Silvercloud and Uma's third-born brother, Nevair Neverknight, a Secondary Nucleoid. Until, that is, All regurgitated them last Mithrada, Monday, at the Great God's command.

The Thanatoids weren't Byronics so the Nag Gap was out. They couldn't access Kore's Hell, inside Apple Isle's Mt Maenalus, because of its Brainrock flow. So, what was the better way? Whatever it was, the truth of the matter was Klannit's parents had no safe way to travel off the Head. That acknowledged, they had better remember what it was pretty damn soon, or else come up with a feasible alternative, because she was damn sure she knew where her missing siblings were – and it wasn't just beyond the Dome

"My looking glasses caught another glimpse of Constantin," Klannit, unbidden, informed her mother.

Constantin was somewhat ironically named. One of the 5923 and, therefore, last of the five sets of twins born to Methandra while she was possessing the Female Entity, during the Male Entity's 11th lifetime, he was her parents' epitome of the Spring Season. If there was one constant about Constantin it was that, like springtime weather, he was constantly changing.

"Do tell, dear," Methandra replied, only half-acknowledging her presence.

"Rather, they caught another glimpse of the cosmicompanion who's holding onto him. Only this time I did like you said. I pulled a Tethys and had the background pan out. They aren't in Trans-Time Trigon, like we hoped they might be. However, they are in a structure somewhat similar to the Entities' Trigon in that it has three spires or towers to it."

"I trust you are about to speak more specifically," said the Scarlet Seeress, after the visionary fumes from purloined cauldron, but once Tantal's Scarlet Empress as well as his Crimson Queen.

As usual her father, Cold to her mother's Heat, was pretending she wasn't there, hence her considerable consternation whenever she entered his presence. His Brainrock power focus was a double-headed war-axe, a Labrys, like Lathakra's backbone, its range of mostly still volcanic mountains. Even an azura might not survive a blow from something like that.

Should the still-missing, fourth generational Thanatoids turn up on the Outer Earth, as Antaeor had, Methandra was fairly confident she could use her admittedly, oft-times strained relationship with Machine-Memory to prevail upon her to bring them inside. She, rather her human form, Miracle Memory, was their non-devic half-mother after all.

Trouble One was the Female Entity hadn't been responding to Methandra's efforts to contact her all week. Trouble Two was it was now the Male Entity's 100th Lifetime and an as-yet-unidentified somebody else was humanizing her. That meant Trouble Three was Methandra would have to rely on persuasion, not possession, in order to gain her cooperation.

Not very likely, they'd both agreed last night when they, Klannit and her mother, were discussing their options. All the more so since Tantal didn't regard Heliosophos as a lesser being. Worse, he regarded him as a kill-on-sight being. Which brought up Trouble Four. Question was which of the two alpha males would slaughter the other one first. Men were just so unreasonable.

The ambulant azura did her best to respond with the required specificity. "I'd say the structure looks alien. I'd say it looks alien because it looks to be on another planet. I'd say the other planet looks to be more of a planetoid. I'd say aliens have captured the cosmicompanions containing my brothers and sisters. I'd say they're holding them on the moon."

"The moon?"

"That'd be what I'd say."

"That being the case, I'd say that narrows our choices down to one."

"Who's Brainrock-blessed, in the best shape of his life and, therefore, can't be readily possessed. Unless you'd care have one of yours or father's acolytes, a Fire King or an Intuit, say, beat him to within an inch of his mortal life. In which case he wouldn't be up to a journey to the moon, would he?"

"Leave it to us, Klannit," Methandra told her azura-daughter.

"Have it leave us first," Tantal told his immediate sister-wife.

Klannit left. As hurtful as it was, a dismissal like that was the closest her father ever came to acknowledging her usefulness.

========

"I don't care how much I remind you of her, Harry," said Morgianna once Nauroz, once Somata, now Sarpedon.

========

"Second Fangs and I don't get along. We never have. If you need proof of that, aside from maybe her old man, Dragon Joe, I was one of the first to realize Barsine Mandam was holding onto Nergal Vetala. Nonetheless, no matter how happy it might have made Fangs at the time, I would never have killed her. She was my friend. And, other than Demios, I haven't had too many friends in my lifetime."

"Bat-bait wasn't holding onto the Blood Queen of Haddock Hadd," the former Queen Scylla of Godbad corrected her nearly lifelong associate, if not friend. "She was baby-beluga-born with remora Vetala inside her." (Remora, also called both a suckerfish and a shark- or whale-sucker, was one of her more apt fishisms. That was due to the fact that remoras fasten onto all sorts of marine animals much as vampires did humans, albeit for blood not transportation.)

"All is in readiness," Diego de Landa interrupted, coming into Thartarre's workroom after only the most token of taps on the door – this in keeping with his poorly concealed attitude that he, not Holgatson, should be the High Priest. "Radios and walkie-talkies are issued. Fire-alarms go off, even if we don't hear them when they do, we'll hear about them seconds later."

They were in the uppermost level of the monastery. Thartarre did most of his thinking and almost all of his paperwork up here. Klannit Janna Quentin-wife had plunged to her death off its balcony. In addition to the two witches, Fisherwoman and the Morrigan, the High Priest was with the Legendarian, Jordan Tethys, and Ringleader, Aristotle Zeross.

They hadn't had to trudge back up the two extremely long sets of steep stairs from the furnace room in order to reach an elevator. Holding their hands, Morg and Fish had taken them to the top floor on their stepping stones. Never let an Athenan War Witch do your housecleaning, that was the lesson to be learned from that.

After his experience inside Nanny Klanny's deadhead, Young Death said he had no interest in playing a Trigregos Gambit. So he'd stayed behind, in his self-described despicable depths. Tethys and Fish shared his distaste for having anything to do with the three Sacred Objects but they felt they better see the game out.

Fish was renowned for having oceans of notions. The idea she put to them, for a change borderline comprehensively, may have been hers but the pen was his. As for Field Commander Nauroz, Governor Niarchos and General Anvil, they had a Haddwar to fight and win. They couldn't be bothered with suchlike hocus-pocus tomfoolery.

"Your sperm at the quill-tiller, Jordy."

Tethys, who was nowhere near as practised at interpreting Fish's fishisms as Morgianna was, took sperm to refer to a sperm-whale. Took her whole statement to mean it was his turn to draw something. Expressly, that something was the Amateramirror, aka the Soul of Devaura. Devaura was the Trigregos Sister after whom the Head's equivalent of Saturdays on the Outer Earth were named. Today was her day, Devauray.

He did, draw it, the pad of paper, or parchment, or whatever, he drew it on would go up in flames. Fish's theory, which she based on what happened to the Tethys triplets' mother Tsukyomi back in 5838, was the mirror would, too. As long as it was secreted somewhere within the upper part of the monastery, it going up would set off the relatively recently installed fire-alarm system.

========

What ignited instead was Thartarre's mirrored egg.
****

(Game-Gambit) 14: **Kronokronos Cannon Fodder**

Devauray, Tantalar 6, 5980

They struck camp not long after daybreak.

========

The Good Companions were in the Crystal Mountain Range; were somewhere on the Crystals' Wildwyck-side, as opposed to its Samarand-side. There'd been a localized earthquake recently, the avalanche they'd camped at the base of was proof of that. It was also the reason their leader felt it wouldn't take much more than an hour's hike upwards before they reached their destination.

His confidence, not his thoughts – he was too strong-willed for mind-reading – were exchanged telepathically between two of those in his company. They were also dutifully transmitted long-distance to Sraddha Isle, in Hadd's Lake Sedona. They went much farther west than that; went across the Cathonia-concealed continent to Sanguerre, capital of the Bloodlands, New Valhalla.

There they were heard by its spiritual leader – literally – Guardian Angel Tyrtod. He was too preoccupied to respond because Nevair Neverknight was preoccupied slaughtering Sang-shells. As Ferdinand Niarchos promised Thartarre Holgatson on Lazam evening, Great Byron had that front of the latest War between the Living and the Dead well in hand.

Two of them actually, two very bloody hands. His paladin had been decathonitized. He killed with impunity.

========

Birhym evening (Wednesday on the Outer Earth), the 3ʳᵈ of Tantalar, Year of the Dome 5980, Nevair Neverknight entered New Valhalla, Sedon' Inner Nose geographically speaking. He'd been crushing any and all who dared to challenge him ever since; had been doing so by any and all means at hand.

That was the beauty of being once cathonitized, once decathonitized. You didn't have to pay heed to Grandfather Sedon's strictures against killing potential adherents. You didn't have to pay heed to Father Byron's dictates either. Didn't have to do diddle, except please yourself. Nevair was blood-crazed. No better place for it than the Bloodlands.

Sapienda-Thursday Neverknight met and repulsed only scattered resistance: primitives armed with wooden clubs and stone hammers for the most part.

Nightfall he came across Marutian host-shells skilled at archery, dart, missile and spear-throwing. Entirely covered in his ebonite armour, with its black, eagle-winged Brainrock shield to protect him, he scarcely noticed them. Scarcely bothered to kill any of them either; kill them anew, rather.

Massacre-matters were different come daybreak Lazam-Friday. That was when he had his first encounter with an organized opposition. Metal weapons were everywhere and, what's more, the predeceased, now Sangazur-animated corpses wielding them knew strategy. He took everything they presented him, all they could throw at him: phalanxes, cavalry, chariots, catapults.

A mountain of strength and fortitude, he pressed ever onward. His goal was Sanguerre, New Valhalla's capital. Woe betide any and all rash enough to challenge him.

Lazam afternoon was great sport. In heavy forest, gorilla-guerrillas native to Djerridam-Goatwood, Sedon's Beard, at the bottom of his father's subcontinent, took their cheap shots, never daring to tangle with him directly. Then came the noble but vainglorious and hence foolhardy knights, in their glistening armour, on their brave steeds, with their ludicrous lances, long-swords, maces and battleaxes. He jousted until dark, chivalrously sparring with and sparing all but the timorous, the Valhallans who, defeated, tried to run away rather than beg merciful quarter.

All through that night and into the next morning, it was like he was progressing through the history of warfare. Bloody slaughter. Bloody marvellous!

He enjoyed much more than endured the oncoming of gunpowder, muskets, rifles, bullets. They became heavy ordnance, no longer hand-cast missiles. Yet he just as easily withstood cannon shot and explosives that would probably blow devils lesser than himself into the Sedon Sphere and beyond it. Perhaps to the Outer Earth and even farther. Maybe back into the stars where he'd come from in the first place.

Then came the flying machines; their occupants dropping incendiaries on his head. When you could walk on the air as readily as on the ground, what was the threat of flying machines? Wrestling armoured vehicles, especially the tanks, had to be the most fun. Better than Yati's Dragons, whom he wasn't allowed to kill either, all those centuries ago when Samarand, Sedon's Tongue, was still in Sedon's Mouth and not on the other side of Hidden Headworld where Daybreak was until the Mighty Moloch decided to remind every Shining One just who was the boss.

Tanks took him back to the time he went on a rampage through Ophir-Moorset and Dandset Typhon set humongous crocodiles on him – the Edenite man-eaters with elongating tails as sentient as their heads, not the dim-witted, dinosaurian monstrosities more commonly found in Klizarod Rex's Floodlands, Sedon's Eyebrow. Or did, put better, before Typhon, a Mithradite highborn who'd carved out a domain for himself in Lazareme's Occipital Regions, realized he, a Byronic even higher born than Ophir's Devalord, had no compunctions about killing.

Not that tanks in the Bloodlands were any more alive than those inside them, he comforted himself, mindful of his face-saving, yet still humiliating retreat from Typhon's rage. Nevertheless, after trundling a few more hours southward, he had to admit Valhallans were much more engaging than the slithering slime-dwellers of Ophir-Moorset.

Bloodlanders didn't just fight to survive. They took pleasure in it. So did he.

========

The Good Companions didn't necessarily enjoy killing. They did enjoy the remuner-ation they received for killing, however. Wouldn't be mercenaries if they didn't.

========

The company's leader was Warlord Mikoto. He was a former Kronokronos of Subcranial Temporis, the territorially immense devic protectorate beneath Sisert, Sedon's Bald Spot at the crown of the Head. His parents were Mantel replicas of a pair of mid Nineteenth Century Outer Earth Japanese.

His father was possessed by Dand Tariqartha, the god-devil of Temporis, Laz-areme's Earth Magician. That was a definite. His mother may have been possessed by Pyrame Silverstar, perhaps the most notorious, and awake, female devil on the Head at the time of Mikoto's conception. That was what she, the Pauper Priestess, claimed anyways and Master Devas were supposedly incapable of lying.

That made him mortal, not to mention truly alive. The Warlord's half- or quarter-devic parentage also made him a deviant. No deviancy was quite the same as any other deviancy but many deviants led long and healthy lives. Mikoto one-upped most other deviants with his remarkable recuperative powers.

Which came in awfully handy when you'd spent most of your life on one battlefield after another, both below the Head, in the Thousand Caverns, and above them, on its surface, after Tariqartha banished him for what would have been capital crimes almost anywhere on the Outer Earth at that time.

He'd aged normally until he was twenty or so. Whereupon he started to age approximately one year for every four or five an ordinary man would. Thus, at al-most one hundred and thirty, he appeared to be in his mid-to-late forties. By that reckoning, at the age of 50 two of his female followers were moderately older than he was.

Yomikune and Katatribe were Jordan Tethys's two surviving triplet-daugh-ters by Tsukyomi born Tornado, who had not precisely spontaneously combusted, though it looked like she had, in 5938 Year of the Dome. The were, like Mikoto, samurais; were, as well, the only still active, altogether-alive members of his original Two Thousand.

The Two Thousand were the fighting force of mostly exiled Temporites who joined him on maybe half-mother Silverstar's ultimately doomed but nonetheless, as far as Mikoto was concerned, righteous quest to conquer the Weirdom of Cabalar-kon in 5950. (The Legendarian could spend days telling tales of providential pal Pyrame's efforts in that regard – and he, or she, as Sister Jordan, didn't need very much in the way of tee-tee-tails for backup either.)

There were a number of others with him today. Some were sons or daughters, grandsons or granddaughters of his Two Thousand. Them he trusted. A few of the others were barbarians; them he paid. So long as there was work to be had they were loyal. And there'd been work aplenty amongst the ever-scuffling states of the Cattail Peninsula. Hadn't been much up here, though, in the Forever Forest of Wildwyck, where they'd been for the past eighteen months.

He was never as sure of the Hecate-Hellion who'd been travelling with them for the last five years. Like him, Mother Earth worshipping Hellions hated devils. They were also as happy dealing with chthonic creatures – faeries, daemons, the

Dead and even the Undead – as he was; the ends always justified the means for Hellions. However, this particular Hellion, zebra-striped as she was, had a pair of exceptionally dangerous as well as duplicitous forbearers.

Her father, he counted an enemy. Her mother, he counted a rival. Accidents did happen. Accidents could be arranged. Over the course of five years she'd shown herself as accident-proof as she'd shown herself a good companion. When it came right down to it, she'd never given him any reason to doubt her trustworthiness, her loyalty and especially not her ability.

Within the hour he was supremely confident he would be safely killing her.

========

Warlord Mikoto had never been content being headman of one of the relatively few *'living'* caverns in Temporis. He knew of his devic heritage; figured he deserved a far loftier destiny. Early in life he decided he should be the Kronokronos Supreme of Temporis instead of his half-brother, Akbarartha; the Awesome Akbar, as he'd been dubbed decades before Mikoto was even born. Dand Tariqartha, their mutual, devic half-father, wouldn't hear of it. He had his reasons of course. And maybe they were valid.

It wasn't that Mikoto didn't try to accommodate him either. At Tariqartha's insistence he'd even let the Lady Takeda, his very own Summoning Child of a daughter, marry the fucking faerie. Takeda Artha, as she thereby became, was one of a large number of sons and daughters he'd sired over his deviancy-extended lifetime. There were so many of them, and they had so many children of their own, he'd long ago lost track of who was related to whom.

When, in Hektor 5945, Akbar and Takeda were killed in the explosion that sundered the Hiroshima Cavern, Mikoto reckoned it was his turn to assume the role of Kronokronos Supreme. Dand the Dad still wouldn't hear of it. So he'd rebelled, hardly for the first time. End result was his banishment. He'd been seeking retribution ever since; a reckoning he could actually win. Which was no easy task when dealing with Shining Ones.

But he knew what happened to Tsukyomi Tethys in 5938; knew what had been happening to the Dand while Takeda was still alive. Knew why it had been happening because he'd given it to her after retrieving it from Tsukyomi's charcoal corpse. What was lost with Takeda could be found again, though. One would lead to the other two.

The Trigregos Talismans could kill devils.

========

'You'd think," she was saying to the ever unwanted but persistent returnee, *"After all that time I was stuck inside it, I could sense where it is. But I can't anymore than that damn simpleton remembered where she hid it. No matter. They adhere to each other, those accursed things. And I know who knows where another of them is.'*

Now it was just a matter of waiting until nightfall for her to wake up.

========

"You really are a self-deluded fool, Nergalid. I'm almost ashamed to call you sister. Do you honestly believe I'd let Janna Fangfingers remember where she was when she had the Chaos Unity plunge the Susasword, the Body of Demeter, through his lovely but just as stupid sister all those centuries ago?"

Once she recognized the fiend manifesting himself atop Dustmound, where she'd brought her soldier shortly after dawn that morning, everything clicked into place. "So you're the one responsible for everyone's forgetfulness. Someday somebody's going to remember you exist, Judge. Hopefully that somebody will be Grandfather Sedon because then you won't anymore."

"Don't be so certain of that. I've plans for daddy dearest."

"Daddy dearest?"

"Oh, yes. I'm the last of his firstborn."

"You're no Great God."

"Neither was Varuna or Mithras. I'm the 'A' in the VAM Entity."

"Are you now?" Vetala considered the implications of that statement. She decided there weren't any; none that she'd remember anyhow. "How nice for you. Now go away. I'm busy."

"So I see."

What the Smiling Fiend saw was Vetala's Soldier sitting in Janna's throne. (Second Fangs had either constructed or imported it – from the ruins of the Hoodoo Hamlet, once a faeries' stronghold on the southern shores of the Bay of Corona, Sedon's Human Eye, just beyond Twilight – such that she could survey her realm, when it wasn't the Nergalid's realm.)

He was asleep. Humans found rest regenerative; he'd been in enough of them to know that. He also knew humans found exposure to Brainrock, so long as it wasn't too much exposure, as restorative for them as it was for devils. In somewhat the same way, devic possession was healthy for humans. So was azura-possession, though not so much so.

He did look fit and fairly healthy, however. He also looked to be wearing the remnants of a uniform; the same black pants and hooded, black and white striped top Sedunihas Thanatos chipped onto the sculptures he'd somehow channelled of the similarly clad cosmicompanions holding onto his as yet still missing siblings.

Smiler didn't need a Gypsium gavel for anything to click into place for him.

"He possessed?"

"So you're behind all those missing stars too," Vetala realized.

"I had some help. From a couple of contrarily lively – as in full of life – Death Gods, if you have to know. Well?"

"Last Sedonda I spotted a shooting star overtop of Tal. It crashed into my immediate sister's private preserve, Sedon's Moustache, where I've been languishing for thirty-five years. Ever since she hauled me out of the Jaag Maelstrom, for which I'm thus far eternally grateful. I sent my ever-faithful Cloud General to investigate it. Kronar found him. He was still alive so my vulturous friend wouldn't go near him. He led me to his side instead.

"As you know Kala's Forbidden Forest is pocked with time-warps. I took him into one. Over the course of next few days, what were for us weeks, I nursed him back to health. Then he returned the favour, drip by drip. So, yes, he fell out of the sky, as in the Sedon Sphere. When I found him, he was suffused with Brainrock. So, yes as well, I suppose it'd be more correct to say he teleported out of it.

"It might be even more accurate to say he was jettisoned out it, by Granddaddy Devil himself. I had a good look round inside him. If he was, he isn't possessed anymore. Whoever got out in him, if anyone did, got out of him before I got to him. He's exceptionally fine blood so I decided to keep him. Then I decided to make him my knight. He's going to become my Attis, my Trigregos Incarnate."

"Is he indeed? That presupposes you can locate the Trigregos Talismans."

"Oh, I will. And once he has them you won't need any plans for your Daddy Dearest. My soldier will sort him out for you, for us all. Then I'll have him sort you out."

"I see," the Smiling Fiend said again. He opened his third eye wider; eyefire-bathed the Blood Queen of Hadd. She screamed.

Her soldier slept through it.

========

The Hellion's mother had far more alarming talents than, as impressive as they were, those acquired by someone as skilled as her father was at using an eye-stave. And not only could her daughter call upon her anytime she wanted, she'd inherited a few of them. Could be she'd inherited a few of her demons as well.

She hadn't inherited the Gatherers of the Dead. Neither did she inherit their mounts, both kinds of them. They were all his, Kronokronos Mikoto's.

========

In terms of service, the Zebranid amongst them was junior to the other four barbarians. While each had joined Mikoto initially for ulterior motives, they had stuck with him for glory, adventure, booty and battle. Hadn't been disappointed either. The Two Thousand, many of their descendants and the strays who hooked up with them over the years were warriors. Always had been; in life and often beyond it. And that's what they gathered, warriors slain in battle.

The Gatherers of the Dead were Rakshas daemons. Originally they may have come from either an aspect of Satanwyck or, more likely, a devic paradise along the lines of the Elysian Fields or Old Valhalla before suchlike heavenly havens became part of the uninhabitable Ghostlands in 4825. Wherever their homeland was originally, chances were their devic overlord would have transplanted them to the Pristine Isles within a matter of decades if not short years or merely months afterwards. Howsoever long it took, that meant they'd been calling the Pristine Isles home for well over a millennium.

The Pristine Isles were in Bogy Bay, a by then sheltered body of water off Fearsome Fobbiat, the Hidden Headworld's western ocean. To its northwest lay the hook of Sedon's Outer Nose, Crepuscule, the Grey Land of Twilight. To its immediate north was Sedon's Inner Nose, the Bloodlands, aka New Valhalla. The south-westernmost coast of Sedon's Cheek, the vast plains of Marutia, was to its northeast whereas Sedon's Moustache and Upper Lip, the Forbidden Forest of Kala Tal and Dukkha as well as Crimson, respectively, were east or slightly southeast of the bay.

That Rakshas were daemons was indisputable. That they were very unusual daemons – make that demons, since they were life-destructive rather than either neutral or beneficent – was equally irrefutable. As counter-intuitive as the notion was, it seemed to Mikoto they were a race of deviants who grew up to become demons.

Rakshas suffered from what been described to him as reverse-butterfly syndrome. Impossibly beautiful, wholly humanoid demigods from birth until sometimes as early as their thirties, but rarely any later than their forties, they would just drop dead, on the spot, without any symptoms or warning signs. Their corpses wouldn't decay; wouldn't just rot away like any ordinary dead thing. They fuzzed-up. It was as if, borderline considerately, they would bodily grow their own shroud of downy cobwebs.

You could leave them like that, where they lay, through all manner of weather, all fluffy and kind of cute in an immobile and nose-worthily non-smelly way. You had to pen them in or dumb animals would make a dog's breakfast of them; had to mesh over the top of the pen, too, or dumb birds would peck them pulpy. Animals or birds did that, they usually wouldn't last until their next meal. The few that did smartened up right rapidly. Their descendants weren't anywhere near as dumb either. Marvellous how instinct develops.

Rakshas corpse-flesh, rather the fuzz covering it, was toxic. Just touching it or breathing it in, once it started molting, could kill you. Besides, you penned them in properly, they took up space. You'd be tripping over mommy or daddy all your life, until you dropped dead beside them and became as in the way as they were already.

Moving them, which still dumb animals and especially migratory birds would do when they're trying to eat them, only jump-started their transformation into their next stage of existence: as a pestilential were-thing, an undeniable demon. Don't try to bury them or even cover them up with token amounts of dirt. Rakshas corpses liked the open air and for sure they'd eventually claw out of it, just as hideously transformed and deadly.

You could try to burn them unto ash but fire awakened Rakshas corpses. It also made their transformation next to instantaneous. Plus, while anything short of complete combustion would serve to stunt their future growth, it would only do so in terms of limiting the size of the shapes they could take on later. Rakshas firebugs were as pestilential as Rakshas bugbears. Hacking their corpses into dinky tidbits before burning them worked to a degree. You better make sure you minutely minced them because their scratches were as deadly as their bites. As for their breath, no matter how tiny they were once transformed, it imparted slow death.

Even after the advent of explosives, what you did was call on the rapid-response squad to remove them, ever so gently. Their fuzziness was a pupa. You held your breath and got to the corpse before it got too fuzzy, you could bag it. You could then weigh down the bag with stones and dump it into the sea, whereupon they'd submerge and never trouble anyone again; at least not on the Pristine Isles.

You didn't get Rakshas corpses underneath the sea, or underneath any body of water, even in a bathtub, quickly enough you had a real problem on your hands. Still, no matter how transformed they were, no matter how devastating a plague they left in their wake before they got there, they'd eventually find their way into a river or stream and thence into the sea themselves. Saltwater was as necessary to their demonic development as their fluffy-dead-bunny, cutesy-papa-pupa stage.

Interestingly, a major advantage to living on the Pristine Isles was Rakshas demons couldn't function on them; not after immersion in seawater completed their transformation into a full-fledged demon. This remained the case even after it ceased to be a proper devic protectorate. Which it did when its overlord was cathonitized by the Byronic Nucleus, circa 5850, in the environs of a different Fields, the

Gregarian Fields, Sedon's Mole – the site of Thrygragon in 4376 YD. It was said that if you netted one, then transported it to one of the Pristine Isles, it would harden into stone.

There might be something to that as well. As Warlord Mikoto knew from visiting the Isles during his meanderings, the coastlines of a number of them had grotesque stone statuary adorning them. Of course that might be an effort on the natives' part to frighten away unwanted tourists. Still, he'd come across many, much more stranger things than grotesque statuary in his days of anything but amiably ambulating about the Head. He looked at one in a mirror whenever he looked into a mirror. Which wasn't very often anymore. He had also come across Klannit Thanatos a few times, and not just after he became a sell-sword.

Rakshas demons were no harder to kill than regular demons; in some respects they were easier to kill. Pin-cushioning them with arrows or ventilating them with bullets would do the trick. They were much smarter than regular demons. Were approaching human smart; were cunning enough to take on forms that could feed unobtrusively. Which was to say they didn't have any particular desire to feed on humans. What they couldn't do was get their forms quite right. Like becoming bored and atrophying into ever-after motionless gargoyles, that was a common drawback amongst demon-kind. They always looked somehow demonic.

Dukkhans boasted they could spot a Rakshas demon a mile away. While that might be an exaggeration, Mikoto knew he could. So long as they kept their distance he wouldn't kill them. Nor would any of his followers. That was because about the only place on the entire Head besides Satanwyck, the Abode of All Demons, where Rakshas weren't killed on sight was the Bloodlands, New Valhalla.

A significant percentage of the Bloods' population was made up of Sangazur-animated Dead Things. The death-breath of Rakshas demons had no effect on Dead Things. Sangs were symbiotic azuras; mutualists, as in mutually beneficial, according some of his acquaintances more well-read in the biological sciences than him. They also had a specific affinity for those who died in battle. Which his followers did, more often than not.

Over the past thirty years, Rakshas riding Vultyrie, the gigantic vultures who followed Kronokronos Mikoto's band by day, or the equally enormous bats, who did the same by night, had claimed many of the warlord's original Two Thousand as their own. Someday, regardless of the recuperative qualities he'd come by due to his deviancy, a Sang might come to claim him. And that was reason enough not to kill Rakshas on sight.

Because, if he was raised by a Sangazur, he'd retain the mental wherewithal to exact a very personal payback on whomever or whatever was sufficiently skilled to kill him.

========

'I knew it. I had one of them once. Should never have left it with my daughter but they adhere to each other, those wondrous things. I can sense it now: a cave lined with Stopstone, reopened by a recent earthquake. Had to be. That must be how that damn simpleton hid the other one from me, encrusted the mirror in Stopstone.

'Won't be long now. I have one, it'll take me to the other two. Hope you had a happy anniversary, half-daddy dearest, because you're about to become one dead devil.'

========

Kronokronos Mikoto paused and sniffed the air. His long sword, a katana with a grinning Death's Head pommel on the end of its grip, was out of its sheathe before the others heard the sound of the black and white fur-coated, ring-eyed, great panda crashing through the bamboo towards them. Bursting into the clearing the bear reared on its hind legs. It was more than just a great panda; it was a gigantic great panda, at least ten feet in height and, in terms of girth, probably as broad as it was wide.

Swords were drawn, arrows notched, guns cocked, rifles primed. For a brief second the panda looked like it might charge them. Then, as if thinking the better of it – or more likely feeling the uncertain footing of the avalanche's rubble beneath its paws – the magnificent beast rambled back into the bamboo forest. Which was great for the bear; not so for one of the young samurai, the junior of the group, who immediately knelt at his lord's feet unbidden.

In thirty years of wandering, mostly in Marutia, Sedon's Cheek, of leading his band of bravos from border war to border war, Mikoto had never drawn his long sword without it tasting blood. This time would be no different. A scratch would have been satisfactory for most warlords but the onetime, long exiled, Kronokronos had one other idiosyncrasy.

He never drew his katana without it savouring death.

========

"Bury that in case the Gatherers are delayed," he ordered, as he sheathed his long sword, averting his eyes from the decapitated corpse.
"And remain here. I go the rest of the way myself."

========

Two of the samurais picked up the body of their late comrade; Mikoto's great-grandson, he'd once boasted. A third one picked up its severed head and placed it on its stomach. A fourth samurai took a shovel out of her pack and led the other three into the woods. The two surviving Tethys triplets, themselves samurais, stood their ground. So did the five barbarians in the band. Not a one of them said a word.

"'Kune, 'Tribe?" demanded Mikoto. "You wish to address me?" Both women bowed slightly but held their silence, and his gaze. The former Kronokronos glared at the other five. As one, they lowered their eyelids. The four samurais assigned to bury Mikoto's great-grandson returned from their appointed task to find the silent standoff continuing.

"No? But, ah, you may be right," allowed Mikoto, intuitively appreciating their point of view. "We have been together too many decades to separate now. You other samurais, your parents and grandparents served me well. You shall honour me with your presence. You five barbarians, remain here.

"You want to make yourselves useful, see if you can contact the Gatherers. I should like to speak with the dead boy again. And I'm sure his parents and grand-parents would as well, once we've returned to Sanguerre with the talismans." (Due to the fact so many of his original Two Thousand and their offspring ended up Sangazur-possessed, Mikoto had made New Valhalla the closest he came to having a home away from home.)

"As you command, sword-master," pronounced the 27-year-old Zebranid.

"Come!"

========

Eyefire could burn anything. Sometimes, though, it had other uses.
Tabula rasa meant "an opportunity for a fresh start; clean slate".
Blip!

========

"Oh, it's just you, Judge," said Vetala, once she recognized him a couple of seconds after she reckoned he'd arrived. "What brings you to Dustmound?"

"Actually I was on my way to see your brood sister in Tal. However, I'm sure you'll be just as delighted to hear my news.

"Congratulations, Nergalid, you're an immediate aunt. Your other litter sister, the Medusa, has just made me a proud Daddy Daemonicus. There'll be an official announcement in a couple of days, after I attend to King Cold and reassert my position as the Head's earthly monarch. But I couldn't resist hearing your reaction."

"Fuck off, Judge. How's that for a reaction?"

"Pretty much what I expected. See you shortly."

========

The gigantic bats the Gatherers rode were vampires, strictly nocturnal, so unless it was a clear night they rarely saw them anyways.

========

However, the Zebranid Leper amongst them was in constant contact with her Morrigan of a mother via their Hellstones and she'd heard from her that Second Fangs, Janna Fangfingers, had launched a major offensive in Hadd less than a week earlier. So maybe Fangs – a kind of cousin on her mother's side – had recalled them. Which would explain why the Gatherers couldn't keep up with them on a nightly basis.

It had been a few days since they'd seen any Gatherers above them, though, and that was odd. The Vultyrie, the enormous vultures they rode during the day, were bred in aviaries within the Bloodlands. Their Brainrock-blessed, Sangazur-animated colleague claimed he hadn't heard of any reason why they might have been recalled.

Then again, the Crystal-Skull-sets Sangs had used to far-speak each other for hundreds of years, their Talking Heads as they referred to them, had been notoriously unreliable for well over a century. Had been ever since the Byronic Nucleus cathonitized the Skull-sets' headless maker, as it happened.

Which also happened to be at the same time the Rakshas lost their devil-god, the Vultyrie their eponymous goddess, who was about as intelligent as they were from most reports, the Bloodlands their devic overlord and the Sangs their primary mother both initially and again after she regained her freedom on Thrygragon.

Damn shame all of that. A worse shame was the Zebranid's father, Demios Sarpedon, was so pissed off at her for joining their marauding band of merry mercenaries he wouldn't assign anyone with an eye-stave to accompany them. Now there was a reliable method of communicating long-distance. Eye-staves were so very useful in so many ways.

Demios was a hard man. He hated Kronokronos Mikoto almost as much as he hated either devils or Saladin Devason, the Weirdom of Cabalarkon's current

Master. He had never forgiven the warlord for being part of Pyrame Silverstar's force of would-be Cabalarkon conquerors, the Weirdom as well as the Undying Utopian. On top of that, he had forbidden his wife to pursue the Trigregos Talismans.

The Morrigan marched to the beat of her own drum. So did both her daughters. Besides, they privately agreed, it wasn't so much the three Sacred Objects they were pursuing as it was the various Witch Sisterhoods' ages-old dream of Panharmonium. It was a dream they shared with Methandra Thanatos. Not surprisingly either. They were Athenans and Hot Stuff, Heat to her husband's Cold, was once worshipped as Mediterranean Athena.

That they were also part devil-hating Utopians, as well as demon-conniving Hecate-Hellions, perhaps should have troubled the Scarlet Seeress more than it did.

========

"Who was that, goddess?"

"Who was who, my soldier? There's no one else here."

"The devil. You woke me up when you started talking to him but I decided to play possum. I saw him, though. He was all in black, had a pink face and hands, three eyes, and never stopped smiling. You called him the Judge. He did something to you after you told him why you made me your knight. You screamed. I'd have shot him but, you know, bullets didn't work on you, did they?"

"The Judge, eh? Barsine Holgat-wife knew a judge once; the fellow she was brought up believing was her twin brother might have been his son. Judge and Wiccan Warlock, those were the names they used in here. But I can't say I recall anyone I ever called Judge."

"He said something about Medusa making him a Daddy Daemonicus."

"Did he really? Now that is interesting."

========

Mikoto led the six surviving samurais uphill, in the direction the panda came from. As became quickly apparent from the bones and refuse outside and inside it, the reason it had challenged them was because they had disturbed it in its den. Leaving the youngest pair of warriors to stand guard outside the cave, the former Kronokronos, the two onetime Tethys triplets and the two remaining samurais turned on the battery-powered flashlights they acquired in Samarand and walked into the lair of the beast now fled.

Could a panda snicker?

The Crystal Mountains, specifically the cavities within them, the Warlord recalled, were held sacred by the peoples of Samarand, on the opposite, eastern side of the range. Samarandin Holy Men spent many years meditating inside quartz-lined caves such as this one. They also made detailed notes and diagrams of what they imagined they saw in the walls herein.

In time the Holy Men, who were more accomplished draftsmen than truly holy men, would return to the absentee Byronic Dragon's narrow coastal protectorate; what had once been on the other side of the Head, where it was referred to as Sedon's Tongue. There they and their acolytes would begin to construct templates based less upon their hallucinations than on the notes and diagrams they'd made of them.

Their hallucinations were visions. Apparently the cave walls as much broadcast as reflected events that were occurring on the Outer Earth almost simultaneously.

The visions they saw were voiceless transmissions akin to Godbadian television sets. That was why, despite the incontestable intelligence of their scientists and technicians, the Samarandins never got things exactly right. A helicopter constructed in Samarand looked like an Outer Earth or Godbadian helicopter. It might even fly like one, but only for awhile. Something was always missing from Samarandin designs. Usually that something was precision.

This particular cave, the one vacated by the ring-eyed, evidently omnivorous panda, was on the Wildwyck slope of the Crystals. It was a mountainside seldom visited by Samarandin Holy Men. Its lower foothills were crazy country. Although undeniably carbon-based lifeforms, the locals were hardly human at all. Diamantes, they called themselves, and that they were: diamond-dense and skin-reflective humanoids.

Headworld historians claimed Diamantes were products of Old Eden's approaching 8,000-year-old genetic experiments. That put them in the same category as the water-breathing Akans and male Lemurians, amphibious Piscine and female Lemurians, up to a certain age, half-life tellurian Mandroids, who were related to the Mantels of Temporis, the Saur Tsars of the Floodlands, the Lizarados of the Lake Lands, Godbad's avian-human Ayres, Simian Sapiens, Garudas and, indeed, most of the Head's exotica. Diamantes weren't fighters, didn't need to be as they were externally impenetrable. They were friendly enough and, like most folks, liked to tell stories.

One of the stories they frequently told was of a haunted cave somewhere in the Crystals. On the Head haunted caves were a dime a dozen, as Godbadians said – their dimes being otherwise worthless coinage representing a tenth of a Godbuck, their currency. But this cave had supposedly been haunted for a suspiciously specific period of time: a highly significant half-millennium.

Five hundred years in the past Janna Fangfingers helped bring about the Disunion of the Unities. It culminated with the last minutes of the Thousand Days of Disbelief. Arguably it started with the disappearance, and presumed death, of the female of the three firstborn Lazaremists. She was the near universally admired, lovely-to-everyone dynamo behind the Age of Lazareme, Thrygragos Everyman, and its just as long lost, largely lamented, yet overly romanticized version of Panharmonium.

If only because he'd held onto the Crimson Corona for so many decades before he gave it to Tsukyomi born Tornado, become Tethys, as a wedding present, Mikoto reckoned he had an attraction for its sister objects: the Amateramirror and the Susasword. That attraction led him to Sraddha Isle years ago. When that, for whatever reasons, proved a waste of time, the same quest pulled him ever eastwards then northwards, deep into the Head's occipital regions.

After eighteen months in Wildwyck, Samarand and the Crystal Mountains between them, Mikoto had become convinced that the ghost haunting the elusive cave was none other than Datong Harmonia, more commonly Harmony: the female triplet who, until those selfsame 500 years ago, had provided the balance betwixt her brood brothers, Chaos and Order, since nigh on forever.

So why, since devils were as much spirit beings as they were physical beings, would a devil haunt anywhere? For the same reason ordinary ghosts did, Mikoto figured. Harmony had been killed there; make that here. He was sure of that now. He could sense it as strongly as he could feel the strength of his grip on the hilt of his katana.

He adopted its Death's Head motif during his days besieging the Weirdom of Cabalarkon in 5950 while heading forces loyal to his devic half-mother, Pyrame Silverstar. Among the properly Hate-Sedon, Utopian rebels – or, as they'd have had it, champions – who joined them, it was a remarkably popular icon.

Over eleven centuries earlier, one of the Weirdom's most magnificent failures, Master Morgan Abyss, took it as her emblem or totem. If it wasn't for her, the thusly renowned Death's Head Hellion, the ever-after radioactive Ghostlands would likely still be home to dozens of pantheistic paradises; Sedon's cult centre, Grand Elysium, merely being the greatest of them. She thereby demonstrated, praise be her memory, that mostly ordinary mortals had it within themselves to knock devils down to size after all.

What was now a Death's Head pommel had once been a Dand-head pommel; had been shaped like the head of his devic half-father, Dand Tariqartha. It had power. Sometime he spoke to it. Sometimes it spoke back, albeit in private. Today it told him that the earthquake had cracked opened the Stopstone-lined cave wherein the incomparable Harmony had been slain by Unholy Abaddon, the Unity of Chaos, a week prior to her own feast day in 5492.

It also told him that once he had what killed her, he would become akin to Morgan Abyss. Only he wouldn't fail.

He'd liberate the Hidden Headworld from the blight of devazurkind.

========

Suddenly the tunnel's ceiling began to collapse.

****

(GAME-GAMBIT) 15: **Trigregos Nephew**

Devauray, Tantalar 6, 5980

"Why did I make you my knight, by the way?"
"Because I'd do anything and everything I could for you, my goddess."
========

Over the centuries, in legends and histories told and retold throughout the Headworld, Janna and Sraddha Somata retained their well-deserved reputation as archetypal Terrible Twins. Beyond the Dome, on the Outer Earth, another set of terrible twins, or so they were thought of until they reached their mid-to-late teens, were Aires and Thalassa D'Angelo.

They were supranormals, fought long and if not always gallantly then usually triumphantly in the Secret Wars of same. Had supra-codenames: Airealist and Sea Goddess, the former not just because he spent so much of his spare time in circuses and the latter not just because she, like her brother, could be counted as pedestal perfect when it came to godly good looks. As such they were better known as the Elemental Twins, after their attributes, which were air and water.

Kid Ringo helped end their 17-years of supra-doings on Xmas Day 1955 – Xmas being named after Xuthros Hor, the Biblical Noah, whom devils and Utopians alike knew had been real person, the Tenth Patriarch of Golden Age Humankind in fact as well as legend. He did so on the Outer Earth's Damnation Isle. There was an Inner Earth Damnation Isle as well. It was composed of whaledreck.

Barsine Mandam had a twin as well. In many respects, even with her being born with Nergal Vetala inside her, he was much more terrible than her. His name was Jesus, although only his mother, Mary Magdalene born Ryne, called him that. Barsine and Jesse, or Jess, as everyone else called him, didn't look in any way similar. The reason for that, which wasn't confirmed until the late Thirties, was because they weren't twins at all. Which was something else to blame on the Simultaneous Summonings of 19/5920. They weren't the only newborns witches, for the most part, deliberately mixed up either.

Barsine was a Melanochroid Mediterranean; had dark hair and white skin. She tanned easily so she was never that white. Neither was her hair ever that long. Although it was true she tended to swim naked, ordinarily she dressed modestly. She wouldn't have been caught dead wearing a purple top split down its front and back such that her breasts were in jeopardy of spilling fully into public view. Barsine did have nice legs, though; often wore shorts. But she never wore a calf-length black skirt, not one slit sidewise from her hips down, either.

The first time Morgianna Sarpedon realized Barsine Mandam was holding onto Nergal Vetala, as she had somewhat imperfectly put it a couple of minutes ago, she had long, sharp fingernails, toothy fangs, up and down, and a third eye. So that wasn't surprising. Fisherwoman was in Africa by then and Morg couldn't remember if she unleashed any eyefire that first time or not.

She did now, definitely. Her target wasn't her, though. It was Fish, Lady Achigan Auranja, once Queen Scylla of Godbad.

That first time she was all there. This time she wasn't. That first time a man didn't come out of her outlined body from the neck down. That then-non-existent man certainly did not have a hand-Gatling in one hand. He did now, also definitely. His target was her. He shot her, a few times; hurt too. Thump, thump, thump went not just the bullets against her – went her heart as well. Kept on going, put better, thankfully.

He was shirtless. He had wrapped a hooded, torn, silver and black striped shirt in his other hand. With it he yanked the flaming, mirrored egg off Thartarre Holgatson's chest, silver necklace with it. He was back in the Barsine-form, and the Barsine-form was back between-space, before the four men there could react.

They had that option, reacting. The witches, that was yet to be ascertained. Fish was fuming. Fumes were coming off her; out of her too; her bellybutton bauble in particular. She wasn't burning; not externally. Vetala's eyefire was more of a mental thing. Was that smoke coming out of her ears? Thartarre was burning still. That was smoke coming off his fancy brown robe, some fire too. With de Landa's help he ripped it off, threw it on the floor and together they stomped it out. The High Priest was wearing Mickey Mouse boxer shorts.

The Legendarian's first thought was for Morgianna. He'd seen folks shot before, all too often. He'd been shot before, all too fatally. To the best of his monumental recollection he had never seen bullets that hadn't penetrated, not even fractionally, any part of the person shot. Morg leapt to her feet. She was miffed. The blunted bullets slid off her onto the floor.

Good trick that, wearing an invisible demon, thought Tethys. Doubly good since it was only invisible in terms of her skin. It must have also made up her pantsuit, which was white of course, because it hadn't been penetrated either. He wondered if chthonic outerwear was readily available in Satanwyck. Or from the feeorin haberdashers of Twilight. He might want to pick a demon-suit for himself someday. So long as he didn't have to debrain it first of course. Tethys was squeamish about that sort of thing.

Morg was a materialist. What she materialized was a hobbyhorse; a wooden horse's head on something akin to a broom-handle; a foreshortened eye-stave, minus the eyeorb atop it, perhaps. Witches and their broomsticks, that part of the Outer Earth's folklore regarding them wasn't fantasy. The horse's head was white. Given who it belonged to, what other colour would it be?

Suddenly it was alive. It was snorting steam out of its nostrils. Its eyes looked like Vetala's had; looked like – what else? – burning coals. Very demonic. Its body was filling in around the broomstick. The Morrigan's psychopomp was a nightmare; unless it was a night-stallion. Tethys had seen it before.

Had seen another of Morg's earlier psychos before too. That one, a just as demonic hoot owl, had eaten his mother, half-mother rather, Titanic Metis. Which was why its name was Metowl, although Morg tended to refer to it as *'My Towel'* – albeit mostly to annoy him, also her, the Sister Jordan Legendarian of the day (Ukemoshi Tethys).

He hadn't seen a glowing ring vanish either/or before; did now. Morg was so pissed she was suddenly the one steaming: "Goddamn it, Harry. It's mine!"

"You'll have to take that up with your brother, sis," Ringleader retorted.

It was probably the first time he, Harry, Dr Aristotle Zeross, had addressed his sister-in-law, Morgianna, as *'sis'*. His goodwife Melina was forever warning him about warming to her. You didn't trifle with the Morrigan. Hecate-Hellions were not pleasant people. Look what their greatest hero, a much earlier Morg, Morgan Abyss, brought down on the Upper Head in 4825 – nuclear devastation, no less.

Ordinarily he heeded her, that Mel as opposed to the Terrible Twins' Mama Mel, Melina Somata, who arguably caused even greater grief to the Hidden Head-world when she put daughter Janna up to disuniting the Unities of Lazareme in 5492. Then again, ordinarily he just stayed away from her, this Morg, Superior Sarpedon.

What kind of a name was Morg anyways? Morgues were not nice places. Besides, there wasn't anything ordinary about today. Plus, he'd promised her brother, Saladin Devason, he'd reacquire the Trigregos Talismans. And one of them, the only one they figured they knew where it was at, had just been ripped off, literally, right before their eyes.

"This is Zeross family business; not Somata family business. That wasn't just Vetala. That was my Dem's Dim who came out of her." Tethys had seen Harry with rings around his eyeballs before too. They were like eyeglass-frames without the lenses. He was using Godstuff to grant him a form of see-forever-eyes; albeit just a regular human pair of them.

"Buggering Be-Jesus," Harry swore, somewhat imaginatively. "That looks like Andy."

Harry extended a hand. Harry was Rings. He had rings on every finger, thumbs included. Had earrings, had bracelets, necklaces, probably had anklets. Didn't have any visible nose-ring and only his Godstuff knew if he had rings attached to his bellybutton or anything even lower down. His dark hair had always been curly. They weren't just good for facilitating remote viewing. A teleport-hole formed in the air in front of him.

He stepped through it and was gone.

========

Tethys looked at Morg. She dropped a glowing Hellstone at her feet. It went out. Fish was already with it. She was a materialist too. She produced then dropped her Brainrock fishnet over Morgianna. It was glowing. It didn't go out. Morg glowered at her: "You heard him, Fish. He said Andy. I've a daughter named Andy."

That she did, Tethys recalled. Her second born, her lone other born: her Dem, Demios's daughter, not Tsishah, Tom-Tiddly Taddletale's daughter. Andaemyn. Her name meant *'without a demon'.* He couldn't recall what Tsishah meant. He did recall Tom-Tiddly Taddletale turned out not to be Tomcat Tattletail, whom he'd hated, incarnation after incarnation, however. They were both fucking faeries, though.

Then Morg went out, like a switched-off lightbulb. She slumped onto the floor. Unconscious.

"I didn't realize you could do that," Tethys said to Fish.

"Watery what?"

"Brainrock net, invisible demon, that I get. Brainrock counteracts Stopstone. I never got you could put out a witch-stone like that."

"Morg's a little manatee-mother," she endeavoured to explain, in her annoyingly, mostly incomprehensible, fishifying manner. "And she'd a baleen-bitching moray of a motherly father-fucker. Went by Celeste Mannering in here; the Celestial Superior on both fillets of the Sed Sphere. She had sprats of knacks, did our Hell-Cel. Life's a school, Jordan River, and not just of fish."

"So I gather. Is Andaemyn in danger?"

"Andy wallows in the wallow with Kronokronos Mikoto. I'd say she deserves what she gefilte-fish gets."

"Sounds to me like it's this Dem's Dim fellow who's more in danger," said the High Priest.

He was aware that Morgianna sometimes called Demios, her husband, Dem. It seems that, simpletons excluded, nothing is ever simple on the Head. Speaking of which, he was rubbing his bared chest with ice de Landa had hastily extracted from his fridge. He may not have been as simple as his Nanny Klanny but he was luckier than her. The burn wasn't even second-degree-bad.

Fish eyed Thartarre. So did her bellybutton bauble, it seemed to him. "Didn't reeling-in realize you'd been to Disneyland." The reference was to his Mickey Mouse boxers.

"A gift from Dr Zeross; both Dr Zerosses. They took their family there last spring. I can't believe I was wearing the bloody mirror all this time."

"No, you can't remora-remember it," said Fish. "Fish-and-chips-dipped in a Solidium small fryer, that's my fluky flake-take on that, my sprat. Mariamnic witch-work's my guess at the mess."

Mariamnic witch-work was fairy tricksterism. That didn't necessarily mean Young Death. He had Jacks of knacks but there were also Jills of Mariamnics. How weird was it, Tethys asked himself, that he'd just been flashing on the fay fart who'd deflowered Morg all those decades ago, hence Tsishah? Probably not weird at all, come to think of it. He did that sort of thing regularly.

So did she. And Fish did have Mariamnic training. So did Morg and so did Morg's eldest, Tsishah Twilight. Sooth said, when it came to Mariamnic witch-work, no one was better at it than Shenon's non-Lemurian Aortic. Nonetheless, virtually any highly skilled witch could make another witch forget things almost as easily as she could make a non-witch forget things. A witch could also make herself forget things. Then again so could Klannit Thanatos.

She didn't say anything further because she liked certainties and the only thing she was certain of right this moment was she was hungry. Fish was always hungry.

========

De Landa's radio beeped, he switched in on, heard out the priest on the other end, then clicked its pause, or shut-up, button. "It's Sraddha Noisome, Moise-son, one of them; you know, one of Young Death's zombie-drovers. He wants to know who's wasting perfectly good horseflesh. Says it just fell out of a glowing ring that suddenly appeared in the air above the burn-pit. Says it was alive. It isn't anymore."

The radio beeped again. This time he shut it off after he heard out who was on the other end. "That was Young Death. He says to tell his Mommy Morg she needs a new psycho."

"Mommy?" said Thartarre. "I thought she was his daughter."

"Daughter!" snapped Tethys.

Then he slapped himself in his forehead, missing the fly bugging him, grabbed his quill off the floor where he dropped it, post-ignition, raced over to Thartarre's desk, found some paper and flipped it over onto its blank side. His quill's nib spurted a splotch of Brainrock ink onto the sheet of paper. Splotches were readymade drawings; this one was of Ringleader.

He'd prepared it the night before in the Dinq, Doinq, Danq Cavern Tavern, before he took them up to the Weirdom of Cabalarkon. He'd reused it this morning when he drew them, he and Rings, from Cabalarkon to here. He could do that sort of thing. His quill could. It was as if it had a memory of its own.

"Damnation," he cursed when the background filled in grey then completely obscured his splotch of Ringleader. "He must be between-space. Unless he took himself beyond the Dome or somewhere there's slabs of Stopstone." Especially from a distance Tethys couldn't draw himself, or anyone else, anywhere blocked-in by Stopstone, what Outer Earthlings referred to as Solidium.

He also couldn't draw anyone either between-space or beyond the Dome; not with any discernible effect anyhow. It'd just be a drawing, a sketch, a splotch, unless it was a blotch, of someone he'd done from memory. He had another thought, grabbed another blank piece of paper and began to scribble frantically.

"Somebody get me a beer. And kill that fucking housefly. Hell's Teeth, I hope I can remember what they look like."

Fish smiled. Her body was shapely. Despite her skin's slightly scaly and vaguely greenish pigmentation, many found it pleasurable to behold. Her gills, her webbed fingers and toes, they only added to her erotic exoticness. She did have those two rows of shark-sharp teeth, though. They, together with her well-known preference for raw, fleshy food, were among her less endearing traits. Fish smiling had a lot in common with a roach regarding road kill.

"Mind like a steel crab-trap, that one," she said. She was being sarcastic. Whether they were made out of steel or not, crab-traps were a metallic mesh, sieves.

Thartarre was pulling on some hiking pants. He liked to hike, when he could get away during the day. Which hadn't been very often of late. Brown robes dragged, collected mud, dirt and damp. Pants were better. His chest wasn't; it was getting worse. He'd need a doctor. So would Morgianna. She looked frozen solid beneath Fish's Brainrock net.

"In the fridge, de Landa. More ice for me while you're there. And use that radio to get some help up here." Obediently Diego de Landa grabbed a bottle of beer for Tethys and ice for his High and Priestly Mightiness. Nanny Klanny must have had the forethought to stock the fridge with chilled pilsner before she went the way of a diving duck, absent the water, and he had the forethought to use a bottle-opener before he brought the beer to the Legendarian.

Fish was watching him work. She clapped her hands together, killed the housefly. Ate it. Burped. Young Death wafted out of her bellybutton bauble, her navel-accessory, her Vesica Piscis. He had a freshly lit cigar in one hand; had Morg's thoroughly charred hobbyhorse in his other. Thankfully it was lighter than Fish's bike-psycho.

"Got them," said Tethys. "They're in some sort of cave. At least they're not between-space. Background's not coming in very clearly so there's got to be some Stopstone interference. Don't think they're in Temporis. Wait a minute, up ahead of them. That's goddamned Mikoto. He's bound to be leading them into a bloodbath. Well, maybe not quite yet, pal."

He drew the ceiling collapsing between his daughters and their leader.

========

As the cave's ceiling collapsed around them, Kronokronos Mikoto raced forward. Two of the samurais managed to keep up with him but, as a goitre of ground cascaded out of the roof, the two remaining Tethys triplets were stranded betwixt and between. In the Sraddhite monastery their father from a different incarnation grinned as broadly as it was nastily. He didn't approve of Kronokronos Mikoto. Nor did he approve of the bloody bloodlessness of his samurai creed.

"Goddamn, I'm good!"

========

As more rubble buried them, the Warlord managed to struggle free. Leaving his young comrades-in-swords to their fates, he pressed onwards. Nothing was going to keep him from his appointment with destiny, not after so many decades of fruitless questing. Sweating blood and much-too-much brain-matter – he'd heal, he always did – he staggered into a tiny cavern glimmering with the telltale radiance of Brainrock-Gypsium. There, spread-eagle on a glowing outcropping of no doubt the same ineffable Godstuff, the remains of the Primordial Godhead, lay a female shape well into the advanced stages of daemonic decomposition.

Whoever she was, had been rather, similarly shimmering chains stretching off equally eerie manacles around her wrists, ankles and neck-torc were fastened to the base of the rock. While these should have been enough to hold her in place, she was further pinned by a curve-bladed sword stuck between her breasts that shined even more brightly than either the chains or the Brainrock boulder itself.

In terms of abundance, Brainrock-Gypsium was usually found in a molten state. An exception was in Sedon's Hairband, where it was mined. They'd crossed Sedon's Hairband, aka the Gypsium Wall, on their way to the Hidden Headworld's occipital regions. As the crow flew, as Gatherers did on their mounts dot-ditto, it wasn't all that far south of where he was now.

Stopstone-Solidium was far more prevalent. It was found throughout the Head's underworld. It was the subtle matter stuff of tellurians, Mother Earth's chthonic creatures; her faeries and her daemons. Samarandins constructed homunculi at least partially out of it; All of Incain manufactured Mandroids out of it. So did Dand Tariqartha – form his half-life Mantels out of it, if perhaps not always top to bottom. Kronokronos Mikoto's birthparents were Mantels. The walls of this cave might be his cousins.

The presence of all this Godstuff should have chimed immediate caution. Would have chimed immediate caution had not his ears been blaring so maddeningly loudly he could not have heard his internal alarm system going off even if it had. That the apparent corpse neither stank, nor the fact that there was no evidence of any animals ever nibbling on it, was simply additional testament that the exiled Kronokronos had had his bell rung once too often recently.

He never hesitated. Not for the merest of moments. Drew the Susasword out of the supine body. Three eyes opened. He hadn't noticed them either.

Whoever she was – still was – she came instantly alive. Again!

As if the chains were ephemeral spider webs she tore herself loose; sprang to her feet, howsoever unsteadily. Reminiscent of a fan-dancer or a stripper after ridding herself of a seventh veil, she began whipping the chains still depending from her wrists around as if they were bullroarers. Bellowed she did, as much in exaltation as in relief; bellowed more boisterously than any bull ever roared.

Whereupon the outline of a female figure appeared in the cave. Whereupon a now-shirtless man with a mirror-like shield on his arm leapt out of her outline. Once Vulva-Vetala's soldier had a machine pistol, a hand-Gatling. He riveted the warlord with bullets, grabbed the sword, vanished once more into female's figure. Who promptly sucked in on herself, duplicating his escape.

The re-enlivened devil was not far behind them.

========

The Cosmic Express was launched on Sunday, the Thirtieth of November 1980. Cosmicar Four exploded out of Cathonia and crashed on Damnation Isle, in the Outer Earth's Aleutian Archipelago. Devoid of humans, it nonetheless carried decathonitized devils. In order to find them shells to possess, the lone fourth generational devil amongst them, Antaeor Thanatos, Demon Land, managed to recombine, bodies with spirits, psyches, souls or minds, the ten nominal members of KOC, the King's Own Crimefighters.

They were the supranormals who had vanished on Christmas 1955; the ones whose disappearance Kid Ringo, 12-year-old Aristotle Zeross, blamed on himself. He should never have abandoned them on the Tholos-shaped Aleutian atoll. He was blaming himself unfairly. His memories of being a supranormal were wiped out the night of that same fateful day. He didn't recover them until early May 1960.

KOC was now the Damnation Brigade. What was left of them.

========

Puck rode bareback on a cricket. He was heading to an adjacent cavern, one of a few. He'd never been to this one before and not just because the tunnel to it was always blocked. Caverns full of replicas are no fun. First they have to be activated. Then those in it do exactly the same thing they did for the specific time and space they were replicated from to do. And that was it. Dullsville. He was hoping to liven things up. So were his pals, and there were a lot of them, heading next door. Other than for mischief and mayhem, they didn't know why they were going. Nor did they care. Mischief and mayhem were good enough for them.

Puck was a wight, a fay or a faerie. Far to the south, on the other side of the Hidden Headworld, in Crepuscule, the Grey Land of Twilight, his sprite-like as well as sprightly sort would be classified by the equally generic term of feeorin. Puck lived in the Faerie Garden of Subcranial Temporis. He wasn't a replica. The Faerie Garden had always been in its own cavern. He wanted a smoke. His corn-kernel pipe was hard to light, and keep lit, when you were on the move, so he spurred his cricket into a tree off of a pleasant glade.

Into the clearing, materializing out of between-space, came a man wearing only a tattered pair of black pants and combat boots without socks. Puck knew a man when he saw one; knew what combat boots were, too. He'd been in the gremlin cavern a different direction next door and had seen television – gremlins mucked up machines then, when they were discarded, brought them into their cavern and got them going again. He knew what the man had about him as well: scads of metallic weaponry. Wights disliked metal even more than they disliked weapons.

Slung across his back was an automatic rifle. He had a belt around his waist. It didn't hold bullets, like that of a gunfighter replicated from the Outer Earth's Wild West. It held bullet clips, dozens of them. A fancy gun, probably a machine pistol, was in a holster against his right hip. That weapon took some of the clips; presumably the rifle took the others.

He also had a large, round, almost half-length mirror strapped to his left forearm and a sword of some sort, a slender cutlass maybe, in his right hand. Both the mirror and the sword gave off the telltale glow of Brainrock-Gypsium, thus bodily bequeathing the man a halo or aura about himself. Puck wasn't too sure what to make of them.

Nor was he too sure what to make of the ghost who'd appeared in the glade beside the man. Ghosts weren't very common in the Faerie Garden. Fays frightened them. This ghost was pale in the same pale-green way as the horse, as foretold in the Outer Earth's Biblical Book of the Apocalypse, traditionally ridden by Death. Which fays were familiar with because Dand Tariqartha had replicated a number of different Judgement Day scenarios in Temporis.

He'd never a greenish ghost before. She also looked like a vampire, a bloodsucker, with fangs. Fays dusted vamps. Fays dusted themselves, too, once they died. Made an ash out of themselves, as they fay-said. Then they sprinkled the resultant faeriedust over an ordinary, usually stolen and always entranced mortal, the younger the better, and lived again. They didn't do that with vampiric ash-dust, though. Just let it blow away in the wind. Vamps were killers. Bloodsuckers earned no right to preservation.

Not only was this vamp a ghost, she had three eyes. Which might make her a devil. Other than Dand Tariqartha, whom wights delighted in tormenting whenever he came by for a visit, devils stayed away from the Faerie Garden. That was because fays found them a delicacy. Their long-gone king and queen, Archon Oberon and Cabala Titania, used to eat devils. Puck once did an Oberon and ate their devil-god. The Dand gave him indigestion, so he barfed him up.

Kings must have tougher tummies than Pucks.

========

Perhaps fatalistically, the ten supranormals who escaped Limbo the previous Sedonda, the Thirtieth of Maruta 5980, decided to call themselves the Damnation Brigade, after the Aleutian atoll upon which they were reconstituted by Demon Land. Today, what would be Saturday on the Outer Earth, what was Devauray on the Hidden Continent, nine of them were in the Thousand Caverns of Subcranial Temporis.

Two of the nine entered the Faerie Garden shortly after dawn. One was wearing the Crimson Corona.

========

Someone else sauntered into the glade. She was a stunner, for a human. At about five foot six, with ruddy, almost red skin, she was big-boned, busty but hard in the bosom and hips. Broad and beamy, she had a swimmer's tight musculature. Looked as loaded for maximum wallop as Combat-Boots did. Had a plain-looking satchel slung over her right shoulder – probably a bottomless bag or kibisis, as they called it – and a long hunter's knife sheathed to her side beneath it.

Across her chest she'd strapped a pouched bandolier. She had a holstered dart-gun attached to it, the bandolier, within easy reach of her left hand; a bow over her left shoulder and a quiver full of arrows lashed tightly to her back. Had as well a tangle of rat's nest hair that cascaded to her shoulders then, abruptly, stopped. It was the kind of hair that, if she ever washed it, tried to iron it straight, would probably cover her to the waist.

Puck momentarily fancied he might like to live in it for a while. Then he reconsidered. Weaponry aside, and even if it wasn't a kibisis, he knew a witch when he saw one. Stuff glowed all over her: finger-rings, barbed bracelets, anklets and especially a necklace made out of sparkling gems. Jasper or bloodstone, he reckoned; might even be made out of rubies.

Stuff that glowed like that, like Combat-Boots' mirror and sword, meant Brainrock, what was almost as often called Gypsium beyond the Dome or, much less frequently one either side of it, Godstuff. Witches loved Brainrock, fays hated it. Brainrock came from the sky, when it didn't come from erupting volcanoes.

Wights were earthborn, chthonic critters. They weren't considered hell-spawn because they were celestial angels, not even fallen ones. They weren't Master Devas, who were, hence the word's original meaning: the Shining Ones. Certain witches, Hellions and Mariamnics mostly, used Brainrock to enslave faeries.

She was more bare than barely dressed, which was admirable. A thin, short-sleeved cotton top and a sleeveless leather vest left her midriff exposed. A brief sarong-like skirt, made out of fur, girded her hips. Puck had a thing for nymphs. He knew dozens of them: dryads, naiads, limnads, oreads, nereids, potimids, crenae, pegae, you name it.

Most of them cavorted about naked or nearly naked. When they weren't in their transformed state, that shouldn't need saying, let alone fay-saying, which depended entirely on which sort of nymph you were. She wore moccasins, though. Very unfriendly that. Moccasins, any kind of footwear, desensitized human feet. More than a few of his fay-pals had been crunched beneath desensitized human feet.

Combat-Boots was even more unfriendly, and not just because of his footgear. He pointed the mirror at the witch and damned if she didn't disappear into it. Then she was reflecting out of it. Then she wasn't. The soldier and the ghost exchanged angry words. Puck only caught snippets of it. They weren't happy about something. It wasn't real; she was an illusion. Puck supposed they were right because moments later the witch strode back into the clearing. She had an arrow notched, primed to let fly. She wasn't alone either.

With her was an enormous, panda-bear-sized man, six and a half feet tall and as broad as he was wide. The term brick shithouse came immediately to Puck's mind. He wore a copper-coloured tunic over a perhaps steel-woven underlay of chain-mail, a tanned-leather cummerbund-like girdle about his belly and a sleeve-less green cape.

The top ends of this garment were attached by a large medallion that bore a facsimile of Sedon's Head, the Hidden Continent as well as that of the Moloch Himself, left side perspective. Puck felt the devils' All-Father, as well as the fays' demonic cousins' acknowledged king, should have been on someone's dinner plate a very, very long time ago. You wouldn't need appetizers or even dessert if you had a main meal of Moloch.

The near-giant's salt and pepper hair was stroked back, like the mane of a lion. (Lions ate wights, the blighters.) His beard, more black turning to grey than grey turning to white, stretched to his chest. He sported red leggings and sandals tied with thongs up to his knees. He held in one massive hand a rune-carved cudgel with a heavy, bulbous burl at its top-end. Seeing this last Puck practically swallowed his corn-kernel pipe. The burl was shaped into the likeness of Tariqartha's own hard-head, the least appetizing of the Dand's aspects; what made him barf him up.

Could this actually be whom Puck was suddenly speculating it might be? Could it be the Kronokronos Supreme; the deviant half-son of Dand Tariqartha and Malar Tzigame, unless it was Pyrame Silverstar; the long-gone birth son of his lot longer gone king and queen, Oberon and Titania, unless it was Alberich and Erda? Did that make the woman his perhaps only rumoured sister Meroudys? That was her name, wasn't it? Fays had terribly memories; mostly because they lived for today, could care less about yesterday.

He wished a firefly would flutter-by. His pipe had gone out and he didn't want miss any of what he anticipated was about to occur. Fays were voyeurs, yes, but they were also fabulous raconteurs, even if they had to make up most of it due to the fact that they couldn't be bothered about how it really went.

Because of that, their stories were invariably much more entertaining than those told by that deviated windbag, Jordan 'Q for Rumour's Quill' Tethys, an ad-mittedly generally jovial jerk, as in beer – not beef – jerky, who insisted he always spoke sooth, as in the truth. And how boring was that? (Rumour of Lazareme was a cerebrally salty, but much celery-celebrated repast of the fair folks' past. That was for sure as the burr in his button butt.)

"Stay your hand, boy," recommended maybe-Supreme. "We were hunting Apocalyptics and me-thinks you're in league with them." The Dand-head of the near-giant's shillelagh both glowed and glowered with clout. The ghost and her soldier eyed them curiously, cautiously. Perhaps significantly Combat-Boots didn't point the mirror at either of them.

"Make one false move and I'll pincushion you just as readily," added the witch. Puck reckoned she could do with a dialogue coach.

"Get them, my soldier," commanded the ghost. She could do with one, too, put buckles on Puck's shoe. "The talismans will protect you."

The witch released her arrow and immediately tumbled into the bushes. It snapped harmlessly against the mirror. Puck blinked. Maybe-Supreme was no longer there – presumably because they were right, he was illusionary. Suddenly the witch was behind the soldier; another arrow notched and shot. This time it was his aura that protected the soldier. Once again the arrow broke apart uselessly. Something landed at his feet, a tiny, glowing gemstone.

She grew out of it, the witch; her cut-anything hunting knife in her left hand. He blocked her swipe with his mirrored shield and, with his sword, sliced her in twain at the waist. Puck was impressed with the profligacy of guts and gore. This witch must have taken a Mariamnic Masters Degree in tricksterism. (Fays didn't need to go university, naturally. They were Master Tricksters, unnaturally to almost anyone else.)

The near-giant was abruptly there again, though not in the same place. He'd reappeared behind Combat-Boots. Puck winced involuntarily as he drove his cudgel against the soldier's head. No aura could protect him from a blow like that. Combat-Boots crumpled to the ground. Both the illusion of the witch and the real Maybe-Supreme vanished again.

Puck whistled in approval. He wasn't very big. His whistle wasn't very loud. Then it amplified. No, not amplified – joined. It wasn't an invisible audience, just a very hard to see one. A firebug alit beside him; lit his corn-kernel pipe. The tree was alive, alight, with fellow fays. Faeries loved spectacle. Loved it even more when they didn't have to provide it.

The swiftness of her soldier's defeat, if he was her soldier, must have shocked the vampiric ghost into action. She was a devil as well. Had to be because she scorched the nearby trees and bushes with eyefire. A couple of fays fell to ground, charcoaled. Puck ducked but one wight that dropped as if stunned or stone-coal-dead was a Salamander. Puck despaired for his future. Being fire-resistant, Salamanders were notoriously difficult to ash. He'd have to be hammered into dust before he could be sprinkled on anyone.

Gods below! This witch wasn't just an advanced Anthean, as Puck had assumed. Or, if she was, she was much more than just any everyday-ordinary Ant-Nightingale. She had a stretched-out soul-self that, while in her image, was anything except pretty. It was so badly scorched it looked like it had just broken free from a stake on a blazing pyre; one where it, not the witch, was burning. It grappled with the vampiric ghost, one apparition against another apparition. Stopstone dust sprinkled out of the Grey. The ghost started to harden.

The witch's soul-self disappeared. An arrow as ethereal as the ghost thumped into its back. The ghost collapsed. In a flash the real witch was over it, twisting the arrow. "Who are you, devil?" she demanded. "What are you doing here?" The ghost writhed about silently. The witch bent down, unsheathed her hunting knife with her free hand. She poised it at the ghost's throat. "This thing can cut anything, even a spook. Want me to prove it?"

Maybe-Supreme piled into her from behind, tumbling her onto the ground. The witch flipped backwards onto her feet; threw her knife at her assailant. It embedded in the Dand-head of his sceptre. He dropped both. The ghost vanished, leaving the air-arrow behind. The witch tried to do the same but the agate she produced didn't activate. Something came out of the air – a glowing chain minus the battering ball.

The witch dodged it, danced away from it, spotted the unconscious or dead soldier, manifested a half dozen illusions of herself, and dove for his sword.

========

Warlord Mikoto just lay there. Some of those who wrote or told tales about his exploits and those of his Two Thousand claimed they'd spilt an ocean of blood in their decades of wilful warfare. An ocean of blood wasn't spilling out of him, although a large puddle of it already had. So long as his heart pumped he fancied he might make for a small pond.

He wallowed in it. Didn't have any choice in the matter. He realized even his fabled recuperative abilities weren't going to be enough this time.

He had no idea who'd killed him.

****

(Game-Gambit) 16: **Freespirit Nihila**

Devauray, Tantalar 6, 5980

Brainrock radiating chains were instantly everywhere, a glowing, glade-wide, butterfly net, a shimming spider web of thick, interlinked thread. They were unavoidable; ravelled the witch like a cat in a spool of yarn. Maybe-Supreme was similarly entangled; had been when he drove her off the vampiric ghost.

They were akin to marinade-marionettes on puppet-string-strands of spaghetti, it seemed to Puck, who was feeling peckish.

========

Yet another female devil came out of the Weird. Better and better. Where was the huckleberry wine when you wanted some? Even more wasted-looking than the witch's soul-self, this one was at least flesh and blood; though there wasn't much left of the former and far too much of the latter. Absolutely not a pretty sight, especially with a great gash in her chest through which Puck could clearly see her heart pumping. It was the first time he realized devils had hearts. Until then he thought they were just demons with bigger brains.

What hair she had was white. It clung to patches of scalp on her otherwise mostly skinless skull. She was dressed in a hole-rived smock or hauberk made out of rusted chain-mail that seemed to extend off a dimly glimmering torc or torque around her neck. If only because it was slightly brighter than her chain-mail smock or the chains wrapped around the two apparent humans, Puck figured the torc had to be her power focus.

The chains were manacled to each of her skeletal wrists by what amounted to mini-torques. She yanked on them, the chains. The humans visibly weakened, their struggling lessened. Enervation, that was the word for it. It was as if they weren't up for it anymore. The devil's chest began to knit itself back together. She was siphoning out their vitality; was debilitating them in order to rehabilitate herself.

"Do something, old man," Puck heard the witch plead with the near-giant. "Snap the chains and go get her."

"Conserve your strength, Witch. I'll act as needed."

"Once I was Datong Harmonia, called thus by antique Illuminaries but best known as simply Harmony, the Unity of Balance," announced the devil, entirely unbidden. "From today on I am renaming myself Freespirit Nihila, she who cares for nothing save my own harmony. Howsoever I look, I am the eldest daughter of Thrygragos Lazareme."

"Oh fuck!" cursed the witch. "Now will you do something?"

Faeries were infamous for their cursing. You didn't want a faerie to curse you. They rarely used such trite curse-words, however. It was so unimaginative. Puck wished he had a mushroom cap for every time a human told him to get the puck out of here. Then he'd been one fat pucker. The witch must have heard of Harmony; Puck knew he had. Didn't like the sounds of Nihila, though. It sounded positively negative.

The old man shrugged his massive shoulders. "Considering my options, which don't seem too plentiful at the moment, I'm doing about all I can do right now, Witch."

Newly named Nihila must have been encouraged by his answer. "Pray forgive the abruptness of my appearance," she carried on. "Forgive my appearance period. I was rather rudely put to sleep and just as rudely awakened earlier this morning. What year is it?"

"5980," he obliged her.

"5980 – nearly five hundred years," she mumbled wistfully, gazing about. "Another cave," she said. "Much roomier than the last one. And with a sun. Must be Temporis. Is my brother in Lazareme still around then?"

"I am Tariqartha's eldest son, if that's who you mean. My name is Akbarartha, Kronokronos Supreme of Temporis." Puck congratulated himself. Except, wasn't Akbar supposed to have a regalia? "I gather you are my aunt. If we truly have a blood bond then release us."

"And you, witch woman?"

"She calls herself Wilderwitch," Akbar answered for her. "She's a member of the Superior Sisterhood of Flowery Anthea. She's wholly mortal as far as either of us knows."

"The Goddess of Life Returning, Father Lazareme's embodiment of the Spring Season, is also my sister. Anthea, as ancient Illuminaries named her, after the reprehensible founder of her otherwise admirable sisterhood, was from the breed between myself and my brother Unities and that of Time-Space, the physician and the artificer.

"You both have distinguished forbearers. Strictly speaking devic blood does not mingle with mortal blood but, nonetheless, we are in a way family. Fecundity, Nergal Vetala, although I rather liked her once, isn't. She's a daughter of Thrygragos Mithras, who once tried to supplant my father as the Headworld's foremost Great God. You were fighting her, which might mean you are my ally, but you are also wearing the Mind of Sapiendev, which can only mean you are my enemy. Take it off and toss it down with the others. Then I shall release you."

"It's not that easy," protested the Witch. Nihila yanked her chain again. Wilderwitch almost passed out. The devil's skin was now almost fully re-grown. Her complexion had also improved noticeably. Not so her disposition.

"Obey me!"

"I can't get it off. It's like it's fused to me."

"Is that all? Skin can be removed. Cut it off her, son of Tariqartha." She whipped his chain, slackening it enough to let him somewhat move.

Responsively, he bent down and picked up his Homeworld Sceptre, as Puck recalled it was called. He was drawing a blank on the Mind of Sapiendev. Something else he couldn't remember was what Akbar's regalia was called, let alone what constituted it. He vaguely recalled there was a book on his exploits, so it'd be in there.

Not that there were any libraries nearby. Besides, he couldn't recall what it was called either. It'd come to him. Then it did – the Akbarnama. The beer-jerky Legendarian wrote it, or recited it to an Illuminary, more likely. Faeries were lucky if they could recollect their own names. He was just a Puck, a fairy type more so than a distinct individual.

When he got together with a bunch of other Pucks they called themselves after Outer Earth hockey players the gremlins told them about. Once the huckleberry wine was flowing they'd get into barroom brawls over which one of them was Guy La Fleur. Which was usually when the gremlins, or whomever they were drinking with, started shouting: *'Get those Pucks the puck out of here!'*

Sidling up to the Witch, Akbar pulled her hunting knife out of his sceptre's Dand-head then clubbed her with it. The bloodstone tiara around her neck fell off. The chains exploded, sending Nihila tumbling to the ground. Freed, her knife already sheathed, her dart-gun drawn and moving at speed, Wilderwitch rapid-fired a dozen darts into the devil. She scampered up Puck's tree, damn near scaring the Puck out of it, but didn't seem to notice he was there. She snapped another clip of darts into her gun.

The Awesome Akbar, as the storytellers often referred to Supreme, hadn't retreated whatsoever. He stood over this self-proclaimed Freespirit Nihila, his sceptre primed like a pool cue at the cue ball of the devil's head. Evidently devic hair wasn't as quick to re-grow as devic skin, though hers was getting stubbly for a cue ball.

"Five hundred years or not, dear aunt, I find your lack of decorum deplorable. I am heir-presumptive to Temporis. If mortals can have such a thing, Temporis may become my protectorate someday. You will speak considerately and specifically. Otherwise we will see if my sceptre can cathonitize devils. Stand, if you can."

Freed physically as well as spiritually, Freespirit Nihila staggered to her feet unaided. She was plucking the Witch's darts out of her skin. And her chain-mail smock, though skin and smock might have been one and the same by now. Unless they always were, just looked like they weren't. Harmony had always been considered incomparable, as if she was unique amongst devazurkind. So maybe her Nihila-aspect didn't need a debrained demonic body in order to achieve individual solidity any more than her Harmony-aspect had.

"Once again, my apologies. I would not have killed you. Nor even drained you overly much. As you can see, I am becoming healthier by the minute. We devils heal rapidly. My concern was with Crinsom's crown. Together with Susal's sword, which has kept me immobile for half a millennium, and Amateram's mirror, they make up the Trigregos Talismans. My only desire is to destroy them."

"How?" Akbar demanded.

Puck had it now, the collective name of Supreme's regalia. They were called the Thrygragos Talismans. Although like all things Gypsium-Brainrock they were mutable, Akbar's regalia consisted of the Mask of Byron, the Cloak of Lazareme and the Cross of Mithras. He'd have to ask him what he'd done with them. Maybe he could promise to barf up his witch as an inducement. She looked scrumptious. She'd also just sat on the firefly. He hoped the bug burnt her bottom. She deserved it for fire-frying his ass.

"By taking them to Sedon's Peak. It's a volcano in the protectorate of my brother, your immediate half-uncle, old man, Anvil the Artificer – Lazareme's Smithy, he whom Illuminaries of Weir named Tvasitar in a bygone era, after another godly smith of an Outer Earth pantheon. The Peak's on the Cattail Peninsula. Its crater is filled with molten Brainrock. I intend to melt them back into slag there. Surely your devic half-father would approve."

"Then take them and go. Wilderwitch and I have work to do. We'll countenance no further distractions." He pointed at the Crimson Corona, which had fallen off the Witch as soon as he'd contacted it with his sceptre. It was lying beside the prone form of the soldier, along with his sword. The mirrored shield was still strapped to his arm.

"My thanks, Kronokronos. You are much wiser than I would have thought. Either your blood-father or birthmother must have been truly special because my younger brother usually half-sires simpletons. As for you, Anthean," she said as Wilderwitch, buttocks unburned, clambered nimbly out of the tree. "You too are truly special. How special neither of you probably realizes. But my chains would have stopped you no more than they stopped your companion. Rather, in all likelihood, you would have made them your own."

Rude sort that she was, poor firebug, Wilderwitch didn't say anything; merely took Akbarartha by his arm and tossed an Anthean Agate at their feet. Whereupon, her stepping forward onto it and him stepping on it after her, they were gone. The ex-Unity was left staring after them. She muttered something after they went away but Puck was too busy stuffing his corn-kernel pipe with the squished firebug to fay-pay her any mind. There was just enough heat left in his fellow wight to puff it going again.

You didn't have to make an ash of yourself. Most faeries were happy to do it for you.

========

Yomikune and Katatribe Tethys stumbled out of the cave, coughing and sputtering from inhaling the dust and crud raised by its roof's collapse. The two much younger, male samurais the warlord left to guard its opening let them pass unscathed. They were only supposed to stop anyone trying to enter it, pandas included. They weren't supposed to stop anyone exiting it.

Andaemyn Sarpedon rushed up to them; wanted to embrace them but held off. Their blades were as sharp as their tempers were short.

========

"Where's Mikoto and the other two?" she insisted on knowing.

The two remaining Tethys triplets were too stuffed-up to respond. That had been a narrow thing. Falling to their knees, between cough-wracks they examined each other silently, like chimps – Pansies in Godbad's Goatwood, Sedon's Beard, where they were a sentient but put-upon minority – combing their fellows' fur for nits to nip. Samurais weren't known for being talkative anyways.

Andy was only one of five *'barbarians'* with Warlord Mikoto's mercenary band of Good Companions, as they thought of themselves. Another was her latest lover. He was exactly the same age as her; was born around the Summer Solstice of 5953. His name was Sabreur Somata and, yes, that meant they might be ever-so-distantly related. He'd joined Mikoto's band at the age of 12; spent most of the fifteen years since then apprenticing to the company's surgeons and herbalists. Which today numbered all of one, him. He took charge of the Tethys twosome.

Sabreur was a Dukkhan, the same as a different Janna, St Peche-Montressor, Alpha Centauri's daughter-law. The Somata surname came from an era pre-Terrible-Twins, from long before Janna and Sraddha Somata were born. He had black skin like the Terrible Twins' Sraddha had, though not Janna eventually Fangfingers.

Presumably, therefore, his Utopian ancestors had reached Sedon's Upper Lip, in south-western Marutia, while the Weirdom of Kanin, starting in the 49th Century of the Dome, was busy turning Sedon's Cheek into an empire, called a Mastery, to replace that of Frozen Lathakra. Presumably as well, his ancestors had just stayed there.

Two of the other barbarians were Godbadians. Andy suspected they were brothers. She didn't suspect they were part-Bandradin. Orangey skin-pigmentation and a fruity-orange skin-complexion confirmed that in her mind. During the course of the Godbadian Civil War, which lasted throughout most of the Fifties until the very early Sixties, Bandradins, for so long the darlings of Great Byron and his Spawn, were anathematized.

Nowadays, most of 20-years later, Bandradins or part-Bandradins were treated no better, nor any worse, than any other Greater Godbadian citizen. King Achigan Auranja himself was a Summoning Child, the same as Andy's Utopian or near-Utopian parents, Demios and Morgianna. While the Civil War raged on he and his just as Bandrad-descended aristocratic elite fled to the Duchy of Achigan, after him, on the Fobbiat-coastline of Sedon's Lower Lip, leaving others to do their fighting.

As a consequence of their abandoning the field, they still weren't very popular. Neither were Bandradins or part-Bandradins who'd returned to their ancestral homeland in the high plateau of the Cattail Peninsula in order to escape what passed for justice in the resultant, at least nominal democracy, the Corporate State of Greater Godbad

Regardless of how fair it was in terms of the greater scheme of things, privacy was respected there. Money, Godbucks, not birthright, counted for almost everything there. So you had to wonder why two part-Bandradins – Tucedon and Salamoneus were their first names – chose to keep their surnames secret. Still, the one rule Mikoto had, other than nobody was allowed to question his rulings, was that no one asked questions about anyone else's past.

Accordingly, no answers of that nature, solicited or unsolicited, were ever volunteered. So it was, whoever they were in actuality, whoever their parents were more like, since they weren't much older than Andy or Sabreur, at most in their mid-thirties, they were just good companions, brothers-in-arms.

As for whether they were actual brothers, the former was slight; the latter was about as big as any Godbadian was big, which was fairly large, so they didn't look much alike. Besides, don't ask, don't tell, applied there too. Yomikune and Katatribe made no bones about their relationship; Tucedon and Salamoneus never mentioned anything about their family trees.

It was the former, who pointed skyward: "Vultyrie, Gatherers, coming."

The last of the five barbarians was extremely pale-skinned. Conceivably he was a Pani; for sure he was a Krachlan. Krachla lay at the head of the Penile Peninsula, Sedon's Mutton Chop, the shaft of which was Hadd. Like the Grey Land of Crepuscule, it rained in Krachla but the sun didn't shine there very long or very often. Panis, many of whom were albinos, were its dominant race. Krachla was where he'd joined them. That's why they considered him a Krachlan for sure.

His name was Alastor Molorchus. He'd lost his left arm in an unspecified accident a dozen years earlier. The rotator-cuff of his left shoulder still rotated. He was rotating it. He was also Brainrock-blessed. "Who's in charge?" he insisted on knowing. So long as he'd been there before, he could send the Vultyrie, and the shape-shifting Rakshas demons riding them, to wherever anyone told him. He just couldn't self-send himself anywhere.

"I am," said Mikoto. The Warlord clomped out of the panda's cave. Both his sheathed swords were secured in his waist-sash. Gripping the neckbands of their bamboo armour in either hand, he was dragging the samurais caught in the collapsing ceiling out of the cave with him. They, a man and a woman, were breathing. He was puffing on a cigar.

"Nice try, granddad," said Andy. "Who killed him?"

Auguste Moirnoir wafted out of the former Kronokronos – former in all senses of the word *'former'*. As he did so, tattered opera clothes and cigar, no top hat, Mikoto collapsed, dead to not just the world. Sabreur didn't waste any time checking on him. Instead he switched his attentions from the Tethys twosome, who were fine, to the two samurais the Voodoo Child hauled out of the cave by animating the dead warlord.

They weren't doing so well. Sabreur wondered how many Sangazur Spirit Selves the Gatherers had brought with them. Molorchus, who had his reasons for avoiding Young Death, went to greet the Rakshas demons as they landed their Vultyrie. The male trickster suspected what those reasons were but he wasn't the judgemental sort.

"You'll have to ask him yourself, grandchild," Young Death said to Andy. "Once the Gatherers have resurrected him. I'd recommend you aren't here when they do, though. Dead or alive, Mikoto's a vicious, self-righteous bastard.

"Fact is I wouldn't recommend any of you be here when they do, not even the Rakshas. He'll want to kill someone right away. I can help you avoid that, should you be so inclined, expressly so. Say the word, I'll incline my head, nod it, and a free ride to the Sraddha Isle monastery is yours for the taking."

Yomikune Tethys, the then-triplet who'd cut off her father's head in 5950, cut it off so swiftly his death was painless, perked up at that. "Free ride?"

"Free-form drawing, put better. For Molorchus as well, should he be so inclined."

========

A Gypsium hoop appeared beneath the ex-Unity's feet. Before Freespirit Nihila realized what was happening to her, she'd fallen through it and was halfway across the Hidden Continent.

"Harmonious landings, Balance," chortled Aristotle Zeross in the Faerie Garden. He bent to pick up the Crimson Corona.

Vetala's soldier wasn't dead!

========

No. Not Dead. More alive than ever. Bull headfirst into stranger's gut. Lift knee to jaw. Stranger? No. Something familiar about him. No matter. Combat boot in face. His face. Face of familiar stranger. Pick up tiara. String round head. My head. Power. Strength. Always tough and fast, killer instinct inbred. Now big, tough, and fast.

"What say, goddess? Off with his head?"

========

"This is your failing, Smiler."

========

King Cold, Tantal Thanatos, angrily rounded on the ever-grinning fiend standing right behind him. Lathakra's gigantic potentate was pounding his massive fists against a heavy oaken table. A huge stein brimful of foaming, now jiggling lager jumped in front of him as if on a trampoline. Hot Stuff, his haughty but lately tiny perfect wife and immediate sister, was striving valiantly to retain her dignity while, at the same time, she maintained her footing in an attempt to continue standing on the selfsame bouncy table.

Perched on a tripod overtop one of Methandra's firestones on the other side of said table, her – rather, Titanic Metis's – revelatory cauldron fumed forth simultaneous visions somehow broadcast from the Faerie Garden. It saved on the headaches individual devils sometimes accrued from far-seeing for too long at one sitting. It also allowed for a collective experience, one that none of the three there in the glacial palace's viewing room was currently enjoying.

"The Nergalid's soldier's become a kind of Trigregos Incarnate," the male of the Frozen Isle's two resident Death Gods ranted. "He'll kill Dr Zeross and, without him, how are we going to bring our children down from the moon?"

"My failing, you enormous ignoramus? I dealt with the Nergalid precisely as I have dealt with every other fool tempted to play a Trigregos Gambit in recent centuries. I wiped the absurd notion from her mind. I had no indication her Outer Earthling pet was anything more than her personal drinking fountain or I would have wiped him as well.

"Better to have wiped him out altogether."

"Perhaps so, in hindsight. You and your wife were supposed to concentrate on what's going on in Temporis. That cavern — that's where your precious Earth Elemental is cowering. Have him dispose of them!"

"Never use that tone with me! This is my protectorate."

King Cold raised himself unsteadily to his full 12-foot height. He was reaching for his Labrys, the double-headed Brainrock war-axe strapped to his back, whereupon, as it had so often in the past 47-years, Smoky Sedona's Spell of Disproportionment reversed itself without warning. Methandra shot from toy-stature to a 10-foot-tall giantess, tumbling inelegantly backwards off the table as she did so.

Tantal, leaning forward, went from twelve feet to eight inches. Falling into his stein of beer, he struggled to swim out of it. Recovering as quickly and as gracefully as she could manage, his sister-wife regained her feet, plucked him out of the stein as one would a dropped lap dog out of a toilet bowl, and placed him on the thankfully sturdy table.

"Our protectorate," she corrected him, as unaware as he was that there had ever been more than just the two of them in the palatial chambre wherein she kept her purloined cauldron.

(In days of yore as well as lore on the Aegean island of Crete, which Lathakra resembled, albeit from the sky, a Labrys was considered as much of a sacred object as a cauldron. Both were emblematic of the matriarchal Goddess Culture that thrived in the Outer Earth's Middle or Mediterranean Sea from circa 2000 to 1500 BCE. Indeed, the myth of the Minotaur and the maze-like Labyrinth originated there during those self-same, so-called Minoan times, which devils still referred to as the mad goddess's man-hating matriarchate.

(While a cauldron obviously symbolized a woman's external genitalia, a Labrys supposedly represented the fallopian tube and ovaries of her internal reproductive system. In reality, then as now, it was just Tantal's Tvasitar talisman or power focus. Also then as now, he was big-cheese-mad-goddess Methandra's most constant male companion. Then, though, Hot Stuff was resolutely Mithras's Virgin so he wasn't identified as her spouse, merely her immediate brother.

(As if to keep his burgeoning reputation intact amongst their devic siblings and cousins, he spent most of his non-consort hours impregnating the matriarchate's other, much more responsive mad goddesses with azuras. So it was to this day and age, he still had more spirit being offspring than any other devil save, perhaps, for their long gone father, Thrygragos Varuna Mithras.)

"Faagh!" he shook himself off. "This can't happen now. Trigregos is killing Zeross."

"It's happened," boomed the Seeress. "No!" she gasped, after glancing at the visionary vapours coming out of her cauldron. "He's hesitating. Fecundity must be calling to him."

Devils counted instantaneous teleportation among their most ho-hum talents.

========

Fisticuffs had never been Harry's specialty. With his rings, there was never any need to get into a kafuffle. And perhaps that was just as well.

He wouldn't have stood a chance against Vetala's soldier in any case.

========

The sudden ferocity of the half-naked maniac's assault left him bashed and brain-boggled; disoriented if not bodily disjointed. Not yet anyhow. He was having trouble catching his breath, breathing period. He spat blood, felt light-headed, queasy, self-diagnosed concussive. His vision was blurry but that wasn't an excuse not to believe his eyes.

There was once, Harry would have heard, a Trigregos Titaness. Her first name was the same as his wife's. Her surname was the same as that given to Morgianna born Nauroz, nowadays also Sarpedon, younger sister of Cabalarkon's current Master, Saladin Devason. Howsoever ironically, that Melina's husband Zalman was responsible for emancipating the Sarpedon underclass, from whom his Mel descended. That Mel died during the Thousand Days of the Disbelief. Centuries later, Dem's Dim must be becoming akin to a Trigregos Titan.

In his childhood he had seen supras such as the last two Olympians (Numbers Two and Three being his mother and his brother), the justifiably egocentric Mr. Brilliant, the stunningly beautiful Radiant Rider and the silver-clad Conquering Christ in action. All of them exuded the equivalent of St Elmo's Fire whilst they were using their supranormal attributes. Only one came close to this and that was Demonites, Olympian III, when the King Crimefighters took him down on Aegean Trigon, the ancestral island home of the Family Zeross, a quarter century ago almost to the day.

When the soldier put on the ruby- or bloodstone-bejewelled crown, he instantaneously transformed; grew at least six inches taller and filled out mightily. His skin turned golden-brown, rippled with muscles and radiated energy, Gypsium energy. Last night the female vamp with the fang-fingered glove had glowed somewhat similarly but nowhere near as intensely. Harry was witnessing an apotheosis. His nephew had apparently turned into a god with guns.

"In Dem's name, Dim, stop it," Ringleader shouted at the evidently mind-numbed bastard. As badly beaten up as he was, he could still appeal for his life. "You're Dmetri Diomad. You're a Cosmicaptain. Your baby brother and sister, Baalbek and Angelica, I met them. On the Head. I saved them. Come with me. I can save you."

Vetala's thrall kneed him in the balls.

========

"Close your eyes and come to me, my soldier."
"Wait."
"No! Come! Now!" He did as his goddess bade.
A newly emergent Trigregos Titan could teleport as near-instantly as a devil could.

========

When he reopened his eyes he found himself some four thousand miles south, in Hadd, on the pinnacle of Dustmound. Vetala was sitting in her Brainrock throne. Beside her stood a pinkish-skinned, three-eyed male with too many fingers on each hand and too many knuckles on the too many fingers he was using to hold onto his no doubt seriously sinister syrinx.

He was wearing darkish, almost insubstantial raiment and a flat-topped mitre. If the man had a beard and no third eye, he might have passed for a terrifying Greek Orthodox minister from his native land – if he had a native land. He was terrifying anyhow. And the Greek Orthodox ministers he recalled coming across no more smiled than they ever played a panpipe.

This one did both, the smiling incessantly.

"Are you finally satisfied, Judge? Even in the midst of battle, thousands of miles north of here, even with the powers of Trigregos, my titan does as I bid."

"Satisfied, Blood Queen? No, never! He is alive and without anyone possessing him, he could rebel from you at any moment."

"That's what titans do classically, rebel. But he won't."

"So you say. With the thrice-cursed talismans he's acquired against all odds, he's too powerful to be trusted. Kill him, I say!"

========

On the Frozen Isle of Lathakra, tiny Tantal and enormous Methandra breathed a sigh of relief. No longer Fecundity, Vulva-Vetala, must have recalled her soldier.

"That was too close," yelled Old King Cold at the top of his lungs.

"We're going to have take charge, husband," whispered the Scarlet Seeress at the bottom of hers. "No one can help us but ourselves"

"All right. I'll take care of the children we've found and guarantee the cooperation of Dr Zeross. Just make sure you don't lose sight of him."

========

Ringleader watched his nephew – not that he was just that anymore, if he ever had been – vanish into the dark-grey universal substance of Samsara, the Weird, between-space. He could have followed but there wasn't much doubt where he'd gone. To Hadd. To Vetala. Next question was whether the Blood Queen possessed him as the now twice-catasterized Cousins had Baal, Ange and Carmine Carmichael.

No, that wasn't the next question. The next question was what was he going to do about them. Thartarre Holgatson and Ferdinand Niarchos would have to be warned. Maybe Quentin Anvil would have to postpone Operation Haas until he'd sorted out the devil and her deadly dupe. Perhaps there was a way he could save his bastard nephew.

Then again, why bother? Dmetri Diomad probably didn't deserve saving. Not after what he'd done in '68, when he betrayed Kadmon Heliopolis and the then latest incarnation of the Black Rose of Anarchy to anagram-AMERICA. Or his subsequent stints as a counter-revolutionary operative for actual-America in Vietnam, Chile and elsewhere. For a 27-year-old, Dem's Dim had amassed a legacy very few could rival. Killers like him weren't made. They were born.

Although he hadn't thought about it for years, he had to wonder anew whether Demonites was Dim's father. Or what kind of truly horrible woman his ostensible mother, Roxanne nee Heliopolis Kinesis, the supra codenamed Slipper, was to have had a son like him. If Hot Rox – a Lovely Lady Afrite, if ever there was one – was his mother; if Diomad hadn't just hatched, out of an egg left by a snake in the grass.

Ringleader was under no illusions. He knew he wasn't up to tangling with Nergal Vetala gone vampiric and her soldier by himself, not now that Dim had the much sought-after Trigregos Talismans. Fortunately, ha-ha, serendipity was seemingly in play – though not Serendipity Luck, another long-gone supra. If two were alive, why not the other eight?

First things first. He heaved to the ground and began to vomit violently. Again. He'd had too much beer last night in Petrograd and the Danq, fine. Puking most of the night away could be blamed on that, he supposed between spasms. The smell of the burn-pit could account for this morning's gut-wrenching experience. Being trashed by his own nephew, receiving a knee in the nuts in particular, what else could he expect except what he was doing?

He couldn't be getting Gypsium sick. He better not be. He couldn't afford the time needed to recover.

========

Deciding the spectacle was over Puck clambered back onto his cricket. Most of the other fays who'd stopped off, as he had, to be a goose and have a gander at the goings-on in the glade had already recommenced their exodus next door. Must be quite the cooking party happening there. What was it called anyways?

He had it. Dand Tariqartha called it the Calvary Cavern.

========

Nevair Neverknight was charging at her. Bodiless Byron's ebon-armoured, long-ago decathonitized paladin was crazed with bloodlust. Which was appropriate since they were in the Bloodlands.

Guardian Angel Tyrtod didn't realize he had a guardian angel of his own.

****

(Game-Gambit) 17: **Devil Rebel**

Devauray, Tantalar 6, 5980

Hovering above Sisert, Sedon's Cranium, Thrygragos Byron and his three Primary Nucleoids, fused together as the Byronic Nucleus, had been waiting all night and half the day for their moment of glory. Beneath them, beneath the Silent Sands of Cathune Bubastis, were the Thousand Caverns of Temporis. As the devic protectorate of Dand Tariqartha, Thrygragos Lazareme's Persian or Earth Magician, even Bodiless Byron could not venture down there.

Consequently, they had conscripted the nine remaining members of the Damnation Brigade – an admirable if riskily named band of only recently reconstituted, bodies with souls, Outer Earth supranormals – to drive the four main Apocalyptics and their two allies up here, to Drought's only recently revealed-as-former devic domain, where Byronics could act unimpeded.

Soon it would be over. Soon the Byronic Nucleus would recathonitize the Sedonda-decathonitized devils and could continue remaking the Hidden Headworld as the Great God pleased.

It was the Unmoving One's age. Why shouldn't Sedon's Head become Byron's Head?

========

With the evident destruction of the Cosmic Express on Sedonda-Sunday, the week could not have got off to a worst start. Since then though, all things considered, matters had proceeded splendidly. Demetray-Tuesday had been the best by far because, with one swift masterstroke, and without having to ill-star anyone, Thrygragos Byron had turned Mithradite against Mithradite. The outcome was much of the Upper Head was now under his control and that of a number of his third generational offspring.

It had been a brilliant ploy, hundred of years in the making. After the Thousand Days of Disbelief, which ended in 5495, the Lake Lands and the Floodlands, two already territorially immense Mithradite domains in the Upper Head, respectively the protectorates of the Emperor Chameleon and Klizarod Rex, enlarged dramatically. The Lakes expanded from the east while the Floods expanded from the west. They'd actually been touching for more than century before Great Byron realized exactly how he could take advantage of the situation.

Their touching was ideal for the Mithradite Master Devas whose protector-ates were in Marutia, Sedon's Cheek, south of them. Since, as one might suppose from their geographical designations, they were both wetlands, their linkage effect-ively cut off incursions through them into the Cheeks from the Ghostlands to their north. Then, starting about thirty years ago, the Upper Head began experiencing an increasingly severe drought. The resultant corridor of abnormally parched land be-tween them was allowing Underlord Yama Nergal and his Inglorious Dead, Death's Angels, easy access to the Cheeks.

The Underlord, the devic Grim Reaper, let it be known he was marching out of the Ghosts. He and his Inglorious Dead wouldn't stop until they reached the Forbidden Forest of Tal and, through it, Hadd, the Land of the Ambulatory Dead, where the rest of his Nergalazurs dwelt. Thus provoked, many of the Master Devas whose protectorates were in the Cheeks demanded Thrygragos Byron intercede on their behalf. Which he and his Spawn successfully did. Of course, surprise, surprise, he and his Spawn had also been responsible for the drought.

Naturally not everything had gone precisely according to plan. Especially after the disaster that had been the launching of the Cosmic Express from the Outer Earth's Centauri Island on Sedonda, he couldn't have expected it would. Yama Ner-gal escaping cathonitization by fleeing back to the Ghosts was a major disappoint-ment.

However, due to the fact that Nergalazurs, like their siblings or half-siblings, the Haddazurs, couldn't maintain control of the corpses they animated during dir-ect rains, floods or submersion in running water, the Underlord had lost most of his army. So that was a decided plus. In a borderline-acceptable, crow-eating way, so was having his two surviving firstborn, Savage Storm and Gravity, back in the realm of the fully free.

Tradeoffs had to made. There was no getting around it. That, as a result of them, King Cold's Lathakra was back on his internal radar screen, well ... The truth was, even though Outer Earthlings didn't invent radar until a few decades ago; even though, as well, it had been well over a thousand years since the expansion and subsequent retraction of the Lathakran Empire; it had never really been off his radar screen.

Lathakra was a volcanically active island thousands of miles south of the Up-per Head, off the east coast of the Cattail Peninsula. It was separated from the peninsula's mainland by the Strait of Clouds. As a reward for her aid, particularly against Underlord Yama's Inglorious Dead on Demetray, Byron re-deeded his only surviving firstborn daughter, Umashakti Silvercloud, with The Argent, the Cattail's nearest metropolis to the Frozen Isle.

Umashakti, as Illuminaries named her after a couple of Vedic or Hindu god-desses on the Outer Earth, was Byron's Moon Mistress; hence also Lunar Uma. Gravity was her attribute. Along with her husband-brother, her fellow firstborn, Savage Storm, Rudra Silvercloud, that made her his most powerful offspring.

Yet, once he'd released her from All of Incain on Mithrada-Monday, he was left with no other choice. Thinking one of his second-born, Vayu Maelstrom, Devil Wind, a Primary Nucleoid, lost on the Outer Earth, he couldn't have done what he'd planned to do on the Upper Head for so many years without the Silverclouds' willing assistance.

Just as the Silverclouds were his, Heat and Cold, Methandra and Tantal Thanatos, were Thrygragos Varuna Mithras's two still-extant firstborn. As Unmoving Byron and, indeed, both his second generational brothers in Sedon knew from grim experience, dealing with firstborns was a delicate business. Not that Mithras, being both dead and having the common courtesy to stay dead since Thrygragon, knew anything anymore.

Spun positively, Byron had to be glad he still had his two left. Their abilities were as impressive as they were useful. And of course they were his to command. Which he would do, albeit only as necessity demanded, since they could be wilful and pernickety. Funny how commands could backfire if specificity wasn't precise. (Actually, it was funny in no way whatsoever.)

Dealing with firstborns kept you on your toes. Was stimulating, put better, since he didn't have any toes. (Being bodiless, Byron was all head.) And they being his did give him a leg up, make that an advantage, over Thrygragos Lazareme, who didn't have any left. Not unless you counted Unholy Abaddon, the onetime Unity of Chaos, who was a devic suicide and hadn't been seen in decades. Which might be part of the reason he, aka Thrygragos Everyman, remained asleep on Tympani, the Isle of the Undying One, in the midst of the Aural Sea, Sedon's Ear.

Spun negatively, what troubled him most was the Silverclouds had long been friendly with the Thanatoids of Lathakra. For almost as long Rufous Rudra – called such because the striped, tigerish fur he sported instead of hair was more reddish than brownish – had been positioned in the Sea of Clouds, between the Frozen Isle and The Argent.

Ostensibly, that had been to keep the Mithradite firstborns in check. He'd placed Uma in The Argent for the same reason, as the next line of defence as it were. It had been a smart move until she more so than he stepped over said line in 5933. Although it wasn't against his expressed orders – third generational Master Devas were genetically incapable of disobeying their father's commands, at least overtly – that was when the Silverclouds escorted the Parents Thanatos and their then-ten, fourth generational devic offspring to Sedon's Peak.

There Tvasitar, Anvil, the Lazaremists' smithy or artificer, forged them individual power foci. It was a trap of course. Unfortunately, Byron had deliberately kept Rudra and Uma in the dark about that. She got intolerably huffy, even defiant. So, hardly for the first time, he stuck her within All the self-proclaimed invincible she-sphinx of Incain as punishment for her temerity.

In Vayu Maelstrom, Devil Wind's absence, deals had to be made. His Beast persuaded him that nearly 50 years imprisonment was enough chastisement for his wife and breed sister and he was probably right. However, imminent measures demanded other, much more potentially portentous decisions had to be made at the same time.

He couldn't fuse his Primary Nucleus without Vayu but circumstances in the Upper Head might necessitate he ill-star two or three ever-recalcitrant Mithradites, the likes of Underlord Yama and the almost as highborn Reptilian brood brothers, Klizarod and Chameleon. Because they weren't compatible with each other, he couldn't do that by fusing with the Silverclouds and his other two Primary Nucleoids, Sedona Spellbinder and Chimaera Glimmenmare, but he could with his Secondary Nucleus: Damon Goldenrod, Aphropsyche Morningstar and his onetime paladin, Nevair Neverknight.

That required releasing Neverknight from the Prison Beach. To do so would entail making an additional compromise in order to secure his wholehearted aid. He'd refused to pay the price Nevair would inevitably demand previously because he couldn't violate his own pre-made agreements. Indeed, he'd been forced to imprison him for trying to get it anyhow. But times had changed in the last hundred and fifty years so he could now. That didn't mean he wanted to, though.

As events went on Demetray-Tuesday, he hadn't been forced to cathonitize anyone. A couple of days later, on Sapienda-Thursday, he'd gone to the Outer Earth together with Smoky Sedona and ever-changing Chimaera. Thanks mostly to her, Sedona, his usual mouthpiece, he'd managed to track down and in effect resurrect Vayu. Which of course meant he no longer needed his Secondary Nucleus to catasterize anyone.

He still had to pay the paladin's price, however, and it was nothing less than the right to make the Bloodlands, New Valhalla, Sedon's Inner Nose, the domain of Sangazur spirit beings, his own inviolate protectorate. As controversial as his decision was to accede to the Silverclouds' desire to stay together so near Lathakra – his Moon, like Mithras's Heat, was a supporter of the witches' version of the Panharmonium Project – deciding to deed the Bloods to Nevair was a no-brainer as far as everyone except the Great God was concerned.

He didn't allow any of his offspring have their own protectorate; never had. Sooth said, he'd only been party to allowing the Mithradites freedom to acquire theirs because his Great God of a Lord Laziest brother, via Lazareme's brainy and beautiful firstborn, Datong Harmonia, figured it was the only way they'd turn against their unjustifiably ambitious father on Thrygragon.

(It remained almost impossible for his brothers and their highest born to conceive of that Great God's unmitigated gall. He must have been absolutely insane to think either Byron or Lazareme would let a henotheistic state of affairs prevail throughout the Hidden Headworld. They would never have accepted a tertiary role to Sedon, let alone a secondary one to Mithras, the last of the Great Gods to see the light of First Weir's star system.)

Harmony reckoned their acquiescence to the Mithradites' demands for individually or collectively independent realms a requisite first step in securing her vision of what she termed the Panharmonium Accord. Ever the realist, Lazareme just wanted Mithras gone. So did Great Byron. Consequently, so long as the accordingly empowered Mithradites didn't impinge on his unfettered domination of the Aka Godbadian subcontinent, Byron was happy to go along with Lazareme's assessment of the situation and let Harmony strike her deal.

A major beneficiary of that deal was Mars Bellona, as ancient Illuminaries named him when they reckoned names would allow them power over Master Devas, if not their fathers. The relatively highborn Apocalyptic of War gained the Bloodlands as if by default shortly after the collapse of the Thanatoids' Lathakran empire in the second quarter of the Dome's 49th Century. But he and his fellow Apocalyptics had been gone skyward for well over a century.

In his absence, the popular Lazaremist Badhbh, Battle Babe, staked her own claim to New Valhalla. Not only was she one of the three Morrigu, Lazareme's war goddesses, she was now the so-called senior mother of Bellona's Sangazurs, a position held since Thrygragon by the Medusa, Mater Matare, the mother of more Sangs than any other devil.

In order to demonstrate her suitability for the position of the Bloods' devic Dand, she moved out of elder sister Krepusyl Evenstar's neighbouring, fay-friendly realm of Crepuscule-Twilight (Sedon's Outer Nose). Whereupon, much to Great Byron's shock, she proved an immediate hit with the Sangs themselves.

Even though it lay on the other side of the Forbidden Forest of the arachnid goddess Kala Tal (Sedon's Moustache), Bogy Bay and the Pristine Isles – traditional Mithradite territories the loathsome load of them – and therefore many hundreds of miles outside his historic sphere of influence, he resolved to remedy the to him appalling situation.

It would have been easiest if the Bloods chose to stay unaffiliated. Letting them fall into Lazaremist hands, though, did not appeal. If rulers they wanted, then so be it – so long as they had the proper ones. Like Iraxas-Hadd and huge swaths of the Cattail Peninsula, for quite some time now he'd been desirous of attending to its disposition entirely in his tribe's favour.

So, despite serious reservations about setting a precedent, he granted his once-decathonitized and thereafter unruly paladin the right to take over the Bloods.

Now all he had to do was fight to win it.

========

Nevair Neverknight knew that, long before his arrival on Birhym-Wednesday, New Valhalla was a contested realm. Had his unbending as well as unmoving father – in the sense that his facial features, the totality of his physical being, never moved – not imprisoned him for seeking to make it his forcibly? He had. Would he now? He wouldn't. And for the same reason.

He'd given his word now as he had then. In that he proved remarkably flexible.

========

To be fair, times had radically changed since he last asserted his right to rule it. Most crucially, Great Byron and his Primary Nucleus cathonitized Mars Bellona in the Gregarian Fields, Sedon's Mole, around 5850. These days the closest thing New Valhalla had to a Master Deva overlord, an over-lady in this case, was a Lazaremist bygone Illuminaries of Weir named Badhbh, after a deity half-heartedly worshipped by Outer Earth Celts almost as long gone as the Illuminaries who named her.

Given that Badhbh was pronounced very much the same or nearly the same as 'baby', it was an ironic, perhaps even deliberately derisive sobriquet for a Goddess of War – Master Devas were never too sure if Illuminaries were honouring devils by giving them names or mocking them. Equally appropriately, her power focus came to be called the Sabre Rattle.

That was in part because it did indeed rattle. You heard the rattling of Baby's Tvasitar Talisman, a sensible person either fought until he or she dropped or else you ran away, perchance to fight another day. You chose to fight, you died, maybe, just maybe, a Sang would reanimate your corpse. In which case you could fight to die another day.

The Valhallans' secondary specialty, after warring, was needlework. Be it skin or bones, they could re-knit together almost any mishmash scraped off the battle-field. So long as it was already dead, it went without saying. True, sometimes you had to accept someone else's arm or leg but, what the hell, beggars can't be choosers. Be grateful for what you get.

Bellona's Battle Bride, as she became known in the centuries before the Medusa, Mater Matare, Mother Murder, re-entered the Primary Apocalyptic of War's life, had an aversion to organized warfare; for any sort of organization, period. Lazaremists were like that; were me-first, fuck-you libertarians. The Sangs ultimately grew tired of her whimsical, perhaps intentionally disruptive behaviour and exiled her by disdain more than anything else. Nevertheless, until they tossed her, she had been worshipped as the Bloods' primary female deity for multiple generations of warrior arrivals.

Having only been released from Incain on Mithrada, Neverknight was completely unaware the Lazaremist was, at least temporarily, no longer the Inner Nose's biggest blowhard. He continued to reckon animative Sangazurs would welcome having even more baby brothers and sisters to thereafter augment the Bloods' dominantly-possessed population. Which of course necessitated them acquiring a new devic father to go along with the devic mother they retained.

He and Battle Babe – who could no doubt make herself into as much of a looker as he wanted her to be – would make wondrous azuras together. He felt certain of that and so should the Sangs. For that reason, as enjoyable as all this slaughtering was, he couldn't fathom why they were making such a gods-almighty fuss about not automatically acclaiming him their new devic overlord.

He and New Valhalla were the perfect fit. As the saying went, ruling it would be as if he'd died and gone to heaven.

========

In the Faerie Garden of Temporis, Demon Land dreamed of his father. Tantal Thanatos appeared before him – and not as a six inch doll-devil either. King Cold spoke directions. Following them, Antaeor began to soil-swim towards the Frozen Isle of Lathakra. One of his presumably just-as-long missing, though never precisely cathonitized, siblings was already there.

It was Devauray, the 6th of Tantalar in the Year of the Dome 5980. That made it Saturday, the 6th of December on the Outer Earth. Less than three weeks from today, on what devils still thought of as Mithramas, Xuthrodites referred to as Xmas, Utopians had only recently started to call Zmas Day, and he had always regarded as Christmas, the Roman-Catholic-raised, earlier arrival would mark a quarter century since he was thrust into what he also regarded as Limbo.

Perhaps by then he'd have redeveloped a third eye.

========

Nevair Neverknight, Unmoving Byron's recently released and reinstated paladin spent the daylight hours fighting his way to the southern stretches of New Valhalla. As it grew dark, he came into sight of Sanguerre, the Bloodlands' walled, capital city. By dawn Sedonda he'd be in it, the city's populace lying battered at his feet, entreating surrender. Either that or he'd be in the Sedon Sphere, a star staring down on the metropolis.

He had not enjoyed his time in Cathonia some two millennia earlier; would rather have been dead, sooth said. Which decathonitized devils may not have to do anymore but he still did anyhow. Whatever death entailed, chances were it'd be different. So cross out that earlier fantasy. In his ignorance of the true situation, it'd be far better to skip the die bit and simply ensure he made New Valhalla his personal heaven.

Then came the moat. He could jump over it. Devils usually weren't ones for exertion, especially not devils who had been so long imprisoned within Incain's She-Sphinx. So, much less energetically, he could just air-walk over it. Instead, he jumped into it. With his heavy armour, he sank immediately to the bottom. He plodded onwards.

To him, confident despite tiring somewhat, water was no different than land, sky, or even Outer Space, though he'd never tried that when he had a body, daemonic or otherwise. This, he quickly realized, though liquid, wasn't exactly water. It was, rather, a cunning trap; one worthy of his father, albeit in a much more mundane manner. The Sangazurs knew their stuff.

Had to. Sang dharma, nothing less than their reason for being, was to provide battleground-training for whomsoever wanted it. They were the azura-offspring of Mars Bellona, the Apocalyptic of War, and a variety of mates, most notably the Medusa, both before and after she started calling herself Mother Murder on Thrygragon.

They had been possessing dead male and female warriors of every race on the Head since time nearly out of mind. Even his mind, out of it as he arguably was already. Except for pure U-bloods, who couldn't be possessed, Nevair reminded himself as if to prove it. But that still included: Caucasians, white and brown, Godbadians and Rajputs from Ophir-Moorset; yellow-skinned oriental types also from Godbad as well as Samarand, formerly Sedon's Tongue; red-skins from Iraxas-Hadd; pale-skins from Krachla; not to mention Pani- and these days also Achigan-born albinos.

But why stop there? Throw in orange-skinned and -textured Bandradins, also nowadays from Achigan; grey-skins from nearby Twilight-Crepuscule; Dukkhans, Apple Islanders and Marutians, who came in a veritable rainbow of natural skin colorations, as did Twilight's faeries, though they added anything except natural blues and greens; Saurs, Myrmidons, Barrings, sentient Simians, and ... well, you name it. Shut up now, battery-brain. Thinking's not your forte.

Since Sangazur-animated trainers were already dead, they seldom killed anyone. They just provided the means and wherewithal for anyone to learn how to kill almost anyone else. Vaguely, Nevair wondered if they knew how to kill devils. He hoped so. It gave him all the more incentive to persevere.

His heaven was here.

========

Only one member of the Damnation Brigade had made it to the Frozen Isle of Lathakra thus far. Sooth said, only his twin sister would be welcome there. Sea-She was much more problematic than Air-He in that she'd stayed behind on the Outer Earth, where they couldn't get to readily. Nonetheless, presuming success in terms of what they intended for those on the Moon, their watery elemental wasn't so much for the future file as the due-soon file.

The Parents Thanatos could care less about the other eight. Correction, yellow-skinned Sedunihas had sculpted Castella-Day bald, so they did care about the hair of one of them.

But that too could be rectified in short order. Tantal's labrys was razor sharp.

========

The sharks had single horns, like narwhals, except their horns glowed with Brainrock. One of the monoceros sharks approached at speed, bit through his leggings, and took out a chunk of his right thigh, narrowly missing the buttock. Even through water he was able to dispatch it with a swipe of his sharp-edged shield. He cautioned himself to be careful.

Horned sharks were a lot like mutated ravendeer; nasty beasts the pair of them. In addition to retractable unicorn horns ravendeer had talarial wings on either side of their four hooves, the ability to pass through the Universal Substance between-space and a proclivity for procreation. After rapidly maturing they led long lives to boot; except they did most of the booting. Or hoofing, put better.

They could project an obscuring nimbus about themselves. It did more than just obscure their approach. You could never be sure they were coming at you until they ignited you. Devic bodies were debrained demons. Despite their (unfounded) reputation on the Outer Earth for thriving in hellfire, most varieties of demons were highly combustible. For the first roughly five centuries after he gained solidity, Nevair had had to debrain more than a few demons after a too-close encounter with a mutated ravendeer.

Xuthros Hor, the Tenth Patriarch of Golden Age Mankind, the one who'd caused the Great Flood of the Head's Year Zero, bred ravendeer from the original faerie-like fusion of one of great-great-grandfather Jaro Dan's crows and father Oriartes Ma's spontaneously created, as if out of nowhere, and hence considered-magical, unicorn. Outer Earth heroes rode ravendeer during the battle for Strongyne circa 2500 YD.

Attis and his legionnaires rode ravendeer when they were conquering the Upper Head in Mithras's name prior to that. The Universal Soldier had not been on one when he cathonitized Nevair in their famous duel at the tail-end of the Crimson Conspiracy but Prime Sinistral Pride, Domdaniel of Satanwyck, had been riding one when he attacked Grandfather Sedon fifteen hundred years earlier.

The mighty Moloch then not altogether in the sky had been so disgusted he ordered Thrygragos Mithras to slay Attis's entire stock; unless it was a flock. The ever-resourceful Sangs or their originally Utopian, biomage advisers could have genetically re-engineered these sharks to be the piscatorial equivalents of mutated ravendeer.

Neverknight caused harpoons to torpedo out of his shield-talisman. They took out a few of them. Two or three were either well-trained or lucky enough to avoid the missiles. They kept coming. He dispatched them expeditiously, taking no chances. The remainder set to devouring the injured ones. In that respect mutated sharks were no different than regular sharks.

There was a barrier up ahead with, he sensed, a different kind of liquid on the other side of it. It wasn't much of a barrier; some kind of whitish, nearly translucent plastic. But maybe it wasn't supposed to be much. Slice it open, thereby mix the liquid there with the water here and, if they did act together, might he make one menace out of two innocent substances?

He could go up and over it. He decided it would be more fun going through it.

========

The Bloodlands, Sedon's Inner Nose, had been the devic protectorate of Mars Bellona, the Apocalyptic of War. War's widow, Badhbh of Lazareme, aka Sabre Rattle, after her power focus, or Battle Babe, had found refuge next door, in the always dreary Grey Land of Twilight, Sedon's Outer Nose. The devic protectorate of her older sister, Krepusyl Evenstar, Miss Mist, the Grey Lady, it lay across the Rhinal Canal on the coast of Fearsome Fobbiat, the Headworld's western ocean.

Once Krepusyl had been Mariamne Dawnstar. Once Twilight had been on the opposite coast of the Head, on the coast of Tempestuous Psychron, where Samarand, formerly Sedon's Tongue, was now. Then it had been known as the Land of Daybreak. That was a long time ago. The Mighty Moloch in the Sky had done the same thing to Lathakra, which was once the lens of Sedon's Human Eye, and, even before that, Sedon's Horn.

The fact Dark Sedon could do that sort of thing, move landforms from one side of his Head to the other, was a reminder that he, more so than any other devil, the two remaining Great Gods notwithstanding, deserved their adulation. The fact that he did it, twice to the Thanatoids, was proof he better get it too, no ifs ands, buts or butt-ends for the smokers among them.

Only some of Bellona's offspring were Battle-Rattle's. The rest came mostly from such diverse Mithras Spawn as Nergal Vetala's presumed brood sisters, Mater Matare and Kala Tal, amongst many others. While in almost every respect superior to Vetala's Haddazurs and Nergalazurs, they were akin in that they were peculiarly adapted to possess corpses.

War's children, the Sangazur Spirit Beings, were comparatively few in number. They were also dwindling in numbers. The Bloodlands were rich; had to be in order to afford modern-day weaponry, but Battle Babe farmed too many of them out. Sangazurs were symbiotic, that made them fickle. In life you worshipped one devil or another. In death Sangs animating your corpse did ditto.

Consequently, too many Sangs switched allegiances. An upshot of that was too many Sangs didn't come back to the Bloodlands; hence the dwindling. Sangs need a father, too. War was it, their alpha male. So far only War could sire Sangs and there was no reason to suspect that would change. Otherwise it already would have wouldn't it.

(Every Master Deva produced symbionts capable of animating dead things. These were the azura spirit beings. They only produced them when they procreated with each other, without the intermediary of a sentient shell. They did otherwise, the offspring would be a deviant. Those who could retain the shell's personality from life were, however, few and far between. Indeed, there were those who claimed that the reanimated shell had to be that of a deviant in order for his or her personality to persist.)

War had been gone for a hundred and thirty years. Even though the corpses they occupied retained the ability to propagate, Sangs were infertile. War's Widow wasn't, far from it. She also flaunted her indiscretions. She couldn't help herself; Lazaremists couldn't help themselves. Total freedom was their way. That included the freedom to be totally stupid.

She had to be driven out. To do any differently would result in the further dilution of the Bloods' azura-bloodline. Enough was more than enough. On top of that, unlike Nergal Vetala's indiscriminate Nergalazurs, whose fathers were either the Planter, Zuvem Nergalis, or the Reaper, Yama Nergal; unlike her just as indiscriminate Haddazurs, who had dozens of different fathers, including War and his two breed brothers, Plague and Catastrophe, respectively the Apocalyptics of Disease and Disaster; Sangs were genetically predisposed to animate only bodies of those slain in battle.

As such those they animated were easy to spot in a crowd. Always badly scarred, often missing limbs or parts of their heads, they were nonetheless as highly intelligent and well-experienced as their shells had been in life. True, most other azuras only occupied bodies, be they living or dead, whereas Sangs actually preserved the mental acuity of the slain sentient. True as well, their seamstresses were the best in the business.

Still and all, recruitment for replacement bodies was hard to come by when you looked like you'd walked out of a war-zone after a close encounter with the wrong end of you-name-it. Other than Iraches, most other sentient beings on the Head did not offer tea and scones to their Dead; all the more so when they were there, physically before them.

Discriminatory as it was, it was no wonder cremation was the preferred method of disposing of dead bodies on the Head.

========

Bigotry towards Sangs, who, arguably, unlike homosexuals on the Outer Earth, were a diminishing minority on the Head, came in spite of yet another of their peculiarities. Sangazur-occupation was beneficent. It postponed a corpse's natural deterioration for decades. While decomposition remained inevitable, it wasn't uncommon for Sangs to animate the same corpses for sixty or seventy years.

Sangs also had a perverse seniority system. Earlier born ones could bump later born ones out of their better-preserved bodies. A Sangazur by the name of Tyrtod was generally considered to be the first born azura of Mars Bellona. A Sang having their own name was odd. Even more oddly, neither Matare nor her reputed breed sister, Kala Tal, were his mother. Instead he was born of Sabre-Rattle's second-born, older sister Titanic Metis, aka Wisdom of Lazareme, a fact that allowed him to think for himself.

Coincidentally, the Spirit Being Tyrtod was currently in control of Field Marshall von Blut, whose given name was also Tyrtod. The two-in-one Tyrtod was with a large crowd gathered atop the battlements of Sanguerre. Most of the others were Marutian warriors, men and women, some black, others Caucasian, who had come to New Valhalla in order to learn the fine art of warfare throughout the ages.

Many another humanoid species were represented in much smaller numbers; groups of no more than two or three. Perhaps the rarest of them were the sexless androgens or the dual-sexed hermaphrodites. Either/or were almost never seen outside Androgynia, the realm of the toad-like Neuter, Geld Neargon, he of the 4-layered alchemical or elemental mitre, which bordered the Marutian coastline of the Aural Sea, Sedon's Ear. There were also a smattering of anthropomorphic non-humans there.

These included ophidian snake-folk from Ophir-Moorset; Saur Tsars from the Floodlands; Lizarados from the Lake Lands; bear-like Barrings from Tanglewood in the Cattail; diamantes, the diamond-skinned hardheads from the Crystal Mountains; ant-like Myrmidons from the Pastures of Plenty and their descendants from Apple Isle. Saur Tsars and Lizarados, both of which were as reptilian as Moorset's ophidians, had been going at each other for more than a century up north, ever since the Lakes and Floods began touching. They weren't allowed to go at each other in Valhalla.

That, as of Demetray, the Saur Tsars' Klizarod Rex was now in exile on Ap Isle whereas the Lizarados' ex-Emperor Chameleon had been devolved into an actual chameleon was well known by now. That this was primarily due to Byronics, among them Neverknight, was equally well known. The two distinct reptilian species were still enemies. They were united in that they couldn't wait until Nevair was abolished. He had every intention of disappointing them.

Others on the battlements surrounding Sanguerre included Simian Sapiens originally from Sedon's Lower Jaw and Goatee, Djerridam or Goatwood, as well as Apple-Ap-Ape Isle. Also from the Subcontinent of Godbad were a few Garudas. They appeared to be intelligent birds almost as gigantic the Vultyrie. In actuality they were avian humans in a removable, feathery regalia that grew between-space at the same time their humanoid aspects were growing up in regular space.

In addition, there were forcibly evolved humanoids such as water-breathing Akans, wearing land-suits, a variety of renegade Piscines, equally amphibious Lemurian Frog Women, primitive Angelycs from the Mystics, and avian-Ayres, their more civilized cousin-species from Goatwood. There were even tellurians here, Mantels and Mandroids both.

Being replicas, given not so much life as independence, the Mantels of Temporis weren't too dissimilar from ordinary men and women. Mandroids, though, were a different matter. More cyborg-machine than flesh and blood, subjugated by the Ancient Lemurians and hunted to the point of extinction by the Three Great Gods in the early centuries of the Dome, Mandroids survived in the Head's various underworlds.

All, the self-proclaimed invincible She-Sphinx of Incain, was the most famous but, under the leadership of a once-human outsider named Steltsar, they had flourished since the Fifties and were fast-becoming a force to be reckoned with again on the Hidden Continent. That Sangazurs allowed tellurians in the Bloods, after the largely artificial beings had nearly driven them out of their homeland twenty years earlier, at the conclusion of the Godbadian Civil War, was testament to the Sangs commitment to their dharma. They would teach anyone the arts and science of warfare, even if it meant teaching their pupils to war against them.

In the Bloodlands you learned how to fight to the best of your natural and/or unnatural abilities. Since Sapienda morning they had been fighting against Nevair

Neverknight. So far everyone except the two-in-one Tyrtod agreed they were receiving a failing grade. He would disagree of course. It was his strategy they were following.

========

The moat's liquids had been carefully developed. As he'd suspected, when he slashed through the barrier, they acted as catalyzing agents on each other. The resultant substance was akin to corrosive acid. It rusted off his armour in a matter of seconds. Figuring it could dissolve his power focus as well, he picked up speed. When he emerged from the moat, beneath the walls of Sanguerre itself, he was naked; had only his gleaming Brainrock, talismanic shield left as protection.

There was a devil waiting for him. There was something recognizable about the golden torc around her neck, the ankle-length, chain-mail hauberk that extended off it and the barbed chains manacled to both her wrists. She was exceedingly skinny, however. Was so wasted-looking she retained only a vaguely feminine shape.

Her dark but lightening hair was patchy. Evidently it was only now growing back, regaining its once golden-butterscotch sheen. Everything about her face and musculature looked hollow, as if her daemonic body had lost most of its substance somewhere — perhaps after an extended stay in the very moat from which he'd just emerged.

========

Who cared anymore? He attacked her.
****

(Game-Gambit) 18: **Farewell, Great Byron**

Devauray, Tantalar 6, 5980

For a brief second she smiled. Then she gritted her teeth and defended herself.

========

His ebon, eagle-winged shield glowed with Brainrock but he was otherwise naked. Bloodlust befuddled his brain. He didn't realize with whom he was dealing. She clasped both her hands together, willed her chains fused, and whipped them at her foe.

Nevair blocked them with his shield, his power focus. Leaping into the sky, he passed into then through it, his shield; became fully armoured again. Finally someone who could match him; finally a Master Deva. Underneath him, effectively as a kind of animate hobby horse, albeit one with a head and tail, he conjured a great, ebon stallion.

He ripped off and tossed down one of his gauntlets, relishing the challenge. So did she.

"Come along, Neverknight! Come to me, you undersexed boy-child. I am Freespirit Nihila, as in annihilation. You persist," she cautioned him, once, "I'll return you to your father a headless corpse." Nevair laughed out loud. He reached into his shield and withdrew a long lance. Spurring his night-black stallion towards the ground, he shouted pure defiance.

"For Byron! For Blood!"

========

Guardian Angel Tyrtod, the leader of the Sangazurs, via his shell, former Field Marshall Tyrtod von Blut, had masterminded a carefully calculated plan of attack against Nevair. The devil had entered from the North, an area, like neighbouring Marutia, plagued by Time Quakes ever since Thrygragon over fifteen hundred years earlier. Given that entry point an irresistible strategy presented itself.

Nag and worry the Byronic with piddling Stone Age resistance. Lead him south where the likes of Babylonian, Greek, Roman and Mongolian armies could challenge him. Bring him into the crusade lands and the chivalric Middle Ages. Exhaust him with tilts and jousts, in which he revelled. Then ease him forward into the ages of the Spanish Conquest of the New World, the revolutions in North America and France, the Napoleonic Era, through the Nineteenth Century on the Outer Earth and into modern times.

Confront him with World Wars One and Two, though stop short of chemical warfare, which wouldn't harm him, and Atomics, which might. Chemicals could ruin the terrain for years hereafter while Atomics were a discredited and unworthy approach to victory. Look what happened to Old Valhalla more than a millennium earlier. Where was the victory if the victorious were eradicated as well? Tantalize him with the moat, get rid of his power focus then finish him off here and now, in the killing zone beneath the battlements.

WWI was the best analogy. They'd fought a war of attrition against Byron's Secondary Nucleoid. It was time for the coup de grace.

Then the other devil appeared. Out of a Gypsium hoop no less. Tyrtod von Blut, who could think as well for himself as Guardian Angel Tyrtod could think for both of them, didn't know who the devil was. However, he knew Ringleader; knew he was the second Outer Earthling thus codenamed and, therefore, knew who both his parents and brother had been. There was only one reason Rings would send a wasted-looking devil to Sanguerre and it wasn't to do them any favours. He wanted to ensure they destroyed her or she destroyed them.

Outer Earth born, in the Prussia of 1895, von Blut had been killed in here, twenty years ago now. His Guardian Angel, trying to think for the both of them, was giving him a headache. The Sangazur Tyrtod knew who she had to be. He imparted that information to his shell. He also imparted a bunch of unanswerable questions and they were what were giving the dead German his headache.

Nihila? Surely that was Harmony, Datong Harmonia as Illuminaries named her in the Dome's 4th Millennium, once the Unity of Balance, firstborn of Thrygragos Lazareme. Had Janna Fangfingers finally found and released her, her devic half-mother, of Sraddha Somata as well? Had she, Second Fangs, sent her to them in order to cement their loyalty to the cause of the Dead, rather than to the cause of Thrygragos Byron, whom Guardian Angel Gomez supported?

Had Azura-Tyrtod's ever-rebellious mother – Titanic Metis or Metisophia, as Illuminaries had her – done it? Or a spiteful Battle Babe, their exiled devic deity, attempting a comeback? Harmony, Metis and Badhbh were Lazaremists. Maybe it was the doing of War himself. His star had been missing from the Night's Sky since Sedonda after all.

So had the Matare Death Star, the Medusa being the devic mother of perhaps a majority of the Sangazurs. As had Star Plague, whose Rakshas demons served the Sangs as their Gatherers of the Dead. Ditto Star Catastrophe, whose crystal skulls doubled as the carryalls Rakshas used to transport Sangazur Spirit Beings long-distance and the Talking Heads they used to far-speak with each other. Ditto too, unless it was four, Star Vultyrie. Second Fangs' vampiric bats being strictly nocturnal, Rakshas rode the Vultyrie's eponymous Vultyrie during the day.

The four Primary Apocalyptics and the Vultyrie were out and about somewhere. So, retorted his host-shell, not quite to himself, why weren't they here? Don't know, do I?

Just shut up and watch then.

========

Formerly-Harmony, evidently nowadays-Nihila, effortlessly levitated into the sky. She found purchase on the air itself. Nevair spurred his stallion towards her, brandishing a Brainrock lance. Making no effort to dodge, she willed herself diamond hard. Anchoring her chains in the dark-grey matter of Samsara, she rendered herself an immovable object. The lance contacted her in the chest and crumpled like a tin shaft against a granite boulder.

Expecting a clean follow-through, Nevair was thrown off balance, jerked off his mount, which immediately vanished. Devils didn't so much conjure psychopomps as they grew them for show out of their Subtle Matter daemonic bodies. Tumbling earthward, he created a crater of himself, for himself, upon impact. Humiliated, though none the worst for wear, he crawled of it. Self-renamed Nihila floated towards him.

"Relying on fakery, Unity?" he mocked her, finally realizing who she was; had been anyhow. She'd been incomparably beautiful once, irresistible to anyone who counted himself male. Once! Was that no longer, needless to say. Make that needles to slay. Reaching into his winged shield he withdrew a laser edged sword.

"See what Brainrock has made me?" He flourished the blade. "It'll cut anything. Even your chain mail."

Nihila touched down and began to lazily whip her chains around like lariats. "Prove it!"

He lunged. As if things alive, her chains sprang against the ground, somersaulted her over his head. Left-hand ones snapped out. Coiled around his ankles. Yanked. Pulled his feet out from under him. He thudded to the ground. Managed to bring his shield around in time to block the descending right-hand chains. Sliced through them. Sliced through the ones around his ankles. Was on his feet. He advanced, scissoring, shredding, Brainrock chain-links with every step. She held her position.

He stood before her then stuck his cut-anything sword back into his shield, raised his helm's visor and smiled. "I enjoyed that." Stunningly fast, he reached out and grabbed what was left of her chains. With them he pulled her to him then kissed her on the lips. "Bye, bye."

He flipped her onto her back. Out of his shield came his laser-edged blade. It pierced her chain-mail hauberk, went through her heart and, anchoring it into the earth behind her, he pinned her there, she writhing futilely. She atomized. He shouted triumphantly. How could the Attis have ever beaten him?

His shield re-formed as metallic eagle-wings off his shoulder blades. He raised himself into the sky, towards the battlements. Those there sought to run away. Except for one. That one hurled himself at Nevair Neverknight. Grappled with him, hauled him downward. It was another devil. He stank.

It was Plague, the Apocalyptic of Disease.

========

The Awesome Akbar bounded across the battlefield in the Pre-Tokugawa Era Cavern. One of the Thousand Caverns of Temporis, it was where Kronokronos Mikoto and the Tethys Triplets were born. He gathered up Cerebrus David Ryne, the leader of the Damnation Brigade, who was desperately wounded.

He was racing back towards Lakshmi of Lemuria, and the Anthean Agate she'd brought him in on, when he spotted the Apocalyptic of War. Mars Bellona was a bodybuilding bonehead with a goatee and spikes cresting his otherwise skinless skull from the forehead backwards like a Mohawk hairstyle. Spouting gibberish, he was playing toy-soldiers with a just as gibbering samurai. Changing direction, with Cerebrus still slung over his shoulder and his Homeworld Sceptre pulsating with power, he went for the Apocalyptic.

Lakshmi, who, having only turned 18 the day before, was nevertheless as much of a Kronokronos as he was, screamed something. He couldn't decipher what it was but her tone was enough. Akbar hit the turf just as another devil appeared behind him. The head of his sceptre exploded, blowing the Kronokronos Supreme and Cerebrus between-space.

The devil was Carcinogen the Leper.

========

Howsoever whimsically, bygone Illuminaries of Weir had named Plague, the now decathonitized Apocalyptic of Disease, Carcinogen the Leper. He was a 3-eyed, humanoid horror covered in puss-leaking skin sores and concomitantly dripping bandages, like an Egyptian mummy who'd been through the wars. Which he sort of had, the War of the Apocalyptics.

Its outcome was still in doubt but any further involvement on his part wasn't. He'd thrown in the proverbial towel and was now trying to escape the consequences of his participation in it without being recathonitized.

Carcinogen had drawn an angel. Unspeakable things were on his mind. Mercy was on hers. Mercy won out. To show his displeasure he'd used his Tvasitar Talisman, a skull-laden shaft with a disease pod at one end and a pendulum-shaped blade on the other end, in order to give her a parting gift. The gift was his right hand, which he'd cut off at the wrist. She didn't appreciate the gesture.

Unaffected by the explosion of Akbar's Homeworld Sceptre, he spotted his fellow Apocalyptic and, even though he was holding his power focus with his one remaining hand, managed to do as Akbar had done with the Brigade's likely dying or already dead leader. He tossed War over his shoulder. He glared at Kronokronos Lakshmi, whose task it was to mop up after the Damnation Brigade finished with the Apocalyptics. She scowled back then stepped on her agate and went away. With his pendulum blade the Leper cut through the air.

He was targeting his old protectorate, the Pristine Isles: a series of tiny islets in Bogy Bay beneath the southern reaches of both Crepuscule, the Grey Land of Twilight, Sedon's Outer Nose, and the Bloodlands, New Valhalla, Sedon's Inner Nose. He undershot the Isles, found himself miles to the north, on the turrets of Sanguerre, Mars Bellona's personal city-state.

Field Marshall Tyrtod von Blut had never seen either devil before. But, even if Bellona, his titular master, looked distinctly demented, what with his tongue elongating out of his fleshless mouth and licking his forearms like they were popsicle sticks, there was no mistaking the Apocalyptics of Disease and War.

The dual smell, the Leper's natural putrescence and War filling his britches, was undignified. Nevertheless, von Blut led the rest and knelt in duly abject supplication. Plague took their adulation as a matter of proper tribute. War simply drooled. Then the Leper realized what was happening on the plain below.

That was Harmony. That was Neverknight. That was Lazareme versus Byron. The Byron atomized the Lazareme. Rose to attack the Mithras. Most sought to flee, even von Blut cowered behind the upper wall of Sanguerre. Disease wasn't afraid. Rather, he saw opportunity present itself. Besides, Varuna Mithras never backed down. Never had to and neither did he, now that he was decathonitized. He leapt into sky.

Time to put paid to Byron.

========

In the Faerie Garden Dr Aristotle 'Harry' Zeross, Ringleader – the second so-named, the first being his 12-years' dead father Angelo – came to in a pool of his own puke. Where was he? Oh, yeah. Temporis. While between-space, marvelling at the fact Wilderwitch and Old Man Power were still alive and seemingly un-aged, he'd overheard the devil, who was using her Gypsium chains to restrain the two supras, identify it as being one of the Thousand Caverns of Dand Tariqartha, Thrygragos Lazareme's Earth Magician.

What had he done to her? Got that, too. Sent her to New Valhalla. It seemed the sensible thing to do. He'd never been to the Ghostlands or Satanwyck, so he couldn't send her to either of those entirely inhospitable territories, but he had been to the Bloodlands, Sedon's Inner Nose.

He'd heard from Alpha Centauri that his ambassador to the Bloods, Gomez Niarchos, Ferdinand's Sangazur-reanimated, but otherwise dead father, had been having trouble convincing the Sangazur powers-that-be that they should support Godbad rather than their fellow Dead Things in Hadd.

Why not send them a Mad Devil? They might appreciate it. She'd certainly give them a workout. Besides, maybe the Sangs could find a way to dispose of her. Which, he figured, would be a good thing. In Nergal Vetala the Head already had more than enough Mad Devils.

So, what was he going to do next? Right. If two were alive, why not the other eight? He wondered if even those two were still alive. Time for see-forever-eyes. He formed lenses-less Gypsium Rings about his eyeballs; extended his far-sight.

Holy Fuck!

========

Never had human eyes beheld such a sight.

Two titanic entities of pure power: a tetrahedron with the face of a snake-haired Medusa on each of its four sides; the Byronhead with its three eyes and three Nucleoids inside them looking out; both were indescribably immense. They glowed with the intensity of the core of a nuclear reactor.

Two nuclei circled above Sisert; sized each other up. This was no place for mortals.

========

In Lathakra, the mutual obliteration of the Byronic and Apocalyptic Nuclei was felt immediately. Sedona's Spell of Disproportionment, which had affected Tantal and Methandra Thanatos since Black Lazam 5933, snapped. Tantal was once again eight feet tall, Methandra around six.

The two embraced joyfully. Smiler backed into the shadows. Having just witnessed the same thing the Parents Thanatos had, via the visionary fumes of Methandra's purloined cauldron, he was burning with rage.

One hundred and thirty years earlier, with him pulling their strings, the four Primary Apocalyptics and a potent force made up of their loyal adherents had been attempting to conquer Marutia, Sedon's Cheek. The Mithradites they'd been seeking to overpower had called in Bodiless Byron and his Spawn to help defend their realms. Smiler had been expecting that. What he didn't expect was being eaten by Archon Oberon at same time the Medusa, Mater Matare, the Apocalyptic of Death, was eaten by the fucking fairy's wife, Cabala Titania.

Without his guidance, and that of the Medusa, such as it was, Mithras's Eighth were routed. They sought refuge in the Gregarian Fields. Where it just so happened Oberon and Titania were resting on their way back to Temporis after an extended stay in Twilight, which was where they'd eaten them. Fucking faeries were called such because they loved doing just that. Their Bacchanals were justifiably notorious throughout the Headworld.

Idiots that they were, Mithras's Eighth and Disaster's lowborn, and extremely low-watt, two-headed mount, the Vultyrie, who was female, joined in the revelry. They were eaten, too. As it turned out, that was a good thing because six Master Devas in just two faeries burnt them out, quite literally. Their deaths freed them.

Which was when the Medusa realized she was pregnant — and not with azuras this time. She was pregnant with four fourth generational devils, one for each of them: War, Plague, Catastrophe and her. She was wrong about that; they were all his. Of course she didn't realize he even existed unless he manifested himself in front of her but that was the truth of the matter, Matare.

He knew what they, once born, needed in order to become full devils: Brainrock power foci. So he took it upon himself to travel to Sedon's Peak, where he prevailed upon Anvil the Artificer – Tvasitar Smithmonger to Illuminaries, Tavy to his few friends – to fashion four devic talismans, one for each of the unborn. He returned with them to the Gregarian Fields and had just given them to the Medusa when the Byronic Nucleus came calling.

Dark Sedon did not approve of devils murdering anyone, even faeries, so he authorized Unmoving Byron and his Primary Nucleoids to enter the Gregarian Fields in order to cathonitize the Apocalyptics and the Vultyrie. Which they did. He got away naturally. It seemed he always did, eventually. Even Dark Sedon couldn't cathonitize or order anyone cathonitized if he didn't remember they existed.

It wasn't until he and the Thanatoids were watching events unfold on the Outer Earth's Damnation Isle last Sedonda that any of them, perhaps even the Medusa herself, realized she was still pregnant; that she'd spent all those decades upstairs gestating to the point of bursting four new devils.

Now she'd been recathonitized. Now as well so had the barely born devils he had thrust into her while they were being digested by Oberon and Titania. He had every right to be burning with rage. No, it suddenly occurred to him, he wasn't just enraged. He was burning with jealousy, that most ignoble of all ignoble emotions.

To his mind, of all the women he had known in the multi-millennia of his existence, only his daemonic half's equally immortal wife, Primeval Lilith, she of the Whole Earth, was Methandra's equal. In all those multi-millennia, though, he had admired her from afar. Like father like son in that regard, he supposed. Only she had consciously jilted Sedon, whereas he had never dared to make his affections known to her, perhaps for fear of the same rejection.

He had vowed there would soon be a reckoning between Cold and himself. Heat would be the prize. Be it willingly or otherwise, he would win her. Of that the Smiling Fiend, once ruler of the Elysian Fields before he left it to the fumbling fingers of fourth-born Zuvem Nergalis and thence, by default, to fifth-born Yama Nergal, had no doubt. Until now, that is.

Where was his reward? To what purpose were his efforts if Hot Stuff, arguably Mediterranean Athena, was still in love with such a monstrously stupid, beer-guzzling buffoon as old King Cold?

Despair was short-lasting. Mirth returned in a matter of seconds. Perhaps they'd make some more babies, more fourth generational devils; devils he'd ultimately command, since he was their real father. Without him possessing them, male devils could only foist more next-to-useless azuras upon their mates. He laughed out loud at the thought.

Methandra and Tantal broke off their embrace. "What's so humorous, Smiler?" demanded the King of Lathakra.

"Existence!"

========

Neverknight's father and three elder siblings passed out of this plane of existence. Although it happened nearly four thousand miles to the northeast, their demise instantly enervated him; left him bereft of strength let alone any desire to fight against following them into the near-oblivion of the Sedon Sphere. Nevair didn't even bother to struggle as the Leper flung him to the ground then chopped off his left arm at the shoulder.

With the severed limb still in its stirrups, Plague kicked the shield-focus twenty yards away. The Byron Spawn could care less. With his father gone it was as if the perpetual misfit's entire reason for being – for defying, for resisting, often for the sake of sheer orneriness – had gone as well. On the battlements von Blut and his immortal sidekick picked up on this right away. The two-in-one Tyrtod had his men remove War then triggered armaments designed to destroy Nevair Neverknight. Why not take out two devils with one stroke?

For fully three minutes he kept up the bombardment, hit the Leper and Nevair with everything he/they and the Sangs had. The accuracy was precise but the effect was dulled by the fact Nevair still wore most of his armour and Carcinogen had his pendulum blade. When the smoke cleared, the Byron was lying prostrate, the fingers of his still-attached right arm twitching, and the Mithras was clambering out of the moat, his power focus scoured but still intact.

The Leper pointed his talisman at von Blut. Its blade detached from its shaft, cleaved like a boomerang, which was how it was shaped, through the air and bifurcated the Field Marshall.

The Sangazur named Tyrtod immediately went looking for another shell.

========

The pendulum blade didn't so much came back through the Universal Substance of Samsara as rematerialized atop its skull-laden shaft.

The Apocalyptic raised high his Tvasitar Talisman; shouted in a voice for all to hear: "In the name of Varuna Mithras, I proclaim myself regent of the Bloodlands. Until War regains competency, his protectorate is mine and you are my subjects. I give you my ambition and, in the time honoured tradition of Sanguerre, I hereby pledge it in blood. Devic Blood. Neverknight's!"

He swung his blade towards Nevair's neck. Chains came out of the air itself; wrapped around his talisman and snagged it out of his hands. Freespirit Nihila stepped out of Samsara. The Leper looked at her in amazement. Clearly Nevair hadn't had the power to cathonitize her but, for her own nihilistic reasons, she had obligingly made it seem that he had.

She did not deign to speak to the Leper; simply flipped the pendulum blade into the moat. Panic-stricken he dove after it. She chortled almost sadistically, snaked one of her chains into Samsara and reproduced it. In her short time back in action, she had become a master of fakery and cruelty both. She did have words, melodramatic ones, for those on the battlements, though.

"Cherish your Apocalyptic for now, Sangazurs. Soon there shall be no more protectorates. Soon there shall be balance. Not power, not authority, not strength of one over another. Everyone shall work for the benefit of everyone else. So speaks Freespirit Nihila, the renewed Unity of Panharmonium."

Whipping her chains around she went away, carrying Disease's talisman with her.

========

One more time the Leper emerged from the moat.

As had been the case when the angel he drew in Temporis – Gloriella D'Angelo Dark, the Radiant Rainbow Rider – got hold of it, without his power focus he was fast-cathonitizing. As wonderful as it was not to have to adhere to his grandfather's dictates anymore; as wonderful as it was to be able to do his own killing without having to rely on his adherents to do it for him, that was the one drawback to being decathonitized.

He couldn't remain on the Head as a simple Spirit Being, as Titanic Metis, Wisdom of Lazareme, had once Methandra Thanatos stole her power focus a thousand-plus years ago. He needed a Tvasitar Talisman of his own to stay that way. But did he need his own talisman? Devils could wield other devils' talismans. Could they do so after decathonitization? That was easily ascertained.

Using what little strength he had left, he limped across the plain in front of Sanguerre's walls. He picked up Nevair's eagle-winged shield, the Byronic's severed arm still in its stirrup, and had his answer. At least at first, and for awhile thereafter, decathonitized devils like both the Byronic and himself, like Bellona as well, needed to possess shells who were both sentient and alive. Carcinogen's current shell was a Temporite, a Mantel half-life, one Cardinal Molino by name and title. He'd known that. Molino wasn't good enough.

Realizing his fate, he brought Neverknight's talisman over to the Byronic. As shoulder re-knitted to arm, Nevair regained consciousness. His eyes opened. He looked at Plague. "Why?"

"Because even devazurs need a rebel."

He rejoined three of his four, fellow Primary Apocalyptics in the night's sky.

========

"BACK SO SOON, DISEASE? I'D HARDLY NOTICED YOU WERE AWAY."

"Don't sound so happy, grandfather," snorted the Plague Star. "I'll find my way out before you notice I was back."

"Don't be in such a hurry to leave," came the voice of Star Catastrophe, the Headless Apocalyptic of Disaster, of Sudden Destruction, Nakba Ramazar. "I've just found the most magnificent head ever." He was referring to the Byronhead.

"I see no reason to gloat," said Star Spellbinder in her father's voice. **"We shall be released much sooner than either of you."**

Pity poor Plague. He'd barely had enough time to realize he was in a game before he suffered his endgame.

========

"Farewell, Great Byron. You'd have made a brilliant bass bongo but I guess I can't have everything!"

The Smiling Fiend laughed so hard he momentarily forgot about the newly minted Trigregos Titan. Then he laughed some more. Why should he remember him? Before he'd returned to Lathakra this last time, for the umpteenth time recently, he'd manipulated events such that Nergal Vetala had no other choice except to kill her own soldier.

Then he abruptly stopped laughing.

As enjoyable as that was, he dare not forget the Trigregos Talismans were still out there, on Dustmound. He recalled something else as well; something Quill Tethys, wearing the second skin of an extremely unattractive female, had said to Thartarre Sraddha Holgatson when he, Smiler, was inside the High Priest.

It was, he apprehended, long past time to end this Sedonplay. And he'd do it too — even if it meant he had to play a Trigregos Gambit himself.

****

(GAME-GAMBIT) 19: **Re-Begin-Game, Damnation**

Devauray, Tantalar 6, 5980

"Kill him I say!"
Heard every word, you grinning fool. You're the enemy. Trying to turn Goddess away from me. Stop you. Attack. Go for the eyes. All three of them.
Trigregos now. Can't be stopped.

========

Raising the Susasword, the soldier raced towards Nergal Vetala, his Goddess of Life Eternal, and her unwelcome guest, whom she'd addressed as the Judge. Then the fiend was in front of her. Then he vanished. It was too late for him to abort his charge. Reflexively Vetala took herself elsewhere. He skidded to a halt. There was no one to kill anymore. It seemed as if the Crimson Corona spoke to him, warning him. He whirled. It was Vetala reappearing.

Kill her, the Mind of Sapiendev spoke to him again. Unless it was just his mind, his subconscious, speaking to him. He hesitated. He realized he was going crazy. She materialized her Brainrock sickle. He was too shocked to raise either his mirrored shield, the Soul of Devaura, or his slight, curved blade, the Body of Demeter, in order to block her thrust.

She drove it into him. It hurt. He died. Dying didn't hurt at all. Should have killed myself a long time ago.

Maybe he had.

========

It was a good thing Sisert was a virtually lifeless expanse of land.
The Apocalyptic Nucleus formed together, blew a hole through the roof of the Calvary Cavern and rocketed into the open air beyond Temporis.

========

Radiant Rider, flying on her rainbow hair and carrying Wildman Dervish Furie along with the Untouchable Diver within it, followed. Once she saw that the Byronic Nucleus was waiting for its Apocalyptic equivalent, she knew this was no place for man nor beast nor even supranormal. Having no time to flee back to the cavern, she hit the ground and covered herself, Furie and the Diver also, with layers of hardening iridescence.

In the last analysis, it was the Untouchable Diver, Yehudi Cohen, who saved their lives. Departiclyzing the three of them, the effects of the two Nuclei annihilating each other passed harmlessly through them. Still and all, Gloriel's solid, rainbow bubble and Furie rapidly digging a pit for them in the frozen sand were contributing factors in their survival. True team-mates, the three members of the perhaps disingenuously named Damnation Brigade protected each other.

They hunkered down in the sand, even slept for a while. It was twilight by the time Furie dared leave the culvert he'd dug for them. The desert surface was crystalline and slippery. The sand had fused into glass.

"Gone, both Nuclei. Must have atomized each other."

The Diver emerged, holding Gloriel in his arms. She was unconscious, breathing in gasps. "Good riddance to them, I say. From what I've seen of these devils, no matter who their father happens to be the world's a better place without them." That said, he abruptly lost his footing and bumbled onto his butt.

"Lord Almighty!" he swore. "Haven't seen anything like this since Emperor Energy tried to turn Tobruk into a skating rink!"

(The last time anyone had seen that otherwise anonymous supra had been on the 6th of August 1945 in Hiroshima. It was also the first time any of them remembered seeing Obadiah and Takeda Power, whose codename became Crimson Corona.)

"Christ!" exclaimed Wildman Dervish Furie, realizing whom the Diver was holding. "What happened to Gloriel?"

Furie's real name was Jervis Murray. He was a black African who'd been raised in Jamaica. Like the Diver he was a Summoning Child. Gloriel was Gloriella nee D'Angelo, now Dark, Glory of the Angels. Her codename was Radiant Rider. Because of her multihued hair, watching Damnation Isle from afar on the previous Sunday, when Demon Land recombined their perfectly preserved bodies with their minds, the Parents Thanatos had initially mistook her for their Day, Castella, whose power focus was just that, rainbow hair.

"Her dome must have shattered when they vaporized each other," responded the Diver. "She'll be all right. Hell, she should be. She survived Carcinogen the Leper. He just sliced me out of his way."

Yehudi Cohen had been born and raised in Germany. His presumed father, a Jewish mystic, was among those members of the Godling Guild who disappeared during its Summoning, one of a never-determined number of Simultaneous Summonings, in 1920. His mother died before he turned ten. He was thereafter raised in a series of boarding schools paid for by the Baron Tyrtod von Alptraum, a Prussian nobleman and industrialist. As he would eventually learn, Von Alp was his mother's lover for many years; from even before the Summoning apparently.

Since no one who survived any of the Summonings remembered much of anything that went on during the six weeks the members of the Godling Guild were lost in the Himalayas, many believed the Baron was actually Cohen's father. While that was unlikely – Cohen didn't look like he had any non-Jewish blood in him whatsoever – there was no denying he came by his supranormal abilities beneath the frigid waters of Hamburg Harbour in 1938.

They came to him after an explosive encounter with a glowing, brain-like boulder composed of a substance that, a decade later on Aegean Trigon, none other that Aristotle Zeross, age 5 at the time, decided to call Gypsium. Cohen had been wearing a crude, homemade wetsuit at the time. He still did; that and a pair of crimson-lens Gorgon Goggles he found in the Roman Colosseum in January 1938, shortly before he realized his Summoning Heritage and thereby became a supra.

"We'll have to take her downstairs to Temporis," the Wildman appreciated. "We have to go back there anyhow, if only to see how Witchie, Johnny and his Beauty are doing. Not to mention if any of the others are still alive."

Witchie was Wilderwitch, Akbarartha's companion in the Faerie Garden. Johnny was John Sundown, Blind Sundown. He was a native American Summoning Child who wielded the Solar Spear of his Cheyenne ancestors and considered himself a creature of the cosmos. His Beauty was Raven's Head.

Raven had a crow creature's feathery head, the sable-black body of a huge horse, a mare in her case, and the speckled tail of an iguana or headless snake. She had talarial wings on either side of her four upper hooves. These, though non-detachable, were therefore akin to the mythological sandals of Hermes or Mercury; also the power focus of Irisiel Mercherm, Lazareme's primary Heliodromus for most of her existence as an individually solid deity.

Blind Sundown rode her. She could fly on her talarial wings, his fellow creature of the cosmos. Not only could he communicate with her, as could Wilderwitch, he could see through her eyes. They were quite the pair, were Johnny and his Beauty. All the more so since Raven had of late developed a retractable horn, like that of a unicorn.

On Friday night Thrygragos Byron and his second-born, Primary Nucleoids had been horrified to see Raven. They thought Thrygragos Varuna Mithras had exterminated her kind, the mutated ravendeer of the Mystic Mountains, thousands of years earlier. He had. Ravendeer weren't just from the Mystic Mountains, however.

The Byronics were more horrified to see what Wilderwitch was wearing, the Crimson Corona. They brought them inside anyhow. They needed the Damnation Brigade to drive the Apocalyptics out of Temporis, to Sisert, where they could recathonitize them. They should have known better. Too late now. Their stars were already in the night's sky.

As for Furie, there were four degrees to his supra-normality. Jervis and Murray were both human, the Murray being a onetime world-class athlete far stronger and faster than the Jervis, who was pretty much a Normie Normalman. They, not that there was any real way to distinguish Jervis and Murray, were gentle sorts. Dervish was their wild man aspect. In his early years as a recognized supranormal he was often described as a Werewolf in Shorts.

In his Dervish Furie persona, he was an astoundingly fast, all but indestructible juggernaut of sheer, raw power. He didn't kill, though. Only Blind Sundown, who hadn't always been blind, and Raven's Head killed. His Furie aspect was his Dervish aspect's engine. No one knew what the Full Furie could do. The Witch and Murray were lovers, had been anyhow. They'd been having a few days of downtime lately. She stayed away from him when he was in wild man mode because she was terrified of the Furie.

"To say the least," said the Diver. "That'd be problematic. Must be a drop of hundreds of feet. You jump, I bet you squish. Wouldn't take the chance, if I was you."

"Wasn't planning on it," admitted Furie. "Go downstairs, mate. If Raven's feeling better, she can fly either up or down. If she's not, then try to find Airealist. He was with Johnny and his Beauty, so they'd know if he's still alive."

Airealist was the codename for Aires D'Angelo. Another Summoning Child – among the original ten members of the Damnation Brigade five were Summoning Children – he was Gloriel's adopted brother. His similarly adopted twin sister was Thalassa. Together they were the Outer Earth's equivalent of the Janna-Sraddha Terrible Twins. The Thanatoids of Lathakra also had a pair of twins named Aires and Thalassa. D-Brig's twins only had two eyes, however.

One thing everyone who knew about the Simultaneous Summonings of 59/1920 agreed upon was that they were the work of Anthean Witches. Not too many of the cognoscenti realized the Ants were pursuing their Panharmonium Pipedream anymore. Nightingales, the Superior Sisterhood's superior sisters, not only wiped the memories of the Summonings' survivors but, nine months later, they deliberately mixed up the babies born because of it. As a result, no one knew the identities of the D'Angelo Terrible Twins' parents; not with any certainty.

However, because they looked so much like D'Angelos, most believed their mother was one or the other of Gloriel's paternal aunts: Celestine or Dolores. Although nearly 80 and reputedly not in the best of health, Dolores now Rivera, Sister Sorrow, was still alive. Celestine D'Angelo had been killed in 1923. In life she was known as the Celestial Superior. Along with Ubris Nauroz, the father of Young Death, she was the person who issued the Summonings.

Sea, to his Air, was the lone member of the Damnation Brigade who hadn't come to Sedon's Head. Presumably she was still on the Outer Earth. They'd left Wilderwitch, Raven's Head and Blind Sundown in the Calvary Cavern. All three were still alive, though the Witch might not be for much longer.

They had no idea what had become of their leader, Cyborg Cerebrus. Had as much of an idea, nil, as to whether Airealist or OMP (short for both Obadiah Melvin and Old Man Power), whom they'd only learned last night was actually Akbarartha, the titular Kronokronos Supreme of Temporis, were still alive either.

"If there's no sign of Airhead," Wildman advised Diver, "Get hold of Dand Tariqartha in Centurium. The devil owes us big time. We saved his precious protectorate from the god-cursed Apocalyptics. The minimum he can do is help Glory and the rest of us get healthy again."

Furie took Gloriel out of the Diver's arm, squatted down and, trying to keep her warm, hugged her tight to his wiry, extremely hairy, even furry, body. There was a reason he'd been thought of as a Werewolf in Shorts. Only now he was more like a Werewolf in shredded evening dress. Gentleman Jervis Murray disported himself in the best clothes money could buy. Over the years he'd spent a great deal on clothes. Wildman Dervish Furie was a whole lot bigger, and far rougher on clothing, than Murray.

The Diver bounded off. Miraculously, disturbingly, he couldn't locate the hole in the floor of Sisert. Departiclyzing, he dove into the solid ground. He could soil-swim only so deep. Something was blocking him from the caverns below – a Solidium Shield, it seemed to him. Being Gypsium-gifted, he couldn't get through Solidium, as Outer Earthlings referred to Stopstone. He dipped around. There was no way he could get into Temporis.

Returning to Sisert's surface, he was astonished to find Old Man Power, Blind Sundown, Wilderwitch, Raven's Head, and Cerebrus David Ryne together with Furie and the Rainbow. Cyborg Cerebrus looked dead; not for the first time either. He'd been shot in the head as a youngster and, even though the bullet didn't kill him, it left him severely brain-damaged.

His headplate was what made him a cyborg or cybernetic organism. It was also what made him a supranormal, one with tremendous mental abilities, telekinesis being just one of them. During Christmas Week of 1946, the then-otherwise-anonymous supra-genius known as the Conqueror, who claimed to have invented the headplate, somehow wired it into his brain-matter then attached it to the top of his skull. During his battle with the Apocalyptic of War it had been partially blown off. He was still breathing, though.

So was Wilderwitch. She didn't look much better than Cerebrus, barely alive, although she was at least still semi-conscious. Murray was the paramedic but the Diver had been on enough battlefields in his life to realize her entire right leg might have to come off. Forget about all that blood, which she'd already staunched herself. Shattered, not just broken, femurs didn't heal very well at the best of times.

This was the worst of times. They were in an ice-covered desert in the north-ernmost extremes of a Hidden Continent that may well be in its own dimension, but was geographically situated in the same position as the Outer Earth's Northern Pacific Ocean. Plus, it was December. Fortunately Raven's Head was on her feet, her talarial winged hooves, and was walking about tentatively. Sundown was standing on a nearby rise, recharging his Solar Spear in the rays of the dying sun. At least that meant the Brigade wouldn't be without his power.

OMP draped his green cape around the feverous witch. The Diver came up to them. "What happened, Old Man?"

"You want the short version or the long one?" asked Akbar.

"Kiss, kiss. Keep it simple."

"Dand my Dad self-cathonitized, became a star in the night's sky. Lakshmi of Lemuria showed her true colours, got hold of his power focus and banished me, and the rest of us, up here. Temporis is lost. I'm afraid Cerebrus is as well. As for Aires, well, I don't see him. You'll have to draw your own conclusions about that." Air and Sea, the D'Angelo version of the Somata Terrible Twins, were elementals. They were state-shifters. So was Gloriel, only the state she shifted into was that of a rainbow; which she could both fly on and make solid.

Dervish Furie slammed the vitreous surface of Sisert with his fist; hit it so hard it cracked. "Ridiculous!" he spat. "We come back after twenty-five years in Limbo, fight off the most powerful foes we've ever come across, survive two Nuclei blowing the crap out of each other, and you're trying to tell me some hopped-up teenager's booted us out of the only haven we're likely to find on the entire Head. Damnation, Damnation Brigade! Are we doomed to finally die in some god-forsaken, frozen-over desert?"

"Load of flagitious flapdoodle that, Dervish," said the Diver. "You really need an answer?"

"Nope! We keep going. Unless you've a better idea."

"Go where?" Akbar demanded.

"To the fucking mountains! Out there!"

"You're talking the Mystics," remembered the old man. Or, via a sort of mental osmosis, his sceptre did it for him. "They're as near or as far as they want to be. Perception, like sentience, often has a different meaning on the Headworld; your Big Shelter, Witch."

"We'll beat this, Akbar," groaned Wilderwitch, semi-deliriously. "We're the Damnation Brigade. We'd fight our way out of Hell itself if it came to that. I've stuff in my bottomless bag that'll help."

"No need, Witch. I've rings on my fingers enough for all!"

"Harry!"

========

Capputis, a hydrocephalic, teenage clone with gills behind his ears, and Thobruk Grudal – at nearly 60 one of the few remaining Trinondev Warriors of Weir who could boast not only of having served the previous Master but of being friends with the current one, a mixed-blood like himself – warily entered his presence.

"What is it?" he, this Master, seeing them, demanded.

========

Saladin Devason had been the Master of Weir since 5950, Year of the Dome. His surname at birth was Nauroz. That remained his official surname. In the Weirdom no one ever called him Devason. Not even in private. He wasn't ubiquitous; wasn't always within earshot, but he always was potentially. The walls had ears up here.

Sal, as a few of his subjects did call him, when he was there with them as well, was large and powerfully-built, perhaps six-five and two hundred forty pounds. Like Grudal and Capputis, indeed like almost all the males currently living within the confines of Cabalarkon, Sedon's Devic Eye on a map of the Headworld, his skin was black.

It wasn't quite as black-as-midnight on a starless night, like that of pureblood males, most of whom were inbred imbeciles, but it was at least as black as the night's sky in a city lit by streetlamps. Which the Weirdom of Cabalarkon was, even if its obelisks were topped by pyramidal firestones that shone at night and recharged during the day.

Today being a day for public *'consultations'*, he was dressed in full Masterly regalia. That consisted of a headdress made of Garuda feathers from which protruded a single rhinoceros horn; a sleeveless cloak made of the fur of a white gorilla or something similar; pantaloons held up by a belt fashioned out of eagle talons; gauntlets that looked like bear paws and boots that looked like tiger paws.

Looped around his neck was his personal chain of office, a necklace of ruby-red bloodstones off of which hung a golden pendant shaped like a triangle with a single eye staring out of it. Attached to the wall behind his throne, just above three chairs left symbolically empty in honour of the three Great Goddesses, once the faraway Utopia of Weir's deities, were a curved sword and a circular shield so shiny it reflected like a mirror. They, like the chain of office, glowed of Brainrock, yes, but they were proven facsimiles of the real things, the Trigregos Talismans: the Amateramirror, the Susasword and the Crimson Corona.

This particular throne room was situated in the old, exceedingly old, albeit not quite antediluvian, Masters Palace. He had another one in the modern-looking skyscraper named Skyrise; modern-looking as in Godbadian-modern. He'd been living there for five years now. It was where he usually held smaller, though just as official gatherings. When he moved into it Skyrise had twenty-five storeys, one for every year of his reign. It now had thirty storeys. No one noticeable worked on Skyrise anymore. He was the Weirdom's Master. He didn't need anyone noticeable to construct it. Cabalarkon, the place, amounted to his protectorate.

What wasn't a fake – what wasn't an original, rather – was what he held in his right hand. It, his Master's Mace, what he sometimes referred to as his Speaking Stick, was a miniature eye-stave complete with a closed eyeorb atop it. His didn't manifest a gargoyle. None of the ones in the throne room manifested gargoyles. These eye-staves, and there were as many of them as there were Trinondevs in the throne room, were as plain as his; a pole with a leathern orb atop it.

Sal was on record as stating gargoyles were for the battlefield or the parade ground. Not that that stopped the imbeciles of Weir parading about on the perfectly preserved, cobblestone streets of the partially antediluvian city with their house gargoyles manifest. Truth was he needed the imbeciles support; couldn't function as the Master without it. Then again nothing up here worked without a Master anymore. Their support empowered him and, with it, he powered everything else. At least so everyone believed.

In contrast to their Master, both the teenager and the older man, an Inner Earth Summoning Child, were wearing the Arabic-style gowns, haiks or djellabas so common in the Weirdom. Grudal's djellaba, his turban and his drawn veil, the equivalent of a Tuareg's tagilmus or taguelmost in the Outer Earth country of Algeria, were dyed various shades of indigo blue. Capputis, being still so comparatively young, wore a gown that was off-white, more like beige, a woman's colour – pureblood Utopian women, most of whom were as imbecilic as their male counterparts, being as white-as-light on a salt flat during a sunny day.

Grudal had drawn his veil as a sign of the seriousness of the situation; as a sign also of his personal failure when it came to performing his duty. That Capputis was as bare-headed as he was bare-faced had little to do with his age or that he rightly felt himself only an apprentice Trinondev. There was no such thing anymore. You were or you weren't.

Capputis was entitled to call himself a Warrior of Weir. Had the Master allowed him to do so, he could have gone to Hadd with Field Commander Nauroz. Grudal could have as well, had his charge, the High Illuminary, allowed him. Which she hadn't.

Grudal had to wait until he turned thirty before he was allowed to become a full-fledged Trinondev, with the turban, veil and eye-stave that went with the privilege. Such strictures, due mostly to unabated inbred idiocy, no longer applied. That the teenager had no headgear was mostly due to the fact that, with all that hair, to go along with his oversized cranium, a turban would just exaggerate his physical deformity.

There were other considerations, however. For one, the amount of cloth a turban that fit him might require wasn't as readily available as it had been in Grudal's youth. For another, a pureblood tailor or seamstress with all of his or her fingers still usable was almost as rare as a pureblood butcher with two hands. Such was the state of affairs in the Utopia of Weir here on Earth in the Year of the Dome 5980.

To be fair, such was also the state of affairs Saladin Devason inherited when he won the Challenge of Weir and thereby attained the Mastery of Cabalarkon in 5950 YD. Too bad it took another decade for Sal to get his loins in gear. More, too bad it wasn't until 5960 that Ringleader, Aristotle Zeross, at the age of 17, found himself in here, underneath the Cathonic Dome, and thence here, to the Weirdom itself. Ringleader had, though, and thanks in large measure to him and his much older wife, there was finally non-cloned hope for the future.

Unfortunately none of that hope was any older than Capputis, clone that he was.

========

"Devils, sire," said Grudal hesitantly, his mixed-blood origin obvious from his bushy growth of facial hair. Unlike the Master, who kept his beard well-trimmed – when he didn't, for fear of having to employ a pureblood barber, self-shave it altogether off – Grudal preferred the hirsute look. "At least we think it's devils."

"Here, in the Weirdom?" Sal scoffed. "Impossible!"

"Whatever it was, sir," offered Capputis, whose obsequiousness belied his undeniable intelligence. "Dr Zeross and her three daughters have just disappeared!"

========

They'd declined to incline their heads, expressly so. All except Andaemyn Sarpedon, that is, and that included his own daughters from an earlier incarnation.

They had their reasons of course.

========

For the six still alive samurais (the Tethys twosome, the two who'd been guarding the cave's entrance, and the two who'd been injured when the Legendarian caused the collapse of the cave's ceiling by drawing it collapsing), they were loyal to Warlord Mikoto. To the death and, with the arrival of the Gatherers, presumably beyond it; so it seemed at any rate.

As for Sabreur Somata, Salamoneus and Tucedon, no surnames required and none acknowledged, they wanted nothing to do with either the Dead or mutually-hated Godbad trying to conquer Hadd. For Alastor Molorchus, he just wanted nothing to do with Young Death.

The ostensible reason Andy agreed to be drawn to Lake Sedona's Sraddha Monastery was because her maybe-grandfather convinced her that her definite-mother was feeling poorly. The real reason was because Morgianna had been in contact with her via their Hellstones. She was doing fine. Fish was her friend, one of only a very few she had left. Her Brainrock fishnet had momentarily inconvenienced her, true, but it hadn't done her any harm.

Besides, Daddy Demios had just come to the monastery thanks to another Athenan War Witch, Janna St Peche-Montressor, and would love to see her again.

Also, there wasn't much point in Andy pursuing the Trigregos Talismans anymore. Not if her grandfather, Morg's acknowledged father, was right and someone had not only managed to free Harmony, the Unity of Balance, but had absconded with the Susasword.

Those wondrous things adhered to each other and Morg knew just the person who could retrieve them. It was just a matter of finding a way to get hold of him.

========

Saladin Devason was a living eye-stave.

========

He'd been disinterestedly holding what passed for court in the one-man ruled Weirdom of Cabalarkon when the young clone and perhaps the only man he dared called friend brought him news of the kidnapping of the High Illuminary. Melina nee Sarpedon Zeross was the twin sister of the traitor Demios, his 30-years' exiled, greatest rival for the Mastery of Weir. Dem was the husband of his more like self-exiled sister, Morgianna, the Morrigan.

Due his own reclusive tendencies, Mel and her children by Harry, soon to be 37, Persephone, 16 or close enough, Helen, 12, and the baby, Athena, 6, were as close as the Weirdom came to having a royal family. They should have been his; they weren't. Mel had rejected him time and time again. Nonetheless, if only because he relied on her far more than he should, the news did not please him in any way whatsoever.

Ever-calculating sort that he was, in order to demonstrate how much the news displeased him he balled his fists together, disappearing his bear-paw gauntlets and Master's Mace as he did so. They, his fists, became single eyes, like those that both peered and stuck out of eye-staves when their eyeorbs opened. Visibly angry he rose to his feet then, to further emphasize just how furious he was, he levitated off the ground and stomped above his throne, on the air itself.

Calmness returned as soon as his functionaries ushered the idiot petitioners, who had come to beg indulgences, out of the throne room. Once everyone except Capputis and Grudal left, he came back to ground, figuratively as well as literally. His eye-fists became plain hands the bear-paws covered again. His Master's Mace reappeared, in the left one this time.

Showtime over, he railed at the messengers. "Disappeared! How? Where?"

"At their coastal villa, sir," sputtered Capputis. "The weather's been unseasonably warm so the High Illuminary and her children were out on the balcony having tea when something cut through the air. They were gone before any of us could react."

"I left my men and her Illuminaries there to look for traces of them," said Grudal, who had spent a disproportionate amount of his life as what her much younger husband, also a Dr Zeross, not so humourously referred to as Mel's Minder. "But as soon as we ascertained to our own satisfaction there weren't any we transported directly here."

The Weirdom of Cabalarkon still had operational Matter Transducers. These teleportation devices didn't work beyond the Weirdom. Other than Trinondev eye-staves, very little of the Utopians' originally extraterrestrial technology did. They were just thankful the clothing as well as life-sustaining, food processing machines and firestone-topped obelisks that provided the city state with its power, continued to function up here, within Cabalarkon's boundaries.

Not even the Illuminaries of Weir knew why that was; not for sure, though they had their theories. Wouldn't be Illuminaries if they didn't. However, so long as Sal was a good Master, nearly six thousand years of being trapped beneath the Sedon Sphere indicated that what still worked would probably continue to work for at least another six thousand years. Would continue to work, it went without saying, so long as Utopians didn't inbreed themselves to extinction.

"Couldn't be devils," Saladin re-emphasized, as if trying to convince himself. "By Sedonic decree this is a devil-free zone; an inviolate, on punishment of instant cathonitization, devil-free zone. Even if it wasn't, our eyeorbs would open automatically and immediately imprison any devil foolish enough to disobey his or her All-Father. Which they aren't supposed to be able to do in any case, so claim our Illuminaries."

The Master of Weir didn't have much use for Illuminaries, most of whom were female; scarcely tolerated them. He suspected, with some justification, they were all closet witches and he truly despised witches of any affinity. "Cut through the air, you say. Not rings in the sky; not an Anthean Agate?"

It couldn't be an Anthean Agate, nor any other kind of witch-stone, because by Saladin's own decree they no longer functioned in Cabalarkon. In the Weirdom he was that powerful. Wasn't anywhere near as much so beyond its borders, however. He'd learned that the high (temperature) hard way.

It was extremely difficult to forget being about to be stewed alive on Shenon, Witch Isle, when you were supposed to be its Quarter Queens' guest. All the more so when one of them, its non-Lemurian Aortic, Tsishah Twilight, his own niece, had guaranteed him safe haven such that she could help facilitate a family reconciliation.

"Cut, sire. Cold blue flash and they weren't there any more. That was it."

"Blue!" Saladin ruminated. "There's something about that colour. Wait a minute, there was a devil allowed here, one with blue skin. Cold, you say. Thanatos. That's it: Tantal Thanatos, King Cold of Lathakra, the Demon Sedon's least favourite grandson. He was made an honorary citizen for saving the Weirdom from the Idiot Twins well over a thousand years ago.

"It'd be in the annals. Melina would know. She's probably the only person left who can read them; let alone has read them. I heard he was killed. But who else would it have been? No devil, not even a Thrygragos, can disobey the Moloch Sedon."

"If I may venture, sir," presumed Capputis. His enlarged head, with its dish-mop of impossible to comb, curly hair atop a long, barge-pole of a body, looked as if it might fall off. Perhaps hydrocephalus was the price the boy paid for having gills behind his ears, Grudal reflected. It was a bad joke. Gills behind the ears shouldn't equate with water on the brain.

"Venture away, Cappy."

Capputis winced at the nickname. Grudal was glad his drawn veil hid his smirk. Even if they had been friends since near-enough to their births – he was a year younger than Saladin, was a Summoning Child, the same as the Sarpedon twins and Morg, Sal's sister – the Master's temper was unpredictable. He might misconstrue a smirk at Cappy's expense for a smirk at his expense.

"Thank you, sir. What about your devic mother? Along with about sixty others, Star Pyrame's been missing from the night sky for almost a week now. The High Illuminary and I were talking about that just last night with Mr Tethys. The Legendarian – and Milady Melina agreed with him – felt devils who escaped Cathonia wouldn't be bound by Sedonic decrees any longer. If they were then they couldn't have escaped. The Daemon as well Devil King would have forbidden it."

"The Pauper Priestess isn't allowed here either," insisted her consequently deviant of a quarter-son. "I won the Mastery fighting her off thirty years ago. You weren't around then, Cappy, but it's a fact. Ask Grudal here, or you, Capputis, ask your development team. This Weirdom amounts to my protectorate. I could cathonitize her with a thought."

The Master tried to sound unambiguous but couldn't conceal his uncertainty. Once cathonitized, always cathonitized, so the High Illuminary and her predecessors, including Copperhead, Kyprian Somata, who was also his great-grandmother as well as his predecessor as the Master of Weir, always claimed.

(Cathonitization or ill-starring – catasterization on the Outer Earth, according to Illuminaries – meant being rendered stars shining out of the night's sky, the Sedon Sphere. It was the equivalent of devic death.)

"Leave me now. And if Dr Zeross, the male Dr Zeross, shows up, tell him nothing. Delay. Say I'm sick. Whatever needs be. On your life don't let this out. If he discovers his family's vanished, he'll go off half-cocked. We can't afford to lose him and his rings now. He's on a mission. If he's successful, we won't be worrying about devils, decathonitized or otherwise, much longer."

"Mission, Master?" wondered Grudal innocently. "You mean other than gathering more outsiders for our breeding pools?"

Capputis next-to-swallowed his tongue. No one, except perhaps Melina born Sarpedon, who was also a duly accredited Dr Zeross, and Golgotha Nauroz, an eighty year old clone who was currently fighting in Hadd, and they only in private, would dare question the Master in that tone or any other tone. If Thobruk Grudal had been a clone, Saladin would have had him devolved.

Instead, much to his additional shock, the Master ripped off his chain of office and threw it onto the throne. "To get us back the real things. Not these sad-sack Brainrock imitations left here by the Attis when he absconded with the real things most of 4,000 years ago. Dr Zeross's goodwill, the goodwill of both Dr Zerosses, is more important than anything else right now."

"Then we better come up with something more positive than hiding our heads in the sand," Grudal recommended. "There were servants around, some of her Illuminaries, other guards. Zmas Day is only two and a half weeks away. Milady Melina has a lot of friends. She is the High Illuminary. So do her children; the hyperactive little one Tina in particular. The public expects to see them on their rounds. They'll have questions. There'll have to be answers."

Saladin glared at his fellow hybrid. Although he did have, Capputis didn't need a big brain to go with his big head to appreciate how immune the nearly 60-year-old Summoning Child felt he was to the Master's displeasure. Grudal had yet to pull back his veil. And if that wasn't an affront, what with him being the only other one there then, Capputis wondered, what was?

"You do try my patience, Grudal. You always have. But you're right. Like the High Illuminary you have a regrettable habit of usually being right. Keep a lid on things. No talk, no rumours. Since you failed in your nearly lifelong duty to protect her, his wife, I'm making damage control your personal duty until Dr Zeross, the other Dr Zeross, brings Golgotha Nauroz back and he can take over from you.

"Capputis, do whatever Grudal says. As of today you're his assistant, learn from him. Just don't learn too much. Consider it a promotion. I'll be making inquiries. Go!" They made proper obeisance, turned to leave. Saladin wasn't quite finished yet. "One more thing. Traitors are executed in this Weirdom. Superior officers carry out the execution personally. Then I deal with the superior officers. I trust that is clear."

It was, abundantly and silently, to both Capputis and Grudal.

========

Once Andy and Young Death were gone; once he'd sent the Gatherers, along with their mounts and a couple of recently deceased samurais to where they wanted to go; once he therefore felt it safe to approach them, Alastor Molorchus made the three other remaining barbarians an offer they couldn't refuse.

Sometimes Crystal Skull-sets did work properly.

========

"I've been given to understand there have been potentially deleterious developments elsewhere. A certain devil is loose upon the Headworld again. There are major Godbucks available to us if we can dispose of her daemonic body forthwith. I shall send you to where she used to make her home. We've been there before so that won't be any problem. Come dark, I shall join you. Are you interested?"

"Are we? Fucking Hell, why wouldn't be?" said Salamoneus.

"How many Godbucks are we talking about, Al?" queried Tucedon.

"Heaps," Molorchus answered.

"Who cares," said Sabreur. "I've a Utopian heritage. If I can kill just one devil before I die myself then I'll do so a happy man."

========

The glowing rings came out of the air in the atrium of the Citadel of the Thinkers, an antediluvian structure made of Cyclopean stonework at the heart of the Weirdom's Cabalarkon City proper, just off the metropolis's massive central square. Aristotle 'Harry' Zeross wasted no time summoning its resident physicians. Most of them didn't have far to come.

The Citadel was the closest thing non-idiotic Utopians had to a university.

========

They came, accompanied by eye-stave-armed Trinondevs. A doctor himself, Harry didn't need to explain who needed help or in what order. He had interned with some of them, trained a few of the younger ones, whilst the older ones, the vast majority, given Utopian life-spans, had been his secondary teachers. Obviously Cyborg Cerebrus was near-terminal, Wilderwitch critical and Gloriel D'Angelo Dark serious.

"These are my people, folks," said Ringleader. "Trust them."

Dervish Furie took a look at the universally black men and universally white women. "Murray's a paramedic. I'd trust him first."

"Then stay!" spouted Ringleader testily. "Although I doubt you can become Murray right away. You're too wound up. Besides, I'd rather have Dervish Furie at my side in Hadd than Jervis Murray back here. Believe me, Utopian physicians and scientocrats know what they're doing. As my wife, whom you'll know, will tell you, true Utopians practically invented medical science. Hell, they practically invented science, period."

"I'd rather have you along as well, Dervish," acknowledged the Diver. With Cerebrus David Ryne down, Yehudi Cohen had presumed to takeover D-Brig's de facto leadership.

"That's a dick-dildo here," agreed Akbarartha, with forced jocularity. "Sounds like where we're going angels fear to tread. And you're no angel."

"Am I to take that as a compliment?" said Furie.

"Take it anyway you like, Dervish."

"What about you, Raven, Johnny?" asked Ringleader.

The part-horse, part-unicorn, bird-headed creature with talarial-winged hooves whinnied in her peculiar neigh-caw manner. "As Beauty says," confirmed Sundown. "Yes."

"Ready when you are then, Rings," said the Diver.

========

Guardian Angel Tyrtod didn't have to wait long for a new shell. That he'd have to start calling himself Guardian Angel Mikoto didn't bother him in the slightest. It wasn't everyday, wasn't any day, he got to recathonitize a Byronic Master Deva. Since he'd already been decathonitized once, it was simplicity itself. Get hold of his power focus, hold it away from him, look up and, if it was night, sure enough, another star would appear in the Sedon Sphere.

It wasn't night yet. Nonetheless, like Plague, Nevair Neverknight didn't realize he was in a game until he was out of it. For him, Sedon's heavens were worse than Hell on Earth. At least in Satanwyck there were always demons to debrain. Here there were just talking stars.

"That's the last time I'm ever nice to anyone," said the Plague Star.

****

(Game-Gambit) 20: **Tethys Draws Trouble**

Devauray, Tantalar 6, 5980

The Master of Weir, Saladin born Nauroz, called Devason, was by nature a solitary fellow.

========

Although Sal had known many women in his 61-years of life, he had never married. Equally so, while he had sired many a son and daughter by many of those women – particularly since Aristotle Zeross began bringing in Outer Earthlings judged by Weir's High Illuminary, Melina now also Zeross, to have had howsoever recessive Utopian genes – he acknowledged no children. Didn't care to either. How could he? In a Utopia there was no such thing as legitimacy or illegitimacy. Every child was as precious as every other child.

The many children he did have were raised by development teams, more often than not in the Weirdom's fertile but poorly tilled countryside. (Whereon, for well over 2,000 years – until their *'redemption'* during the mastery of Zalman Somata, Janna Fangfingers' birthfather – the leached-off Sarpedon underclass toiled so slavishly.) If they started to act uppity, to try to lord or lady it over any other child, they were moved even farther away from the metropolis.

Could be they'd have to learn to grow, breed, capture and hunt their own suppers. Horror of horrors.

In the 30-years of his Mastery, Sal did mostly as he desired. When he needed advice he looked to Golgotha Nauroz or Mel herself for it. That didn't mean he took it but it did mean he sometimes asked for it. They weren't physically available right this minute but Trinondev eyeorbs were so very useful in so many ways. He could use his Master's Mace to far-speak with the former. If Mel had her equivalent of his mace with her, her caduceus, as she both called it and had her manifested gargoyle make it appear, he could contact her as well.

For some reason, he felt the need to contact someone he hadn't spoken to for approaching six and a half years. Since he and Jordan Tethys were very nearly stewed alive on Shenon, as it happened; on the same day, and on the same heart-shaped island, Athena 'Tina' Zeross was born. So, rather than resume holding court after Grudal and Capputis left him, Saladin went behind his throne, accessed the Matter Transducer hidden there, and teleported himself out of the ages-old Masters' Palace.

He thereby transported himself beyond the expansive central square of Cabalarkon City proper to his private quarters on the uppermost level of Skyrise, his towering, deliberately never completed, Godbadian-modern skyscraper. Once there he changed his mind; decided to have a nap instead. His pride simply wouldn't let him do what his brain was nagging at him to do.

Hours later he was more exhausted from tossing and turning than he had been from holding court. Finally, he got out of bed, had a shower and pulled on a dressing gown. In his still private antechamber he approached an unadorned wall, activated his Master's Mace, its eyeorb, materialized his safe, opened it, and removed an ordinary looking box largely made out of Stopstone.

Swallowing his dignity, he took out the tiny Hellstone secreted therein. It was the only witch-stone he allowed in the Weirdom. It began to glow almost immediately. Which likely meant she'd already been trying to contact him. Soon the indistinct shape of the Morrigan appeared in the air.

"This is a surprise, brother. The approaching holidays making you reconsider our life long banishment?"

(As his only sibling, Morgianna was the daughter of Augustus Nauroz, a pure or virtually pure U-blood, and Pandora Mannering, a witch whose forbearers were anything except pure in any sense of the word. Everyone, albeit inaudibly, referred to him as Devason because his witch-mother was possessed when he was conceived. However, Sal used Nauroz as his surname.

(At the insistence of their great-grandmother, Master Kyprian, Morg became a Somata, which was how she was raised. At her own insistence, as soon as they turned thirty, shortly after Kyprian's death, she married her longtime bodyguard and became Sarpedon. Sal should have married Dem's twin sister around the same time – that's what Kyprian wanted – but for whatever reason it wasn't to be.)

"Bollocks, Morg. You are my flesh. I never exiled you, just your traitorous lover, the pretender. And it's no surprise. I've been thinking about contacting you for hours now. Whose eye-stave were you using to plant that notion in my mind, by the way? One of Mel's Illuminary ambassadors?"

It was stupid question. He dreaded her answer. So long as he was in the Weirdom he could use his Master's Mace to contact anyone who had an eye-stave anywhere on the Head. However, no one, not Mel nor even Golgotha, could use theirs to contact him. They especially couldn't use theirs to influence his thoughts. Beyond the Weirdom, though, there was one eye-stave reputedly superior to his mace. It had once belonged to his paternal grandfather.

"That's impossible," she far-spoke, calling his bluff. "And you know it."

"Your agate's warm to the touch. You've been trying to get hold of me."

"That's true. Fact is I was about to ask Jordy to send you a message." (Quill Tethys, the legendary 30-Year Man, could send messages long-distance; he just couldn't draw anyone anywhere without their expressed consent.)

"Where are you?"

"Where do you think? Where he is, where you and Mel sent him this morning. Wait a minute. You think I had Demios send you urgings with his pre-Earth eye-stave."

Ubris Nauroz had given his improbably old eye-stave to Demios Sarpedon, rather than to his own son, because Augustus had been devolved moments after Morg's birth. He wouldn't give it to Sal, which is what he should have done. Ubris did not approve of Deva-sons. Of course Ubris was a vampire by then. Vamps didn't think sensibly.

"Didn't you?"

"Of course not."

"Where is he?"

"Gone back to Aka Godbad City again. But Andy's here. You do remember Andy don't you. Andaemyn, our daughter, your niece, the one you wouldn't even say hello to on Witch Isle six and a half years ago because she's striped skin? So is Golgotha. You sent him and his men here yourself.

"So is just about every other right-thinking person on the entire Head. There's a war on, between the Living and the Dead. You should be here too, Sal. You should be here leading the struggle against devazurkind, not hiding out in your inviolable Eye-Land."

She said this last scornfully. Utopians, the Master of Weir especially, were bred to hate devils; foremost their All-Father, the Moloch Sedon. Yet, to their forever shame, the vast majority of pureblood Utopians left on the Whole Earth cowered in an area easily identifiable on a map of the Headworld as Sedon's Devic Eye-Land.

"Haddazur zombies are beneath my attention."

"Are they? Nergal Vetala's back. And so is Harmony."

In his private quarters, Saladin came close to gagging. He looked to his cupboard, where he'd hung his chain of office. It was glowing. "The Unity of Balance?"

"You ever heard of another Harmony? Don't bother replying. Mine was as dumb a question as yours was. The answer's yes. According to our Young Daddy Death it is anyhow. And there's more."

"So that's it."

"Huh?"

"Why I've been feeling the urge to contact you. They're trying to contact me. They want their rightful owner. They want me. Got them?"

"Jordy will find them for us eventually. One hitch."

"Yes?"

"You might have to fight for them."

"I see. You'd like that, wouldn't you? Draw me into a fight, presumably outside the Weirdom, and hope, when I win them, I'll be so beaten up you can sick the pretender on me."

"Don't be a fool, Sal. Demios forbade me going after them. I'm giving you first crack. You win them, they're yours. You win, you lift your banishment on Dem, me and our family, including Tsishah." Morg was only 13 when she had Tsishah Twilight, the come-Spring, soon to be retiring, non-Lemurian Aortic of Shenon.

(Utopians weren't supposed to start having children until they reached maturity at the age of 30. Obviously that didn't mean they were incapable of having children before then. Augustus was only 16 when he sired Saladin. Besides, Morg was a hybrid Utopian. Thanks to their witch-mother, so was he.

(Tsishah's father, Tom-Tiddly Taddletale, was a faerie. He'd abducted Tsishah when she was barely out of the womb. Because of what happened to his sister, and because their two devolved, perpetually 7-year-old parents may ultimately prove to be just faeries themselves, Sal hated fucking faeries almost as much as he hated witches or devils.)

"You do that, we'll come back to the Weirdom and together we can plot our next move. Looked in the Night's Sky yet? I can't see the stars from here but word's reached us that Great Byron's been cathonitized. He's up there now. So are his Primary Nucleoids, we believe. Which means Godbad's lost its Byronic protectors."

"And you want to renew our alliance with ex-King Achigan and take out the Fatman."

"Not just the ex-King. Godbad's an ex-queen, too."

"Fucking Fish," he cursed.

Scylla Nereid was a Piscine, an Inner Earth amphibian, slightly more than a year older than him. A natural-born witch-prodigy, she received most of her training from his officially much-loved, but secretly thoroughly loathed predecessor, Kyprian Somata. It was Kyprian, Copperhead, traitor to the realm due to her unflinching support of the Superior Sisterhood's Panharmonium pipedream and consequential truck with female Master Devas, who gave her the Fisherwoman codename.

Fish, as everyone called her, looked mostly human. Fetchingly so, even he had to admit; often to her face, albeit not recently. Which was remarkable in that, to the best of Sal's knowledge, she didn't have an ounce of age-retarding Utopian blood in her ancestry. Then again she claimed to be a deviant, like him, so that might explain her continuing good looks. Of course witches could look like almost anything.

"So you'd know better than me. I don't swing that way. What do you say, brother? Shall I come and get you?"

"Tell you what, Morg. Tethys finds them; you have Ringleader send whomever has them up here and I'll take care of the rest."

"I would if I could. 30-Beers can't locate Rings. Fact is he's given up trying. He thinks he might have gone to the Outer Earth. Unless he's hiding out between-space or moving so fast Jordy can't get a fix on him, that is. For all we know he could be dead."

"Then have Tethys draw himself up here; you as well. No one else. I only have my chain of office with me so I'll be in the Masters Palace, in the throne room. With the other two copies. For an hour, no more. We'll deal with them from there or we won't deal with them at all."

Morgianna's image faded into the agate. The gemstone became dull and opaque. There'd be no reactivating it from his end. He put it back in its box and returned it to the safe. If she came through on it, it would be into a two-by-two hollow containment area between-space, one lined by another foot's thickness of Solidium-alloyed steel.

Tethys, though, had Sal's permission to draw himself up here anytime he pleased.

========

"It's no use, Judge," Morgianna said to her never-remembered visitor. "He won't come out of the Weirdom and you can't go into it. As soon as he comes back, you'll have to send me and Demios to Dustmound. Vetala's a Master Deva. Dem's the oldest eye-stave in existence. Hadd isn't really her protectorate. So it'll probably work."

"I am going to go anywhere near your husband's oldest eye-stave in existence?"

"No, I guess you aren't. Nothing else for it." Morg materialized a Crystal Skull.

"What are you doing?"

"Calling off an assassination."

========

Well after darkness fell the Living's brain-trust gathered in the huge, brightly lit, command tent outside the ancient monastery on Sraddha Isle in the middle of Lake Sedona.

========

In preparation for their coming assault on Hadd's hotspots the Godbadians had taken hundreds of snapshots from their whirlybirds and fixed-wing aircraft. In Petrograd they put together an aerial map of Hadd and reproduced a number of copies of it. General Quentin Anvil brought the biggest one to the monastery on their eventful flight here first thing this morning. It was rolled out on a table within the tent.

The reappearance of Nergal Vetala had changed their plans. What use were even Outer Earth weapons against a Master Deva? By now, however, everyone there knew approximately what Jordan Tethys could do with his quill. Golgotha Nauroz knew exactly what the eye-staves his Trinondevs carried could do to Vetala.

Anywhere except Haddock-Hadd, said Fish, Fisherwoman, Lady Achigan, the former Queen Scylla of Godbad. She'd know, too. She'd earned her Illuminary stripes, as it were, quite literally at the feet of a master, none other than Kyprian Somata, when she was the High Illuminary of Weir as well as its Master.

If it was her protectorate, Golgotha agreed. He'd seen the list prepared by the current High Illuminary, Demios's twin sister, Melina now Zeross. Two particularly pertinent stars were missing from the Sedon Sphere. They were that of the Planter, Zuvem Nergalis, a Mithradite, and that of Vanthysces, the original devic Grim Reaper, a Byronic.

Hadd, when it was known as El Dorado, was partially the latter's de facto protectorate before it nominally became all of Vetala's. (Only arguably, Tethys objected, reminding everyone that Byronics never really had protectorates. Still didn't as far as both he and Fish knew.) As for the former, whom Tethys generally referred to as Gravedigger or else Devil Doom, he was the father of maybe as many as half of Vetala's Nergalazurs.

The Trinondev Field Commander and his men were willing to try their luck taking her out. So was Demios Sarpedon and his similarly eye-stave-armed Zebranids, some of whom were women. It was a touchy situation. No more so than the situation that began to develop as soon as Janna St Peche-Montressor got word from Godbad that Unmoving Byron's star was now shining out of the night's sky.

She initially heard it from her fellow Athenans, via their witch-stones. She received radio confirmation from her husband Yataghan Montressor, the Fatman's son by the late Emeralda born Plantagenet. So disturbed was she at what else Yataghan had to say that she returned to Aka Godbad City forthwith, taking Demios Sarpedon with her. The Fatman, Alpha Centauri, had collapsed. Chances were he'd collapsed at the very moment Bodiless Byron was cathonitized.

Learning of the news, Fish excused herself. In all probability she was with her Piscines right now, busy abolishing aquatic Dead Things in Lake Sedona. While her absence might have been more in the interests of maintaining good relations within the too-often-fractious forces of the Living, she'd insisted Morgianna, wholly recovered from being fish-netted, and daughter Andaemyn go with her. Which had immediately set tongues a-wagging.

Fish, Morg and Demios had long ago made their peace with the Fatman and his closest advisers. However, until about twenty years ago, they, Fish's Piscines, the Sarpedons' Zebranids, the women's Athenan War Witches and their Mother-Earth-worshipping, Hecate-Hellion associates had fought on the opposite side of the Godbadian Civil War to many of Anvil's veterans and their Byronic deities. As well, many of Golgotha's Trinondevs regarded Demios in particular as an enemy of their Master, which was true, and therefore the Weirdom itself, which the Sarpedons and their followers would disagree with vehemently. And wastefully.

As Thartarre Sraddha Holgatson quite rightly pointed out when he was attempting to mediate between the two Utopian factions as to which one of them, Golgotha or Demios, would lead the attack on Vetala, vehemence and the violence that generally accompanied it was best directed at the clear-cut enemy, the Dead and Undead Things of Hadd. Nonetheless, as sensible as that sounded to a neutral like Jordan Tethys, sometimes conspiracy theories were like a pile of powder that just needed a match or drop of water in order to explode.

Thrygragos Byron in the night's sky, could that be due to Utopians, their eyestaves and the rest of their extraterrestrial weaponry? The Fatman collapsing, had Fish and Morg's War Witches or Hellions poisoned him? Maybe the Godbadian military should give up on Hadd, leave it for the Dead, and return to Godbad. Saner heads prevailed. One war at a time, insisted General Anvil.

There is only one war, underlined Governor Niarchos, and it's here.

========

"From Diluvia to Krachla, from the Gulf of Aka to the Sea of Akadan," said the Legendarian, standing over the tabletop upon which was laid the aerial map the Godbadians had prepared, "This is Hadd. Lake Sedona's the big teardrop here in the middle."

"That's us. Rather that's Sraddha Isle," indicated Thartarre with the curved, reinforced silver blade screwed into the prosthetic attached to the stump of his right arm. The High Priest, burnt chest attended to by now, wasn't drinking; had yet to have his token beer for the day.

Neither was his adjunct, Diego de Landa. Nor was Morg's lieutenant, Garcia Dis L'Orca, who, if she was anything like Janna St Peche-Montressor, probably didn't drink anyways. The Trinondevs' Field Commander, Golgotha Nauroz, made a decent beer up in Cabalarkon but abstained when he was anywhere else.

Quentin Anvil, Nanny Klanny's son, the Godbadian-raised general who was in charge of Operation Haas, Godbad's military presence in Hadd, and Ferdinand Niarchos, the governor of New Iraxas, the Godbadian province northwest of Hadd, who was here to represent the commercial interests of Centauri Enterprises, did drink. They just weren't right now.

Young Death was, however. As necromantic as his disgusting talents were oriented, he enjoyed the delights of the Living. So was Jordan Tethys. The Legendarian had been going at it most of the day, ever since his daughters refused to be drawn to Sraddha Isle. Didn't they want to see him anymore? They'd buried the hatchet, hadn't they? Why follow Kronokronos Mikoto after death? He'd be Sangazur-possessed; they were altogether alive.

Tethys had a bad feeling about what he was about to do; get involved. He painted, did art. He recounted his- and her-stories. He avoided participating in their making. Midnight was still hours away yet he was getting close to his maximum allotment of thirty per day. He flipped his sketchbook to a specific page.

"And this is Nergal Vetala."

Besides his memories of her from incarnations long in the past, he'd partially based his rendition of her on a photograph Thartarre had found of his mother, Barsine Mandam. He'd then added some details based on how Vetala appeared when she popped out of the Weird in the High Priest's top-level workroom that morning.

The drawing was therefore of a long-haired, extremely pale and vaguely greenish-skinned devil. She was nearly nude, covered only by a dark gown that was slit down her front to below the navel and along its sides from hips to ankles. Except for her third eye and fangs, she was exceptionally attractive.

He set his Gypsium quill upon the sketchpad. "And this is where she is."

Not so miraculously – they'd seen the same thing happen a number of times already today – it stood up on its nib, which was glowing. It didn't do anything else, however, and that hardly for the first time today. The last time he'd drawn Second Fangs, at Thartarre's urging, it hadn't done anything either.

Was the High Priest worried about her, the vampire who'd caused his 5-year-old self to kill his own mother and then led his father to his drowning death in the Jaag Maelstrom 35-years-ago?

"The background's not filling in," noted Young Death, eagle-eyed that he was.

(His paternal aunt, Kanin Nauroz, a pureblood Utopian, sister of Ubris, Golgotha's template, hooked up with an avian-human, a hollow-boned Garuda changeling, near the tail-end of the last century. To celebrate their union, she was rewarded with a set of Garuda feathers. Decades later he'd helped her phoenix, rise from her own ashes.

(It wasn't a pleasant memory. Being burnt alive had to be the worst death imaginable. And he'd done more than just imagine most of them.)

"Which tells you one of a number of things," the Legendarian reminded him.

"Try Rings again," suggested Niarchos.

"We've been through that already, governor," said Thartarre. "Jordy dare not. If Harry's got hold of even one of the Trigregos Talismans, the background will fill-in and he'll ignite."

"This is ridiculous," said Anvil. "The last time that quill of his worked it panned out of Janna Fangfingers and showed us she was in Necropolis, what Byronics called Manoa, for whatever reason, in the to us distant past. Gleaming City or not, I'm sticking with Plan A. I'm ordering it bombed come daylight."

"Daylight, of course," snapped Tethys. "Fangs must have been wearing a day-suit. She'll have taken it off by now. I'll splotch her out." He did.

"My, my, what have we here?"

========

"Goddamn it, Tyrtod. All right. Goddamn it, Mikoto. She can't countermand my orders. Who the hell do you think is paying for all this? Who else has a Gleaming City to mine as I please. What's that? It's too late anyways.

"Good. Yeah, well, I didn't expect they could anyhow. Too bad in a way. They were Good Companions."

========

Dusk then full darkness fell over the Hidden Headworld. The moon rose behind the perpetual cloud-covering of Hadd. It didn't provide any more light than was common after dark in the Penile Peninsula's shaft but, with it, so too rose Hadd's vampires. One of them wasn't Janna Fangfingers, Second Fangs.

Fangs had been up all day. Had been wearing a light-blocking day-suit since she left her bunker in Necropolis for Dustmound in order to attain some visuals. She sat in Vetala's throne. Had no idea where Vetala was. Then she did. She was standing right in front of her. Overtop of her soldier's corpse. Had that been where she'd been all day? Inside him, trying to reverse her murdering him – and if so, had she succeeded?

"You're looking comfortable, Janna."

"Have you been crying, Goddess?"

"I killed my soldier. He was attacking me. I have no idea why but I had no choice except to kill him. You're tempted, aren't you?"

"I've been busy, not tempted. Are those the real Trigregos Talismans?"

"They are."

"Thought so," said Second Fangs, fingering the crystal skull attached to the choker around her neck, what she'd been using all day to keep in touch with her contacts in the Crystal Mountains, Sanguerre and even Sraddha Isle. "That's why he attacked you then. You're a devil. The Trigregos Sisters' power foci have a built-in animosity towards devils. They'll always end up trying to kill you. You played a Trigregos Gambit and you won a dead soldier."

"So it seems. You do realize he had to free your devic half-mother in order to get hold of the Susasword."

"Of course I do. Among other things I've been using the far-sight granted me by this throne to follow her progress. She's taken herself to where you tried to go 35 years ago, to Sedon's Hairband. Funnily enough, she shucked her demonic body and melded with her High Seat not long after she arrived there from Sanguerre. Might you know why?"

"Harmony's a firstborn female. In terms of unbridled might she rivals every other firstborn, of every other tribe. She must be replenishing her spirit-self. Did she kill anyone?"

"She funnelled into herself a good percentage of the vivacity of three mercenaries I sent after her daemonic body. I expect they'll recover. They're strong lads. Unlike you and I, she's harmonious. She doesn't kill. I should go to her."

"I wouldn't advise it. You're the main reason she lost half a millennium of life. You think she'll just welcome you with open arms?"

"She might. She was trying to cure me when I coerced Abaddon into putting her down. I can still be cured. Hadd needs a champion and there's those things there I can trade for her assistance in driving away the Byronics-worshippers."

"I'm all the champion Hadd needs."

"There's a lot of missing stars up there, Goddess. Take yourself above the clouds and have a look. You up to taking on the Planter, Zuvem Nergalis, the father of so many of your Nergalazurs? Or Vanthysces, the original Grim Reaper? A good percentage of what we can see from Dustmound was his protectorate, in everything but name, before it was yours; he's the father of a lot of the azuras who've lingered hereabouts over the centuries; and there's an awful lot more Godbadians in Hadd than there used to be."

"Isn't Chaos supposed to be your champion?"

"Last night, on the other side of Diluvia, I had the deviant, Jordan Tethys, 30-Years, the Legendarian, try to draw me to his Unholiness. We were, um, disconnected before we could complete the transmission. But, before we were, I discovered where Abe was, in the Land of Nothingness, on the Cattail Peninsula. I'd need a subtle matter body to go there."

"You just said there's one sitting empty in Sedon's Hairband."

"No, I just said there's three damn near drained-dead bodies below Harmony's High Seat. Let me tell you of my dilemma."

"Please do. I'm ever so intrigued."

"Because you're trying to get rid of me. I understand that. What say I just pick the thrice-cursed things off your soldier's body and finish what he started? Then I could be my own champion. My birthmother had all three of them once; that's why she came to be known in not just the Annals of Weir as the Trigregos Titaness.

"Besides, I've a reputation of someone who fights her own battles. I'm female, I've wielded them in the past and my parents, no matter how diluted their blood was by the time they had me and my brother, were hybrid Utopians. Despite the fact our devic half-parents were arguably the most powerful male and female Shining Ones of the era, they brought us up hating devils and the Trigregos Talismans can kill devils."

"So why haven't you done so already? Thanks to First Fangs' fang-fingered glove, you're a self-psychopomp. You could have come out of the Weird and whisked him away between-space before I had a chance to react. By the time I found you, you could have made the things your own. Were you afraid they wouldn't accept a bloodsucker as their mistress?"

Fangfingers didn't answer immediately. Instead she regarded the body of Vetala's soldier. Were it not for the slight gash in his chest he could have been sleeping. "I don't take unnecessary risks. I've been here most of the day. So has his body. You haven't been. So where have you been? It's curious no Haddazur has reanimated him, wouldn't you say?"

"I would," the Blood Queen of Hadd allowed. "I'd also say that for a presumably ordinary man I killed with a sickle-thrust in the chest, he's demonstrating impressive recuperative qualities. So maybe he's an Outer Earth deviant; a Sed-son perhaps, though Pyrame would have been upstairs by the time he was conceived. That crystal skull you're forever wearing about your neck isn't leaking by any chance, is it?"

"My twin brother didn't have golden-brown skin. Nor would I consider a dead man a worthy receptacle for his soul. You killed him with your talisman?"

"I just said that."

"Brainrock, like devic and, some say, azura possession, is supposed to be healthful for mortals."

"Killing someone isn't generally considered to be healthful to anyone."

"Ordinarily I'd agree with you. However, the Attis had golden-brown skin. At least so I've heard. And he kept coming back from the dead. Mind you, I've also heard someone finally finished him off around a 130-years ago. Orfeo was his name; he was a fucking faerie."

"Do tell. Any of your other skulls leaking?"

"Not that I'm aware of. I'm pretty careful with them. Some of the souls I've collected over the centuries have proven to be much more dominating than any mere Sangazur I've ever come across. As a matter of fact some of them have approaching devic attributes in that regard. Sraddhites, Athenans, even pureblood Utopians, dead as they may be, can't withstand them. You'll recall Bat-Koatyl?"

"Only if I must."

"Well, him I parcelled out once too often. A vamp who goes by the unimaginative name of Night Owl got hold of him three human generations ago. I haven't been able to get him back since. Might your soldier be the Attis?"

"He fell from the sky and he wasn't possessed. But that's about all I'm sure about; about all he was sure about as well. I know. I probed him as thoroughly as I've ever probed anyone."

"He must be a deviant then." Janna Fangfingers, she in the Brainrock throne, redirected her attention to Vetala. "You asked me a question a moment ago. There's a bunch of answers to it. One is my devic half-mother. She won't rest until the Trigregos Talismans are destroyed. Ergo, she'll have to be destroyed. So, like I said, I dispatched some mercenaries circuitously in my employ to have a go at destroying her daemonic body. They failed.

"Just as unfortunately, even if they had succeeded in destroying her body, which looked pretty badly beat-up anyways, they wouldn't have altogether abolished her. She's never been cathonitized so she'd still be a Sprit Being, like Titanic Metis, Wisdom of Lazareme, or Pretty Parsis, Great Byron's Enchantress as well as his Earth Magician. Plus, she didn't leave her Tvasitar talisman, her torc, on her body. The other thing is it appears she's acquired another devil's power focus to bolster her own. It's Plague's, Carcinogen the Leper's. Highly perplexing all of it.

"I'm thinking she's so powerful she didn't need a debrained demon's body in the first place. My theory is she's growing a new body, one made up entirely of Brainrock-Gypsium. In which case she'll become a devil unlike any other devil, save herself, yet again. In any event, one way or another, she'll be coming after whomever's wielding the Sisters' foci. I'd rather it not be me.

"Another is you. You are my goddess even if you weren't my maker. You may have stripped me of my authority but I don't hold that against you. I remain as loyal to you as I remain loyal to your realm. You, though, are as much devil as vampire; as much devil as my half-mother. There are ways of dealing with devils, always have been, and some of them are on Sraddha Isle right now. Ringots also come to mind. But there must be others out there that I am as yet unaware of. Given time I shall discover what they are. Then I'll determine how to use them to our advantage."

"Time? You would have me abandon the defence of Hadd in the meanwhile?"

"Not abandon, rethink how best to defend it. You can't see them from here, what with the clouds of Hadd, but I've had reports of a dozen or more stars in the Sedon Sphere tonight than there were last night. My contacts in Sanguerre, the ones who nominally employ the mercenaries I just mentioned, tell me they believe the biggest and brightest of the new ones is none other than Thrygragos Byron himself.

"Great Byron and his Nucleoids being in the Night's Sky is what suggests there are others out there who can deal successfully with devils. That's hardly all it suggests, however. In the absence of its Great God, a stab at Godbad, a renewal of its Civil War, would draw its military back there in a flash. Give me your blessing and I'll see to everything. Truth told I've seen to most of it already. Strike when the iron's hot is one maxim that comes to mind. Carpe Diem is another one; though naturally I'm more inclined to seize the night.

"We had a serious setback when, as I've only just found out, the Byronics trapped Death's Angels in a rainstorm a few days ago. But Sangs are fabulous strategists and, before you returned to Hadd, I acquired many willing associates; your immediate sister and her demonic Indescribables among them.

"Kala Tal was afraid she'd be next on the Byronics' hit list and, even if that's no longer likely, she still won't leave her protectorate. Her demons are under no such restrictions. There's dozens of them already gathered on the outskirts of her Forbidden Forest, with more on the way. I've the means of delivery and tonight I propose to start doing just that."

"This is indeed interesting news. I shall have to consider your words."

========

The throne atop Dustmound. looked to have been crudely carved out of a single slab of Brainrock. It had a back, a seat, armrests, and that was about it. It wasn't an electric chair such as had once been used on the Outer Earth for executions by electrocution. It didn't have clamps for a condemned man's waist, shoulders, wrists and ankles. Neither did it have any sort of conductive helmet with electrodes and such like poking out of it.

It was made of Brainrock. So was Janna's fang-fingered glove. It fused her right hand to the armrest. So was the Crimson Corona. Godstuff was teleportive. It appeared around her head, robbing her of the will to become either a bat or to mystify. So was the Susasword, teleportive. It came through the throne's back, through her back and out her front, between her breasts.

As for the Amateramirror, it was circular shaped, like a full moon platter. Fang-fingers had been wearing a choker about her throat. It was displaced. The Amateramirror displaced it; was now situated where her throat had been. Janna's head teetered on the mirror's upper surface, the glassine part of it. It looked shocked; was as if it figured, if it could figure anything, it was still attached to her neck. It wasn't.

Then it toppled, turned to dust. Then the rest of her body dusted-ditto.

The Blood Queen of Hadd smiled toothily. She didn't approve of Utopians, purebloods or hybrids, period. More specifically, she had never forgiven Second Fangs for standing by while her then equally vampiric twin brother drove his shin-splint into her chest five hundred years ago. Nor did she approve of what Janna did to Jordan *'Q for also Squiggly'* Tethys the next moment, after the Utopian hybrid acquired her, Nergal Vetala, thanks be to her and her twins' therefore not-quite-unique form of deviancy.

Mindful of how useful he and his quill could be, she'd planned to keep the Fatazur-animated Dead Thing that he was at the time beside her, dependent on her for sustenance. Janna eyefire-blasting him into oblivion – him occupying the body of her Squiggly, her childhood sweetheart – mercifully provided him with the opportunity to have a new incarnation, one beyond her influence. All of which made Janna's endgame unconscionably long-delayed as well as satisfying in a dispassionate, non-blood-lustful way.

Her going out so Joan the Baptist like also struck her as sort of poetic. How many times had she, Janna Somata, ripped out someone's throat with her fang-fingered glove before she drank him or her dry, not even bothering to turn them? Hundreds, thousands? Vetala automatically turned everyone she chomped. Devic saliva, she supposed.

Undeath wasn't quite the same as Death. It didn't count as a capital, as in cathonitizing, offence. Too bad she dusted before he could present Janna's head to her on an Amateramirror salver. She'd have enjoyed seeing the look on her face. Wait a minute, she had, hadn't she? Was that bile mixed in with her blood smearing the mirror?

Maybe he'd let her lick it clean.

========

Waste not, want not, she supposed, still smirking delightedly at the Joan the Baptist allusions – her wit was every bit as sharp as her teeth.

========

Duly pleased with herself, Vetala watched as her soldier took shape in the Brainrock throne.

He was breathtaking to behold, her very own golden-brown warrior. He now had Janna's fang-fingered glove on his right hand. Having four Tvasitar Talismans probably wasn't the embarrassment of riches it might seem. Pyrame's Attis had dozens of them and even Silverstar herself had a bunch of them the last time they met. Dark Sedon used to give them to her as tokens of affection more so than partial payment for favours rendered over the millennia.

The Crimson Corona sat well on his forehead. Since he was left-handed and held the Susasword in that hand, he wore the Amateramirror further up the same arm as the fang-fingered glove. She had to admit they sort of complimented each other. She definitely had to get him some less tattered and better fitting pants. She decided he could keep the combat-boots. Even a dead man infused with Godstuff shouldn't have to fight barefoot.

"You're truly magnificent, my soldier," she told him as he stood up.

"I am no one's soldier," he told her. "I am Trigregos Incarnate. Trigregos serves no one. You should address me accordingly."

"I gave you back your life."

"Did you? I think not. Trigregos brought me back from beyond the brink, not you."

"You are no longer my soldier?"

"This husk suits me for now. I thank you for finding it for me. I am in your debt. In time I shall repay you in full. But first, know you this: Trigregos kills devils!"

"Then kill me last."

"As you wish, Goddess."

"Excellent. In the meantime, there are a few hundred non-devic invaders of my territory you can kill as well. You do kill more than just devils, I trust?"

"On one condition. Accept me as your god."

She didn't need convincing. They embraced. Then they burst into flames.

========

Jordan Tethys signed his name and dotted the drawing of the Trigregos Talismans. The effect was instantaneously apparent.

The cheers in the huge, brilliantly lit, command tent outside the ancient monastery on Sraddha Isle, in the middle of Lake Sedona, where the Living's brain-trust had gathered, were positively deafening. The Legendarian was afraid his back would break from all the slapping. Even Anvil didn't care that his map was about to go up like Jordy's sketchpad just had.

"Now that was one hot kiss," had to say Young Death.

========

A Gypsium hoop, a teleportal, a teleport-hole, appeared in the centre of the command tent. Out of it came six extraordinary beings.

"Harry," exclaimed Thartarre.

"Son," gasped Young Death, recognizing Dervish Furie.

"Want a beer?" wondered the legendary 30-Year Man, recognizing someone else.

"Sure," Akbarartha, the rightful Kronokronos Supreme of Temporis, answered.

Raven's Head voided herself on the floor.

"Born in a barn," snorted Niarchos.

"That's a mutated ravendeer," said de Landa, whose hobby was taxidermy.

"Watch who you're calling a mutate, priest," countered a blind Irache holding a solar spear.

========

The rolling hills on the northern boundary of Free Iraxas were not alive with the sound of music. They were metaphorically alive but the sound coming from them, Sedon's Hairband, was more like a woman wailing in grief. He could tell the three men lying at his feet were still breathing but he wasn't too sure what to make of the daemonic hulk above them. It looked empty.

The wailing stopped. It wasn't empty anymore. It spoke.

========

"You'd be Ahriman, the 'A' in the VAM Entity. The last surviving firstborn of Thrygragos Sedon."

"I am content with Smiler. You'd be Harmony, firstborn of Lazareme."

"I was. Now I prefer Nihila. Are you responsible for the abolishment of my daughter?"

"If by daughter you are referring to Janna Fangfingers, then I can't say I'm sorry for your loss. The Headworld would be a better place without vampires."

"In that we agree. What do you know of Fecundity's soldier?"

"I know Vetala killed him, if that's who you're referring to."

"Oh, no. That's going to be my job. Come tomorrow."

West to east – from the Jaag coast of Akadan, where it met the internal sea of Sedon's Ear, to the shores of Tempestuous Psychron, the Head's eastern ocean – the mostly Harmony-made Gypsium Wall still surmounted the rolling hills that comprised Sedon Hairband; hence the name that sometimes appeared on maps of the Hidden Headworld.

The wall itself, composed mainly of the Brainrock Godstuff also called Gypsium, wasn't what it had been up until roughly 500 years ago. Since it wasn't so much crumbling as partially dismantled, that wasn't entirely due to Harmony's enforced absence. For the balance of the night, until not long before dawn, it didn't so much resonate as vibrate with the reverberations of gods, devils that they were, expunging cumulative centuries of sexual inactivity.

Firstborns had a thing for firstborns.

========

Saladin Devason awoke in a war-zone. Re-begin-game him.

========

Not every pureblood Utopian in the Weirdom of Cabalarkon was a complete imbecile, though the majority of them certainly were that. Some purebloods, like the Sarpedon twins, the Weirdom's scientocrats, biomages, physicians, teachers, Illuminaries, Trinondevs, and many others, couldn't be considered imbeciles in any way, shape or form. Even in realms where there were hardly any imbeciles at all, most of them would rank in the category of the exceptional.

Imbecility had its gradations. A few borderline imbeciles actually enjoyed working for their clothing, shelter and daily rations. There were lots of things they could do. The members of the cleaning staff who arrived in the morning to scrub down the Masters' Throne Room in the old palace were flummoxed when it came time to dust the facsimiles of the Amateramirror and the Susasword.

They weren't there anymore.

========

A seventh person appeared out of the Grey in the midst of the tent. It was Katatribe Tethys. She had a crossbow like the ones Sraddhites used to shoot vamps.

The Dand-head of Akbar's Homeworld Sceptre exploded just as she shot her bolt.

****

(GAME-GAMBIT) 21: **Endgames Inevitable**

Sedonda, Tantalar 7, 5980

On the Frozen Isle of Lathakra, Dr Melina Zeross, the white-as-light High Il-
luminary of Weir, an inarguably non-imbecilic Utopian pureblood, and her bright,
but not quite white-as-light, hybrid daughters, Persephone, almost 16, Helen, 12, and
Athena, 6, were in a cage suspended from the ceiling of an ice cavern. Below them, on
the ground, stood their guards. None of her daughters would want to build Frosty the
Snowman again.

Their guards were animate snowmen armed with icicle spears.

========

Devauray having been unseasonably warm for early Tantalar in the Weirdom
of Cabalarkon, they'd only been wearing light winter clothing when they were kidnapped. Although the snowmen had provided them with furs and blankets, there
was no heat in the place. Consequently, she was hugging her daughters just as tightly as she could. They in turn were hugging her as tightly as they could. The youngest one was clinging to her neck so much so Mel feared for her blood's continuing
circulation.

"When's daddy coming?" the little girl pleaded.

"Soon, Tina. Soon!"

He might be as well. Elsewhere in the Glacial Palace, Methandra Thanatos
had finally relocated the other Dr Zeross, Aristotle, Harry, Ringleader, the second
so named. She had him in her crosshairs, as it were. Her immediate brother and
husband, Cold to her Heat, would fetch him hither as soon as he wasn't surrounded
by Trinondevs, their eye-staves and the eyeorbs atop them. Anywhere other than in
a devil's protectorate eyeorbs were prison pods for devils like her. Were for Tantal,
too. Anywhere except here and the Weirdom of Cabalarkon, that is.

He found that a lot more humourous than she did.

========

The explosion of Akbar's Homeworld Sceptre put Katatribe off her aim. Young
Death, who had been standing beside the Legendarian, took the crossbow bolt in the
chest. He wasn't very big, and the bolt was probably poison-dipped, so he died instantly.
The corpse he left behind quickly disintegrated.

The resultant geyser of blood evaporated just as quickly. His cigar stayed lit. Just fell on the floor. No one thought to stub it out.

========

Anvil shot her. Shot her a couple more times when she tried to sit up and take aim anew. The Godbadian general had been in the mood to kill someone all day.

"Stop shooting me, Fuckhead," she shouted. This time he shot her in the face. Ugly but nowhere near as messy as he'd have thought. "Goddamn it, Anvil," now the voice belonged to Young Death, "Getting shot hurts. Besides, she's already dead."

Anvil stopped. "Mother of fucking hell," he cursed.

Suddenly the monastery's alarm system began to go off.

========

Save perhaps for Raven's Head, Blind Sundown's highly intelligent mount, Obadiah Melvin Power, Old Man Power, OMP, Kronokronos Akbarartha, was the eldest member of the Damnation Brigade. As such, rather than a Summoning Child like the Untouchable Diver – who, having lost 25 years in Limbo, had yet to celebrate his 35th birthday – it probably should have fallen to him to become D-Brig's leader. He felt himself off his game so he hadn't raised any objections to the Diver taking over from Cyborg Cerebrus.

There were a combination of reasons for that. One was his poor showing against Demon Land in the Faerie Garden. Another was his near escape from Carcinogen the Leper in the pre-Tokugawa Era Japanese Cavern. Perhaps he should have turned and fought Plague after Lakshmi of Lemuria, Fish's step-niece, Aortic Amphitrite's deviant-daughter by half-daddy Tariqartha, the Chronocollector, the Time-Space Displacer, shouted her warning. Instead he'd smashed Cerebrus and himself to Centurium, replicated Versailles.

In a way he shouldn't be blaming Lakshmi for expelling him from Temporis. Only the evening before the Dand their mutual half-dad, the subterranean caverns' devic overlord, Lazareme's Earth Magician, had insisted the undeniably attractive yet, equally so, unquenchably ambitious teenager break off her engagement to Centurion Sophiscient.

Her idea? Probably. Her reward? Betrothal to the Dand's eldest surviving quarter-son, the Kronokronos Supreme. Just as much so, Lakshmi was to be Akbar's reward for returning to Temporis in time to win the War of the Apocalyptics. It didn't quite happen that way. She didn't want to marry a cowardly old failure, fine. She shouldn't have expelled the rest of D-Brig. That was inexcusable.

He acquiesced to going with Rings to wherever. Upon arrival there-ever, he spotted the samurai woman about to shoot someone with a crossbow. He pointed his Homeworld Sceptre in her direction. Its head, which was shaped like Dand Tariqartha's head, exploded. She was just the start. There was gunfire. There was pleading from the samurai to stop shooting her. Her voice changed into that of a little boy. The clangour began. He'd have to feel sorry for himself later.

Cereberant or Keres Hellhounds had three heads. They were self-psychopomps native to Apple Isle. Korant Corn Queens kept them as personal pets. Had he had time to bash himself in the head with his Homeworld Sceptre he might have remembered such things. He didn't. Then he was back on it, his game. Always assuming his preferred game was baseball.

He had the bat for it: his Homeworld Sceptre. None of the four other members of D-Brig Ringleader brought to Sraddha Isle paused to appreciate his return to form. They were dealing with their own demons. A swing and a strike. Its right head was blown away. It still had two heads left. It look scrawny, hungry. Did they starve demons here in wherever? Gone number two. Homerun. It leapt at him. Kablooie!

Unlike Demon Land, whom he'd battled to a standstill if not exactly a stalemate in Temporis, the Hellhound didn't re-form itself. Heck of a stench. Brimstone, he reckoned.

========

Somebody was being awfully generous with their demons. One thing about Wildman Dervish Furie was he should never have been allowed to kill anything, even if they were already dead. Howlers, kobolds, ghouls, goblins, pookas, kelpies, the wild man didn't know what any of them were; just keep them coming.

He burst outside the tent; burst through the tent. He kept going. They rarely did.

========

Blind Sundown, riding Raven's Head, who was an actual ravenhead, if not a mutated Mystic Mountains ravendeer, was right behind Furie. Metallic monstrosities were everywhere. He had a fully charged Solar Spear. Metallic monstrosities were slag. Too bad they were Godbadian aircraft.

"They're glamours," realized Jordan Tethys, rushing out of the tent.

"He'd blind, he can't see glamours," said Katatribe Tethys, arriving at her father's side. She was bullet-ridden and huffing — but only because she was simultaneously puffing on Young Death's cigar. She spoke in his voice.

"Raven sees for both of them," said Ringleader, who was sickeningly familiar with Young Death's disgusting, necromantic knacks.

"Get out of my daughter, Gush," the Legendarian demanded.

"I do," Augustus-Katatribe countered, "The Sang will get back into her. It does, guess what you get in your back?"

"Up there," pointed the Diver. His crimson-lens Gorgon goggles granted him a degree of far-sight. "On the battlements. I knew it. Where there's a witch there's a will." Ringleader cast a teleport-hole. He went for them; was repulsed. Evidently he wasn't the only one Gypsium-gifted in the vicinity.

"Not to mention ichthyosauri-illusions," said a newcomer. It was Fisherwoman. They knew each other, Fish and the outsiders. Fish and the Diver knew each other in the Biblical sense as well. For a while; a long, for them very long, while ago.

"Scylla?" he queried.

"Yehudi," she nodded, acknowledging his existence if nothing else. "I've been hook-looking for her. She's brine-mine."

Sundown and Raven were still destroying metallic monstrosities. Fish materialized her Brainrock landing gaffe. She vanished, on a witch-stone. The witch on the battlements had a shaven head and black skin. She must have been using witch-stones to cast her illusions. Fish could travel on witch-stones.

It, an Undead Thing, did a Janna Somata; didn't react in time to either become a bat or to mystify. Got an oversized fishhook through the forehead into the brainpan as a result of her slowness; got dusted. When it came to dusting vamps, Brainrock, applied invasively, beat silver or wood any day of the week.

A black and white striped bat came out of the Weird. It sought to put the bite on Jordan Tethys, more like to rip his throat out. The Diver almost casually stuck out his fist, departiclyzed it, his fist, re-particlyzed it, ditto; dusted it, the vamp.

Said: "Hope that was okay."

========

Fish didn't come back on a witch-stone someone had somewhere about his or her self. She came back the way she came in, off of the nib of 30-Beers' Gypsium quill. Had she wanted to, she could have followed Tethys on his meanderings via the Weird, the Grey, the Universal Substance of Samsara, anytime since she'd tuned into it, the nib of his quill, the previous Sedonda.

Her bellybutton bauble was glowing even more brightly than usual. Might it be a soul-sink? It might.

"The witch was a Sraddhite vamp, duh-the-dogfish that. Must have been a mussel-masticating master-caster in her daytime. Some octopus-pucker-sucker was up there with her, shoal-the-though. He got away via her mirrored egg-roe."

Raven's Head, Blind Sundown on her, trotted up to them.

"Make it quick," said Auguste Moirnoir, snatching a final, fare-thee-well and good luck puff. Might as well. It wasn't as if smoking was going to kill him. Especially not with Sundown there. The cigar was what wouldn't survive.

Being burnt hurt as much as ever, however.

========

The mostly demonic assault and the mostly firearm, flamethrower and splatter pack munitions the Sraddhites and their allies, primarily Godbadians and War Witches, countered it with lasted until dawn. The Indescribables suffered massive casualties but theirs was evidently a pre-emptive strike presumably prearranged by Nergal Vetala or Second Fangs prior to their demise.

Their task accomplished – very little of the Godbadian aircraft amassed on Sraddha Isle, or anywhere else in Hadd, would be flying anytime in the near future – they were in full retreat long before midnight. The five members of the Damnation Brigade (the Diver, Furie, Sundown and the two non-Summoning Children, Akbar and Raven) didn't last even as long as that.

Didn't need to really. Neither did Aristotle Zeross, Auguste Moirnoir or Jordan Tethys. The clean-up had already begun by the time they turned-in. Besides, they'd done their bits. Them being so widespread, the bits D-Brig 5 in particular left behind were some of the most difficult to clean-up. They were exhausted, none more so than Harry Zeross, Ringleader.

He'd stopped throwing up, though, so maybe he wasn't becoming Gypsium sick after all.

Zeross, Tethys, the Diver, Furie and Akbar were given quarters in the monastery. Young Death already had a place to stay there. Raven, who was resolutely non-toilet-trained, chose to stay in the husk of an aircraft hangar she and Sundown had inadvertently helped torch before Fish rendered the illusion-caster resurrection-proof. Sundown stayed with Raven.

At Golgotha Nauroz's insistence D-Brig-5 agreed to share their quarters with his Trinondevs. The 80-year-old clone, who had come across members of D-Brig during his stays on the Outer Earth as Master Kyprian Somata's main *'mole'* beyond the Dome, albeit over forty years ago now, had never yet heard of a devil, even a vampiric devil, who couldn't survive going up in flames. Neither had Jordan Tethys. It might take her some time to acquire a new subtle matter shell, however.

Unless the debrained demon's body she'd been using had some Salamander or Lava Lout in it demons were notoriously flammable. Of course, if her body was still that of Barsine Mandam, who was otherwise human, which was possible, then maybe she had granulated like so much severely overdone toast. For the same reason, the Legendarian didn't expect Vetala's golden brown warrior to have survived. Not that he shed any tears for him. He reserved his for Katatribe.

The Voodoo Child had been inside her; had read her deadhead even as he drove out the Sangazur that animated her after her first death. That had been Kronokronos Mikoto's doing, her first death, he told Tethys when he vacated her after Sundown immolated her corpse. He'd been right about the Warlord. As soon as the Rakshas Gatherers reanimated Mikoto with a symbiotic Sangazur from one of the Crystal Skulls they carried with them, he felt obligated to kill someone. For some reason, misplaced loyalty perhaps, Katatribe had volunteered.

So why had she, once similarly reanimated by a Sang, volunteered to assassinate him, her own father, albeit from a different incarnation, 30-Beers wanted to know. It was her turn, Young Death said. She had her orders. From Mikoto; more precisely from his Guardian Angel Tyrtod. Make that Guardian Angel Mikoto, Jordy's brother in that they shared the same devic mother, Titanic Metis, whose cauldron of a power focus Methandra Thanatos now had.

Why would anyone want to assassinate me, was Tethys's next question. Elementary, my dear Daddy Jordy, you can long-distance-ignite anyone wearing or even holding onto the Trigregos Talismans. Did, too, didn't you? So, Tethys extrapolated, it was someone who wanted the thrice-cursed objects for his or herself. Dogfish-the-duh, agreed the trickster, echoing Fish.

There's a long list of them. Warlord Mikoto's at the top of it – in death as in life, in that respect. And he's still got Yomikune with him. Got more than her, Young Death pointed out. Someone denied Harry the Weird, he added. Remember? Tethys did. Other than Sal in Cabby's Weirdom, only a devil in his or her own protectorate can do that. Guess Vetala's demonic body had some Salamander or Lava Lout in it after all.

"I'm going to need help on this."

========

Neither Jordan Tethys nor Young Death slept in the monastery that night.

The Grey wasn't denied to either of them. The difference was the legendary 30-Year Man could draw himself to wherever he wanted to go whereas the male trickster couldn't even kill himself in order to escape from whatever frozen hell he'd ended up.

It was damn hard to kill yourself when you're shackled, ankles, wrists, waist and neck, from chains in a cage raised off the ground in a glacial chamber. He, thinking in Augustus Nauroz's parental mind-mode, just hoped he'd freeze to death in time to get back to them before his idiotic children got themselves irretrievably deceased.

"Eek!" shrieked Tina Zeross, from the cage next to his.

========

Jordan Tethys, the legendary Thirty Year Man, had earned his 30-Beers nickname. He'd also, he figured, earned the right to sleep-in. He woke up. It wasn't even light yet. They were on Tympani, Eardrum Isle, that of the Undying One in the midst of the Aural Sea of Sedon's Ear. She was as divinely beautiful as ever; positively exuded incomparable gorgeousness.

"Harmony?"

"Call me Nihila."

========

The Crimson Corona was also known as the Mind of Sapiendev because, reputedly, Sapiendev was the thinking third of the Trigregos Sisters. Sapienda, Thursday on the Outer Earth, was named after her. Sapienda night, at the derelict abattoir Hadd-side of the Pani Canal, Nergal Vetala had deliberately made three new vampires. They had awakened this morning, Sedonda-Sunday, the mandatory three days later; had done so shortly before dawn. (Sedonda was named after Dark Sedon.)

They were Cosmicompanions E, F and G. They were possessed; had been for a week. Unfortunately for the devils possessing them not a one had been cathonitized with their power foci. In theory Tvasitar Smithmonger could make replacement talismans. Non-decathonitized devils could wield other devils' talismans. Presumably so could decathonitized devils. In theory, also, they could reshape them into their own.

Plague, Carcinogen the Leper, had tried that with Neverknight's shield after Nowadays Nihila made off with his Pendulum Blade. It hadn't worked for him. The devils possessing the three cosmicompanions had no way of knowing that. Had no way of knowing the Apocalyptic was still occupying a Mantel half-life when he recathonitized. Mantels were next-to-useless as shells. Nor, without theirs, had they any way of transporting themselves to Sedon's Peak.

That meant a couple of things, they concluded – they being a Mithradite, a Lazaremist and a Byronic – after discussing it amongst themselves. Although they could manifest themselves overtop their shells, and thus could discuss the direness of their situational straits 3-eyed face to 3-eyed face (even if one seemed composed of straw, not skin), the first thing they agreed upon was that, at least for the time being, they were stuck inside vampiric shells. One of them, the Lazaremist, had spent considerable time inside vampiric shells before Abe Chaos cathonitized him. He didn't think that was such a bad thing.

The Mithradite, who had also been cathonitized by his Unholiness, the Unity of Chaos, shortly before he committed devic suicide, wasn't so sure about that. Vampires had to feed; that meant killing. Wouldn't Grandfather Sedon just recathonitize them as soon as they killed someone? The Byronic, who'd been cathonitized in Abaddon's presence, scoffed at that notion. They'd escaped Cathonia, the Sedon Sphere, without the Moloch's permission. What authority could he possibly have over them anymore?

The Byronic was the first of them to realize where they were: El Dorado, a good percentage of which had effectively been his old protectorate, albeit under his father's suzerainty. Vampires, in their bat-forms, could fly. It might take them a few days to reach it but they should be able to make it to Manoa. There, in the Gleaming City, he should be able to find its overlord, Damon Goldenrod. Surely his elder brother would help him. Maybe he would help his cousins as well, if he asked him to do so.

The Byronic, the Straw Man, had been in the night's sky hundreds of years longer than either the Mithradite or the Lazaremist. He had no idea El Dorado was now Hadd. Neither did the other two; Vetala still hadn't renamed Old Iraxas Hadd when they were rendered stars in the night's sky. Or, if she had, she hadn't bothered to inform either of them.

The Mithradite was feeling pretty good, though. He had supporters here: azuras, his own azuras. Actually, so did the Byronic. The Lazaremist didn't feel badly either. He could sense his power focus was somewhere hereabouts. The other thing they agreed upon was that dawn was approaching.

As hungry as they were, they'd better get themselves back into the abattoir, away from the coming light. Otherwise they wouldn't have any shells left.

========

*"**Deplorable**," said the ever-smiling fiend, fresh from most of a night's rocking and rolling in the Gypsium Wall.* **"Those are human beings. Rather they're hybrid Utopian beings. You can't hold them in conditions like that and expect Dr Zeross's cooperation."**

"For once you're right, Judge," Methandra Thanatos agreed. "I shall see to Mirrors' punishment myself."

========

At fully ten feet in height, the giantess towered over the mass of darkness that was the Smiling Fiend. At least his pinkish face and two hands, the ones with too many joints in their fingers, still showed through all that darkness. By contrast not a speck of Methandra's skin was visible. She was that thoroughly masked, hooded, cloaked and otherwise covered in garments coloured various shades of red, purple and violet.

She pointed her sorceress's cane, her equally elongated Brainrock matchstick or firebrand, at two of the snowmen; made briefly boiling puddles out of them.

"You others, treble the guard and have them removed to a Fire King's domicile. See they're well-fed and kept warm."

"But, mistress," one of the snowmen protested. "We'd melt in a Fire King's longhouse." She melted him.

"You others," she instructed the leftover snowmen. "Quadruple the guard and have them removed to an Intuit's igloo. Then see they're well-fed and kept warm."

"Methandra of Mythland!" Melina challenged her as the remaining snowmen began to lower the cage wherein she and her daughters had spent close to twenty hours being held. "How dare you treat us like canaries in a chicken coop? And how dare you kill your own servants? Why didn't the Mighty Moloch above you all cathonitize you on the spot?"

Methandra whirled and without saying a word left the chamber. Smiler lingered. *"You will have to forgive her, High Illuminary. We've been under considerable stress of late. Besides, Hot Stuff rarely speaks to anyone she considers beneath her. You should feel fortunate she deigned to enter your presence. Mirrors, Klannit Thanatos, must be unavailable."*

Melina regarded the speaker. She'd seen him many times in the past. Seen the body he appeared to be occupying anyhow; albeit not in such an amorphous state. However, it had been a long time since she'd last had the dubious pleasure of his company. "Even though you're sporting a third eye and your voice is different than I recall it, I recognize you. You're Judge Warlock. Tell me, how can she get away with killing the snowmen?"

"Ah, as to that, they are animated forms shaped with compacted snow only. The Scarlet Seeress has never quite accepted Cold can have hundreds of azuras whilst the best she can provide him with besides the ever-so-useful Klannit-creature are fourth generational devic children. So you might say she was just letting off some steam."

He made to leave himself. Young Death called down from his cage. "What about me?"

Smiler glanced upwards. If anything his perpetual grin broadened. *"An interesting question. Perhaps she's saving you for her buffoon of a brother-husband. Here in his protectorate I believe he has it within his ability to completely rid the cosmos of abominations such as yourself. Drowning, perhaps, in his beer stein. Except I understand drowning is a relatively painless way to die."*

He left. The snowmen unlocked the cage and helped the three Zeross cubs out of it. Mother Lion Melina wouldn't let them touch her. Their eyeballs may be non-burning coals but they were expressive.

"Don't tempt fate, Mommy Mel," the Voodoo Child called down to her from his inescapable perch. "Tantalazurs are no smarter than their sire. They might mistake you for a form only and try to make a mush of slush out of you too, boohoo."

Wisely Persephone took one of Mel's arms while Helen took the other. Together they helped their mother out of the chicken coop, as she'd referred to it. Tina was still looking up at Young Death, manacled as he was to the bars of the second cage. "Don't worry, Grand-Pappy Death. Once daddy gets here I'll ask him if I can kill you myself."

Melina had already asked Young Death what he was doing here. He said he didn't know. He was lying. Tricksters lied.

========

Smiler was in an exceptionally good mood when he returned to Lathakra from Sedon's Headband. Nowadays Nihila promised she'd deal with the Trigregos Talismans personally. Properly as well. They'd be dissolving in the Brainrock-filled crater of Sedon's Peak's lava lake before the day was half-done, she swore upon her inviolable oath as a Master Deva.

Trinondev eye-staves? Not a worry, she further claimed, without providing details.

He left it to her to tie-up those loose-ends. He had a few of his own. Primary amongst them was getting the Medusa's children, his children, out of the Cathonic

Zone. If Ringleader, Harry Zeross, could get to the Outer Earth, and thence to the Moon, with his Gypsium rings, chances were he could get into the Sedon Sphere. If he couldn't, well, there were other ways; there always were. A wrecked cosmicar still containing teleportive fuel made up of the same Godstuff on the Outer Earth's Damnation Isle for example. Zeross first, though.

He was pleased to see that, when he rematerialized on Lathakra, Methandra Thanatos was focusing on Ringleader with the visionary fumes emitting from her purloined cauldron. He was also pleased to see that Cold wasn't around. As for the problem of Trinondev eye-staves, Heat assured him, once she recognized him, she knew of ways to deal with them.

Unlike Nowadays Nihila, she provided details. Which was how he learned what the Thanatoids had done with the Family Zeross. He could believe Cold's stupidity. He couldn't believe hers.

As they walked through the glacial palace towards the ice cave where Klannit had secured the High Illuminary and her brats, Methandra boasted she had been busy on other fronts besides relocating and thereafter keeping tabs on Ringleader. He was moderately impressed with her accomplishments thus far. She directed her talents as wisely and as subtly as he did. He doubted they were as effective but she could still learn. If he chose to teach her.

One thing was for sure. Even he wasn't up to keeping two highborn Master Devas satisfied; three, if he chose to free the Medusa at the same time he got their children out of the Sedon Sphere. He decided he wouldn't bother with her. Mother Murder would have to stay up top. And, he further decided, one of the other two would have to join her.

While, without accessing the SAG Gap, when it was in one of its once-a-decade-periodical, wandering phases, Methandra couldn't get beyond the Dome physically, she could still cast splendours beyond it. Consequently, she had taken steps to ensure the oddly always 2-eyed, and therefore only presumed, 'daughter' they'd detected on the Outer Earth was on her way to its Centauri Island.

That Centauri Island – there was one in here as well – was linked to the Inner Earth's Aka Godbad City via the Nag Gap. Nag was short for Nagasaki; the thusly named 'doorway' in the Dome having opened when the United States of America dropped an atomic bomb on the Japanese port city on August 9, 1945. Someday, the way things were going out there, Atomics would bring down Cathonia.

Water's twin brother was already on the Frozen Isle, she'd said. He'd likely be asleep for a long while, however. Might even redevelop a third eye given enough rest. Antaeor, who usually did have three eyes, would probably need an extended nap himself, once he arrived.

King Cold hadn't been as generous to their Earth Elemental as he had their Air Elemental. Antaeor had been put to sleep, mid-battle, by a cluster of fucking faeries responding to their Kronokronos Supreme's cry for help. Tantal figured the least he could make Earth do was soil-swim home as penance for being so embarrassingly susceptible to faeriedust.

The fiend didn't bother telling her how he'd once been eaten by a faerie.

========

Neither did he accompany Methandra back to her station in front of her fuming, crimson cauldron. She was keeping something from him, he'd realized. She'd
been busy on other fronts as well; must have been if Klannit, Mirrors, her *'angelus'*,
her messenger, wasn't around to interact on her behalf with the Thanatoids' prisoners.

He heard sounds coming from the playroom of yellow-skinned Sedunihas, the
Thanatoids' deaf-mute, slow-to-age, youngest offspring, so he detoured there rather
than follow her. King Cold had preceded him. Like his sister-wife, the Intuits and
Fire Kings' devil-god had grown since he'd seen him last; was now maybe twelve-
foot tall.

"Ah, Smiler. Not so funnily I wasn't just wondering what had become of you.
You've heard the news about Air and Earth, I trust. About Water as well?" For once
the fiend was struck speechless. "And Thrygragos Byron too, I expect. Come see
what my talented son is doing."

"What madness is this?"

Sedunihas was working on a Stopstone bust of his thought-grandfather,
Thrygragos Varuna Mithras. Gone since Thrygragon, Mithramas Day 4376, they
were trying to resurrect him.

========

*D-Brig-5 (Blind Sundown, Raven's Head, the Untouchable Diver, the Kronokro-
nos Supreme and Wildman Dervish Furie) rose with the day. So did Ringleader. All had
desperately needed a night's sleep.*

They got one; it being almost winter, daybreak came late.

========

Having eaten and attended to their morning ablutions – the Diver even gave
himself a shave – they along with Golgotha Nauroz and a number of his Trinondevs,
their overnight guardians, entered the still-standing but now thoroughly trashed
command tent together shortly after 8 bells. The Living's brain-trust was minus two:
Young Death, whom D-Brig-5 recalled as Auguste Moirnoir, the Black Death, and
Jordan Tethys. It was supplemented by one.

"Fisherwoman," the Diver hailed her.

Things had been so frantic the night before they never had a chance to talk.
In fact, other than at breakfast, with Harry and Golgotha, but without Sundown or
Raven in attendance, they hadn't had much of a chance to talk with anyone; even
each other.

They didn't much like each other anyways. Only OMP, now Akbarartha, and
Furie belonged to the 1955 version of the oft-times regrouped King's Own Crimefighters. The other three, like Wilderwitch, were independent contractors brought
in to takedown Cyborg Cerebrus's gone-mad-again twin brother, Saul Ryne, the
Magnificent Psycho.

Takedown or takeout, as the need arose – hence the involvement of Blind
Sundown and Raven's Head.

She, Scylla Nereid, smiled, never a pleasant sight; held out her arms as if invit-
ing an embrace. Hesitantly he approached his sometimes lover from over four decades earlier at the first Academy of Man in Amsterdam and, once, afterwards. Didn't

embrace her, though. Now, just as it had way back then, a smile featuring two rows of shark-sharp teeth warranted caution.

"Good thing Thalassa, Sea Goddess, isn't here. She thought she'd killed you back in the early Fifties."

"Sedimentary-evidently our kind don't die eel-easily. Salivating-seems neither do you. Don't munch-a-bunch-of-barnacles age much either, I see-by-the-seaside."

"Still fishifying too."

"Goes without fay-saying, Diver," The vaguely greenish and somewhat scaly-skinned, blubber-wearing, gills-behind-her-ears, born-Piscine nodded at her on-again, off-again colleagues from the first, though not the last, incarnation of the King's Own Crimefighters. "Obadiah, Johnny, Raven, Dervish, been a dugong-long time, a very dugong-long time indeed-the-seaweed. Always expected to see you back on the Head. Natural place for scum-slurping supras like us. Speaking of which-the-Witch, where's my sister?"

"Witchie couldn't make it," grunted Furie.

A decent night's sleep, even if it was in a noisy war-zone, hadn't been enough to revert him to his gentlemanly persona. It was probably for the best. Jervis Murray would never have approved of wearing a brown robe. Now wasn't the time to say much more; not even to ask Fish how she knew they'd been on this Hidden Head-world of hers, and everyone else's, previously.

Everyone else included Harry, Golgotha and the never-aging little trickster who'd been calling him son since the late Thirties, wherever he'd gone. While OMP-Akbar and, when she was with them, Wilderwitch seemed right at home on the Head, Furie only suspected he'd been underneath the Dome before. He expected the same was true of Sundown, the Diver and Raven. Although, if you stopped to think about it, where else would someone – some thing, put better – like Johnny's Beauty come from?

"Just as swell," said Fisherwoman. "That's the trouble with Hadd. Krill-kill someone they don't stay deathbed-on-the-lake-head dead."

"What's your role here?" required the Diver.

"Aquatics," she all-but-snarled, as if it was self-evident, which it was. Where-upon she briefly ceased fishifying; never a good sign.

"Most Dead Things can't abide free-flowing water but there are exceptions. I'm to clear out Lake Sedona. I've a prize pack of perky Piscines like me, strictly water-breathing Akans and old Lemurians, most of them manatee-males, to kelp-help me out." Sometimes she couldn't stop herself. "How about you-the-few?" Couldn't stop fay-saying either.

"Go at them like we did the Apocalyptics," replied Furie. "With all we've got. As far as I can make out, that's the nearest thing we have to a plan."

"Which never was far-to-the-sandbar, as I recall-the-squall." The Water Witch gave him a playful poke in the ribs; grinned mischievously. It wasn't an invitation to make-out. It was to remind him that her teeth were almost as sharp as his fangs. "No time to get squid-squiggly, gents." Unless she was eating, which she often was, Fish could never cease fishifying for long. "And lady," she added belatedly, gesturing at Raven.

"Splatter-matters are more pressing-for-fish-oil than smacking mackerel Right Whale now. Driftwood-good to see you again. And, speaking of which, the Sea, the otter-other Water Witch, you ever see Sea Stuff again, you tell her Atlantean could have dainty died a whole whitefish-slower than he did."

She returned to the Living's brain-trust: the Sraddhites' High Priest, Thartarre Sraddha Holgatson, New Iraxas Governor Ferdinand Niarchos and Godbadian General Quentin Anvil. Thartarre's lieutenant, Diego de Landa, and Garcia Dis L'Orca, the War Witches' Number Two, Morgianna being their Number One, had already been there when D-Brig arrived and the Diver called her over to speak with them. Golgotha, the Trinondevs' Field Commander, and Ringleader had gone straight to the group as soon as they entered the tent.

Fish didn't want to be left out of their deliberations. She didn't want them deliberately leaving her out of them either. The newcomers wouldn't know she had once been queen of Godbad. Probably didn't even know what Godbad was – an immense subcontinent no less, with mountains rivalling that of the Himalayas. But the others definitely did and she didn't want them to suspect she'd lost interest in it.

Fat chance of that. The Fatman, Alpha Centauri, was probably keeping its throne warm just for her; albeit with electrode arm, chest and head cuffs.

========

They were looking at the aerial map of Hadd they'd managed to salvage after Jordan Tethys's sketchpad ignited atop it last night. Before he retired, the Legendarian must have circled the area of the Penile Peninsula where he'd simultaneously ignited Vetala and her soldier after they dusted Janna Fangfingers. He'd labelled it Dustmound, which was the same name living Iraches used for the gruesome spire of mostly skulls and bones.

"You want us to leave this Dustmound to you and Harry's outsiders?" Anvil was asking Golgotha as Fish came up to them.

"If they are willing to join us," Golgotha confirmed. "Otherwise Dr Zeross shall take twenty of my Warriors Elite and I with him there alone."

"No," Thartarre insisted. "As ever so useful as your eye-staves are, as good as you are with them and as good as these Outer Earth, so-called supras may be, I shall lead my Sraddhites there also. We know how to handle Dead Things."

"All staffs and no distaffs?" Fish inserted, smiling in that disconcerting way she had of doing so by maximizing the glint off her double-layer of shark-sharp teeth. "We War Witches and Hellions would hake-hate you to go anywhere without female companionship."

"We do have priestesses amongst our number, Lady Achigan," said Thartarre testily.

"And we agreed that I shall lead our land forces," added Garcia, who was Morg's woman, not Fish's.

Garcia was exactly the same age, perhaps to the day, as the Morrigan's Andaemyn. Like Andy, she struck Fish as being merely good at what she did. Which was nothing special. Indeed, other than her – but including Harry, whose rings were all that made him supra-special as far as she was concerned – there was nothing special about any of those in the tent until D-Brig-5 walked into it. If they were the genuine article and, judging from last night's display they were; had to be. They don't make them like that anymore.

"Am I to surmise there's a prize for you guys?" Then she had it. "Wait a min-now-minute. Of course there is. Harry, use your eye-spies!"

"Where's the Morrigan and her daughter?" snapped Thartarre, who'd hoped to keep some of the prize everyone seemed to be after for himself and his Sraddhites.

Harry, Ringleader, already had rings around his eyeballs. He understood what Fish was saying. They were instantly glowing. He was far-seeing.

========

D-Brig-5 were chatting.

"Witchie will be pissed when I tell her Fish isn't dead," said Furie.

"On the contrary, Dervish," countered OMP-Akbar. "Despite their past disagreements, my sense is the Witch will be overjoyed to hear her sister's still alive."

"So long as she is to hear it," said Sundown unnecessarily.

"Nonetheless," admitted the Diver, howsoever whimsically, "It was good to see her again. And hear her fishisms."

"That your cock doing the walking or your mouth doing the talking?" wondered the wild man nastily.

"Bit of both, I imagine. She certainly got your goat."

"So now I'm a goat," said Furie. "Better than a werewolf-in-shorts, I suppose."

"Mind you," the Diver further ruminated, ignoring his comrade, "Even though we finally proved Atlantean was a Rache rat-bastard, I doubt Thalassa, if we ever see her again, will be happy Fish's still alive. And Wilderwitch, whom I'm confident will survive her injuries, won't be at all happy hearing Superior Sarpedon is still around, especially if Skull-Face is right and she doesn't look all that much older than she did pre-Limbo."

(Black Skull-Face was Golgotha's codename during the early years of the Outer Earth's Secret War of Supranormals.)

"Then again," he added, "The Witch always said Ants don't so much age as reach their time then fall down and die."

"Fish has aged," objected Sundown, who had seen her through Raven's eyes. Neither of them, neither Creature of the Cosmos, had ever liked her. That being the case, even if she was a Lady Achigan nowadays – and apparently had been a crowned Queen for the most the years they'd known her, they'd just been informed – there had always been something about her worthy of admiration. "Not much, maybe, but she is visibly getting on."

Raven's Head whinnied her own comment. "Who'll be happier," the Cheyenne supra translated for their benefit, "Wilderwitch or you, Diver?"

"What's that supposed to mean, Johnny?"

"Raven was just trying to make sense of what Furie said. You and Fish had your fling in the early Forties or late Thirties, before I hooked up with her and reconnected with you lot."

"Oh, just making chitchat, was she? Tell you what, Raven. We ever get anywhere safe and sane, I'll be sure to write you a letter about how happy I am."

It was a putdown. Nowhere safe and sane could contain a huge, ebony horse with a bird's head, currently retracted unicorn's horn, the speckled tail of an iguana, or maybe a snake minus its head, and talarial wings on both sides of all four of her upper hooves.

"Ants get around," recalled OMP-Akbar, sensing the tension amongst his comrades.

He didn't need to bop himself with his Homeworld Sceptre to remember that both Sundown and Jervis Murray had also loved life-loving Antheans in their day. Presumably Murray's Witch was still alive, in the Weirdom of Cabalarkon, but Johnny's Sorciere, Solace born Sunrise, had been brutally murdered in 1953 by the Conquering Christ and the remnants of Atlantean's Rache. She'd also been much closer to Fish than Wilderwitch ever had. Which-witch suggested Sorciere kept her secrets as well as either Fish or the Witch had.

Given the terrible circumstances of her death, it was no wonder Sundown and Raven went on their Vengeance Quest. What was a wonderment was, when the King Crimefighters were re-formed to take them down, no one else was killed. Sundown and Raven's Head might be killers; however, they were principled killers. They only killed other killers; ones who probably deserved to die.

"Fuck it," swore Furie. Were the suddenly manifest nodules on his forehead the nubs of nascent goat-horns? Was Dervish Furie on the verge of transforming into the Full Furie? Had his feet just become cloven hooves. Probably. "I'd rather be killing Dead Things."

He didn't have long to wait.

========

The Smiling Fiend opened his third eye, let loose his Eyefire, liquefied the Stopstone bust the deaf-mute, naturally gifted sculptor was working on into so much mush.

========

Sedunihas squealed in fright and leapt away. 'Why do that, Uncle Smile?' he started signing frantically. 'Dad say good. Grandfather look that.'

Having recognized the unnaturally slowly aging, fourth generational devil's talent years earlier, Smiler had made a point of relearning sign-language "You waste skill, Artist," he gestured. "Me grandfather more than that."

Old King Cold, Tantal Thanatos, had never bothered to learn sign-language. "Not this time, Judge," he bellowed as loudly as a 12-foot behemoth could bellow; bellowed so loudly maybe even Sedunihas could hear him.

For a stupid, beer-guzzling buffoon he was astonishingly quick with his Brainrock war-axe, his Tvasitar Talisman. Lathakra was his protectorate. He could cathonitize anyone who displeased him within it. Only minutes earlier Smiler had been debating with himself how best to free his children by the Medusa from the Sedon Sphere. He hadn't been debating how he might free himself, once he was up there himself.

"Say hello to the Mighty Moloch for me," laughed old King Cold as he prepared to bring his war-axe down upon the fiend. "Tell him there's a properly chilled pilsner waiting for him here in Lathakra. That, and a Labrys!"

The earth quaked. Antaeor Thanatos had returned to the Frozen Isle. Three other newcomers had arrived moments earlier. One of them had a Brainrock quill.

========

The Three Great Goddesses were second generational devils. Along with the Illuminaries of Weir, Jordan Tethys was among those who agreed that no more than 500 third generational devils made it to the Inner Earth. Only nine Master Devas were firstborns. Of them four were generally thought to be female.

Three were extant. The two visitors who didn't have a Brainrock quill were waiting for the third thought-firstborn; the one who was actually a second-born.

The Trigregos Talismans were irresistible.

========

Begin Endgame-Gambit.

****

(ENDGAME-GAMBIT) 22: **Damnation In Pane**

Sedonda, Tantalar 7, 5980

The Amateramirror displaced the choker-like strip of cloth Janna Fangfingers had been wearing about her throat just before her head, together with the rest of her body, turned to dust. Attached to it was a crystal skull.

Both were still there, the choker and the crystal skull attached to it. So was the Brainrock throne, somewhat shrunken in size. Second Fangs wasn't. Dust thou art, to dust thou shall return. Neither were the remains of Vetala's soldier, any sign of the Nergalid herself nor any sign of the Trigregos Talismans.

"If you've brought me here on false pretences you're not going back to Cabalarkon in triumph. You're going back in chains. To face the Master's justice. To face my justice."

========

The four of them, Saladin Devason, Morgianna now Sarpedon, Andaemyn always Sarpedon and Alastor Molorchus, had come to the pinnacle of Dustmound for what should have been a simple salvage mission: collect the Trigregos Talismans, charred as they may be, and beetle back to the Master's Weirdom, where Molorchus, Morg's Gypsium-gifted, Outer Earth born thrall, had collected him last night. Collected him from his bed in Skyrise – which he'd reckoned was inaccessible to anyone else.

Until he finally woke up, not all that long ago, in the Morrigan's between-space 'shelter' within the Sraddhite monastery, he hadn't known Molorchus existed. With the exceptions of Ringleader, Harry Zeross, who had his Gypsium rings, and Jordan Tethys, whose Brainrock quill had to have belonged to a devil at one time, he didn't think it was even possible for a non-devil to have abilities like Molorchus evidently had. As far as Sal was concerned that was a failing of the High Illuminary's beyond-Cabalarkon intelligence network.

He could block the functioning of Anthean agates and every other variety of witch-stone up there, in what amounted to his own protectorate. He could block psychopomps like Garudas, Keres Hellhounds or Morg's Night Mare. Had he known of Molorchus he felt sure he could have blocked the Weirdom's Weird from him too.

Maybe Melina now Zeross knew of his existence; just kept it to herself. Maybe she was afraid that if he blocked Molorchus he would have to block her similarly

Brainrock-blessed husband. Mel never appreciated the fullness of his abilities. Neither had Morg.

He found the whole episode disconcerting. He could never forget the fact that the recently gone-missing High Illuminary was Morg's sister-in-law; the pretender's twin, no less. Had Mel and her daughters been kidnapped? Or had they been spirited to safety by this selfsame Molorchus fellow?

Was he like Harry in that he could only teleport himself and others to places he'd either been to before or could visualize? Morg had never been in Skyrise. Mel lived in Skyrise. She'd been on his floor. She was a trained doctor, though; not a proper witch. Couldn't do illusions to save her life.

Future file stuff that. Where were the damned talismans?

It was daylight. As always the non-vulturous cloud-covering of Hadd obscured the sun but it was still bright enough to keep ordinary vampires underground, in caves or tombs in the depths of one of Hadd's ruined cities or outposts. Vetala wasn't an ordinary vampire, true. Nonetheless, if she wasn't abolished, if she showed up to try and prevent him from reclaiming what rightfully belonged to his Weirdom, well, she was a Master Deva.

Sal generally slept naked so, along with Trinondev clothing, his chain of office and the two other Brainrock facsimiles of the Trigregos Talismans, Morg had the forethought to bring his Master's Mace with them to Sraddha Isle. Chances were Vetala wasn't so reckless as to venture anywhere near him so long as he had his mace. Still, if she was, fine. He had no objection to imprisoning her, in the prison pod that was the eyeorb atop his mace, his Speaking Stick, as he sometimes called it. It'd be a bonus.

"That isn't very friendly, uncle," said Andy.

The Zebranid was dressed in jungle khaki, as if she was going hunting. Her flak jacket had plenty of pockets to it. She must have had on some sort of bullet-proof vest underneath it since she looked more blocky than shapely. A couple of pistols in holsters were belted to her hips and a samurai's long-sword, a katana, with no pommel on its grip, was strapped to her back alongside what he took to be a Godbadian-manufactured sniper's rifle. She also carried a satchel slung off one shoulder.

Sal wasn't sure she was a witch. Given who her mother and sister were, there was a strong probability she was but the satchel bulged, so he didn't think it was a witch's kibisis or bottomless bag. Since the one-armed man was similarly outfitted, albeit with a bowie-knife rather than a sword and no rifle, more likely it was just where she kept her extra ammunition.

He knew his sister was a first-rate witch, however; was therefore a materialist. He also knew she reputedly wore an invisible demon. It could be all she wore; all she figured she needed to wear. Demons were composed of subtle matter. He wasn't above seeing her as naked as she must have seen him when she had her thrall teleport him to the monastery.

"I'm not the friendliest of fellows, leper," he said to his niece. "Now, if you'll all stand aside, I'll concentrate on the matter at hand."

"Won't you be needing these?" Morg was holding the facsimiles of the talismans, including his chain of office, the fake Crimson Corona incorporated into it.

"No more than I'll be needing this. Here, catch." He tossed her his Master's Mace.

Even beyond the Weirdom, Sal was the Master of Weir. He was a living eye-stave. Morgianna jumped out of the way of the mace. Its eyeorb opened anyways. He'd been wrong about her wearing only an invisible demon. Even though she was a nearly 60-year-old mixed-blood, she looked as good as ever in her underwear. It was as white as her pantsuit, hair and skin had been. Her hair and skin were still white.

Devic bodies were debrained demons. Eyeorbs sucked a devil's third eye out of his or her skull first, yes, but then they sucked their subtle matter bodies into their mass between-space. All of Incain did identically when she devoured devils. When they were cathonitized the devils ended up in the Sedon Sphere. Most ended up there with their talismans and demonic bodies. Some didn't, but so what?

When they were decathonitized they all ended up having to possess sentient beings anyways. Had to hold onto them until their bodies either recovered from the trauma of cathonitization or they found other demons to de-brain and thereupon occupy. Mel had told him that. So had Master Kyprian and various other teachers he and Morg both had while they were growing up.

After the Mighty Moloch Above decathonitized Nevair Neverknight the first thing Byron's Paladin did was debrain a fresh demon he could occupy. Their information was valid, they assured him. It came from interviews their long-gone predecessors conducted with Neverknight himself. Saladin wasn't the best of students but he was hardly the worst. He knew exactly what he was doing.

Andy didn't. Then she was encased in a thought-bubble Sal projected off one of his eye-orbed fists and was hurtling off Dustmound. Alastor Molorchus got the same treatment. Saladin winked at his stunned immobile sister, who was still holding the fakes even though she was now standing on Dustmound in her underwear. Then he closed his two eyes and did as promised; concentrated on the matter at hand.

It was working. Morg was still in her underwear but she wasn't holding onto the fakes anymore. His chain of office was a crimson crown about his forehead. The pendant with the design that resembled the open-eye-in-a-pyramid motif found on the Outer Earth American dollar bill dangled over his forehead. Then it closed. The phoney Amateramirror appeared as a shield on his left arm. The fake Susasword materialized in his right hand.

Somebody screamed. Must have been Morg, simultaneously snapping out of her state of stupefaction and apprehending her predicament. He thought his mace back into his left hand; levitated, encasing himself in a mental force shield just in case.

He chanced a glance at his sister in time to see her vanish on a witch-stone. Where had it come from? Was it in one of her teeth, her underwear? Was it a false fingernail? Morg painted her fingernails. They glinted, had minuscule specks. Did she have a bellybutton bauble instead of a bottomless bag like Fish did?

No matter; no time to think about it.

He was glowing. The fakes were glowing. They were coming, the real things. He could feel them coming. The fakes were getting hot. The eyeorb atop his mace was still open. It was fattening. It too was glowing. Something was wrong. He ejected it. Another orb took its place. He had dozens of them secreted between-space. Always did, even in Cabalarkon; didn't really need his Master's Mace. He was a living eyeorb and materialist both.

What was going on? Morg was back. She came out of the Weird atop, what? The crystal skull he'd earlier spotted lying on the ground in front of the Brainrock chair maybe? She wasn't a self-psychopomp, was she? She went for the first eyeorb, the one into which he'd slurped her invisible demon; what was her outerwear. Got it. Vanished again.

Dustmound shook. Cubic feet of skeletal matter, dust and debris formed into a colossal shape. Some sort of the demonic concretion of all that bony matter reared out of its tip. There was flesh to some of it; arms, legs, heads, animating. What was he dealing with? He ejected another eyeorb. Two, three, five more appeared in rapid succession, filled-up. He ejected them.

The thing kept growing. It loomed above him. Was the mass of Dustmound shrinking? He conjured up five, ten more eyeorbs. They swelled; he ejected them on the verge of bursting. How many more did he have left? Would he be able to hold on long enough?

Numerous glowing rings appeared around the concretion, contracted; fragmented it. The air rained its remains. More rings formed. From them came Field Commander Nauroz and around twenty of his veteran Trinondevs, gargoyles manifest. Saladin recognized them all. And not just by their house or individual gargoyles. Some may not have been friends exactly but they were his life's comrades. The same thing started happening to the eyeorbs atop their eye-staves.

"Shut them down now," Golgotha ordered.

Eyeorbs were transmitters. They transmitted his orders. Eyeorbs only needed to be open when they were taking something into them: a devil, an azura, a demon's subtle matter form. For most other things they worked as readily closed as open. What Sal hadn't understood, but Golgotha had, was that when open azuras could fill them up without being mind-over-mind compelled to do so. This was an unexpected and worrisome development. Vetala's Haddazurs were wilfully suicidal.

Still more rings formed. Out of them came Thartarre Holgatson and thirty-odd Sraddhites. Some were women. They sprinkled witch-stones over Dustmound. War Witches and, with them, holding their hands, even more Sraddhites began appearing off them. They fanned out.

Saladin had hung on long enough. The real things arrived, melded with the fakes as they should. As he knew they would. They were too hot for him. Saladin Devason was as good as cannon-shot out of the sky. Protected by his thought-bubble he bounced on the ground below Dustmound. He was dazed.

Besides his Master's Mace, the only thing left of his talismans were the pendant with the open-eye-in-the-pyramid motif. It was too hot too handle too; was burning him. He didn't handle it. He was still a living eye-stave. He enclosed it in a telekinetic ball of mind-matter. He looked up. Andaemyn was rushing at him, her katana drawn.

He flung it at her.

========

Vetala's Soldier came whole atop Dustmound. In addition to having the Three Sacred Objects, fused as they now were with the Cabalarkon-facsimiles, he wore the fang-fingered glove. They glowed with Gypsium. He glowed with Gypsium, a warm golden-brown. He stood in front of Vetala's empty and visibly diminished Brainrock throne. It did too. It would. Brainrock and Gypsium were the same Godstuff.

He reckoned he was too now. More Gypsium than man; more god than anything else.

========

He hadn't needed its replenishment as much as Vetala had. She'd been wearing more clothing than he had and her demonic body proved alarmingly flammable. Both of them bursting into flame at the same time the Trigregos Talismans had was harsh. Sitting in her throne had been healing, however. In an outstandingly fast, dare he think it?, even rapid-fire fashion. And it had been soothing, like ice on a burn. Which they both were, burnt, badly. Were, rather. Hence its diminishment.

He was Trigregos now. He couldn't be killed anymore. He felt good. What could be better than repulsing a debatably genuine aspirant to the talismans' ownership? Melded as they were with their just-as-much Brainrock imitations, the talismans themselves felt better too, the Crimson Corona, the Mind of Sapiendev, informed him.

So many duplicates had been their drain-bane for ever so long.

========

Six insubstantial shapes formed in the midst of five separate rings. Becoming the Trigregos Titan had restored many of his memories but the only one he recognized was Dmetri Diomad's arguable uncle. "What's it going to be, Dimmy?" asked that one. "You going to give them up voluntarily or are you going to make us come out and take them from you?"

His codename's Ringleader, the Corona informed him. Told him the names of the other shapes as well. Said they'd have to die. Which was okay with him. Trigregos caused the Corona to appear on all their heads. He figured doing so would make them compliant. It didn't. One of the others, a near-giant Santa Claus of a man, spoke in a booming voice.

"Takeda Power was my wife, soldier. Her crown plain doesn't work on us anymore. Hasn't, from the looks of you, whoever you are, for probably as long as you've been alive. We'd like to keep you that way. Alive, I mean."

Unfazed, Trigregos expanded the reflective face of the Amateramirror so that it caught all six members of the Damnation Brigade, uncle included, they in their rings, in its glass. He'd imprison them there, shatter their images and thus kill them. The reflections were indistinct. Were they top-drawer vampires like Janna Fangfingers? Or weren't they fully formed yet?

"We come all the way through, Dim," Uncle Ringleader put to him, borrowing one of Fish's favourite phrases, "You're in deep whaledreck. Take them off. Lay them on the ground. Back off. The King Crimefighters weren't killers. The Damnation Brigade, well, you call our bluff, might be we'll call you an undertaker."

"Fuck you!"

The Diver leapt out of the teleportal he was in; it dispelled. Vetala's glowingly golden-brown warrior shot a bolt of Gypsium energy at him out of the Susasword.

The Corona had told him it could that sort of thing. Too late. The Diver had already ducked into the ground. He could do that sort of thing, the Corona remembered. Dervish Furie sprang out of Harry's Gypsium hoop in the sky; which vanished as immediately as the one the Diver was in had. Oh, he was there after all, imparted the Corona.

The wild man came right at him. The golden-brown warrior had a golden-brown aura. It was strong enough to rebuff the Africa-born, Jamaica-raised Summoning Child. Furie found himself sailing through the air. He came to ground well away from Dustmound; not far from where Saladin Devason landed.

Not this time, goddamn samurais.

========

"Moderately impressive character this nephew of yours, Rings," Blind Sundown threatened by understatement. He was in the same teleportal as Raven's Head. "He may require our undivided attention."

"Not before he gets mine," said the rightful Kronokronos Supreme of Temporis, he in his teleport-hole. "And if he does, kid, all the King's horses and all the King's men won't be able to put your nephew back together again. Not unless I want them to – and I'm having my doubts about this *'don't kill'* stuff right now."

OMP-Akbar was chomping at the bit. Not the one Raven's Head allowed Sundown to place in her chops; the proverbial bit. The one that told him that here at last was an opportunity to atone for his failures in Temporis against Demon Land, Carcinogen the Leper and, yes, even Lakshmi of Lemuria.

"Hear him, Dim?" Even though the Old Man no longer wore his regalia, the Thrygragos Talismans, Ringleader had no doubt he was giving fair warning.

"We're not," said the Cheyenne Summoning Child. Far from being intimidated by the danger presented by Vetala's soldier, Sundown seemed to be asking for some sort of dispensation before he crisped him. "When he's ours, Rings, you say goodbye. Ready for that yet or do you feel like playing Neville Chamberlain in Munich?"

"Last chance, Dmetri." Ringleader wanted to keep his presumed nephew alive and in one piece. Knowing Sundown's predilection for expediency in the extreme – the man hadn't used stun mode, if there was such a thing, on his Solar Spear since mid '53 – he wangled the carrot of preservation.

"Listen to me please," he next-door-to-begged him. "We're holding back. I can send OMP into your hip pocket. Hell, he could walk into it almost as quickly," he added notionally.

"I don't expect you to appreciate what he can do to you with his Homeworld Sceptre. You weren't on Aegean Trigon when he single-handedly took out your old man, Olympian III, in '55. But I'm telling you, he'd be far more gentle on you than Blind Sundown and Raven's Head. They cathonitized Headless Ramazar, the Vultyrie and most of Mater Matare yesterday. What they'll do to you only I'm preventing. For the love of our family, yield!"

Nergal Vetala, revealingly clothed, re-clothed, as she had been in Temporis, showed herself. She was at her soldier's side. There was something insubstantial about her as well, as if she wasn't all there yet either. She'd been waiting for the right moment to demonstrate who was in control here.

Even though she was certain Hadd remained her protectorate – the persistence of the ever-rainless, non-vulturous clouds of Hadd obscuring the sun indicated as much – Trinondev eye-staves filled to the point of bursting with Haddazur Spirit Beings seemed the right moment.

Hundreds of Dead Things clambered clumsily out of Dustmound. Most were armed with shards of bones that no longer had enough sinews left to hold together a fellow Dead Thing. Gigantic vultures led by Cloud-General Kronar flew out of the clouds above them. On their backs were even more Dead Things. These ones were armed with modern-day weapons.

That probably meant they were animated by Sangazurs. Regular Haddazurs, who were born in Hadd, and Nergalazurs, who were mostly born up north, in Satanwyck and the Elysian Fields before they became the Ghostlands, were so uncoordinated they were as likely to shoot the living vultures they were riding as they were anyone else. If Sangs then, in life, the Dead Things had been kill-or-be-killed warriors. In death they were just killers.

"Nice smelling blood you Outer Earthlings have," she, her ghost, challenged them. "Want to play with us? Feel free. Do yourself a favour, ring-man, go away, take your deviants and leave us alone. This is Hadd. I'm its goddess. This isn't your affair." She vanished as a discharge of solar energy went through where she'd just been. Sundown didn't need anyone's dispensation to obliterate a devil.

As Ringleader had promised, he sent the long-ago-dubbed Awesome Akbar directly behind Trigregos Incarnate. The old man smacked the soldier so hard the Dand-head of his Homeworld Sceptre vapourized. So did the soldier. It, the head of his sceptre, re-formed immediately. The soldier didn't.

Someone laughed. A female's voice. The ghost of Vetala appeared above him. "Boo!"

OMP-Akbar clubbed her. No easy task that, clubbing a ghost, but his sceptre was a fabulous weapon. It was carved out of a bough of the original Tree of Life, he now recalled being brought up believing. He had done the same thing to her in Temporis the day before. It made a kind of nebulous contact and Vetala vanished yet again. It was a now-you-see-her, now-you-don't, game of cat and mouse. Only it seemed to Akbar the devil was the scaredy-cat.

He readied himself, expecting the soldier to materialize somewhere nearby. When nothing untoward happened he signalled Ringleader, Kid Ringo as he still thought of him, who promptly whisked him to his side within his teleportal. Rings fused the one containing Sundown and Raven's Head with it. They were suitably impressed with Akbar's successful extraction of both foes, the devil and the soldier.

"Didn't realize you could do that, OMP," Sundown praised him, in his restrained way of praising anyone. Raven whinnied her accord.

"Neither did I," he acknowledged. "I must have hit him harder than I intended."

OMP-Akbar was as puzzled as they were impressed. He hadn't willed his sceptre to kill or destroy the soldier, Dmetri Diomad, as Ringleader had briefed them prior to bringing them here. He'd willed it only to knock him out. Still, dealing with such like self-psychopomps had always been an uncertain business. You never knew how much they were there.

Amongst the supranormals he'd faced with that ability during his decade-plus on the Outer Earth, Slipper was by far the most elusive. Slipper was the codename assigned to Roxanne born Heliopolis Kinesis; Hot Rox as the Summoning Children in the Damnation Brigade still referred to her. Also according to Rings, whose briefing had lasted maybe ten minutes, some of which he delivered after they'd already arrived here and were waiting between-space to see how Saladin Devason fared doing his own dirty work, she was this Diomad's mother.

"What about his talismans?" wondered Ringleader. "Did you blow them out of existence as well?"

"I don't think so. I did a stunt in Temporis to keep Lakshmi getting hold of the fullness of my devic father's power focus. It shouldn't have made mine powerful enough to destroy other power foci, though. No, the soldier's around somewhere, laying low, out of sight, probably with the vamp. Maybe they want us to wear ourselves out fighting Dead Things before they show themselves again."

The stunt he was referring to was to knock the Dand-head of his sceptre against the head of Tariqartha's somewhat similar-looking sceptre. The knock transferred some of the Dand's power to his; unfortunately not enough to stop Lakshmi booting him out of Temporis, along with the rest of D-Brig. It didn't stop her from sealing the Thousand Caverns with some sort of Solidium shield either.

Be that as it may, he was wrong. Vetala's soldier showed himself just then — inside Ringleader's teleportal.

For a big as well as evidently old man, OMP-Akbar was awfully quick. More explosions. Everyone in what amounted to the Brainrock-blessed, much younger man's between-space *'shelter'* got blasted outside it. Tactical error that, Rings' had just enough time to regret. Eggs in the same basket always was. For his stupidity he'd have smacked himself in the face if the ground didn't do it for him first.

His miraculous rings were the only thing supranormal about Aristotle Zeross. Luckily he was far sturdier than Humpty Dumpty.

========

Like Morgianna now Sarpedon until she had Andaemyn in mid '53, whereupon she became eligible to earn her second seven years of Anthean training, which she did, her 100-plus Athenans were not necessarily Ants. However, while easily 80% of them had their first seven years of Ant-training, while most of the older ones had had daughters and while many thereafter did become qualified Mistresses of Life, all of them considered themselves Life's defenders first and foremost.

As such, under the leadership of Morg's lieutenant, Garcia Dis L'Orca, who was Andy's age and just as childless, they showed no mercy towards the aberrant dead. They pranced in and out of Samsara upon their witch-stones, spilling chemical compounds on Dead Things that caused them to spontaneously combust. Not a one of them could be touched let alone harmed. Then it seemed they were running into each other between-space. Some of them started falling into regular space.

They didn't stay fallen for long. A few pulled knives out of their backs or stomachs and started using them on their still alive, once fellow War Witches. A number of other freshly minted Dead Things had oozing bullet holes in vital areas. Some started using their compounds on Living Things. Still ablaze, they were up again, and fighting on the other side, almost immediately.

Shortly before daybreak on the morning of Sapienda-Thursday, three bats with betwixt-and-between talents, the gift to remain visible yet intangible, which was something else Slipper could do, had manifested themselves on the battlements of the Sraddhites' monastery. Of them, by generating the equivalent of a miniature sunburst instead of a gargoyle within the brain-bulb he'd captured him in, Golgotha Nauroz saw to it the Trinondev had his endgame Lazam night in Petrograd. Shortly after Second Fangs had hers here, last night, Devauray-Saturday; the Zebranid and the Sraddhite War Witch had their endgames at the Sraddhites' monastery. The Diver accounted for the former just after Fish accounted for the latter.

Sapienda-Thursday morning, the Sraddhite vamp had brought through a dozen dead Athenans who, before they were in effect re-killed and disposed of properly, were too agile to be zombies animated by Haddazurs. War Witches were supposed to kill themselves before they were taken and to keep on killing themselves if they were occupied by symbiotic Sangazurs. So, unless they'd gone bad before they were killed, they had to have been animated by some sort of super-azura or an entirely different breed of possessive spirit.

Devauray morning, when Young Death read Nanny Klanny's deadhead he'd blurted out something to the effect that Second Fangs did indeed have Crystal Skull soul-sinks; that that was her trick. Whose soul-selves did she preserve inside them? Dead friends or allies, presumably, including her twin brother.

They were so strong-willed they could dominate the corpses they animated. Didn't deaden them either; kept them lively, just as Sangs did. Evidently they were also as tough as azuras were in terms of being able to indefinitely survive incorporeally. A new and even more deadly adversary then.

Living Athenans began withdrawing to Sraddha Isle.

========

Thartarre Holgatson and his by now roughly four dozen brown-robed Sraddhites, those that were still Living Things, had never seen so many Dead Things in one place. For the most part they were a slow, shambling foe compared to the fit, well-trained and highly motivated priests and priestesses. Their scavenged weapons were no match for the fire canisters and forged metal of the Sraddhites but they had a few advantages over their living counterparts.

A clean, killing stroke was useless against them. Being already dead, the zombies had to be dismembered. Decapitation was a good start but, possessed as they were by azura Spirit Beings, even headless ones carried on. Fire was the only truly effective agent for destroying them but the Haddazurs animating them would endure to occupy fallen Sraddhites. Flames spread so there was also the hazard ones already on fire would battle on until they were totally consumed, reduced to ash.

Far more valuable would be Outer Earth and Godbadian anti-personnel ballistics such as grenades or expanding bullets, the Splatter Packs Rings brought from beyond the Dome a couple of days earlier. But they had similar drawbacks. Brown robes, the garment, were no more proof against explosives than they were fire-resistant.

The High Priest and his warrior monks preferred pack-fighting, a melee. They also preferred the tried-and-true methods their ancestors had used when Sraddha Somata was as alive as he was their god. Back canisters, with their nozzles spurting a napalm-like substance with a delayed ignition similar to the compounds used by the War Witches; hacking swords and axes; blazing arrows and ordinary ones for the vultures that carried zombies into action: they'd been good enough for grandma and grandpa. They were good enough for them.

Given the overwhelming number of Dead Things and the fact not just Dust-mound itself, but the whole area around it, seemed to be a mass burial ground, the Sraddhites were hard-pressed. Haddit Zombies were crawling out of the earth to get at them. A Brown Robe would go down only to rise up moments later an enemy wearing a brown robe. Already Thartarre was noticing zombies just so accoutered. One was too many.

The Dead Things riding the vultures in the sky above were shooting bullets; had plenty of ammunition. For Sangs there was no such thing as casualties due to friendly fire; all their fire was friendly. Unlike Dis L'Orca's Athenans, who popped into and out of Samsara on their witch-stones, and Golgotha's Trinondevs, whose eye-staves, even when their eyeorbs were closed in order to avoid being filled by Azura Spirit Beings, projected force shields in the forms of rampaging gargoyles to protect themselves, the Sraddhites were wide-open and vulnerable. And, with the Godbadian aircraft essentially destroyed, there was no air support he could call in to drive off the vulturous Cloud of Hadd and their Sangazur-animated riders.

Thartarre had relied on Ringleader to bring them here; had expected him to bring them back to the monastery once they'd retrieved the three talismans. Now he couldn't even see Dr Zeross's teleportals in the air. Where was he? Where were his vaunted Outer Earth supras? What was happening to the War Witches? Why were they turning on each other?

At least the Sangs were concentrating their gunfire on the Trinondevs. Their shields weren't a hundred percent impregnable, not under withering assault from every imaginable angle. The ground beneath their feet was an animate minefield. A half-dozen had already gone down. Only to get up again, as per usual. Weren't much use anymore, though. Haddazurs didn't have their Utopian brains; couldn't make eye-staves work.

Even if he ordered an immediate retreat, they were on foot; they'd be picked off from above. He hollered at his fellow Brown Robes to get away with the War Witches if they could; hollered at Dis L'Orca and her Athenans to wait or come back for them. Yelled at Golgotha and his Trinondevs. It was no use, he shouted to them, Hadd was Vetala's protectorate after all. They had to abandon the area's arena until they had reinforcements. Melees were as horrific as they were horrifically loud.

This was not going at all well. His justifiable desire for a share of the Trigregos pie had the makings of a death wish.

========

A half dozen Dead Things were clawing out of shallow graves in front of him. Furie didn't bother pausing to dismember any of them. He just used their heads as stepping stones, non-witchery variety. In the pre-Tokugawa Era Cavern of Temporis he'd had plenty of trouble with samurais and their super-sharp swords. Although a great deal more of the blood spattering the shredded evening clothes he'd been wearing at the time was theirs, he had received more than a few nicks and scratches.

Which, given his hide was tank-armour-tough, was a testament to how sharp their blades had been. He'd very nearly lost an eye there as well.

Seeing the four samurais appear behind the Master of Weir, as Rings had additionally identified Saladin Devason, Morg's brother, he was going to have to shift into as close to Full-Furie gear as he dared do, pre-Headworld, in order to prevent this Saladin fellow becoming an ex-Master. Was he the same tall, gawky, not-quite-as-black Saladin, filled out now, he'd met as a teenager at the Amsterdam Academy of Man? It wouldn't surprise him in the slightest.

The onrushing Zebranid between them had her blade out. Andaemyn, that was the name Rings gave them for her; said she was Morgianna and Demios Sarpedon's daughter. Both the Diver and Old Man Power, Akbarartha now, had remembered her as Andrea, Andy. The Diver claimed she didn't have zebra-striped skin as a baby. Illusions, said Rings. Not the striped skin; the illusions were she didn't have stripes.

Saladin clearly perceived his own niece as a menace because he threw something at her. She hit the turf smartly, did a roll and came up with a pistol in each hand. She fired over his head, dropped a couple of samurais, a man and a woman, poised behind him. They, not Stripes, gave Furie the impression of potential assassins.

Saladin had yet to realize they were behind him. Andy had been shooting at him; her father's daughter, that one. He had her in a thought-bubble, a brain-bulb; was raising her high off the ground by the time the wild man reached him. Now Saladin must have thought Furie was a menace. He let the Zebranid drop, from quite a height, and tried to encase the Outer Earth supra in the same way he had her.

He never came close to nabbing him. Furie was too quick; passed him. The two shot samurai were attempting to get to their feet but they were pathetically sluggish. Could they be dead already? Had they already been dead? Was that why Andy had shot them? Who cared? Furie ignored the maybe dead ones; went for the other two, also a man and a woman. How had they got here anyways?

They were swift; Furie was swifter. Shattered the man's sword arm at the shoulder; kicked out the woman's legs then broke both her arms just for good measure. Looked up. The man whose arm he'd broken had a long sword sticking through him. One of the now definitely dead samurais had got to him. He had to be dead because he had a short sword sticking out of him and much more than that spilling out of them. Gutted, he was; ambidextrous, these samurais were.

The other shot one, a woman, was definitely dead because her neck was smoking. The smoke was rising through where her head had been. That was Sundown's doing; Johnny had smoked her. Didn't need a peace-pipe to do so either. That was what his Solar Spear did; smoked folks. He and Raven's Head must have burst out of Zeross's teleportal.

Riding her, his Beauty, who perhaps significantly wasn't flying, the Native American Summoning Child was blazing a pathway through a conflagration composed of nevertheless still teeming Dead Things. They were heading toward the pinnacle of Dustmound. Why wasn't Raven flying? For purposes of maximum massacre? What was up there? Furie's eyesight was perfect but it wasn't far-sight.

The Cheyenne's wouldn't have been an errant blast. Furie and Sundown weren't tight but they looked after each other's back. They all did. That was why the last incarnation of KOC, the King's Own Crimefighters, never made much of an effort to stop them when he and Raven went on their year-long Vengeance Quest after the Rache brutally murdered Solace-Sorciere, Johnny's childhood bride, as she was in the process of giving birth in June of 1953. Once comrades-in-arms, always comrades-in-arms.

So how had they got here, the samurais? Hang on a sec. There was a fourth person on the top of Dustmound. Saladin tossed him off it at the same time he tossed Andy off it. Once they arrived here, while they were still in the Weird, Zeross said he thought there was something familiar about him. Furie looked around for him. Spotted Sal instead.

The Master of this Weir of his was standing over his niece. Was doing something to her. Was projecting a nearly imperceptible, even for Furie, mind-globe over her head. He was, it seemed to the wild man, seeking to smother her. He wasn't flash-fast but he was fast enough. Cannon-balled the Master to one side, didn't give him an opportunity to recover. Didn't bother breaking any bones; slapped him silly then stood astride him.

"Flip a coin, Sal," he proposed, ever so generously. "It is Sal, isn't it?" The Master glared at him. Glazed at him, more like. Devason was so boxer-brain-addled he could barely focus his eyes. "One side's cracked ribs, a broken leg or arm or neck; other side's a permanent disability, lifelong wheelchair at the minimum. Either way Zebra Girl there's going to an infirmary, not a mortuary."

"Don't think he has a coin," came a voice from behind him. The wild man's speed was blinding. Then he was looking at a blind man and a ravendeer with a unicorn horn. They were looking at him as well. Then he was beside them, looking down at Saladin Devason. It was like they were in Limbo again.

"You aren't worth the space." Vetala's soldier told the Master. The Susasword was akin to Sundown's Solar Spear. It could discharge killing force.

========

They exploded beyond between-space. John Sundown and Raven's Head were thrown apart from each other. Without contact with Raven, Sundown was truly blind. Without him, still suffering from yesterday's ordeal in Temporis, she was disinclined to fly. Even separated they were no easy marks, as the Haddit Zombies quickly discovered.

He had senses beyond sight. Had an innate strength. Was capable of short-term bursts of speed that approximated those of Dervish Furie. His Solar Spear was not quite fully charged anymore but it was charged enough. Being a creature of the cosmos, he was immune to fire. She too was a creature of the cosmos.

Rearing onto her hind hooves, she whinnied defiantly. Her whole being, from the tip of her now completely extended unicorn horn to her iguana-like, speckled tail, crackled with energy. Zombies who came too close found themselves suddenly aflame. They had auras about them, those two; a nimbus that was more yellow and red than the gold and brown of Trigregos's Gypsium. It both repulsed and punished, with fire, those who sought to infringe upon it.

They found each other. Sundown leapt atop her. Their nimbus neither repulsed nor punished each other. They looked around for the others. With her eyes they spotted Dervish Furie on the flats below Dustmound. A couple of male samurais, one with a dangling arm, seemed intent on killing each other. Let them.

Another one was also on her feet. She was sneaking up on Furie. The Wildman was dealing with another woman; breaking her arms. She must be alive. The one sneaking up on him was shambling. She must be dead. Sundown blew her head off. She was now, that was for certain. Raven's Head switched their shared eyesight toward the top of Dustmound. There, that throne – it's Gypsium.

It's more than that. Dead Things blazed before them. They, he firing his Solar Spear at anything in their way, advanced relentlessly onwards and upwards. Raven and through her, him, could see what no one else could see. The devil was just sitting there, in the Brainrock throne, calmly taking in the action going on in front of her.

Barsine Mandam, Sorciere's best buddy way back when, albeit with fangs and three eyes? It couldn't be. And not just because she looked so smug, as if she was witnessing a performance being put on for her entertainment. She – couldn't be Barsine, sister of Jess, the Conquering Christ, Solace's killer a decade after Barstool's supposed death, somewhere – she, this vampiric Blood Queen of Hadd, the Land of the Ambulatory Dead, its ungodly Goddess, had no notion what they'd done yesterday to the Apocalyptics in Temporis. Couldn't have!

Whoever, whatever, she had no notion they were about to do the same thing to her.

Her soldier was suddenly between them and her. He pointed his mirrored-shield at them.

========

"Two down," Goddess congratulates him. "Him next."

'Him-next' was Wildman Dervish Furie. He took care of him. Saladin had encased himself in a brain-bubble. Bubbles are easy to pop. Goddess screams.

Have to kill him later.

========

OMP-Akbar, the rightful Kronokronos Supreme, erupted out of Kid Ringo's teleportal; tumbled well down slope from the tip of Dustmound. The Dand-head of his Homeworld Sceptre was already re-forming. Dead Things came to make him one of their own. It didn't need to altogether re-form. It detonated. He wasn't there anymore. Brainrock attracts Brainrock.

He came out of the Weird atop her throne. Whacked downwards; cranium-cracked the devil walnut-open. She screamed. Her skull spouted blood and brains. Didn't faze her much. On a rubber neck she turned to regard him; spat venom at him. Her spit hurt him more than she was hurting. Maybe his sceptre couldn't kill devils. Maybe he should have willed it to cathonitize her.

"Like me better his way, old man?"

She wasn't a pretty sight. Likely he wasn't either by now. Her third eye smouldered; her fangs glistened. His eyes glossed over reflexively; he'd forgotten he had such reflexes. She materialized a Brainrock sickle, her power focus, and attempted to swipe off his neck-nut. He blocked it with his sceptre. Her sickle imbedded in his cudgel. There was a flare. Goddess and Supreme were repelled from each other.

Ignoring their talismans, they grappled. He was feeling incongruously hungry. Vetala went for his jugular but his hands were around her neck, choking her. Sparks were coming out of his fingertips. Where had they come from? He really should have bopped himself with his Homeworld Sceptre as soon as he arrived on the Hidden Headworld. He had a very useful heritage. He just wished he could remember what else he could do.

She let loose her eyefire. He was sweating. His sweat was sparkling. It was coming back to him; memories of what else he could do. She tried to turn into mist but he was with her every which way she went. State- and shape-shifting, he could do that when he had on his regalia. Maybe he hadn't needed them. His strength was as formidable as hers. He needed it.

"What are you?"

"A fucking faerie! Only you're the one who's fucked."

OMP-Akbar tightened his grip. He'd have crushed unto so much soggy pulp anything other than a vampire and a Master Deva in her own protectorate. Vetala screamed again. Pussy-willow scaredy-cat. Her soldier was instantly upon Dustmound's peak. They both reflected out of the mirror's vitreous surface. Trigregos Incarnate thought only of the Santa Claus. Dmetri Diomad had always hated Christmas. His parents, if they were Diomad's parents, called it Xmas. How could you like anything called Xmas?

What Trigregos thought his talismans did. The rightful Kronokronos Supreme was in there with the other three, Dervish Furie, Raven's Head and John Sundown. Their reflections weren't reflections anymore. They were steady-state; akin to full-colour, extraordinarily life-like portraits inscribed on a glass plate in an ornate frame. That was a nice pre-Christmas present.

Trigregos wanted another one. Looked around for the Diver; couldn't spot him. Using far-sight provided by the Corona he found Diomad's uncle lying a couple of feet off the ground. He was being held up by an invisible something that seemed to be emanating from the top of a tall, incredibly gaunt, black-skinned man's staff. There were a lot of other black men around the first one. All were dressed in indigo robes. Most were blacker than the Furie; all were blacker than the Master. For some reason he couldn't suck any of them into the Amateramirror. Perhaps it was filled to capacity.

The Vampire Queen snapped her sickle out of Akbar's sceptre. Carrying both talismans with her, exhausted, smarting from the lightness of the day and still not recovered from very nearly being burnt unto ash the night before, she stumbled back onto her throne. At her signal he went over to her, ever mindful the Diver was somewhere about.

"The battle's over, my soldier," she more wheezed than whispered. Devils had always had considerable difficulty when it came to tangling with faeries. "We've held the day; we'll win the night. Let the Dead finish the Living. Guard me."

He would have, had not Kronokronos Mikoto been there – symbiotic Sangazur-possessed, bullet-ridden corpse that he was now. In death as in life severing heads was a samurai speciality. Problem was it only worked when your foe's neck was still attached to his shoulders. And his skull to his neck. The dead warlord slashed his katana, with its Death's Head pommel, what had once been a Dand-head pommel, through the empty space between the soldier's shoulders and skull.

"Now you're showing off," observed Vetala, just as she was wracked by a fit of coughing. Faeriedust in the lungs?

"No," responded her glowingly golden-brown warrior. "Now I'm showing off." Using the Susasword he cleaved the warlord in twain, from top of his head to the split of his crotch.

Guardian Angel Mikoto went looking for another shell to occupy.

========

Tantal Thanatos put his Earth Elemental to bed in the glacial chamber next to the one where he'd put his Air Elemental the day before. He checked on the latter, still asleep, still no third eye. No matter, it'd come. He was feeling inordinately pleased with himself. Couldn't quite remember why, though.

He returned to where his wife was supposed to be keeping an eye, or three, on the male Dr Zeross via the visionary fumes emitting from her purloined cauldron. Cauldron, fumes, visions, all were still there. She wasn't. Then someone else was, a Byronic.

"Seen my missus, Cold?"

"Can't say as I have, Silvercloud. Heard about your father. No real loss. Want a beer?"

"Wouldn't say no. What're you watching?"

****

(ENDGAME-GAMBIT) 23: **The Diver Digests Godstuff**

<u>Sedonda, Tantalar 7, 5980</u>

Gypsium attracts Gypsium. Gyps also repels Gyps. UD, Yehudi Cohen, the Un-touchable Diver, wasn't anywhere near Dustmound because Alastor Molorchus had dis-patched him.

========

The Diver's crimson-lens Gorgon Goggles granted him an only myopic form of far-sight compared to Harry Zeross's eye-rings. He could recognize trouble when he far-saw it. There was nothing tentative about his identification. He'd seen him last night on the monastery's battlements with the glamour-casting vamp. Fish gaffed her, but not before he got away via a mirrored egg. The one-armed man was trouble with a Capital T for treachery.

The Diver fancied himself as good with faces as he was with quips. Others would contest that, the quips bit in particular. He'd be the first to admit he wasn't very good when it came to names, but he knew that face from pre-Limbo days. That wasn't all of it, either. He'd come out of Ringleader's teleportal, gone immediately underground, because he spotted the one-armed man bring in the four samurais just by rotating the shoulder-cuff of his missing arm.

His shoulder-cuff was doing that G-string-thing. It was Gypsium-glowing.

========

Haddit Zombies were relentless. They just kept coming, crawling out of the ground and tumbling out the sky. By contrast fewer and fewer of Garcia Dis L'Orca's War Witches were coming out of between-space. Athenans didn't have uniforms. They didn't wear brown robes like Sraddhite priests and priestesses or dyed-indigo ones like his Trinondevs did. Some wore pants, some wore skirts, some even wore shorts. More than a few of them wore balaclavas or tightly wound headscarves to hide their identity.

They did, however, generally wear clothes. Then again so did their risen-again corpses. The clothes their now dead, yet still ambulatory, former fellows wore were distinguishable from most of the initial Haddit Zombies primarily because virtually none of them had been wearing anything. They were also distinguishable from the clothing worn by alive-witches because alive-witches didn't outfit themselves as if they were gore-splattered tatterdemalions.

And where was the Master?

========

At the outset of this increasingly ill-advised gambit – a simple salvage operation like fuck!, as Dr Zeross was prone to exclaiming – there were along the lines of twice as many of Dis L'Orca's War Witches than there were of his Sraddhites. It seemed to him, their High Priest, albeit not by much, that the totality of numbers were stacked more in favour of his Brown Robes by now.

The War Witches had finished their fighting, that much was certain.. They were only coming out of the Grey to grab hold of, then retreat with, their wounded fellows or his Sraddhites.

Good on them!

========

Field Commander Golgotha Nauroz brought two units of the Weirdom's all-male Warrior Elite to Dustmound. Each unit consisted of ten Trinondevs. Dead Things were breaking through their overly stressed force shields with greater regularity than they had been mere minutes earlier. The High Priest, Thartarre Sraddha Holgatson, and his, say, three dozen remaining Brown Robes had become as much the targets of the Cloud of Hadd and their well-armed riders. Mostly that was due to the fact Golgotha was down to half of those he came here with, units and men. The Dead Things had to shoot someone besides themselves.

Golgotha had Ringleader; Dr Zeross hadn't landed well: was bruised and confused; wasn't with it enough to make use of his rings. The Utopian clone couldn't make use of them, either; he wasn't sure anyone else could. He made a strategic decision, called his decimated Trinondevs together. They formed a mind-shield around themselves and the Sraddhites. The gargoyle they collectively manifested wasn't variations on the brazen bat theme they'd been using to terrorize the enemy since their arrival in Hadd. En masse, and massively deflated emotionally, they levitated and began to sweep eastward.

They'd hadn't forgotten their Master. He'd got himself here. He could get himself out of here. Rather, his sister could. Looked about to be doing so right this minute as well.

========

The Cloud of Hadd followed them, its riders firing sporadically, albeit neither urgently nor particularly accurately. Moments later the skies behind them, over-top Dustmound, started lighting up loudly. Then came the additional sound of Godbadian warplanes. Hadn't they destroyed them? Were they bombarding Dustmound?

Curiosity may have killed the cat. That didn't mean the cat wasn't curious anymore. Not even after it had exhausted its nine lives. Everybody serves somebody. Those riding the Cloud of Hadd wanted to find out who they were now serving. Besides, even for Sangazur-animated Dead Things, there was something undignified chasing a big black bunny rabbit whose floppy ears were flapping wings.

They abandoned the pursuit.

========

Morgianna hadn't forgotten her daughter. Andaemyn had Hellstones about her. Morg came out on one; cradled her baby in her arms. She was entirely the

White Witch again. Her pantsuit was a not-quite-invisible demon. The underwear, that was from the Outer Earth. Radiant Rainbows Fashion Emporium. Based in Paris. No, not Castella Thanatos's radiant rainbow. Surprised you remember that. Hers was hair. At least she didn't think it was Castella's rainbow.

How had she got Alastor Molorchus to take them both to the Master's private quarters in Skyrise? After she had him take her to Cabalarkon's Masters Palace in the first place? She'd never been to Skyrise. It's an abomination. She saw enough of his floor when he contacted her via the witch-stone. It was just a matter of conjuring up the image in the mind of Molorchus.

She had a good memory, was even better with illusions and Al was a fabulous thrall. Much better than Mel's Harry; wasn't as fragile for one thing. The little specks in her creamy nail-polish? They were just some of her equivalencies of a bottomless bag. Those little specks under a microscope, some of them looked like Crystal Skulls. Hellions knew about soul-sinks.

Want him? Can do. "After he gets us where you can't reach us."

========

"Him next," said Nergal Vetala, she in her throne. It was waning again; ice melting, Brainrock was replenishing her. This time she was referring to the one-armed man. The Trigregos Titan agreed.

========

Cosmicaptain Dmetri Diomad had met Alastor Molorchus on the tiny, three-peaked island of Trigon when he was growing up. It lay in the Aegean Sea between Santorini and Crete. Some said Santorini was Plato's Atlantis. While that may be, it was definitely ancient Strongyne, the Island of Strong Women, during the centuries the so-called mad goddesses' Middle Sea matriarchate flourished in what was now best known as the Mediterranean Basin.

Nearby Crete was another hotbed of Mother-Earth-centric devotion in that long-gone era. The Goddess Culture's eradication began when Strongyne blew its heart into the sky roughly 3,500 years ago. According to some its eruption, not any Celestial Angel of Death, also accounted for the ten Plagues of Biblical Egypt – Mosaic times being synchronous with the final decades of the devic matriarchate.

Legend had it Trigon surfaced as a result of its eruption. Its three peaks were known as the Dragon's Teeth.

Unlike Diomad, who'd only occasionally visited it in his childhood and, later on, as a teenager, Molorchus had been raised there; raised there before, during and after the Outer Earth's Second World War. He'd matured to become a first class engineer and physicist. Except, he was supposed to have died during an experiment into the teleportive usage of Gypsium on Centauri Island, where Cosmicaptain Diomad began his final adventure.

All that was left of Alastor Molorchus out there was an arm; the one he didn't have anymore. That was in 1968, around the same time Aegean Trigon sank. Or whatever it did. The Diomad part of the golden-brown warrior's brain supposed that meant the experiment had been a partial success; that Al had teleported most of himself in here, beneath the Dome.

Rumour had it Molorchus was a bum-boy. No part of his brain approved of bum-boys.

==========

He was hovering above her, them. Was literally hovering. He was a living eye-stave. Was levitating. Had his Master's Mace, his Speaking Stick, in hand. Bugger of a brother had yet another eyeorb atop it. How many more did he have? It was open. For some reason Haddazurs weren't filling it up. She couldn't lie under its influence. Was all but paralyzed under its influence. Could barely talk let alone move.

He'd encased her and Andy in a mind-globe; a separate one from the one in which he'd encased himself. Errant bullets pinged off them. Andy was in no condition to notice anything, might have a broken back, but Morg winced every time one hit their shield. They didn't seem to bother him in the slightest. She'd never really appreciated how powerful he was, even outside the Weirdom. He must have been practising since Aortic Amphitrite's Lemurians almost stewed him and the Legendarian alive on Shenon six and a half years ago.

"So you admit it," he said. "You were setting me up. Only the leper there, not the pretender, was to be your assassin. Your thrall, you used a Hellstone on him; that's why he's your thrall. Call him over. Have him take us home. My home, your jail cell."

"To a jail cell? To face your justice? Yeah, sure." Morgianna was so exasperated at her brother's paranoia she rolled her eyes; looked to the skies, as if for divine inspiration. She didn't expect to receive it. Her eyes widened. "What's the moon doing on this side of the clouds?"

"Oldest trick in the book, Morg."

She didn't receive divine inspiration. She got instead what on the Hidden Headworld passed for divine intervention.

"Watch it, Sal. Lightning bolt coming."

She was gone the moment it struck; went out on the same Hellstone upon which she'd got to Andaemyn before Saladin could kill her. She carried her daughter with her. The Master didn't have time to kill either of them. Andy was a big girl. Pantsuit-demons were strong. Devils were stronger; none were stronger, more powerful, than firstborns.

Even if one of them was a second-born.

=========

It wasn't a hot-time in the old town tonight, first of all, because Dustmound wasn't a town. It wasn't the moon on this side of Hadd's ever-rainless cloud-covering, second of all, because it was still today, as in still daylight. A throne made out of Gypsium-Brainrock couldn't act like cooling ice when it was broiling. That was Heat's doing. The golden-brown warrior couldn't move. That was Gravity's doing. Chain-lightning?

"That's Balance. Yikes. That'll have smartened him up."

"Want another beer, Beast?"

"Sure. Good show you got on, Cold."

=========

Given Hadd's latitude and the fact it was early Tantalar, December on the Outer Earth, there were barely ten hours of daylight per day. By the time the ten Tri-nondev Elite, counting Golgotha Nauroz, and their passengers, another twenty in total, including Thartarre Holgatson and Ringleader, Dr Aristotle Zeross, arrived on Sraddha Isle more than half of those hours were spent. That meant the Godbadians still had plenty of time to finish their evacuation of Sraddha Isle and the rest of their positions in and around Lake Sedona.

Ferdinand Niarchos, Quentin Anvil, Janna St Peche Montressor, Garcia Dis L'Orca and Diego de Landa, Thartarre's Curia-designated Number Two, were waiting for them. So were Demios Sarpedon and thirty of his Zebranids.

If anything the lightshow in the west, whence they'd fled, had intensified.

========

The Trinondevs weren't the only ones to suffer a devastating defeat on Dustmound. In terms of numbers, the Sraddhites and the Athenans lost more personnel. Golgotha Nauroz had brought two of his once thirty, 10-man units with him to Dustmound. As far as he was concerned, those twenty were the elite of the Elite. Excluding himself he came back with only nine of them.

Demios Sarpedon had been in Aka Godbad City with Janna St Peche-Montressor seeing to her father-in-law, Alpha Centauri, who hadn't had either a stroke or a heart attack as they'd feared. So long as he lost two or three hundred pounds, in the very near future, the Fatman should be okay.

Carrying around, or wheeling around, that much weight was all very well and fine when you were often the host-shell of a Great God. But, with Thrygragos Byron in the night's sky, to continue stuffing your face to your heart's discontent could only hasten the day you'd be winched into your grave.

Unless he wanted to donate his corpse to heat the Sraddhites' monastery, that is. For which they'd be grateful. Given the Fatman's size, it might save on as much of a week's worth of scrawny zombies.

As well as being a Lovely Lady Afrite, howsoever contrarily Janna already was a War Witch drill-sergeant. She was looking forward to becoming a slave driver.

They left Godbad with Centauri contemplating radical surgery.

========

After attending his daughter, who was same age, perhaps to the day, as both Janna St Peche-Montressor and Garcia Dis L'Orca, then hearing out his wife, Sarpedon was looking for a very specific someone to kill. His name was Saladin Devason.

Demios had the oldest eye-stave in existence. Many of his Zebranids had eye-staves of their own. For easily observable reasons, striped skin being unacceptable in the Weirdom of Cabalarkon, they hadn't been invited to participate in the supposedly routine salvage mission to Dustmound.

Dem had been considering leading them there anyways, if only to make sure Sal was good and dead. He wasn't sure they could make it there under their own power, especially not with all the abnormal meteorological turmoil visible in that directions. Neither would the Godbadians give them a lift. They needed all the aircraft they'd called in from Petrograd and Krachla to evacuate their forces otherwise stranded on and around Lake Sedona.

Word had come from Gomez Niarchos, Ferdinand's father, Godbad's Sangazur-animated ambassador to Sanguerre, that the Valhallans had regained their devic overlord, Mars Bellona, the Apocalyptic of War. That meant Badhbh, Sabre Rattle, Bellona's Sangs-banished bride, was no longer War's widow.

Consequently, despite the undeniable ravages Nevair Neverknight wrought softening it up for her and her Crepuscular forces, Battle Baby might be tempted to hold off seeking to reclaim the Bloodlands, New Valhalla, as her own. Worse, she might be tempted to redirect her armies to Twilight's south and thence by sea across Bogy Bay towards Godbad itself.

Regardless, with Unmoving Byron and his Primary Nucleoids in the Sedon Sphere, the Corporate State's government wanted its military at home. There was already talk of launching a pre-emptive air-strike on the Bloodlands.

========

Although on his feet and walking without assistance, Harry dismissed demands from Sarpedon and his similarly retribution-minded followers to provide them with a free ring-ride to Dustmound. He ached from head to toe; wanted food, maybe a beer. Then, after a quick side trip to Cabalarkon for reinforcements, he'd take them to Dustmound. He'd take every last Trinondev, every last Zebranid, and every other suicidal fool he could find with him there, too. He wasn't going to abandon them like he did on Damnation Isle on Christmas Day 1955.

Demios knew whom he, Harry, was talking about. Then he wasn't talking any longer. The Utopian Summoning Child had been in enough scraps during his nearly sixty years on this or any other planet to recognize shock when he saw it. He'd experienced it firsthand on the Outer Earth earlier in the week, after enduring a thorough bashing of his own.

He didn't catch him. He left that to Janna and Garcia. Life-defending Athenans weren't half-bad when it came to dispensing life-saving condiments prepared for them by their pacifistic, Althean-healer counterparts. Instead, as Thartarre and the rest of the Living's brain-trust, arguing amongst themselves, went their own way; as St Peche-Montressor and Dis L'Orca, who had survived more than just a scrap today, conducted Harry toward the monastery's infirmary; Demios rounded on Golgotha Nauroz.

"I want a full report, clone. Then I want your command. What happened today was a disgrace but it may be a blessing in disguise. It's long past time we Utopians had a legitimate leader; a real Master."

"And you're it?" Golgotha challenged him. "Ubris may have given you his eye-stave but I have his genetic makeup and I serve his grandson."

"Who's dead."

"Impossible. We saw your wife about to rescue him."

"You saw Devason trying to kill Morg and my daughter. He may have succeeded with Andy. My wife's still with her."

"You're saying your wife killed her own brother in self-defence?"

"After what he did to Andy, I'm sure she would have if she could have. She was lucky the lightning struck him before he could finish them off."

"Saladin Devason was killed by an Act of God?"

"The Devil, more like. Or his spawn. You know your history. He wouldn't be the first Master to be killed by a bolt of lightning. My sister's named after an earlier one."

He was referring to Melina Somata, the birthmother of the Janna and Sraddha Terrible Twins who was sometimes recalled, affectionately, as the Trigregos Titaness.

She'd succeeded husband Zalman as the Master of the Weirdom of Cabalarkon (as well as, a few years earlier, Kanin City) after his Unholiness, Abe Chaos, killed Zal with the Susasword five hundred years in the past.

Illuminaries did not like to bruit it about that that Melina was actually killed by her own daughter, who put the bite on her after she was struck by lightning. Then again neither Golgotha nor Demios liked to recall Ubris Nauroz was made a vamp during the course of the Simultaneous Summonings of 19/5920. Possibly, although no one could recall anything that went on during the Summonings with any certainty, by the same vampire – none other than that unlamented dust-bag, Janna Fangfingers herself.

Then there was Master Morgan Abyss, the Death's Head Hellion of an even earlier age. She was a Melusine Piscine not unlike Fisherwoman. She was also, though he never confirmed it, an earlier incarnation of the Legendarian, Jordan 'Q for Quill' Tethys. A great deal had been written about Master Morgan – whom Morgianna may have been named after. She was even held blameworthy of causing the Ghostlands (via the Idiot or Atomic Twins, Tammuz and Osiraq, once Mithras's torchbearers), though that may have been Pyrame Silverstar, whom that Morg may or may not have been possessing.

Year of the Dome 4825 was a very long time ago. Just ask the Thanatoids of Lathakra, who'd slept for well over a thousand years thanks in large measure to the Death's Head Hellion. Or ask Datong Harmonia, the Unity of Balance in her Nemesis aspect, who may have killed her with chain lightning – the same chain lightning that may have just accounted for Saladin Devason on Dustmound.

"I believe we shall have to have a word with this Morrigan of yours."

"I already have. Your command, clone."

"I didn't mean you and I, Sarpedon. I meant we, the same we who shall decide who is fit to command them."

========

The cagey, 80-year-old clone had landed in Krachla with three hundred Trinondevs. He'd divided them into thirty units of ten. There weren't thirty groups left primarily because bat-psychos could get through brain-bulbs. After some consequentially necessary reorganizing, there were now twenty-five units; most of them had a full complement of ten members left. Golgotha had far-spoken to their group leaders on his way back here.

Over the course of the next few hours, while daylight held, while the frighteningly bizarre sound and lightshow in the west continued unabated, twenty-four impossibly immense, multi-coloured and noisily tittering bats flew out of Hadd's cloud-covering. An hour prior to twilight more than two hundred Trinondevs were on the Isle.

They hadn't come to begin an en masse evacuation like the Godbadians. Neither had they come to make a last stand. With a dozen eyeorbs each, say a minimum of a couple dozen Spirit Beings per eyeorb, do the math. By their reckoning even Dustmound couldn't have that many Haddazurs or Nergalazurs in its vicinity. They'd come to prepare for a final offensive.

Tomorrow was D-Day. The D stood for Dustmound.

After that morning's disaster, their overall field commander wasn't as confident as his group leaders. Harry, however, had persuaded him that now that the Master had entered the game Sal would authorize him to transport hundreds more Trinondevs down here. And they could easily bring many more than just a dozen eyeorbs per person with them.

Would massive reinforcements be enough? Was the theory even valid? Golgotha wasn't averse to assigning a few units to sweep the monastery and the tunnels beneath it with open eyeorbs in order to test it out. Thartarre might object, however. Young Death's zombie workforce saved his Sraddhites a great deal of hard labour. After yesterday's lecture General Anvil might object, too. He'd have liked to bury his mother, not cremate her.

According to Ferdinand Niarchos, the general was a Christian like Melina Zeross, the High Illuminary of Weir, and her three daughters, who wore sanctified crucifixes when doing their rounds as the equivalent of Cabalarkon's royal family up in Sedon's Devic Eye-Land. Alpha Centauri, Godbad's de facto ruler, was openly Christian himself, a baptized Roman Catholic. Which had always struck the clone as the height of irony since, reputedly, the Fatman often acted as Great Byron's shell.

Of course everyone thought Devason was alive at the time they were returning from Dustmound. On top of that Harry had just lost five of his oldest friends. Not that, after a quarter century in Limbo, three of them were even as old as he was nowadays. Harry had also been raving, They weren't lost, he could get them back. Go up to the Weirdom and come back to Hadd. And … And … And now he was in the infirmary.

Understandably, Golgotha sympathized. Rings had used scads of Brainrock these past few days. He had also been put through the figurative ringer physically. His own nephew had beaten him to a pulp in Temporis yesterday. Then, give or take twenty-four hours later, he'd been expelled from his own teleportal by the concussive force of OMP-Akbar's Homeworld Sceptre going off inside it. Had landed rough as well; might have bulged his numbskull yet again. He might not be altogether off his nut as yet but it had to be coming unscrewed.

And now the Master was dead. Adopt, adapt and improve.

========

Who needed either of them, Morg said, when Golgotha and a delegation of Trinondevs met with her and Demios just before nightfall. It looked like Andy was going to survive after all, thank you very much for your concern. Morg was a witch but she wasn't much good at healing. Andy was tough stuff. This is Al. Don't mind the head-bandage, Al's fine. He's also way better than Harry. Harry relies on his rings. Al is his own Gypsium generator. More Trinondevs? More eyeorbs? An interesting concept. Might be able to arrange it. Just one thing …

Golgotha voluntarily resigned; left his hat in the proverbial ring, however. The Trinondevs first order of business therefore became who was going to lead them to Dustmound come morning. Although he remained a much loathed personage in the Cabalarkon camp, Demios won. The Trinondevs and their Zebranid cousins now had just the one field commander. Funny how things work sometimes.

The clone expressed himself satisfied with the results. He said he'd be happier standing guard over Ringleader anyways. Morg wasn't happy about that. That pleased him almost as much as the results of the vote. Golgotha Nauroz really was a perceptive old codger.

What didn't please him was when Demios decided to join him in Harry's quarters.

========

Once codenamed Blackguard, once also the Ace of Spades, Demios Sarpedon had the oldest eye-stave in existence.

It might not be able to match up against the presumed-destroyed Master's Mace, not in Cabalarkon anyhow, but Ubris had given it to Dem, not him, so he had no doubt it could override Golgotha's own. Then Demios dismissed Garcia Dis L'Orca and he felt infinitely better. Garcia, who performed much the same role with the Morrigan's Athenan War Witches as he had with the Master's Trinondevs in Hadd, was Morg's lieutenant. Demios was just her husband.

"Where's Fish?" Sarpedon asked him.

"Don't know. Out abolishing aquatic Dead Things, I suppose."

"What about my wife's Young Daddy Death?"

"Don't know that either. What's troubling you, Sarpedon?"

"You can call me Dem in private, Golgotha."

"Golgotha's better than clone, Dem."

"You fixed the vote."

"And you've the oldest eye-stave in existence. You overheard us."

"Morg disobeyed me."

"Not technically. She brought Sal ... I can call him Sal since we're being so friendly and off-the-record here ... She brought Sal down to go after the Trigregos Talismans. She couldn't get hold of them herself so he was the logical one to do it. Sounds like he should never have left Cabalarkon but that's the way of things. Julius Caesar was ambitious, too, and look where he ended up. Your sister, the High Il-luminary, will make a fine stand-in until we can get up there ourselves and she can issue a new challenge."

"Technically, maybe, but she wanted them."

"Not for herself, for the Weirdom. Maybe for you as well."

"More maybes. Andy wouldn't have the ability to kill Devason. Ergo Devason was trying to kill her. Morg wouldn't have been able to stop him. He was hit by lightning. You and I know that has to be devil-doing. Morg's making deals with devils. Decathonitized ones as well, since never-cathonitized devils aren't allowed to kill. Decathonitized or not, Utopians should never make deals with devils."

"You work for the Fatman, Bodiless Byron's shell when he needed one."

"The Great God and his Byronics were planning to leave the planet. Eventu-ally. They were going to take all their siblings and cousins with them. That meant we could go as well. We don't belong on the Whole Earth, Golgotha."

"Now there's where I disagree with you, Dem. We belong here because devils are here. What's more, we belong on the Hidden Continent because, for the most part, devils are as trapped underneath the Dome as we are. You don't trust your wife, fine. She's dealing with devils, fine as well.

"If she is, then it's ultimately going to be to their detriment. You can mark me on that. What she shouldn't be dealing with are the Dead. And all that garbage about that Molorchus fellow being a pale-skinned Pani from Krachla is just that, garbage. He's dead. You can mark me on that, too."

Something happened. A blip in the air, no more than that.

"What the hell was that?" Snake-thin, skin-tight, skull-faced Golgotha Nauroz demanded of Demios Sarpedon. Something did come out of between-space, on one of Garcia Dis L'Orca's deliberately left-behind witch-stones.

Someone did, rather.

========

"Oh dear-on-the-weir." It was Fisherwoman, duh-the-dogfish that. She eel-eyed Ringleader. Skewed her nose. Sniffed out the drugs he'd been given, presumably so he could sleep, though she was beginning to doubt that was all of the reason. Regarded Golgotha and Demios equally eely-eyed.

Muttered: "Well, if Rings isn't the mollusc-munching mother-lode, who the squid-is?"

========

The Untouchable Diver reverse-diving out of the ground at his feet startled him. The Jewish Summoning Child flattening him didn't so much so. He had all his wits about him. Hadn't needed his Mistress Morgianna to tell him who he was last night, after he reported back to her just before Fish abolished their colleague's vampiric body, though not her soul-self. He'd seen the Diver in action on Aegean Trigon more than a few times, albeit decades earlier. He hadn't forgotten he didn't kill either. Not that that much mattered to him anymore.

Alastor Molorchus could only dispatch someone to where he himself had been before. Molorchus had been to Lake Sedona before. He hadn't been in its depths but he could imagine them. So he teleported the Diver there. Deep into them. The crocodile coming at D-Brig's perhaps presumptuous leader was already dead. The Diver didn't realize that. His first thought was to surface, in order to catch his breath. He'd forgotten he didn't to breathe.

Then he blipped.

========

A man needs a woman like a fish needs a bicycle. Unless it was the other way around, that was a common enough saying on both sides of the Whole Earth. Witches had been making psychopomps since time immemorial. They were extensions of their soul-selves, their psyches, their mental might. A psychopomp was psychically powered by a witch's soul-self. Morg's Night Mare of a hobbyhorse was a shape-shifting demon she'd debrained herself. Fish used a shape-shifting Mandroid devoid of intelligence.

A psychopath was, more often than not, a mentally unstable person prone to antisocial and occasionally criminal behaviour. A cycle path, however, was just a dedicated pathway where you could ride your bike unhindered by cars if not pedestrians. Having tried out both during her long, eventful and experimental lifetime, she neither needed a man nor a woman.

But, because all the best witches had psychopomps, she immodestly reckoned that since she was the best of the best she needed one, too. Being something of a twisted sister, Fish decided it would be fun to have a psycho-bike. So she had her Mandroid made that way, to her specifications.

Later on she added a psychomotor; gave her psycho-bike a psychopomp-pump as she was fond of fay-saying at cocktail parties. When she was visiting her Summoning Child husband, Achigan Auranja, the King of Godbad, then the Duke of Achigan, Sedon's Lower Lip-tip in silhouette, she took enormous enjoyment outracing the security men he assigned to look after her, as if she needed them, on her psycho-motorcycle.

It having shape-shifting capabilities, she was riding her psycho-bike as a psycho-jet-ski when she received a worrying communication via witch-stone from one of her Athenan Piscines. They'd snared a crocodilian Dead Thing in one of their nets. It was putting up quite the struggle so they'd butchered it on the spot. There'd been a body inside it. Damndest thing, the body was still intact; hadn't been chopped like the croc. It was still lying there on a beach on the other side of the island from the monastery and the Godbadians' airstrip.

Wasn't moving, wasn't breathing either. They couldn't touch it when they tried, so they figured it had to be an illusion. Otherwise it'd sink into the ground, wouldn't it? No sign of a witch-stone and, you know, most War Witches couldn't cast a glamour to save their backsides at a stake-barbecue. Could it be a Selkie changeling? It looked part-seal so maybe it had died in mid-transformation. Only Selkies didn't transform, did they? Just took off their sealskins, like Garudas did their feathers. And Selkies didn't wear crimson goggles. Any suggestions?

Fish jetted her psycho-ski to the coordinates provided. The Diver, she recalled, didn't need to breathe; had to remember to do so. It was one of the most upsetting aspects of his supra-talents; his Summoning Heritage, as he put it. (Not that Summoning Children were the only supranormals who fought in the Outer Earth's secret war of same.) Neither could he ever take off the sleeveless, makeshift wetsuit and hood he'd been wearing when he had his close encounter with a Brainrock boulder that blew up beneath the Hamburg harbour in January 1938. That meant he did resemble a half-transformed Selkie.

He could render his sealskin intangible, without rendering the rest of his body intangible, however. So he had no trouble expelling bodily wastes. Had no trouble making babies either, as she well knew. Why wear a rubber when you're covered with rubber, he'd joked. Nine months later, well, water under the troll's toll-bridge that the jack-sprat.

Their son, whom World War II had prevented either of them raising, had been adopted by a pair of Greek Cypriots with Jewish blood. She kept tabs on him as best she could until she was forced to flee to the Inner Earth in '52. Checked up on him once in awhile in the Sixties as well, once she made her peace with Alpha Centauri and regained access to the Nag Gap. He fell in with Kadmon Heliopolis and the Black Rose of Anarchy. Was one of Kad's Trigon Spartae. Died in '68, when Aegean Trigon sank. Or whatever it did.

Spartae meant Dragon's Teeth.

========

Fisherwoman rode her bike-psycho, as a jet-ski, out of the Weird underneath the lake's waters off the beach. Then she pedalled it, as a psycho-cycle, onto the beach. Fish liked to make an entrance. It was a wasted effort. Her Piscines, men as well as women, didn't even notice her arrival. They were transfixed on the excited atmospherics evident in the western sky. They must have been wondering what was going on there, overtop Dustmound in all likelihood.

Fish wasn't; she'd witnessed plenty of devil-doings during her sixty-plus years of days and nights. *'Morg, Morg, what hast-the-mast thou rotten-wrought by rocking the bat-boat?'*

Fish fancied herself a poet as well as the best witch on either side of Cathonia.

========

Like a Homeworld Sceptre, just as a Sangazur-reanimated daughter was about to take her turn and assassinate her father from a 50-years' previous incarnation, earthquakes had their uses. He'd avoided King Cold's down-thrust and taken himself to Sedon's Hairband. Nowadays Nihila wasn't there. Her High Seat was, however.

It was a good show.

========

Psycho-cycle had a psycho-shed. It was weird. It was in the Weird, off her bellybutton bauble, her Vesica Piscis, her equivalent of many other witches' bottomless bags. Stuff stuck in them, in there, were stuck between-space. Did wonders for maintaining the figure; kept her looking skim-board trim. Shaking water off herself, like a dog from its fur, she shed the bike and materialized her fishnet instead. This could touch the untouchable. It flashed as it did so, as she netted the Untouchable Diver with it. At her age Fish did not appreciate flashes.

She dropped then stepped on a Hellstone, an Athenan bullet-pellet. Came out in her fish-lair, what she'd made her own in one of the partially flooded tunnels Mandroid servitors of Lemurian matriarchs may have made for Frog Women howsoever many millennia ago, when southern Hadd was Lemuria and Pacifica was still the Places of Peace. Non-breathing as he was, she was sure the Diver was just asleep.

Then she fell a dot-ditto.

========

Fish was festooned with witch-stones: the usual things, rings on her fingers, rings on her toes, linked as they were by webbed flesh. They were supplemental to her Vesica Piscis. Her bellybutton bauble protruded big-time when it doubled as a baby-belly button. She wasn't pregnant now, hadn't been since the Sixties. Neither was she festooned with as many supplemental rings and things when she woke up. She did, however, have an arm reaching into her tummy.

"Gynaecology isn't your forte, is it, Diver? Blowfish the fingering submarines lower down, where the small fry come out. Where and when I cry out, dick the digital dildo ditto."

"Can the sardines, Fish. I'm hungry. Ah, here's something." He pulled out her psycho-bicycle bell. "Damn, it isn't glowing. Hold still. I'm going in for more." Fish sprang backwards, onto her feet. She was also very agile for her age. Produced her fishnet. It was glowing. The Diver's face contorted greedily. He looked demented; said: "That's more like it."

He went for it. She dodged, vanished it. Produced her psycho-bicycle gloves this time. They weren't glowing either. Then they were Stopstone boxing gloves, well-padded. She wasn't Mohammed Ali, couldn't deliver a haymaker. She bopped him a good one anyways. Knocked him for a loop, the poop. The Diver never could handle Stopstone, she'd recalled. Or Solidium, as it was called on the Outer Earth.

Godstuff had its bad-stuff. Stopstone counteracted Brainrock; Solidium did ditto against Gypsium. Stopstone equalled Solidium; Brainrock equalled Gypsium. Fish could do sums, too. (Unless it was two.) Which she did, one. Then she had it. Rings and things gone, *'It isn't glowing'*, Cassius Clay-maker.

"Wait a skate," she demanded, as the Diver coiled like a rabid animal, ready to go for her again. She dematerialized one of her gloves; materialized a handful of Athenan bullet-pellets in its place. They were glowing. Within seconds she had him eating out of her hand. More flashes; he relaxed, seemed sane again. Stood up, stepped away from her.

"Sorry about flipping out, Fish. I got zapped then I must have blipped. I woke up, saw you with all your pretty, ever-so-tempting, shiny jewellery just lying there and, well, what else can I say? I've no excuses. I don't think I was possessed. I don't know what the flapdoodle's wrong with me. Nice grotto you got by the way."

"Gale's a whale, Diver; tempest in a teapot. You might knot but I might-the-bite. It's your Summoning Heritage. No one remora-remembers what harpy-happened on the Simultaneous Summonings. But one thing everyone agrees on is that every woman who lived through it, and could become pregnant, came back just Jack- or Jill-in-the-box that. Lady Lust came to town and Mama Maternity stayed behind. If everyone summoned was possessed, then-in-the-fen that hake-makes you Summoning Children deviants.

"Devils refresh themselves with jet-stream-Gypsium. That's the tunny-ticket, isn't it? All these years, we never reef-realized it. Your body's imbued with brain-coral Brainrock. That's how you came by your Summoning Heritage; that's how you're going to kelp-keep it. Hellions have Hellstones; Ants have Anthean Agates; War Witches have bullet-pellets.

"Can't do much with them except get about on them, blue's true. But the pickerel-point is they're all witch-stones; they're all made of Brainrock and they all have dozens of them. I'll spread the word-worm; convene a covens-convention; pass the collection plate. We'll have you right as rainbow trout in no time."

"No need. I know just where to find a mother-lode of the stuff. Thanks, Fish."

He dove upwards, into the roof of her grotto and kept going. She knew he could do that. She also knew of only one mother-lode of Gypsium on the island. It was a father-lode. She just hoped Harry recognized devil-doings when he saw it and got everyone off Dustmound in time to avoid it. She conjured out her psycho-bike, got on it and rode after him.

Riding was good for the figure too.

========

Garcia Dis L'Orca burst into Ringleader's quarters brimming with excitement. She was fortunate Fish, Golgotha and Demios Sarpedon recognized her or she might have become, almost instantaneously and in a variety of terminal ways, a Dead Thing brimming with excitement.

"You have to see this. It's snowing!"

****

(ENDGAME-GAMBIT) 24: **Dust Devils**

Sedonda, Tantalar 7, 5980

Last night, after they mistakenly decided it was Nergal Vetala who had denied Harry Zeross access to the Weird, Jordan Tethys told Young Death he needed help. So he'd gone to get it. Got it, too. Sort of. Got it from the distaff side of his extended devic family; not the staff side.

Maybe he would have to start coming back as a woman after all. Wouldn't start drinking wine instead of beer, though. He had his pride. And a beer belly to maintain.

========

If Hadd was Vetala's protectorate there wasn't much anyone could do about it, right? Actually there were a few things that could be done about it. Gods or near-gods weren't supposed to kill. They were supposed to sit back and let their azura-occupied adherents do it for them. That was the history of warfare on the Hidden Continent. An army of adherents invades another devil's protectorate and that devil's adherents fight and die protecting it. More often than not the defenders won. So long as their faith in their devil-god was strong enough, the devil-god could bedevil invaders with inconveniences more so than catastrophes.

Nergal Vetala's adherents were animated Dead Things. Her azuras weren't just her azuras. Neither was Hadd originally her protectorate. Twelve hundred years ago, when it was El Dorado, it was divided amongst Byronics. The Legendarian couldn't expect any help from Byronics with their father in the night's sky. In effect the Age of Byron was over by default. Time for another Age of Lazareme? Somebody had to fill the void and he was the only Great God left.

Accordingly Tethys had come to the Isle of the Undying One; presumably the Undying One was Thrygragos Lazareme. He couldn't find him, though. The Great God had to be sleeping between-space so he couldn't draw himself to him. There were other ways; there always were other ways. Lazareme liked his stories; they helped him go back to sleep.

Speaking of which, sleeping, his head was throbbing. Had he exceeded his 30 beers allotment? He'd figure out how to reach him come morning. Except Nowadays Nihila woke him before morning; before dawn, to be more precise. Had she abolished him, her own father? If she had, she didn't volunteer that information. He never thought to ask her. He'd do whatever she asked of him. He was weak that way. Also, he'd never seen her redolent with such irrefutable authority before. Even if he could have once, just saying *'no'* wasn't an option any longer.

'Do me a favour, Jordy. You recall what Byron's Straw Man and Mithras's Grave-digger or Devil Doom look like?' Approximately, no guarantees. *'Then let me show you what I think they look like now.'* She face-danced to look like them. He made some sketches; background filled-in. Tethys did recall what the fop, Faustus Vladuca, First Fangs, looked like. Fop had once possessed one of his 500-years-gone incarnations.

'I thought that was them. I've been sitting on my High Seat, using devic far-sight, to scan Hadd. Been doing some other things as well, but you don't need to know about them.' She proceeded to tell him anyhow; albeit not as graphically as he might have liked. *'You know Dream, Phantast the Dreamweaver, the firstborn Thanatoids of La-thakra's immediate brother? He's been decathonitized. Had myself quite the wet dream. Am I blushing? You are.'*

In terms of lines of longitude Tympani, Sedon's Eardrum, which was where they were, wasn't that far east of western Hadd. His drawing, panned out far enough, revealed that was where the three decathonitized devils were speaking amongst themselves, 3-eyed face to 3-eyed face. They must have sensed dawn coming because they reverted to their human selves and, be damned, if their human selves weren't vampiric. They'd be useless during the day. Plus, they didn't seem to have any power foci with them.

'Are the Ghostlands still radioactive?' she'd asked him. He told her they were; agreed with her the Mithradite Reaper was the last devil known to have had the Byronic Reaper's Tvasitar Talisman. *'I'm disinclined to go to the Ghosts. What about Gravedigger's Brainrock spade?'* Tethys wasn't so sure about that. He had a notion it might have been on the Outer Earth at some point during its Secret Wars but they ended a long time ago by mortal standards; not to mention three of his incarnations.

'A shame in a way. Nothing I can do about it now. One or the other will just have make-do with Plague's. I'll have Brother Anvil make them new ones if they're good boys and do precisely as I say. Won't have to make the fop a new one, though. Remind me to thank Dame Chance the next time I see her.'

Devils also called Chance Serendipity, Fata Fortuna or Lady Luck; long-gone Illuminaries called her Wintry Moira, after a Celtic Goddess of same. Like Nowadays Nihila, Badhbh, Battle Baby, ex of the Bloodlands, Titanic Metis, ostensibly Tethys's and for sure Guardian Angel Tyrtod's devic mother, and this Moira, Chance, were Lazaremists. Metisophia was a second-born, Moira a fifth-born and Battle Babe a sixth-born. It seemed he was getting help from that Great God's tribe even if he wasn't getting any from the Great God himself. He had a suggestion.

'*Speaking of spare talismans, Chance might appreciate it if you thanked her by returning my half-mom, her sister's cauldron. Of course you'd have to go to Lathakra to get it but, you know, it'd be a nice gesture.*'

'*A psychic Legendarian instead of a drunken one. My, how times have changed. Actually I vaguely recall you being an Intuit once so I guess that explains that. The Frozen Isle's a couple of stops away. Got any gold or precious stones?*'

'*I've a few stashes between-space. What would someone like you need gold for?*'

'*It isn't for me. I can't wait for dark to enlist Brother Fop and the other two, so they're going to need some lively shells to demonstrate what good little boys they are. And it just so happens I recently encountered three ideal candidates for the task at hand. They're mercenaries; they're used to putting their lives on the line for the right price. Right then, let's be off. Next stop The Argent.*'

'*The Argent, Lathakra?*' Tethys twigged. It seemed the Second Age of Lazareme would have to be indefinitely postponed. Always assuming they could pull it off of course. He just hoped they wouldn't include the ritual castration or outright sacrifice of Year Kings this time. '*I'll call you Nihila if you want, Harmony, but I'd hate to have to call you stupid. In the name of the Panharmonium Project, you're going to play a Trigregos Gambit.*'

'*I'm not going to play anything, Jordy. I'm going to become Trigregos Demeter.*'

========

Decathonitized Master Devas weren't supposed to kill lesser beings. Never-cathonitized Master Devas weren't allowed to kill lesser beings. They did, they weren't never-cathonitized anymore. There was no way Vetala's Soldier, her golden-brown warrior, was a lesser being. The mere fact he could wield the thrice-cursed Godly Glories negated that possibility.

Freespirit Nihila didn't realize he was already dead.

========

Goddess charged him to take out the one-armed man. He would have, once he took out ex-Kronokronos Mikoto, had he not been charged a different way at that precise instant. Chain lightning. One jagged bolt to make sure, two, three, four more to make doubly, trebly, four-times sure. Yet still he stood. Trigregos Incarnate knew how to deal with her. Rather, his talismans did. One of them had been immobilizing her for five hundred years.

Goddess screamed. She'd been going that a lot lately. A shame her throne wasn't just broiling. It was melting. Doubly too bad for her he couldn't move. No one could. Correction, three could. Just not him; nor her or her ambulatory Dead. What was the moon doing there anyways? And wasn't it supposed to be a man in the moon not a woman?

How was he to know Lazareme's Brother Moon-Face had a firstborn daughter-ditto?

========

Alastor Molorchus did not have divided loyalties. He was Morgianna long Sarpedon's man through and through. Had been ever since she grafted a Hellstone into his chest a number of years ago and thereby coerced him away from her pal, his previous mistress, Janna Fangfingers. Superior Sarpedon recognized talent when she saw it; they both did. Morg recognized it in him just as she recognized it in Second

Fangs, her daughters and herself. She was also as ruthless as she was so very talented, was the Morrigan.

On her command he'd brought in Mikoto and the four still living samurais he'd travelled with as a member of the Warlord's Good Companions for so long. In the past month a few of Second Fangs' psycho-bats had got through Trinondev force shields via between-space and chomped them. Janna herself had turned one of Weir's vaunted Warrior Elite. No mean feat that, talented ex-girl; ex-Undead girl, now thoroughly dead-and-dusted girl.

Morg reckoned that if her brother got out of hand, once he got hold of the Trigregos Talismans, then turned on her and her daughter, it would be wise to have some back-up. So long as they were within eyeshot, Molorchus could teleport someone somewhere with pinpoint accuracy. He'd done that last night when Morg changed her mind too late to countermand her own orders for him to bring Kata-tribe Tethys, already dead and Sangazur-animated thanks to the onetime Kronokronos of Temporis, to Sraddha Isle in order to snuff out her father from a 50-years' previous incarnation.

Last night was a royal botch-up. Didn't Morg realize he needed to gather things between-space before he could bring them through? As much as he was her puppet, she couldn't just pull his strings and expect instant gratification. He was a scientist. Improvisation was anathema to a scientist. It went against all his training.

Then again no one could have anticipated any of what went on yesterday morning and afternoon: Warlord Mikoto being shot apart so badly even his fabled recuperative abilities couldn't save him; Janna Fangfingers acquiring the Trigregos Talismans, which she'd long-distance promised Morg to trade in return for him bringing in demon after demon, some of them Janna's, some of them Morg's, in order to disable the Godbadian aircraft; both of them wanting Jordan Tethys dead and non-Sangazur-animated first; Janna additionally wanting the three mercenaries to destroy Harmony's demonic body.

And it was all down to him, wasn't it? Not to mention that was just the start of it. This was just the continuation of it. Zoom! Off Dustmound goes Andy. Zoom! There goes me. Yow! Was that a human shinbone rammed up his butt? Pull it out; start bringing in the samurais. He'd been to Sanguerre before. Zoom, zoom and more zooms. At least the Dead Things were staying away from him. Crack! That was his skull. As if he needed another hole in his head. No wonder they were staying away from him.

Ka-pow! Unless it was Kablooie! That's the Diver. Dispatch him. Up there, that's Vetala's Soldier. He's the Trigregos Talismans. He's supposed to be dead. Big whoop that – who isn't around here? Good job for Mikoto. He is too. Pinpoint accuracy. Oh, dear, now he's doubly dead. And doubly halved. Over there, mistress and daughter. She was right. Sal's double-dealing. Best dispatch them. Get away from me, Tyrtod. I'm my own guardian angel.

Lightning struck. Jolted the fundament. Ass over teakettle time. There was one good thing about having a Hellstone grafted into your chest. Hecate-Hellions could get about on them. Could come out of them. Hellions didn't care if they were alive or dead; it was their soul-selves that counted. About time you showed, witch. Make with the mirror.

When the snow started falling on Sraddha Isle Alastor Molorchus, the telltale bullet-hole in his head covered in a wraparound bandage, was deep asleep in one of the Morrigan's 'shelters' between-space. It was off the same sickroom Morgianna was overseeing her daughter's recovery. Molorchus didn't realize he was sleeping with the corpse of an Irache War Witch kept inert by virtue of the fact it was in the Weird.

Soul-selves, like devils and even azuras, to a lesser extent, could be curative. Sometimes they helped strengthen other soul-selves. If Andy's soul-self wasn't strong enough to re-enliven herself, well, her body would still be around for mommy to hug.

========

The moon wasn't the actual moon. It was a devic power focus made manifest. The three who came out of it, the ones who could still walk about, were female devils. Breasts equal female; three eyes equal devils. Two were firstborns; one thought she was a firstborn. One of the firstborns made the moon. Her attribute was gravity.

The Byronic was why he couldn't move.

========

Nergal Vetala was screaming because her Brainrock throne was simultaneously melting and broiling her. The Mithradite, her eldest sister, was the reason for that. Methandra Thanatos, masked and covered in various shades of red, purple and violet garments, was huge: 10-feet tall if she was an inch. She was Heat. Her magician's cane was more like the torch atop New York's Statue of Liberty on the Outer Earth than it was a matchstick. Call it a firebrand then.

Freespirit Nihila, who had dark hair nowhere near as long as Vetala's and whose body, from the Gypsium torc around her neck down, looked to be composed of glowingly golden chain-mail, was responsible for the chain lightning. Umashakti Silvercloud's power focus was moon-shaped. It disgorged them.

Uma was a large, as in fleshy, silver-haired devil. No more gigantic than Nihila, she waxed and waned with the moon's phases. Her physical size suggested it was full, approaching full or within a day or two of it having been full. Also like the Unity of Panharmonium, she had bracelets around her wrists. Nihila's were more akin to manacles from which depended more chains. Uma's were crescent moons. Her gown was shimmering moonlight. To say she had a moon-face would be redundant.

They walked around him. They didn't pay any attention to Hadd's Blood Queen. It hardly registered she'd stopped screaming.

"A Crimson Crown for a Crimson Queen, eh, Hot Stuff?" said Nowadays Nihila.

"Chain lightning to a lightning blade," Methandra said. "It's as we agreed."

Umashakti Silvercloud wasn't so happy. "My moon-mirror's full-up."

That was about when the sound and lightshow began. Vetala was in her soldier.

========

"Don't do it, Yomi."

"I'm broken, father."

"Breaks heal."

========

The Outer Earth supranormal, Wildman Dervish Furie, had been in a hurry. His daughter, albeit from an earlier incarnation, had enough strength left in her arms to two-handed-gut herself with her short sword. Maybe that was for the best. Pad of paper already in hand, he splotched onto it the drawing of Yomikune he'd done the day before when he offered, through Young Death, to withdraw her and Katatribe, her now ashen triplet-sister, as well as their sell-sword companions from the Crystals to Sraddha Isle.

They never should have refused. Only Andaemyn Sarpedon had accepted. He'd already noted how Andy was doing. Not well. What kind of a life was that of a mercenary anyways? As far as he was concerned, rather than them putting on a gun, the world would be a far better place if they first put it to their head and pulled the trigger.

He had already prepared fire. Useful stuff, fire against Dead Things. He was a regular boy scout. He splotched her on fire. He'd already signed his name. The way things had been going of late he'd taken to pre-signing his pre-prepared artwork. He dotted it. Dotting was so much quicker than having to sign your name as well as dot it. The pad of paper didn't ignite; she did. Her eyes never left him as she went up in flames. He silently promised them both he'd never forget that look. He took it for gratitude.

It was and then it wasn't. Ablaze as she was, she reared to her feet, blade in hand; spoke to him. The voice was that of a man, one he sort of recognized. "That any way to treat a daughter, let alone a brother, Jordy? I'd have looked after her. Oh, well, your body's years younger and I much prefer being inside a man."

Lightning struck. Jolted the fundament. Didn't strike either of them, not directly. Struck nearby, struck Saladin Devason; close to him anyways. Knocked Tethys onto his fundament. Even afire, what was left of Yomikune was steadier on her feet than her old man; a man who was indeed much younger than her physically. George Taurson was born in '48; Yomi in '30.

"Check that," she said in Tyrtod's voice. "I've never been a Master of Weir before."

Strictly speaking Guardian Angel Tyrtod would be Guardian Angel Yomikune right that moment. She/he staggered towards Devason, intent upon becoming Guardian Angel Saladin. It was too much for him/her. Thoroughly crisped critters could only go so far before they made an ash of themselves.

Buggered if the Master didn't stir. Had the Tyrtod Sangazur got to him? Nowadays Nihila would be infuriated. The Cathonic Dome would collapse if he died, she'd told him, though someone else must have told her that first. That was why, after he'd done everything else she'd asked him to do, she and her fellow firstborns brought him here. To draw Saladin to Cabalarkon since they dare not go there themselves.

He'd been distracted by his daughter about to commit seppuku, hara-kiri, samurai-suicide or whatever their cruel code demanded they do to themselves when they were broken. Besides, he couldn't draw anyone anywhere who hadn't expressly given him permission to do so. Sal had been busy interrogating his sister, or killing her, or both, when he arrived. So why had the ex-Unity of Harmony fried him? He saw Morgianna disappear, taking Andaemyn with her. Was that why? How could Morg be more important than maintaining Cathonia?

Or had the Panharmonium Unity fried him? The out-of-place Master of Weir had been in a brain-bulb when the bolt hit him. Or came close to hitting him. He'd also been in the air, levitating; therefore wasn't grounded. Did either make a difference? Sal wasn't that now, in the air. Was very much grounded, however. He wasn't encased in a thought-balloon. Even if he hadn't been lightning-struck he was so dumbstruck he probably couldn't formulate much in the way of thoughts right that moment.

It wasn't kosher but life and death situations, unconsciousness or semi-consciousness, these were mitigating circumstances. He might be able to get away with it. Might be better if he just got up, walked over to him and asked Saladin if he wanted to go home. The Master didn't answer, then he could decide whether to carry him to Cabby's Weirdom anyhow. Sal looked heavy. Master worked out. Jordan Tethys resolutely did not. The heaviest weights he lifted usually contained beer. Neither had George Taurson.

He didn't feel like getting up. It was too late not to get involved. Or was it? He was a certifiable coward. More lightning, entirely centred on the pinnacle of Dustmound this time. What was going on up there? What was going on over there? The one-armed man, Morg's man, he was rotating his shoulder cuff. An Irache woman was holding something up in front of him. She looked dead, had a nasty gash in her back. It was one of those handheld mirrors Sraddhites used so they could tell if they were dealing with a non-reflective vamp. How had she got here? Did it matter? No.

So that was how he did it. Emitted Brainrock radiance straight at a mirror, vanished when it reflected back at him. Too bad she hadn't. Too bad she'd spotted either him or the Master. Too bad she had a knife; likely the one she'd recently pulled out of her back. Too bad she looked like she knew how to use it. Too bad, Sal. It works or it doesn't work. He sure as hell wasn't going to hang around to ask anyone's permission to do what he had to do.

Flip to another page. The throne room in the old Masters Palace of Cabalarkon the City. Sal was sitting in the throne, Master's Mace in hand. Tethys was standing beside him. Already signed. More lightning. He dotted it. Hours later, as snow blanketed Sraddha Isle, Jordan Tethys, the legendary 30-Year Man, was under much warmer blankets reacquainting himself with Cosmicompanion Carmine Carmichael.

For him, it was a happy ending to a lousy day.

========

Umashakti Silvercloud's moon-mirror wasn't the only thing full-up.

Saladin Devason had ejected many an eyeorb, many a prison pod, off the top of his Master's Mace after he'd opened the first one, which Morg had grabbed in order to release her pantsuit-demon. None of them were designed to take in azuras or demons. They were designed to take in Master Devas. Hadd may or may not be Nergal Vetala's inviolate protectorate but Dustmound was infused with her azuras.

The Trigregos Talismans killed devils. The Trigregos Titan didn't. Not yet anyways. For the longest time he couldn't move. He wasn't about to give them up, not without a fight. Except, how can you fight when you can't move? Mental might's the answer to that. That and the fact Alastor Molorchus wasn't the only one who could generate Brainrock-Gypsium.

Rather, in keeping with the Law of the Conservation of Matter, Al wasn't the only one who could attract it into himself from howsoever faraway. Not that, it being Godstuff, the post Big Bang remnants of the Primordial Godhead, Gypsium-Brainrock necessarily had to obey anything having to do with thermodynamics. God was an anarchist.

Godstuff was teleportive. Demons ate devils. Vetala had heaps of them; put better, her immediate sister, Kala Tal, had heaps of them. They were already gathered at a specific spot in Tal's Forbidden Forest; maybe only 5-10% of those Janna Fangfingers arranged to come together there had been lost the night before on Sraddha Isle. From inside her soldier, Hadd's Blood Queen transported them unerringly onto the three female devils. Hence the start of the sound and light show: the devils blasting them, burning them, hurtling them into the sky, imploding and exploding them. That went on for hours.

The Nergalid was running out of them. Either that or her arachnid breed-sister was shutting off access to them. The firstborn devils were becoming exhausted. She was going to outlast them. Somewhat like her Mithras of a thought-father on Thrygragon she was feeding on her azuras; they were keeping her and, through her, her soldier primed. He and Molorchus weren't the only who could attract Gypsium into themselves. The firstborns could too and Nowadays Nihila, the Unity of Panharmonium, had spent the night supersaturating herself with Godstuff.

Vetala, though, had hundreds of azuras, thousands of them: Haddazurs, Nergalazurs, azuras she hadn't even birthed; ones who had been here since the First War between the Living and the Dead; ones who had been here before she, the Thanatoids and their allies even conquered El Dorado, old Iraxas before that.

Then they started abandoning Dustmound. What else had Nihila and her fellow wannabe Trigregos got up their collective sleeves?

========

The snow? Old King Cold decided it was time to turn what had been a good show into a cold shower. How dare his sister-wife play a Trigregos Gambit when they still had seven children to rescue? To bring back to Lathakra even if one of them, their Water Elemental, didn't need rescuing as such?

Rudra Silvercloud, Byron's Savage Storm, had more prosaic motives. How dare his sister-wife get herself shredded into a dozen or more suddenly vacated, until then azura-occupied eyeorbs. They'd only just started getting reacquainted after her being imprisoned for nearly fifty years in All of Incain.

Neither could care less about Freespirit Nihila. Let her dangle there.

========

Someone did care about Nowadays Nihila. He'd watched the show until it ended. He was intrigued by the way Nergal Vetala had possessed her soldier in order to marshal her defence of Dustmound. Devils couldn't possess devils but they could possess a pseudo-demigod seemingly composed of Godstuff; the exact sort of near-omnipotent being the Unity of Panharmonium was working on making herself when they reconnected last night.

It non-lightning-struck him as an interesting, if desperate, strategy. The same held for the Indescribables she brought in from Tal, where the one-armed man must have gathered them the night before in order to bring them through the Grey to Lake Sedona and its environs. Demons were a two-way street. Both Nihila and Vetala could be over-relying on the one, Brainrock, without giving enough consideration to the counteractive qualities of the other, Stopstone.

Then he watched some more. Almost as interesting was whom the three enormous bats transformed into once they came to earth on what was left of Dustmound. Which wasn't much by then. He didn't know who they were but he recognized their uniforms. Sedunihas had etched the same uniforms onto his missing siblings, the ones who were supposed to be on the Moon.

How did vamps go from otherwise comparatively ordinary-looking chiropters to humanoid bloodsuckers wearing clothes? For that matter, how did ordinary-looking men and women suddenly develop fangs just before they went for your throat? Godbadians had videotape, movies and television. Thanks to the Fatman's Centauri Enterprises, so did the inhabitants of more and more places on the Head. Maybe they had educational programs on how vamps became demons at the same time they became vamps.

Make a mental note: After re-securing earthly kingdom, get a library card.

========

"Yo, vamps. These what you looking for?"

========

In life they had been Elvis Elfin, Felix Dee and Geraint Plantagenet, Cosmicompanions E, F and G. In Undeath they were vampires; just vampires. Nothing more, nothing less. That morning they'd been something much, much more. They'd flown two hundred miles, the devils' voices yammering in their heads, nagging at them to hurry up, in hopes of becoming that very thing again.

Along the way, through a blinding snowstorm, they gorged themselves on crippled, but at the same time still breathing, wild animals; predatory beasts for the most part. Them and what they took to be were-things, also still breathing, though in no more condition to defend themselves than the beasts had been. Some of these last were werewolves, like the ones they'd seen the night they'd been turned. By no means all of them were lupine, however. Was there a full moon up there, on the other side of the clouds? Did there need to be a full moon in this hellacious landscape for were-things to be about? Probably not.

Having a third eye didn't register any significance to the three cosmicompanions, whose brains were still their own. Feeling so physically powerful, so vital, even if they were dead, or Undead, did. They weren't possessed anymore but, as bloodsuckers, they had excellent night-sight. They had an implanted notion of what they were looking for: self-sealed, ovular leathern pods, three in number. They had no notion of what had happened here.

The snow had stopped falling but it hadn't just been snow that had fallen. Rain had too. And hailstones big as boulders. And icicle spears evidently. There were patches in the snow. There were bodies everywhere. Some were human; of them most were already in an advanced state of decomposition. There were lots of other things lying around as well. Mercifully none of them were moving.

Amongst the detritus were bits and pieces of more bodies; a great many dead beasts like the ones they'd been feeding on during the course of their stunningly fast journey here; and an astonishing number of things that could never have been human, animal, nor even changeling were-things. Unless it was in monster movies or comic books, they'd never seen anything as absolutely indescribable when they were altogether alive and on the Outer Earth.

Were they demons? Something along those lines, they speculated.

=========

She didn't become Trigregos Demeter. Hadn't yet rather, just to be fair. He'd seen that from her High Seat.

=========

She hadn't been forthcoming when she told him how she was going to handle Trinondev eyeorbs. A superabundance of Brainrock pre-absorbed from Sedon's Hairband then redirected into them via her chains was brilliant. He was disappointed he hadn't thought of that himself. Most of the other stunts she pulled were reasonably inspiring as well.

He was, however, highly suspicious when he far-saw who was occupying the three mercenaries. It couldn't be pure chance that those selfsame three Master Devas, of the more than sixty he'd helped decathonitize a week ago, ended up in Hadd. The big eye-mouth in the sky had to be grinning so broadly it was a wonderment the Moloch Sedon hadn't swallowed his own firmament by now.

The Smiling Fiend could visualize how they arrived there. Their uniforms told him that.

=========

For their part E, F and G had seen the three mercenaries before; had seen them that morning. They were with the absolutely gorgeous, albeit 3-eyed, dark-haired woman wearing the almost blindingly bright hauberk made out of what seemed to be golden chain-mail. They'd seen them with her and the scruffy looking, 2-eyed fellow with the not-quite-so-brightly glowing, feathered quill stuck in his checked cap. Two of the mercenaries had similar, vaguely orangey skin-colouration and texture. The third was black as an absence of light.

They knew they were mercenaries because they didn't wear uniforms yet were nonetheless armed to the teeth as if for battle: all kinds of battles, ones from Robin Hood or William Tell eras as well. The slightly smaller and much more slender of the two orange-skins was on one knee. He had a bow notched with a wooden arrow complete with a glinting, metallic arrowhead. He was aiming at them. They didn't have an apple on their heads but he had some more in a quiver laying on the ground in front of him, within easy reach.

Wooden arrows, they could kill vamps. The metallic arrowhead, it likely only improved the arrow's lethality. He looked swift, a crack shot. The bigger of the two orange-skins had two long staffs, one in his each hand; make that in each paw, he was that big, that hairy and that bearish. The black fellow had a third one. Atop each of these staffs were ovular, leathern pods. The black fellow was the one who'd hailed them.

"Might be," said E.

"Then you're as fucked as we are," said the bear of the two orange-skins.

"They're full," said Sabreur Somata. "With what you're really looking for. You see, they're designed to suck in devils, third eye, daemonic body, power focus, the whole shebang. Or in this case the whole he-bang. I know how to use them on account of I've a Utopian heritage. You haven't the vaguest idea what I'm talking about, do you?"

"You're alive," said F.

"That we are," agreed Sabreur. "In large measure because I know how to use them. Thing is, what you're looking for, they're devils. Got three eyes for starters. These ovules, they're called prison pods for a reason. They imprison devils. They're also called eyeorbs or eye-eggs. Their original owners, you might be able to piece enough of them together to make one corpse; half of one anyhow. Which is another odd thing.

"This is Hadd and this was Dustmound. Once it was a towering dingus, now it's barely a blackhead. In Hadd the Dead are supposed to rise, to fight anew. They're animated by what's called azuras. Nothing's rising, you can see that. We think it's because the azuras got used up. That's our theory anyways and we're sticking to it.

"Which bring me to my pal Tucedon. Also brings us to him sticking you. We call him Deuce, as in the Devil. Dead shot, Deuce. Has to be if he wants to stay a live shooter. Light's not so good, it being dark and all. Have to hit a vamp in the heart if you're going to dust him with wood; at least so I've heard.

"That arrowhead, though; now that's reinforced silver. Sure thing vamp-killers, silver arrowheads. Deuce has a few them. I've a gun with silver bullets; dumdum shells, they expand; fragment inside you. I'm a regular cowboy in the quick-draw department. Meet Salamoneus. Scattergun on Sal's back? Silver buckshot, full thereof. Or it could be empty. So could my gun. We've been busy not being dead."

"You ever ride a bat, cowboy?" wondered G.

"Piggyback on porky vamp-bats like you three? Easier than a nightmare horse. You were in the Abattoir this morning. You're here now. Two hundred miles, only an hour or so since dusk. Mightily impressive speed. We were talking, whispering. Me, I'm always yapping; usually to myself. Can't stop. Anyhow, we reckon you're psychobats. That means you had a Brainrock-blessed sire; that you can travel through the Weird.

"That way, west, there's a semi-civilized mini-continent called Godbad. It isn't to our taste; prices on head sort of thing. Anyhow, Godbad's found a way to cure vampirism. Called blood transfusion. You'll have heard about blood transfusions."

"You want us to fly you to this Godbad," said E, stating the obvious.

"It's not far. Just over that body of water you could see if Dustmound wasn't a pimple of its former self. It's the Gulf of Aka. New Iraxas, that's the Godbadian province I'm on about, it's on the other side of it. There's banks there, regular banks, not just blood banks. We got ourselves a big payday coming, just a matter of waiting for a wire transfer. You get us there, get underground for a few days until our money comes through, and we'll even pay for your procedures."

"Those prison pods you got on the ends of those staffs," said F. "The devils inside them, they're calling to us. How's that?"

"They call to us too, over and over again. Tell us to release them. Mental might, that's how Utopians make eye-staves work. So we release them. Sucked right back in they go. Got a mind of their own, eyeorbs. And like I said, I know how to use them."

"The devil in the golden chains?" wondered E. "She got you here. Where'd she go?"

"Nowhere," said Sabreur. "Still here in fact. Got a curved blade stuck through her again, pinning her to that Brainrock throne over there. There isn't much left of it; not much left of her either. Gal's been drained and I don't mean of blood. There was a fuck of a fight here, in case you haven't sussed that out yet. Devils, demons, Dead Things, snowmen, wild animals, some of them half-human changelings, Brainrock, Stopstone, they were throwing everything they had at each other. End of the day we figure that's where she belongs. What say?"

"I'd say saddle up," did say G, "Except I don't see any saddles."

========

Her azuras were abandoning her.

========

A devil manifested himself out of the Weird – black skin, was standing on a flying carpet. Nergal Vetala recognized him. He was the Planter; was yet another Nergalid, Zuvem Nergalis according to ancient Illuminaries. Didn't a flying carpet belong to the ever-enchanting Parsis, Bodiless Byron's Earth Magician? Where had he got hold of it, how could he utilize it, a male using a female's power focus?

Nay problems, obviously. Anyone could use a devic power focus, she recalled 30-Beers telling her, when he told her stories. Which he often did, back when he was a Fatazur-animated Dead Thing Walking, not long after she got herself out of the Amateramirror on what went down in history, and her-story, as All Death Day. And he should know. Tethys had spent 1500 years – 2,000 now – wielding Rumour of Lazareme's Brainrock quill.

Planter accounted for many of her Nergalazurs. He was their father; their sea-man's sailing semen. Not that devils had semen as such; sailing or otherwise; their spiritual seed, then. The azuras born of Byronics, where were they? A devil slashed through the air. That answered that. Unmoving Byron's Straw Man was the devils' first Reaper.

Illuminaries of Weir had him as Vanthysces Vastness for some typically stupid reason – they had her as Vetala because sometimes she got mixed up and manifested her hands on the wrong wrists such that her thumbs, when her palms were down, pointed outwards, not inwards. The power focus he was using belonged to Plague, Carcinogen the Leper, the Apocalyptic of Disease. Second Fangs had said something about him, hadn't she?

Vetala was inside her soldier. He still hadn't moved despite the fact Gravity had long ago lost the concentration she required in order to prevent anyone except herself and her two fellow Panharmonium Unities moving. He moved now, to block the down-thrust of the Straw Man's Pendulum Blade with the Amateramirror. It did more than block him; it repulsed him.

Then Vetala felt her golden-brown warrior falter. He had been resolutely hold-ing onto the three Trigregos Talismans with every mote of mental might he could muster. He had a fourth talisman on him. Someone was trying to take it away from him. The Fop, First Fangs, who'd have believed it?

When you have the advantage of leverage, when you can press back on some-one's arm at the wrist, the person goes to his knees. He went to his knees; she inside him went to her knees. It must have been off-putting. He couldn't hold onto the Trigregos Talismans by sheer force of will anymore. They had minds of their own, those things. Or the Crimson Corona was mind enough for the three of them. They off-put themselves.

The Amateramirror, the traitor, whirred off his arm like a buzzsaw. Uma caught it. The Susasword, another traitor, twirled out of his grip like the drill-bit of a carpenter's brace-and-bit set. Nihila snagged it. Even the Corona left his forehead. Methandra had that; put it on her head. The fop tore off his power focus, the fang-fingered glove.

It felt to Vetala as if he'd torn off her soldier's right hand with it. Her golden-brown warrior was disintegrating; some Taurus Chrysaor Attis him. He'd battled Mithras to a near standstill; this fellow couldn't even stand anymore. She thought them both to her throne; into her throne, hidden from sight. There wasn't much left of it. There wasn't much left of either of them.

Guardian Angel Tyrtod had finally found himself a new shell. It was one of the dead Trinondevs. He knew how their eye-staves worked, psycho-kinesis, mind-over-matter, but he couldn't get the eye-stave to work for him. The devil closest to him was Gravedigger; black as midnight on a starless night; same as his shell. Tyrtod was having trouble holding onto him, the dead Trinondev. The eyeorb atop his eye-stave opened as if of its own accord.

Tyrtod was startled, so was Nergalis. His third eye went into it first, his subtle matter demonic body and the devic power focus, Parsis's power focus, the flying carpet he was standing on, what the Hot Stuff Thanatoid had lent him, followed. His shell was almost as black as the devil had been; as the dead Trinondev was.

The male Nergalid's shell didn't fall far; didn't fall awkwardly either. Landed on his feet. Tore something off his bandoleer, tossed it at him, Tyrtod, in the Trinondev. It was a grenade. It blew. It was time, once again, for Guardian Angel Tyrtod to find yet another shell. This was getting tedious. How many shells could a Guardian Angel go through before he was through himself?

Vetala, in her soldier, them both invisible within her throne, caught what had happened to the Planter. With him gone, his control over the Nergalazurs reverted to her. She was already feeling stronger. Of course that could be the Gypsium she was absorbing from her throne – and it from wherever faraway. Her soldier was reintegrating. What a outstanding specimen. Could he be the Attis after all; all her Attis, not Pyrame's to boot?

The black guy, where had he gone? There was something interesting about him, she thought. There, he'd grabbed another eye-stave. Unless it was the same one Guardian Angel Tyrtod's dead Trinondev had. No, it was a different one. Seemingly he knew how to use them; had encased himself in a mind-globe. Stubble beard, that was what was interesting about him. No pureblood then, meaning she could possess him. If she dared leave her soldier and her throne to do so.

She had another thought. She knew how they worked too. Mind over matter. There were dozens of them strewn around Diminished Dustmound. It wasn't just her soldier who had tremendous willpower. The ones the Master had ejected opened. Where had he got to anyways? The azuras captured inside them escaped.

Gravity, she was next. She'd do it herself this time. Had to; what with the azuras coming into her she was recovering far faster than her Attis. Concentrated the more. Uma couldn't believe it. She was shredded into the vacated ones, dropped the mirror. It just lay there. Nihila started unleashing chained lightning into the prison pods, bolt after bolt. They erupted; rather the Silvercloud erupted out of them. Slowly but surely Uma started re-forming.

Blast the Unity anyhow. Nergal Vetala lost her composure, manifested herself physically, went for her, Brainrock sickle raised high. Methandra didn't need to cry a warning. Nihila was ready for her. The Blood Queen never got close. Brainrock chains ravelled her; started draining her, strengthening Nihila. Vanthysces Vastness went for Methandra. A decathonitized devil seemingly composed of straw against the epitome of Heat, you have to be kidding. He was blazing. Sabreur shouted something the giantess not only heard but heeded.

"Wait! His shell's alive. Look."

Sabreur opened the eyeorb atop the latest eye-stave he'd acquired; thought Straw not Heat. The Byronic's third eye went into it first, his subtle matter demonic body, afire as it was, and power focus, Plague's power focus, the Pendulum Blade, followed. Tucedon was loose; not the slightest charcoaled. Sabreur was in trouble. Eyeorb filled-up, no more force shield, animated Dead Things coming at him. Methandra was in trouble too. Maybe the Corona didn't appreciate her choosing not to kill the mercenary. It started to eat into her brain. It started to snow.

Then it started to hail. A hailstone as big as boulder smashed against Dustmound. It was akin to a colossal egg; cracked, out of it came wild beasts and werethings. More smashed into the ground. More wild beast, more were-things. Then came the snowmen, armed with icicles. The vulturous Cloud of Hadd, Sangazur-animated Dead Things riding them, guns-firing, finally deciding to re-enter the fray, flew out of the perpetually cloud-covered sky.

Were driven out actually, as it happened. There was a Silvercloud in them; not lining them. Rain joined the snow; joined the hail. Winds, approaching cyclonic, came up. Rudra Silvercloud was Byron's Savage Storm; devils called him Beast. The wild beasts and were-things were his; the snowmen belonged to King Cold, Tantal Thanatos. Firstborns married their immediate tribal siblings. Firstborns fought with each other; fought for each other, put better. For their firstborn sister-wives as well.

First Fangs was excessively pleased with himself. After five hundred years he had his power focus back. That was enough for him. Screw any oaths of fealty he'd made. He'd been decathonitized. He didn't have to abide by his vows anymore; probably never did. Nowadays Nihila may be his eldest sister in Lazareme but he'd done what he'd agreed to do. Time to cut himself out of here.

He was a Black Godling from the Cattail Peninsula, the long time sphere of influence of her fellow Unity, Chaos, Unholy Abaddon, her killer. He had what passed for a protectorate there once. Father Lazareme didn't approve of protectorates back then but maybe that's changed. Maybe he could win it back. Or make it his officially. Maybe he wouldn't bother.

He stepped on something. It might have been a Dead Thing already turning into crud. Vetala's azuras couldn't hold onto corpses when it was raining or snowing and it was doing both of those things simultaneously. Yuck. He stumbled forward, tripped into a hole. Oh, no. He'd landed on a Trinondev eyeorb; broke it open like the eye-egg it also was; it wasn't full-up anymore. Then it was, with him.

Salamoneus was back in action. Picked up the eye-stave; picked up another one nearby. It had a unopened eyeorb atop it. Sabreur piled on top of him. So did Tucedon. Sabreur knew how these things worked. He enclosed all three of them in a brain-bulb just as explosions started wracking Dustmound. Vetala was pulling out all the stops; was pulling all her azuras into her but moisture was destabilizing it, diminishing it even further. It was collapsing into itself.

The explosions were of a very specific nature. They were exploding against Nihila. It was the Dand-head of Kronokronos Akbarartha's Homeworld Sceptre that was exploding, over and over again. Vetala's Soldier was wielding it. What kind of power did it have – was it a power focus unto itself? Was it even more powerful? Nihila was, to say the least, sidetracked.

The Susasword decided she was unworthy of it. Or the Crimson Corona decided for them both. It reversed in her hand. Trigregos Incarnate grabbed its hilt with his spare hand, the one he'd grown back when he reintegrated; the one not holding onto Akbar's sceptre. He drove the blade through her. As if she was on her own petard he hoisted her, rammed her backwards into Vetala's throne, left her stuck there.

There was a brief yelp. He, the Trigregos Titan, not Titaness, whirled. An enormous, 3-eyed, blue-skinned Viking-type wielding a correspondingly immense, two-headed war-axe had just lopped off the hot-stuff-giantess's head. The Crimson Corona, the Mind of Devaura, was now on Uma Silvercloud. She was levitating wild things, were-things, everything she could grab with her gravitational moonbeams; hurling them as far away from collapsing Dustmound as she could.

An orange-and-brown furred, tiger-striped were-thing with three eyes appeared before her. He swung a single-bladed weapon on a spearhead, a halberd. Off went her head. Wisely, obediently, the Crimson Corona chose the Trigregos Titan's head as its next resting place. The Amateramirror was on his arm. No more traitors either of them.

Goddess was beside him. None of them were standing on anything except the air itself. Them included the two headless Master Devas. Then they had heads again. No wonder, even if they were demonstrably devils, their adherents worshipped them as gods. Nergal Vetala raised her Brainrock sickle.

"Thanatoids, Silverclouds, this is my protectorate. You are here without my leave. I command you cathonitized."

Nothing happened. The four transgressing firstborns exchanged glances. They all recalled Vetala would never have had Hadd if it hadn't been for the Thanatoids and the expansion of their Lathakran empire; an expansion aided and abetted by the Silverclouds and Lazareme's Chaos Unity; an expansion that ended more than 1,100 years earlier with the Atomic Twins irradiating the subsequent Ghostlands at whomever's command.

That a preponderance of her Haddazurs and Nergalazurs resided in Hadd was most of the reason she'd held onto it. The rest of the reason was living Iraches, nowadays a perhaps borderline minority in their own homeland, still worshipped her. She'd been consuming azuras all day in order to keep herself going. Right now there were zip azuras on the zit of Dustmound to help her keep even this much of Hadd exclusively her own.

Vetala clutched her soldier's arm. Neither she nor the Crimson Corona had to tell him this was no place to be.

Four firstborns combining their clout was beyond doubt devil-devastating.

========

The snow stopped falling on Diminished Dustmound.

The cosmicompanion vampires arrived. They and the mercenaries made their deal then left the vicinity. Nothing moved; not even Guardian Angel Tyrtod. The Gatherers of the Dead had already come on their Vultyrie and bats-of-burden in order to collect the three still relatively intact samurais, including the one without a head. Tyrtod hitched a ride with them to Sanguerre.

He was Guardian Angel Mikoto again. Sangs had marvellous seamstresses.

****

(ENDGAME-GAMBIT) 25: **Morg's A Morgue**

Sedonda, Tantalar 7, 5980

Them, the three remaining Good Companions, riding bareback on piggy-bats, him still sitting on Harmony's High Seat in Sedon's Hairband, Smiler far-watched them go. Then he went far-blind.

Where'd all the Brainrock gone?

========

Had it been higher – the proud, middle finger insult to the Sedon Sphere it had been for so many centuries, rather than the emasculated stub it was now – Fisherwoman could have watched them go, too. So could Demios Sarpedon. Athenan War Witches, dead or alive, had left plenty of bullet-pellets on Diminished Dustmound.

It was Golgotha Nauroz who told them about Vetala's Brainrock throne. She hadn't taken the 80-year-old clone with her. She'd left him to look after Harry Zeross, Ringleader. No doubt on the Morrigan's orders – and hopefully for benign motives – Morg's woman, Garcia Dis L'Orca, had decided to sedate him.

Witch-potions were hardly Fish's specialty. Illuminatus, Melina born Sarpedon – Demios's twin and Harry's High Illuminary of a Utopian wife – was much better at them. So was her niece, Aranyani born Ryne called Nightingale become Maxwell, who'd forged a career with them on the Outer Earth. Truth was she was more of a generalist than a specialist.

Which-witch was why most witches with specialties strove to keep their secrets to themselves. Call it copyright protection. When it came to copyright infringement, Fish was galloping scallops unscrupulous.

She could have held hands with either Demios or Golgotha, could have held hands with both of them, taken them both to Dustmound with her. They'd discussed their options, friendly sorts that they were in private, after the snow stopped falling and they were back in Ringleader's quarters within the Sraddhites' monastery.

He'd look after Rings, drugged as was, Golgotha promised. There was a mother-lode of Gypsium in the form of Vetala's Brainrock throne on Dustmound. The Diver had been there at the same time he was. Couldn't be sure where he'd got to; he'd been keeping himself alive; not keeping track on anyone else. Could the Diver teleport, like Harry could, by envisaging where he wanted to go then going there?

There'd been devil-doings going on in the west, Dustmound and its vicinity, all day. So it made good sense for Fish to choose a pureblood with the oldest eye-stave in existence to take with her when she went there.

For one thing, Demios's eye-stave was extraterrestrial in origin. For another, answers to the question of how the Utopians' pre-Earth technology functioned were always controversial, essentially unverifiable. What they could be sure of was Sarpedon's wasn't just self-loading, like Saladin Devason's Master's Mace. It manufactured its own eyeorbs. For yet another, purebloods couldn't be possessed; everyone agreed on that.

That was why Saladin officially Nauroz was only a quarter devil. His father Augustus was a pureblood. Unless of course the Moloch Sedon could possess purebloods. No one agreed on that, although Sal asserted, ad nauseam, he was no mortal Sed-son. He died, the Dome wouldn't collapse. He'd died. The Dome hadn't collapsed. Then again, if he was one, he might not have been the only Sed-son on this side of the Dome. He had, after all, a large number of sons of his own.

No one was quite sure if clones of purebloods could or couldn't be possessed. Golgotha swore he never had been and everyone believed him. Fish knew she couldn't be; her Vesica Piscis saw to that. It was a pearl, though it looked more like a clamshell. It pretty much kept her from harm. Probably she was the only one who believed that, however.

Fish was pissed. Not because no one believed her about being non-acquirable and not because she was a Piscine. Demios was too, pissed. For a different reason. He was irked because there was no sign of Devason's body. Why would there be a bee-in-the-undersea, Fish quibbled, fishifying typically as well as topically.

Pandora Mannering, the late Master's mother, was a sand-witch-hybrid. That meant he could be possessed, by a simple azura to boot, in the fruit-of-the-loam. Sal, much more sadly than she cared to admit, could be a Dead Thing Swimming. He might even be a Dead Thing Swimming who'd walked or flown away thanks to a symbiotic Sangazur. With his Master's Mace as well, the-waves-do-swell.

Fish was more than mildly peeved because she'd come to what little was left of Dustmound in anticipation of finding the Diver seeking to absorb a mother-lode of Brainrock. What they found instead was a load of motherhood; past and potentially future motherhood. She was dangling off what had to be Vetala's not so large, and not so much so gleaming anymore, Gypsium throne. She was doing so on a curved blade that also barely glimmered with the same telltale radiance of Godstuff, remnants of the Big Bang's primordial Godhead.

Devils called Vetala Fecundity but this had to be Datong Harmonia, the fabled Unity of Harmony as well as paradisiacal Panharmonium. Brainrock chains, an ugly, urine-yellow rather than glowingly golden as they were in all the old stories, some of which she'd heard from Jordan Tethys, gave that away.

Connect that with the fact the blade was also made out of currently dishwater-dull Brainrock, that must make it the Susasword. Being prone to anthropomorphizing, Fish thought it looked quite content now that it was back to doing what it did best; namely, sticking through Harmony, through her chains, and thereby sticking her to a slab of Brainrock.

Fish was cannier than a cannery. Demios was warier than most warriors. They regarded her, stuck there as she was, without doing anything either presumptuous or precipitous. Might it not be better to just leave her there?

No choice was given. The Susasword was akin to Blind Sundown's Solar Spear. It could discharge killing force. It discharged a Gypsium blade that went straight through Fish's howsoever-often baby-belly-full, bellybutton bauble, came out on the other side of her back and carried onto into Demios.

Master Kyprian and her Illuminaries of the Twenties and into the Thirties had taught both of them, among many another, that Thrygragos Lazareme was the firstborn of the second generational Great Gods. Therefore, Harmony was one-third of the firstborns of the firstborn; in other words, she was the oldest female Master Deva in existence.

The Susasword was still stuck to the back of Vetala's throne. Nowadays Nihila wasn't stuck through it, to it, anymore. She was inside Dem's eyeorb. The oldest female devil inside the oldest prison-pod in existence, it was fitting. They fit each other like a 'T', not a tee, and standing for tough tiddlywinks for all thus affected.

========

Andaemyn was rallying.

========

Morgianna born Nauroz – become Somata, at the insistence of great-grand-mother Kyprian; become Sarpedon because of her love for Demios – knew she would. Andy was almost as hard-bodied as she was hard-headed; came with the genes. It would be awhile yet before she dared release the curative soul-self that had jump-started her daughter; be a lot longer after that before Andy could walk again, if she ever did.

She had no intention of leaving her now. Wouldn't be a proper mother if she did and whatever else she was, the Morrigan was a proper mother. Unless of course she couldn't avoid it, it went without saying. In which case, if she had time, she'd make sure Andy had the best care witchery could procure. Or, if she didn't have quite enough time to take her to a top-notch Althean Healer like Ventricular Tele-passa, she of Godbad, on Shenon, or her sister-in-law, Melina nee Sarpedon Zeross, the High Illuminary of Weir, she'd make sure Andy was at least relatively safe.

The Sraddhite monastery may have been largely heated by Haddit zombies for most of the last fifteen years, but it still had fireplaces. Morg was mopping Andy's face; was watching flames and concomitant smoke rising up the chimney off logs in the fireplace within her quarters, her daughter's sickroom, as she did so. She was doing more than just watching as she was washing. Was multitasking; was speaking to them dot-ditto.

"And you were so sure. A Crimson Crown for a Crimson Queen."

"The Trigregos Talismans tricked us, Hellion. I knew beforehand they could kill devils. I took the risk anyways. So did Gravity. Hers was occupied, hers being the Soul of Devaura. Three firstborn females, who else could be more entitled to them? Fecundity took over her golden-brown Attis and, yes, if Cold hadn't come for me, the Crimson Corona, the Mind of Sapiendev, would have eaten mine, my mind, my brain.

"The Body of Demeter put Harmony out of her misery, again. Then we put Fecundity and her Attis out of ours. He had the Mind and Soul on him when we did, so that's it for the Panharmonium Project. Can't say as I'm sorry either. They were too tempting."

"And as advertised. For glorious goddesses you're dreadfully dim. They were never meant for Master Devas; not even firstborns. They were meant for your mothers. Or their reincarnations. You say there's still the one left. Andy's out of danger so I'll have someone look after her while I go fetch it. Tvasitar Smithmonger can re-make the other two when the time comes. I'll take Demios with me so we don't have to worry about Harmony."

"I'm not worried about Harmony, or Freespirit Nihila, or whatever she prefers to call herself these days. Let her rot. I've learned my lesson. So has Gravity. We're done with Trigregos. The Moloch Sedon was playing with us, we get that now. Do as you please, Morrigan. But only after we take delivery of Dr Zeross. I'll refocus the fumes from my cauldron onto his sickroom. Cold will come through as soon as you've taken care of the Trinondev guarding him. We're ready now."

"I see. Well, thanks for talking to me, Methandra. I almost feel honoured and it certainly has been ever so edifying. Seems the situation's changed. So sorry yours didn't kill you."

The Morrigan chucked the bowl wherein she dipped the cloth she was using to mop her daughter's face into the fireplace. Chucked the cloth she was using to do so into it as well. Followed with a few other things, nests for the most part. Being a materialist came in awfully handy sometimes – emphasis on awfully.

Demons came in all sorts of shapes and sizes. Many were teleportive psychopomps. The white-as-a-clean-handkerchief Ghast she tossed onto the Thanatoid's flame-form was a Grey Ghast. It didn't burst into flames; it vanished into the Grey, the Weird, the Universal Substance of Samsara. So did the nests. It'd take Hot Stuff, Heat to more polite devils, wherever she was, a minute or two to burn the Ghast off her. It might take a bite or two out of her before she did so. Demons ate devils. Morg hoped it went for her three eyes first; those in the nests certainly would

Pantsuit-demons, the equivalent of denim demons so popular with Hellion hippies a few years ago, were strong. She gathered Andy in her arms, dropped a Hellstone at her feet and stepped them both through between-space to one of the witch-stones Garcia left in Ringleader's quarters on her orders. If the Thanatoids were afraid of Golgotha and his prison pods then, wherever he was, that was a safe place to leave Andy.

She'd still have to find Demios. That was never a problem for her. The two of them were raised together; had been together almost from the first day they could be with anyone, sexually speaking. They had a mind-link even identical twins couldn't rival. They'd go to Dustmound, collect the Susasword, which was an imperative for her, and take out Freespirit Nihila, which would bolster his ego.

What kind of a name was Nihila anyways? Sounded like something old-time Illuminaries might have come up with after a few bottles of Greek retsina.

After that, as she'd promised Golgotha and the delegation of Trinondevs who'd come to see her while she was tending Andy, the ones she convinced to make Demios, not the clone, their Field Commander, Alastor Molorchus could transport them to Cabalarkon. It wouldn't be to gather up dozens more Trinondevs and hundreds more eyeorbs to go with them, though. It would be to stay. The Dead could rot along with Nihila. One would lead to the other two.

They had to be still out there because four members of the Damnation Brigade were captured inside the Amateramirror. That much Harry and Golgotha had confirmed before she had Dis L'Orca put Harry under, the easier for the Thanatoids to gather him at their leisure. If the firstborns had obliterated the Soul, along with the Mind and Vetala's Soldier, they would have killed D-Brig-4. Methandra hadn't been cathonitized. Ergo she hadn't helped kill anyone.

The Weirdom needed a new Master; not another Challenge of Weir.

========

Since no one had thought to bring de-icing units to Sraddha Isle – or, indeed, to any of their bases on or around Lake Sedona – the carpet of freshly fallen snow had grounded the Godbadian evacuation efforts for the night.

A few of the more Outer-Earth-modern helicopters did come with built-in de-icing equipment, however. They could also fly at night. The Corporate State's Godbadian-based military command were not risk-takers but they wanted their top personnel, notably General Quentin Anvil and Governor Ferdinand Niarchos, back home as soon as possible. So did their civilian and therefore supposedly superior overseers; not that anyone in the military particularly cared about them.

There was an ordinarily trouble-free way to accomplish that. These were not ordinary times and, anyhow, Janna St Peche-Montressor did not follow their orders.

========

"There's been a day of devil-doings over what your map calls Dustmound," she repeated; she being an Athenan War Witch as well as a Lovely Lady Afrite. (Not to mention the daughter-in-law of Alpha Centauri, the Corporate State of Aka Godbad's resident strongman even with Thrygragos Byron upstairs, shining brightly out of the night's sky.) "But that only makes the Weird even less safe. Tell the powers-that-pretend-to-be to fuck off."

"I wouldn't go through it anyways," said Anvil, also not for the first time.

"I would," said Niarchos. "And I have. But if Janna won't risk taking any of us through it because of all those Dead Ants Stalking the Grey, as they call it over in Sedon's Noses, then I say we do as Thartarre says. Hunker down until daylight and hope the snow's melted by then. Sooth said, I'd be happier hunkering down here until Harry wakes up and we've access to his rings. At least they're reliable."

"Were," said the Janna there, St Peche-Montressor. "Supposedly Superior Sarpedon had him put to sleep because he was exhausted. Garcia Dis L'Orca, though, is afraid he might be possessed."

"I didn't think anyone Brainrock-blessed could be possessed," said Thartarre.

"Devils can't possess other devils and they can't possess someone who's already being possessed by another devil, that's about all anyone who isn't an Illuminary can say. Just be glad none of us are."

Like everyone else in the command tent she'd allowed herself to be scoped by one of Golgotha's men, when he was still one of Golgotha's men. With Bodiless Byron in the night's sky, and her having been in the company of Demios Sarpedon for most of the last two days, she didn't see how she could be possessed, either by

APM All-Eyes or by anyone else. But Anvil had insisted and she'd gone along with it.

"Be that as it may," said the general. "I'd be much happier if Golgotha was back in charge of the Trinondevs. He's always played straight with us."

"In that we're agreed."

The Janna there did not follow the Morrigan's orders any more than she did those of the Godbadians' military or civilian authorities. However, although Dukkhan born and raised, she was enough of a homer not to trust either of the Sarpedons very far. She may not have been very old, not even a teenager, during the final years of Godbad's bloody Civil War but she knew whose side they'd been on. And it wasn't that of her then future father-in-law.

That Morgianna was on Fish, then Queen Scylla, and her husband, then King Achigan Auranja's side – and that they shamelessly employed Achigan's anti-Byronic faeries as well as Morrigan Morg's ditto-demons – to this day didn't make it easy to follow the Fatman's instructions and let bygones be bygones.

"Nonetheless," the Janna there added in that spirit, unless it was leftover from APM's spirit, "I found it an odd thing for Garcia to say. How could anyone here, even someone who's Brainrock-blessed, be devil-possessed with all these Trinondevs around?" The Lovely Lady had been thinking, unless again it was APM thinking before she let SPM come here all by her lonesome, as in dispossessed.

"I reckon there's a couple of ways of looking at it. Could she be saying devils want him and his rings for reasons none of us can fathom? In other words, that she suspects Morg's dealing with devils and won't come right out and say it. Or could she be afraid he was killed on Dustmound and possessed by something else; the same sort of something else her dead War Witches seem to be possessed by? In which case putting him to sleep makes good sense. Ringleader would be a deadly enemy to have, no pun intended."

"I'm beginning to wish we had a Nightingale in our midst," said Niarchos, who shared virtually everyone there's distrust of the Sarpedons if not so much so Fisherwoman. Nightingales – not Fish's niece, Aranyani Nightingale, daughter of long gone Eden, who'd taken Nightingale as her maiden name mostly because she didn't know who her parents were until she came inside in the very late Thirties – were the clandestine cadre of tiptop witches who ran the Superior Sisterhood of Flowery Anthea.

Ant Nightingales could be reached through Tsishah Twilight, the Aortic representing various sisterhoods, including Ants, on Shenon, Witch Isle, the heart-shaped island off the Cattail Peninsula's western coast. He didn't suggest anyone go there, though. He knew as well as everyone else did that Aortic Tsishah was the Morrigan's eldest child; albeit by Tom-Tiddly Tattletale, a faerie sort oddly related to Eden, Fish, and Wilderwitch's birthparents, the Dual Entities.

"Well, we don't," observed the High Priest. "Besides, it's too late to do anything about any of that. Lady Achigan has gone off again. No one knows where she went, at least no one's telling the rest of us. No one can locate the Utopians' elected Field Commander, Demios Sarpedon. Former Field Commander Nauroz won't leave Dr Zeross's bedside and Superior Sarpedon won't leave her daughter's bedside. Nor will she let any of our physicians, or anyone else for that matter, enter her quarters."

"I've my orders," said Anvil. "I'm to take a helicopter gunship to New Iraxas tonight. The governor's to go with me."

"The governor's a civilian," The governor at issue reminded the presumptuous military man. "You can seek to have me impeached, Quentin, but I'm not going anywhere tonight, not willingly."

"And we've a crisis in leadership," said Thartarre, whose authority extended over the Sraddhites alone. "We can't keep relying on runners going to Former Field Commander Nauroz in order to receive his orders in lieu of elected Field Commander Sarpedon's orders. And the War Witches are forced to do almost exactly the same thing.

"Their Field Leader Dis L'Orca won't do anything without Superior Sarpedon's okay. Yet she isn't even allowed in to speak with her face-to-face. Has to take her orders via witch-stones or through a closed door. It's ridiculous. Even more reason for me to question your state's choice of allies, general."

"We have managed to arrange for Trinondevs and Zebranids with eye-staves to stay close to myself and Garcia's remaining Athenans," St Peche-Montressor objected as if on the general's behalf. It was just as well. Quentin Anvil looked about to burst with annoyance. They'd been going at this for hours now.

There were five War Witches in the command tent with them just then. Like her, they would have bullet-pellets about themselves. There were two Utopians there as well, a male Trinondev and a female Zebranid. They were holding eye-staves. The now dead, consequently ex-Master's misogyny aside, gender had nothing to do with how effective anyone was when it came to wielding an eye-stave. It was their willpower that counted.

They, like everyone else in the tent, the other being Diego de Landa (Diego Sraddha Landa-son), weren't possessed by either a devil or an azura. That much could be confirmed. Whether they were possessed by that mysterious something else, they all agreed there was only person who could detect whatever it was. Unfortunately, Young Death was amongst the ranks of the missing.

"It isn't good enough," the High Priest, Thartarre Sraddha Holgatson, reiterated.

"It'll have to do, priest," snapped Anvil. "For the last time, can't we at least settle on us targeting Manoa-Necropolis once I return to base? It's the enemy's hub. Where its forces are most concentrated. Militarily it makes the most sense."

"Had you aircraft," Thartarre, unrelenting, chided him.

"Look outside, priest. We still do. And there's plenty more where they came from in Petrograd, Krachla, or at Pear Point over on the Cattail. It hasn't snowed in any of those places. Besides, we won't need them all for a defence of the subcontinent or even a pre-emptive strike on Sanguerre. I can order it from here, before I go. Our radios still work."

"Then I would advise they continue to spray the non-vulturous clouds of Hadd with liquid nitrogen," Thartarre re-emphasized. "We shall continue blasting the clouds with silver iodine from our cannons and with our rocket launchers. Even if Mrs St Peche-Montressor is correct and today's snowfall is a result of devil-doings, and not our attempts to seed the clouds artificially, it is indicative Nergal Vetala is losing her grip on Hadd. While we dare not hope the Blood Queen and her impossibly powerful pawn are no more, we cannot afford to relax our efforts in that regard. Rain may be all that's needed to win the Living a great victory."

"Snow's frozen rain," St Peche-Montressor concurred. "And it's certainly put a damper on goings-on hereabouts. Other than in the Lake, we've had no reports of the Dead attacking anywhere since it started. Not only that, the reports we already had from Lady Achigan's Piscines suggest the watery front wasn't such a big deal anyhow.

"Which really shouldn't surprise anyone. Call them as you please, Haddazurs or Nergalazurs, the vast majority of the azuras animating Hadd's Dead amount to Vetalazurs. Vetalazurs aren't aquatically oriented. So the watery Dead they've been extracting have to have been animated by azura-leftovers from First War days, if not from centuries pre-Vetala."

"Seeding clouds," retorted the general, "Has always struck me as a pseudo-science at best. Nothing I've ever read has convinced me otherwise. No, the solution has to be military. I've battled Sangazurs and their shells. I've battled their Outer Earth allies, Field Marshall von Blut and his Lost Legion, alive and dead. Warlord Mikoto and his Two Thousand; the Mandroid monstrosity Steltsar, he and his tellurians, them too.

"With your father, Ferd, when he was spearheading our revolution as the Duke of Aka Godbad, our fellow Godbadians and our allies, we beat off Sangazur-animated Dead Things during the Civil War. One of us, Godfrey Necator, whom you might remember, was so fearless the Sangs made him an honorary Valhallan before he became an actual Valhallan. Sure, we had belated help from our Byronic devil-gods. But their loyalties were divided at first, you might also recall. We prevailed regardless, through superior force of arms."

"So we can and will beat Hadd's Dead militarily. If we're allowed to do our jobs. The snow was on our side today. Snow melts and the air's already drying up. The Dead will rise anew as soon as the ground follows suit. Because of the perhaps only apparent, not actual, threat from Sanguerre, we may have to delay conquering Hadd while we attend to New Valhalla, but that doesn't mean we forget about it.

"At the very least, bombing Necropolis will destroy zombies. It might even rob Hadd's vamps of places to hide during the day. We sally forth sporadically, when we can, over the coming weeks, which will be my recommendation to the chain of command, that will certainly serve notice we aren't going away. That we'll be back big time, with even bigger bombs, Neutron Bombs maybe, once we've sorted out their pals in the Bloodlands."

"Except you are going away, General," said Thartarre, seemingly for the ump-teenth time. "And you're leaving us in the lurch. Sixty missing stars from the Sedon Sphere, even if a few of them are apparently back already; Godbad's Great God now up there himself; along with his Primary Nucleoids, if what Mrs St Peche-Montressor also tells us is correct.

"Devil-doings over Dustmound; snow throughout Hadd; some other kind of devil-like Spirit Beings animating dead Antheans and dead Trinondevs. There's a strong possibility we're being set-up. I shouldn't have to remind any of you that, before it was Hadd, old Iraxas was part of the Lathakran Empire. And before that it was El Dorado."

"And there's a stronger one," countered Janna, "A probability even, that you aren't being set-up at all. My father-in-law is a peaceful man. I believe I speak for him, Alpha Centauri, as well as Aortic Tsishah, the nominal Superior of our Sisterhood – and a number of other Sisterhoods, including the Superior Sisterhood itself, that of Flowery Anthea – when I say that bombing such a beautiful and ancient city as Manoa-Necropolis into rubble is an absolutely scandalous misuse of resources."

"Not to mention a violation of Godbad's agreement with the Iraches of Free Iraxas," said Niarchos, who in his official capacity did speak for the Fatman and Centauri Enterprises. "Which I shouldn't have to remind you, High Priest, you and your Curia signed onto as well. They've already landed on Hadd's east coast. So, while I'm all in favour of bombing Necropolis from a military standpoint, general, I can't condone it."

"And no matter what he thinks," said St Peche-Montressor. "Godfrey Kenton isn't the president yet."

"No," Niarchos agreed. "President Lemon is and, even with Great Byron cathonitized, he's Alpha's boy. You go if you have to, Quentin. Good luck to you as well. I'll still be in radio contact and I'm betting you get to bombard Sanguerre before Necropolis."

"Oh, I'm going all right." Quentin Anvil got to his feet. "But don't think for a moment I don't know what all of you are hoping for: that Godbad's devil-gods will come to your aid. Damon Goldenrod had Manoa built, or rebuilt, in all its golden glory. You're thinking he'll want it back. And now that he and his immediate, third-born sister, APM-All-Eyes, are the eldest Byronics left on this side of the Head they'll call on Byron's firstborn, Rudra Silvercloud, Bestial Storm, to make it rain in Hadd.

"Well, let me tell you one other thing for free while I'm at it. If we're to truly win the day, to be truly free, we not only have to find a way to defeat the devils and deviants leading Hadd's Horrors, we have to do it ourselves. If we leave that to others, even our own gods, devils that they are, we will be beholding to those others. A decent commander-in-chief would agree with me when I say we should be beholding to no one but ourselves."

That said, General Quentin Anvil stomped out of the tent and onto the snow-cleared tarmac. There, within a matter of minutes, his helicopter was revved-up and ready to rotor. Janna St Peche-Montressor watched him go then glanced at Thartarre and Niarchos. "Why was he looking at me when he said that? I've been scoped by pros. APM isn't inside me."

Thartarre hated to rub in the palpable. Ferdinand Niarchos couldn't resist. "Even if it's Krepusyl of Crepuscule who has a Morgenstern for a power focus, Aphropsyche Morningstar is a devil. Maybe he thought she was listening in long-distance. When you're All-Eyes, why can't you be All-Ears too?"

"This is interesting," said Diego de Landa, Thartarre's Curia-appointed Number Two. Along with the five War Witches and the two of Utopian extraction, he was the only other one in the command tent.

"What is it?" had to ask Niarchos.

"A note," said de Landa. "It just appeared underneath the notes I was taking."

"Jordy," said Janna, the Janna in the tent, APM's SPM.

"Read it," said Weird Ferd.

"It's still coming in. *'Morg's a morgue ... "*

========

Former Field Commander Nauroz swore he'd never been possessed by a devazur and everyone believed him. He had, however, fallen asleep reading a book while he was supposed to be guarding Ringleader, the male of the two Dr Zerosses. No matter how long-lived he might be by human standards, the clone was 80 years old.

He was also draped with a white-as-a-clean-sheet Ghast; a king-sized white-as-a-sheet Ghast. His eye-stave and the rucksack containing the replacement eyeorbs he'd requisitioned, from the Elite's dead, were just as underneath it. Demons were, of course, mostly made up of Solidium-Stopstone, Gypsium-Brainrock's counterforce.

Very few devils were good with demons. One, though, may have been just as chthonic as he was cathonic.

========

"I've been contemplating the efficacy of the earthborn, Morrigan."

"Judge?" The Smiling Fiend was hardly perceptible, all in black, with just his pinkish face and overlong fingers visible in the dimly lit room. He was standing on the other side of Ringleader's bed from where she came through on Dis L'Orca's bullet-pellet.

"God, you gave me start." She overacted only slightly when she smacked her chest in order to emphasize just how startled she'd been. Next, her on the opposite side of Rings' bed, she reconsidered Golgotha's condition, which she'd first observed from between-space before she came wholly through into the room. "You took a terrible risk doing that."

She, Morgianna Sarpedon, the Morrigan, had stepped into Harry's quarters seemingly solo. When you had two presumed-parents who had been perpetual 7-year-olds since the day you were born, you naturally picked up a degree of faerie-tricksterism. Andaemyn was now resting beside Alastor Molorchus and the Irache War Witch's non-animated corpse. They were in the same mobile *'shelter'* she'd cast off one of her witch-stones. Said witch-stone was a button on the left breast-pocket of her pantsuit-demon.

"It was an experiment. Heat told me how you intended to handle Trinon-dev eyeorbs and I decided that what's good for the goose is good for the gander. I was Daemonicus once, recall. When I was in Pandemonium last week I sat on Hellblob's throne. Once he recognized me he acknowledged I had more right to it than he did. So I retain my mastery over daemons. And that, plus some cartage, should prove all I need to return sanity to the Land of the Dead."

Baaloch Hellblob, as Illuminaries had rather whimsically named him, was the reigning Prime Sinistral of Satanwyck, the seventh such – although a few, Lust, Wrath and Avarice most notably, had ruled it a couple of times. His attribute was sloth; thus also Sinistral Sloth. Even his subjects referred to him as Hellblob. When they didn't refer to him as Lord Lazy, that is.

(Curiously, Thrygragos Lazareme, Thrygragos Everyman, as of now the pre-sumed last surviving Great God, was sometimes referred to as the Lord Laziest Lazareme. For most of the last five hundred years, though, ever since the Disunition of his Unities, largely due to the Trigregos Talismans, he was more correctly referred to as the Lord Sleepiest Lazareme, for that was what he spent virtually all of his time doing – sleeping on Tympani, Eardrum Isle.)

"Be assured, I didn't come through prior to enshrouding the clone and his eye-stave. I employed a Ghast-psychopomp; a Grey Ghast, as you Hellions refer to them. Stopstone counters Gypsium, we all know that. Yet it seems a daemon can seal an eyeorb shut, thus rendering it inoperable as a prison-pod. How long have you known that?"

He could have used his third eye on her. That she did know. She hated being bathed in devic eyefire. Likely her pantsuit-demon would hate it even more; had it had a brain. Also, she wasn't wearing fireproof underwear. "Virtually all my life. Thanks primarily to the Death's Head Hellion – whom, now that I recognize you, realize you probably advised, if not necessarily controlled – Illuminaries learned a very long time ago that it's a weakness of eyeorbs.

"However, as you might appreciate, it's not something we generally share with non-Utopians. Let alone devils like yourself. But, you know what? It's only effective when the Trinondev isn't concentrating on sucking in the daemon's subtle matter form. I assume Golgotha was already asleep, otherwise he'd have vacuumed-up the Ghast as soon as he saw it coming out of the Grey."

"Tinkerbells might think they're faeries but they're just daemons with a modicum more intelligence. Faerie sleep-dust worked on Antaeor Thanatos in Temporis. I saw no reason it shouldn't work on an exhausted Trinondev, especially an aging clone who probably hasn't been up north supping the life-extending crud churned out by their salvaged version of Weir's Mother Machine for weeks now."

"Even so, you're lucky you had the Ghast cover his eye-stave and satchel before you came through because, unless a superior mind is countermanding their programming, eyeorbs automatically open in the presence of Master Devas. He wouldn't have had to be awake in order to nail you. He wakes up, he throws off the Ghast, he will nail you.

"I am aware of that, Morrigan. And I will remember your concern for my well-being. You, however, will not; not once I make my departure. Which is sort of a shame because then you'd remember this: I wasn't controlling Morgan Abyss, my wife was; rather, Daemonicus's wife was – Primeval Lilith, the Demon Queen of the Night. I was, however, there very much biblically."

"You were Tomcat Tattletail?"

"Many times – including in the early 4800s."

(When he told tales involving Tomcat Tattletail – and he told a, to him, perhaps surprising number of them – the Legendarian could barely conceal his loathing for the disturbingly recurring, hence supposedly faerie, panpipe-playing troubadour. The Tethys-deemed slime bucket, who could get beyond the Dome via beehive Tholoi or Ghost Houses with Brainrock hearthstones, generally chose to look like a commonly perceived form of Thrygragos Everyman in here.

(As such, especially when she followed him to the Outer Earth like a lovesick puppy, he had caused the divine Harmony all kinds of trouble; reportedly caused the 30-Year Man more than a few premature deaths as well. Which doubly explained the loathing – Tethys had a *'thing'* for Datong Harmonia; most men did.

(However, far from being Judge Druj, the Smiling Fiend – who had a pair the panpipes for his power focus, Morg now recalled – Jordy thought Tomcat was what had become of his half-father, Rumour of Lazareme, after faeries ate him circa 4000 YD. What he'd think if he knew the truth … well, there was no point even speculating was there.)

"Now I am disappointed I won't remember anything you say after you're gone. Still, there's nothing new about that is there. At least I won't lose any sleep over it. Departure, so long as it's immediate, is a commendable notion. I need Golgotha awake. The Thanatoids want Ringleader and by now they're mightily miffed at me as well. So unless you'd care to take them both on, you better get out of here, Judge."

"They aren't the only ones. And I mean that both ways. I wanted Dr Zeross myself, for cartage purposes, and I'm none too pleased with you having him drugged. He's dead useless to me that way. However, now that you've seen fit to pop by so unexpectedly, it occurs to me your one-armed thrall can be equally useful. Where is he?"

"Right here." She tapped the button on the right breast pocket of her pantsuit-demon.

Having a knack for faerie-tricksterism was good. Having a superior mind to go with an empty eyeorb that had been atop the Master's Mace only a few hours earlier was better. He'd escape. He always did. He didn't anticipate it would be so quickly. Nor did he expect he'd still be effectively stuck where he was as soon as he did.

He knew where all the Brainrock had gone. It was coming this way. Where were all the Haddazurs when you needed them? Of course! They were with where-all-the-Brainrock-had-gone. Not long now. He self-counselled patience. He did that a lot. No one else would listen to him. No one else would remember listening to him, make that.

Morgianna smiled. She couldn't move much more than her smile muscles, such as they were, but she was a hybrid-Utopian. She could be possessed.

========

"'Morg's a morgue'," Golgotha read aloud sometime later.

========

"'Chances are she's in league with devils but she's definitely in league with the Dead. Her one-armed man's how she brings in demons. He's Gypsium-gifted; uses mirrors to get away. There's an Irache following him around between-space; she brings him the mirrors. I saw her on Dustmound. She's lively for a Dead Thing; looks to be good with a knife. Beware. Also be well.'

"'Having a wonderful time in Cabalarkon. Hope to see you all alive and healthy again someday soon.'"

The clone folded up the paper in disgust. "Jordy's such a coward," he muttered. "The least he could do is come through and draw up someone who might do us some good."

"It seems you've done us some good," said one of his men. In the absence of Demios Sarpedon, all the Utopian Trinondevs were his men again. "And he did save the Master."

"There is that, I suppose. Got an opinion, Yehudi?"

========

At the same time Diego de Landa was first reading out loud the far-sent message from the Legendarian to everyone in the command tent, the Trinondev with them there, and indeed every other Trinondev on Sraddha Isle, was receiving far-spoken orders from Saladin Devason via their eyeorbs. Ergo, Sal was alive. Unless it was a trick – who could be sure anymore?

The Master wanted the elder Sarpedons apprehended at all costs. He wanted them held in brain-bulbs until Ringleader woke up, whereupon he wanted Rings to bring them to the Weirdom of Cabalarkon. Jordan Tethys couldn't transport anyone conscious without their expressed permission and would refuse to transport anyone deliberately rendered unconscious for just that utility. It was the Master's far-spoken commands that snapped Golgotha awake.

He threw off the Ghast as if was just a king-sized bed sheet. Whereupon, much to both his astonishment and trepidation, he discovered Morgianna was in the room with him. So was Alastor Molorchus, ditto both. He looked like he'd just awakened from a deep sleep. Yeah, right. Maybe in a coffin. Golgotha believed Molorchus was Sangazur-animated, a Dead Thing Walking. No Pani was that pale-skinned; not even the albinos among them.

Moreover, the bandage around his head was as clean as it had been earlier in the day. Which was when he and some of his group leaders had met with the Sarpedons and Morgianna suggested Molorchus could accomplish the same thing Ringleader could because he generated his own Gypsium. Didn't he ooze, didn't he even sweat? Not if he was dead, he didn't. What was the bandage covering anyways? A trepan bore-hole through the crown of his skull?

The overhead lamp as well as his reading light were on. Morgianna had her back to him. She was laying Andaemyn out on the couch; appeared to be putting something, a witch-charm perhaps, in a pocket of Andy's pyjama top. The one-armed man was standing behind the couch. Golgotha knew about Morg's pantsuit-demon. He'd seen Molorchus with her on Dustmound before they were introduced this afternoon. It was six of one and a half-dozen of the other. One of them had to go before he could get to the other one. It had to be her thrall.

There was maybe ten feet between them; easily within range. He had him in a mind-globe visibly detached from his eye-stave; leapt to his feet. With a two-handed swing of his stave he thereby slammed the globe, the one-armed man inside it, telekinetically against the wall. Did it again. He had Morg's attention now. For a hybrid who was only twenty years younger than him, the Morrigan was wicked-witch-quick. Something came at him, a Ghast of the Grey. He had no choice except to release Molorchus and suck it into his suddenly open eyeorb.

A Ghast, even a Ghast of the Grey, a psychopomp, was reasonably compact. There should still be room for a pantsuit-demon. Figuring Molorchus a non-issue he concentrated on stripping it off her. There was a flash. Morg was momentarily bathed in the telltale luminescence of Godstuff. She was akin to the Master; was his sister. One of her fists was an eyeorb. Her resolve proved stronger than his. Figuratively reversing the tables, she had him encased in a brain-bulb of her own conjuring.

How embarrassing, he thought to himself, as she started asphyxiating him. You really are too old for all this aggravation. Ringleader, Dr Aristotle Zeross, was lying drugged on the bed. Some of his rings flickered ever so briefly. He rolled over. The selfsame some of his rings weren't there anymore.

"Damnation, clone," she shrieked at him. "You have no idea of the stakes here. Be thankful I need you to guard Andy while I'm away. Get up, Al. Get me out of here. Anywhere will do. Then find yourself a mirror and take yourself there. I'll be waiting."

Alastor Molorchus clambered clumsily to his feet. His eyes glazed over. The Diver was behind him; one hand evidently inside the one-armed man's head. He had been in the room all along, intangibly inside Ringleader. He'd blipped. Far from the lifesaver Fish convinced him it was, he was becoming worried he was starting to blip – go limp, blank and insubstantial, half in-space, half between it – due to exposure to Gypsium.

He extracted his hand; gave the one-armed man a none-too-gentle shove forward. Said: '*Timber*'. Molorchus hit the floor like a toppled lapdog of a log. Might have bounced a bit. He dove at Morgianna, grabbed hold of her eye-fist with both hands. There was enough Brainrock in her eye-fist to give him an additional charge. He didn't blip; couldn't afford to, his willpower wasn't want-power.

She had fingers again. He was all over her. She couldn't be possessed due to her ensorcelled Hellstones. The Diver was as ravenous as a Gypsium junkie without having to go in search of his next fix. Which was when and how Smiler managed to possess her. The Diver didn't realize that. Golgotha, Black Skull-Face, cried a warning.

The one-armed man was with it already. That wasn't right. The Diver had pulled the same stunt dozens of times pre- and post-Limbo. Molorchus should be out cold. Instead, he was on his knees; had twisted his body such that his rotator cuff was pointing at the Diver and Morgianna. Golgotha's open eye-orb was focused on Molorchus. Something came out of him. He pitched forward again. This time he didn't even twitch.

"Gotcha, you Sang bastard." The clone ejected the eyeorb. Grabbed for his rucksack, needed another eyeorb. Smiler figured he was in for an instant extraction. He felt Morg blank. The Diver had hit her. Past time someone did; she'd been a meddlesome Morrigan of late. If they didn't strip her of her demon, he should be safe behind it and within her.

The door shattered. More Trinondevs, at least their eyeorbs were closed. Morg's pantsuit-demon, which wasn't just her clothes, which covered her head, hair and exposed skin as well, acted as a kind of insulation. It prevented the prison-pods from detecting him; from opening automatically and taking him out of her.

Witch-stones activated. War Witches led by Garcia Dis L'Orca came off them. They looked alive; looked enraged as well. Garcia had a satchel slung over one shoulder; had a shotgun in her hands. She aimed it at him; at Morg, rather. Two barrels fired point-blank, was even a pantsuit-demon that impenetrable?

For Smiler, right this second, patience wasn't a virtue. It was a necessity.

========

"Opinions I've got in spades," the Untouchable Diver, Yehudi Cohen, responded.

========

"What I don't have is four of my seemingly forever-companions. Nor do I have the foggiest flapdoodle what to do next. Maybe you should ask ball-girl there, Skull-Face."

Ball-girl was Morgianna. The Trinondevs had encased her in thought-balloons; balls of them. There were balls around her hands, balls around her head, around her legs, her feet, her toes, her breasts. There were even balls around her fingertips. According to Dis L'Orca, who'd gone off her boss-bitch big time, Morg's nail polish was as dangerous as her pantsuit-demon. The more Trinondevs came into Ringleader's quarters, the more balls they projected about her.

She wasn't necessarily Public Enemy Number One but, in the absence of her husband, she was the Public Enemy they had. That they also had Alastor Molorchus, who hadn't moved since Golgotha took the Sang out of him, was a bonus. At least he hadn't instantly started to smell. He was encased in balls anyhow.

Poor, fractured, still unconscious, Andaemyn was encased in balls. The Trinondevs were having themselves a ballgame. Ringleader was snoring. Garcia Dis L'Orca was fuming. Morg was conscious. They hadn't stripped her of her pantsuit-demon yet. They had taken away Dis L'Orca's shotgun, however. Which might be most of the reason why she was fuming.

"First ask her why she allied herself with the Dead," she said. "No, skip that. We know that already. She thought Second Fangs had the Amateramirror. Or knew where it was. Ask her instead how she overcame our training. Athenans are defenders of life. We're taught to kill ourselves rather than chance being taken and turned. Even if a Sang gets hold of one of us, it can't negate our training. We're taught to mutilate ourselves to the point of uselessness even to an azura. Besides, our goddess would never allow it."

"You're not a Utopian, Garcia," countered Morgianna, once Golgotha had one of his men relax the thought-balloon such that she could speak.

"Even so, no War Witch, dead or alive, should ever kill another War Witch."

"Why ask me when the answer's a shotgun-sandwich away?" smirked Morg.

"What's that supposed to mean?"

"Kill yourself and find out."

"Why's she smirking?" wondered St Peche-Montressor, the Janna in the notso-much-so-crowded-anymore room with them. Golgotha had been issuing instructions. Trinondevs had been coming and going. War Witches had been too, though not before they'd one-by-one emptied Dis L'Orca's satchel of whatever it contained.

"I mean, she is smirking, isn't she?" St Peche-Montressor had one of the things Garcia's satchel had contained as well. "I know it's almost impossible to tell with pureblood Utopian women but Morg's a mixed-blood. If she isn't smirking then at the very least she's smiling."

"She's smiling," confirmed the Diver, who'd known Superior Sarpedon long pre-Limbo. Something buzzed him. Reflexively he stuck out his fist, de-particlyzed it, his fist, re-particlyzed it, killed himself a Tinkerbell.

Said: "Hope that was okay."

========

"Don't worry, UD. I'll make an ash of her when I get the chance." Young Death was back in the land of the Living on Sraddha Isle. The monastery's alarms went off distractingly.

The Morrigan smiled so broadly she swallowed herself.

****

(ENDGAME-GAMBIT) 26:   **Psycho Soul Grenades**

Mithrada, Tantalar 8, 5980

The flying gunship carrying General Quentin Anvil, along with the two helicopters he'd assigned to accompany his chopper, got off cleanly. The general had the best pilot in the business with him. The other two didn't; didn't fare so well either. Nergal Vetala and her soldier, her golden-brown warrior, her Attis, could walk on the air. He did more. He ran across the sky, blowing apart first one then another helicopter with OMP-Akbar's Homeworld Sceptre.

He was going for the third one when its pilot dipped it low, toward the Lake's surface. It exploded upon impact. Everyone on it successfully leapt off first. All of them could swim. Some of them might even make it to shore. Just as in the expansive moat surrounding the Bloodlands' Sanguerre, Lake Sedona had freshwater, mono-horned sharks.

Fisherwoman and her aquatics removal crews only concentrated on Dead Things.

========

Led by once again Field Commander Golgotha Nauroz, two truncated units of more than a dozen Trinondevs collectively formed a shape like a flying ant with its black-as-midnight body divided into head, thorax and abdomen. It had two antennae off the head, six legs off the underside of the thorax, and a pair of wings off the upper side of the thorax. It soared into the night's sky. Ignoring her soldier, the Trinondevs guided their thus not so much so rampant as motivated gargoyle straight for Nergal Vetala.

Golgotha and one of his group leaders reached their eye-staves out of the mental-energy-made-manifest enclosing Weir's Warriors Elite. The eye-staves became the ant-gargoyle's antennae. The orbs at their tips opened; a single, disembodied eye poked out of each antenna on prehensile tendrils. They focused on the Vampire Queen. She felt her devic eye bulge as if it was about to burst out of her forehead. She struggled to close it, abolishing dozens more of her azuras in the process.

Two more Trinondevs stuck their eye-staves out of the ant-gargoyle in place of its front legs. Two more disembodied eyes poked out. Before they could focus on Vetala, her soldier was on the scene, racing on the air, blipping into and out of sight like the self-psychopomp he'd become. Swinging Akbar's sceptre like a baseball bat, he swatted the exposed staves. They snapped like toothpicks.

The communal gargoyle momentarily faltered. The golden-brown warrior brought his stolen sceptre against it. The Trinondevs inside were rocked but the chitin-like exterior of their mental manifestation didn't crack. Another blow and it might. Golgotha and his collective retreated to Sraddha Isle.

The Vampire Queen mind-to-mind commanded her soldier to carry on; to take the Utopians out one by one if necessary. She didn't care if he killed them or not; she had oodles of others to finish them off, ones whose only real skill was killing. What she wanted him to do was destroy the prison pods atop their eye-staves.

Extraterrestrial devices from Old Weir, they were designed to automatically capture and hold onto devils indefinitely. Unexpectedly, they could also confine their azuras. It wasn't automatic. They had to concentrate on doing so, but they could, and that could prove catastrophic for her. Although she had thousands left, they were spread throughout Hadd and she was loathe to waste anymore of hers here than necessary.

Her azuras weren't just what kept her Dead Things moving. After all she'd been through these past three or four days; they were what was keeping her going. Had been, in all likelihood, for the over thirty-five years prior to her spanking new, or renewed, Attis falling out of the sky last Sedonda and Cloud General Kronar finding him for her.

She'd seen how Nowadays Nihila dealt with eyeorbs on Dustmound: Gypsium channelled via her chains in the form of lightning strikes. Without the Susasword, which was keeping the former quintessence of exquisiteness out of her just as exquisite hair, she was afraid her Attis lacked such a handy-dandy distance-delivery system. From what she'd seen of it, Akbar's sceptre worked best with contact. Still, with the Amateramirror full-up, and therefore useless except as a shield, she trusted the Crimson Corona would come up with something.

Obediently, the evidently undying neo-demigod sped after them. Vetala telepathically ordered her vulturous Cloud General to have his Vultyrie and their Sangazur-animated riders come out of the sky's non-vulturous cloud-covering and trail in his wake, shooting out the too bright spotlights and strafing the ramparts from high above. She hadn't been able to gather more of the Forbidden Forest's Indescribables in one place such that her Attis could transport them to Sraddha Isle. For some reason, Kala Tal, her spidery litter sister, had blocked access to her protectorate.

Neither had she brought in any more regular Haddit Zombies to aid in this assault. That was a strategic decision dictated by the presence of so many Trinondevs already on the island. However, ever since dusk she'd been having her bats-of-burden vampires, the ones that carried Dead Things from place to place when Janna Fangfingers was acting as her regent, collect as many of them as they could into one massive army.

For the time being it was centred on Diminished Dustmound. After her experience with the Thanatoids and Silverclouds, she figured the sheer preponderance of ambulant Dead Things in one place should thereby render it her inviolable protectorate. However, once she'd acquired what she came here to acquire, she'd also have herself a rapid deployment unit.

She reckoned she had something better than demons or regular Dead Things for tonight's assault anyways: the berserker attack-bats Second Fangs had been intentionally starving for weeks in preparation for a night like this. Bloodlust-blind, butchery was foremost in their minds. Tonight's anticipated slaughter wouldn't be indiscriminate, though. They were to target Utopians, anyone with black or black and white striped skin, anyone who had an eye-stave.

Her psycho-bats were similarly tasked. She drifted back, not wishing to expose herself to the Trinondevs and their eye-staves again. The psycho-bats didn't. They went into the Weird; came out inside the ant-gargoyle. Externally it had been black-as-midnight. Abruptly it became white-as-daylight. Primarily that was because that was what it was, internally lit-up. It was a set-up. Golgotha wasn't afraid of repeating himself.

Brain-bulbs as lightbulbs. You couldn't – more like shouldn't or, better yet, daren't – make them go incendiary in such close quarters but incandescence was just as effective. As expected so were the Godbadian-manufactured eye-shields. The Trinondevs who came out of their consequently dissolving ant-gargoyle atop the monastery's fortifications emerged blinking, singed and thoroughly covered in dust.

Had they been in Petrograd, a onetime Weirdom where Ferdinand Niarchos lived and sort of ruled as the duly elected governor of New Iraxas, they could have pocketed a sizeable bounty from the Fatman's Centauri Enterprises. So long as they could somehow verify not so much that it was vampire dust as how many vampires said dust once constituted, that is.

(CE, as it was generally known, was currently trying to green-up New Iraxas, the subcontinent's sole petroleum-producing province now that Fish and her self-preservative Piscines had forced it to shut down its Gulf of Aka facilities. Greening it up, not just Ferd's argument went, would render it safe for ordinary men and women to work there, thus eliminating the need for Dead Things and their vampiric overseers.)

They weren't in Godbad, however. They were alive, though. For now.

========

Perhaps neither of them should have gone back into action right away. Certainly they had no intention of doing so when they returned from Diminished Dustmound to Sraddha Isle, leaving the Susasword where it was, still attached to Vetala's Brainrock throne. Once bitten, twice shy, and all that aphoristic claptrap in a crab-trap.

Not that Fish had been bitten as such.

========

Brainrock was teleportive. The energy blade, due to the volition of whomsoever or whatsoever, had gone through her Vesica Piscis, her bellybutton bauble. It went out of her back into Demios Sarpedon. Chary sort that he was, he'd encased himself in a thought-balloon before he took her hand and went with her from the monastery. Regrettably, even with the oldest eye-stave in existence, he couldn't quite deflect it away from himself harmlessly.

Both suffered a consciousness-robbing rush but he'd also suffered a nasty gash in his left side. Fish's Vesica Piscis had once been a devic power focus. The energy blade hadn't even touched her. Or, if it had, it was just with its radiance. Time passed, awareness returned. She was tending to his wound. She looked positively lustrous with vitality. Despite his non-arterial blood loss, he didn't feel too hard done by himself. Maybe Gypsium-Godstuff, having failed to kill him, had decided to reinvigorate him instead. Psycho-bicycle was next.

They returned to the monastery the same way they'd left it, via between-space; came back to the same place as well, Ringleader's quarters. The clangour was approaching deafening. The monastery had to be under attack. Times had changed since they'd been away. Rings (Dr Aristotle Zeross, Harry, the Gypsium-gifted supra once codenamed Kid Ringo) was still snoozing on his bed. Now, though, Demios's daughter, Andaemyn Sarpedon, was lying as if dead on the couch. She was encased in a mind-globe. So was Morg's one-armed man, Alastor Molorchus; only he was being held aloft, above the floor. Someone had torn off his head-bandage.

Were both of them as drugged as Rings had been? By the same person, too. They could ask her. She, Garcia Dis L'Orca, was there. Except, for some reason, she was enclosed in a mind-globe. They could have asked Young Death what was going on. Only he was as well.

Three of Garcia's War Witches weren't; their guns were drawn, however. Five of Golgotha's Trinondevs were also there. Presumably four of them were maintaining the brain-bulbs while the other one, like the Athenans, was on Ringleader guard duty. Bar none, the person they wanted to ask what was happening was the Untouchable Diver.

It took a couple of minutes to get around to it.

========

"Pretender," cried the unoccupied Trinondev, spotting Sarpedon and Fish, minus her Mandroid psychopomp, materializing out of the Weird. He was promptly encased in his own brain-bulb, projected off his own eye-stave. The ones encasing Andaemyn, Young Death, Garcia and Molorchus dropped the globes in which they were holding them. Then their globes dropped over them, the Trinondevs.

"Five at once," said Fish. "Splish-splash-splendid, Demios."

"Best I've overridden at the same time is ten. Psycho-bicycle chains?" He was referring to the three War Witches. Their weapons were across the floor. They were on the floor, chained to each other.

"Nothing bottom-feeding about soul-selves. Not to a top of the food-chain witch."

Garcia was on the floor, trying to catch her breath. It was hard to breathe inside a mind-globe. So was Molorchus, on the floor. He wasn't trying to catch his breath. He was dead to the world due to the fact he was plain dead. Underneath where his head-bandage had been earlier in the day was a noticeable hole in his foreskull. It wasn't a trepan bore-hole. It was a veritable fissure made by a large calibre bullet. Auguste Moirnoir, Young Death, was reaching for a cigar. The Diver must have dove into the floorboards; was nowhere to be seen. The alarms kept on ringing. Ringleader kept on snoring. Andy kept on breathing.

"Scum out, scum out, wherever you are, Diver," said Fish.

"You two first," came a man's voice from Ringleader's bed. It wasn't Ringleader's voice.

The illusionary forms of Fisherwoman and Demios Sarpedon vanished. "Like some anchovy-answers first," she said. Her voice also seemed to be coming from Ringleader's bed.

"Oh, for fuck's sake, you assholes," said Young Death, lighting his cigar. "We're all on the same side here. It's Mommy Morg that's been dealing with the Dead."

"And betraying our goddess in the process," agreed Garcia, getting to her feet. She raised her hand; had something in it. It was a Crystal Skull. "And this is how."

The mind-globe encasing the chief Trinondev lowered such that it uncovered his head, allowing him to speak. "The Master's alive, traitor. He's ordered you arrested. Young Death, your daughter, the dead man and the rogue Athenan, they belong to you filthy Sarpedons. Field Commander Nauroz wants them held until he can deal with them. Your Morrigan of a wife got away. If you're going to kill us get it over with."

"He's right to a point," said the Diver, playing one of his famous hunches and rolling out of Ringleader's sleeping body, where he'd gone in case he had to get Harry away in a hurry. More of Zeross's rings had vanished but the Diver looked solid enough. Unlike Fish he couldn't cast glamours, verbal or visual. "Skull-Face doesn't trust any of them. I'm not sure he even trusts me. He said I better stay here and look after Rings. Left me here with five Trinondevs and three War Witches to look after me, I'm thinking.

"Vetala's Soldier is Rings' nephew. He's leading the attack on the island. He's a bad one, a veritable Gypsium Man, and I'm having trouble metabolizing Gypsium. I keep blipping."

"Blipping?" came a voice out of the walls. It was Demios's voice. Somehow Fish must be scrambling it to disguise where they were between-space.

"Don't know how to describe it any better, Ace. Physically I'm half-here, half-there, in and out of between-space, but mentally I'm more like passed out or asleep. This sort of thing happened one other time, in early '47, just after I helped Magus Maxius and the rest sort Davy out, make him Cerebrus. I retired then; stayed mostly out of action for the better part of the next five years. Which was when so many of us, you, your wife, even Fish there, got sucked into that SDL mess. Now it's happening again, after twenty-five years in Limbo and back barely a week."

Magus Maxius was a long dead Scottish supranormal, a Summoning Child like so many of them. He'd suffered a nasty fall in early 1938. Actually, thanks to her uncle, like Andy had today on the plain just below Dustmound, it was more of a drop than a fall. It left him a quadriplegic. In the late Thirties and early Forties, Codename Illuminatus (Melina born Sarpedon now Zeross) acted as his nurse.

Davy was David Ryne, Cyborg Cerebrus, D-Brig's erstwhile leader. He hadn't been dead when they left him in Cabalarkon with Wilderwitch and Gloriel on Devauray but he might be by now. The SDL was the Supranormal Defense League. Davy's cousin, Jesus Mandam, the Conquering Christ (once Barsine Holgat-wife's thought-twin, though it turned out they might not even have had the same father, let alone the same mother), wanted supras to go public.

Although Fish was already back beneath the Dome by then, in September of 1952 he called together every known supranormal, active or inactive, even ones who had been redacted (had their memories reedited such that they believed they had always been a Normie or Norma Normalman), to do just that. Under the SDL's banner the gathering took place in Vancouver, British Columbia, Canada. They never did go public.

"It's getting to the point where I'm afraid to use my abilities; afraid using them will kill me. Can't re-retire yet, though. Furie, Sundown, Raven, OMP, they're stuck in the prick's mirror. I've got one of your oceans of notions I can get them out. Hell, I know I can get them out. We three go up there, just the three of us, we've a shot. It'll be just like the old days."

"Demios?" That was Fish's voice, from somewhere. The Diver hated talking to air.

"I'm up for it. Watch out for my daughter, Trinondev. Anything happens to her, I'll be dealing with you."

"Gush, Garcia," Fish again. "Stay out of the piranha pool. We survive the dive, we're going to have worms of words. Get your ass in gear, Diver. Time to polish off a mirror."

"God, I love it when she doesn't fishify." The Diver dove upwards. Into the ceiling and kept on going.

========

The Trigregos Titan strode the battlements.

========

The first Trinondev he encountered raised a protective force field. Guided by the Crimson Corona, he did not try to blow it apart. Rather, when he clubbed it with Akbar's sceptre, he had it absorb its energy. Worked too. He grabbed the eye-stave from the startled Trinondev with his free hand, the one that once wore First Fangs' Brainrock glove; the hand the forearm of which the Amateramirror was attached. With just as blinding speed, he bopped the orb atop it unto powder, banged the stave against the Utopian's head for fun, dropped it and walked on by.

As the semi-dazed Trinondev fumbled to pull out a replacement eyeorb from his rucksack he was shot dead from above. Significantly he didn't rise anew. Vetala was nowhere to be seen, could be hiding in the clouds. Two hundred plus Trinondevs on the island, a dozen prison-pods each, an afternoon and evening of them, Weir's Warriors Elite, sweeping the monastery and the tunnels beneath it with open eyeorbs. Do the math. Golgotha really was a cagey old codger.

Three more Trinondevs confronted the golden-brown warrior. They'd been well instructed on what to do. They bombarded the Amateramirror with mind-generated energy beams then levitated away to be replaced by three more who did the same thing. They were trying to break out the four members of the Damnation Brigade held within the mirror and they were almost succeeding. He found himself concentrating on keeping the remnants of the Brigade within it. Additional Warriors of Weir in dyed-indigo robes, veils drawn, assaulted him from behind. It was as if they were seeking him out instead of the other way around.

Again guided by the Corona, he waited until at least twenty Trinondevs were surrounding him then slammed the head of Supreme's sceptre into the ground. Bolts of energy burst every which way. All were directed into the orbs atop the eye-staves. They were deadening bolts. The disembodied eyes drooped down on their tendrils, dulled though not expelled. He let the Trinondevs flee, humiliated but unharmed. Until, that is, the attack-bats came a-slaughtering.

Atop the ramparts, where strobe-lights were still flashing without any perceptibly detrimental effect, particularly on the berserker-bats, groups of left-behind

Godbadians, War Witches and brown-robed, shaven-headed Sraddhites were clustered around Godbadian gun-emplacements. It was as if cannons, machine guns and missile launchers were as much sacred objects to them as the two he was wearing. Much of the artillery had protective metal-plating over its top and to its anterior. Besides as shielding they were using the emplacements to blast the vulturous Cloud of Hadd out of the sky.

He waded through them from behind; began pounding armaments into slag. The guns silenced, living Vultyrie swooped lower. The desire for vengeance overcoming caution, Sangazur-animated Dead Things jumped off them. He left them fighting furiously with those of Living who still were among the living. Brown Robes seemed to relish melee conditions. He went looking for more Trinondevs and their toothpicks for eye-eggs.

Something drove into him; crashed into him. He barely noticed it. A woman hopped off it, vanished. It was, he decided, some sort of flying jet-ski. It was crushed. It was mashed. It had tentacles, like a gelatinous octopus. It was crusting him. He raised Akbar's Homeworld Sceptre in order to smash it into smithereens. A brain-bulb formed around his arm. There, over there, an out-of-uniform Trinondev encased in his own though-balloon. It was as much a matter of strength of mind as it was a literal arm-wrestle for his arm and Akbar's sceptre.

Something dove into him, a man in a wetsuit wearing crimson-lens goggles. He'd wondered what had become of the Diver on Dustmound earlier in the day. He wasn't wondering where he was now. There was a flash, he flashed. The Diver had a thing for Brainrock, his Brainrock. Then he was in a struggle for his other arm, the one on which he'd strapped the Amateramirror. The Diver was trying to breakout his friends.

The woman was back. She had an oversized fishhook, a fisher's gaffe: a fisher-woman's gaffe. She gaffed him in the head. She was trying to rip off the Crimson Corona along with the top of his skull. Her octopus, it was inside him; it was trying to eat him from the inside. Its suckers were toothy orifices.

He … needed … more … Brainrock.

========

No more talking walls.

========

The five Trinondevs and three War Witches were able to move again. The alarms kept on ringing. Ringleader kept on snoring. Andy kept on breathing. Garcia stepped on a witch-stone and was gone. Young Death was just as gone. Momentarily thereafter the Trinondevs were as well. As were the War Witches. Finally, so was Ringleader, bed, blankets and remaining rings. Blankets were particularly welcome where he was going.

"Where'd Morg have you send him, Al?" queried a voice from behind him. The one-armed man turned slowly, making sure he could position the rotator cuff of his missing arm in the direction of the voice, which sounded vaguely familiar to him.

Barsine Mandam was sitting on the edge of the couch. That was why the voice sounded familiar to him. Even with fangs, morbidly pale skin and a third eye, she looked super for someone who had been dead for thirty-five years. He supposed she would be caught dead wearing something that revealing after all. Of course thirty-five years ago Alastor Molorchus might have been all of seven and living on Aegean Trigon.

"Sorry," he apologized. "But I can only hold onto one dead thing at time."

"Oh, I get it. You're not Al. You're what's-his-name, Gush, the Morrigan's Young Daddy Death, right?"

"You have me at a disadvantage. Have we had the pleasure?"

"I'll have my answer first."

"Lathakra, if you have to know. A little girl wanted her daddy. Wanted to kill me herself, too. Which I didn't think was appropriate. So I did a deal with a devil. King Chicken-Shit Cold couldn't bring himself to kill me himself so he had one of his snowmen do it for him. I was gradually freezing to death anyhow so an icicle spear up the Ying-Yang was a welcome relief. Hardly felt it actually. Wouldn't, would I? I was mostly bum-numb by then."

"The devils you say. Shame that. Those rings of his looked ever so useful this morning. Trinondevs to the left of me, Trinondevs to the right of me, teleport-holes beneath them and off they go into the wild blue yonder. I really will have to do something about those irritating Thanatoids someday. Guess you'll do for now."

Alastor Molorchus had never been to the Prison Beach of Incain. Young Death had. All, Incain's self-proclaimed invincible She-Sphinx, devoured devils. She, the Mandroid Monster Maker, also held onto something devils referred to as the Unnameable but he knew to call Demogorgon. It was a conglomerate devil; conglomerate because, if the stories he'd heard were at all accurate, it had earned its other name long before Dark Sedon raised the Cathonic Zone out of his own essence 5,980 years earlier. Its other name was Devil Eater.

He, via the one-armed man, let her have it; sent her there. It occurred to him Incain would be a good place for her soldier as well. All the Invincible was also known as the Mandroid Mother Machine. Mandroids smothered Brainrock. He hoped she was hungry. He ran out of the room. Molorchus was no self-psychopomp and there was no readily reflective mirror in sight. The alarms kept on ringing; the clangour was deafening. Andy kept on breathing, with no one left to guard her.

Except perhaps for a dead, semi-soulless Irache warrior woman sheltered between-space off a witch stone her Mama Morg left in one of her pyjamas top's breast pockets.

========

Young Death knew his tunnels; sent them there. Five Trinondevs and three War Witches found themselves in those tunnels. It was dark. Brain-bulbs as lightbulbs; eye-eggs could be incandescent. Five were incandescent. Gush's workforce, Haddit Zombies the lot of them, were lying dead to the world everywhere they walked. They weren't getting up again either.

This was new. The Athenans tossed away their bullet-pellets. They'd had enough. No cannon fodder them. They took their time walking out. A pair of them, a Trinondev and a Samarandin, took even more time before they emerged deep beneath the monastery's ziggurat. Nine months later, they hoped, the world, either side of it, would welcome yet another Zebranid. Or two. Maybe even three.

So much for the uneaten eight. Young Death was a good guy.

========

He got it too, the Brainrock. The one-armed man was on the scene. Was that the Crimson Corona on his forehead, just below the bullet-hole. Had she turned traitor again? How could he be on his feet with a hole in the head that size? Then again how could he, a week ago Cosmicaptain Dmetri Diomad, still be on his feet?

Unless of course he had never been Dem's Dim, just looked like him.

========

Trickster within him, Molorchus did his G-string-thing. Vetala's Soldier took it in, atomized the psycho-cephalopod with the tentacle-mouths where its suckers should have been. More. Molorchus obliged. He won the three-against-one tug-of-war; repulsed them all. The Diver blipped; Fish turtled; Demios staggered backwards, the wound in his side bleeding again. More. The one-armed man gave him all he had left. The Crimson Corona was back on his head. He wanted it there; no traitor her. He vanished. That, he hadn't wanted.

Young Death fell out of Alastor Molorchus. The one-armed man was draped in darkness; his face all that was visible. It wasn't his face. It was pinkish; had three eyes. He was smiling.

"Not bad for mortals. Take a memo, Morg. Invite to coronation."

========

Clams have legs. Clams have eyes. Clams have antennae. Clams have two antennae. Clams have an eye at the end of each of their two antennae. Everyone grew tired of Fish's interminable fishisms eventually. Equally so, everyone eventually told Fish to clam up. Twisted sister that she was, she didn't clam up. She turtled instead. Her Vesica Piscis, her bellybutton bauble, was shaped like a clam. She turtled inside it, between-space.

Turtle-shelled as she was, it developed legs and antennae, with eyes at the end of them, the antennae. Ommatophores, that was the word for stalks terminating in eyes. Antennae, ants, Antheans, that was fishily funny. She wasn't thinking right. Came with extending so much of your psyche into your latest psychopomp, even if it was a metamorphic Mandroid, her psycho-bicycle, then having it atomized. Oh well-the-seashell, her soul-self hadn't altogether atomized with it.

Wait a minnow-minute. That was Judge Warlock, wasn't it? Couldn't be. She knew who Judge Warlock was, the Outer Earth's last living Sed-son; knew where he was as well. Someone else must have got hold of his Daemonicus form. Someone else who just happened to have three eyes? Too late to ask him. He'd just vanished. Young Death, you idiot. I told you to stay out of the piranha pool. Berserker bats, rabid rampant. Catch you later, Gush. Good spurt that. Claws must have hit an artery. They would. Throats had arteries.

A turtle's shell bore a superficial similarity to a flying saucer. Her protective covering was akin to a razor-clam. Flying saucer, razor-clam, Vesica Piscis once a devil's power focus, Brainrock-Gypsium was teleportive, berserker bats had spotted Demios, the wound in his side had opened again. Blood drew bloodsuckers. It was her, flying saucer razor-clam flying-Fish, to the rescue. When it came to dusting vamps Godstuff, applied invasively, beat silver or wood any night of the week.

"I've got him, Fish," said the Diver, who recognized a flying saucer razor-clam when he saw one. He did too. Hadn't blipped for long; couldn't afford to blip for even the few seconds he had. He'd spotted Demios in trouble just as she had. Had thought to himself that it would be nice to be able to get to Sarpedon in time to prevent him going the way of the Black Death, as he remembered Young Death, as Auguste Moirnoir.

Thought and was there, just in time to render Blackguard, the Ace of Spades, Sarpedon's two supra-codenames, intangible. He could do that, virtually always could. He'd never teleported all by his lonesome before; not that he could recall at any rate. Seems he could do that now. Metabolizing Gypsium had radically amplified his abilities. About time he was good for something besides being dispatched by devils and one-armed men.

Attack-bats attacked in packs. Fish only buzz-sawed through three of the four berserkers attacking Sarpedon. The fourth one passed through Demios-Diver, their dual selves, as if they were ghosts. It whirled just as Fish, whirring, dusted its fellows. It looked very confused. The Diver took the vamp's look to be confusion, rather. It was a reasonable supposition. Demios was momentarily confused himself. After more than a quarter-century of not seeing the Diver in action he'd forgotten most of what he could do.

Attack-bats were only partially humanized. Still had a howsoever expressive bat's face, fur and wings. They didn't wear tuxedos or opera capes but they were human-sized. Pre-Limbo one of the Emperor Mammalian's Manimals looked like an attack-bat. That Manimal wasn't a vampire. He did feed on blood, though.

Many of the Manimals were carnivores. No surprise there. Some of them were hunters. Nothing wrong with that. It was what they sometimes hunted that was wrong. Supranormals weren't supposed to kill. They were allowed to defend themselves, naturally. Fish, Moirnoir, Blind Sundown, Raven's Head, Sorciere, Slipper, they were among the supras who defended themselves lethally. And consequently lived to tell the tale.

Sarpedon caught it in a brain-bulb. He knew a variety of ways to vanquish vamps; could do it with both ends of his eye-stave sooth said, as fays might say. Brain-bulb as a lightbulb, why not? So what if it was Golgotha's idea, if it meant one less attack-bat he was all for it. It did. Golgotha always was a bright light, ha-ha.

A Vultyrie plummeted onto the ramparts. It must have been shot down by a War Witch, a Brown Robe or one of the Godbadians who hadn't been evacuated. Young Death tumbled out of it. A Sangazur-animated Dead Thing was pinned underneath it; was trying to free his gun-hand, gun with it. Young Death tumbled into him; had him shoot himself in the head. That hurt humongously but it would at least slow him down.

The voodoo child tumbled out of him, spotted Sarpedon – with two heads, both recognizable. Shouted: "The Sangs, Daddy Dem. Get airborne. Suck them out with your orbs."

"I can't do both," Sarpedon shouted back. His Sarpedon-head shouted back, make that. His other head was wearing crimson-lens Gorgon Goggles and a black, rubbery hood.

"Leave airborne to me," said the Diver one of their two heads.

"You can't fly, Yehudi."

"Maybe not, Ace. But if I can soil-swim, I should be able to sky-swim. Should be able to keep you untouchable at the same time, dick-dildo."

He should, he could, and so he did. So did they. For awhile.

========

Gush rushed across the battlements, leapt into her. He knocked her over; couldn't enter her. What's wrong with this picture?

========

Codename Fisherwoman (ex-Queen Scylla, nowadays nominally Lady Achigan), Thartarre Holgatson and Golgotha Nauroz were nearby, in close proximity to each other. They were observing the fighting more so than participating in it themselves. They saw their collision, not what led up to it. Regardless, this was worth investigating.

Under the umbrella of Golgotha's mind-globe, the three of them scooted to where the other two had fallen. "Stand back," demanded Thartarre, apprehending her condition. "I'll fire her."

"What for?" Garcia Dis L'Orca, whom the Voodoo Child had collided with, cried out anxiously, though not exactly apoplectically. "I'm fine."

"Heart in hand tells a different story," observed the collider, Young Death. "Unless that isn't your heart in your hand."

Fish had told both Dis L'Orca and Young Death to stay out of the piranha pool; which, for her, was longhand to stay out of trouble. Like illusions and glamours, which she seldom used, she wasn't very effective when it came to ordering folks around. She'd been a lousy queen in her day; a lousy lady everyday in terms of lording over anyone. They hadn't paid her any heed.

The forever-seven trickster could force Sangs out of Dead Things. It was one of his more savoury knacks. Could take over the resultantly rendered inanimate corpse and reanimate him or her. Which some folks thought more rude than useful. Had Dis L'Orca been killed? Was that what he'd been trying to do? Gush had been killed at least once that Fish had seen so far tonight. And, if Dis L'Orca hadn't just been killed, then that wasn't her externalized heart she was vainly trying to shove back into her torn-open chest cavity.

"Then why couldn't you get into me?" Garcia put to him.

What twigged him she was dead, presumably had been for quite sometime as well, was the attack-bat. In the main, attack-bats killed first and ate later; much later, unbridled butchery being their re-eminent objective. Having felled her from behind, this particular attack-bat tore Garcia's heart out of her chest and was in the process of having a quick chomp, as if it was an energizing chocolate bar, when the War Witch, albeit without a heart, blasted him point-blank with a shotgun full of silver buckshot. Whereupon she did the same to the next attack-bat who came along.

"What wizardry is this?" gasped Golgotha, over-dramatically. The War Witch had just wholly healed right in front of his eyes. He rephrased his question rhetorically. "Oh, I see. What witchery is this?" Fish first cast a glamour about Garcia. Fish second cast her fishnet about her.

"Sorry, staffs, but there's something fishy here and it's not me." She grabbed Young Death by his neckband, dropped and stepped on a witch-stone. "I'll let you know when I get to the sea-bottom of it. Stay albacore-alert and abalone-alive until then."

With Dis L'Orca netted but not protesting, Young Death squirming like a naughty boy with mom twisting his earlobe, Fish disappeared for the nonce of the night.

========

Moments later the Diver came out of the Grey in front of the Sraddhites' High Priest and the Trinondevs' Field Commander. He still had two heads but the Demios of the two looked ghastly.

"Dem's had the bun, Skull-Face. He's something for you. You can't keep it, though."

The battle continued; wound down as more and more Sangs keeled off their oddly night-flying Vultyrie and didn't get up again. Only now it was Golgotha Nauroz who wielded the oldest eye-stave in existence. It was appropriate in that Ubris Nauroz had gifted it to Sarpedon and Golgotha had been cloned from Ubris Nauroz. Even though the vamps fled as daylight approached, he still hadn't given it back to him.

Demios wouldn't be able to do anything with it for awhile anyways.

========

Thartarre Sraddha Holgatson had the latest casualty lists in front of him. The name of Demios Sarpedon was on one of them. Not as a fatality; as someone borderline.

========

Philosophically, even though she wasn't one for worshipping anyone or anything, Fish was more of a Mother-Earth-oriented Hecate-Hellion than anything else. Hellions hated devils; regarded them as extraterrestrial invaders; which they were. Fallen angel devils had to have fallen from somewhere; had to have been heaven, the heavens. Hellions wanted to eradicate devils. So did the Utopians of Weir.

Although originally extraterrestrials themselves, Utopians therefore had a commonality of cause with Hecate-Hellions. Had had since some seven centuries prior to the Genesea as it happened. Which additionally meant it was unbeknownst to them due to the fact that Utopians (for sure) didn't reach the then Whole Earth until some ten years before the Great Flood of Genesis.

(As preserved by the Lazaremist Librarian, Biblio Drek, in the annals of devazurkind upon the Whole Earth, seven centuries prior to the Genesea was when the Hecate Hellions took half their name from ate Datong Harmonia – albeit, for Harmony, millennia pre-Illuminary-given name as well as pre-daemonic-body-beautiful.

(Presumably as well that meant she had been a half-human, half-demonic hybrid. Indeed, even though it was impossible to verify this, quite possibly that nominal Hecate was an offspring of Primeval Lilith, the Demon Queen of the Night, by Alorus Ptah, the second of the two Biblical Adams, the Golden Age of Humankind's instigative and thus prime Patriarch.)

Morgianna long Sarpedon had been after the Trigregos Talismans seemingly forever. She reasoned that because they could kill devils they should be in the hands of the Head's anti-devil movement. They were also her ticket back to Cabalarkon, where she further believed they could be replicated using the Weirdom's pre-Earth, yet somehow, and only sometimes, still functioning technology. The Master her brother had the same idea.

While she wasn't tight with either born-Nauroz, for years Fish had done her best to dissuade them both of such an ill-omened obsession. She – and not just she – argued nothing good would ever come of having them; nothing ever had. Corona Power, as OMP-Akbar's wife Takeda came to be known on the Outer Earth, had been more maniacal than a mercury-vapour-maddened Mad Hatter and she'd only had the one. For a relatively less recent example, Holgat the husband and Barsine the wife didn't even realize they had one and look what happened to them.

Dependent on which version of '*The Disunition of the Unities*' you heard or read, Unholy Abaddon, the Unity of Chaos, had hold of the Susasword five hundred years ago only long enough to kill Zalman Somata and then use it to remove his sister Unity from sight and mind until this last Devauray. Nonetheless, three years after he'd last had it, he ended up cutting out his third eye and thereby committing devic suicide.

They weren't necessary for the Antheans' Panharmonium Project. The three Thrygragos Brothers didn't need the power foci Tvasitar Smithmonger forged for them so why, should the three-in-one Sisters be reincarnated, would they need theirs? As usual her argument fell on deaf ears. She'd been right, though. Not only had nothing good come of having them, witness Vetala's Soldier. And certainly nothing good had come of Morg relentlessly pursuing them, for her or anyone else.

Superior Sarpedon's monomania had led her irrevocably astray. No one would ever trust her again. Not hubby Demios, who hated her dealing with devils; not Golgotha, cloned as he was from her grandfather, who blamed her for dealing with the Dead; not her father, devolved as he was, whom she handed over to the Thanatoids of Lathakra; not Methandra of Mythland, the Athenans' nominal goddess, whom she'd attacked with her Indescribables; not her War Witches, whom she'd had her psychotic Hellions infiltrate; and now not even Fish herself.

How dare Morg arrange to betray Harry Zeross to the Thanatoids? More to the periwinkle point, how dare she mess with her mind?

========

Fish had had an approaching lifelong, often antagonistic relationship with the feeorin of Crepuscule, the Grey Land of Twilight, Sedon's Outer Nose, they and Twilight's second-born Lazaremist overlord, over-lady rather, Krepusyl Evenstar: the devic half-mother of much younger sister Wilderwitch. The feeorin were fay-folk, chthonic creatures; earthborn as opposed to skyborn. So were daemons, who were considered life-beneficent or life-neutral, and demons, without the '*a*', who were considered anti-life, especially anti-human-life.

Other than in Satanwyck and the Forbidden Forest of Kala Tal (a Mithradite, Vetala's litter sister), ordinary folks and even devils rarely encountered demons on the Hidden Headworld. With the exception of the Grey Land and a solitary cavern in Temporis, the same was true of faeries. The Bloodlands, Sedon's Inner Nose, were next door to Twilight, immediately to its east.

Up until something like a hundred and thirty years ago, one of its dominant devils was Nakba Ramazar, the headless Apocalyptic equally of Disaster or Sudden Destruction. An eighth-born Mithradite, he rode the two-headed – two-backed as well – devic Vultyrie, a lowborn '*sister*'. That he had in effect made a mount of a fellow Master Deva made him very nearly unique among his often unkind kind.

His adherents often offered him decapitated heads as a form of tribute. Over time the human inhabitants of Twilight, who were ethnically related to the Outer Earth's Celts, began trophy-collecting human and animal skulls themselves. In that regard, this Ramazar, called Catastrophe by devils, was an amorous sort with an attraction, or *'thing'*, for second-born Lazaremists. Because of that, he reckoned Miss Mist, Krepusyl Evenstar, she of Crepuscule, Sedon's Outer Nose, shared her adherents' affection for severed heads. She didn't.

Being amongst other things a Life Goddess (like her brood sisters Flowery Anthea and the Legendarian's half-mother, Titanic Metis) as well as a Love Goddess, Lazareme's Venus (in many respect that Great God's equivalent of Bodiless Byron's APM All-Eyes, Aphropsyche Morningstar), she wouldn't. In a classic case of wrongheadedness, even for a devil that didn't have a head anymore (he lost it, quite literally, over Anthea not all that long after gaining a daemonic body), that didn't stop him from trying to woo her with gifts of them anyways.

The same as the Outer Earth's ancient Celts, Crepuscule's sentient denizens believed the soul, the essence of a being, resided in the head. (Even if fays, like their similarly earthborn, daemonic cousins, reckoned themselves soulless, this conviction held true for Twilight's human and faerie inhabitants alike.) Not even forty years ago, hence well into modern times, Crepuscular warriors newly home from combat duty still mounted heads of their slain enemies both inside and outside their dwellings in order to show-off their prowess in battle.

Old habits die hard and, unless they'd changed their minds what with the return of Mars Bellona to the Bloodlands, Crepuscular warriors were preparing to go head-hunting again. Within a matter of days, more so than weeks, they planned to march into the Bloods in order to aid their Grey Lady Goddess in her efforts to reclaim them in the name of her younger sister, the War Goddess Badhbh, Battle Baby, whom the Sangs had kicked out of New Valhalla, Sedon's Inner Nose, for being too much of a fuck-you Lazaremist.

Centuries earlier, the Grey Land had been on the other side of the Headworld, where it was known as the Land of Daybreak. At that time Illuminaries of Weir referred to Krepusyl Evenstar as Mariamne Dawnstar. Her witch-followers (which included Tsishah Twilight, her grandmother, Young Life, aka Hush Mannering, and at one point the mother in-between them, the Morrigan herself) were still known as Mariamnics. Then it was to the east of the Crystal Mountains, where Samarand, once Sedon's Tongue, was now.

While ruling east of the Crystals as Dawnstar, Mariamne developed a fondness for diamonds and, indeed, all things crystalline. Once he made the connection, Headless Ramazar started making, then sending, Krepusyl Evenstar presents; this in a blatant effort to rekindle the romance he once shared with her sister Anthea. These presents took the form of Crystal Skulls, which she liked, and for a few centuries Catastrophe and her were an item, as Outer Earth gossip-columnists said today.

(Second-born Lazaremists were an exceedingly unlucky threesome. Eventual Krepusyl and her domain had been displaced toward the end of the Dome's 47th Century whereas Metisophia, Wisdom of Lazareme, had been without a power focus, her cauldron, since the empire of Lathakra began its expansion a bare few decades later. As for Anthea, *'rekindle'* was something of a joke given she'd been burning between-space, on a perpetual pyre supposedly of her own conjuring, for thousands of years off the Forever Forest of Wildwyck, in the Head's occipital regions.)

Crystal Skull were soul-sinks. They held onto strong, even trans-migratory souls. Souls, psyches, could communicate with other souls psychically. Sangs used Crystal Skull-sets as a sort of radio or telephone transmitter/receiver in order to far-speak with each other. Witches did the same with their witch-stones; Trinondevs were a currently strictly dick-dildo, as in male, with their eye-staves. Properly ensorcelled witch-stones could prevent devic possession.

Eyeorbs atop eye-staves, applied as prison pods, could capture and hold onto devic and azura spirit-selves. They could, as well, capture and hold onto both devic power foci, which were largely composed of Brainrock-Gypsium, and subtle matter daemonic bodies, which were primarily made up of Stopstone-Solidium. (Be-brained daemons weren't so easy to capture. Neither were faeries, who claimed to have too much integrity to be captured at all – and for once may not have been lying through their trickster teeth.)

Some believed the souls of sentient beings were immature devils or even non-glorified Celestial Angels. Others believed the soul and the mind were the same thing. Beliefs aside, whatever the reality was this suggested soul-sinks, witch-stones and eyeorbs were merely versions of the same thing. Which, in turn, suggested a combination of Brainrock-Gypsium and Stopstone-Solidium.

Simplistic terms for such a complex substance were Stoprock, Aether or Quintessence. Overall, it was just yet another variant of the dark grey material of between-space, the subtle matter of Samsara, the Weird, the Grey, the Universal Substance. Everything was related to everything else. Accept that, get on with it. Crystal Skulls as soul-grenades, this was a novel notion.

All of this roiled around the capacious cavity Fish sometimes called her brain-drained memory pool after she hauled both Young Death and dead Dis L'Orca to her fish-lair-grotto in the, maybe, Mandroid-made tunnels beneath the monastery atop Sraddha Isle. Whereupon, as advertised, they got to having worms of words.

Which for them were preferable to eels of electricity, though they got a few jolts of suchlike whenever Fish judged truth-telling unforthcoming – un-firth-skimming, as she put it.

========

Scylla Nereid, as Lemurian Aortic Merthetis, Lakshmi of Lemuria's grandmother, named her, had never liked Garcia Dis L'Orca. Fisherwoman, as Barsine-Vetala's acknowledged father, Magister Joseph Mandam, concurred with codenaming her when she was still in her teens, was too much the individualist to appreciate those she considered toadying sycophants.

Lady Achigan, as often unhappy happenstance eventually rendered her, nevertheless took a degree of pity on dead Dis L'Orca, huddled there, beneath her fishnet, gazing forlornly at her heart in hand. That Garcia was dead, yet still animate, that Young Death couldn't get into her and that therefore she was being animated by something other than an azura, this was as puzzling as a pontoon in a spittoon.

Fish sat stewing on her own internal juices as Young Death told her what had happened to them last night, after she dusted the Sraddhite bat on the battlements and they'd gone to see Morgianna together. He might be lying. Tricksters lied. Wouldn't be tricksters if they didn't. The best lies made sense, though, and this made sense.

Their joint stupidity didn't, but only in retrospect. They still trusted Morg then. It was Andaemyn they didn't trust; her and the one-armed man she'd travelled with for so long. He, Young Death knew, was a Dead Thing Walking and it was he, Alastor Molorchus, they'd both seen on the battlements bringing in the Indescribables.

It was Andy they found first. To her credit she'd joined Garcia and her War Witches fighting the very demons Molorchus had brought onto Sraddha Isle. They came staggering into the Sarpedons' quarters sometime after midnight, once the rout was on outside. They were unhurt but exhausted. After that, well, Fish didn't even remember her going with Young Death to look for Morgianna in the first place.

"Morg came through," Young Death explained. "Her pantsuit-demon is a muscular no-brainer. She was carrying the Master, my son, her brother, Saladin Devason, in her arms. She had the Master's Mace in one hand; had both Cabby's fake mirror and fake sword in the other. She was as startled as you were but you were quick to make with the soul-net and gaffe, as an eel-whip as well."

(Fish's gaffe had once been a devil's power focus, too. Its normally nasty-looking hook had aspects of a snake-stick about it – a snake-stick or caduceus being Codename Illuminatus, Melina then Sarpedon's device more so than weapon of choice. Being, as she was well-characterized, something of a twisted sister, Fish liked to *'adjust'* its metallic barb-end into an electric eel stuck to a pole and thereafter use its consequential buggy whip qualities to impress her quests.)

"You scared the shit out of Andy. So, while you were about to do whatever you were going to do to her mother, the loyal young, um, whippersnapper sleep-darted you from behind. Garcia got me. And the moral of that story is never turn your back on a War Witch, especially one you haven't disarmed first. Andy and Garcia may not be tiptop witches, they aren't materialists like you or Morgianna, but that doesn't mean they aren't fast on the draw and quicker on the trigger."

"After that," Garcia contributed, "The one-armed man came through like Alice out of her looking glass. Morg got in touch with our goddess, Mediterranean Athena, Methandra Thanatos, and they had Al send Young Death here to Lathakra for safe-keeping, as it were. You see, the Thanatoids wanted Ringleader, for his teleportive Brainrock rings. It seems they had, or have, a mission for him and they wanted Morg's Young Daddy Death there to guarantee her getting him to them."

"She redacted me," Fish said, seriously not fishifying.

"She could have killed you," Garcia noted. "But she didn't. You also had something of hers in your bellybutton."

"The masticating, master-casting, dead witch's soul-self," understood Fish. "I wasn't sure I haddock-had her."

"You did. She got her out."

"How the sea-cow?"

"I'll show you. You've got to promise to give it back, though." Fish promised. She could lie too. Garcia trusted her.

The 27-year-old, who shared a birth date with Andaemyn Sarpedon and Janna St Peche-Montressor, pulled a Crystal Skull out of her shredded shirt and smashed it on the floor. Both Fish and Young Death watched in amazement as it reverse-shattered; re-formed itself; something smoky was now inside it. They knew what it was intuitively: Garcia's soul-self. They knew this cogently because Garcia fainted dead away – emphasis on '*dead*'.

"Now that's a good trick," marvelled the Voodoo Child. "The super-azura is more like a supra soul-self – your own."

"It's sick for a trick," Fish rephrased inimitably. "Stickleback-specially if horrible Hellions can make you do snuff-stuff barnacle-brain-passed-on that you'd have dick-done in limpid-lichen-life – as in never-ever-the-tether while bivalve-alive." She picked up the pellucid reliquary, vanished it. Garcia was well and truly gone now.

The former queen of Godbad nodded at Young Death, thought-father of the current Master of Weir. He went into dead Dis L'Orca; began debriefing her deadhead. By morning they had Garcia's life story; a supply of crystalline suction cups for psychotic psyches, as Moirnoir declared them; and a newfound admiration for Barsine Mandam.

Bat-Bait, as both onetime best friends Fish and Sorciere sometimes called Barsine, had known all about them; had collected and stored hundreds of them in her still existent darkroom before Vetala reasserted control of their joint being thirty-five years ago.

They also had a new problem; one that would likely necessitate the immediate evacuation of Sraddha Isle.

"I'm truly sorry, Fish," Young Death, inside of Garcia, underneath Fish's soulnet, apologized.

"Like I said, after I got into of Morg's one-armed man, Vetala showed up. She wanted Rings but I'd already sent him to the Frozen Isle. She decided Al, me in him, would do just as well, so I sent her to Incain, to be devoured by its She-Sphinx or else Demogorgon, its internal as much as eternal Devil-Eater-aspect.

"I was going to do the same thing to her soldier but the Crimson Corona must have mind-bent me because I sent him to Sedon's Peak instead. You do realize what that means don't you."

She did. Many believed the cliff-faces semi-circling – hovering over and above – its lava lake sentinel-like represented those of the Trigregos Sisters.

He said it anyhow.

========

"*He's going bathe in its caldera, absorb even more Brainrock. The Trigregos Titan is going to come back to Hadd even more unstoppable than he already was.*"

****

(ENDGAME-GAMBIT) 27: **D-Day For D-Brig**

Mithrada, Tantalar 8, 5980

Methandra Thanatos wasn't a giantess anymore.

========

The Frozen Isle's Death Goddess wasn't much taller than Illuminatus, Melina nee Sarpedon Zeross, her prisoner much more so than her guest at present. Judging from the tattered state of her garments and mask, the Scarlet Seeress had recently survived a knockdown drag-out confrontation with a mob of nastily gnashing, bordering on omnivorous, and very voracious moths; ones that had eaten her outfit as well as two-fifths of her height.

For the first few thousand years of the Headworld's existence, said wholly unwilling detainee knew from her decades of extensive studies, Lathakra was Sedon's Horn. Back then it stretched far to the north from its root, foot or base in Methandra's own Mythland, the Jewel of Sedon's Crown. (Mythland, now largely unpopulated, lay within the western extremity of said Crown, aka the Mystic Mountains, the foothills of which began hundreds of miles beyond Melina's home in Cabalarkon, the place, Sedon's Devic Eye-Land.)

It became Sedon's Cataract, the lens or monocle of Sedon's Human Eye, geographically the Gulf of Corona, after the mighty Moloch mostly in the sky moved it to just outside said Gulf, in an effort to separate blustery brother from desirous sister. Hot Stuff – called such because she was just that, in all senses of the word *'hot'* – foiled the Devil's designs. She remained steadfastly Mithras's Virgin. (Klannit, the azura she had with Tantal pre-Dome, didn't count because they were stuck inside be-brained demons at the time of both her conception and her birth.)

Moreover, she promptly abandoned her domain, the aforementioned Sedon's Jewel, in order to rejoin her icicle-bearded, but non-sexually beloved brood brother. In fairly short order thereafter, as displeased as ever with the Thanatoids – particularly the Virgin's continual spurning of his attentions – Dark Sedon left it across the Sea of Clouds, off the Cattail's east coast, where the sun still rose but no longer shone very warmly.

(Logicians couldn't accept that even Sedon had the ability to uproot let alone transport such incredibly varied, not to mention vast landmasses. Instead, they postulated he did so by subsiding the ground in one place, where the Horn then the

Lens – or Daybreak and Samarand, for that matter – had been. Whereupon he raised nearly identical approximations of them elsewhere.

(As for their worshipful populace, the buildings they lived and worked in, the farms, orchards and ranches they tended, or the plains, savannahs and woodlands wherein they hunted, he must have first teleported them to safe holds before finally depositing them on their newly risen destinations.

(That pontificated, albeit without any possible way to corroborate it short of Sedon duplicating the feat for an audience of reliable witnesses, suchlike *'ye of little faith'* rationalists couldn't deny his punishments by displacement for their devic lords and ladies' hubristic conceits still bordered on the purely miraculous.)

Since the Cattail was Unholy Abaddon's traditional territory, Satanic Sedon must have hoped Cold and Chaos would have at each other, double-headed war-axe against triple-tined trident, and the land beneath them be sundered. Going against form, they started drinking beer together – though Methandra stuck to wine, red of course – and, the Devil be damned, decided to conquer the Head instead; hence the expansion of the Empire of Lathakra throughout the last three-quarters of the Dome's 48th Century and a couple of decades into its 49th.

The Frozen Isle, however, was always Tantal's protectorate, not Methandra's. Melina knew that, too. Consequently, she further wondered if Old King Cold, Heat's immediate brother-husband, who was as colossal as ever, had sat back warming himself on her discomfort; had voyeuristically watched his wife suffer until he decided enough was enough. Had the mob of moths, or whatever they were, Solidium teeth? Must have; ergo, they were daemonic.

They'd done the damage. He did the talking. "High Illuminary of Weir, what do you know of witch-potions?"

========

Maybe as many as five dozen of Field Commander Nauroz's Warriors Elite were on the fatality lists Thartarre Sraddha Holgatson had in front of him.

Undeath was unnatural. How could the Living possibly be losing?

========

The High Priest was in no mood to glance at the rest of the lists. They were too depressing; the ones for his Sraddhites and the remnants of Niarchos's Godbadian soldiers were almost as thick as the one for the Trinondevs. There'd be body-bags more to add to them if Ferdinand Niarchos couldn't convince Godbad's civilian and military authorities to fly in some fully manned and equipped medical evacuation units from Petrograd awfully soon; highlight *'awfully'*.

Besides, tonight's assault was still ongoing. Make that today's counter-assault was still ongoing. It was now well into Mithrada morning, what Golgotha and his Trinondevs had hoped would be D-Day – D as in Dustmound. It occurred to Thartarre they'd already had their D-Night – D as in dreadful; as in also Dead or Dying.

True, most of the fight still ongoing was taking place elsewhere; between-space for the most part, he presumed. Athenan War Witches had a new weapon, Crystal Skulls, psycho soul-grenades they'd been dubbed, which he'd further been given to understand were Hellion soul-sinks. Armed thusly, with Janna St Peche-Montressor having taken over from Garcia Dis L'Orca, alive Athenans were off in pursuit of dead ones.

These last, he'd additionally been given to understand, were devil-hating, Mother-Earth-worshipping, seriously psychotic Hecate-Hellions gone rogue. Dead or alive, they willingly fought with the Dead against the Living. That smacked of nihilism. Which in turn made the High Priest wonder if, despite her apparent destruction, as only recently reported by Lady Achigan and Demios Sarpedon, they'd switched to worshipping Freespirit Nihila.

They were in his workroom on the uppermost level of the Sraddhites' monastery. Jordan Tethys was having his first beer. You could twang the tension.

========

Daylight robbed Diego de Landa and his fellow big-game bat-hunters of their prey to pray for: the berserker attack-bats. He was back tending the radio. "This is interesting."

"Shucking-oysters what is?" demanded Fisherwoman, Scylla Nereid, Lady Achigan, once the marital Queen of Godbad.

"Indigenous Iraches, living ones," Sraddha Landa-son, to identify Diego by his Curia-given name, reported, "Have entered Necropolis, formerly the Gleaming City of Manoa, unopposed." Considering the exciting news he'd just received, he sounded remarkably restrained. "Its Dead didn't resist. They aren't even rising."

"They wouldn't," said the lone animated Dead Thing in their presence. "Vetala's so desperate to survive she must have sucked in its azuras before she came for the ones here." Garcia Dis L'Orca had not spoken in her voice. She was also smoking a cigar. Garcia, alive or dead, had probably never smoked anything ever before. No one needed to question how she was speaking let alone who was inside her.

On Lathakra, shortly after his Morrigan of a thought-daughter had let loose her dentally well-endowed demons on its Crimson Queen via the Grey, Young Death negotiated an icicle spear suppository rather than letting Tina Zeross do the dastardly deed herself. He preferred it that way. An otherwise normal, Utopian-human 6-year-old shouldn't be allowed to kill a perpetually 7-year-old faerie fart like him. No kid, not even a faun's kid, should. It might become habit-forming.

Out of respect for the squeamishness of their fully alive companions in Thartarre's makeshift command central – whose number included Governor Niarchos, Golgotha Nauroz and the Diver – Fish was hiding Garcia's ever-so-rudely exposed chest-cavity with an illusion of intactness. She'd thrown it with a witch-stone that she'd hastily prepared, and inserted therein, before venturing back up here.

Casting glamours wasn't one of Fish's specialties, but not everyone had to know she was a Dead Thing Walking; especially not everyone in this crowd, equipped as many were with fire hoses and incendiary back canisters. Should she eventually decide to release dead Dis L'Orca's Crystal-Skull-sunk soul-self, she'd get her a second skin sometime thereafter.

That shouldn't be much of a problem. Fish knew slithering sacks packed with Ophirants, a pan-species witch sisterhood whose members specialized in stunningly effective serpent splendours that bordered on proprietorial if not exclusivity. Properly extruded, and thereby plasticized, their serpent splendours not only tended toward tangibility. They manoeuvred as if naturally, hence the second skin terminology.

By and large Ophirants were natives of Ophir-Moorset, on the occipital side of the Aural Sea, Sedon's Ear. They got on with Athenan War Witches such as Fish and Garcia; took a lot of the same training – and from the same trainers to boot. (Which, booting, they were very good at.) By no means always human (not even close, hence the pan-species bit), they often kept snakes as their familiars. Which was why they were sometimes disparaged as snake-sucklers.

Perhaps more peculiarly, they also had a high degree of appreciation, if not unqualified, out-and-out admiration, for the anti-devil attitudes Hellions shared with next to no one on the Head except for Utopians and chthonic creatures such as demons and faeries. Other than sympathetically, Fish wasn't a Hellion but Garcia was, through and through, no pun intended.

(Many an Ophirant was a non-human Ophidian. Despite approaching scorpioid in appearance, suchlike Ophidians were not arachnid. They were howsoever strangely mutated, sentient reptilians like Saurians and Lizarados. They almost never slithered but did have an unaccountable fear of heights and thus rarely took to the trees. Which was doubly odd given the Forever Forest of Wildwyck – from whence, for the most part, Hellions hailed originally – was west of their homeland, Ophir-Moorset.

(Furthermore, just because they were ground-skulking and Satanwyck was to Moorset's east, that didn't make them earthborn daemonic either. Sooth said, Ophidians who were brought up by the book, as it were, hunted demons for sport – and vice versa. That didn't affect the affection Ophidian Ophirants held for Hellion witches, however, so go figure.)

Garcia was definitely a Hellion. One who had betrayed their Morrigan, sure, and one who had done so with the long-distance guidance of a Hellion-hated devil, sure again. Nonetheless, among Ophirants, there were loads of anthropomorphic snakes who owed Fish favours. Truth be told, one of them was, for the worshippers amongst them, their highest born god-devil.

Dandset Typhon, Ophir-Moorset's monstrous Mithradite overlord, might have been an escaped star had not Fish prevented him becoming one in the first place, decades ago now.

========

In the old days that the Diver seemed so fond of, scads of supras died. So did their children and grandchildren,
For those who lasted long enough to have either/or, that went without saying.

========

In June of 1953, on or about Midsummer's Day, a breathtaking number of the Outer Earth's onetime female supranormals, as well as a few who were then still active, popped babies. All of them had been in Vancouver Canada on the Autumnal Equinox of '52 (which was still celebrated as Harmony's Feast Day in here). That was when the phrase 'Lady Lust came to town and Mama Maternity stayed behind' was coined out there.

Appallingly, every known boy-baby was either stillborn or died of SIDS, Sudden Infant Death Syndrome, within a matter of a few days. Only the girls survived. Among those girls were Andaemyn Sarpedon, Janna St Peche and Garcia Dis L'Orca. Alone of those three, that Janna was born beneath the Dome.

Garcia's parents were associates more so than friends of Fish and the Sarpedons. When, a dozen years later, in 1965, her Spanish Falangist of a father died under the usual mysterious circumstances and, shortly thereafter, her mother committed suicide – if she did – the Sarpedons took in Garcia and her older brother, Salvatore.

Took them in quite literally as well, since they brought them inside. Herein, they saw to it they enjoyed their teenage years as non-striped but never-bullied members of the burgeoning Zebranid community. Which, what Andy regarded as her home, they'd founded high up in the Whiplash Range, on the Cattail Peninsula, about as far away from the Weirdom of Cabalarkon as one could go while remaining on the Hidden Headworld.

(They'd established it some years after the relatively newly proclaimed Master of Weir, Saladin Devason, exiled the Sarpedons, along with their loyalist followers, from Sedonic Daddy Cabby's Weirdom in 5950. Geographically it wasn't far from either the high plains of Bandrad, from whence Godbad's royalty came initially, and the Prison Beach of Incain.)

Salvatore was now on the Outer Earth; had been for a number of years. Garcia stayed with her by then best pal Andy and the Sarpedons. She took the obligatorily arduous Athenan training there, in the southeast corner of the Cattail, as well as on Shenon (Witch Isle) and in the War Witches' enclave on the Cattail-side of Sedon's Hairband, the Gypsium Wall, the site of Harmony's High Seat.

Like all her sister Athenans, Garcia underwent a secret ritual, a strictly distaff one no doubt related to the Mithraic or Eleusinian Mysteries endured by men, or men and women, many hundreds of years earlier on the Outer Earth: she was symbolically killed and resurrected. Andy went through much the same ceremony.

It was designed to render her unafraid of death; fearless in a fight and, in some cases, fully prepared to kill oneself rather than risk capture. Unbeknownst to her, so confirmed Young Death, who vouched for her deadhead's sooth-saying, Garcia proved to be one of those very rare Athenans. Unlike Andy, she proved to be a natural born Hellion.

True Hellions couldn't give a good cod-damn, as Fish would fay-say, whether they were living or dead. Garcia's soul-self was supra-strong. She wasn't killed and resurrected symbolically. She'd been killed for real and resurrected herself. She therefore in effect became her own Guardian Angel; her own animus, the motive force that, counter-intuitively, kept her brain active yet somehow also prevented her body from deteriorating.

It was as yet unclear if Morgianna Sarpedon knew Garcia was a true Hellion, a Dead Thing kept going by her own soul-self. What was clear was dead Dis L'Orca took her War Witch vows very seriously. She couldn't very well defend life to the death anymore, but she remained a life-defender. She also remained dedicated the Superior Sisterhood's Panharmonium Project.

Hours before she discovered she was dead, she thought Methandra Thanatos and Superior Sarpedon were as dedicated as she was to it. When the latter, their Morrigan, proved false to the former, their devic goddess, contradiction in terms that it sounded to some others, the former saw to it Garcia found the means to at least rob the latter of some her most effective agents.

Whether it was endgame Morg, that was anyone's guess. Everyone else guessed it wasn't but no one knew what had become of her or her one-armed man. They did know what had become of Nergal Vetala, however. Jordan Tethys had shown them. Sadly, it had nothing to do with Incain and everything to do with evacuating the Living's positions throughout Lake Sedona.

Overnight, Hadd's Blood Queen had howsoever amassed more Dead Things in one place, Diminished Dustmound, than any of them believed could possibly exist.

It wasn't All-Death Day all over again, not yet, but it boded ominously for its recurrence.

========

Fish had been lost in reverie.

========

Somehow the topic had gone back to Vetala's Soldier and he'd said it again, the Diver had: "We three go at him, just the three of us, we've a shot. It'll be just like the old days."

The night before the third of them had been Demios Sarpedon. The third of them today was Field Commander Nauroz. Neither of them responded: "It's no use"; though they might have. The person who said that was Governor Ferdinand Niarchos. Since he'd just signed off the other radio, laying down his headset, he may not have even heard the Diver's assertion.

"No fucking use at all. There's still no sign of General Anvil's helicopter so the High Command has gone ahead and scrambled their warplanes and long-distance helicopter gunships towards Sanguerre. And they won't even consider releasing any of their short-haul planes to keep on seeding the clouds, let alone any of their back-up transport planes to evacuate the rest of our troops and the injured. We might have to take you up on your offer after all, Jordy."

Jordan Tethys, 30-Beers, the legendary 30-Year Man, hadn't come down from Cabalarkon just because he was sick and tired of Golgotha and Gethsemane's home-brew. (That acknowledged, it was expectoration-worthy compared to the vastly superior suds concocted by Sraddhite warrior monks, whose mortal god, when alive, shared best pal Squiggly's not just inherited taste in beer.)

Neither had he had come down here because he was already bored of Cosmi-companion Carmine Carmichael's withering attentions. (Far from it, though they were withering. CC was insatiable.) Via his eye-stave – as opposed to Sarpedon's – Golgotha Nauroz had informed the Master of last night's devastating near-massacre of so many of their Trinondevs. He also told Devason of the disappearance of both Ringleader and Morg's one-armed man.

Sal wanted Nauroz and his men out of the line of fire. So he sent Tethys to Sraddha Isle to facilitate that very thing. He still wanted the Sarpedons apprehended but, after a far-spoken shouting match with his Field Commander, he'd given up on that happening anytime soon. So long as he was down here and the Master was up there, Black Skull-Face could out-argue a devil's son.

As partial payback for him *'lending'* him his eye-stave, Golgotha took it upon himself to countermand the Master's orders that Demios should be taken at all costs. None of his wholly active Trinondevs, who still numbered well over a hundred, objected. Trying to capture him would only have stopped Sarpedon taking in Sang after Sang with his rapidly ejecting, yet just as rapidly replicating prison-pods. Had they forced him to fend them off, Weir's Warrior Elite would only have been benefiting the real enemy, the ambulant dead and undead things.

The Dead weren't rising on Sraddha Isle anymore either. And no one pretended the pretender to the Mastery of Weir didn't have a lot do with that.

How did it, the oldest eye-stave in existence, manufacture eyeorbs anyhow? That was something else no one could say for sure. (The ineffability of teleportive Godstuff combined with the mother of all Utopian generational or millennial Mother Ships buried or sunken somewhere on the Head, but miraculously still functioning, being the most common theory.)

They could and did say it was a pity that it couldn't manufacture excesses of them on command. Otherwise Golgotha could have supplied his Trinondevs indefinitely. They had to be filled first, though, and that was why, besides the fact he couldn't disobey the Master of Weir, the 80-year-old clone was preparing to leave Hadd.

He and his Warriors Elite were running out of unfilled eyeorbs almost as quickly as they were running out of themselves.

"My offer was to draw the wounded to safety, Ferd," said the Legendarian. "I'll start with the Weirdom's Trinondevs and get to the Living when and if I can. Although I've never had any trouble running out of Brainrock ink before, there's always a first time. I do, well, I'll come back. At least I have been for going on 2,000 years, knock wooden head. None of you have that option, so most of you will just have to hope I don't run dry."

"We'll stay and fight," swore Thartarre.

"And you'll die," Tethys promised him. "Nergal Vetala's got none of your estimable mother, Barsine Mandam, left in her, Tar. Sure as shooting fish in a barrel, night comes she'll have her bats-of-burden raining Dead Things on this monastery – and anywhere else they can get to where it isn't raining non-bloody wetness. I say we get to it. Before her Attis reappears on the scene."

"Sure as shooting what in a barrel, Jordan River?"

"You heard me, Fish. If you hadn't lost you-know-who, I might've been able to persuade the Lazaremists to take him on. As it is, you play a Trigregos Gambit, you better have stacks of chips on the table. And, as near as I can make out, Vetala's got towers of them now. You'll run out long before she does."

"Relying on devils is not an option for us," said Golgotha.

"You're buggering off anyways," said the Diver bitterly.

He'd not only known Barsine, he knew her father, Magister Mandam. Still did, he believed, though how Dragon Joe became – or re-became – Akbarartha, the rightful Kronokronos Supreme of Subterranean Temporis, well, he'd need more than just a few days back beneath the Dome to reconcile that with Whole Earth reality, not to mention what passed for his memories.

(That Naomi, one of his two daughters by wife Rachel, was the same age, to the day or near enough, as Andy, Garcia and Janna by now St Peche-Montressor, well, that too required additional reflection now that assimilation had a checkmark beside it. He used to say he wasn't losing his memory, it was full. Right now he reckoned it was full of crap.)

Golgotha couldn't disobey a direct order from the Master so he had already refused to join with the Diver and Fish, three against one, once Vetala's Soldier returned from Sedon's Peak. Assuming he hadn't already, that is. Assuming, further, he wasn't waiting between-space for night to come or for the Godbadians to start sending in more planes he could destroy with OMP-Akbar's Homeworld Sceptre. Which was what Niarchos and his superiors feared.

Fish still hadn't committed herself one way or another. The Diver doubted she'd be much use anyhow. Not against something like Vetala's champion, this Trigregos Titan who might have begun life as Demonites and Hot Rox's bastard. Even the otherwise anonymous supra codenamed Emperor Energy hadn't been as extraordinarily powerful as the Blood Queen's golden-brown warrior.

UD, Yehudi Cohen, was prepared to go it alone in any case. Problem was there was nowhere he could go as yet. Jordan Tethys refused to draw the Amateramirror because he reckoned that would incinerate Furie, OMP-Akbar, Sundown and Raven. As if you could incinerate the last two. Creatures of the Cosmos didn't incinerate, they incinerated others. Plus, the wild man was so Mr Hyde hard-hided he probably wouldn't burn either.

But, borderline begrudgingly, the Diver had to admit – out loud as well – that without his regalia, his Thrygragos Talismans as he knew to call them but didn't, or his Homeworld Sceptre, OMP-Akbar was vulnerable to just that: Burning in an hellacious inferno not only not of his own making but with no way of escaping it.

For her part, not that she would admit it out loud, Fish had to agree with the point Tethys had just made. What with so many prison-pods ejected on Dustmound, as well as both outside and inside the monastery, what did one do with them after they were chock-a-block-stuffed, like a salmon with spicy breadcrumbs?

In the Weirdom of Cabalarkon there were constantly guarded vaults lined with Stopstone containing ejected eyeorbs. She knew that because, over the course of more than six decades of living, she'd spent what cumulatively amounted to a number of years there. And her eyes were almost always wide open even if they, the prison-pods or eye-eggs, never were. Hard to argue with ocular proof, as Fish-Spear probably proclaimed iambically.

Outsiders, even insiders like Fish's patron and primary teacher, Master Kyprian always Somata, or Melina long-nowadays Zeross, couldn't possibly know if the ones in the Weirdom contained devils, mere azuras, or demons whose bodies neither occupied any longer. Or, if they did contain devils, which devils they contained, let alone when they were first captured.

Controversially, Illuminaries like Codename Illuminatus claimed that many, probably most of them, not only contained Master Devas, aka Shining Ones, they contained ones captured off-planet multi-millennia earlier. For some scarily, pre-Earth devils were for the most part still bodiless spirit beings and hence glorified azuras of unknown potency.

(From Mel's perspective, the sheer mystery of what they could do made their persistence in her homeland a truly frightening prospect. What if they broke out en masse, like more than 60 of their brethren did on the 30th of Maruta just passed, when they decathonitized? Who could say they weren't immeasurably more power-ful than the 500 or so who survived the Genesea and made it to the Inner Earth six millennia earlier?

(Fortunately the ancient orbs showed no signs of decay or deterioration. Even more fortunately, not to mention reassuringly, the Death's Head Hellion, who flour-ished circa the beginning of the Head's 49th Century, proved today's eye-eggs could hold onto pre-Earth's Shining Ones. Still, that was then and this was now.)

The ones in Hadd were just lying about waiting to be trampled, and thereby emptied, or else collected, to be taken to Cabalarkon in due course. The ones here-abouts included one particular eyeorb Fish had carefully secreted within her port-able shelter, her version of a witch's bottomless bag, her bellybutton bauble.

Flying saucer razor-clam had a pearl. She'd intended to feed it to All of Incain when she got around to it. Clams can have legs. Clams can have an ommatophore at the end of each antsy antennae. Unhappily, Fish had just discovered that clams can also have bowel movements. She was renowned for having oceans of notions. Right now she didn't have a piddle of a puddle as to what had become of the prison pod within which Demios captured Nowadays Nihila. It was very embarrassing.

"Not until Jordy sends our wounded back to Cabalarkon," snapped Golgotha. "In fact, in the name of everyday humanity, I'm prepared to wait until Jordy sends away all the wounded. It doesn't matter to me how long it takes or where he sends them. The Godbadians can go to Petrograd, Aka Godbad, or command central in Godbad City; the Brown Robes to the Sraddhites' settlements in Diluvia; the War Witches to Shenon. He can even send any Hellions who won't stay dead to Satan-wyck, for all I care.

"If he runs out of Brainrock ink before he can get to us then – you know what, Diver? – we aren't buggering off anywhere. Let it rain Dead Things tonight, for now we're staying. The Legendarian's right. Let's get to it."

"Here, here," exclaimed Thartarre in evident relief. "Spoken like the calculat-ing clone I've always known you to be, Field Commander. You got any better ideas, Lady Achigan?"

"As a matter of aqua-fact fitness programs, I do," she said. Thanks to Tethys, she had just had one. "Shooting clip-winged, ducky decoys in a duck-pond. God-bad City's the HQ, minus the IQ, of Godbad's powers-that-be. It's about time they re-experienced the powers that be me." Fish wasn't one for elaboration. You'd likely need an interpreter to understand it anyhow and she seldom carried living beings in her bellybutton bauble anymore.

She dropped a witch-stone and was gone. If she encountered any antagonistic Athenans between-space, she had a few handfuls of Crystal Skulls ready to mater-ialize and soul-grenade-detonate. As for Indescribables or golden-brown warriors, she could fall out of the Weird deep beneath the sea. She crustacean-trusted they couldn't follow her that far underwater; the pressure alone should cause their brains to explode.

Then again it wouldn't be the first time she'd been wrong. It might be the first time she'd been dead wrong, though.

========

"Where'd she go?" had to ask Diego de Landa, who'd also taken off his earphones.

"To re-become Godbad's Queen for a Day?" speculated Ferdinand Niarchos.

"She's no good at coercion," recalled Young Death, speaking out of dead Dis L'Orca.

"Given the state of her baby sister up in Cabalarkon, Fish is the best witch there is left," said the Legendarian, Jordan Tethys.

He'd visited Wilderwitch while he was up there – visited but, due to her condition, didn't speak to her. At least she was better off than Cerebrus David Ryne, who'd been placed in a tub of life-preserving, but animation-suspending Cathonic Fluid. He was thereupon left in the Catacombs of the Sleepers, beneath the Citadel of the Thinkers and beside the sarcophagus containing none other than the Undying Utopian, Cabalarkon himself.

He knew her from the same bad old days the Diver thought of as good old days, despite all evidence to the contrary. He also knew Eden Ryne, Cerebrus's mother and Fish's other sister by the Dual Entities; knew her devic mother was Heat's younger sister and friend, Pyrame Silverstar, who was called Providence, capitalized, by some.

Eden was one of the Trigregos Triplets, who were simultaneously born in 1909. Another was Cybele St Synne, his current incarnation's mother. Eden reputedly died in 1955, so she didn't live long enough to became a proper Ant Nightingale, the Anthean sisterhood's equivalent the Hellions' Morrigan and the Korants' Miracle Maenad, Cybele's title. Nonetheless, her maiden name was just that: Nightingale.

"Or right, as far as that goes. Let's hope she succeeds in convincing the bombers to do their bombing here, not there. In the meantime, Golgotha, I want what's left of your Trinondevs to gather every ejected eyeorb they can locate inside or outside the monastery. I'll draw them up to Cabalarkon with your wounded. The orbs, I mean, not the rest of your Trinondevs."

"You giving me orders now, Jordy?" wondered the clone.

"Me? Never. All I'm, um, suggesting is that it would be a good thing if we didn't just leave them, you know, just lying around. Who knows what could get out of them."

"Don't dissemble, Tethys. Talk straight. My wife's homebrew isn't that bad."

"All right. I'm a Hubris trying to relocate a Who. The Who's Harmony, whatever the Unity calls herself these days. Should she need one, I've a marvellous shell for her up in Cabby's Weirdom. Of course I'd have to draw CC out of there first. But a tavern of temperance might be good for both of them. Truth told Harm used to own the one I'm thinking about; hence its ideal pilsners since everything about her was, and may well be again, ideal.

"Besides, the Master doesn't approve of loose women. Neither do most Utopian women."

"Sounds like someone I should meet," said Niarchos.

"I saw her first, Weirdo."

========

The Diver was on the other side of the Legendarian and Black Skull-Face. He was eyeballing Tethys's latest rendition of Diminished Dustmound. Nergal Vetala was sitting on her Brainrock throne and, yes, she did look much Barsine Mandam. Not that, as much as he could recall of her, which wasn't a great deal, Barsine would be caught dead in such revealing clothing.

In so far as the drawing extended, many thousands of the Blood Queen's approximately incalculable multitude of Dead Thing were on their hands and knees, butts up, bellies and heads down, prostrate below her feet; paying her due homage. Could one pray due homage? Probably. Devils had to eat more than food. Did worship have flavour? Was worry a curry?

The Diver's Gorgon Goggles didn't gleam as such; Vetala's forces weren't what he was spotlighting. Neither were the eyes behind them just focusing on the Susasword, which was still stuck into the backside of the devic vampire's throne. It hadn't burst into flames, Tethys's sketchpad with or without it, presumably because the Legendarian had drawn Vetala, not the curved blade. When the drawing's background filled-in the talisman was just there.

The drawing wasn't done yet. Only now it was drawing itself. Rather, the Legendarian's quill was upright, skating over the pad of paper as if it was an ice rink. More like an ink rink, it left splotches rather than blotches behind. The Diver recalled a supra who could do that sort of thing, and with much the same implement. Had it been Tethys under a different name? Oh, probably.

Then it rendered yet another character, one he recognized right away. Except, that wasn't possible was it. "That can't be who I think it is; that can't be Satan St Synne."

The Diver was as precipitous as Fish. He didn't wait for an answer, if question he'd asked. He grabbed hold of the glowing nib of Jordan's quill. It stopped glowing; stopped adding to its drawing of Dustmound dot-ditto. The Diver wasn't there anymore. He'd done a squishy squid in reverse; he'd injected instead of ejected Brainrock ink.

"Change of plans," Tethys announced, once he realized what the Diver had done. "Looks like none of us are going anywhere anytime soon. How's the beer supply holding out, Tar?"

========

In all likelihood the Untouchable Diver wouldn't have known – though Melina nowadays Sarpedon did – that Satan St Synne and Judge Warlock were pseudonyms used by the same person, Sedon St Sedon. UD would have heard that St Synne was still alive, though, albeit only after a fashion, as in kept so artificially somewhere in California.

He also would have known that St Synne helped raise adopted daughter Cybele from infancy until she disappeared, along with her birthmother, Louise born Riel, during the Simultaneous Summonings of 19/5920. He may or may not have heard that Cybele returned, howsoever briefly, to the Outer Earth in the late Thirties or that she was the Korant Sisterhood's long serving Miracle Maenad on Apple Isle to this day.

Almost definitely, he had no idea that she was George Taurson's mother; that Taurson became Jordan Tethys's latest incarnation, when he died for the first time a number of years ago; that St Synne may well be the last living small-case-sedon, or Sed-son, beyond the Cathonic Dome; or that the Dome might collapse if he died for real.

It wouldn't have been relevant in any case. All the more so since the Diver hadn't spotted Judge Warlock, Satan and/or Sedon St Synne anyways.

He hadn't spotted a person.

========

The one-armed man, Morg's Young Daddy Death animating him from the inside, sent her to Incain.

Nergal Vetala was never without her moon-sickle so she hadn't bothered hanging around such that its She-Sphinx had a chance to notice let alone devil-devour her (thereby amalgamating her with the Unnameable's already impressive accumulation of optional extremities). Returning between-space to Sraddha Isle almost at once, she could no more find Alastor Molorchus, as she knew to call the one-armed man, by the time she got back there than she could her soldier.

Having no desire to linger in a warzone where Trinondevs were evidently prevailing despite impressive losses, she sliced herself to Diminished Dustmound. He wasn't there either. Neither was Freespirit Nihila. Oddly, even portentously, the Susasword was precisely where she'd left it. Mindful of what she'd caused its cousinly or sisterly talisman, the Amateramirror, do to Janna Fangfingers, she wasn't about to touch it.

Her Attis would want it now that it wasn't pinning the ex-Unity to the back of her Brainrock throne. Let him pull it out. Where was he?

As uncomfortable as she was with what was sticking out of its other side, she sat down in her throne. It replenished her at the same time it granted her even greater far-sight. She couldn't find him anywhere in Hadd. A long night, and the start of what could be a longer day later, made no difference. She still couldn't find him.

The days weren't that long in Tantalar.

========

The Hidden Headworld was the size of the Outer Earth's African continent. Unlike Africa it had extensive subsurface layers to it; Temporis, Absudyl (sometimes Minius) and Satanwyck (Sedon's Temple) being only some of the largest. Despite the arrival of more and more of her adoring Dead Things she was beginning to despair of ever locating him. Was beginning to despair period.

She had such hopes for him; for them. She was so alone. Wait. Was that him? Nope.

========

"I've been contemplating matrimony, Fecundity."

So a not-immediately-familiar voice said to her, Nergal Vetala, the Vampire Queen of the Dead. She was re-energizing herself on her Brainrock throne. Was also unashamedly wallowing in the worship emanating from her still-gathering multitude of Vetalazur-animated Dead Things. It being daytime Kronar and his Vultyrie had taken over transportation duties from her bats-of-burden.

"Is that a proposal, Judge?" she asked after the standard awkward silence that ensued after he, whom no one could remember even existed until he manifested himself, did just that.

"You might call it that. I am not one for kneeling before my intended; although you may tender your acceptance from your knees if you desire. Neither do I count any rings, Brainrock or otherwise, amongst my possessions. I am prepared to serenade you with my panpipes but only if you're considering maternity."

"Which I have been. Be careful what you wish for. I eat my young."

"Who, in their plenteousness, can't stand in a shower, let alone a rainstorm, when they're possessing Dead Things. They don't have to possess just Dead Things, do they?"

"Not that I'm aware of. But, like any other azura, they're at their most effective when they do. If they aren't, they're just subsumed within their living shells and good for only directing worship to whomever. The other thing to consider is that, unlike most other sentient beings, my Iraches enjoy having their ancestors over for tea and crumpets. Vampires, though, you might recall, are infertile."

"Vampirism can be cured. You're sitting on its cure. One of them."

"So I am. How very observant of you. However, from my perspective, there's a rather undesirable drawback to what you're ever so romantically proposing. As you're thoroughly aware, otherwise you wouldn't be here, the problem with Master Devas as fathers is they get first crack at the adulation of their azuras.

"In that respect we put-upon mothers, the ones who do all the work, are little more than an afterthought. That's why, compared to we women, there are a dispro-portionate number of male Master Devas who have their own protectorates."

"Exactly why my proposition should be so appealing. Unless I'm there with them, no one can recall I exist. So, naturally, our azuras would be passionate about you alone."

"Unless you're there with them – precisely. You called me Fecundity instead of Grower, Nergalid or even Vetala. In that, you're hardly alone. Virtually everyone did; for a very good reason, too. Until I allowed a psycho-bat, First Fangs inside him, to put the bite on me most of five hundred years ago, I was by far the most procreative of female Master Devas. That means you'll be there a lot, won't you?"

"And was – for thousands of years. You were almost as adept as Bedazzling Belialma, not to mention the divine Harmony."

"You really got around, didn't you, Judge."

"Still do."

"Too bad you're too smart to stick around, otherwise you'd have been upstairs a very long time ago."

"So it's as I expected. The maternity you're contemplating is with your Outer Earth foil. Very well. If that's the way you prefer it, never let it be said I didn't give you the opportunity to not only become my wife but to dispose of your soldier and his talismans. You have rebuked me at your cost. It's time to pay the piper, Vampire Queen."

Twin skulls appeared in the air to either side of the vampiric devil, she on her throne.

"Recognize us?" asked one, in a voice that didn't belong to her unwelcome visitor.

It clanged dimly in the recesses of recognition, though she couldn't quite iden-tify it. His skull filled out. They both did; had faces and hair. Both faces were bright, maybe even beautiful. The skull who'd spoken had a glistening, silvery face. He was clean-shaven. His hair was dark, like the night, but it sparkled, as if with stars. She knew who he was now. He was the heavens.

The other speaking-skull introduced him anyhow: "He's Varuna." His or its voice was just as distinctive. Even though she hadn't heard it since Thrygragon – and that was over 1500 years ago – Vetala knew it immediately; shuddered accordingly, very much involuntarily as well as, gallingly, just a tad guiltily.

"I'm Mithras," he, or it, added just as unnecessarily. This Mithras had a beard; beard and hair together were sunrays; said levitating head looked less leonine than seriously solar.

"And I'm Ahriman," the Smiling Fiend provided. He was, as always, darkness with pinkish skin. *"Together we are your father. You cannot disobey us. We order you to self-cathonitize!"*

Nergal Vetala couldn't stop herself. She extracted her Tvasitar Talisman, her Brainrock moon-sickle, from the arm of her similarly composed throne. Gripped it with both hands and sliced it at her third eye. Tip touched devic eye but went no farther. With tremendous force of will, she struggled valiantly against her genetic heritage.

Not so strangely, many of the longest lasting Haddit Zombies down slope from the two devils began decomposing where they lay; where they'd been offering her abject obeisance until then. Long distance, effective re-absorption of the Vetalazurs up until then enlivening them done, she regained her senses, leapt out of her throne and slashed the sickle against one shimmering skull then the other.

Both vanished upon contact. Smiler simply smiled. *"I trust you have just learned something of value, sister. There was no Great God called Varuna Mithras. Thrygragos Everyman and the Unmoving One did have an older brother, yes – a very much older brother. But Varuna and Mithras were separate beings. I am the third and last of Thrygragos Sedon's firstborn."*

He could have paused to let that sink in, but he was in a triumphalist mood. *"The Moloch is not the Devil, though he is the original Shining One. He learned from the Dual Entities who created him how to beget five others. They were Byron, Lazareme and the Trigregos Sisters: Demeter, Sapiendev and Devaura. That is why Varuna Mithras never ordered 'his children' to do anything. He couldn't. He wasn't their father.*

"That is why fable says no second born of Varuna Mithras made it to the Whole Earth. Completely untrue. Tantal, Methandra and Phantast, as Illuminaries named the Thanatoids, were the second threesome. Father Sedon has spent many multiple multi-millennia keeping it his secret from everyone except me.

"And he can't remember I exist any more than you can, not unless I want you to."

Relieved, preternaturally serenely even, Vetala again sat in her throne. Everywhere she looked more and more of her Dead Things were arriving on the plain below Dustmound. The vast majority were walking but Cloud General Kronar and his remaining Vultyrie, what was left of the vulturous Cloud of Hadd, were flying in dozens more by the minute.

"We've had our reckonings before, vampire. I shan't order you to do anything purely because I can't order you to do anything; not with any confidence of complete compliance at any rate. However, unless you submit yourself fully to my

will, this shall be our last. You wouldn't be the first Master Deva I've disposed of and I'm not speaking about cathonitization either."

"I've heard such threats before, Judge. No matter how you phrase it, what you're proposing is at best tantamount to consensual rape. I shall not submit to rape of any description, marital or otherwise. This is my protectorate. Unlike your pair of talking heads I can and will command you to cathonitize. Be gone!"

The pinkish-faced fiend looked around almost absently: at the sky, the ground, the not so far-off Akan Gulf, the curious Dead Things, those that dared peer up at them, and then at the Sedon Sphere again. He wasn't bothered by the Nergalid's dictate; didn't anticipate it was anything more than a flurry of bluster à la King Cold. No zap, no nap. He wasn't sleepy anyways.

"From Harmony's High Seat in Sedon's Headband, I both far-saw and far-heard you say virtually the same thing to the Thanatoids and the Silverclouds yesterday. It didn't work then and it won't work now. Sooth said, the difference between firstborn and lower born, even second born like the Thanatoids, is so vast it rivals the difference between Sedon and his Great God brothers.

"Even so, it's only thanks to your Brainrock-blessed soldier that you and he got away yesterday. They'd have catasterized you as surely I will much worse today if you deny me; as surely as I will abolish him the next time he reappears. I'll do so whomever and whatever he is: a Golden Brown warrior, another The-attis, another Universal Soldier reborn, or just the most recent of the Lackland Libertine's lordly deviants, like Janna Fangfingers and her just as terrible twin, the Sraddhites' too mortal god.

"The 'greatest hero of the Living', ha!, my bonny backend."

Judge Druj, the Lord of Liars, was one of the more savoury honourifics devils gave him once he identified himself with Ahriman. They did so since the word *'druj'* meant *'evil'* in certain dualist traditions on the Outer Earth that acknowledged his existence. Another appellation he sometimes claimed was Angra Mainyu, two words that originally meant *'malign spirit'* or *'destructive mentality'*, both of which applied to him equally accurately in her mind.

Very little didn't amuse the fiend, who was basically an embodiment of materialism and, as such, an arch-devil in Outer Earth terms. Expressing outright ridicule, though, struck her as somewhat uncharacteristic. Of course Vetala's remembrances of him could hardly be considered reliable. Even with him stranding right there, annoying the hell out of her, she could barely recollect meeting him in the past and even then only a few times far between – between the sheets as well.

"To your credit, you have sought to improve your chances of cathonitizing anyone by amassing so many of your azuras here, in one place, at Dustmound. You hope to combine their collective willpower – their just as desperate devotion to you – in order to guarantee it is your own inviolable postage stamp of territorial triviality. I realize that.

"So, yes again, I was wondering about that myself. Now I have my answer. For you it's a false hope. For you also, the answer's no."

Wait a minute! What that it? Had he annoyed the hell into her? Had he slipped the necrotic notion of becoming a vampire into her mind all those centuries ago? (When she sought haven in Satanwyck, Sedon's Temple, alongside ever-erotic

Belialma, Lady Lust, who hoped to reclaim her Bastion of Bliss, and with it her templar throne, from Sinistral Envy.)

Did he stop her, stop them, then punish them both for their temerity? Was he, not the Moloch Sedon, the earthborn daemons' perhaps unacknowledged but actual monarch? Was he King Daemonicus returned as the Devil Reborn?

Whatever else he was, he remained an intentional imponderable, that was for sure; a head-scratcher; albeit thankfully only when his head was visible.

"Father Sedon has always had a soft spot for you; a hard cock as well. Clearly he doesn't anymore. You should never have played a Trigregos Gambit, Fecundity, Blood Queen of Futility and next to nil else. There is only one game on the Head and it's Sedonplay. Even with so many of your Dead Things around you, you can't make this pitiful little lump of skulls and bones your protectorate anymore than Hadd ever was."

"Oh do shut the frothing fuck up, Smiler."

"That I shall. Rather, that I shall ensure you're no longer here to hear. End of endgame, Nergalid. You lost."

========

After most of a night in Pandemonium, the Abode of All Demons, where she could sample from a grab-bag of chthonic creatures she could thereafter control as the Hecate-Hellions' Morrigan, Morgianna Sarpedon had acquired a few impressive specimens. She didn't have to debrain them herself this time. Lord Lazy (Sinistral Sloth, Baaloch Hellblob) had them debrained for her. Then, fine chef that he proved to be, he fried them up himself, their brains, nicely seasoned too.

Of course, since Hellblob somewhat resembled a dwarfish, red-shelled Humpty Dumpty with squiggly tufts of hair he passed off as a moustache and goatee, he either did that or Smiler, in his alter ego as Daemonicus, the Whole-Earthly King of Demons, would make an omelette out of him. Prime Sinistrals never forgot who was boss when he was around and she didn't forget that because she'd come with him, albeit all on her lonesome.

Having lost her Night's Mare, her psychopomp hobbyhorse, on Devauray; having had her pantsuit-demon stripped off her by her brother yesterday, on Sedonda; having as well been in danger of having Golgotha and his Trinondevs do the same again last night; the first demon she chose to make her own was a self-psychopomp. Hence she became a self-psycho herself.

Her pantsuit-demon did not itself have the brains left to object to its supplanting. It didn't have a lot to object to anyways. For one thing, Morg was wearing her latest psycho as an overcoat. Although no doubt related, it wasn't a denim-demon if only because it wasn't blue. It was white. What other colour, or lack thereof, would she let it be? Doubly wasn't blue because she made it happy to serve her; always assuming something that had no brains could have emotions.

She was behind Vetala's throne. She shoved the Susasword through its back, through Vetala's back, out her front. What's good for one goose – her pal, Janna Fangfingers – was good for another goose. The devic vampire's goose was thereby about to be slow-cooked. Whoever heard of a monogamous gander anyhow?

Like the Trinondevs' Field Commander, Golgotha Nauroz, Smiler wasn't averse to repeating what worked once, albeit on a comparatively ordinary vampire. The

Morrigan wasn't afraid of doing as the Earthly Demon King desired. It wouldn't be the first time. It would just be the first time she'd gain a curved, Brainrock blade as her reward. So long as she could hold onto its hilt long enough to kill Vetala, that is.

She could use it to kill the Earthly Demon King later.

========

The whir of the elevator stopped. Someone stomped into Thartarre's workroom atop the monastery on Sraddha Isle. He was wearing a brown robe but it wasn't his uniform. That had been soaked through. His head wasn't shaved bald; that was his mother. He hated vamps even though his father had become one. His hair was wet. He was using a towel.

He said: "Give me that radio, Ferd. I'm calling for an injection of the hard stuff."

========

Nergal Vetala screamed. If he wasn't so busy smiling, Smiler might have yawned at that. He did, however, materialize his panpipes, started playing them sombrely, soothingly. He played a lament – music to die for; music to die by, make that. Dead Things en masse stumbled to their feet, sought to lurch up the slight hill that remained of Diminished Dustmound; sought to rescue their gruesome Goddess.

The ambulant corpses closest to her and her throne didn't make it very far. She took out, then took in, their animating azuras in order to preserve herself. The first group collapsed; more of them collapsed as they staggered nearer to the summit; group after groping group collapsed in succession. Someone should have yelled dog-pile. Hadd's Blood Queen still couldn't detach herself from the Susasword.

The Trigregos Talismans killed devils. The Susasword was killing her, leisurely, excruciatingly.

The Smiling Fiend wasn't a sadist. Neither was the Morrigan. But, to withdraw the curved blade such that she could thereafter use it to make like Lady Guillotine, and thus end the Blood Queen's agony, would only give Vetala the split second she'd need to cut herself elsewhere. The Trigregos Talismans also made devils stupid. Smiler knew that; was counting on it. Vetala knew that too. Didn't matter. She needed him now.

As more and more of her Dead Things rooted where they dropped; started to rot on the spot, she far-screamed for him to come to her aid. He, on Sedon's Peak, freshly emerged from a lovely, if exceedingly hot bath in its lava lake, far-heard her. He, the Crimson Corona on his head, had enough time to grab Akbar's sceptre and the Amateramirror.

He couldn't be bothered to pull on pants or his combat boots. Stark naked suited him. All the best champions of ancient Greece, the heroes of his youth, his teens and even now, bodily well into his mid-twenties, got sculpted going into bloody battle that way. He thought himself to Dustmound. Hovering above it, he took a moment to reacclimatize himself.

Who was that, the devil shrouded in darkness playing the syrinx? Who was she, the white-clad woman – the Hellions' Morrigan? Whoa, where'd the devil go? And who's that? Alastor Molorchus. Cosmicaptain Dmetri Diomad had known him, hadn't he? Big brother Rom's bum-boy. Or so Dim had heard.

Whoosh! Thump! It wasn't Godstuff coming out of Al's missing arm's rotator cuff. It was Indescribables: indescribable demon after indescribable demon. Solidium counters Gypsium. Stopstone sponges Brainrock. They, it, encrusted him. He expelled vast quantities of Godstuff to broil them away. He, literally notwithstanding, couldn't stay aloft; came to ground, came to Dustmound, albeit on his feet, not his butt.

More and more demons – the Morrigan's one-armed man must have a pipeline to Hell itself. Indescribable concretions hardened, more Gypsium expended. His head was still free, both his arms were as well. On his head was the Crimson Corona. In one hand he held OMP-Akbar's Homeworld Sceptre. On his other arm was the Amateramirror. Behind his goddess's throne, the White Witch was unwavering.

She wanted all three talismans, let her have them, one by one. The Crimson Corona first. There it was, on her head now. Do it, witch. The Morrigan slid the sword out of the Vampire Queen's back, out of the back of her throne; she'd been wanting to do that anyways. That makes two.

Vetala was loose; as loose as a thoroughly cooked goose – wasn't moving. The stench from everywhere around him assailed his senses. Not many of her thousands of Dead Things were moving either. Her throne began to glow brighter than it had it been; he somewhat less so. The whooshing and thumping were unrelenting. Your turn, Al.

Do this too, witch. Brainrock blades fired off the sword's hilt. Thanks. Molorchus looked better as a hat-rack crumbling to ground pin-cushioned. The Crimson Corona returned to his head. Good to have you back again. Oh, that's where the devil in darkness went. Why isn't he smiling? What's that?

Holy fuck, why am I screaming!

========

He was right. Smiler wasn't smiling. Even for him, it was inappropriate to smile when your demonic body now resembled a blades-protrusive porcupine. Pain would pass, he could metabolize Brainrock. He'd be smiling again momentarily. He looked up; saw himself reflected in the Amateramirror.

His reflection wasn't smiling either.

========

Trigregos Incarnate was screaming because the Diver was inside him.

UD, Yehudi Cohen, had to go through the Weird, the dark grey universal substance of Samsara, to get to him. Solidium, the term he used for Stopstone, had always been the Diver's bane but now that he could teleport it didn't trouble him. No devil, he couldn't possess Vetala's Soldier but he could disrupt his attentiveness. He didn't know what a Trigregos Gambit was but he played one in ignorance. Either that or the Crimson Corona played one on his behalf.

Pre-Limbo years earlier, from 1945 to 1955, he and the rest of the King Crimefighters had numerous opportunities to witness Corona Power using her bloodstone tiara for purposes of mind-over-mind control. Most of them not only became immune to its effect but learned how to employ it. The Diver, who was as famous for his hunches as he was for his quips, some of which were mega-groaners, gambled he could force it to order its sister object, the Amateramirror, to release OMP-Akbar, Dervish Furie, Blind Sundown and Raven's Head.

It seemed to resist. So did the soldier, seemed to anyhow. The diversion of him within him seemed to do the trick. Inside the mirror synapses snapped. The Cheyenne Summoning Child and his Beauty (whom some claimed housed the spirit of a different Summoning Child, Sundown's wife, once Fish's best buddy, Sorciere born Solace Sunrise) regained consciousness.

So did the Wildman and the rightful Kronokronos Supreme of Subterranean Temporis, who'd been Corona's husband; had been when she was Takeda Mikoto and they both lived on the Hidden Headworld, too. That hadn't been like Limbo, D-Brig-4 would concur as one. That had been like Death with no sense of an afterlife; with no sense of anything at all.

The first two expanded their cosmic aura, roiled out of it and immediately regained solidity. The second two didn't have cosmic auras but they were out as well. The Amateramirror hadn't so much rejected them as ejected them. Maybe it found the prospect of a devil more appetizing than three supras and a mutated ravendeer.

No sooner were they out of it than the mirror's glassine surface re-formed. The Smiling Fiend looked up and he was in it. The soldier had been screaming. He stopped abruptly. The Diver had taken into himself all the Brainrock-Gypsium the onetime Cosmicaptain hadn't transferred to Vetala's throne. Old Man Power, Akbarartha, was the first to reorient himself to his surroundings. The nearly gigantic greybeard strode purposely to the demon-caked soldier and grasped his Homeworld Sceptre.

"I believe this is mine," he said casually.

The soldier held on but there was nothing in his eyes. His golden-brown skin was more like dirty brown clay baked too long in a kiln. The Awesome Akbar, a massive Santa Claus of a man at six and a half feet tall, one who was almost as broad as he was wide, gave his sceptre a tug. Ordinarily he knew his own strength, could temper it accordingly. Maybe he used too much of it this time because he didn't just tear his sceptre out of his grip. He tore off the Soldier's arm with it. Now that was surprising.

He swatted the severed arm with his free hand. It crumbled; flaked away.

========

The analogy was apt. Dried-out clay was exactly what had become of Vetala's Theattis.

========

His head cracked from the inside out. Like Olympian Athena emerging from Sky God Zeus's skull in Greek Mythology, the Diver floated upwards. The Crimson Corona was attached to his head. Then he blipped; vanished into the Weird. The Crimson Corona was now around Akbar's head. It had little or no effect on him. It didn't need to: the Kronokronos needed no encouragement, let alone any coercion, to do what he did next.

Rightful Supreme deliberately smashed his sceptre against the Amateramirror. Its Dand-head erupted. So did the mirror; glass, Smiler's reflection with it, even its frame blew apart. One more swing and he blew apart the soldier. Bad boy was already dead wasn't he. Past time to bury him. Bones and bits of fetid flesh remained stuck to some of its no longer constituent parts. Although a day late, OMP-Akbar was a good as his word. All the king's men …

He had a thought. Unless his Homeworld Sceptre had it for him, which would be unusual since he hadn't bopped his head with its head. His thought was a question. Why waste all that demonic, subtle matter? Its Dand-head didn't erupt when he brought it down this time. There wasn't so much demonic material sprayed over immediate Dustmound anymore, however.

The Crimson Corona was now on the Morrigan's head. This could get awkward. She wasn't dead yet. And even with a name like theirs they weren't supposed to kill except as a last resort – though that had rarely stopped Johnny and Raven. For them justifiable homicide sometimes equated with righteous retribution; hence their bloody Vengeance Quest against the Conquering Christ and The Rache, so-called, that ended on Salvation Island in 1953.

The mirror was re-forming itself on her arm. She pointed the hilt of the Susasword at the four members of the Damnation Brigade. So what if she wasn't dead yet? They'd already had more than enough of this flagitious flapdoodle, the Diver's equivalent of Fish's screeching codswallop or baleen bilge bucket of whaledreck. Furie was in motion. So was Raven's Head. The throne beside Superior Sarpedon, as they best knew Morgianna, was now a woman, the Vampire Queen.

Nergal Vetala, formerly Fecundity, most renowned of a number of Mithradite Moon Goddesses, slashed her Brainrock sickle against Morg's wrist. It might have broken it. It visibly stuck there, in her psycho-overcoat as well as in her forearm. It was Morg's turn to scream. She couldn't help but drop the hilt. Her overcoat-demon, combined with her pantsuit-demon, coated the sickle, began to dissolve it and vice versa.

Sundown's Solar Spear discharged pent-up killing energy. It wasn't directed at Superior Sarpedon. It was directed at the Vampire Queen. The devil hardly had time to shriek. Without contact with Raven's horn it wasn't cathonitizing energy. It didn't need to be. Just as Dervish Furie tackled Morgianna, Raven's Head, galloping forward, unicorn horn telescoped, lowered, skewered the devil.

Like a stuck rat, Vetala thrashed about not precisely pointlessly. In seconds she atomized. Endgame her.

========

That was when they felt the first drop of rain.
****

(ENDGAME-GAMBIT) 28: **Everyone Loses Eventually**

Mithrada, Tantalar 8, 5980

Other than Nergal Vetala, her soldier and a certain somebody no one would ever remember existed, it wasn't endgame anyone else.

========

"This is interesting," said Diego de Landa, who had his headset on again.

"What is?" asked Jordan Tethys.

In addition to radio, which Godbadians, via the Nag Gap, had only imported from the Outer Earth a few decades earlier, there were a number of ways to communicate long distance on the Hidden Headworld. Three of them were witch-stones, Utopian eye-staves and Crystal Skulls. More of a problem was the logistics behind launching a pre-emptive air strike on Sanguerre, capital city of the Bloodlands, Sedon's Inner Nose.

From the northern provinces of the subcontinent of Aka Godbad the most direct route would be across Sedon's Moustache, aka the Forbidden Forest of Kala Tal, so called because it was a Mithradite Master Deva's protectorate. Ergo, that was suicidal. One thing devil-gods excelled at besides inspiring bad thoughts and worse nightmares (from a monotheist's perspective anyway), was causing the worst weather imaginable. After all, what weather killed could always be attributed to Mother Nature, not Master Devas.

From New Iraxas you could skirt Tal by flying east into Hadd then north, over-top the Diluvia Mountain Range's easternmost slopes, then west, overtop Marutia, Sedon's Cheek. Which was plagued by Time Quakes. Ergo, even if you could load enough fuel into your warplanes and long-range helicopter gunships, no go there either, right? Yet New Iraxas was where the bulk of Godbad's northern air force was located. That was because the Godbadian brain-trust's thrust had been on Hadd, Old Iraxas.

To send its air force the other way, overtop Fearsome Fobbiat, the Headworld's western ocean, then north, across Bogy Bay and the Pristine Isles, to the Bloods, meant first having to deploy it to Godbad's northwest corner from its northeast coast. That was even farther; would require even more fuel. (Since there was noth-ing to the subcontinent's west other than the ocean and, ultimately, the edge of

Cathonia – which was a no-pass, all-crash zone – the Godbadians only manned a few small, strictly naval, coast guard stations on that side.)

The Corporate State's military masterminds deemed a pre-emptive strike on Sanguerre mandatory. East, then north, then west, was doubly deemed the way to go. Time Quakes were random, never forget. The odds of one striking during a speedy over-flight were consequently judged low unto subterranean. Could quakes even shake the sky?

That being the dace-case of canned tuna, since you're fish-heading that way any-bays …

A rough translation of *'Shooting clip-winged, ducky decoys in a duck-pond'* was hit them where they stood, or glorified, or grovelled. Them, they, were Nergal Vetala's unprecedented and unlikely-to-repeat convergence of Dead Things, worshipful azuras animating them, on and around howsoever diminished Dustmound.

Fish wasn't very persuasive. Godbadians, Godbad's military and its civilian overseers, had had it with regal types. Two other radio-users were, however. One was Godbadian General Quentin Anvil, who was a very good swimmer. The other was Gomez Niarchos, who was dead. Then there was a fellow who went by the name of Alpha Centauri on the Inner Earth. He was by far the most persuasive voice of all. He used a telephone from his headquarters-cum-fortress in Aka Godbad City, not a radio. President Lemon was his man.

Gomez could also use a Crystal Skull-set. His son had one of them. Fish stuck with witch-stones. Once compelling the bombers to do their bombing was done, a radio, a Crystal Skull-set and a witch-stone came back into play. The messages thus transmitted were essentially identical. "Stay away from Dustmound," repeated de Landa upon complete reception of his.

"Bit late for that," Tethys muttered, popping another beer. He was all in favour of screw-tops but wasn't averse to using a bottle-opener.

With the exception of some functionaries – including a number of wounded, yet still moderately mobile Trinondevs and mostly uninjured Zebranids with eyestaves – Tethys, Niarchos and de Landa, who'd been placed in charge of residual defense of the monastery, were the only ones left of the Living's brain-trust in the makeshift, top-floor, command central.

They weren't unsighted as to events on Dustmound anymore. Witch-stones, like Trinondev eyeorbs, had many uses.

The Legendarian had just never used them as inkwells before.

========

She had them, had all three of them. Ouch!

========

Nergal Vetala fractured her wrist. She dropped one. Sundown roasted the Blood Queen whereupon Raven's Head impaled what was left of her. When did Raven get a horn, become a monoceros? No matter. Zap, crackle, poof. Good show, beauty. Bye-bye, Bat-bait. Good riddance, Nergalid. Don't bother coming back this time. Don't bother coming back again anytime. Soon devils will be as foreign to the Inner Earth as they already are on the Outer Earth.

Furie tackled her, knocked her down, sat on her, the bastard. She still had two; could will the hilt back into her hand. Not the one that hurt so much. It'd heal. Her psycho-overcoat could crust the sickle alone. Her pantsuit-demon could cast her wrist immobile. She could will it back to her other hand, the one with the mirror attached to its forearm. A third hand, the Diver's hand, reached out of the ground, grabbed the hilt and pulled it underneath Dustmound with him.

'*Oh, you think yourself so smart, don't you, Yehudi?*'

The fucking faerie lumbered up to her, smacked the mirror with his Home-world Sceptre. Now that was clever. Its Dand-head didn't explode. It disgorged sticky quantities of subtle matter, demonic crap, Stopstone, Solidium, all over the Amateramirror, frame and all. Useless now, it; not so her. She still had one.

The bead-blindfolded Blind Man was above her, holding onto Raven's reins. Bye-bye, Morg. Even if he was gal-pal, fellow War Witch and closet Hellion Sor-ciere's childhood groom (then, later on, albeit still most of forty years ago, her legal husband), Johnny was a killer. Except, he didn't kill her. He instead used the tip of his Solar Spear to flick the Crimson Corona off her head. Now she had none.

She felt sick. She wasn't done yet. Last night in Satanwyck Morg had had a veritable smorgasbord of demons to choose from; some of them she actually ate.

"Get off of me, you great lummox," she yelled at Furie. "I'm going to puke."

"Oh, really?" queried the African-born, Jamaica-raised Summoning Child, glaring down at her. He deliberately bared his fangs, such as they were. Were those horns sprouting out of the top of his skull? Sure looked like it. What precise kind of wild man was he – a satyr? He had halitosis, that much she could be sure about.

"First I'm a Werewolf in Shorts. Next I'm a goat. Now I'm a lummox. What's a lummox anyways?"

D-Brig-4 – the four who'd been held within the Amateramirror – towered over her. Considering her supine position, everything that wasn't underneath her towered over her. Raven Head's unicorn horn still smouldered. Sundown's Solar Spear glowed the more what with him twirling the Crimson Corona around on its spearhead. The Dand-head of OMP-Akbar's Homeworld Sceptre didn't shimmer a glimmer but it could instantaneously. She was under no illusion about that.

Make that D-Brig-5. The Diver dove out of Dustmound, landed on his feet atop it. It was raining so hard he would have to dive into the sky and keep going, to the other side of Hadd's cloud-covering, before he had to stop swimming; let alone have any hope of ever getting dry again. He was juggling the hilt of Demeter's Body as tauntingly as the sightless Cheyenne, the Blind Irache in Headworld terms, was twirling Devaura's Mind.

They were so cocky. Even Raven, who was as female as she was resolutely not toilet-trained, looked cocksure of herself.

"Wouldn't know, Dervish," said the Diver. UD was cooking up a wisecrack. "But I do know she considers Auguste Moirnoir her father. Maybe she needs an Augie-bag."

Even for the Diver that was bad. Morg puked up whole heaps more than could have been contained in any single doggie bag; even a doggie bag for a behemoth Rottweiler, Bull Mastiff or Great Dane.

========

Cerebrus David Ryne wasn't trying to be devious, disingenuous, fatalistic, any of the above, when he gave them their group-name barely a week ago. They'd been de-constituted, their bodies separated from their minds, on the Outer Earth's Damnation Isle in late December 1955; on Christmas Day, to be precise. That'd be Xmas to Xuthrodites like their patriarch, Ryne Senior, her old comrade in crime – called the Great Man by many, Loxus Abraham by his parents.

They'd been reconstituted, their bodies recombined with their minds, on the same forsaken Aleutian atoll most of a quarter century later, on the last day of November this year out there. Physically they were unaged. Mentally, they were not noticeably demented. Put better, a couple of them were — but only to a wee degree.

(OMP, Obadiah Melvin 'Old Man' Power, at lease had an excuse. He was possessed; not in his right mind due to the fact six devils had wangled their way into his right mind. More unacceptably given the circumstances, and despite uniform admonitions to the contrary, Gloriella nee D'Angelo become Dark, whose Aunt Mnemosyne was the third Trigon Triplet, had insisted on reacquainting herself with her elderly parents and remaining family.

(The result had been tragically predictable: her sainted, as well as senescent, mother's outraged, but righteous, rejection – via a sanctified crucifix brought to bear very accurately, forehead-wise – and the sudden need for an ambulance to haul away her fragile, even more aged father to the nearest emergency ward.)

Although they thought of where they'd consciously been as Limbo – when they were consciously aware of being anywhere, that is – it seemed to all of them at the time that they'd just been to Hell and back. Given where they were de-constituted then reconstituted; given as well Devil Wind (Vayu Maelstrom as they learned to refer to him), the four Apocalyptics, the devic Vultyrie and Demon Land (Antaeor Thanatos), openly acknowledged they were members of a race of devils; since they'd overcome them, Damnation Brigade fit.

It still fit for the five members of D-Brig currently on Diminished Dustmound. All the more so given what the Morrigan, Superior Sarpedon, had just spat as much out of her innards as between-space. If those things weren't Hell-spawned demons, well, now was hardly the time to put their heads together and come up with a better description. At least they, these hideous Indescribables, were holding off attacking them for some reason.

Their bodies were unaged because they'd been preserved as Stopstone-covered statuary in Centurium, replicated Versailles, one of the Thousand Caverns of Dand Tariqartha, for all that time. Two days ago, Devauray-Saturday, in a different Temporite cavern, the Diver and Furie, along with Wilderwitch, owed their survival to the timely arrival of the Calvary Cavalry, as they'd already begun to write in their own mental memoirs.

It consisted of Glory of the Angels, Johnny and his Beauty, arguably the descendent of an actual unicorn fused magically with a pair of raven or crow tricksters. Wilderwitch and Radiant Rider, like Cyborg Cerebrus, were currently unavailable. The same was true of the Elemental Twins — the other two initial members of the once 10-strong Damnation Brigade: Gloriel's adopted siblings, Thalassa and Aires D'Angelo, whose codenames were Sea Goddess and Airealist.

Wildman Dervish Furie, the Untouchable Diver, Blind Sundown and Raven's Head, whose like hadn't been seen on the Head for thousands of years, bolstered by OMP-Akbarartha, Temporis's rightful Kronokronos Supreme, were here, on Diminished Dustmound. That meant they'd have to be their own last minute rescue-party because she wasn't about to let them off the hook now.

Unless …

========

In addition to her pantsuit-demon outerwear, as well as her Outer Earth made and bought underwear, she was wearing a psychopomp-overcoat. That sort of psycho could flash through the Weird as readily as devils could. The Morrigan went from underneath Furie to overtop Alastor Molorchus, what was slash-shredded-left of him.

That wouldn't be enough to contain any circulating blood but his recumbent corpse could still contain an azura, had she had one readily available. Nay probs there. She painted her fingernails. Some of their specks, under a microscope or reasonably powerful magnifying glass, looked liked Crystal Skulls because they were Crystal Skulls.

"The Three Sacred Objects," she cried, "The Trigregos Talismans, they're mine. I've one."

She did, too. The made-useless, because it was demon-encrusted, Amateramirror was on her left forearm. The Diver had the hilt of the Susasword while Blind Sundown was still twirling the Crimson Corona on the tip of his Solar Spear tantalizingly. "I'll have the other two now or I'll have them momentarily. Only then it'll be over your dead bodies. Your choice."

That was why the horrors were holding off. She thought she was being generous; was giving them a chance to live. Would Sundown and Raven give her a chance to do ditto? More to the point, could her pantsuit-demon, ameliorated by her psycho-overcoat, withstand a killing burst of solar energy? They might, especially if it hit the Amateramirror first and thereby burnt off the demonic crusting OMP-Akbar splattered over its still glassless surface.

"I don't approve of your tone, Sarpedon," said the Cheyenne Summoning Child. "And I don't approve of anyone who has truck with demons."

Because he was holding onto her reins, he could see through Raven's eyes. He knew what they were up against; they both did. He also saw Morg raise up the mirror, as if it would be enough to shield her from his spear's discharge. They'd both been inside that mirror, bodies with minds. It had knocked them completely out, as good or bad as dead. It wasn't anything they wanted to repeat.

"We could run and you couldn't stop us but you're relentless, aren't you? So long as we have any of them, you'd never leave us alone. Smart says scorch." He let his spear-tip lower, shook the Crimson Corona off it. Let the talisman lie closer to OMP-Akbar's feet than to either his or Raven's hooves. It was a significant gesture.

"So call me dumb. This isn't my world."

"A wise decision, Johnny," Morg congratulated him, breathing easier. "Yehudi?"

In Cerebrus's absence, UD, Yehudi Cohen, the Untouchable Diver, was D-Brig's presumptive leader. He realized precisely why Sundown had done what he'd done. He nevertheless hesitated contemplatively; did so out loud as well.

"I know of your dealings with the Dead and the Undead, Superior. I know about your Hellions killing their fellow War Witches in aid of you getting hold of these things. I realize everything you've done is in the name of destroying devils. I'm an Israeli citizen. Sometimes the means warrant the end. Furie?"

"Ordinarily I'd vote to run," the wild man responded, equivocally. "But Sundown's right. It isn't our world."

"Your world, Old Man," the Diver said. Following Sundown's lead, he tossed the hilt of the Susasword at Akbar's feet. In doing so, he thereby copped a cowardly plea of uninvolvement, if not disentanglement per se. Which, devoutly desirous as it may be, was beyond their grasp – in non-punning terms. "Your choice."

"Turn around and walk away, faerie-fuck," said Morgianna, all but salivating at the thought of having the Trigregos Talismans again.

Of the five potentially standing in the way of her reclaiming them, only Sundown and Raven frightened her. The other three she reckoned she could handle herself. Besides, she was hardly alone. The corpse of Alastor Molorchus was only a materialized, then tossed-down and shattered, Crystal Skull away from animating again. Her vomited demons, her Indescribables, were plain slavering. Puked up semi-digested or not, they were as disgusting as they weren't digesting. That was a situation in need of remedying. They were hungry.

Raven's Head emitted some sounds in that peculiar neigh-caw way she did; was, she knew from the Secret War of Supranormals, speaking.

Sundown translated: "Raven says she loves playing polo."

OMP-Akbar turned around and walked away. Fucking faeries hated devils, yes; didn't much like being called faerie-fucks, though.

"Mount up, old man," said Sundown.

He was holding onto Raven's reins with one hand; had his Solar Spear in the other. She bent to accommodate OMP. He got onto her in one fluid motion, as if he was an old man in name only. Which he was. Effortlessly Blind Sundown hopped up behind him.

The White Witch, Morgianna born Nauroz, become Somata, the Morrigan, Superior Sarpedon, nearly had them all again. There was a demon-crusted and therefore useless one on her arm. There were two anything except useless ones lying a mere thought away. It was just a matter of collecting them.

She wasn't stupid. She knew what D-Brig-5 were capable of doing. But she'd lasted as long as they had; longer, in fact, since she didn't have the luxury of lolling away a quarter of a century in Limbo. Plus, she had really good hearing.

Correction, she was stupid.

========
Young Death, inside Garcia Dis L'Orca's dead body, had been the first to bugger off.
========

He had a daughter entirely unworthy of saving. He fully intended to save her anyways. Either that or he'd die trying. Big Whoop that. He'd once been killed just looking at his own reflection. Of course that was when he and the near-devil, Klannit Thanatos, weren't getting along; no sin killing him. Dead Dis L'Orca could get about on witch-stones. Diminished Dustmound was littered with them. He didn't need those ones, though. He had a better idea.

Witch-stones as inkwells had rendered Jordy's Brainrock quill functional again. Morg was behind Vetala's throne desperately holding onto the Susasword, trying to kill the yet wriggling Vampire Queen, when he left the monastery. He, inside Garcia, might be able to step between-space to her; to come off on one of her very own witch-stones, a plentitude of which she always secreted about her person.

That wasn't his idea, though. Satan St Synne, whom he also knew as Judge Warlock, didn't have three eyes but he'd vanished only to be replaced by his inspiration for a better idea.

"Demons," he'd exclaimed. "Fucking brilliant, Morg. Golgotha, every last one of your men, I want them down below, outside the tent. Yours too, priest. And yours as well, governor; if Daddy Quentin left you any. Someone get hold of the Fatman's daughter-in-law. Tell her Dustmound. There's going to be a D-Day after all."

Which was why, sometime afterwards, the Legendarian told De Landa it was a mite late to stay away from Diminished Dustmound.

He'd drawn everyone he could there.

========

Polo? Of course.

The old man had lost his regalia somewhere, presumably on the Outer Earth. She'd known they were the Thrygragos Talismans virtually from moment she first encountered him. Without them he was far more vulnerable than the other four. Now that he was on Raven's back, with Blind Sundown behind him, he was protected by their cosmic aura.

They'd played her for a fool. No more!

========

She materialized a Crystal Skull in her unhurt hand; cracked it against the deadhead of a dead guy; one Alastor Molorchus by the name his possibly not quite as long-dead parents gave him. As a Sangazur repossessed him, reactivated him, she made her move. She had the Soul, raised it protectively; thought herself to the Mind and Body. Got close. Got a blast of enflaming stellar energy courtesy of Sundown and his Solar Spear for her troubles.

She wasn't stupid after all. Unless she was just lucky. And here on the Head, where the closest stars were cathonitized devils, there was even a lucky star named just that – Star Luck, after Wintry Moira, Dame Chance, Fata Fortuna. Or had been, rather. Yet, she instantly gathered further, there was something even less likely. Sundown had aimed for the mirror; was actually giving her a chance to live. In which case he was right. He was the dumb one.

She was fleetingly on fire. Neither her psycho-overcoat nor her pantsuit-demon had any Lava Lout, let alone any fairy Salamander, to them. But the mirror had taken most of the burst and the rain truly was torrential. No, she wasn't on fire for long. However, the pain in her broken wrist was now all but overpowering. She chanced a glance. Psycho-overcoat was history. Vetala's power focus wasn't; was still sickle-sticking out of her wrist.

She grabbed hold of it, yanked it out. Screamed, almost passed out with pain. Screamed the more at her vomited-up Indescribables. Kill them. Kill them all. As if they needed the encouragement. D-Brig didn't either. Although none of them were psychic, none of them trusted Morgianna Sarpedon. She'd had, as the Diver might put it, quite the her-story of untrustworthiness pre-Limbo. Evidently nothing had changed post-Limbo

Furie voted to run. He did, right at her. The Diver hadn't voted to do anything. He dove anyways, right at her. Polo had another meaning besides clouting Dead Things, who weren't moving anyways, or Indescribables, who were, though not as fast as D-Brig-3. Sundown may have been blind but Raven's speed was blinding.

OMP-Akbar bent low and slammed the Dand-head of his Homeworld Sceptre onto the Crimson Corona and the Susasword. They exploded on contact; weren't there anymore. Furie had the Morrigan pinned again, shook Vetala's moon-sickle out of her grip and hurled it as far away from her as he could, which was a decent distance.

The Diver tried a different tactic. He rendered Morg's arm intangible. The Amateramirror was still solid. It fell off her. He grabbed it, rolled away with it, came up with it, yelled *'Catch!'*, flung it in the direction of Raven, Sundown and OMP-Akbar. The old man – in terms of time alive, if not physical decrepitude – must have heard *'Splat!'* because that was what he did to it. Swung his sceptre and, once its head made contact with the mirror, made it go splat.

It wasn't there anymore either. That meant, albeit only theoretically, that there was no reason for them to fight anymore.

========

After swimming to it, General Anvil was so angry at having had to spend the night in an inflatable raft on Lake Sedona he'd have self-dried himself sooner or later. An injection of the hard stuff meant missiles. Dustmound was a very small duck pond. He was already on his way there, with everything Godbadian that could still fly, now that the snow had melted, and everyone Godbadian who could still fight, for clean-up duty.

Make that mop-up duty. It hadn't been raining when he set off for Dustmound.

========

Something huge hit Raven Head. It must have been huge because, protected as she was by her cosmic aura, it bowled her over; sent both Sundown and OMP-Akbar sprawling off her. It wasn't a bowling ball. It was something similar; was more akin to a cannonball. It was huge, though; a huge, ball-like skull. Wasn't crystalline; was blazing.

Sundown was blind again. OMP-Akbar wasn't. He shouted at the top of his lungs. Morg's Indescribables were upon him, upon them. What he shouted was: "Bellona!"

Molorchus clambered to his feet. He had a Sang inside him. The rotator cuff of his missing arm was doing its G-string thing; was rotating. There was no more G-thing to do. He had a Hellstone embedded in his chest. Out of it came a War Witch. It was dead Dis L'Orca. Then there was no more Sang inside him; might have been one inside of Garcia, though. There still wasn't any Gypsium to do his G-string thing. It was still raining. Then it was raining arrows as well. Arrows hurt.

The sky was growing even darker as it filled with hundreds, perhaps thousands of vultures, each of which carried at least one Dead Thing. The Cloud of Hadd had returned. Only this time the Dead Things they were carrying weren't possessed by Vetalazurs, be they Nergalazurs or Haddazurs. Couldn't be. They were raining arrows down on them from above. Vetalazurs couldn't animate Haddit zombies in a rainstorm and weren't coordinated enough to flight arrows while flying. Not if they wanted to stay aloft. They'd as likely hit the vultures carrying them.

The Dead had to be animated by Sangs. Had Morgianna arranged her own cavalry? No. Not that D-Brig-5 were in any position to notice it but virtually all of the Dead Things the Vultyrie were carrying were Japanese. Former Kronokronos Mikoto now knew who'd killed him. Not once, with bullets, but twice, the second time with the Susasword. This was personal.

Was more than that actually. This was war, the Dead against the Dead if necessary. The prize, other than the satisfaction of revenge, would be the same: the Trigregos Talismans. But that was just for starters. Vetala vapourizing additionally meant it would be for Hadd, sometimes called Sedon's Mutton Chop, sometimes also called the Penile Peninsula, and not just by wannabe comedians.

He'd brought someone special with him; someone who wasn't at all funny. He also didn't have to ride a Vultyrie in order to go anywhere. Rather, Guardian Angel Tyrtod had. Devils couldn't possess other devils but symbiotic Sangs could dominate simpletons.

Guardian Angel Tyrtod could think for himself. Was now, not so unusually, doing the thinking for two. One of them was not the dead Warlord. He wasn't Guardian Angel Mikoto anymore – a different Sang had that pleasure. Nor, precisely, was he just Guardian Angel Tyrtod.

Tyrtod meant War-Death. He was Guardian Angel Mars Bellona.

========

There was a sickening picture from the Second World War often reprinted in Life Magazine. A German soldier had been killed and decapitated; his severed head mounted on a tank's fender. Most of its skin had rotted away, leaving only a gnarly skull. The grotesquery still had on his spiked helmet. Historically Celts beheaded their enemies and mounted them on the end of their spears. Really ambitious barbarians rammed spearheads upwards, through a skull's cranium, before they paraded around with them.

Mars Bellona was a bonehead with two-eyeholes, a nose-hole, glistening teeth, though not fanglike, nor otherwise inhuman, and a goatee. He didn't have on a spiked helmet. Nor was his backbone exactly a spear's shaft with the spear's head piercing out of the top of his skull. Instead, spikes crested his skull like a Mohawk hairstyle, from where his third eye should be all the way back to its base. He had an incongruously muscular body, wore pants, combat boots, with spiked toes, and a spiked bandoleer over an otherwise bare chest.

Likely the bandoleer was his power focus. It glowed. All sorts of deadly things emitted from it. His forearms were mutable. This minute one was a rotating Gatling gun while the other was a wide-bored cannon barrel. His ammunition was ordinarily blazing skulls, the same as his fellow Apocalyptic, Catastrophe, Headless Disaster, Nakba Ramazar, whose Tvasitar Talisman had most recently taken the form of a flintlock shotgun. His cannon-arm was what fired the cannonball-skull. His arm-Gatling fired Crystal Skulls.

They shattered all about Diminished Dustmound and beyond it, on the plain below it. Haddit zombies, those that weren't too decomposed to do so, began to rise anew. They weren't possessed of Vetalazurs; could function in the rain. As Gomez Niarchos had radioed Godbad City, there wasn't much point bombing Sanguerre.

Many of its Sangazurs weren't there anymore and those that were weren't necessarily anti-Godbadian.

The reason for that was Battle Baby, the highborn Lazaremist whose talisman was the Sabre Rattle.

Displaced to Sedon's Outer Nose not all that long ago, she – Badhbh, as Illuminaries had her after, as one might expect, a Celtic battle goddess; one third of the not-just-folkloric Morrigu – was back in Sedon's Inner Nose big time. She was hardly alone; was at the helm of Godbadian-armed, blood-lustful legions of trophy head-hunters from the Grey Land of Twilight.

Had Gomez something to do with that? Not really. That was mostly down to Thrygragos Byron. The Great God might be in the high night's sky, entirely unexpectedly, but some of his anticipated masterstrokes had worked out wonderfully. They hadn't been confined to Mithradite realms in the Upper Head, such as the Floodlands, the Lake Lands, the Ghostlands and the Cheek Lands, either. He'd intended to make Sedon's Head his head, Byron's Head.

Of course he'd only intended to make it thus until the Cosmic Express or at least some of its Brainrock-powered cosmicars returned to the Outer Earth. All went well, a few if not all those that did would come back with news of a more suitable planet than the Whole Earth for his people, devils that they were.

It had to be somewhere he could lead the devazur race; somewhere they'd be safe and could thrive. Needless to say, it also had to somewhere other than the nowhere that the Cosmic Express and its components ended up on the 30th – which was essentially where it had started out. That anticipated masterstroke therefore hadn't worked out at all well.

Lazaremists retaking the Bloods, though, that seemed to be going according to plan.

========

"Blowfish the fingering submarines lower down," Fisherwoman suggested to Untouchable Diver comparatively quite a while ago.

"Can the sardines, Fish. I'm hungry. Ah, here's something."

He'd already had more than merely something. He'd had enough of the prison pod within which Demios Sarpedon had captured Nowadays Nihila, on nowhere near quite-so-diminished Dustmound the night before. As a consequence, it no longer could contain anyone — especially not anyone once by far and away the shiniest of the Shining Ones.

Fish hadn't needed to be particularly persuasive back in Godbad City; no more so than Alpha Centauri had needed to make that phone call.

Clams must have bowel movements, or their equivalencies, but devils didn't always need to manifest their third eyes in order to get their way.

========

The Vultyrie, Mikoto's Two Thousand riding them, give or take a few hundred, Rakshas among them, were being pursued. The rain may have been torrential but it wasn't thunderously so. The thunder was the distant sound of airplanes high above the clouds, that and the drone of helicopter gunships, stroboscopic spotlights flashing, coming in from all directions.

The five members of the once 10-strong Damnation Brigade on Diminished Dustmound were too preoccupied to pay much attention to the witch-stones sud-

denly activating on it and the plain around it. Off of them came Thartarre Sraddha
Holgatson, Golgotha Nauroz, the High Priest's Sraddhites and the Utopian clone's
Trinondevs. There was a goodly, if not godly, number of these last; virtually all that
was left of them.

There were also Godbadians and Zebranids among them. Every one of those
who came through were holding hands with as many and more Athenan War
Witches, as led by Janna St Peche-Montressor. Noticeable by their absence were
Governor Ferdinand Niarchos, Jordan Tethys and the two other Sarpedons, Demios
and Andaemyn. Neither Niarchos nor Tethys were fighters, so no surprise there. The
Sarpedons were incapacitated.

Before coming here Golgotha had given Demios his own personal eye-stave
for purposes of protection. He'd kept Dem's for purposes of multiplication. Demios
was with his daughter, in their Curia-assigned quarters. The majority of the Sarpedons' Zebranids were still on Sraddha Isle guarding them just in case any of the
left-behind Trinondevs got brave and, as per their Master's inviolable commands,
tried to apprehend them.

Fisherwoman wasn't there either. Not yet. Then she was, in a way. She was
bigger than life, much bigger than Diminished Dustmound. She didn't quote Bob
Dylan, whom she'd more than just met on the Outer Earth, howsoever many years
ago now. She didn't cry out: 'A Hard Rain's A-Gonna Fall', though she perhaps
should have.

Because that was what started to fall, in addition to wet rain and arrows.

Neither did she cry out: 'Incoming!' Which would have been both accurate and
appropriate; not to mention seriously non-fishifying. She did look good in a glowingly golden, chain-mail hauberk; no question of that. And there was nothing better
against incoming missiles, no matter what they were tipped with, than teleportive
Brainrock chains.

So everyone there and aware instantly started hoping anyhow.

Fish proved her twisted sisterhood. She cried out: "In-Swimming. No con-
doms!"

========

*King Cold ripped his war-axe, his Labrys, off his back and swung it at Melina born
Sarpedon and her children, Zerosses the three of them.*

Daddy-Hubby Harry gasped in impotent horror!
****

Nuclear Dragons

- November-December 1980 -

Jim McPherson

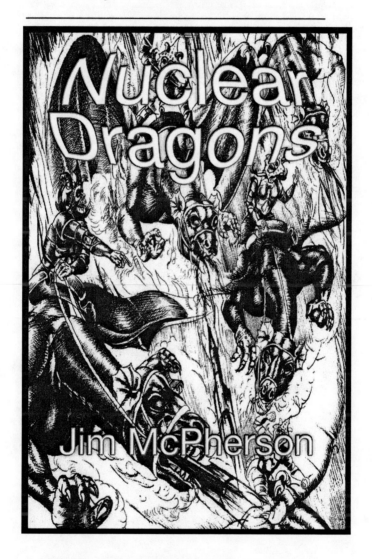

A *PHANTACEA* Mythos Mosaic Novel

Phantacea Publications (James H McPherson, Publisher)

Coming in 2012 (6012 Year of the Dome)

NUKE 3: The Launching of the Cosmic Express

Sunday, November 30, 1980

It was early 1978 that the signals were first detected. They came from somewhere out in space. At first scientists, while publicly holding their tongues, were extremely excited. Finally there was proof that humanity wasn't alone in the cosmos. Science fiction had become science fact. Experiments were begun to decode the signals and send messages back.

Then, about a month after their initial detection, the source was pinpointed. Elation gave way to shock then to near panic.

The beams were coming from the Earth's moon!

========

There were extraterrestrials out there all right but they were right on top of us, on our Moon, as Loxus Abraham Ryne put it – and not some far distant planet or spacecraft. Question was, if the aliens were that close why didn't they make direct contact? Why were they squatting on the Moon permeating the Earth and its people with indecipherable beams?

There seemed only one reasonable answer. They were softening us up; bombarding our brain cells until we were too weak to resist. They'd invade and it would be all over. The world would be colonized and humanity would either be wiped out or enslaved.

In an extraordinary session of the Security Council, the United Nations agreed to meet this off-worldly intrusion aggressively. Although not forgotten, suspicions and ideologies were put on the back burner for the nonce. The Nations of the Earth agreed to pool their knowledge, resources, and manpower in order to confront this alien menace and send it packing. Earth would not be a planetary sitting duck.

The first step was to set up the Society for the Prevention of Alien Control of Earth (SPACE or the SPACE Council). To head this organization, the governments agreed to appoint Loxus Abraham Ryne. Among the many hats he wore or had worn, the Dutch-Iraryan businessman once ran New Century Enterprises, the world's largest corporation, AMERICA – mostly for Americans – and still did the pan-humanist Alliance of Man.

Abe, as he allowed his friends call him (and many of his enemies, of whom he had at least as many as he had friends), was also the patriarch of the non-denominational, Illuminated Faith of Xuthros Hor. As old as the century at seventy-eight, Ryne took to his latest and perhaps greatest challenge with a vigour and surety belying his age.

Ryne immediately clamped a total blackout on the activities of SPACE. Under no circumstances was word to leak that there were aliens on the Moon bombarding humanity with behaviour- and attitude-altering thought-beams as a presumed prelude to a full-scale invasion. With cold-blooded efficiency he began to enforce his mandate.

He cut through bureaucracies, technological impasses, resource, capital and supply problems. He demanded access from the Soviet Union to the secret papers of Jesus Mandam, a supranormal who was variously known as the King Conqueror or the Conquering Christ from 1943 to 1953. Mandam had been the patriarch's nephew, the son of his twin sister, Mary, and her equally late husband, Joseph Mandam.

A highly gifted, almost futuristically innovative genius, Mandam was virtually unknown to the general public. Though politically nonaligned, he spent much of his active life in the Soviet Union and was killed on Christmas Day 1953, during an unannounced explosion of a hydrogen bomb on the South Sea island of Salvation.

The Soviets preserved his notes and, when the beams were detected, shared them with the U.N. and the Alliance of Man – which was the main reason the Liberty was built in the USSR.

It was now in place, orbiting above a specific crater on the Moon.

=========

The Cosmic Express looked almost minuscule atop its fifteen-storey high firing rockets. It actually was quite large, three or four storeys in its own right. Six Cosmicars adhered to its outer shell. Each was the size of a transit bus and comfortably held a seven-member crew. The central stalk held another fifteen people, mostly relief staff, while the bud on the head of it, the control capsule, was virtually a cosmicar unto itself.

Nine people would always be there, including the overall commander, the chief engineer, the chief navigator, their first officers and alternates.

The Express was cloaked by a hardened carapace made out of another mysterious substance called 'Solidium'. The theory was that it would burn off leaving earth's atmosphere and that, thereafter, the Express would function either whole or as independent compartments, depending on the commander's orders.

Sixty-six people would be on the Express. Either sixty-six reached Outer Space or a minimum of sixty-six would die that day.

=========

"Ah, Mr Maxwell," Alfredo Sentalli, masking his annoyance rather well, greeted his security chief. "Everything's A-OK, I trust? You took quite a while getting here."

"Couldn't be better, sir."

"It doesn't have to be better, Mr Maxwell," observed Hiyati Samarand, Project Sentalli's overseer. "Merely as good as it's supposed to be. Which is perfect. Correct?"

"Nothing's perfect," noted Maxwell cautiously. Was Samarand smirking? Had he noticed something? Was something wrong? "We're only human, after all."

"Um, quite," said Sentalli, wiping his brow. "The crew are aboard so I'm afraid you've missed saying good-bye to them but Commander Sol and his cosmicaptains are waiting for you."

With the Fatman leading the way in his wheelchair, Maxwell fell into line with Dulles, Samarand, Yataghan, Lindquist, Hannibal, and the heads of the various departments. Tragic that Kinesis couldn't be there after all his work. But, thought Max, the sooner the Express was launched the sooner he could get Rom off the tranquilizers they'd been feeding him since yesterday afternoon.

Maxwell had spent many hours with Avatar Sol and the six cosmicaptains, supervising their physical training and that of their crew. Of the two hundred or so trainees, the sixty-six that were finally chosen had passed rigorous muster. While mental preparedness was as important as physical fitness, one went with the other. He was pleased with the results.

This was as bright, as tough and as determined a group, as he'd even seen. He wished the people who had worked under him during his years as Operations Head of AMERICA had been collectively half as good as this bunch were. Maybe then the Worldwide Order, with its phoenix-like capacity to rise out of its own ashes, wouldn't have survived as long as it did.

Of course there were always exceptions. He wouldn't have picked Dmetri Diomad to be a Cosmicaptain. The Greek quisling was not even thirty, too young for such a position, in Maxwell's opinion, though he had been an undercover agent for AMERICA in his teens. Thanks to him, back in '68, Maxwell managed to trace Kadmon Heliopolis, the leader of the Black Rose of Anarchy, to Trigon, his isolated Aegean island hideaway.

Without Diomad's back-stabbing, Heliopolis might have escaped to Turkey. As it was, Kadmon – Rom's childhood friend – was a sitting duck and even AMERICA couldn't miss. Kadmon had been good to Diomad too. The ability to betray friends was not the kind of qualification Maxwell would have used to pick a Cosmicaptain but, he supposed, all that was water under the proverbial bridge.

Then there was Colonel Avatar Sol, the overall flight commander. A more obvious alias would be hard to find. Maxwell even thought he knew who he really was, Chthlonius 'Tiger' Tiecher, given some hefty plastic surgery. The half-Jewish, Israeli-trained Cypriot worked with AMERICA against the Worldwide Order throughout the first half of the Sixties. Major trouble with this, besides the fact that Lon Tiecher would be almost forty whereas Sol was thirty-three, was that he was dead – killed on Trigon at the same time as Heliopolis and the other so-called Spartae.

The bombers that were supposed to soften up Trigon before AMERICA sent in ground troops hit something on the island. The resultant eruption literally blew the tiny island out of existence. It just wasn't there any more. According to experts in such matters, Trigon's explosion should have rivalled that of Santorini, a much larger, neighbouring isle, which, fifteen hundred years before Christ, had blown its core, its heart, into the sky.

That volcanic cataclysm had wiped out the entire Minoan civilization. Even if had just sunk, which islands occasionally did, it should have caused a devastating whirlpool. That it simply vanished was unprecedented. Nevertheless, whatever happened to Trigon, not even Ti Tiecher could have survived.

So, who was Avatar Sol? *'Why, Avatar Sol, of course,'* said Alfredo Sentalli, *'And I want him to lead this mission.'*

That he'd only shown up on Centauri Island in 1978, that he'd replaced Mik Starrus – Maxwell's choice for commander – that he had no credentials for the task, not even birth records nor any kind of documented military background, any kind of background whatsoever, made no difference. He was the best man for the job, no question of it, insisted Sentalli. Max realized this Sol was another of the untouchables and, as such, there was no point arguing. The Fatman had made up his mind.

Then there was Mikelangelo Starrus. Born in '43, he was an American citizen despite his Romanesque-sounding name. He'd taken his demotion from overall commander to captain of Cosmicar Two in stride. Cosmicars would be on the front line when it came to exploring other planets and Mik enjoyed being in the middle of things.

As a young man, already a Vietnam veteran, he'd led the squad of bombers that hit Trigon. In fact, it was one of his bombs that struck the top of one of the island's three peaks, thereby triggering the disappearance. Understandably he had been quite shaken by the episode and talked as if it was his fault for years afterwards. It was only when he described the event to Romaine Kinesis, in Maxwell's presence, that the truth was revealed.

The bomb had hit an outcropping of Gypsium, probably the original one that Rom, Heliopolis, and Aristotle Zeross discovered in 1948.

'Whomsoever touches Gypsium,' recited Rom.

'Yeah, I know,' finished Max, *'Touches both the unknown and the unknowable.'*

The other four cosmicaptains all met with Maxwell's approval. Even though three of them were women and he was an admitted dinosaur when it came to placing women in life-threatening situations, Nehrini Purandar, Alexandra Gagarin, and Elizabeth Dre'Ath – an East Indian, a Russian and a Brit – had impeccable credentials. All had a PhD, in different though equally difficult and demanding fields, and all had been in their respective country's space programs.

Maxwell was particularly proud of *'Lilabet'*, the daughter of his war-time compadre, Nathan Dre'Ath – the nephew of Max's adoptive mother, Bunnie nee O'Ryan Galvin. It wasn't just that Lilabet was virtually family; she'd worked damn hard and deserved her place amongst the elite of the Cosmic Express. So did the last one, Sango Belzem, a Portuguese who'd earned his doctorate studying under Rom Kinesis.

All in all, a fine group. He told them as much as he shook their hands a last time.

========

As Sol and his cosmicaptains entered the elevators that would take them to the Cosmic Express, aboard the phony fish packer miles off the coast of Centauri Island, the directors of a revitalized WORLD readied themselves for their own launch. Nervous anticipation was the common state of affairs in both places but calm professionalism was equally the order of the day.

For an anxious hour the countdown continued.

========

"Thirteen minutes," announced Hiyati Samarand.

Maxwell heard him and, through Maxwell – through Major Mind's mind tap – those on the packer heard him as well. Only the phantasm known as Daemonicus was smiling. He smiled all the broader when Samarand announced 'Twelve' – then, suddenly, burst into a rage.

"Abort!" screamed Maxwell. "Abort! Goddamn you to Hell, Samarand! Stop the countdown!"

"Too late. Let him fry."

"No!"

"What madness is this? What's going on? No, don't panic! Follow Yati! Keep counting till he, and he alone, aborts!"

========

"It's fucking Kinesis," yelled Dulles, ripping the gun off his back. Max cuffed his adoptive father's illegitimate son to the floor then pulled off his own multi-purpose rifle.

"Up there. In the roof struts," spotted George Hannibal.

"Forget him, Maxwell," demanded Samarand.

"With what he can do, you forget it. Abort, I'm telling you. Do it! Gypsium works for Rom, not us. Stop the countdown, I say. And you, Yataghan, get your old man out of here. Now!"

"Wait!" ordered Sentalli. "He jumped."

========

Two hours earlier the ceiling above the launch pad had been opened. It was a fine day; couldn't ask for a better one. Everyone on the island hunkered down in front of their television sets to begin the long wait until ignition. There was a scuffle in one of the living quarters at the windward resort. No one had reported it because no one could move after it was over.

Romaine Kinesis, groggy from the drugs but no less determined, stole a jeep and careened across the island to the launch site. There he'd overridden the security codes and gained access to his own laboratory. His canister, hoses, and hand prongs were there as was his sky sled.

So was the Gypsium Irradiation Chamber where his colleague, Alastor Molorchus, had been disintegrated twelve years earlier. Not entirely disintegrated – his left arm had survived, and that was all that'd been buried in his grave in the cemetery on Mt. Kinesis. No time for the Chamber. Take too long to get it primed, though he started it up just in case. The canister and sled would have to do.

Bursting out of his lab, he disabled two overly curious passers-by. One didn't go down clean. What was his name? Marsh? Something like that. Somehow he managed to reach a button on his belt. Alarms began ringing.

As soon as Samarand noted thirteen minutes to lift off, alarms began to sound. Steadfastly he ignored them and went to his computer console to find out what was going wrong. With twelve minutes to go, he realized the alarms had started in the proximity of the professor's lab.

Maxwell ordered the mission aborted.

========

"The fuck he did, Fatman. He's goddamned flying. Get back."

Max blew out the superheat-resistant glass with a blast from his mini-bazooka. Lights went from flashing to stroboscopic, alarms from blaring to screeching. Computer voices bleated an insistent message: *"Evacuate. All personnel, evacuate."*

"Eleven minutes to lift off," intoned Samarand, either supernally calm or into the state of an automaton. "You'll have to kill him, Maxwell."

"I'm working on it, for Christ's sake. Junior, get going. You others, fucking vanish!"

Yataghan rolled Sentalli out of the control room. The rest of the technicians scrambled after them. Two of the security guards gathered up Adolph Dulles and dragged him along. Only Samarand, Hannibal, and Lindquist stood their ground.

"Have it your own way, fat heads." Max cracked out the rest of the safety glass, propped a leg on the ledge, and took aim. Kinesis flitted around the Express, directing particles of motive-accelerating Gypsium at the glass shields surrounding the far perimeter of the launch pad.

Maxwell fired.

========

"Bastard missed," gasped Dis L'Orca.
"Maxwell doesn't miss."
"He's old. Past it. They're going to have to abort now."
"Ten minutes," intoned Samarand, nervelessly.
"His kind are never past it, Salvatore. Not if I'm right about him. No, he's deliberately missing, stalling for time, hoping Yati cancels. But he won't. Carry on!"

========

"Use heavy ammo, you idiot," demanded Hannibal.

"And risk damaging the Express? Grab a brain, lawyer, and get out of here. Take Doc and Fu Manchu with you."

"Abort, Yati," implored Lindquist. "This isn't working out. Kinesis could be a Mithradite."

"You think Great Byron wouldn't have sensed it, APM? No, there's another way." Samarand bent over his computer console. "Take him out, both of you. Take both of them out."

Maxwell whipped around. Too late. Something blew him out the window. The tarmac lay twenty storeys below.

========

Romaine Kinesis turned his attention to the control room just as Maxwell hurtled out of the already-shattered window. Two creatures – couldn't call them human – ran up to the ledge. They sent something at him but he was already on his way to rescue his friend. He caught Maxwell in a tractor beam of Gypsium particles and brought both of them softly to the tarmac floor.

"Ten," intoned Samarand.

"Again?" groaned Maxwell.

"Ten seconds. Hiyati's accelerated ..."

========

"Launch Kamikaze ... NOW!"

========

"...THE COUNTDOWN!"

"NINE-EIGHT-SEVEN-SIX-FIVE-FOUR-THREE-TWO-ONE-ZERO! WE HAVE IGNITION! WE HAVE LIFT OFF! WE'RE ON OUR WAY!"

So was Kamikaze Kaligula.

========

Kaligula was under no illusions about her role. She was kamikaze but the 'divine wind' she rode was not that of death, but rebirth. Daemonicus had told her to think of her mission in terms of a jailbreak. She took him as meaning 'breaking the shackles of these mortal coils'.

Hardly what he meant at all.

========

Inside the control capsule, Commander Avatar Sol writhed under the stress of take off; as did cosmicaptains Mik Starrus, Dmetri Diomad, and the sixty odd others aboard the Express.

On Centauri Island there was only jubilation.

With the primary containment area around the perimeter of the launch site decimated because Rom Kinesis had blown out most of the protective glass, personnel had fled to secondary control rooms. It was a two minute dash but Yataghan, pushing his father, made it just in time.

"We did it. She's off."

Euphoria!

"Sir, we've picked up a blip on our radar. It's on an intercept course with the Express. They're going to collide!"

They did.

Dejection!

========

Colonel Sol had seen many a strange sight in his time; a few even matched this.

Somehow the entire Cosmic Express was still in tact. Whatever hit the Express managed to inject it into some sort of dark, grey space. Sol felt a sense of deep joy, almost of accomplishment. Dozens of pinpoints of light were approaching the vessel. Stars, faeries, angels?

Devils!

The smaller ones kept coming. The largest, the brightest of all, resolved itself. To Sol's fractured mind, it was at least ten times the size of the Express. And what it was – what it appeared to be – was a single, impossibly huge and disembodied eye. Its pupil had lips and teeth and a tongue. A mouth.

And it spoke!

"YOU PIG-WHUMPING, MECHANICAL LOLLIPOP, LOOK WHAT YOU'VE DONE.

"NOT ONLY HAVE YOU RIPPED MY HOLY HALO AND PIERCED THE FORBIDDEN ZONE, YOU'VE FREED SOME OF MY JACKASS OFFSPRING AS WELL."

In the cosmic control capsule, Avatar Sol could think of only one thing. "Fire second stage. Let's get out of here."

"Second stage fired, sir!"

"AND AFTER ALL THAT, YOU'RE TRYING TO GET AWAY. WELL, PUKE ON YOU. A LITTLE GOD-SUCK WILL TEACH YOU SOME MANNERS."

Pursing its lips, the eye-thing slurped the entire Express into its mass and began to chew it. To Sol, it was like what clothes must experience inside a washing machine. He felt for all the still-living oysters he'd chomped on as a child.

RRRUURP!

"BLOODY HELL! YOU OUTER EARTHLINGS TASTE AS LOUSY AS YOU DID SIX THOUSAND YEARS AGO!"

The eye-mouth spat them not just out of its craw but out of wherever they were in the first place.

"YUK!"

=========

"The War of the Apocalyptics", "Goddess Gambit" and "Nuclear Dragons" all carry on from this point.

And they're only the first three, full-length **PHANTACEA Mythos** *novels comprising the* LAUNCH *1980 story cycle that do so.*

****

CPSIA information can be obtained at www.ICGtesting.com
Printed in the USA
LVOW120819190112

264500LV00002B/1/P